THE FORSYTE SAGA

Complete Three Volumes

JOHN GALSWORTHY

THE FORSYTE SAGA

THE FORSYTE SAGA

PREFACE

"The Forsyte Saga" was the title originally destined for that part of it which is called "The Man of Property"; and to adopt it for the collected chronicles of the Forsyte family has indulged the Forsytean tenacity that is in all of us. The word Saga might be objected to on the ground that it connotes the heroic and that there is little heroism in these pages. But it is used with a suitable irony; and, after all, this long tale, though it may deal with folk in frock coats, furbelows, and a gilt-edged period, is not devoid of the essential heat of conflict. Discounting for the gigantic stature and blood-thirstiness of old days, as they have come down to us in fairy-tale and legend, the folk of the old Sagas were Forsytes, assuredly, in their possessive instincts, and as little proof against the inroads of beauty and passion as Swithin, Soames, or even Young Jolyon. And if heroic figures, in days that never were, seem to startle out from their surroundings in fashion unbecoming to a Forsyte of the Victorian era, we may be sure that tribal instinct was even then the prime force, and that "family" and the sense of home and property counted as they do to this day, for all the recent efforts to "talk them out."

So many people have written and claimed that their families were the originals of the Forsytes that one has been almost encouraged to believe in the typicality of an imagined species. Manners change and modes evolve, and "Timothy's on the Bayswater Road" becomes a nest of the unbelievable in all except essentials; we shall not look upon its like again, nor perhaps on such a one as James or Old Jolyon. And yet the figures of Insurance Societies and the utterances of Judges reassure us daily that our earthly paradise is still a rich preserve, where the wild raiders, Beauty and Passion, come stealing in, filching security from beneath our noses. As surely as a dog will bark at a brass band, so will the essential Soames in human nature ever rise up uneasily against the dissolution which hovers round the folds of ownership.

"Let the dead Past bury its dead" would be a better saying if the Past ever died. The persistence of the Past is one of those tragi-comic blessings which each new age denies, coming cocksure on to the stage to mouth its claim to a perfect novelty.

But no Age is so new as that! Human Nature, under its changing pretensions and clothes, is and ever will be very much of a Forsyte, and might, after all, be a much worse animal.

Looking back on the Victorian era, whose ripeness, decline, and 'fall-of' is in some sort pictured in "The Forsyte Saga," we see now that we have but jumped out of a frying-pan into a fire. It would be difficult to substantiate a claim that the case of England was better in 1913 than it was in 1886, when the Forsytes assembled at Old Jolyon's to celebrate the engagement of June to Philip Bosinney. And in 1920, when again the clan gathered to bless the marriage of Fleur with Michael Mont, the state of England is as surely too molten and bankrupt as in the eighties it was too congealed and low-percented. If these chronicles had been a really scientific study of transition one would have dwelt probably on such factors as the invention of bicycle, motor-car, and flying-machine; the arrival of a cheap Press; the decline of country life and increase of the towns; the birth of the Cinema. Men are, in fact, quite unable to control their own inventions; they at best develop adaptability to the new conditions those inventions create.

But this long tale is no scientific study of a period; it is rather an intimate incarnation of the disturbance that Beauty effects in the lives of men.

The figure of Irene, never, as the reader may possibly have observed, present, except through the senses of other characters, is a concretion of disturbing Beauty impinging on a possessive world.

One has noticed that readers, as they wade on through the salt waters of the Saga, are inclined more and more to pity Soames, and to think that in doing so they are in revolt against the mood of his creator. Far from it! He, too, pities Soames, the tragedy of whose life is the very simple, uncontrollable tragedy of being unlovable, without quite a thick enough skin to be thoroughly unconscious of the fact. Not even Fleur loves Soames as he feels he ought to be loved. But in pitying Soames, readers incline, perhaps, to animus against Irene: After all, they think, he wasn't a bad fellow, it wasn't his fault; she ought to have forgiven him, and so on!

And, taking sides, they lose perception of the simple truth, which underlies the whole story, that where sex attraction is utterly and definitely lacking in one partner to a union, no amount of pity, or reason, or duty, or what not, can overcome a repulsion implicit in Nature. Whether it ought to, or no, is beside the point; because in fact it never does. And where Irene seems hard and cruel, as in the Bois de Boulogne, or the Goupenor Gallery, she is but wisely realistic—knowing that the least concession is the inch which precedes the impossible, the repulsive ell.

A criticism one might pass on the last phase of the Saga is the complaint that Irene and Jolyon those rebels against property—claim spiritual property in their son Jon. But it would be hypercriticism, as the tale is told. No father and mother could have let the boy marry Fleur without knowledge of the facts; and the facts determine Jon, not the persuasion of his parents. Moreover, Jolyon's persuasion is not on his own account, but on Irene's, and Irene's persuasion becomes a reiterated: "Don't think of me, think of yourself!" That Jon, knowing the facts, can realise his mother's feelings, will hardly with justice be held proof that she is, after all, a Forsyte.

But though the impingement of Beauty and the claims of Freedom on a possessive world are the main prepossessions of the Forsyte Saga, it cannot be absolved from the charge of embalming the upper-middle class. As the old Egyptians placed around their mummies the necessaries of a future existence, so I have endeavoured to lay beside the figures of Aunts Ann and Juley and Hester, of Timothy and Swithin, of Old Jolyon and James, and of their sons, that which shall guarantee them a little life here-after, a little balm in the hurried Gilead of a dissolving "Progress."

If the upper-middle class, with other classes, is destined to "move on" into amorphism, here, pickled in these pages, it lies under glass for strollers in the wide and ill-arranged museum of Letters. Here it rests, preserved in its own juice: The Sense of Property. 1922.

VOLUME I. THE MAN OF PROPERTY

by JOHN GALSWORTHY
".........You will answer
The slaves are ours....."
—Merchant of Venice.
TO EDWARD GARNETT

PART I

CHAPTER I—'AT HOME' AT OLD JOLYON'S

Those privileged to be present at a family festival of the Forsytes have seen that charming and instructive sight—an upper middle-class family in full plumage. But whosoever of these favoured persons has possessed the gift of psychological analysis (a talent without monetary value and properly ignored by the Forsytes), has witnessed a spectacle, not only delightful in itself, but illustrative of an obscure human problem. In plainer words, he has gleaned from a gathering of this family—no branch of which had a liking for the other, between no three members of whom existed anything worthy of the name of sympathy— evidence of that mysterious concrete tenacity which renders a family so formidable a unit of society, so clear a reproduction of society in miniature. He has been admitted to a vision of the dim roads of social progress, has understood something of patriarchal life, of the swarmings of savage hordes, of the rise and fall of nations. He is like one who, having watched a tree grow from its planting—a paragon of tenacity, insulation, and success, amidst the deaths of a hundred other plants less fibrous, sappy, and persistent—one day will see it flourishing with bland, full foliage, in an almost repugnant prosperity, at the summit of its efflorescence.

On June 15, eighteen eighty-six, about four of the afternoon, the observer who chanced to be present at the house of old Jolyon Forsyte in Stanhope Gate, might have seen the highest efflorescence of the Forsytes.

This was the occasion of an 'at home' to celebrate the engagement of Miss June Forsyte, old Jolyon's granddaughter, to Mr. Philip Bosinney. In the bravery of light gloves, buff waistcoats, feathers and frocks, the family were present, even Aunt Ann, who now but seldom left the corner of her brother Timothy's green drawing-room, where, under the aegis of a plume of dyed pampas grass in a light blue vase, she sat all day reading and knitting, surrounded by the effigies of three generations of Forsytes. Even Aunt Ann was there; her inflexible back, and the dignity of her calm old face personifying the rigid possessiveness of the family idea.

When a Forsyte was engaged, married, or born, the Forsytes were present; when a Forsyte died—but no Forsyte had as yet died; they did not die; death being contrary to their principles, they took precautions against it, the instinctive precautions of highly vitalized persons who resent encroachments on their property.

About the Forsytes mingling that day with the crowd of other guests, there was a more than ordinarily groomed look, an alert, inquisitive assurance, a brilliant respectability, as though they were attired in defiance of something. The habitual sniff on the face of Soames Forsyte had spread through their ranks; they were on their guard.

The subconscious offensiveness of their attitude has constituted old Jolyon's 'home' the psychological moment of the family history, made it the prelude of their drama.

The Forsytes were resentful of something, not individually, but as a family; this resentment expressed itself in an added perfection of raiment, an exuberance of family cordiality, an exaggeration of family importance, and—the sniff. Danger—so indispensable in bringing out the fundamental quality of any society, group, or individual—was what the Forsytes scented; the premonition of danger put a burnish on their armour. For the first time, as a family, they appeared to have an instinct of being in contact, with some strange and unsafe thing.

Over against the piano a man of bulk and stature was wearing two waistcoats on his wide chest, two waistcoats and a ruby pin, instead of the single satin waistcoat and diamond pin of more usual occasions, and his shaven, square, old face, the colour of pale leather, with pale eyes, had its most dignified look, above his satin stock. This was Swithin Forsyte. Close to the window, where he could get more than his fair share of fresh air, the other twin, James—the fat and the lean of it, old Jolyon called these brothers—like the bulky Swithin, over six feet in height, but very lean, as though destined from his birth to strike a balance and maintain an average, brooded over the scene with his permanent stoop; his grey eyes had an air of fixed absorption in some secret worry, broken at intervals by a rapid, shifting scrutiny of surrounding facts; his cheeks, thinned by two parallel folds, and a long, clean-shaven upper lip, were framed within Dundreary whiskers. In his hands he turned and turned a piece of china. Not far off, listening to a lady in brown, his only son Soames, pale and well-shaved, dark-haired, rather bald, had poked his chin up sideways, carrying his nose with that aforesaid appearance of 'sniff,' as though despising an egg which he knew he could not digest. Behind him his cousin, the tall George, son of the fifth Forsyte, Roger, had a Quilpish look on his fleshy face, pondering one of his sardonic jests. Something inherent to the occasion had affected them all.

Seated in a row close to one another were three ladies—Aunts Ann, Hester (the two Forsyte maids), and Juley (short for Julia), who not in first youth had so far forgotten herself as to marry Septimus Small, a man of poor constitution. She had survived him for many years. With her elder and younger sister she lived now in the house of Timothy, her sixth and youngest brother, on the Bayswater Road. Each of these ladies held fans in their hands, and each with some touch of colour, some emphatic feather or brooch, testified to the solemnity of the opportunity.

In the centre of the room, under the chandelier, as became a host, stood the head of the family, old Jolyon himself. Eighty years of age, with his fine, white hair, his dome-like forehead, his little, dark grey eyes, and an immense white moustache, which drooped and spread below the level of his strong jaw, he had a patriarchal look, and in spite of lean cheeks and hollows at his temples, seemed master of perennial youth. He held himself extremely upright, and his shrewd, steady eyes had lost none of their clear shining. Thus he gave an impression of superiority to the doubts and dislikes of smaller men. Having had his own way for innumerable years, he had earned a prescriptive right to it. It would never have occurred to old Jolyon that it was necessary to wear a look of doubt or of defiance.

Between him and the four other brothers who were present, James, Swithin, Nicholas, and Roger, there was much difference, much similarity. In turn, each of these four brothers was very different from the other, yet they, too, were alike.

Through the varying features and expression of those five faces could be marked a certain steadfastness of chin, underlying surface distinctions, marking a racial stamp, too prehistoric to trace, too remote and permanent to discuss—the very hall-mark and guarantee of the family fortunes.

Among the younger generation, in the tall, bull-like George, in pallid strenuous Archibald, in young Nicholas with his sweet and tentative obstinacy, in the grave and foppishly determined Eustace, there was this same stamp—less meaningful perhaps, but unmistakable—a sign of something ineradicable in the family soul. At one time or another during the afternoon, all these faces, so dissimilar and so alike, had worn an expression of distrust, the object of which was undoubtedly the man whose acquaintance they were thus assembled to make. Philip Bosinney was known to be a young man without fortune, but Forsyte girls had become engaged to such before, and had actually married them. It was not altogether for this reason, therefore, that the minds of the Forsytes misgave them. They could not have explained the origin of a misgiving obscured by the mist of family gossip. A story was undoubtedly told that he had paid his duty call to Aunts Ann, Juley, and Hester, in a soft grey hat—a soft grey hat, not even a new one—a dusty thing with a shapeless crown. "So, extraordinary, my dear—so odd," Aunt Hester, passing through the little, dark hall (she was rather short-sighted), had tried to 'shoo' it off a chair, taking it for a strange, disreputable cat—Tommy had such disgraceful friends! She was disturbed when it did not move.

Like an artist for ever seeking to discover the significant trifle which embodies the whole character of a scene, or place, or person, so those unconscious artists—the Forsytes had fastened by intuition on this hat; it was their significant trifle, the detail in which was embedded the meaning of the whole matter; for each had asked himself: "Come, now, should I have paid that visit in that hat?" and each had answered "No!" and some, with more imagination than others, had added: "It would never have come into my head!"

George, on hearing the story, grinned. The hat had obviously been worn as a practical joke! He himself was a connoisseur of such. "Very haughty!" he said, "the wild Buccaneer."

And this mot, the 'Buccaneer,' was bandied from mouth to mouth, till it became the favourite mode of alluding to Bosinney.

Her aunts reproached June afterwards about the hat.

"We don't think you ought to let him, dear!" they had said.

June had answered in her imperious brisk way, like the little embodiment of will she was: "Oh! what does it matter? Phil never knows what he's got on!"

No one had credited an answer so outrageous. A man not to know what he had on? No, no! What indeed was this young man, who, in becoming engaged to June, old Jolyon's acknowledged heiress, had done so well for himself? He was an architect, not in itself a sufficient reason for wearing such a hat. None of the Forsytes happened to be architects, but one of them knew two architects who would never have worn such a hat upon a call of ceremony in the London season.

Dangerous—ah, dangerous! June, of course, had not seen this, but, though not yet nineteen, she was notorious. Had she not said to Mrs. Soames—who was always so beautifully dressed—that feathers were vulgar? Mrs. Soames had actually given up wearing feathers, so dreadfully downright was dear June!

These misgivings, this disapproval, and perfectly genuine distrust, did not prevent the Forsytes from gathering to old Jolyon's invitation. An 'At Home' at Stanhope Gate was a great rarity; none had been held for twelve years, not indeed, since old Mrs. Jolyon had died.

Never had there been so full an assembly, for, mysteriously united in spite of all their differences, they had taken arms against a common peril. Like cattle when a dog comes into the field, they stood head to head and shoulder to shoulder, prepared to run upon and trample the invader to death. They had come, too, no doubt, to get some notion of what sort of presents they would ultimately be expected to give; for though the question of wedding gifts was usually graduated in this way: 'What are you givin'? Nicholas is givin' spoons!'—so very much depended on the bridegroom. If he were sleek, well-brushed, prosperous-looking, it was more necessary to give him nice things; he would expect them. In the end each gave exactly what was right and proper, by a species of family adjustment arrived at as prices are arrived at on the Stock Exchange—the exact niceties being regulated at Timothy's commodious, red-brick residence in Bayswater, overlooking the Park, where dwelt Aunts Ann, Juley, and Hester.

The uneasiness of the Forsyte family has been justified by the simple mention of the hat. How impossible and wrong would it have been for any family, with the regard for appearances which should ever characterize the great upper middle-class, to feel otherwise than uneasy!

The author of the uneasiness stood talking to June by the further door; his curly hair had a rumpled appearance, as though he found what was going on around him unusual. He had an air, too, of having a joke all to himself. George, speaking aside to his brother, Eustace, said:

"Looks as if he might make a bolt of it—the dashing Buccaneer!"

This 'very singular-looking man,' as Mrs. Small afterwards called him, was of medium height and strong build, with a pale, brown face, a dust-coloured moustache, very prominent cheek-bones, and hollow cheeks. His forehead sloped back towards the crown of his head, and bulged out in bumps over the eyes, like foreheads seen in the Lion-house at the Zoo. He had sherry-coloured eyes, disconcertingly inattentive at times. Old Jolyon's coachman, after driving June and Bosinney to the theatre, had remarked to the butler:

"I dunno what to make of 'im. Looks to me for all the world like an 'alf-tame leopard." And every now and then a Forsyte would come up, sidle round, and take a look at him.

June stood in front, fending off this idle curiosity—a little bit of a thing, as somebody once said, 'all hair and spirit,' with fearless blue eyes, a firm jaw, and a bright colour, whose face and body seemed too slender for her crown of red-gold hair.

A tall woman, with a beautiful figure, which some member of the family had once compared to a heathen goddess, stood looking at these two with a shadowy smile.

Her hands, gloved in French grey, were crossed one over the other, her grave, charming face held to one side, and the eyes of all men near were fastened on it. Her figure swayed, so balanced that the very air seemed to set it moving. There was warmth, but little colour, in her cheeks; her large, dark eyes were soft.

But it was at her lips—asking a question, giving an answer, with that shadowy smile—that men looked; they were sensitive lips, sensuous and sweet, and through them seemed to come warmth and perfume like the warmth and perfume of a flower.

The engaged couple thus scrutinized were unconscious of this passive goddess. It was Bosinney who first noticed her, and asked her name.

June took her lover up to the woman with the beautiful figure.

9

"Irene is my greatest chum," she said: "Please be good friends, you two!"

At the little lady's command they all three smiled; and while they were smiling, Soames Forsyte, silently appearing from behind the woman with the beautiful figure, who was his wife, said:

"Ah! introduce me too!"

He was seldom, indeed, far from Irene's side at public functions, and even when separated by the exigencies of social intercourse, could be seen following her about with his eyes, in which were strange expressions of watchfulness and longing.

At the window his father, James, was still scrutinizing the marks on the piece of china.

"I wonder at Jolyon's allowing this engagement," he said to Aunt Ann. "They tell me there's no chance of their getting married for years. This young Bosinney" (he made the word a dactyl in opposition to general usage of a short o) "has got nothing. When Winifred married Dartie, I made him bring every penny into settlement—lucky thing, too—they'd ha' had nothing by this time!"

Aunt Ann looked up from her velvet chair. Grey curls banded her forehead, curls that, unchanged for decades, had extinguished in the family all sense of time. She made no reply, for she rarely spoke, husbanding her aged voice; but to James, uneasy of conscience, her look was as good as an answer.

"Well," he said, "I couldn't help Irene's having no money. Soames was in such a hurry; he got quite thin dancing attendance on her."

Putting the bowl pettishly down on the piano, he let his eyes wander to the group by the door.

"It's my opinion," he said unexpectedly, "that it's just as well as it is."

Aunt Ann did not ask him to explain this strange utterance. She knew what he was thinking. If Irene had no money she would not be so foolish as to do anything wrong; for they said—they said—she had been asking for a separate room; but, of course, Soames had not....

James interrupted her reverie:

"But where," he asked, "was Timothy? Hadn't he come with them?"

Through Aunt Ann's compressed lips a tender smile forced its way:

"No, he didn't think it wise, with so much of this diphtheria about; and he so liable to take things."

James answered:

"Well, HE takes good care of himself. I can't afford to take the care of myself that he does."

Nor was it easy to say which, of admiration, envy, or contempt, was dominant in that remark.

Timothy, indeed, was seldom seen. The baby of the family, a publisher by profession, he had some years before, when business was at full tide, scented out the stagnation which, indeed, had not yet come, but which ultimately, as all agreed, was bound to set in, and, selling his share in a firm engaged mainly in the production of religious books, had invested the quite conspicuous proceeds in three per cent. consols. By this act he had at once assumed an isolated position, no other Forsyte being content with less than four per cent.

for his money; and this isolation had slowly and surely undermined a spirit perhaps better than commonly endowed with caution. He had become almost a myth—a kind of incarnation of security haunting the background of the Forsyte universe. He had never committed the imprudence of marrying, or encumbering himself in any way with children.

James resumed, tapping the piece of china:

"This isn't real old Worcester. I supose Jolyon's told you something about the young man. From all I can learn, he's got no business, no income, and no connection worth speaking of; but then, I know nothing—nobody tells me anything."

Aunt Ann shook her head. Over her square-chinned, aquiline old face a trembling passed; the spidery fingers of her hands pressed against each other and interlaced, as though she were subtly recharging her will.

The eldest by some years of all the Forsytes, she held a peculiar position amongst them. Opportunists and egotists one and all—though not, indeed, more so than their neighbours—they quailed before her incorruptible figure, and, when opportunities were too strong, what could they do but avoid her!

Twisting his long, thin legs, James went on:

"Jolyon, he will have his own way. He's got no children"—and stopped, recollecting the continued existence of old Jolyon's son, young Jolyon, June's father, who had made such a mess of it, and done for himself by deserting his wife and child and running away with that foreign governess. "Well," he resumed hastily, "if he likes to do these things, I s'pose he can afford to. Now, what's he going to give her? I s'pose he'll give her a thousand a year; he's got nobody else to leave his money to."

He stretched out his hand to meet that of a dapper, clean-shaven man, with hardly a hair on his head, a long, broken nose, full lips, and cold grey eyes under rectangular brows.

"Well, Nick," he muttered, "how are you?"

Nicholas Forsyte, with his bird-like rapidity and the look of a preternaturally sage schoolboy (he had made a large fortune, quite legitimately, out of the companies of which he was a director), placed within that cold palm the tips of his still colder fingers and hastily withdrew them.

"I'm bad," he said, pouting—"been bad all the week; don't sleep at night. The doctor can't tell why. He's a clever fellow, or I shouldn't have him, but I get nothing out of him but bills."

"Doctors!" said James, coming down sharp on his words: "I've had all the doctors in London for one or another of us. There's no satisfaction to be got out of them; they'll tell you anything. There's Swithin, now. What good have they done him? There he is; he's bigger than ever; he's enormous; they can't get his weight down. Look at him!"

Swithin Forsyte, tall, square, and broad, with a chest like a pouter pigeon's in its plumage of bright waistcoats, came strutting towards them.

"Er—how are you?" he said in his dandified way, aspirating the 'h' strongly (this difficult letter was almost absolutely safe in his keeping)—"how are you?"

Each brother wore an air of aggravation as he looked at the other two, knowing by experience that they would try to eclipse his ailments.

"We were just saying," said James, "that you don't get any thinner."

Swithin protruded his pale round eyes with the effort of hearing.

"Thinner? I'm in good case," he said, leaning a little forward, "not one of your thread-papers like you!"

But, afraid of losing the expansion of his chest, he leaned back again into a state of immobility, for he prized nothing so highly as a distinguished appearance.

Aunt Ann turned her old eyes from one to the other. Indulgent and severe was her look. In turn the three brothers looked at Ann. She was getting shaky. Wonderful woman! Eighty-six if a day; might live another ten years, and had never been strong. Swithin and James, the twins, were only seventy-five, Nicholas a mere baby of seventy or so. All were strong, and the inference was comforting. Of all forms of property their respective healths naturally concerned them most.

"I'm very well in myself," proceeded James, "but my nerves are out of order. The least thing worries me to death. I shall have to go to Bath."

"Bath!" said Nicholas. "I've tried Harrogate. That's no good. What I want is sea air. There's nothing like Yarmouth. Now, when I go there I sleep...."

"My liver's very bad," interrupted Swithin slowly. "Dreadful pain here;" and he placed his hand on his right side.

"Want of exercise," muttered James, his eyes on the china. He quickly added: "I get a pain there, too."

Swithin reddened, a resemblance to a turkey-cock coming upon his old face.

"Exercise!" he said. "I take plenty: I never use the lift at the Club."

"I didn't know," James hurried out. "I know nothing about anybody; nobody tells me anything...."

Swithin fixed him with a stare:

"What do you do for a pain there?"

James brightened.

"I take a compound...."

"How are you, uncle?"

June stood before him, her resolute small face raised from her little height to his great height, and her hand outheld.

The brightness faded from James's visage.

"How are you?" he said, brooding over her. "So you're going to Wales to-morrow to visit your young man's aunts? You'll have a lot of rain there. This isn't real old Worcester." He tapped the bowl. "Now, that set I gave your mother when she married was the genuine thing."

June shook hands one by one with her three great-uncles, and turned to Aunt Ann. A very sweet look had come into the old lady's face, she kissed the girl's cheek with trembling fervour.

"Well, my dear," she said, "and so you're going for a whole month!"

The girl passed on, and Aunt Ann looked after her slim little figure. The old lady's round, steel grey eyes, over which a film like a bird's was beginning to come, followed her wistfully amongst the bustling crowd, for people were beginning to say good-bye; and her fingertips, pressing and pressing against each other, were busy again with the recharging of her will against that inevitable ultimate departure of her own.

'Yes,' she thought, 'everybody's been most kind; quite a lot of people come to congratulate her. She ought to be very happy.' Amongst the throng of people by the door, the well-dressed throng drawn from the families of lawyers and doctors, from the Stock Exchange, and all the innumerable avocations of the upper-middle class—there were only some twenty percent of Forsytes; but to Aunt Ann they seemed all Forsytes—and certainly there was not much difference—she saw only her own flesh and blood. It was her world, this family, and she knew no other, had never perhaps known any other. All their little secrets, illnesses, engagements, and marriages, how they were getting on, and whether they were making money—all this was her property, her delight, her life; beyond this only a vague, shadowy mist of facts and persons of no real significance. This it was that she would have to lay down when it came to her turn to die; this which gave to her that importance, that secret self-importance, without which none of us can bear to live; and to this she clung wistfully, with a greed that grew each day! If life were slipping away from her, this she would retain to the end.

She thought of June's father, young Jolyon, who had run away with that foreign girl. And what a sad blow to his father and to them all. Such a promising young fellow! A sad blow, though there had been no public scandal, most fortunately, Jo's wife seeking for no divorce! A long time ago! And when June's mother died, six years ago, Jo had married that woman, and they had two children now, so she had heard. Still, he had forfeited his right to be there, had cheated her of the complete fulfilment of her family pride, deprived her of the rightful pleasure of seeing and kissing him of whom she had been so proud, such a promising young fellow! The thought rankled with the bitterness of a long-inflicted injury in her tenacious old heart. A little water stood in her eyes. With a handkerchief of the finest lawn she wiped them stealthily.

"Well, Aunt Ann?" said a voice behind.

Soames Forsyte, flat-shouldered, clean-shaven, flat-cheeked, flat-waisted, yet with something round and secret about his whole appearance, looked downwards and aslant at Aunt Ann, as though trying to see through the side of his own nose.

"And what do you think of the engagement?" he asked.

Aunt Ann's eyes rested on him proudly; of all the nephews since young Jolyon's departure from the family nest, he was now her favourite, for she recognised in him a sure trustee of the family soul that must so soon slip beyond her keeping.

"Very nice for the young man," she said; "and he's a good-looking young fellow; but I doubt if he's quite the right lover for dear June."

Soames touched the edge of a gold-lacquered lustre.

"She'll tame him," he said, stealthily wetting his finger and rubbing it on the knobby bulbs. "That's genuine old lacquer; you can't get it nowadays. It'd do well in a sale at Jobson's." He spoke with relish, as though he felt that he was cheering up his old aunt. It was seldom he was so confidential. "I wouldn't mind having it myself," he added; "you can always get your price for old lacquer."

"You're so clever with all those things," said Aunt Ann. "And how is dear Irene?"

Soames's smile died.

"Pretty well," he said. "Complains she can't sleep; she sleeps a great deal better than I do," and he looked at his wife, who was talking to Bosinney by the door.

Aunt Ann sighed.

"Perhaps," she said, "it will be just as well for her not to see so much of June. She's such a decided character, dear June!"

Soames flushed; his flushes passed rapidly over his flat cheeks and centered between his eyes, where they remained, the stamp of disturbing thoughts.

"I don't know what she sees in that little flibbertigibbet," he burst out, but noticing that they were no longer alone, he turned and again began examining the lustre.

"They tell me Jolyon's bought another house," said his father's voice close by; "he must have a lot of money—he must have more money than he knows what to do with! Montpellier Square, they say; close to Soames! They never told me, Irene never tells me anything!"

"Capital position, not two minutes from me," said the voice of Swithin, "and from my rooms I can drive to the Club in eight."

The position of their houses was of vital importance to the Forsytes, nor was this remarkable, since the whole spirit of their success was embodied therein.

Their father, of farming stock, had come from Dorsetshire near the beginning of the century.

'Superior Dosset Forsyte, as he was called by his intimates, had been a stonemason by trade, and risen to the position of a master-builder.

Towards the end of his life he moved to London, where, building on until he died, he was buried at Highgate. He left over thirty thousand pounds between his ten children. Old Jolyon alluded to him, if at all, as 'A hard, thick sort of man; not much refinement about him.' The second generation of Forsytes felt indeed that he was not greatly to their credit. The only aristocratic trait they could find in his character was a habit of drinking Madeira.

Aunt Hester, an authority on family history, described him thus: "I don't recollect that he ever did anything; at least, not in my time. He was er—an owner of houses, my dear. His hair about your Uncle Swithin's colour; rather a square build. Tall? No—not very tall" (he had been five feet five, with a mottled face); "a fresh-coloured man. I remember he used to drink Madeira; but ask your Aunt Ann. What was his father? He—er—had to do with the land down in Dorsetshire, by the sea."

James once went down to see for himself what sort of place this was that they had come from. He found two old farms, with a cart track rutted into the pink earth, leading down to a mill by the beach; a little grey church with a buttressed outer wall, and a smaller and greyer chapel. The stream which worked the mill came bubbling down in a dozen rivulets, and pigs were hunting round that estuary. A haze hovered over the prospect. Down this hollow, with their feet deep in the mud and their faces towards the sea, it appeared that the primeval Forsytes had been content to walk Sunday after Sunday for hundreds of years.

Whether or no James had cherished hopes of an inheritance, or of something rather distinguished to be found down there, he came back to town in a poor way, and went about with a pathetic attempt at making the best of a bad job.

"There's very little to be had out of that," he said; "regular country little place, old as the hills...."

Its age was felt to be a comfort. Old Jolyon, in whom a desperate honesty welled up at times, would allude to his ancestors as: "Yeomen—I suppose very small beer." Yet he would repeat the word 'yeomen' as if it afforded him consolation.

They had all done so well for themselves, these Forsytes, that they were all what is called 'of a certain position.' They had shares in all sorts of things, not as yet—with the exception of Timothy—in consols, for they had no dread in life like that of 3 per cent. for their money. They collected pictures, too, and were supporters of such charitable institutions as might be beneficial to their sick domestics. From their father, the builder, they inherited a talent for bricks and mortar. Originally, perhaps, members of some primitive sect, they were now in the natural course of things members of the Church of England, and caused their wives and children to attend with some regularity the more fashionable churches of the Metropolis. To have doubted their Christianity would have caused them both pain and surprise. Some of them paid for pews, thus expressing in the most practical form their sympathy with the teachings of Christ.

Their residences, placed at stated intervals round the park, watched like sentinels, lest the fair heart of this London, where their desires were fixed, should slip from their clutches, and leave them lower in their own estimations.

There was old Jolyon in Stanhope Place; the Jameses in Park Lane; Swithin in the lonely glory of orange and blue chambers in Hyde Park Mansions—he had never married, not he—the Soameses in their nest off Knightsbridge; the Rogers in Prince's Gardens (Roger was that remarkable Forsyte who had conceived and carried out the notion of bringing up his four sons to a new profession. "Collect house property, nothing like it," he would say; "I never did anything else").

The Haymans again—Mrs. Hayman was the one married Forsyte sister—in a house high up on Campden Hill, shaped like a giraffe, and so tall that it gave the observer a crick in the neck; the Nicholases in Ladbroke Grove, a spacious abode and a great bargain; and last, but not least, Timothy's on the Bayswater Road, where Ann, and Juley, and Hester, lived under his protection.

But all this time James was musing, and now he inquired of his host and brother what he had given for that house in Montpellier Square. He himself had had his eye on a house there for the last two years, but they wanted such a price.

Old Jolyon recounted the details of his purchase.

"Twenty-two years to run?" repeated James; "The very house I was after—you've given too much for it!"

Old Jolyon frowned.

"It's not that I want it," said James hastily; "it wouldn't suit my purpose at that price. Soames knows the house, well—he'll tell you it's too dear—his opinion's worth having."

"I don't," said old Jolyon, "care a fig for his opinion."

"Well," murmured James, "you will have your own way—it's a good opinion. Good-bye! We're going to drive down to Hurlingham. They tell me June's going to Wales. You'll be lonely tomorrow. What'll you do with yourself? You'd better come and dine with us!"

Old Jolyon refused. He went down to the front door and saw them into their barouche, and twinkled at them, having already forgotten his spleen—Mrs. James facing the horses, tall and majestic with auburn hair; on her left, Irene—the two husbands, father and son, sitting forward, as though they expected something, opposite their wives. Bobbing and bounding upon the spring cushions, silent, swaying to each motion of their chariot, old Jolyon watched them drive away under the sunlight.

During the drive the silence was broken by Mrs. James.

"Did you ever see such a collection of rumty-too people?"

Soames, glancing at her beneath his eyelids, nodded, and he saw Irene steal at him one of her unfathomable looks. It is likely enough that each branch of the Forsyte family made that remark as they drove away from old Jolyon's 'At Home!'

Amongst the last of the departing guests the fourth and fifth brothers, Nicholas and Roger, walked away together, directing their steps alongside Hyde Park towards the Praed Street Station of the Underground. Like all other Forsytes of a certain age they kept carriages of their own, and never took cabs if by any means they could avoid it.

The day was bright, the trees of the Park in the full beauty of mid-June foliage; the brothers did not seem to notice phenomena, which contributed, nevertheless, to the jauntiness of promenade and conversation.

"Yes," said Roger, "she's a good-lookin' woman, that wife of Soames's. I'm told they don't get on."

This brother had a high forehead, and the freshest colour of any of the Forsytes; his light grey eyes measured the street frontage of the houses by the way, and now and then he would level his, umbrella and take a 'lunar,' as he expressed it, of the varying heights.

"She'd no money," replied Nicholas.

He himself had married a good deal of money, of which, it being then the golden age before the Married Women's Property Act, he had mercifully been enabled to make a successful use.

"What was her father?"

"Heron was his name, a Professor, so they tell me."

Roger shook his head.

"There's no money in that," he said.

"They say her mother's father was cement."

Roger's face brightened.

"But he went bankrupt," went on Nicholas.

"Ah!" exclaimed Roger, "Soames will have trouble with her; you mark my words, he'll have trouble—she's got a foreign look."

Nicholas licked his lips.

"She's a pretty woman," and he waved aside a crossing-sweeper.

"How did he get hold of her?" asked Roger presently. "She must cost him a pretty penny in dress!"

"Ann tells me," replied Nicholas, "he was half-cracked about her. She refused him five times. James, he's nervous about it, I can see."

"Ah!" said Roger again; "I'm sorry for James; he had trouble with Dartie." His pleasant colour was heightened by exercise, he swung his umbrella to the level of his eye more frequently than ever. Nicholas's face also wore a pleasant look.

"Too pale for me," he said, "but her figure's capital!"

Roger made no reply.

"I call her distinguished-looking," he said at last—it was the highest praise in the Forsyte vocabulary. "That young Bosinney will never do any good for himself. They say at Burkitt's he's one of these artistic chaps—got an idea of improving English architecture; there's no money in that! I should like to hear what Timothy would say to it."

They entered the station.

"What class are you going? I go second."

"No second for me," said Nicholas;—"you never know what you may catch."

He took a first-class ticket to Notting Hill Gate; Roger a second to South Kensington. The train coming in a minute later, the two brothers parted and entered their respective compartments. Each felt aggrieved that the other had not modified his habits to secure his society a little longer; but as Roger voiced it in his thoughts:

'Always a stubborn beggar, Nick!'

And as Nicholas expressed it to himself:

'Cantankerous chap Roger—always was!'

There was little sentimentality about the Forsytes. In that great London, which they had conquered and become merged in, what time had they to be sentimental?

CHAPTER II—OLD JOLYON GOES TO THE OPERA

At five o'clock the following day old Jolyon sat alone, a cigar between his lips, and on a table by his side a cup of tea. He was tired, and before he had finished his cigar he fell asleep. A fly settled on his hair, his breathing sounded heavy in the drowsy silence, his upper lip under the white moustache puffed in and out. From between the fingers of his veined and wrinkled hand the cigar, dropping on the empty hearth, burned itself out.

The gloomy little study, with windows of stained glass to exclude the view, was full of dark green velvet and heavily-carved mahogany—a suite of which old Jolyon was wont to say: 'Shouldn't wonder if it made a big price some day!'

It was pleasant to think that in the after life he could get more for things than he had given.

In the rich brown atmosphere peculiar to back rooms in the mansion of a Forsyte, the Rembrandtesque effect of his great head, with its white hair, against the cushion of his high-backed seat, was spoiled by the moustache, which imparted a somewhat military look to his face. An old clock that had been with him since before his marriage forty years ago kept with its ticking a jealous record of the seconds slipping away forever from its old master.

He had never cared for this room, hardly going into it from one year's end to another, except to take cigars from the Japanese cabinet in the corner, and the room now had its revenge.

His temples, curving like thatches over the hollows beneath, his cheek-bones and chin, all were sharpened in his sleep, and there had come upon his face the confession that he was an old man.

He woke. June had gone! James had said he would be lonely. James had always been a poor thing. He recollected with satisfaction that he had bought that house over James's head.

Serve him right for sticking at the price; the only thing the fellow thought of was money. Had he given too much, though? It wanted a lot of doing to—He dared say he would want all his money before he had done with this affair of June's. He ought never to have allowed the engagement. She had met this Bosinney at the house of Baynes, Baynes and Bildeboy, the architects. He believed that Baynes, whom he knew—a bit of an old woman—was the young man's uncle by marriage. After that she'd been always running after him; and when she took a thing into her head there was no stopping her. She was continually taking up with 'lame ducks' of one sort or another. This fellow had no money, but she must needs become engaged to him—a harumscarum, unpractical chap, who would get himself into no end of difficulties.

She had come to him one day in her slap-dash way and told him; and, as if it were any consolation, she had added:

"He's so splendid; he's often lived on cocoa for a week!"

"And he wants you to live on cocoa too?"

"Oh no; he is getting into the swim now."

Old Jolyon had taken his cigar from under his white moustaches, stained by coffee at the edge, and looked at her, that little slip of a thing who had got such a grip of his heart. He knew more about 'swims' than his granddaughter. But she, having clasped her hands on his knees, rubbed her chin against him, making a sound like a purring cat. And, knocking the ash off his cigar, he had exploded in nervous desperation:

"You're all alike: you won't be satisfied till you've got what you want. If you must come to grief, you must; I wash my hands of it."

So, he had washed his hands of it, making the condition that they should not marry until Bosinney had at least four hundred a year.

"I shan't be able to give you very much," he had said, a formula to which June was not unaccustomed. "Perhaps this What's-his-name will provide the cocoa."

He had hardly seen anything of her since it began. A bad business! He had no notion of giving her a lot of money to enable a fellow he knew nothing about to live on in idleness. He had seen that sort of thing before; no good ever came of it. Worst of all, he had no hope of shaking her resolution; she was as obstinate as a mule, always had been from a child. He didn't see where it was to end. They must cut their coat according to their cloth. He would not give way till he saw young Bosinney with an income of his own. That June would have trouble with the fellow was as plain as a pikestaff; he had no more idea of money than a cow. As to this rushing down to Wales to visit the young man's aunts, he fully expected they were old cats.

And, motionless, old Jolyon stared at the wall; but for his open eyes, he might have been asleep.... The idea of supposing that young cub Soames could give him advice! He had always been a cub, with his nose in the air! He would be setting up as a man of property next, with a place in the country! A man of property! H'mph! Like his father, he was always nosing out bargains, a cold-blooded young beggar!

He rose, and, going to the cabinet, began methodically stocking his cigar-case from a bundle fresh in. They were not bad at the price, but you couldn't get a good cigar, nowadays, nothing to hold a candle to those old Superfinos of Hanson and Bridger's. That was a cigar!

The thought, like some stealing perfume, carried him back to those wonderful nights at Richmond when after dinner he sat smoking on the terrace of the Crown and Sceptre with

Nicholas Treffry and Traquair and Jack Herring and Anthony Thornworthy. How good his cigars were then! Poor old Nick!—dead, and Jack Herring—dead, and Traquair—dead of that wife of his, and Thornworthy—awfully shaky (no wonder, with his appetite).

Of all the company of those days he himself alone seemed left, except Swithin, of course, and he so outrageously big there was no doing anything with him.

Difficult to believe it was so long ago; he felt young still! Of all his thoughts, as he stood there counting his cigars, this was the most poignant, the most bitter. With his white head and his loneliness he had remained young and green at heart. And those Sunday afternoons on Hampstead Heath, when young Jolyon and he went for a stretch along the Spaniard's Road to Highgate, to Child's Hill, and back over the Heath again to dine at Jack Straw's Castle—how delicious his cigars were then! And such weather! There was no weather now.

When June was a toddler of five, and every other Sunday he took her to the Zoo, away from the society of those two good women, her mother and her grandmother, and at the top of the bear den baited his umbrella with buns for her favourite bears, how sweet his cigars were then!

Cigars! He had not even succeeded in out-living his palate—the famous palate that in the fifties men swore by, and speaking of him, said: "Forsyte's the best palate in London!" The palate that in a sense had made his fortune—the fortune of the celebrated tea men, Forsyte and Treffry, whose tea, like no other man's tea, had a romantic aroma, the charm of a quite singular genuineness. About the house of Forsyte and Treffry in the City had clung an air of enterprise and mystery, of special dealings in special ships, at special ports, with special Orientals.

He had worked at that business! Men did work in those days! these young pups hardly knew the meaning of the word. He had gone into every detail, known everything that went on, sometimes sat up all night over it. And he had always chosen his agents himself, prided himself on it. His eye for men, he used to say, had been the secret of his success, and the exercise of this masterful power of selection had been the only part of it all that he had really liked. Not a career for a man of his ability. Even now, when the business had been turned into a Limited Liability Company, and was declining (he had got out of his shares long ago), he felt a sharp chagrin in thinking of that time. How much better he might have done! He would have succeeded splendidly at the Bar! He had even thought of standing for Parliament. How often had not Nicholas Treffry said to him:

"You could do anything, Jo, if you weren't so d-damned careful of yourself!" Dear old Nick! Such a good fellow, but a racketty chap! The notorious Treffry! He had never taken any care of himself. So he was dead. Old Jolyon counted his cigars with a steady hand, and it came into his mind to wonder if perhaps he had been too careful of himself.

He put the cigar-case in the breast of his coat, buttoned it in, and walked up the long flights to his bedroom, leaning on one foot and the other, and helping himself by the bannister. The house was too big. After June was married, if she ever did marry this fellow, as he supposed she would, he would let it and go into rooms. What was the use of keeping half a dozen servants eating their heads off?

The butler came to the ring of his bell—a large man with a beard, a soft tread, and a peculiar capacity for silence. Old Jolyon told him to put his dress clothes out; he was going to dine at the Club.

How long had the carriage been back from taking Miss June to the station? Since two? Then let him come round at half-past six!

The Club which old Jolyon entered on the stroke of seven was one of those political institutions of the upper middle class which have seen better days. In spite of being talked about, perhaps in consequence of being talked about, it betrayed a disappointing vitality. People had grown tired of saying that the 'Disunion' was on its last legs. Old Jolyon would say it, too, yet disregarded the fact in a manner truly irritating to well-constituted Clubmen.

"Why do you keep your name on?" Swithin often asked him with profound vexation. "Why don't you join the 'Polyglot'? You can't get a wine like our Heidsieck under twenty shillin' a bottle anywhere in London;" and, dropping his voice, he added: "There's only five hundred dozen left. I drink it every night of my life."

"I'll think of it," old Jolyon would answer; but when he did think of it there was always the question of fifty guineas entrance fee, and it would take him four or five years to get in. He continued to think of it.

He was too old to be a Liberal, had long ceased to believe in the political doctrines of his Club, had even been known to allude to them as 'wretched stuff,' and it afforded him pleasure to continue a member in the teeth of principles so opposed to his own. He had always had a contempt for the place, having joined it many years ago when they refused to have him at the 'Hotch Potch' owing to his being 'in trade.' As if he were not as good as any of them! He naturally despised the Club that did take him. The members were a poor lot, many of them in the City—stockbrokers, solicitors, auctioneers—what not! Like most men of strong character but not too much originality, old Jolyon set small store by the class to which he belonged. Faithfully he followed their customs, social and otherwise, and secretly he thought them 'a common lot.'

Years and philosophy, of which he had his share, had dimmed the recollection of his defeat at the 'Hotch Potch'; and now in his thoughts it was enshrined as the Queen of Clubs. He would have been a member all these years himself, but, owing to the slipshod way his proposer, Jack Herring, had gone to work, they had not known what they were doing in keeping him out. Why! they had taken his son Jo at once, and he believed the boy was still a member; he had received a letter dated from there eight years ago.

He had not been near the 'Disunion' for months, and the house had undergone the piebald decoration which people bestow on old houses and old ships when anxious to sell them.

'Beastly colour, the smoking-room!' he thought. 'The dining-room is good!'

Its gloomy chocolate, picked out with light green, took his fancy.

He ordered dinner, and sat down in the very corner, at the very table perhaps! (things did not progress much at the 'Disunion,' a Club of almost Radical principles) at which he and young Jolyon used to sit twenty-five years ago, when he was taking the latter to Drury Lane, during his holidays.

The boy had loved the theatre, and old Jolyon recalled how he used to sit opposite, concealing his excitement under a careful but transparent nonchalance.

He ordered himself, too, the very dinner the boy had always chosen-soup, whitebait, cutlets, and a tart. Ah! if he were only opposite now!

The two had not met for fourteen years. And not for the first time during those fourteen years old Jolyon wondered whether he had been a little to blame in the matter of his son. An unfortunate love-affair with that precious flirt Danae Thornworthy (now Danae Pellew), Anthony Thornworthy's daughter, had thrown him on the rebound into the arms of June's mother. He ought perhaps to have put a spoke in the wheel of their marriage; they were too young; but after that experience of Jo's susceptibility he had been only too anxious to see him married. And in four years the crash had come! To have approved his son's conduct in that crash was, of course, impossible; reason and training—that combination of potent factors which stood for his principles—told him of this impossibility, and his heart cried out. The grim remorselessness of that business had no pity for hearts. There was June, the atom with flaming hair, who had climbed all over him, twined and twisted herself about him—about his heart that was made to be the plaything and beloved resort of tiny, helpless things. With characteristic insight he saw he must part with one or with the other; no half-measures could serve in such a situation. In that lay its tragedy. And the tiny, helpless thing prevailed. He would not run with the hare and hunt with the hounds, and so to his son he said good-bye.

That good-bye had lasted until now.

He had proposed to continue a reduced allowance to young Jolyon, but this had been refused, and perhaps that refusal had hurt him more than anything, for with it had gone the last outlet of his penned-in affection; and there had come such tangible and solid proof of rupture as only a transaction in property, a bestowal or refusal of such, could supply.

His dinner tasted flat. His pint of champagne was dry and bitter stuff, not like the Veuve Clicquots of old days.

Over his cup of coffee, he bethought him that he would go to the opera. In the Times, therefore—he had a distrust of other papers—he read the announcement for the evening. It was 'Fidelio.'

Mercifully not one of those new-fangled German pantomimes by that fellow Wagner.

Putting on his ancient opera hat, which, with its brim flattened by use, and huge capacity, looked like an emblem of greater days, and, pulling out an old pair of very thin lavender kid gloves smelling strongly of Russia leather, from habitual proximity to the cigar-case in the pocket of his overcoat, he stepped into a hansom.

The cab rattled gaily along the streets, and old Jolyon was struck by their unwonted animation.

'The hotels must be doing a tremendous business,' he thought. A few years ago there had been none of these big hotels. He made a satisfactory reflection on some property he had in the neighbourhood. It must be going up in value by leaps and bounds! What traffic!

But from that he began indulging in one of those strange impersonal speculations, so uncharacteristic of a Forsyte, wherein lay, in part, the secret of his supremacy amongst them. What atoms men were, and what a lot of them! And what would become of them all?

He stumbled as he got out of the cab, gave the man his exact fare, walked up to the ticket office to take his stall, and stood there with his purse in his hand—he always carried his money in a purse, never having approved of that habit of carrying it loosely in the pockets, as so many young men did nowadays. The official leaned out, like an old dog from a kennel.

"Why," he said in a surprised voice, "it's Mr. Jolyon Forsyte! So it is! Haven't seen you, sir, for years. Dear me! Times aren't what they were. Why! you and your brother, and that auctioneer—Mr. Traquair, and Mr. Nicholas Treffry—you used to have six or seven stalls here regular every season. And how are you, sir? We don't get younger!"

The colour in old Jolyon's eyes deepened; he paid his guinea. They had not forgotten him. He marched in, to the sounds of the overture, like an old war-horse to battle.

Folding his opera hat, he sat down, drew out his lavender gloves in the old way, and took up his glasses for a long look round the house. Dropping them at last on his folded hat, he fixed his eyes on the curtain. More poignantly than ever he felt that it was all over and done with him. Where were all the women, the pretty women, the house used to be so full of? Where was that old feeling in the heart as he waited for one of those great singers? Where that sensation of the intoxication of life and of his own power to enjoy it all?

The greatest opera-goer of his day! There was no opera now! That fellow Wagner had ruined everything; no melody left, nor any voices to sing it. Ah! the wonderful singers! Gone! He sat watching the old scenes acted, a numb feeling at his heart.

From the curl of silver over his ear to the pose of his foot in its elastic-sided patent boot, there was nothing clumsy or weak about old Jolyon. He was as upright—very nearly—as in those old times when he came every night; his sight was as good—almost as good. But what a feeling of weariness and disillusion!

He had been in the habit all his life of enjoying things, even imperfect things—and there had been many imperfect things—he had enjoyed them all with moderation, so as to keep himself young. But now he was deserted by his power of enjoyment, by his philosophy, and left with this dreadful feeling that it was all done with. Not even the Prisoners' Chorus, nor Florian's Song, had the power to dispel the gloom of his loneliness.

If Jo were only with him! The boy must be forty by now. He had wasted fourteen years out of the life of his only son. And Jo was no longer a social pariah. He was married. Old Jolyon had been unable to refrain from marking his appreciation of the action by enclosing his son a cheque for L.500. The cheque had been returned in a letter from the 'Hotch Potch,' couched in these words.

'MY DEAREST FATHER,

'Your generous gift was welcome as a sign that you might think worse of me. I return it, but should you think fit to invest it for the benefit of the little chap (we call him Jolly), who bears our Christian and, by courtesy, our surname, I shall be very glad.

'I hope with all my heart that your health is as good as ever.

'Your loving son,

'Jo.'

The letter was like the boy. He had always been an amiable chap. Old Jolyon had sent this reply:

'MY DEAR JO,

'The sum (L.500) stands in my books for the benefit of your boy, under the name of Jolyon Forsyte, and will be duly-credited with interest at 5 per cent. I hope that you are doing well. My health remains good at present.

'With love, I am,

'Your affectionate Father,

'JOLYON FORSYTE.'

And every year on the 1st of January he had added a hundred and the interest. The sum was mounting up—next New Year's Day it would be fifteen hundred and odd pounds! And it is difficult to say how much satisfaction he had got out of that yearly transaction. But the correspondence had ended.

In spite of his love for his son, in spite of an instinct, partly constitutional, partly the result, as in thousands of his class, of the continual handling and watching of affairs, prompting him to judge conduct by results rather than by principle, there was at the bottom of his heart a sort of uneasiness. His son ought, under the circumstances, to have gone to the dogs; that law was laid down in all the novels, sermons, and plays he had ever read, heard, or witnessed.

After receiving the cheque back there seemed to him to be something wrong somewhere. Why had his son not gone to the dogs? But, then, who could tell?

He had heard, of course—in fact, he had made it his business to find out—that Jo lived in St. John's Wood, that he had a little house in Wistaria Avenue with a garden, and took his wife about with him into society—a queer sort of society, no doubt—and that they had two children—the little chap they called Jolly (considering the circumstances the name struck him as cynical, and old Jolyon both feared and disliked cynicism), and a girl called Holly, born since the marriage. Who could tell what his son's circumstances really were? He had capitalized the income he had inherited from his mother's father and joined Lloyd's as an underwriter; he painted pictures, too—water-colours. Old Jolyon knew this, for he had surreptitiously bought them from time to time, after chancing to see his son's name signed at the bottom of a representation of the river Thames in a dealer's window. He thought them bad, and did not hang them because of the signature; he kept them locked up in a drawer.

In the great opera-house a terrible yearning came on him to see his son. He remembered the days when he had been wont to slide him, in a brown holland suit, to and fro under the arch of his legs; the times when he ran beside the boy's pony, teaching him to ride; the day he first took him to school. He had been a loving, lovable little chap! After he went to Eton he had acquired, perhaps, a little too much of that desirable manner which old Jolyon knew was only to be obtained at such places and at great expense; but he had always been companionable. Always a companion, even after Cambridge—a little far off, perhaps, owing to the advantages he had received. Old Jolyon's feeling towards our public schools and 'Varsities never wavered, and he retained touchingly his attitude of admiration and mistrust towards a system appropriate to the highest in the land, of which he had not himself been privileged to partake.... Now that June had gone and left, or as good as left him, it would have been a comfort to see his son again. Guilty of this treason to his family, his principles, his class, old Jolyon fixed his eyes on the singer. A poor thing—a wretched poor thing! And the Florian a perfect stick!

It was over. They were easily pleased nowadays!

In the crowded street he snapped up a cab under the very nose of a stout and much younger gentleman, who had already assumed it to be his own. His route lay through Pall Mall, and at the corner, instead of going through the Green Park, the cabman turned to drive up St. James's Street. Old Jolyon put his hand through the trap (he could not bear being taken out of his way); in turning, however, he found himself opposite the 'Hotch Potch,' and the yearning that had been secretly with him the whole evening prevailed. He called to the driver to stop. He would go in and ask if Jo still belonged there.

He went in. The hall looked exactly as it did when he used to dine there with Jack Herring, and they had the best cook in London; and he looked round with the shrewd, straight glance that had caused him all his life to be better served than most men.

"Mr. Jolyon Forsyte still a member here?"

"Yes, sir; in the Club now, sir. What name?"

Old Jolyon was taken aback.

"His father," he said.

And having spoken, he took his stand, back to the fireplace.

Young Jolyon, on the point of leaving the Club, had put on his hat, and was in the act of crossing the hall, as the porter met him. He was no longer young, with hair going grey, and face—a narrower replica of his father's, with the same large drooping moustache—decidedly worn. He turned pale. This meeting was terrible after all those years, for nothing in the world was so terrible as a scene. They met and crossed hands without a word. Then, with a quaver in his voice, the father said:

"How are you, my boy?"

The son answered:

"How are you, Dad?"

Old Jolyon's hand trembled in its thin lavender glove.

"If you're going my way," he said, "I can give you a lift."

And as though in the habit of taking each other home every night they went out and stepped into the cab.

To old Jolyon it seemed that his son had grown. 'More of a man altogether,' was his comment. Over the natural amiability of that son's face had come a rather sardonic mask, as though he had found in the circumstances of his life the necessity for armour. The features were certainly those of a Forsyte, but the expression was more the introspective look of a student or philosopher. He had no doubt been obliged to look into himself a good deal in the course of those fifteen years.

To young Jolyon the first sight of his father was undoubtedly a shock—he looked so worn and old. But in the cab he seemed hardly to have changed, still having the calm look so well remembered, still being upright and keen-eyed.

"You look well, Dad."

"Middling," old Jolyon answered.

He was the prey of an anxiety that he found he must put into words. Having got his son back like this, he felt he must know what was his financial position.

"Jo," he said, "I should like to hear what sort of water you're in. I suppose you're in debt?"

He put it this way that his son might find it easier to confess.

Young Jolyon answered in his ironical voice:

"No! I'm not in debt!"

Old Jolyon saw that he was angry, and touched his hand. He had run a risk. It was worth it, however, and Jo had never been sulky with him. They drove on, without speaking again, to Stanhope Gate. Old Jolyon invited him in, but young Jolyon shook his head.

"June's not here," said his father hastily: "went off to-day on a visit. I suppose you know that she's engaged to be married?"

"Already?" murmured young Jolyon'.

Old Jolyon stepped out, and, in paying the cab fare, for the first time in his life gave the driver a sovereign in mistake for a shilling.

Placing the coin in his mouth, the cabman whipped his horse secretly on the underneath and hurried away.

Old Jolyon turned the key softly in the lock, pushed open the door, and beckoned. His son saw him gravely hanging up his coat, with an expression on his face like that of a boy who intends to steal cherries.

The door of the dining-room was open, the gas turned low; a spirit-urn hissed on a tea-tray, and close to it a cynical looking cat had fallen asleep on the dining-table. Old Jolyon 'shoo'd' her off at once. The incident was a relief to his feelings; he rattled his opera hat behind the animal.

"She's got fleas," he said, following her out of the room. Through the door in the hall leading to the basement he called "Hssst!" several times, as though assisting the cat's departure, till by some strange coincidence the butler appeared below.

"You can go to bed, Parfitt," said old Jolyon. "I will lock up and put out."

When he again entered the dining-room the cat unfortunately preceded him, with her tail in the air, proclaiming that she had seen through this manoeuvre for suppressing the butler from the first....

A fatality had dogged old Jolyon's domestic stratagems all his life.

Young Jolyon could not help smiling. He was very well versed in irony, and everything that evening seemed to him ironical. The episode of the cat; the announcement of his own daughter's engagement. So he had no more part or parcel in her than he had in the Puss! And the poetical justice of this appealed to him.

"What is June like now?" he asked.

"She's a little thing," returned old Jolyon; "they say she's like me, but that's their folly. She's more like your mother—the same eyes and hair."

"Ah! and she is pretty?"

Old Jolyon was too much of a Forsyte to praise anything freely; especially anything for which he had a genuine admiration.

"Not bad looking—a regular Forsyte chin. It'll be lonely here when she's gone, Jo."

The look on his face again gave young Jolyon the shock he had felt on first seeing his father.

"What will you do with yourself, Dad? I suppose she's wrapped up in him?"

"Do with myself?" repeated old Jolyon with an angry break in his voice. "It'll be miserable work living here alone. I don't know how it's to end. I wish to goodness...." He checked himself, and added: "The question is, what had I better do with this house?"

Young Jolyon looked round the room. It was peculiarly vast and dreary, decorated with the enormous pictures of still life that he remembered as a boy—sleeping dogs with their noses resting on bunches of carrots, together with onions and grapes lying side by side in mild surprise. The house was a white elephant, but he could not conceive of his father living in a smaller place; and all the more did it all seem ironical.

In his great chair with the book-rest sat old Jolyon, the figurehead of his family and class and creed, with his white head and dome-like forehead, the representative of moderation, and order, and love of property. As lonely an old man as there was in London.

There he sat in the gloomy comfort of the room, a puppet in the power of great forces that cared nothing for family or class or creed, but moved, machine-like, with dread processes to inscrutable ends. This was how it struck young Jolyon, who had the impersonal eye.

The poor old Dad! So this was the end, the purpose to which he had lived with such magnificent moderation! To be lonely, and grow older and older, yearning for a soul to speak to!

In his turn old Jolyon looked back at his son. He wanted to talk about many things that he had been unable to talk about all these years. It had been impossible to seriously confide in June his conviction that property in the Soho quarter would go up in value; his uneasiness about that tremendous silence of Pippin, the superintendent of the New Colliery Company, of which he had so long been chairman; his disgust at the steady fall in American Golgothas, or even to discuss how, by some sort of settlement, he could best avoid the payment of those death duties which would follow his decease. Under the influence, however, of a cup of tea, which he seemed to stir indefinitely, he began to speak at last. A new vista of life was thus opened up, a promised land of talk, where he could find a harbour against the waves of anticipation and regret; where he could soothe his soul with the opium of devising how to round off his property and make eternal the only part of him that was to remain alive.

Young Jolyon was a good listener; it was his great quality. He kept his eyes fixed on his father's face, putting a question now and then.

The clock struck one before old Jolyon had finished, and at the sound of its striking his principles came back. He took out his watch with a look of surprise:

"I must go to bed, Jo," he said.

Young Jolyon rose and held out his hand to help his father up. The old face looked worn and hollow again; the eyes were steadily averted.

"Good-bye, my boy; take care of yourself."

A moment passed, and young Jolyon, turning on his, heel, marched out at the door. He could hardly see; his smile quavered. Never in all the fifteen years since he had first found out that life was no simple business, had he found it so singularly complicated.

CHAPTER III—DINNER AT SWITHIN'S

In Swithin's orange and light-blue dining-room, facing the Park, the round table was laid for twelve.

A cut-glass chandelier filled with lighted candles hung like a giant stalactite above its centre, radiating over large gilt-framed mirrors, slabs of marble on the tops of side-tables, and heavy gold chairs with crewel worked seats. Everything betokened that love of beauty so deeply implanted in each family which has had its own way to make into Society, out of the more vulgar heart of Nature. Swithin had indeed an impatience of simplicity, a love of ormolu, which had always stamped him amongst his associates as a man of great, if somewhat luxurious taste; and out of the knowledge that no one could possibly enter his rooms without perceiving him to be a man of wealth, he had derived a solid and prolonged happiness such as perhaps no other circumstance in life had afforded him.

Since his retirement from land agency, a profession deplorable in his estimation, especially as to its auctioneering department, he had abandoned himself to naturally aristocratic tastes.

The perfect luxury of his latter days had embedded him like a fly in sugar; and his mind, where very little took place from morning till night, was the junction of two curiously opposite emotions, a lingering and sturdy satisfaction that he had made his own way and his own fortune, and a sense that a man of his distinction should never have been allowed to soil his mind with work.

He stood at the sideboard in a white waistcoat with large gold and onyx buttons, watching his valet screw the necks of three champagne bottles deeper into ice-pails. Between the points of his stand-up collar, which—though it hurt him to move—he would on no account have had altered, the pale flesh of his under chin remained immovable. His eyes roved from bottle to bottle. He was debating, and he argued like this: Jolyon drinks a glass, perhaps two, he's so careful of himself. James, he can't take his wine nowadays. Nicholas—Fanny and he would swill water he shouldn't wonder! Soames didn't count; these young nephews—Soames was thirty-one—couldn't drink! But Bosinney?

Encountering in the name of this stranger something outside the range of his philosophy, Swithin paused. A misgiving arose within him! It was impossible to tell! June was only a girl, in love too! Emily (Mrs. James) liked a good glass of champagne. It was too dry for Juley, poor old soul, she had no palate. As to Hatty Chessman! The thought of this old friend caused a cloud of thought to obscure the perfect glassiness of his eyes: He shouldn't wonder if she drank half a bottle!

But in thinking of his remaining guest, an expression like that of a cat who is just going to purr stole over his old face: Mrs. Soames! She mightn't take much, but she would appreciate what she drank; it was a pleasure to give her good wine! A pretty woman—and sympathetic to him!

The thought of her was like champagne itself! A pleasure to give a good wine to a young woman who looked so well, who knew how to dress, with charming manners, quite distinguished—a pleasure to entertain her. Between the points of his collar he gave his head the first small, painful oscillation of the evening.

"Adolf!" he said. "Put in another bottle."

He himself might drink a good deal, for, thanks to that prescription of Blight's, he found himself extremely well, and he had been careful to take no lunch. He had not felt so well for weeks. Puffing out his lower lip, he gave his last instructions:

"Adolf, the least touch of the West India when you come to the ham."

Passing into the anteroom, he sat down on the edge of a chair, with his knees apart; and his tall, bulky form was wrapped at once in an expectant, strange, primeval immobility. He was ready to rise at a moment's notice. He had not given a dinner-party for months. This dinner in honour of June's engagement had seemed a bore at first (among Forsytes the custom of solemnizing engagements by feasts was religiously observed), but the labours of sending invitations and ordering the repast over, he felt pleasantly stimulated.

And thus sitting, a watch in his hand, fat, and smooth, and golden, like a flattened globe of butter, he thought of nothing.

A long man, with side whiskers, who had once been in Swithin's service, but was now a greengrocer, entered and proclaimed:

"Mrs. Chessman, Mrs. Septimus Small!"

Two ladies advanced. The one in front, habited entirely in red, had large, settled patches of the same colour in her cheeks, and a hard, dashing eye. She walked at Swithin, holding out a hand cased in a long, primrose-coloured glove:

"Well! Swithin," she said, "I haven't seen you for ages. How are you? Why, my dear boy, how stout you're getting!"

The fixity of Swithin's eye alone betrayed emotion. A dumb and grumbling anger swelled his bosom. It was vulgar to be stout, to talk of being stout; he had a chest, nothing more. Turning to his sister, he grasped her hand, and said in a tone of command:

"Well, Juley."

Mrs. Septimus Small was the tallest of the four sisters; her good, round old face had gone a little sour; an innumerable pout clung all over it, as if it had been encased in an iron wire mask up to that evening, which, being suddenly removed, left little rolls of mutinous flesh all over her countenance. Even her eyes were pouting. It was thus that she recorded her permanent resentment at the loss of Septimus Small.

She had quite a reputation for saying the wrong thing, and, tenacious like all her breed, she would hold to it when she had said it, and add to it another wrong thing, and so on. With the decease of her husband the family tenacity, the family matter-of-factness, had gone sterile within her. A great talker, when allowed, she would converse without the faintest animation for hours together, relating, with epic monotony, the innumerable occasions on which Fortune had misused her; nor did she ever perceive that her hearers sympathized with Fortune, for her heart was kind.

Having sat, poor soul, long by the bedside of Small (a man of poor constitution), she had acquired, the habit, and there were countless subsequent occasions when she had sat immense periods of time to amuse sick people, children, and other helpless persons, and she could never divest herself of the feeling that the world was the most ungrateful place anybody could live in. Sunday after Sunday she sat at the feet of that extremely witty preacher, the Rev. Thomas Scoles, who exercised a great influence over her; but she succeeded in convincing everybody that even this was a misfortune. She had passed into a proverb in the family, and when anybody was observed to be peculiarly distressing, he was known as a regular 'Juley.' The habit of her mind would have killed anybody but a Forsyte at forty; but she was seventy-two, and had never looked better. And one felt that there were capacities for enjoyment about her which might yet come out. She owned three canaries, the cat Tommy, and half a parrot—in common with her sister Hester;—and these poor creatures (kept carefully out of Timothy's way—he was nervous about animals), unlike human beings, recognising that she could not help being blighted, attached themselves to her passionately.

She was sombrely magnificent this evening in black bombazine, with a mauve front cut in a shy triangle, and crowned with a black velvet ribbon round the base of her thin throat; black and mauve for evening wear was esteemed very chaste by nearly every Forsyte.

Pouting at Swithin, she said:

"Ann has been asking for you. You haven't been near us for an age!"

Swithin put his thumbs within the armholes of his waistcoat, and replied:

"Ann's getting very shaky; she ought to have a doctor!"

"Mr. and Mrs. Nicholas Forsyte!"

Nicholas Forsyte, cocking his rectangular eyebrows, wore a smile. He had succeeded during the day in bringing to fruition a scheme for the employment of a tribe from Upper India in the gold-mines of Ceylon. A pet plan, carried at last in the teeth of great difficulties—he was justly pleased. It would double the output of his mines, and, as he had often forcibly argued, all experience tended to show that a man must die; and whether he died of a miserable old age in his own country, or prematurely of damp in the bottom of a foreign mine, was surely of little consequence, provided that by a change in his mode of life he benefited the British Empire.

His ability was undoubted. Raising his broken nose towards his listener, he would add:

"For want of a few hundred of these fellows we haven't paid a dividend for years, and look at the price of the shares. I can't get ten shillings for them."

He had been at Yarmouth, too, and had come back feeling that he had added at least ten years to his own life. He grasped Swithin's hand, exclaiming in a jocular voice:

"Well, so here we are again!"

Mrs. Nicholas, an effete woman, smiled a smile of frightened jollity behind his back.

"Mr. and Mrs. James Forsyte! Mr. and Mrs. Soames Forsyte!"

Swithin drew his heels together, his deportment ever admirable.

"Well, James, well Emily! How are you, Soames? How do you do?"

His hand enclosed Irene's, and his eyes swelled. She was a pretty woman—a little too pale, but her figure, her eyes, her teeth! Too good for that chap Soames!

The gods had given Irene dark brown eyes and golden hair, that strange combination, provocative of men's glances, which is said to be the mark of a weak character. And the full, soft pallor of her neck and shoulders, above a gold-coloured frock, gave to her personality an alluring strangeness.

Soames stood behind, his eyes fastened on his wife's neck. The hands of Swithin's watch, which he still held open in his hand, had left eight behind; it was half an hour beyond his dinner-time—he had had no lunch—and a strange primeval impatience surged up within him.

"It's not like Jolyon to be late!" he said to Irene, with uncontrollable vexation. "I suppose it'll be June keeping him!"

"People in love are always late," she answered.

Swithin stared at her; a dusky orange dyed his cheeks.

"They've no business to be. Some fashionable nonsense!"

And behind this outburst the inarticulate violence of primitive generations seemed to mutter and grumble.

"Tell me what you think of my new star, Uncle Swithin," said Irene softly.

Among the lace in the bosom of her dress was shining a five-pointed star, made of eleven diamonds. Swithin looked at the star. He had a pretty taste in stones; no question could have been more sympathetically devised to distract his attention.

"Who gave you that?" he asked.

"Soames."

There was no change in her face, but Swithin's pale eyes bulged as though he might suddenly have been afflicted with insight.

"I dare say you're dull at home," he said. "Any day you like to come and dine with me, I'll give you as good a bottle of wine as you'll get in London."

"Miss June Forsyte—Mr. Jolyon Forsyte!... Mr. Boswainey!..."

Swithin moved his arm, and said in a rumbling voice:

"Dinner, now—dinner!"

He took in Irene, on the ground that he had not entertained her since she was a bride. June was the portion of Bosinney, who was placed between Irene and his fiancee. On the other side of June was James with Mrs. Nicholas, then old Jolyon with Mrs. James, Nicholas with Hatty Chessman, Soames with Mrs. Small, completing, the circle to Swithin again.

Family dinners of the Forsytes observe certain traditions. There are, for instance, no hors d'oeuvre. The reason for this is unknown. Theory among the younger members traces it to the disgraceful price of oysters; it is more probably due to a desire to come to the point, to a good practical sense deciding at once that hors d'oeuvre are but poor things. The Jameses alone, unable to withstand a custom almost universal in Park Lane, are now and then unfaithful.

A silent, almost morose, inattention to each other succeeds to the subsidence into their seats, lasting till well into the first entree, but interspersed with remarks such as, "Tom's bad again; I can't tell what's the matter with him!" "I suppose Ann doesn't come down in the mornings?"—"What's the name of your doctor, Fanny?" "Stubbs?" "He's a quack!"—"Winifred? She's got too many children. Four, isn't it? She's as thin as a lath!"—"What d'you give for this sherry, Swithin? Too dry for me!"

With the second glass of champagne, a kind of hum makes itself heard, which, when divested of casual accessories and resolved into its primal element, is found to be James telling a story, and this goes on for a long time, encroaching sometimes even upon what must universally be recognised as the crowning point of a Forsyte feast—'the saddle of mutton.'

No Forsyte has given a dinner without providing a saddle of mutton. There is something in its succulent solidity which makes it suitable to people 'of a certain position.' It is nourishing and tasty; the sort of thing a man remembers eating. It has a past and a future, like a deposit paid into a bank; and it is something that can be argued about.

Each branch of the family tenaciously held to a particular locality—old Jolyon swearing by Dartmoor, James by Welsh, Swithin by Southdown, Nicholas maintaining that people might sneer, but there was nothing like New Zealand! As for Roger, the 'original' of the brothers, he had been obliged to invent a locality of his own, and with an ingenuity worthy of a man who had devised a new profession for his sons, he had discovered a shop where they sold German; on being remonstrated with, he had proved his point by producing a butcher's bill, which showed that he paid more than any of the others. It was on this occasion that old Jolyon, turning to June, had said in one of his bursts of philosophy:

"You may depend upon it, they're a cranky lot, the Forsytes—and you'll find it out, as you grow older!"

Timothy alone held apart, for though he ate saddle of mutton heartily, he was, he said, afraid of it.

To anyone interested psychologically in Forsytes, this great saddle-of-mutton trait is of prime importance; not only does it illustrate their tenacity, both collectively and as individuals, but it marks them as belonging in fibre and instincts to that great class which believes in nourishment and flavour, and yields to no sentimental craving for beauty.

Younger members of the family indeed would have done without a joint altogether, preferring guinea-fowl, or lobster salad—something which appealed to the imagination, and had less nourishment—but these were females; or, if not, had been corrupted by their wives, or by mothers, who having been forced to eat saddle of mutton throughout their married lives, had passed a secret hostility towards it into the fibre of their sons.

The great saddle-of-mutton controversy at an end, a Tewkesbury ham commenced, together with the least touch of West Indian—Swithin was so long over this course that he caused a block in the progress of the dinner. To devote himself to it with better heart, he paused in his conversation.

From his seat by Mrs. Septimus Small Soames was watching. He had a reason of his own connected with a pet building scheme, for observing Bosinney. The architect might do for his purpose; he looked clever, as he sat leaning back in his chair, moodily making little ramparts with bread-crumbs. Soames noted his dress clothes to be well cut, but too small, as though made many years ago.

He saw him turn to Irene and say something and her face sparkle as he often saw it sparkle at other people—never at himself. He tried to catch what they were saying, but Aunt Juley was speaking.

Hadn't that always seemed very extraordinary to Soames? Only last Sunday dear Mr. Scole, had been so witty in his sermon, so sarcastic, "For what," he had said, "shall it profit a man if he gain his own soul, but lose all his property?" That, he had said, was the motto of the middle-class; now, what had he meant by that? Of course, it might be what middle-class people believed—she didn't know; what did Soames think?

He answered abstractedly: "How should I know? Scoles is a humbug, though, isn't he?" For Bosinney was looking round the table, as if pointing out the peculiarities of the guests, and Soames wondered what he was saying. By her smile Irene was evidently agreeing with his remarks. She seemed always to agree with other people.

Her eyes were turned on himself; Soames dropped his glance at once. The smile had died off her lips.

A humbug? But what did Soames mean? If Mr. Scoles was a humbug, a clergyman—then anybody might be—it was frightful!

"Well, and so they are!" said Soames.

During Aunt Juley's momentary and horrified silence he caught some words of Irene's that sounded like: 'Abandon hope, all ye who enter here!'

But Swithin had finished his ham.

"Where do you go for your mushrooms?" he was saying to Irene in a voice like a courtier's; "you ought to go to Smileybob's—he'll give 'em you fresh. These little men, they won't take the trouble!"

Irene turned to answer him, and Soames saw Bosinney watching her and smiling to himself. A curious smile the fellow had. A half-simple arrangement, like a child who smiles when he is pleased. As for George's nickname—'The Buccaneer'—he did not think much of that. And, seeing Bosinney turn to June, Soames smiled too, but sardonically—he did not like June, who was not looking too pleased.

This was not surprising, for she had just held the following conversation with James:

"I stayed on the river on my way home, Uncle James, and saw a beautiful site for a house."

James, a slow and thorough eater, stopped the process of mastication.

"Eh?" he said. "Now, where was that?"

"Close to Pangbourne."

James placed a piece of ham in his mouth, and June waited.

"I suppose you wouldn't know whether the land about there was freehold?" he asked at last. "You wouldn't know anything about the price of land about there?"

"Yes," said June; "I made inquiries." Her little resolute face under its copper crown was suspiciously eager and aglow.

James regarded her with the air of an inquisitor.

"What? You're not thinking of buying land!" he ejaculated, dropping his fork.

June was greatly encouraged by his interest. It had long been her pet plan that her uncles should benefit themselves and Bosinney by building country-houses.

"Of course not," she said. "I thought it would be such a splendid place for—you or—someone to build a country-house!"

James looked at her sideways, and placed a second piece of ham in his mouth....

"Land ought to be very dear about there," he said.

What June had taken for personal interest was only the impersonal excitement of every Forsyte who hears of something eligible in danger of passing into other hands. But she refused to see the disappearance of her chance, and continued to press her point.

"You ought to go into the country, Uncle James. I wish I had a lot of money, I wouldn't live another day in London."

James was stirred to the depths of his long thin figure; he had no idea his niece held such downright views.

"Why don't you go into the country?" repeated June; "it would do you a lot of good."

"Why?" began James in a fluster. "Buying land—what good d'you suppose I can do buying land, building houses?—I couldn't get four per cent. for my money!"

"What does that matter? You'd get fresh air."

"Fresh air!" exclaimed James; "what should I do with fresh air,"

"I should have thought anybody liked to have fresh air," said June scornfully.

James wiped his napkin all over his mouth.

"You don't know the value of money," he said, avoiding her eye.

"No! and I hope I never shall!" and, biting her lip with inexpressible mortification, poor June was silent.

Why were her own relations so rich, and Phil never knew where the money was coming from for to-morrow's tobacco. Why couldn't they do something for him? But they were so selfish. Why couldn't they build country-houses? She had all that naive dogmatism which is so pathetic, and sometimes achieves such great results. Bosinney, to whom she turned in her discomfiture, was talking to Irene, and a chill fell on June's spirit. Her eyes grew steady with anger, like old Jolyon's when his will was crossed.

James, too, was much disturbed. He felt as though someone had threatened his right to invest his money at five per cent. Jolyon had spoiled her. None of his girls would have said such a thing. James had always been exceedingly liberal to his children, and the consciousness of this made him feel it all the more deeply. He trifled moodily with his strawberries, then, deluging them with cream, he ate them quickly; they, at all events, should not escape him.

No wonder he was upset. Engaged for fifty-four years (he had been admitted a solicitor on the earliest day sanctioned by the law) in arranging mortgages, preserving investments at a dead level of high and safe interest, conducting negotiations on the principle of securing the utmost possible out of other people compatible with safety to his clients and himself, in calculations as to the exact pecuniary possibilities of all the relations of life, he had come at last to think purely in terms of money. Money was now his light, his medium for seeing, that without which he was really unable to see, really not cognisant of phenomena; and to have this thing, "I hope I shall never know the value of money!" said to his face, saddened and exasperated him. He knew it to be nonsense, or it would have frightened him. What was the world coming to! Suddenly recollecting the story of young Jolyon, however, he felt a little comforted, for what could you expect with a father like that! This turned his thoughts into a channel still less pleasant. What was all this talk about Soames and Irene?

As in all self-respecting families, an emporium had been established where family secrets were bartered, and family stock priced. It was known on Forsyte 'Change that Irene regretted her marriage. Her regret was disapproved of. She ought to have known her own mind; no dependable woman made these mistakes.

James reflected sourly that they had a nice house (rather small) in an excellent position, no children, and no money troubles. Soames was reserved about his affairs, but he must be getting a very warm man. He had a capital income from the business—for Soames, like his father, was a member of that well-known firm of solicitors, Forsyte, Bustard and Forsyte— and had always been very careful. He had done quite unusually well with some mortgages he had taken up, too—a little timely foreclosure—most lucky hits!

There was no reason why Irene should not be happy, yet they said she'd been asking for a separate room. He knew where that ended. It wasn't as if Soames drank.

James looked at his daughter-in-law. That unseen glance of his was cold and dubious. Appeal and fear were in it, and a sense of personal grievance. Why should he be worried like this? It was very likely all nonsense; women were funny things! They exaggerated so, you didn't know what to believe; and then, nobody told him anything, he had to find out everything for himself. Again he looked furtively at Irene, and across from her to Soames. The latter, listening to Aunt Juley, was looking up, under his brows in the direction of Bosinney.

'He's fond of her, I know,' thought James. 'Look at the way he's always giving her things.'

And the extraordinary unreasonableness of her disaffection struck him with increased force.

It was a pity, too, she was a taking little thing, and he, James, would be really quite fond of her if she'd only let him. She had taken up lately with June; that was doing her no good, that was certainly doing her no good. She was getting to have opinions of her own. He didn't know what she wanted with anything of the sort. She'd a good home, and everything she could wish for. He felt that her friends ought to be chosen for her. To go on like this was dangerous.

June, indeed, with her habit of championing the unfortunate, had dragged from Irene a confession, and, in return, had preached the necessity of facing the evil, by separation, if need be. But in the face of these exhortations, Irene had kept a brooding silence, as though she found terrible the thought of this struggle carried through in cold blood. He would never give her up, she had said to June.

"Who cares?" June cried; "let him do what he likes—you've only to stick to it!" And she had not scrupled to say something of this sort at Timothy's; James, when he heard of it, had felt a natural indignation and horror.

What if Irene were to take it into her head to—he could hardly frame the thought—to leave Soames? But he felt this thought so unbearable that he at once put it away; the shady visions it conjured up, the sound of family tongues buzzing in his ears, the horror of the conspicuous happening so close to him, to one of his own children! Luckily, she had no money—a beggarly fifty pound a year! And he thought of the deceased Heron, who had had nothing to leave her, with contempt. Brooding over his glass, his long legs twisted under the table, he quite omitted to rise when the ladies left the room. He would have to speak to Soames—would have to put him on his guard; they could not go on like this, now that such a contingency had occurred to him. And he noticed with sour disfavour that June had left her wine-glasses full of wine.

'That little, thing's at the bottom of it all,' he mused; 'Irene'd never have thought of it herself.' James was a man of imagination.

The voice of Swithin roused him from his reverie.

"I gave four hundred pounds for it," he was saying. "Of course it's a regular work of art."

"Four hundred! H'm! that's a lot of money!" chimed in Nicholas.

The object alluded to was an elaborate group of statuary in Italian marble, which, placed upon a lofty stand (also of marble), diffused an atmosphere of culture throughout the room. The subsidiary figures, of which there were six, female, nude, and of highly ornate workmanship, were all pointing towards the central figure, also nude, and female, who was pointing at herself; and all this gave the observer a very pleasant sense of her extreme value. Aunt Juley, nearly opposite, had had the greatest difficulty in not looking at it all the evening.

Old Jolyon spoke; it was he who had started the discussion.

"Four hundred fiddlesticks! Don't tell me you gave four hundred for that?"

Between the points of his collar Swithin's chin made the second painful oscillatory movement of the evening.

"Four-hundred-pounds, of English money; not a farthing less. I don't regret it. It's not common English—it's genuine modern Italian!"

Soames raised the corner of his lip in a smile, and looked across at Bosinney. The architect was grinning behind the fumes of his cigarette. Now, indeed, he looked more like a buccaneer.

"There's a lot of work about it," remarked James hastily, who was really moved by the size of the group. "It'd sell well at Jobson's."

"The poor foreign dey-vil that made it," went on Swithin, "asked me five hundred—I gave him four. It's worth eight. Looked half-starved, poor dey-vil!"

"Ah!" chimed in Nicholas suddenly, "poor, seedy-lookin' chaps, these artists; it's a wonder to me how they live. Now, there's young Flageoletti, that Fanny and the girls are always hav'in' in, to play the fiddle; if he makes a hundred a year it's as much as ever he does!"

James shook his head. "Ah!" he said, "I don't know how they live!"

Old Jolyon had risen, and, cigar in mouth, went to inspect the group at close quarters.

"Wouldn't have given two for it!" he pronounced at last.

Soames saw his father and Nicholas glance at each other anxiously; and, on the other side of Swithin, Bosinney, still shrouded in smoke.

'I wonder what he thinks of it?' thought Soames, who knew well enough that this group was hopelessly vieux jeu; hopelessly of the last generation. There was no longer any sale at Jobson's for such works of art.

Swithin's answer came at last. "You never knew anything about a statue. You've got your pictures, and that's all!"

Old Jolyon walked back to his seat, puffing his cigar. It was not likely that he was going to be drawn into an argument with an obstinate beggar like Swithin, pig-headed as a mule, who had never known a statue from a——straw hat.

"Stucco!" was all he said.

It had long been physically impossible for Swithin to start; his fist came down on the table.

"Stucco! I should like to see anything you've got in your house half as good!"

And behind his speech seemed to sound again that rumbling violence of primitive generations.

It was James who saved the situation.

"Now, what do you say, Mr. Bosinney? You're an architect; you ought to know all about statues and things!"

Every eye was turned upon Bosinney; all waited with a strange, suspicious look for his answer.

And Soames, speaking for the first time, asked:

"Yes, Bosinney, what do you say?"

Bosinney replied coolly:

"The work is a remarkable one."

His words were addressed to Swithin, his eyes smiled slyly at old Jolyon; only Soames remained unsatisfied.

"Remarkable for what?"

"For its naivete"

The answer was followed by an impressive silence; Swithin alone was not sure whether a compliment was intended.

CHAPTER IV—PROJECTION OF THE HOUSE

Soames Forsyte walked out of his green-painted front door three days after the dinner at Swithin's, and looking back from across the Square, confirmed his impression that the house wanted painting.

He had left his wife sitting on the sofa in the drawing-room, her hands crossed in her lap, manifestly waiting for him to go out. This was not unusual. It happened, in fact, every day.

He could not understand what she found wrong with him. It was not as if he drank! Did he run into debt, or gamble, or swear; was he violent; were his friends rackety; did he stay out at night? On the contrary.

The profound, subdued aversion which he felt in his wife was a mystery to him, and a source of the most terrible irritation. That she had made a mistake, and did not love him, had tried to love him and could not love him, was obviously no reason.

He that could imagine so outlandish a cause for his wife's not getting on with him was certainly no Forsyte.

Soames was forced, therefore, to set the blame entirely down to his wife. He had never met a woman so capable of inspiring affection. They could not go anywhere without his seeing how all the men were attracted by her; their looks, manners, voices, betrayed it; her behaviour under this attention had been beyond reproach. That she was one of those women—not too common in the Anglo-Saxon race—born to be loved and to love, who when not loving are not living, had certainly never even occurred to him. Her power of attraction, he regarded as part of her value as his property; but it made him, indeed, suspect that she could give as well as receive; and she gave him nothing! 'Then why did she marry me?' was his continual thought. He had forgotten his courtship; that year and a half when he had besieged and lain in wait for her, devising schemes for her entertainment, giving her presents, proposing to her periodically, and keeping her other admirers away with his perpetual presence. He had forgotten the day when, adroitly taking advantage of an acute phase of her dislike to her home surroundings, he crowned his labours with success. If he remembered anything, it was the dainty capriciousness with which the gold-haired, dark-eyed girl had treated him. He certainly did not remember the look on her face—strange, passive, appealing—when suddenly one day she had yielded, and said that she would marry him.

It had been one of those real devoted wooings which books and people praise, when the lover is at length rewarded for hammering the iron till it is malleable, and all must be happy ever after as the wedding bells.

Soames walked eastwards, mousing doggedly along on the shady side.

The house wanted doing, up, unless he decided to move into the country, and build.

For the hundredth time that month he turned over this problem. There was no use in rushing into things! He was very comfortably off, with an increasing income getting on for three thousand a year; but his invested capital was not perhaps so large as his father believed—James had a tendency to expect that his children should be better off than they were. 'I can manage eight thousand easily enough,' he thought, 'without calling in either Robertson's or Nicholl's.'

He had stopped to look in at a picture shop, for Soames was an 'amateur' of pictures, and had a little-room in No. 62, Montpellier Square, full of canvases, stacked against the wall, which he had no room to hang. He brought them home with him on his way back from the City, generally after dark, and would enter this room on Sunday afternoons, to spend hours turning the pictures to the light, examining the marks on their backs, and occasionally making notes.

They were nearly all landscapes with figures in the foreground, a sign of some mysterious revolt against London, its tall houses, its interminable streets, where his life and the lives of his breed and class were passed. Every now and then he would take one or two pictures away with him in a cab, and stop at Jobson's on his way into the City.

He rarely showed them to anyone; Irene, whose opinion he secretly respected and perhaps for that reason never solicited, had only been into the room on rare occasions, in discharge of some wifely duty. She was not asked to look at the pictures, and she never did. To Soames this was another grievance. He hated that pride of hers, and secretly dreaded it.

In the plate-glass window of the picture shop his image stood and looked at him.

His sleek hair under the brim of the tall hat had a sheen like the hat itself; his cheeks, pale and flat, the line of his clean-shaven lips, his firm chin with its greyish shaven tinge, and the buttoned strictness of his black cut-away coat, conveyed an appearance of reserve and secrecy, of imperturbable, enforced composure; but his eyes, cold,—grey, strained—looking, with a line in the brow between them, examined him wistfully, as if they knew of a secret weakness.

He noted the subjects of the pictures, the names of the painters, made a calculation of their values, but without the satisfaction he usually derived from this inward appraisement, and walked on.

No. 62 would do well enough for another year, if he decided to build! The times were good for building, money had not been so dear for years; and the site he had seen at Robin Hill, when he had gone down there in the spring to inspect the Nicholl mortgage—what could be better! Within twelve miles of Hyde Park Corner, the value of the land certain to go up, would always fetch more than he gave for it; so that a house, if built in really good style, was a first-class investment.

The notion of being the one member of his family with a country house weighed but little with him; for to a true Forsyte, sentiment, even the sentiment of social position, was a luxury only to be indulged in after his appetite for more material pleasure had been satisfied.

To get Irene out of London, away from opportunities of going about and seeing people, away from her friends and those who put ideas into her head! That was the thing! She was too thick with June! June disliked him. He returned the sentiment. They were of the same blood.

It would be everything to get Irene out of town. The house would please her, she would enjoy messing about with the decoration, she was very artistic!

The house must be in good style, something that would always be certain to command a price, something unique, like that last house of Parkes, which had a tower; but Parkes had himself said that his architect was ruinous. You never knew where you were with those fellows; if they had a name they ran you into no end of expense and were conceited into the bargain.

And a common architect was no good—the memory of Parkes' tower precluded the employment of a common architect:

This was why he had thought of Bosinney. Since the dinner at Swithin's he had made enquiries, the result of which had been meagre, but encouraging: "One of the new school."

"Clever?"

"As clever as you like—a bit—a bit up in the air!"

He had not been able to discover what houses Bosinney had built, nor what his charges were. The impression he gathered was that he would be able to make his own terms. The more he reflected on the idea, the more he liked it. It would be keeping the thing in the family, with Forsytes almost an instinct; and he would be able to get 'favoured-nation,' if not nominal terms—only fair, considering the chance to Bosinney of displaying his talents, for this house must be no common edifice.

Soames reflected complacently on the work it would be sure to bring the young man; for, like every Forsyte, he could be a thorough optimist when there was anything to be had out of it.

Bosinney's office was in Sloane Street, close at, hand, so that he would be able to keep his eye continually on the plans.

Again, Irene would not be to likely to object to leave London if her greatest friend's lover were given the job. June's marriage might depend on it. Irene could not decently stand in the way of June's marriage; she would never do that, he knew her too well. And June would be pleased; of this he saw the advantage.

Bosinney looked clever, but he had also—and—it was one of his great attractions—an air as if he did not quite know on which side his bread were buttered; he should be easy to deal with in money matters. Soames made this reflection in no defrauding spirit; it was the natural attitude of his mind—of the mind of any good business man—of all those thousands of good business men through whom he was threading his way up Ludgate Hill.

Thus he fulfilled the inscrutable laws of his great class—of human nature itself—when he reflected, with a sense of comfort, that Bosinney would be easy to deal with in money matters.

While he elbowed his way on, his eyes, which he usually kept fixed on the ground before his feet, were attracted upwards by the dome of St. Paul's. It had a peculiar fascination for him, that old dome, and not once, but twice or three times a week, would he halt in his daily pilgrimage to enter beneath and stop in the side aisles for five or ten minutes, scrutinizing the names and epitaphs on the monuments. The attraction for him of this great church was inexplicable, unless it enabled him to concentrate his thoughts on the business of the day. If any affair of particular moment, or demanding peculiar acuteness, was weighing on his mind, he invariably went in, to wander with mouse-like attention from epitaph to epitaph. Then retiring in the same noiseless way, he would hold steadily on up Cheapside, a thought more of dogged purpose in his gait, as though he had seen something which he had made up his mind to buy.

He went in this morning, but, instead of stealing from monument to monument, turned his eyes upwards to the columns and spacings of the walls, and remained motionless.

His uplifted face, with the awed and wistful look which faces take on themselves in church, was whitened to a chalky hue in the vast building. His gloved hands were clasped in front over the handle of his umbrella. He lifted them. Some sacred inspiration perhaps had come to him.

'Yes,' he thought, 'I must have room to hang my pictures.'

That evening, on his return from the City, he called at Bosinney's office. He found the architect in his shirt-sleeves, smoking a pipe, and ruling off lines on a plan. Soames refused a drink, and came at once to the point.

"If you've nothing better to do on Sunday, come down with me to Robin Hill, and give me your opinion on a building site."

"Are you going to build?"

"Perhaps," said Soames; "but don't speak of it. I just want your opinion."

"Quite so," said the architect.

Soames peered about the room.

"You're rather high up here," he remarked.

Any information he could gather about the nature and scope of Bosinney's business would be all to the good.

"It does well enough for me so far," answered the architect. "You're accustomed to the swells."

He knocked out his pipe, but replaced it empty between his teeth; it assisted him perhaps to carry on the conversation. Soames noted a hollow in each cheek, made as it were by suction.

"What do you pay for an office like this?" said he.

"Fifty too much," replied Bosinney.

This answer impressed Soames favourably.

"I suppose it is dear," he said. "I'll call for you—on Sunday about eleven."

The following Sunday therefore he called for Bosinney in a hansom, and drove him to the station. On arriving at Robin Hill, they found no cab, and started to walk the mile and a half to the site.

It was the 1st of August—a perfect day, with a burning sun and cloudless sky—and in the straight, narrow road leading up the hill their feet kicked up a yellow dust.

"Gravel soil," remarked Soames, and sideways he glanced at the coat Bosinney wore. Into the side-pockets of this coat were thrust bundles of papers, and under one arm was carried a queer-looking stick. Soames noted these and other peculiarities.

No one but a clever man, or, indeed, a buccaneer, would have taken such liberties with his appearance; and though these eccentricities were revolting to Soames, he derived a certain satisfaction from them, as evidence of qualities by which he must inevitably profit. If the fellow could build houses, what did his clothes matter?

"I told you," he said, "that I want this house to be a surprise, so don't say anything about it. I never talk of my affairs until they're carried through."

Bosinney nodded.

"Let women into your plans," pursued Soames, "and you never know where it'll end."

"Ah!" Said Bosinney, "women are the devil!"

This feeling had long been at the—bottom of Soames's heart; he had never, however, put it into words.

"Oh!" he Muttered, "so you're beginning to...." He stopped, but added, with an uncontrollable burst of spite: "June's got a temper of her own—always had."

"A temper's not a bad thing in an angel."

Soames had never called Irene an angel. He could not so have violated his best instincts, letting other people into the secret of her value, and giving himself away. He made no reply.

They had struck into a half-made road across a warren. A cart-track led at right-angles to a gravel pit, beyond which the chimneys of a cottage rose amongst a clump of trees at the border of a thick wood. Tussocks of feathery grass covered the rough surface of the ground, and out of these the larks soared into the haze of sunshine. On the far horizon, over a countless succession of fields and hedges, rose a line of downs.

Soames led till they had crossed to the far side, and there he stopped. It was the chosen site; but now that he was about to divulge the spot to another he had become uneasy.

"The agent lives in that cottage," he said; "he'll give us some lunch—we'd better have lunch before we go into this matter."

He again took the lead to the cottage, where the agent, a tall man named Oliver, with a heavy face and grizzled beard, welcomed them. During lunch, which Soames hardly touched, he kept looking at Bosinney, and once or twice passed his silk handkerchief stealthily over his forehead. The meal came to an end at last, and Bosinney rose.

"I dare say you've got business to talk over," he said; "I'll just go and nose about a bit." Without waiting for a reply he strolled out.

Soames was solicitor to this estate, and he spent nearly an hour in the agent's company, looking at ground-plans and discussing the Nicholl and other mortgages; it was as it were by an afterthought that he brought up the question of the building site.

"Your people," he said, "ought to come down in their price to me, considering that I shall be the first to build."

Oliver shook his head.

The site you've fixed on, Sir, he said, "is the cheapest we've got. Sites at the top of the slope are dearer by a good bit."

"Mind," said Soames, "I've not decided; it's quite possible I shan't build at all. The ground rent's very high."

"Well, Mr. Forsyte, I shall be sorry if you go off, and I think you'll make a mistake, Sir. There's not a bit of land near London with such a view as this, nor one that's cheaper, all things considered; we've only to advertise, to get a mob of people after it."

They looked at each other. Their faces said very plainly: 'I respect you as a man of business; and you can't expect me to believe a word you say.'

Well, repeated Soames, "I haven't made up my mind; the thing will very likely go off!" With these words, taking up his umbrella, he put his chilly hand into the agent's, withdrew it without the faintest pressure, and went out into the sun.

He walked slowly back towards the site in deep thought. His instinct told him that what the agent had said was true. A cheap site. And the beauty of it was, that he knew the agent did not really think it cheap; so that his own intuitive knowledge was a victory over the agent's.

'Cheap or not, I mean to have it,' he thought.

The larks sprang up in front of his feet, the air was full of butterflies, a sweet fragrance rose from the wild grasses. The sappy scent of the bracken stole forth from the wood, where, hidden in the depths, pigeons were cooing, and from afar on the warm breeze, came the rhythmic chiming of church bells.

Soames walked with his eyes on the ground, his lips opening and closing as though in anticipation of a delicious morsel. But when he arrived at the site, Bosinney was nowhere to be seen. After waiting some little time, he crossed the warren in the direction of the slope. He would have shouted, but dreaded the sound of his voice.

The warren was as lonely as a prairie, its silence only broken by the rustle of rabbits bolting to their holes, and the song of the larks.

Soames, the pioneer-leader of the great Forsyte army advancing to the civilization of this wilderness, felt his spirit daunted by the loneliness, by the invisible singing, and the hot, sweet air. He had begun to retrace his steps when he at last caught sight of Bosinney.

The architect was sprawling under a large oak tree, whose trunk, with a huge spread of bough and foliage, ragged with age, stood on the verge of the rise.

Soames had to touch him on the shoulder before he looked up.

"Hallo! Forsyte," he said, "I've found the very place for your house! Look here!"

Soames stood and looked, then he said, coldly:

"You may be very clever, but this site will cost me half as much again."

"Hang the cost, man. Look at the view!"

Almost from their feet stretched ripe corn, dipping to a small dark copse beyond. A plain of fields and hedges spread to the distant grey-bluedowns. In a silver streak to the right could be seen the line of the river.

The sky was so blue, and the sun so bright, that an eternal summer seemed to reign over this prospect. Thistledown floated round them, enraptured by the serenity, of the ether. The heat danced over the corn, and, pervading all, was a soft, insensible hum, like the murmur of bright minutes holding revel between earth and heaven.

Soames looked. In spite of himself, something swelled in his breast. To live here in sight of all this, to be able to point it out to his friends, to talk of it, to possess it! His cheeks flushed. The warmth, the radiance, the glow, were sinking into his senses as, four years before, Irene's beauty had sunk into his senses and made him long for her. He stole a glance at Bosinney, whose eyes, the eyes of the coachman's 'half-tame leopard,' seemed running wild over the landscape. The sunlight had caught the promontories of the fellow's face, the bumpy cheekbones, the point of his chin, the vertical ridges above his brow; and Soames watched this rugged, enthusiastic, careless face with an unpleasant feeling.

A long, soft ripple of wind flowed over the corn, and brought a puff of warm air into their faces.

"I could build you a teaser here," said Bosinney, breaking the silence at last.

"I dare say," replied Soames, drily. "You haven't got to pay for it."

"For about eight thousand I could build you a palace."

Soames had become very pale—a struggle was going on within him. He dropped his eyes, and said stubbornly:

"I can't afford it."

And slowly, with his mousing walk, he led the way back to the first site.

They spent some time there going into particulars of the projected house, and then Soames returned to the agent's cottage.

He came out in about half an hour, and, joining Bosinney, started for the station.

"Well," he said, hardly opening his lips, "I've taken that site of yours, after all."

And again he was silent, confusedly debating how it was that this fellow, whom by habit he despised, should have overborne his own decision.

41

CHAPTER V—A FORSYTE MENAGE

Like the enlightened thousands of his class and generation in this great city of London, who no longer believe in red velvet chairs, and know that groups of modern Italian marble are 'vieux jeu,' Soames Forsyte inhabited a house which did what it could. It owned a copper door knocker of individual design, windows which had been altered to open outwards, hanging flower boxes filled with fuchsias, and at the back (a great feature) a little court tiled with jade-green tiles, and surrounded by pink hydrangeas in peacock-blue tubs. Here, under a parchment-coloured Japanese sunshade covering the whole end, inhabitants or visitors could be screened from the eyes of the curious while they drank tea and examined at their leisure the latest of Soames's little silver boxes.

The inner decoration favoured the First Empire and William Morris. For its size, the house was commodious; there were countless nooks resembling birds' nests, and little things made of silver were deposited like eggs.

In this general perfection two kinds of fastidiousness were at war. There lived here a mistress who would have dwelt daintily on a desert island; a master whose daintiness was, as it were, an investment, cultivated by the owner for his advancement, in accordance with the laws of competition. This competitive daintiness had caused Soames in his Marlborough days to be the first boy into white waistcoats in summer, and corduroy waistcoats in winter, had prevented him from ever appearing in public with his tie climbing up his collar, and induced him to dust his patent leather boots before a great multitude assembled on Speech Day to hear him recite Moliere.

Skin-like immaculateness had grown over Soames, as over many Londoners; impossible to conceive of him with a hair out of place, a tie deviating one-eighth of an inch from the perpendicular, a collar unglossed! He would not have gone without a bath for worlds—it was the fashion to take baths; and how bitter was his scorn of people who omitted them!

But Irene could be imagined, like some nymph, bathing in wayside streams, for the joy of the freshness and of seeing her own fair body.

In this conflict throughout the house the woman had gone to the wall. As in the struggle between Saxon and Celt still going on within the nation, the more impressionable and receptive temperament had had forced on it a conventional superstructure.

Thus the house had acquired a close resemblance to hundreds of other houses with the same high aspirations, having become: "That very charming little house of the Soames Forsytes, quite individual, my dear—really elegant.'

For Soames Forsyte—read James Peabody, Thomas Atkins, or Emmanuel Spagnoletti, the name in fact of any upper-middle class Englishman in London with any pretensions to taste; and though the decoration be different, the phrase is just.

On the evening of August 8, a week after the expedition to Robin Hill, in the dining-room of this house—'quite individual, my dear—really elegant'—Soames and Irene were seated at dinner. A hot dinner on Sundays was a little distinguishing elegance common to this house and many others. Early in married life Soames had laid down the rule: "The servants must give us hot dinner on Sundays—they've nothing to do but play the concertina.'

The custom had produced no revolution. For—to Soames a rather deplorable sign— servants were devoted to Irene, who, in defiance of all safe tradition, appeared to recognise their right to a share in the weaknesses of human nature.

The happy pair were seated, not opposite each other, but rectangularly, at the handsome rosewood table; they dined without a cloth—a distinguishing elegance—and so far had not spoken a word.

Soames liked to talk during dinner about business, or what he had been buying, and so long as he talked Irene's silence did not distress him. This evening he had found it impossible to talk. The decision to build had been weighing on his mind all the week, and he had made up his mind to tell her.

His nervousness about this disclosure irritated him profoundly; she had no business to make him feel like that—a wife and a husband being one person. She had not looked at him once since they sat down; and he wondered what on earth she had been thinking about all the time. It was hard, when a man worked as he did, making money for her—yes, and with an ache in his heart—that she should sit there, looking—looking as if she saw the walls of the room closing in. It was enough to make a man get up and leave the table.

The light from the rose-shaded lamp fell on her neck and arms—Soames liked her to dine in a low dress, it gave him an inexpressible feeling of superiority to the majority of his acquaintance, whose wives were contented with their best high frocks or with tea-gowns, when they dined at home. Under that rosy light her amber-coloured hair and fair skin made strange contrast with her dark brown eyes.

Could a man own anything prettier than this dining-table with its deep tints, the starry, soft-petalled roses, the ruby-coloured glass, and quaint silver furnishing; could a man own anything prettier than the woman who sat at it? Gratitude was no virtue among Forsytes, who, competitive, and full of common-sense, had no occasion for it; and Soames only experienced a sense of exasperation amounting to pain, that he did not own her as it was his right to own her, that he could not, as by stretching out his hand to that rose, pluck her and sniff the very secrets of her heart.

Out of his other property, out of all the things he had collected, his silver, his pictures, his houses, his investments, he got a secret and intimate feeling; out of her he got none.

In this house of his there was writing on every wall. His business-like temperament protested against a mysterious warning that she was not made for him. He had married this woman, conquered her, made her his own, and it seemed to him contrary to the most fundamental of all laws, the law of possession, that he could do no more than own her body—if indeed he could do that, which he was beginning to doubt. If any one had asked him if he wanted to own her soul, the question would have seemed to him both ridiculous and sentimental. But he did so want, and the writing said he never would.

She was ever silent, passive, gracefully averse; as though terrified lest by word, motion, or sign she might lead him to believe that she was fond of him; and he asked himself: Must I always go on like this?

Like most novel readers of his generation (and Soames was a great novel reader), literature coloured his view of life; and he had imbibed the belief that it was only a question of time.

In the end the husband always gained the affection of his wife. Even in those cases—a class of book he was not very fond of—which ended in tragedy, the wife always died with poignant regrets on her lips, or if it were the husband who died—unpleasant thought— threw herself on his body in an agony of remorse.

He often took Irene to the theatre, instinctively choosing the modern Society Plays with the modern Society conjugal problem, so fortunately different from any conjugal problem in real life. He found that they too always ended in the same way, even when there was a lover in the case. While he was watching the play Soames often sympathized with the lover;

but before he reached home again, driving with Irene in a hansom, he saw that this would not do, and he was glad the play had ended as it had. There was one class of husband that had just then come into fashion, the strong, rather rough, but extremely sound man, who was peculiarly successful at the end of the play; with this person Soames was really not in sympathy, and had it not been for his own position, would have expressed his disgust with the fellow. But he was so conscious of how vital to himself was the necessity for being a successful, even a 'strong,' husband, that he never spoke of a distaste born perhaps by the perverse processes of Nature out of a secret fund of brutality in himself.

But Irene's silence this evening was exceptional. He had never before seen such an expression on her face. And since it is always the unusual which alarms, Soames was alarmed. He ate his savoury, and hurried the maid as she swept off the crumbs with the silver sweeper. When she had left the room, he filled his glass with wine and said:

"Anybody been here this afternoon?"

"June."

"What did she want?" It was an axiom with the Forsytes that people did not go anywhere unless they wanted something. "Came to talk about her lover, I suppose?"

Irene made no reply.

"It looks to me," continued Soames, "as if she were sweeter on him than he is on her. She's always following him about."

Irene's eyes made him feel uncomfortable.

"You've no business to say such a thing!" she exclaimed.

"Why not? Anybody can see it."

"They cannot. And if they could, it's disgraceful to say so."

Soames's composure gave way.

"You're a pretty wife!" he said. But secretly he wondered at the heat of her reply; it was unlike her. "You're cracked about June! I can tell you one thing: now that she has the Buccaneer in tow, she doesn't care twopence about you, and, you'll find it out. But you won't see so much of her in future; we're going to live in the country."

He had been glad to get his news out under cover of this burst of irritation. He had expected a cry of dismay; the silence with which his pronouncement was received alarmed him.

"You don't seem interested," he was obliged to add.

"I knew it already."

He looked at her sharply.

"Who told you?"

"June."

"How did she know?"

Irene did not answer. Baffled and uncomfortable, he said:

"It's a fine thing for Bosinney, it'll be the making of him. I suppose she's told you all about it?"

"Yes."

There was another pause, and then Soames said:

"I suppose you don't want to, go?"

Irene made no reply.

"Well, I can't tell what you want. You never seem contented here."

"Have my wishes anything to do with it?"

She took the vase of roses and left the room. Soames remained seated. Was it for this that he had signed that contract? Was it for this that he was going to spend some ten thousand pounds? Bosinney's phrase came back to him: "Women are the devil!"

But presently he grew calmer. It might have, been worse. She might have flared up. He had expected something more than this. It was lucky, after all, that June had broken the ice for him. She must have wormed it out of Bosinney; he might have known she would.

He lighted his cigarette. After all, Irene had not made a scene! She would come round— that was the best of her; she was cold, but not sulky. And, puffing the cigarette smoke at a lady-bird on the shining table, he plunged into a reverie about the house. It was no good worrying; he would go and make it up presently. She would be sitting out there in the dark, under the Japanese sunshade, knitting. A beautiful, warm night....

In truth, June had come in that afternoon with shining eyes, and the words: "Soames is a brick! It's splendid for Phil—the very thing for him!"

Irene's face remaining dark and puzzled, she went on:

"Your new house at Robin Hill, of course. What? Don't you know?"

Irene did not know.

"Oh! then, I suppose I oughtn't to have told you!" Looking impatiently at her friend, she cried: "You look as if you didn't care. Don't you see, it's what I've' been praying for—the very chance he's been wanting all this time. Now you'll see what he can do;" and thereupon she poured out the whole story.

Since her own engagement she had not seemed much interested in her friend's position; the hours she spent with Irene were given to confidences of her own; and at times, for all her affectionate pity, it was impossible to keep out of her smile a trace of compassionate contempt for the woman who had made such a mistake in her life—such a vast, ridiculous mistake.

"He's to have all the decorations as well—a free hand. It's perfect—" June broke into laughter, her little figure quivered gleefully; she raised her hand, and struck a blow at a muslin curtain. "Do you, know I even asked Uncle James...." But, with a sudden dislike to mentioning that incident, she stopped; and presently, finding her friend so unresponsive, went away. She looked back from the pavement, and Irene was still standing in the doorway. In response to her farewell wave, Irene put her hand to her brow, and, turning slowly, shut the door....

Soames went to the drawing-room presently, and peered at her through the window.

Out in the shadow of the Japanese sunshade she was sitting very still, the lace on her white shoulders stirring with the soft rise and fall of her bosom.

But about this silent creature sitting there so motionless, in the dark, there seemed a warmth, a hidden fervour of feeling, as if the whole of her being had been stirred, and some change were taking place in its very depths.

He stole back to the dining-room unnoticed.

CHAPTER VI—JAMES AT LARGE

It was not long before Soames's determination to build went the round of the family, and created the flutter that any decision connected with property should make among Forsytes.

It was not his fault, for he had been determined that no one should know. June, in the fulness of her heart, had told Mrs. Small, giving her leave only to tell Aunt Ann—she thought it would cheer her, the poor old sweet! for Aunt Ann had kept her room now for many days.

Mrs. Small told Aunt Ann at once, who, smiling as she lay back on her pillows, said in her distinct, trembling old voice:

"It's very nice for dear June; but I hope they will be careful—it's rather dangerous!"

When she was left alone again, a frown, like a cloud presaging a rainy morrow, crossed her face.

While she was lying there so many days the process of recharging her will went on all the time; it spread to her face, too, and tightening movements were always in action at the corners of her lips.

The maid Smither, who had been in her service since girlhood, and was spoken of as "Smither—a good girl—but so slow!"—the maid Smither performed every morning with extreme punctiliousness the crowning ceremony of that ancient toilet. Taking from the recesses of their pure white band-box those flat, grey curls, the insignia of personal dignity, she placed them securely in her mistress's hands, and turned her back.

And every day Aunts Juley and Hester were required to come and report on Timothy; what news there was of Nicholas; whether dear June had succeeded in getting Jolyon to shorten the engagement, now that Mr. Bosinney was building Soames a house; whether young Roger's wife was really—expecting; how the operation on Archie had succeeded; and what Swithin had done about that empty house in Wigmore Street, where the tenant had lost all his money and treated him so badly; above all, about Soames; was Irene still—still asking for a separate room? And every morning Smither was told: "I shall be coming down this afternoon, Smither, about two o'clock. I shall want your arm, after all these days in bed!"

After telling Aunt Ann, Mrs. Small had spoken of the house in the strictest confidence to Mrs. Nicholas, who in her turn had asked Winifred Dartie for confirmation, supposing, of course, that, being Soames's sister, she would know all about it. Through her it had in due course come round to the ears of James. He had been a good deal agitated.

"Nobody," he said, "told him anything." And, rather than go direct to Soames himself, of whose taciturnity he was afraid, he took his umbrella and went round to Timothy's.

He found Mrs. Septimus and Hester (who had been told—she was so safe, she found it tiring to talk) ready, and indeed eager, to discuss the news. It was very good of dear Soames, they thought, to employ Mr. Bosinney, but rather risky. What had George named him? 'The Buccaneer' How droll! But George was always droll! However, it would be all in the family they supposed they must really look upon Mr. Bosinney as belonging to the family, though it seemed strange.

James here broke in:

"Nobody knows anything about him. I don't see what Soames wants with a young man like that. I shouldn't be surprised if Irene had put her oar in. I shall speak to...."

"Soames," interposed Aunt Juley, "told Mr. Bosinney that he didn't wish it mentioned. He wouldn't like it to be talked about, I'm sure, and if Timothy knew he would be very vexed, I...."

James put his hand behind his ear:

"What?" he said. "I'm getting very deaf. I suppose I don't hear people. Emily's got a bad toe. We shan't be able to start for Wales till the end of the month. There's always something!" And, having got what he wanted, he took his hat and went away.

It was a fine afternoon, and he walked across the Park towards Soames's, where he intended to dine, for Emily's toe kept her in bed, and Rachel and Cicely were on a visit to the country. He took the slanting path from the Bayswater side of the Row to the Knightsbridge Gate, across a pasture of short, burnt grass, dotted with blackened sheep, strewn with seated couples and strange waifs; lying prone on their faces, like corpses on a field over which the wave of battle has rolled.

He walked rapidly, his head bent, looking neither to right nor, left. The appearance of this park, the centre of his own battle-field, where he had all his life been fighting, excited no thought or speculation in his mind. These corpses flung down, there, from out the press and turmoil of the struggle, these pairs of lovers sitting cheek by jowl for an hour of idle Elysium snatched from the monotony of their treadmill, awakened no fancies in his mind; he had outlived that kind of imagination; his nose, like the nose of a sheep, was fastened to the pastures on which he browsed.

One of his tenants had lately shown a disposition to be behind-hand in his rent, and it had become a grave question whether he had not better turn him out at once, and so run the risk of not re-letting before Christmas. Swithin had just been let in very badly, but it had served him right—he had held on too long.

He pondered this as he walked steadily, holding his umbrella carefully by the wood, just below the crook of the handle, so as to keep the ferule off the ground, and not fray the silk in the middle. And, with his thin, high shoulders stooped, his long legs moving with swift mechanical precision, this passage through the Park, where the sun shone with a clear flame on so much idleness—on so many human evidences of the remorseless battle of Property, raging beyond its ring—was like the flight of some land bird across the sea.

He felt a touch on the arm as he came out at Albert Gate.

It was Soames, who, crossing from the shady side of Piccadilly, where he had been walking home from the office, had suddenly appeared alongside.

"Your mother's in bed," said James; "I was, just coming to you, but I suppose I shall be in the way."

The outward relations between James and his son were marked by a lack of sentiment peculiarly Forsytean, but for all that the two were by no means unattached. Perhaps they regarded one another as an investment; certainly they were solicitous of each other's welfare, glad of each other's company. They had never exchanged two words upon the more intimate problems of life, or revealed in each other's presence the existence of any deep feeling.

Something beyond the power of word-analysis bound them together, something hidden deep in the fibre of nations and families—for blood, they say, is thicker than water—and neither of them was a cold-blooded man. Indeed, in James love of his children was now the prime motive of his existence. To have creatures who were parts of himself, to whom he might transmit the money he saved, was at the root of his saving; and, at seventy-five, what was left that could give him pleasure, but—saving? The kernel of life was in this saving for his children.

Than James Forsyte, notwithstanding all his 'Jonah-isms,' there was no saner man (if the leading symptom of sanity, as we are told, is self-preservation, though without doubt Timothy went too far) in all this London, of which he owned so much, and loved with such a dumb love, as the centre of his opportunities. He had the marvellous instinctive sanity of the middle class. In him—more than in Jolyon, with his masterful will and his moments of tenderness and philosophy—more than in Swithin, the martyr to crankiness—Nicholas, the sufferer from ability—and Roger, the victim of enterprise—beat the true pulse of compromise; of all the brothers he was least remarkable in mind and person, and for that reason more likely to live for ever.

To James, more than to any of the others, was "the family" significant and dear. There had always been something primitive and cosy in his attitude towards life; he loved the family hearth, he loved gossip, and he loved grumbling. All his decisions were formed of a cream which he skimmed off the family mind; and, through that family, off the minds of thousands of other families of similar fibre. Year after year, week after week, he went to Timothy's, and in his brother's front drawing-room—his legs twisted, his long white whiskers framing his clean-shaven mouth—would sit watching the family pot simmer, the cream rising to the top; and he would go away sheltered, refreshed, comforted, with an indefinable sense of comfort.

Beneath the adamant of his self-preserving instinct there was much real softness in James; a visit to Timothy's was like an hour spent in the lap of a mother; and the deep craving he himself had for the protection of the family wing reacted in turn on his feelings towards his own children; it was a nightmare to him to think of them exposed to the treatment of the world, in money, health, or reputation. When his old friend John Street's son volunteered for special service, he shook his head querulously, and wondered what John Street was about to allow it; and when young Street was assagaied, he took it so much to heart that he made a point of calling everywhere with the special object of saying: He knew how it would be—he'd no patience with them!

When his son-in-law Dartie had that financial crisis, due to speculation in Oil Shares, James made himself ill worrying over it; the knell of all prosperity seemed to have sounded. It took him three months and a visit to Baden-Baden to get better; there was something terrible in the idea that but for his, James's, money, Dartie's name might have appeared in the Bankruptcy List.

Composed of a physiological mixture so sound that if he had an earache he thought he was dying, he regarded the occasional ailments of his wife and children as in the nature of personal grievances, special interventions of Providence for the purpose of destroying his peace of mind; but he did not believe at all in the ailments of people outside his own immediate family, affirming them in every case to be due to neglected liver.

His universal comment was: "What can they expect? I have it myself, if I'm not careful!"

When he went to Soames's that evening he felt that life was hard on him: There was Emily with a bad toe, and Rachel gadding about in the country; he got no sympathy from anybody; and Ann, she was ill—he did not believe she would last through the summer; he had called there three times now without her being able to see him! And this idea of Soames's, building a house, that would have to be looked into. As to the trouble with Irene, he didn't know what was to come of that—anything might come of it!

He entered 62, Montpellier Square with the fullest intentions of being miserable. It was already half-past seven, and Irene, dressed for dinner, was seated in the drawing-room. She was wearing her gold-coloured frock—for, having been displayed at a dinner-party, a soirée, and a dance, it was now to be worn at home—and she had adorned the bosom with a cascade of lace, on which James's eyes riveted themselves at once.

"Where do you get your things?" he said in an aggravated voice. "I never see Rachel and Cicely looking half so well. That rose-point, now—that's not real!"

Irene came close, to prove to him that he was in error.

And, in spite of himself, James felt the influence of her deference, of the faint seductive perfume exhaling from her. No self-respecting Forsyte surrendered at a blow; so he merely said: He didn't know—he expected she was spending a pretty penny on dress.

The gong sounded, and, putting her white arm within his, Irene took him into the dining-room. She seated him in Soames's usual place, round the corner on her left. The light fell softly there, so that he would not be worried by the gradual dying of the day; and she began to talk to him about himself.

Presently, over James came a change, like the mellowing that steals upon a fruit in the sun; a sense of being caressed, and praised, and petted, and all without the bestowal of a single caress or word of praise. He felt that what he was eating was agreeing with him; he could not get that feeling at home; he did not know when he had enjoyed a glass of champagne so much, and, on inquiring the brand and price, was surprised to find that it was one of which he had a large stock himself, but could never drink; he instantly formed the resolution to let his wine merchant know that he had been swindled.

Looking up from his food, he remarked:

"You've a lot of nice things about the place. Now, what did you give for that sugar-sifter? Shouldn't wonder if it was worth money!"

He was particularly pleased with the appearance of a picture, on the wall opposite, which he himself had given them:

"I'd no idea it was so good!" he said.

They rose to go into the drawing-room, and James followed Irene closely.

"That's what I call a capital little dinner," he murmured, breathing pleasantly down on her shoulder; "nothing heavy—and not too Frenchified. But I can't get it at home. I pay my cook sixty pounds a year, but she can't give me a dinner like that!"

He had as yet made no allusion to the building of the house, nor did he when Soames, pleading the excuse of business, betook himself to the room at the top, where he kept his pictures.

James was left alone with his daughter-in-law. The glow of the wine, and of an excellent liqueur, was still within him. He felt quite warm towards her. She was really a taking little thing; she listened to you, and seemed to understand what you were saying; and, while talking, he kept examining her figure, from her bronze-coloured shoes to the waved gold of her hair. She was leaning back in an Empire chair, her shoulders poised against the top—her body, flexibly straight and unsupported from the hips, swaying when she moved, as though giving to the arms of a lover. Her lips were smiling, her eyes half-closed.

It may have been a recognition of danger in the very charm of her attitude, or a twang of digestion, that caused a sudden dumbness to fall on James. He did not remember ever having been quite alone with Irene before. And, as he looked at her, an odd feeling crept over him, as though he had come across something strange and foreign.

Now what was she thinking about—sitting back like that?

Thus when he spoke it was in a sharper voice, as if he had been awakened from a pleasant dream.

"What d'you do with yourself all day?" he said. "You never come round to Park Lane!"

She seemed to be making very lame excuses, and James did not look at her. He did not want to believe that she was really avoiding them—it would mean too much.

"I expect the fact is, you haven't time," he said; "You're always about with June. I expect you're useful to her with her young man, chaperoning, and one thing and another. They tell me she's never at home now; your Uncle Jolyon he doesn't like it, I fancy, being left so much alone as he is. They tell me she's always hanging about for this young Bosinney; I suppose he comes here every day. Now, what do you think of him? D'you think he knows his own mind? He seems to me a poor thing. I should say the grey mare was the better horse!"

The colour deepened in Irene's face; and James watched her suspiciously.

"Perhaps you don't quite understand Mr. Bosinney," she said.

"Don't understand him!" James hummed out: "Why not?—you can see he's one of these artistic chaps. They say he's clever—they all think they're clever. You know more about him than I do," he added; and again his suspicious glance rested on her.

"He is designing a house for Soames," she said softly, evidently trying to smooth things over.

"That brings me to what I was going to say," continued James; "I don't know what Soames wants with a young man like that; why doesn't he go to a first-rate man?"

"Perhaps Mr. Bosinney is first-rate!"

James rose, and took a turn with bent head.

"That's it," he said, "you young people, you all stick together; you all think you know best!"

Halting his tall, lank figure before her, he raised a finger, and levelled it at her bosom, as though bringing an indictment against her beauty:

"All I can say is, these artistic people, or whatever they call themselves, they're as unreliable as they can be; and my advice to you is, don't you have too much to do with him!"

Irene smiled; and in the curve of her lips was a strange provocation. She seemed to have lost her deference. Her breast rose and fell as though with secret anger; she drew her hands inwards from their rest on the arms of her chair until the tips of her fingers met, and her dark eyes looked unfathomably at James.

The latter gloomily scrutinized the floor.

"I tell you my opinion," he said, "it's a pity you haven't got a child to think about, and occupy you!"

A brooding look came instantly on Irene's face, and even James became conscious of the rigidity that took possession of her whole figure beneath the softness of its silk and lace clothing.

He was frightened by the effect he had produced, and like most men with but little courage, he sought at once to justify himself by bullying.

"You don't seem to care about going about. Why don't you drive down to Hurlingham with us? And go to the theatre now and then. At your time of life you ought to take an interest in things. You're a young woman!"

The brooding look darkened on her face; he grew nervous.

"Well, I know nothing about it," he said; "nobody tells me anything. Soames ought to be able to take care of himself. If he can't take care of himself he mustn't look to me—that's all."

Biting the corner of his forefinger he stole a cold, sharp look at his daughter-in-law.

He encountered her eyes fixed on his own, so dark and deep, that he stopped, and broke into a gentle perspiration.

"Well, I must be going," he said after a short pause, and a minute later rose, with a slight appearance of surprise, as though he had expected to be asked to stop. Giving his hand to Irene, he allowed himself to be conducted to the door, and let out into the street. He would not have a cab, he would walk, Irene was to say good-night to Soames for him, and if she wanted a little gaiety, well, he would drive her down to Richmond any day.

He walked home, and going upstairs, woke Emily out of the first sleep she had had for four and twenty hours, to tell her that it was his impression things were in a bad way at Soames's; on this theme he descanted for half an hour, until at last, saying that he would not sleep a wink, he turned on his side and instantly began to snore.

In Montpellier Square Soames, who had come from the picture room, stood invisible at the top of the stairs, watching Irene sort the letters brought by the last post. She turned back into the drawing-room; but in a minute came out, and stood as if listening. Then she came stealing up the stairs, with a kitten in her arms. He could see her face bent over the little beast, which was purring against her neck. Why couldn't she look at him like that?

Suddenly she saw him, and her face changed.

"Any letters for me?" he said.

"Three."

He stood aside, and without another word she passed on into the bedroom.

CHAPTER VII—OLD JOLYON'S PECCADILLO

Old Jolyon came out of Lord's cricket ground that same afternoon with the intention of going home. He had not reached Hamilton Terrace before he changed his mind, and hailing a cab, gave the driver an address in Wistaria Avenue. He had taken a resolution.

June had hardly been at home at all that week; she had given him nothing of her company for a long time past, not, in fact, since she had become engaged to Bosinney. He never asked her for her company. It was not his habit to ask people for things! She had just that one idea now—Bosinney and his affairs—and she left him stranded in his great house, with a parcel of servants, and not a soul to speak to from morning to night. His Club was closed for cleaning; his Boards in recess; there was nothing, therefore, to take him into the City.

June had wanted him to go away; she would not go herself, because Bosinney was in London.

But where was he to go by himself? He could not go abroad alone; the sea upset his liver; he hated hotels. Roger went to a hydropathic—he was not going to begin that at his time of life, those new-fangled places we're all humbug!

With such formulas he clothed to himself the desolation of his spirit; the lines down his face deepening, his eyes day by day looking forth with the melancholy which sat so strangely on a face wont to be strong and serene.

And so that afternoon he took this journey through St. John's Wood, in the golden-light that sprinkled the rounded green bushes of the acacia's before the little houses, in the summer sunshine that seemed holding a revel over the little gardens; and he looked about him with interest; for this was a district which no Forsyte entered without open disapproval and secret curiosity.

His cab stopped in front of a small house of that peculiar buff colour which implies a long immunity from paint. It had an outer gate, and a rustic approach.

He stepped out, his bearing extremely composed; his massive head, with its drooping moustache and wings of white hair, very upright, under an excessively large top hat; his glance firm, a little angry. He had been driven into this!

"Mrs. Jolyon Forsyte at home?"

"Oh, yes sir!—what name shall I say, if you please, sir?"

Old Jolyon could not help twinkling at the little maid as he gave his name. She seemed to him such a funny little toad!

And he followed her through the dark hall, into a small double, drawing-room, where the furniture was covered in chintz, and the little maid placed him in a chair.

"They're all in the garden, sir; if you'll kindly take a seat, I'll tell them."

Old Jolyon sat down in the chintz-covered chair, and looked around him. The whole place seemed to him, as he would have expressed it, pokey; there was a certain—he could not tell exactly what—air of shabbiness, or rather of making two ends meet, about everything. As far as he could see, not a single piece of furniture was worth a five-pound note. The walls, distempered rather a long time ago, were decorated with water-colour sketches; across the ceiling meandered a long crack.

These little houses were all old, second-rate concerns; he should hope the rent was under a hundred a year; it hurt him more than he could have said, to think of a Forsyte—his own son living in such a place.

The little maid came back. Would he please to go down into the garden?

Old Jolyon marched out through the French windows. In descending the steps he noticed that they wanted painting.

Young Jolyon, his wife, his two children, and his dog Balthasar, were all out there under a pear-tree.

This walk towards them was the most courageous act of old Jolyon's life; but no muscle of his face moved, no nervous gesture betrayed him. He kept his deep-set eyes steadily on the enemy.

In those two minutes he demonstrated to perfection all that unconscious soundness, balance, and vitality of fibre that made, of him and so many others of his class the core of the nation. In the unostentatious conduct of their own affairs, to the neglect of everything else, they typified the essential individualism, born in the Briton from the natural isolation of his country's life.

The dog Balthasar sniffed round the edges of his trousers; this friendly and cynical mongrel—offspring of a liaison between a Russian poodle and a fox-terrier—had a nose for the unusual.

The strange greetings over, old Jolyon seated himself in a wicker chair, and his two grandchildren, one on each side of his knees, looked at him silently, never having seen so old a man.

They were unlike, as though recognising the difference set between them by the circumstances of their births. Jolly, the child of sin, pudgy-faced, with his tow-coloured hair brushed off his forehead, and a dimple in his chin, had an air of stubborn amiability, and the eyes of a Forsyte; little Holly, the child of wedlock, was a dark-skinned, solemn soul, with her mother's, grey and wistful eyes.

The dog Balthasar, having walked round the three small flower-beds, to show his extreme contempt for things at large, had also taken a seat in front of old Jolyon, and, oscillating a tail curled by Nature tightly over his back, was staring up with eyes that did not blink.

Even in the garden, that sense of things being pokey haunted old Jolyon; the wicker chair creaked under his weight; the garden-beds looked 'daverdy'; on the far side, under the smut-stained wall, cats had made a path.

While he and his grandchildren thus regarded each other with the peculiar scrutiny, curious yet trustful, that passes between the very young and the very old, young Jolyon watched his wife.

The colour had deepened in her thin, oval face, with its straight brows, and large, grey eyes. Her hair, brushed in fine, high curves back from her forehead, was going grey, like his own, and this greyness made the sudden vivid colour in her cheeks painfully pathetic.

The look on her face, such as he had never seen there before, such as she had always hidden from him, was full of secret resentments, and longings, and fears. Her eyes, under their twitching brows, stared painfully. And she was silent.

Jolly alone sustained the conversation; he had many possessions, and was anxious that his unknown friend with extremely large moustaches, and hands all covered with blue veins, who sat with legs crossed like his own father (a habit he was himself trying to acquire), should know it; but being a Forsyte, though not yet quite eight years old, he made no mention of the thing at the moment dearest to his heart—a camp of soldiers in a shop-window, which his father had promised to buy. No doubt it seemed to him too precious; a tempting of Providence to mention it yet.

And the sunlight played through the leaves on that little party of the three generations grouped tranquilly under the pear-tree, which had long borne no fruit.

Old Jolyon's furrowed face was reddening patchily, as old men's faces redden in the sun. He took one of Jolly's hands in his own; the boy climbed on to his knee; and little Holly, mesmerized by this sight, crept up to them; the sound of the dog Balthasar's scratching arose rhythmically.

Suddenly young Mrs. Jolyon got up and hurried indoors. A minute later her husband muttered an excuse, and followed. Old Jolyon was left alone with his grandchildren.

And Nature with her quaint irony began working in him one of her strange revolutions, following her cyclic laws into the depths of his heart. And that tenderness for little children, that passion for the beginnings of life which had once made him forsake his son and follow June, now worked in him to forsake June and follow these littler things. Youth, like a flame, burned ever in his breast, and to youth he turned, to the round little limbs, so reckless, that wanted care, to the small round faces so unreasonably solemn or bright, to the treble tongues, and the shrill, chuckling laughter, to the insistent tugging hands, and the feel of small bodies against his legs, to all that was young and young, and once more young. And his eyes grew soft, his voice, and thin-veined hands soft, and soft his heart within him. And to those small creatures he became at once a place of pleasure, a place where they were secure, and could talk and laugh and play; till, like sunshine, there radiated from old Jolyon's wicker chair the perfect gaiety of three hearts.

But with young Jolyon following to his wife's room it was different.

He found her seated on a chair before her dressing-glass, with her hands before her face.

Her shoulders were shaking with sobs. This passion of hers for suffering was mysterious to him. He had been through a hundred of these moods; how he had survived them he never knew, for he could never believe they were moods, and that the last hour of his partnership had not struck.

In the night she would be sure to throw her arms round his neck and say: "Oh! Jo, how I make you suffer!" as she had done a hundred times before.

He reached out his hand, and, unseen, slipped his razor-case into his pocket. 'I cannot stay here,' he thought, 'I must go down!' Without a word he left the room, and went back to the lawn.

Old Jolyon had little Holly on his knee; she had taken possession of his watch; Jolly, very red in the face, was trying to show that he could stand on his head. The dog Balthasar, as close as he might be to the tea-table, had fixed his eyes on the cake.

Young Jolyon felt a malicious desire to cut their enjoyment short.

What business had his father to come and upset his wife like this? It was a shock, after all these years! He ought to have known; he ought to have given them warning; but when did a Forsyte ever imagine that his conduct could upset anybody! And in his thoughts he did old Jolyon wrong.

He spoke sharply to the children, and told them to go in to their tea. Greatly surprised, for they had never heard their father speak sharply before, they went off, hand in hand, little Holly looking back over her shoulder.

Young Jolyon poured out the tea.

"My wife's not the thing today," he said, but he knew well enough that his father had penetrated the cause of that sudden withdrawal, and almost hated the old man for sitting there so calmly.

"You've got a nice little house here," said old Jolyon with a shrewd look; "I suppose you've taken a lease of it!"

Young Jolyon nodded.

"I don't like the neighbourhood," said old Jolyon; "a ramshackle lot."

Young Jolyon replied: "Yes, we're a ramshackle lot.'"

The silence was now only broken by the sound of the dog Balthasar's scratching.

Old Jolyon said simply: "I suppose I oughtn't to have come here, Jo; but I get so lonely!"

At these words young Jolyon got up and put his hand on his father's shoulder.

In the next house someone was playing over and over again: 'La Donna mobile' on an untuned piano; and the little garden had fallen into shade, the sun now only reached the wall at the end, whereon basked a crouching cat, her yellow eyes turned sleepily down on the dog Balthasar. There was a drowsy hum of very distant traffic; the creepered trellis round the garden shut out everything but sky, and house, and pear-tree, with its top branches still gilded by the sun.

For some time they sat there, talking but little. Then old Jolyon rose to go, and not a word was said about his coming again.

He walked away very sadly. What a poor miserable place; and he thought of the great, empty house in Stanhope Gate, fit residence for a Forsyte, with its huge billiard-room and drawing-room that no one entered from one week's end to another.

That woman, whose face he had rather liked, was too thin-skinned by half; she gave Jo a bad time he knew! And those sweet children! Ah! what a piece of awful folly!

He walked towards the Edgware Road, between rows of little houses, all suggesting to him (erroneously no doubt, but the prejudices of a Forsyte are sacred) shady histories of some sort or kind.

Society, forsooth, the chattering hags and jackanapes—had set themselves up to pass judgment on his flesh and blood! A parcel of old women! He stumped his umbrella on the ground, as though to drive it into the heart of that unfortunate body, which had dared to ostracize his son and his son's son, in whom he could have lived again!

He stumped his umbrella fiercely; yet he himself had followed Society's behaviour for fifteen years—had only today been false to it!

He thought of June, and her dead mother, and the whole story, with all his old bitterness. A wretched business!

He was a long time reaching Stanhope Gate, for, with native perversity, being extremely tired, he walked the whole way.

After washing his hands in the lavatory downstairs, he went to the dining-room to wait for dinner, the only room he used when June was out—it was less lonely so. The evening paper had not yet come; he had finished the Times, there was therefore nothing to do.

The room faced the backwater of traffic, and was very silent. He disliked dogs, but a dog even would have been company. His gaze, travelling round the walls, rested on a picture entitled: 'Group of Dutch fishing boats at sunset'; the chef d'oeuvre of his collection. It gave him no pleasure. He closed his eyes. He was lonely! He oughtn't to complain, he knew, but he couldn't help it: He was a poor thing—had always been a poor thing—no pluck! Such was his thought.

The butler came to lay the table for dinner, and seeing his master apparently asleep, exercised extreme caution in his movements. This bearded man also wore a moustache, which had given rise to grave doubts in the minds of many members—of the family—, especially those who, like Soames, had been to public schools, and were accustomed to niceness in such matters. Could he really be considered a butler? Playful spirits alluded to him as: 'Uncle Jolyon's Nonconformist'; George, the acknowledged wag, had named him: 'Sankey.'

He moved to and fro between the great polished sideboard and the great polished table inimitably sleek and soft.

Old Jolyon watched him, feigning sleep. The fellow was a sneak—he had always thought so—who cared about nothing but rattling through his work, and getting out to his betting or his woman or goodness knew what! A slug! Fat too! And didn't care a pin about his master!

But then against his will, came one of those moments of philosophy which made old Jolyon different from other Forsytes:

After all why should the man care? He wasn't paid to care, and why expect it? In this world people couldn't look for affection unless they paid for it. It might be different in the next—he didn't know—couldn't tell! And again he shut his eyes.

Relentless and stealthy, the butler pursued his labours, taking things from the various compartments of the sideboard. His back seemed always turned to old Jolyon; thus, he robbed his operations of the unseemliness of being carried on in his master's presence; now and then he furtively breathed on the silver, and wiped it with a piece of chamois leather. He appeared to pore over the quantities of wine in the decanters, which he carried carefully and rather high, letting his head droop over them protectingly. When he had finished, he stood for over a minute watching his master, and in his greenish eyes there was a look of contempt:

After all, this master of his was an old buffer, who hadn't much left in him!

Soft as a tom-cat, he crossed the room to press the bell. His orders were 'dinner at seven.' What if his master were asleep; he would soon have him out of that; there was the night to sleep in! He had himself to think of, for he was due at his Club at half-past eight!

In answer to the ring, appeared a page boy with a silver soup tureen. The butler took it from his hands and placed it on the table, then, standing by the open door, as though about to usher company into the room, he said in a solemn voice:

"Dinner is on the table, sir!"

Slowly old Jolyon got up out of his chair, and sat down at the table to eat his dinner.

CHAPTER VIII—PLANS OF THE HOUSE

Forsytes, as is generally admitted, have shells, like that extremely useful little animal which is made into Turkish delight, in other words, they are never seen, or if seen would not be recognised, without habitats, composed of circumstance, property, acquaintances, and wives, which seem to move along with them in their passage through a world composed of thousands of other Forsytes with their habitats. Without a habitat a Forsyte is inconceivable—he would be like a novel without a plot, which is well-known to be an anomaly.

To Forsyte eyes Bosinney appeared to have no habitat, he seemed one of those rare and unfortunate men who go through life surrounded by circumstance, property, acquaintances, and wives that do not belong to them.

His rooms in Sloane Street, on the top floor, outside which, on a plate, was his name, 'Philip Baynes Bosinney, Architect,' were not those of a Forsyte.—He had no sitting-room apart from his office, but a large recess had been screened off to conceal the necessaries of life—a couch, an easy chair, his pipes, spirit case, novels and slippers. The business part of the room had the usual furniture; an open cupboard with pigeon-holes, a round oak table, a folding wash-stand, some hard chairs, a standing desk of large dimensions covered with drawings and designs. June had twice been to tea there under the chaperonage of his aunt.

He was believed to have a bedroom at the back.

As far as the family had been able to ascertain his income, it consisted of two consulting appointments at twenty pounds a year, together with an odd fee once in a way, and—more worthy item—a private annuity under his father's will of one hundred and fifty pounds a year.

What had transpired concerning that father was not so reassuring. It appeared that he had been a Lincolnshire country doctor of Cornish extraction, striking appearance, and Byronic tendencies—a well-known figure, in fact, in his county. Bosinney's uncle by marriage, Baynes, of Baynes and Bildeboy, a Forsyte in instincts if not in name, had but little that was worthy to relate of his brother-in-law.

"An odd fellow!' he would say: 'always spoke of his three eldest boys as 'good creatures, but so dull'; they're all doing capitally in the Indian Civil! Philip was the only one he liked. I've heard him talk in the queerest way; he once said to me: 'My dear fellow, never let your poor wife know what you're thinking of! But I didn't follow his advice; not I! An eccentric man! He would say to Phil: 'Whether you live like a gentleman or not, my boy, be sure you die like one! and he had himself embalmed in a frock coat suit, with a satin cravat and a diamond pin. Oh, quite an original, I can assure you!"

Of Bosinney himself Baynes would speak warmly, with a certain compassion: "He's got a streak of his father's Byronism. Why, look at the way he threw up his chances when he left my office; going off like that for six months with a knapsack, and all for what?—to study foreign architecture—foreign! What could he expect? And there he is—a clever young fellow—doesn't make his hundred a year! Now this engagement is the best thing that could have happened—keep him steady; he's one of those that go to bed all day and stay up all night, simply because they've no method; but no vice about him—not an ounce of vice. Old Forsyte's a rich man!"

Mr. Baynes made himself extremely pleasant to June, who frequently visited his house in Lowndes Square at this period.

"This house of your cousin's—what a capital man of business—is the very thing for Philip," he would say to her; "you mustn't expect to see too much of him just now, my dear young lady. The good cause—the good cause! The young man must make his way. When I was his age I was at work day and night. My dear wife used to say to me, 'Bobby, don't work too hard, think of your health'; but I never spared myself!"

June had complained that her lover found no time to come to Stanhope Gate.

The first time he came again they had not been together a quarter of an hour before, by one of those coincidences of which she was a mistress, Mrs. Septimus Small arrived. Thereon Bosinney rose and hid himself, according to previous arrangement, in the little study, to wait for her departure.

"My dear," said Aunt Juley, "how thin he is! I've often noticed it with engaged people; but you mustn't let it get worse. There's Barlow's extract of veal; it did your Uncle Swithin a lot of good."

June, her little figure erect before the hearth, her small face quivering grimly, for she regarded her aunt's untimely visit in the light of a personal injury, replied with scorn:

"It's because he's busy; people who can do anything worth doing are never fat!"

Aunt Juley pouted; she herself had always been thin, but the only pleasure she derived from the fact was the opportunity of longing to be stouter.

"I don't think," she said mournfully, "that you ought to let them call him 'The Buccaneer'; people might think it odd, now that he's going to build a house for Soames. I do hope he will be careful; it's so important for him. Soames has such good taste!"

"Taste!" cried June, flaring up at once; "wouldn't give that for his taste, or any of the family's!"

Mrs. Small was taken aback.

"Your Uncle Swithin," she said, "always had beautiful taste! And Soames's little house is lovely; you don't mean to say you don't think so!"

"H'mph!" said June, "that's only because Irene's there!"

Aunt Juley tried to say something pleasant:

"And how will dear Irene like living in the country?"

June gazed at her intently, with a look in her eyes as if her conscience had suddenly leaped up into them; it passed; and an even more intent look took its place, as if she had stared that conscience out of countenance. She replied imperiously:

"Of course she'll like it; why shouldn't she?"

Mrs. Small grew nervous.

"I didn't know," she said; "I thought she mightn't like to leave her friends. Your Uncle James says she doesn't take enough interest in life. We think—I mean Timothy thinks—she ought to go out more. I expect you'll miss her very much!"

June clasped her hands behind her neck.

"I do wish," she cried, "Uncle Timothy wouldn't talk about what doesn't concern him!"

Aunt Juley rose to the full height of her tall figure.

"He never talks about what doesn't concern him," she said.

June was instantly compunctious; she ran to her aunt and kissed her.

"I'm very sorry, auntie; but I wish they'd let Irene alone."

Aunt Juley, unable to think of anything further on the subject that would be suitable, was silent; she prepared for departure, hooking her black silk cape across her chest, and, taking up her green reticule:

"And how is your dear grandfather?" she asked in the hall, "I expect he's very lonely now that all your time is taken up with Mr. Bosinney."

She bent and kissed her niece hungrily, and with little, mincing steps passed away.

The tears sprang up in June's eyes; running into the little study, where Bosinney was sitting at the table drawing birds on the back of an envelope, she sank down by his side and cried:

"Oh, Phil! it's all so horrid!" Her heart was as warm as the colour of her hair.

On the following Sunday morning, while Soames was shaving, a message was brought him to the effect that Mr. Bosinney was below, and would be glad to see him. Opening the door into his wife's room, he said:

"Bosinney's downstairs. Just go and entertain him while I finish shaving. I'll be down in a minute. It's about the plans, I expect."

Irene looked at him, without reply, put the finishing touch to her dress and went downstairs. He could not make her out about this house. She had said nothing against it, and, as far as Bosinney was concerned, seemed friendly enough.

From the window of his dressing-room he could see them talking together in the little court below. He hurried on with his shaving, cutting his chin twice. He heard them laugh, and thought to himself: "Well, they get on all right, anyway!"

As he expected, Bosinney had come round to fetch him to look at the plans.

He took his hat and went over.

The plans were spread on the oak table in the architect's room; and pale, imperturbable, inquiring, Soames bent over them for a long time without speaking.

He said at last in a puzzled voice:

"It's an odd sort of house!"

A rectangular house of two stories was designed in a quadrangle round a covered-in court. This court, encircled by a gallery on the upper floor, was roofed with a glass roof, supported by eight columns running up from the ground.

It was indeed, to Forsyte eyes, an odd house.

"There's a lot of room cut to waste," pursued Soames.

Bosinney began to walk about, and Soames did not like the expression on his face.

"The principle of this house," said the architect, "was that you should have room to breathe—like a gentleman!"

Soames extended his finger and thumb, as if measuring the extent of the distinction he should acquire; and replied:

"Oh! yes; I see."

The peculiar look came into Bosinney's face which marked all his enthusiasms.

"I've tried to plan you a house here with some self-respect of its own. If you don't like it, you'd better say so. It's certainly the last thing to be considered—who wants self-respect in a house, when you can squeeze in an extra lavatory?" He put his finger suddenly down on the left division of the centre oblong: "You can swing a cat here. This is for your pictures, divided from this court by curtains; draw them back and you'll have a space of fifty-one by twenty-three six. This double-faced stove in the centre, here, looks one way towards the court, one way towards the picture room; this end wall is all window; You've a southeast light from that, a north light from the court. The rest of your pictures you can hang round the gallery upstairs, or in the other rooms." "In architecture," he went on—and though looking at Soames he did not seem to see him, which gave Soames an unpleasant feeling— "as in life, you'll get no self-respect without regularity. Fellows tell you that's old fashioned. It appears to be peculiar any way; it never occurs to us to embody the main principle of life in our buildings; we load our houses with decoration, gimcracks, corners, anything to distract the eye. On the contrary the eye should rest; get your effects with a few strong lines. The whole thing is regularity there's no self-respect without it."

Soames, the unconscious ironist, fixed his gaze on Bosinney's tie, which was far from being in the perpendicular; he was unshaven too, and his dress not remarkable for order. Architecture appeared to have exhausted his regularity.

"Won't it look like a barrack?" he inquired.

He did not at once receive a reply.

"I can see what it is," said Bosinney, "you want one of Littlemaster's houses—one of the pretty and commodious sort, where the servants will live in garrets, and the front door be sunk so that you may come up again. By all means try Littlemaster, you'll find him a capital fellow, I've known him all my life!"

Soames was alarmed. He had really been struck by the plans, and the concealment of his satisfaction had been merely instinctive. It was difficult for him to pay a compliment. He despised people who were lavish with their praises.

He found himself now in the embarrassing position of one who must pay a compliment or run the risk of losing a good thing. Bosinney was just the fellow who might tear up the plans and refuse to act for him; a kind of grown-up child!

This grown-up childishness, to which he felt so superior, exercised a peculiar and almost mesmeric effect on Soames, for he had never felt anything like it in himself.

"Well," he stammered at last, "it's—it's, certainly original."

He had such a private distrust and even dislike of the word 'original' that he felt he had not really given himself away by this remark.

Bosinney seemed pleased. It was the sort of thing that would please a fellow like that! And his success encouraged Soames.

"It's—a big place," he said.

"Space, air, light," he heard Bosinney murmur, "you can't live like a gentleman in one of Littlemaster's—he builds for manufacturers."

Soames made a deprecating movement; he had been identified with a gentleman; not for a good deal of money now would he be classed with manufacturers. But his innate distrust of general principles revived. What the deuce was the good of talking about regularity and self-respect? It looked to him as if the house would be cold.

"Irene can't stand the cold!" he said.

"Ah!" said Bosinney sarcastically. "Your wife? She doesn't like the cold? I'll see to that; she shan't be cold. Look here!" he pointed, to four marks at regular intervals on the walls of the court. "I've given you hot-water pipes in aluminium casings; you can get them with very good designs."

Soames looked suspiciously at these marks.

"It's all very well, all this," he said, "but what's it going to cost?"

The architect took a sheet of paper from his pocket:

"The house, of course, should be built entirely of stone, but, as I thought you wouldn't stand that, I've compromised for a facing. It ought to have a copper roof, but I've made it green slate. As it is, including metal work, it'll cost you eight thousand five hundred."

"Eight thousand five hundred?" said Soames. "Why, I gave you an outside limit of eight!"

"Can't be done for a penny less," replied Bosinney coolly.

"You must take it or leave it!"

It was the only way, probably, that such a proposition could have been made to Soames. He was nonplussed. Conscience told him to throw the whole thing up. But the design was good, and he knew it—there was completeness about it, and dignity; the servants' apartments were excellent too. He would gain credit by living in a house like that—with such individual features, yet perfectly well-arranged.

He continued poring over the plans, while Bosinney went into his bedroom to shave and dress.

The two walked back to Montpellier Square in silence, Soames watching him out of the corner of his eye.

The Buccaneer was rather a good-looking fellow—so he thought—when he was properly got up.

Irene was bending over her flowers when the two men came in.

She spoke of sending across the Park to fetch June.

"No, no," said Soames, "we've still got business to talk over!"

At lunch he was almost cordial, and kept pressing Bosinney to eat. He was pleased to see the architect in such high spirits, and left him to spend the afternoon with Irene, while he stole off to his pictures, after his Sunday habit. At tea-time he came down to the drawing-room, and found them talking, as he expressed it, nineteen to the dozen.

Unobserved in the doorway, he congratulated himself that things were taking the right turn. It was lucky she and Bosinney got on; she seemed to be falling into line with the idea of the new house.

Quiet meditation among his pictures had decided him to spring the five hundred if necessary; but he hoped that the afternoon might have softened Bosinney's estimates. It was so purely a matter which Bosinney could remedy if he liked; there must be a dozen ways in which he could cheapen the production of a house without spoiling the effect.

He awaited, therefore, his opportunity till Irene was handing the architect his first cup of tea. A chink of sunshine through the lace of the blinds warmed her cheek, shone in the gold of her hair, and in her soft eyes. Possibly the same gleam deepened Bosinney's colour, gave the rather startled look to his face.

Soames hated sunshine, and he at once got up, to draw the blind. Then he took his own cup of tea from his wife, and said, more coldly than he had intended:

"Can't you see your way to do it for eight thousand after all? There must be a lot of little things you could alter."

Bosinney drank off his tea at a gulp, put down his cup, and answered:

"Not one!"

Soames saw that his suggestion had touched some unintelligible point of personal vanity.

"Well," he agreed, with sulky resignation; "you must have it your own way, I suppose."

A few minutes later Bosinney rose to go, and Soames rose too, to see him off the premises. The architect seemed in absurdly high spirits. After watching him walk away at a swinging pace, Soames returned moodily to the drawing-room, where Irene was putting away the music, and, moved by an uncontrollable spasm of curiosity, he asked:

"Well, what do you think of 'The Buccaneer'?"

He looked at the carpet while waiting for her answer, and he had to wait some time.

"I don't know," she said at last.

"Do you think he's good-looking?"

61

Irene smiled. And it seemed to Soames that she was mocking him.

"Yes," she answered; "very."

CHAPTER IX—DEATH OF AUNT ANN

There came a morning at the end of September when Aunt Ann was unable to take from Smither's hands the insignia of personal dignity. After one look at the old face, the doctor, hurriedly sent for, announced that Miss Forsyte had passed away in her sleep.

Aunts Juley and Hester were overwhelmed by the shock. They had never imagined such an ending. Indeed, it is doubtful whether they had ever realized that an ending was bound to come. Secretly they felt it unreasonable of Ann to have left them like this without a word, without even a struggle. It was unlike her.

Perhaps what really affected them so profoundly was the thought that a Forsyte should have let go her grasp on life. If one, then why not all!

It was a full hour before they could make up their minds to tell Timothy. If only it could be kept from him! If only it could be broken to him by degrees!

And long they stood outside his door whispering together. And when it was over they whispered together again.

He would feel it more, they were afraid, as time went on. Still, he had taken it better than could have been expected. He would keep his bed, of course!

They separated, crying quietly.

Aunt Juley stayed in her room, prostrated by the blow. Her face, discoloured by tears, was divided into compartments by the little ridges of pouting flesh which had swollen with emotion. It was impossible to conceive of life without Ann, who had lived with her for seventy-three years, broken only by the short interregnum of her married life, which seemed now so unreal. At fixed intervals she went to her drawer, and took from beneath the lavender bags a fresh pocket-handkerchief. Her warm heart could not bear the thought that Ann was lying there so cold.

Aunt Hester, the silent, the patient, that backwater of the family energy, sat in the drawing-room, where the blinds were drawn; and she, too, had wept at first, but quietly, without visible effect. Her guiding principle, the conservation of energy, did not abandon her in sorrow. She sat, slim, motionless, studying the grate, her hands idle in the lap of her black silk dress. They would want to rouse her into doing something, no doubt. As if there were any good in that! Doing something would not bring back Ann! Why worry her?

Five o'clock brought three of the brothers, Jolyon and James and Swithin; Nicholas was at Yarmouth, and Roger had a bad attack of gout. Mrs. Hayman had been by herself earlier in the day, and, after seeing Ann, had gone away, leaving a message for Timothy—which was kept from him—that she ought to have been told sooner. In fact, there was a feeling amongst them all that they ought to have been told sooner, as though they had missed something; and James said:

"I knew how it'd be; I told you she wouldn't last through the summer."

Aunt Hester made no reply; it was nearly October, but what was the good of arguing; some people were never satisfied.

She sent up to tell her sister that the brothers were there. Mrs. Small came down at once. She had bathed her face, which was still swollen, and though she looked severely at Swithin's trousers, for they were of light blue—he had come straight from the club, where the news had reached him—she wore a more cheerful expression than usual, the instinct for doing the wrong thing being even now too strong for her.

Presently all five went up to look at the body. Under the pure white sheet a quilted counter-pane had been placed, for now, more than ever, Aunt Ann had need of warmth; and, the pillows removed, her spine and head rested flat, with the semblance of their life-long inflexibility; the coif banding the top of her brow was drawn on either side to the level of the ears, and between it and the sheet her face, almost as white, was turned with closed eyes to the faces of her brothers and sisters. In its extraordinary peace the face was stronger than ever, nearly all bone now under the scarce-wrinkled parchment of skin—square jaw and chin, cheekbones, forehead with hollow temples, chiselled nose—the fortress of an unconquerable spirit that had yielded to death, and in its upward sightlessness seemed trying to regain that spirit, to regain the guardianship it had just laid down.

Swithin took but one look at the face, and left the room; the sight, he said afterwards, made him very queer. He went downstairs shaking the whole house, and, seizing his hat, clambered into his brougham, without giving any directions to the coachman. He was driven home, and all the evening sat in his chair without moving.

He could take nothing for dinner but a partridge, with an imperial pint of champagne....

Old Jolyon stood at the bottom of the bed, his hands folded in front of him. He alone of those in the room remembered the death of his mother, and though he looked at Ann, it was of that he was thinking. Ann was an old woman, but death had come to her at last—death came to all! His face did not move, his gaze seemed travelling from very far.

Aunt Hester stood beside him. She did not cry now, tears were exhausted—her nature refused to permit a further escape of force; she twisted her hands, looking not at Ann, but from side to side, seeking some way of escaping the effort of realization.

Of all the brothers and sisters James manifested the most emotion. Tears rolled down the parallel furrows of his thin face; where he should go now to tell his troubles he did not know; Juley was no good, Hester worse than useless! He felt Ann's death more than he had ever thought he should; this would upset him for weeks!

Presently Aunt Hester stole out, and Aunt Juley began moving about, doing 'what was necessary,' so that twice she knocked against something. Old Jolyon, roused from his reverie, that reverie of the long, long past, looked sternly at her, and went away. James alone was left by the bedside; glancing stealthily round, to see that he was not observed, he twisted his long body down, placed a kiss on the dead forehead, then he, too, hastily left the room. Encountering Smither in the hall, he began to ask her about the funeral, and, finding that she knew nothing, complained bitterly that, if they didn't take care, everything would go wrong. She had better send for Mr. Soames—he knew all about that sort of thing; her master was very much upset, he supposed—he would want looking after; as for her mistresses, they were no good—they had no gumption! They would be ill too, he shouldn't wonder. She had better send for the doctor; it was best to take things in time. He didn't think his sister Ann had had the best opinion; if she'd had Blank she would have been alive now. Smither might send to Park Lane any time she wanted advice. Of course, his carriage was at their service for the funeral. He supposed she hadn't such a thing as a glass of claret and a biscuit—he had had no lunch!

The days before the funeral passed quietly. It had long been known, of course, that Aunt Ann had left her little property to Timothy. There was, therefore, no reason for the slightest agitation. Soames, who was sole executor, took charge of all arrangements, and in due course sent out the following invitation to every male member of the family:

To...........

Your presence is requested at the funeral of Miss Ann Forsyte, in Highgate Cemetery, at noon of Oct. 1st. Carriages will meet at "The Bower," Bayswater Road, at 10.45. No flowers by request. 'R.S.V.P.'

The morning came, cold, with a high, grey, London sky, and at half-past ten the first carriage, that of James, drove up. It contained James and his son-in-law Dartie, a fine man, with a square chest, buttoned very tightly into a frock coat, and a sallow, fattish face adorned with dark, well-curled moustaches, and that incorrigible commencement of whisker which, eluding the strictest attempts at shaving, seems the mark of something deeply ingrained in the personality of the shaver, being especially noticeable in men who speculate.

Soames, in his capacity of executor, received the guests, for Timothy still kept his bed; he would get up after the funeral; and Aunts Juley and Hester would not be coming down till all was over, when it was understood there would be lunch for anyone who cared to come back. The next to arrive was Roger, still limping from the gout, and encircled by three of his sons—young Roger, Eustace, and Thomas. George, the remaining son, arrived almost immediately afterwards in a hansom, and paused in the hall to ask Soames how he found undertaking pay.

They disliked each other.

Then came two Haymans—Giles and Jesse perfectly silent, and very well dressed, with special creases down their evening trousers. Then old Jolyon alone. Next, Nicholas, with a healthy colour in his face, and a carefully veiled sprightliness in every movement of his head and body. One of his sons followed him, meek and subdued. Swithin Forsyte, and Bosinney arrived at the same moment,—and stood—bowing precedence to each other,— but on the door opening they tried to enter together; they renewed their apologies in the hall, and, Swithin, settling his stock, which had become disarranged in the struggle, very slowly mounted the stairs. The other Hayman; two married sons of Nicholas, together with Tweetyman, Spender, and Warry, the husbands of married Forsyte and Hayman daughters. The company was then complete, twenty-one in all, not a male member of the family being absent but Timothy and young Jolyon.

Entering the scarlet and green drawing-room, whose apparel made so vivid a setting for their unaccustomed costumes, each tried nervously to find a seat, desirous of hiding the emphatic blackness of his trousers. There seemed a sort of indecency in that blackness and in the colour of their gloves—a sort of exaggeration of the feelings; and many cast shocked looks of secret envy at 'the Buccaneer,' who had no gloves, and was wearing grey trousers. A subdued hum of conversation rose, no one speaking of the departed, but each asking after the other, as though thereby casting an indirect libation to this event, which they had come to honour.

And presently James said:

"Well, I think we ought to be starting."

They went downstairs, and, two and two, as they had been told off in strict precedence, mounted the carriages.

The hearse started at a foot's pace; the carriages moved slowly after. In the first went old Jolyon with Nicholas; in the second, the twins, Swithin and James; in the third, Roger and young Roger; Soames, young Nicholas, George, and Bosinney followed in the fourth. Each of the other carriages, eight in all, held three or four of the family; behind them came the doctor's brougham; then, at a decent interval, cabs containing family clerks and servants; and at the very end, one containing nobody at all, but bringing the total cortege up to the number of thirteen.

So long as the procession kept to the highway of the Bayswater Road, it retained the foot's-pace, but, turning into less important thorough-fares, it soon broke into a trot, and so proceeded, with intervals of walking in the more fashionable streets, until it arrived. In the first carriage old Jolyon and Nicholas were talking of their wills. In the second the twins, after a single attempt, had lapsed into complete silence; both were rather deaf, and the exertion of making themselves heard was too great. Only once James broke this silence:

"I shall have to be looking about for some ground somewhere. What arrangements have you made, Swithin?"

And Swithin, fixing him with a dreadful stare, answered:

"Don't talk to me about such things!"

In the third carriage a disjointed conversation was carried on in the intervals of looking out to see how far they had got, George remarking, "Well, it was really time that the poor old lady went." He didn't believe in people living beyond seventy, Young Nicholas replied mildly that the rule didn't seem to apply to the Forsytes. George said he himself intended to commit suicide at sixty. Young Nicholas, smiling and stroking a long chin, didn't think his father would like that theory; he had made a lot of money since he was sixty. Well, seventy was the outside limit; it was then time, George said, for them to go and leave their money to their children. Soames, hitherto silent, here joined in; he had not forgotten the remark about the 'undertaking,' and, lifting his eyelids almost imperceptibly, said it was all very well for people who never made money to talk. He himself intended to live as long as he could. This was a hit at George, who was notoriously hard up. Bosinney muttered abstractedly "Hear, hear!" and, George yawning, the conversation dropped.

Upon arriving, the coffin was borne into the chapel, and, two by two, the mourners filed in behind it. This guard of men, all attached to the dead by the bond of kinship, was an impressive and singular sight in the great city of London, with its overwhelming diversity of life, its innumerable vocations, pleasures, duties, its terrible hardness, its terrible call to individualism.

The family had gathered to triumph over all this, to give a show of tenacious unity, to illustrate gloriously that law of property underlying the growth of their tree, by which it had thriven and spread, trunk and branches, the sap flowing through all, the full growth reached at the appointed time. The spirit of the old woman lying in her last sleep had called them to this demonstration. It was her final appeal to that unity which had been their strength—it was her final triumph that she had died while the tree was yet whole.

She was spared the watching of the branches jut out beyond the point of balance. She could not look into the hearts of her followers. The same law that had worked in her, bringing her up from a tall, straight-backed slip of a girl to a woman strong and grown, from a woman grown to a woman old, angular, feeble, almost witchlike, with individuality all sharpened and sharpened, as all rounding from the world's contact fell off from her— that same law would work, was working, in the family she had watched like a mother.

She had seen it young, and growing, she had seen it strong and grown, and before her old eyes had time or strength to see any more, she died. She would have tried, and who knows but she might have kept it young and strong, with her old fingers, her trembling kisses—a little longer; alas! not even Aunt Ann could fight with Nature.

'Pride comes before a fall!' In accordance with this, the greatest of Nature's ironies, the Forsyte family had gathered for a last proud pageant before they fell. Their faces to right and left, in single lines, were turned for the most part impassively toward the ground, guardians of their thoughts; but here and there, one looking upward, with a line between his brows, searched to see some sight on the chapel walls too much for him, to be listening to something that appalled. And the responses, low-muttered, in voices through which rose the same tone, the same unseizable family ring, sounded weird, as though murmured in hurried duplication by a single person.

The service in the chapel over, the mourners filed up again to guard the body to the tomb. The vault stood open, and, round it, men in black were waiting.

From that high and sacred field, where thousands of the upper middle class lay in their last sleep, the eyes of the Forsytes travelled down across the flocks of graves. There—spreading to the distance, lay London, with no sun over it, mourning the loss of its daughter, mourning with this family, so dear, the loss of her who was mother and guardian. A hundred thousand spires and houses, blurred in the great grey web of property, lay there like prostrate worshippers before the grave of this, the oldest Forsyte of them all.

A few words, a sprinkle of earth, the thrusting of the coffin home, and Aunt Ann had passed to her last rest.

Round the vault, trustees of that passing, the five brothers stood, with white heads bowed; they would see that Ann was comfortable where she was going. Her little property must stay behind, but otherwise, all that could be should be done....

Then severally, each stood aside, and putting on his hat, turned back to inspect the new inscription on the marble of the family vault:

SACRED TO THE MEMORY OF ANN FORSYTE,

THE DAUGHTER OF THE ABOVE JOLYON AND ANN FORSYTE,

WHO DEPARTED THIS LIFE THE 27TH DAY OF SEPTEMBER, 1886,

AGED EIGHTY-SEVEN YEARS AND FOUR DAYS

Soon perhaps, someone else would be wanting an inscription. It was strange and intolerable, for they had not thought somehow, that Forsytes could die. And one and all they had a longing to get away from this painfulness, this ceremony which had reminded them of things they could not bear to think about—to get away quickly and go about their business and forget.

It was cold, too; the wind, like some slow, disintegrating force, blowing up the hill over the graves, struck them with its chilly breath; they began to split into groups, and as quickly as possible to fill the waiting carriages.

Swithin said he should go back to lunch at Timothy's, and he offered to take anybody with him in his brougham. It was considered a doubtful privilege to drive with Swithin in his brougham, which was not a large one; nobody accepted, and he went off alone. James and Roger followed immediately after; they also would drop in to lunch. The others gradually melted away, Old Jolyon taking three nephews to fill up his carriage; he had a want of those young faces.

Soames, who had to arrange some details in the cemetery office, walked away with Bosinney. He had much to talk over with him, and, having finished his business, they strolled to Hampstead, lunched together at the Spaniard's Inn, and spent a long time in going into practical details connected with the building of the house; they then proceeded to the tram-line, and came as far as the Marble Arch, where Bosinney went off to Stanhope Gate to see June.

Soames felt in excellent spirits when he arrived home, and confided to Irene at dinner that he had had a good talk with Bosinney, who really seemed a sensible fellow; they had had a capital walk too, which had done his liver good—he had been short of exercise for a long time—and altogether a very satisfactory day. If only it hadn't been for poor Aunt Ann, he would have taken her to the theatre; as it was, they must make the best of an evening at home.

"The Buccaneer asked after you more than once," he said suddenly. And moved by some inexplicable desire to assert his proprietorship, he rose from his chair and planted a kiss on his wife's shoulder.

PART II

CHAPTER I—PROGRESS OF THE HOUSE

The winter had been an open one. Things in the trade were slack; and as Soames had reflected before making up his mind, it had been a good time for building. The shell of the house at Robin Hill was thus completed by the end of April.

Now that there was something to be seen for his money, he had been coming down once, twice, even three times a week, and would mouse about among the debris for hours, careful never to soil his clothes, moving silently through the unfinished brickwork of doorways, or circling round the columns in the central court.

And he would stand before them for minutes' together, as though peering into the real quality of their substance.

On April 30 he had an appointment with Bosinney to go over the accounts, and five minutes before the proper time he entered the tent which the architect had pitched for himself close to the old oak tree.

The accounts were already prepared on a folding table, and with a nod Soames sat down to study them. It was some time before he raised his head.

"I can't make them out," he said at last; "they come to nearly seven hundred more than they ought."

After a glance at Bosinney's face he went on quickly:

"If you only make a firm stand against these builder chaps you'll get them down. They stick you with everything if you don't look sharp.... Take ten per cent. off all round. I shan't mind it's coming out a hundred or so over the mark!"

Bosinney shook his head:

"I've taken off every farthing I can!"

Soames pushed back the table with a movement of anger, which sent the account sheets fluttering to the ground.

"Then all I can say is," he flustered out, "you've made a pretty mess of it!"

"I've told you a dozen times," Bosinney answered sharply, "that there'd be extras. I've pointed them out to you over and over again!"

"I know that," growled Soames: "I shouldn't have objected to a ten pound note here and there. How was I to know that by 'extras' you meant seven hundred pounds?"

The qualities of both men had contributed to this not-inconsiderable discrepancy. On the one hand, the architect's devotion to his idea, to the image of a house which he had created and believed in—had made him nervous of being stopped, or forced to the use of makeshifts; on the other, Soames' not less true and wholehearted devotion to the very best article that could be obtained for the money, had rendered him averse to believing that things worth thirteen shillings could not be bought with twelve.

"I wish I'd never undertaken your house," said Bosinney suddenly. "You come down here worrying me out of my life. You want double the value for your money anybody else would, and now that you've got a house that for its size is not to be beaten in the county, you don't want to pay for it. If you're anxious to be off your bargain, I daresay I can find the balance above the estimates myself, but I'm d——d if I do another stroke of work for you!"

Soames regained his composure. Knowing that Bosinney had no capital, he regarded this as a wild suggestion. He saw, too, that he would be kept indefinitely out of this house on which he had set his heart, and just at the crucial point when the architect's personal care made all the difference. In the meantime there was Irene to be thought of! She had been very queer lately. He really believed it was only because she had taken to Bosinney that she tolerated the idea of the house at all. It would not do to make an open breach with her.

"You needn't get into a rage," he said. "If I'm willing to put up with it, I suppose you needn't cry out. All I meant was that when you tell me a thing is going to cost so much, I like to—well, in fact, I—like to know where I am."

"Look here!" said Bosinney, and Soames was both annoyed and surprised by the shrewdness of his glance. "You've got my services dirt cheap. For the kind of work I've put into this house, and the amount of time I've given to it, you'd have had to pay Littlemaster or some other fool four times as much. What you want, in fact, is a first-rate man for a fourth-rate fee, and that's exactly what you've got!"

Soames saw that he really meant what he said, and, angry though he was, the consequences of a row rose before him too vividly. He saw his house unfinished, his wife rebellious, himself a laughingstock.

"Let's go over it," he said sulkily, "and see how the money's gone."

"Very well," assented Bosinney. "But we'll hurry up, if you don't mind. I have to get back in time to take June to the theatre."

Soames cast a stealthy look at him, and said: "Coming to our place, I suppose to meet her?" He was always coming to their place!

There had been rain the night before-a spring rain, and the earth smelt of sap and wild grasses. The warm, soft breeze swung the leaves and the golden buds of the old oak tree, and in the sunshine the blackbirds were whistling their hearts out.

It was such a spring day as breathes into a man an ineffable yearning, a painful sweetness, a longing that makes him stand motionless, looking at the leaves or grass, and fling out his arms to embrace he knows not what. The earth gave forth a fainting warmth, stealing up through the chilly garment in which winter had wrapped her. It was her long caress of invitation, to draw men down to lie within her arms, to roll their bodies on her, and put their lips to her breast.

On just such a day as this Soames had got from Irene the promise he had asked her for so often. Seated on the fallen trunk of a tree, he had promised for the twentieth time that if their marriage were not a success, she should be as free as if she had never married him!

"Do you swear it?" she had said. A few days back she had reminded him of that oath. He had answered: "Nonsense! I couldn't have sworn any such thing!" By some awkward fatality he remembered it now. What queer things men would swear for the sake of women! He would have sworn it at any time to gain her! He would swear it now, if thereby he could touch her—but nobody could touch her, she was cold-hearted!

And memories crowded on him with the fresh, sweet savour of the spring wind-memories of his courtship.

In the spring of the year 1881 he was visiting his old school-fellow and client, George Liversedge, of Branksome, who, with the view of developing his pine-woods in the neighbourhood of Bournemouth, had placed the formation of the company necessary to the scheme in Soames's hands. Mrs. Liversedge, with a sense of the fitness of things, had given a musical tea in his honour. Later in the course of this function, which Soames, no musician, had regarded as an unmitigated bore, his eye had been caught by the face of a girl dressed in mourning, standing by herself. The lines of her tall, as yet rather thin figure, showed through the wispy, clinging stuff of her black dress, her black-gloved hands were crossed in front of her, her lips slightly parted, and her large, dark eyes wandered from face to face. Her hair, done low on her neck, seemed to gleam above her black collar like coils of shining metal. And as Soames stood looking at her, the sensation that most men have felt at one time or another went stealing through him—a peculiar satisfaction of the senses, a peculiar certainty, which novelists and old ladies call love at first sight. Still stealthily watching her, he at once made his way to his hostess, and stood doggedly waiting for the music to cease.

"Who is that girl with yellow hair and dark eyes?" he asked.

"That—oh! Irene Heron. Her father, Professor Heron, died this year. She lives with her stepmother. She's a nice girl, a pretty girl, but no money!"

"Introduce me, please," said Soames.

It was very little that he found to say, nor did he find her responsive to that little. But he went away with the resolution to see her again. He effected his object by chance, meeting her on the pier with her stepmother, who had the habit of walking there from twelve to one of a forenoon. Soames made this lady's acquaintance with alacrity, nor was it long before he perceived in her the ally he was looking for. His keen scent for the commercial side of family life soon told him that Irene cost her stepmother more than the fifty pounds a year she brought her; it also told him that Mrs. Heron, a woman yet in the prime of life, desired to be married again. The strange ripening beauty of her stepdaughter stood in the way of this desirable consummation. And Soames, in his stealthy tenacity, laid his plans.

He left Bournemouth without having given himself away, but in a month's time came back, and this time he spoke, not to the girl, but to her stepmother. He had made up his mind, he said; he would wait any time. And he had long to wait, watching Irene bloom, the lines of her young figure softening, the stronger blood deepening the gleam of her eyes, and warming her face to a creamy glow; and at each visit he proposed to her, and when that visit was at an end, took her refusal away with him, back to London, sore at heart, but steadfast and silent as the grave. He tried to come at the secret springs of her resistance;

only once had he a gleam of light. It was at one of those assembly dances, which afford the only outlet to the passions of the population of seaside watering-places. He was sitting with her in an embrasure, his senses tingling with the contact of the waltz. She had looked at him over her, slowly waving fan; and he had lost his head. Seizing that moving wrist, he pressed his lips to the flesh of her arm. And she had shuddered—to this day he had not forgotten that shudder—nor the look so passionately averse she had given him.

A year after that she had yielded. What had made her yield he could never make out; and from Mrs. Heron, a woman of some diplomatic talent, he learnt nothing. Once after they were married he asked her, "What made you refuse me so often?" She had answered by a strange silence. An enigma to him from the day that he first saw her, she was an enigma to him still....

Bosinney was waiting for him at the door; and on his rugged, good-looking, face was a queer, yearning, yet happy look, as though he too saw a promise of bliss in the spring sky, sniffed a coming happiness in the spring air. Soames looked at him waiting there. What was the matter with the fellow that he looked so happy? What was he waiting for with that smile on his lips and in his eyes? Soames could not see that for which Bosinney was waiting as he stood there drinking in the flower-scented wind. And once more he felt baffled in the presence of this man whom by habit he despised. He hastened on to the house.

"The only colour for those tiles," he heard Bosinney say,—"is ruby with a grey tint in the stuff, to give a transparent effect. I should like Irene's opinion. I'm ordering the purple leather curtains for the doorway of this court; and if you distemper the drawing-room ivory cream over paper, you'll get an illusive look. You want to aim all through the decorations at what I call charm."

Soames said: "You mean that my wife has charm!"

Bosinney evaded the question.

"You should have a clump of iris plants in the centre of that court."

Soames smiled superciliously.

"I'll look into Beech's some time," he said, "and see what's appropriate!"

They found little else to say to each other, but on the way to the Station Soames asked:

"I suppose you find Irene very artistic."

"Yes." The abrupt answer was as distinct a snub as saying: "If you want to discuss her you can do it with someone else!"

And the slow, sulky anger Soames had felt all the afternoon burned the brighter within him.

Neither spoke again till they were close to the Station, then Soames asked:

"When do you expect to have finished?"

"By the end of June, if you really wish me to decorate as well."

Soames nodded. "But you quite understand," he said, "that the house is costing me a lot beyond what I contemplated. I may as well tell you that I should have thrown it up, only I'm not in the habit of giving up what I've set my mind on."

Bosinney made no reply. And Soames gave him askance a look of dogged dislike—for in spite of his fastidious air and that supercilious, dandified taciturnity, Soames, with his set lips and squared chin, was not unlike a bulldog....

When, at seven o'clock that evening, June arrived at 62, Montpellier Square, the maid Bilson told her that Mr. Bosinney was in the drawing-room; the mistress—she said—was dressing, and would be down in a minute. She would tell her that Miss June was here.

June stopped her at once.

"All right, Bilson," she said, "I'll just go in. You, needn't hurry Mrs. Soames."

She took off her cloak, and Bilson, with an understanding look, did not even open the drawing-room door for her, but ran downstairs.

June paused for a moment to look at herself in the little old-fashioned silver mirror above the oaken rug chest—a slim, imperious young figure, with a small resolute face, in a white frock, cut moon-shaped at the base of a neck too slender for her crown of twisted red-gold hair.

She opened the drawing-room door softly, meaning to take him by surprise. The room was filled with a sweet hot scent of flowering azaleas.

She took a long breath of the perfume, and heard Bosinney's voice, not in the room, but quite close, saying.

"Ah! there were such heaps of things I wanted to talk about, and now we shan't have time!"

Irene's voice answered: "Why not at dinner?"

"How can one talk...."

June's first thought was to go away, but instead she crossed to the long window opening on the little court. It was from there that the scent of the azaleas came, and, standing with their backs to her, their faces buried in the golden-pink blossoms, stood her lover and Irene.

Silent but unashamed, with flaming cheeks and angry eyes, the girl watched.

"Come on Sunday by yourself—We can go over the house together."

June saw Irene look up at him through her screen of blossoms. It was not the look of a coquette, but—far worse to the watching girl—of a woman fearful lest that look should say too much.

"I've promised to go for a drive with Uncle...."

"The big one! Make him bring you; it's only ten miles—the very thing for his horses."

"Poor old Uncle Swithin!"

A wave of the azalea scent drifted into June's face; she felt sick and dizzy.

"Do! ah! do!"

"But why?"

"I must see you there—I thought you'd like to help me...."

The answer seemed to the girl to come softly with a tremble from amongst the blossoms: "So I do!"

And she stepped into the open space of the window.

"How stuffy it is here!" she said; "I can't bear this scent!"

Her eyes, so angry and direct, swept both their faces.

"Were you talking about the house? I haven't seen it yet, you know—shall we all go on Sunday?"

From Irene's face the colour had flown.

"I am going for a drive that day with Uncle Swithin," she answered.

"Uncle Swithin! What does he matter? You can throw him over!"

"I am not in the habit of throwing people over!"

There was a sound of footsteps and June saw Soames standing just behind her.

"Well! if you are all ready," said Irene, looking from one to the other with a strange smile, "dinner is too!"

CHAPTER II—JUNE'S TREAT

Dinner began in silence; the women facing one another, and the men.

In silence the soup was finished—excellent, if a little thick; and fish was brought. In silence it was handed.

Bosinney ventured: "It's the first spring day."

Irene echoed softly: "Yes—the first spring day."

"Spring!" said June: "there isn't a breath of air!" No one replied.

The fish was taken away, a fine fresh sole from Dover. And Bilson brought champagne, a bottle swathed around the neck with white....

Soames said: "You'll find it dry."

Cutlets were handed, each pink-frilled about the legs. They were refused by June, and silence fell.

Soames said: "You'd better take a cutlet, June; there's nothing coming."

But June again refused, so they were borne away. And then Irene asked: "Phil, have you heard my blackbird?"

Bosinney answered: "Rather—he's got a hunting-song. As I came round I heard him in the Square."

"He's such a darling!"

"Salad, sir?" Spring chicken was removed.

But Soames was speaking: "The asparagus is very poor. Bosinney, glass of sherry with your sweet? June, you're drinking nothing!"

June said: "You know I never do. Wine's such horrid stuff!"

An apple charlotte came upon a silver dish, and smilingly Irene said: "The azaleas are so wonderful this year!"

To this Bosinney murmured: "Wonderful! The scent's extraordinary!"

June said: "How can you like the scent? Sugar, please, Bilson."

Sugar was handed her, and Soames remarked: "This charlottes good!"

The charlotte was removed. Long silence followed. Irene, beckoning, said: "Take out the azalea, Bilson. Miss June can't bear the scent."

"No; let it stay," said June.

Olives from France, with Russian caviare, were placed on little plates. And Soames remarked: "Why can't we have the Spanish?" But no one answered.

The olives were removed. Lifting her tumbler June demanded: "Give me some water, please." Water was given her. A silver tray was brought, with German plums. There was a lengthy pause. In perfect harmony all were eating them.

Bosinney counted up the stones: "This year—next year—some time."

Irene finished softly: "Never! There was such a glorious sunset. The sky's all ruby still—so beautiful!"

He answered: "Underneath the dark."

Their eyes had met, and June cried scornfully: "A London sunset!"

Egyptian cigarettes were handed in a silver box. Soames, taking one, remarked: "What time's your play begin?"

No one replied, and Turkish coffee followed in enamelled cups.

Irene, smiling quietly, said: "If only...."

"Only what?" said June.

"If only it could always be the spring!"

Brandy was handed; it was pale and old.

Soames said: "Bosinney, better take some brandy."

Bosinney took a glass; they all arose.

"You want a cab?" asked Soames.

June answered: "No! My cloaks please, Bilson." Her cloak was brought.

Irene, from the window, murmured: "Such a lovely night! The stars are coming out!"

Soames added: "Well, I hope you'll both enjoy yourselves."

From the door June answered: "Thanks. Come, Phil."

Bosinney cried: "I'm coming."

Soames smiled a sneering smile, and said: "I wish you luck!"

And at the door Irene watched them go.

Bosinney called: "Good night!"

"Good night!" she answered softly....

June made her lover take her on the top of a 'bus, saying she wanted air, and there sat silent, with her face to the breeze.

The driver turned once or twice, with the intention of venturing a remark, but thought better of it. They were a lively couple! The spring had got into his blood, too; he felt the need for letting steam escape, and clucked his tongue, flourishing his whip, wheeling his horses, and even they, poor things, had smelled the spring, and for a brief half-hour spurned the pavement with happy hoofs.

The whole town was alive; the boughs, curled upward with their decking of young leaves, awaited some gift the breeze could bring. New-lighted lamps were gaining mastery, and the faces of the crowd showed pale under that glare, while on high the great white clouds slid swiftly, softly, over the purple sky.

Men in, evening dress had thrown back overcoats, stepping jauntily up the steps of Clubs; working folk loitered; and women—those women who at that time of night are solitary—solitary and moving eastward in a stream—swung slowly along, with expectation in their gait, dreaming of good wine and a good supper, or—for an unwonted minute, of kisses given for love.

Those countless figures, going their ways under the lamps and the moving-sky, had one and all received some restless blessing from the stir of spring. And one and all, like those clubmen with their opened coats, had shed something of caste, and creed, and custom, and by the cock of their hats, the pace of their walk, their laughter, or their silence, revealed their common kinship under the passionate heavens.

Bosinney and June entered the theatre in silence, and mounted to their seats in the upper boxes. The piece had just begun, and the half-darkened house, with its rows of creatures peering all one way, resembled a great garden of flowers turning their faces to the sun.

June had never before been in the upper boxes. From the age of fifteen she had habitually accompanied her grandfather to the stalls, and not common stalls, but the best seats in the house, towards the centre of the third row, booked by old Jolyon, at Grogan and Boyne's, on his way home from the City, long before the day; carried in his overcoat pocket, together with his cigar-case and his old kid gloves, and handed to June to keep till the appointed night. And in those stalls—an erect old figure with a serene white head, a little figure, strenuous and eager, with a red-gold head—they would sit through every kind of play, and on the way home old Jolyon would say of the principal actor: "Oh, he's a poor stick! You should have seen little Bobson!"

She had looked forward to this evening with keen delight; it was stolen, chaperone-less, undreamed of at Stanhope Gate, where she was supposed to be at Soames'. She had expected reward for her subterfuge, planned for her lover's sake; she had expected it to break up the thick, chilly cloud, and make the relations between them which of late had been so puzzling, so tormenting—sunny and simple again as they had been before the winter. She had come with the intention of saying something definite; and she looked at the stage with a furrow between her brows, seeing nothing, her hands squeezed together in her lap. A swarm of jealous suspicions stung and stung her.

If Bosinney was conscious of her trouble he made no sign.

The curtain dropped. The first act had come to an end.

"It's awfully hot here!" said the girl; "I should like to go out."

She was very white, and she knew—for with her nerves thus sharpened she saw everything—that he was both uneasy and compunctious.

At the back of the theatre an open balcony hung over the street; she took possession of this, and stood leaning there without a word, waiting for him to begin.

At last she could bear it no longer.

"I want to say something to you, Phil," she said.

"Yes?"

The defensive tone of his voice brought the colour flying to her cheek, the words flying to her lips: "You don't give me a chance to be nice to you; you haven't for ages now!"

Bosinney stared down at the street. He made no answer....

June cried passionately: "You know I want to do everything for you—that I want to be everything to you...."

A hum rose from the street, and, piercing it with a sharp 'ping,' the bell sounded for the raising of the curtain. June did not stir. A desperate struggle was going on within her. Should she put everything to the proof? Should she challenge directly that influence, that attraction which was driving him away from her? It was her nature to challenge, and she said: "Phil, take me to see the house on Sunday!"

With a smile quivering and breaking on her lips, and trying, how hard, not to show that she was watching, she searched his face, saw it waver and hesitate, saw a troubled line come between his brows, the blood rush into his face. He answered: "Not Sunday, dear; some other day!"

"Why not Sunday? I shouldn't be in the way on Sunday."

He made an evident effort, and said: "I have an engagement."

"You are going to take...."

His eyes grew angry; he shrugged his shoulders, and answered: "An engagement that will prevent my taking you to see the house!"

June bit her lip till the blood came, and walked back to her seat without another word, but she could not help the tears of rage rolling down her face. The house had been mercifully darkened for a crisis, and no one could see her trouble.

Yet in this world of Forsytes let no man think himself immune from observation.

In the third row behind, Euphemia, Nicholas's youngest daughter, with her married-sister, Mrs. Tweetyman, were watching.

They reported at Timothy's, how they had seen June and her fiancé at the theatre.

"In the stalls?" "No, not in the...." "Oh! in the dress circle, of course. That seemed to be quite fashionable nowadays with young people!"

Well—not exactly. In the.... Anyway, that engagement wouldn't last long. They had never seen anyone look so thunder and lightningy as that little June! With tears of enjoyment in their eyes, they related how she had kicked a man's hat as she returned to her seat in the middle of an act, and how the man had looked. Euphemia had a noted, silent laugh, terminating most disappointingly in squeaks; and when Mrs. Small, holding up her hands, said: "My dear! Kicked a ha-at?" she let out such a number of these that she had to be recovered with smelling-salts. As she went away she said to Mrs. Tweetyman:

"Kicked a—ha-at! Oh! I shall die."

For 'that little June' this evening, that was to have been 'her treat,' was the most miserable she had ever spent. God knows she tried to stifle her pride, her suspicion, her jealousy!

She parted from Bosinney at old Jolyon's door without breaking down; the feeling that her lover must be conquered was strong enough to sustain her till his retiring footsteps brought home the true extent of her wretchedness.

The noiseless 'Sankey' let her in. She would have slipped up to her own room, but old Jolyon, who had heard her entrance, was in the dining-room doorway.

"Come in and have your milk," he said. "It's been kept hot for you. You're very late. Where have you been?"

June stood at the fireplace, with a foot on the fender and an arm on the mantelpiece, as her grandfather had done when he came in that night of the opera. She was too near a breakdown to care what she told him.

"We dined at Soames's."

"H'm! the man of property! His wife there and Bosinney?"

"Yes."

Old Jolyon's glance was fixed on her with the penetrating gaze from which it was difficult to hide; but she was not looking at him, and when she turned her face, he dropped his scrutiny at once. He had seen enough, and too much. He bent down to lift the cup of milk for her from the hearth, and, turning away, grumbled: "You oughtn't to stay out so late; it makes you fit for nothing."

He was invisible now behind his paper, which he turned with a vicious crackle; but when June came up to kiss him, he said: "Good-night, my darling," in a tone so tremulous and unexpected, that it was all the girl could do to get out of the room without breaking into the fit of sobbing which lasted her well on into the night.

When the door was closed, old Jolyon dropped his paper, and stared long and anxiously in front of him.

'The beggar!' he thought. 'I always knew she'd have trouble with him!'

Uneasy doubts and suspicions, the more poignant that he felt himself powerless to check or control the march of events, came crowding upon him.

Was the fellow going to jilt her? He longed to go and say to him: "Look here, you sir! Are you going to jilt my grand-daughter?" But how could he? Knowing little or nothing, he was yet certain, with his unerring astuteness, that there was something going on. He suspected Bosinney of being too much at Montpellier Square.

'This fellow,' he thought, 'may not be a scamp; his face is not a bad one, but he's a queer fish. I don't know what to make of him. I shall never know what to make of him! They tell me he works like a nigger, but I see no good coming of it. He's unpractical, he has no method. When he comes here, he sits as glum as a monkey. If I ask him what wine he'll have, he says: "Thanks, any wine." If I offer him a cigar, he smokes it as if it were a twopenny German thing. I never see him looking at June as he ought to look at her; and yet, he's not after her money. If she were to make a sign, he'd be off his bargain to-morrow. But she won't—not she! She'll stick to him! She's as obstinate as fate—She'll never let go!'

Sighing deeply, he turned the paper; in its columns, perchance he might find consolation.

And upstairs in her room June sat at her open window, where the spring wind came, after its revel across the Park, to cool her hot cheeks and burn her heart.

CHAPTER III—DRIVE WITH SWITHIN

Two lines of a certain song in a certain famous old school's songbook run as follows:

'How the buttons on his blue frock shone, tra-la-la! How he carolled and he sang, like a bird!...'

Swithin did not exactly carol and sing like a bird, but he felt almost like endeavouring to hum a tune, as he stepped out of Hyde Park Mansions, and contemplated his horses drawn up before the door.

The afternoon was as balmy as a day in June, and to complete the simile of the old song, he had put on a blue frock-coat, dispensing with an overcoat, after sending Adolf down three times to make sure that there was not the least suspicion of east in the wind; and the frock-coat was buttoned so tightly around his personable form, that, if the buttons did not shine, they might pardonably have done so. Majestic on the pavement he fitted on a pair of dog-skin gloves; with his large bell-shaped top hat, and his great stature and bulk he looked too primeval for a Forsyte. His thick white hair, on which Adolf had bestowed a touch of pomatum, exhaled the fragrance of opoponax and cigars—the celebrated Swithin brand, for which he paid one hundred and forty shillings the hundred, and of which old Jolyon had unkindly said, he wouldn't smoke them as a gift; they wanted the stomach of a horse!

"Adolf!"

"Sare!"

"The new plaid rug!"

He would never teach that fellow to look smart; and Mrs. Soames he felt sure, had an eye!

"The phaeton hood down; I am going—to—drive—a—lady!"

A pretty woman would want to show off her frock; and well—he was going to drive a lady! It was like a new beginning to the good old days.

Ages since he had driven a woman! The last time, if he remembered, it had been Juley; the poor old soul had been as nervous as a cat the whole time, and so put him out of patience that, as he dropped her in the Bayswater Road, he had said: "Well I'm d——d if I ever drive you again!" And he never had, not he!

Going up to his horses' heads, he examined their bits; not that he knew anything about bits—he didn't pay his coachman sixty pounds a year to do his work for him, that had never been his principle. Indeed, his reputation as a horsey man rested mainly on the fact that once, on Derby Day, he had been welshed by some thimble-riggers. But someone at the Club, after seeing him drive his greys up to the door—he always drove grey horses, you got more style for the money, some thought—had called him 'Four-in-hand Forsyte.' The name having reached his ears through that fellow Nicholas Treffry, old Jolyon's dead partner, the great driving man notorious for more carriage accidents than any man in the kingdom—Swithin had ever after conceived it right to act up to it. The name had taken his fancy, not because he had ever driven four-in-hand, or was ever likely to, but because of something distinguished in the sound. Four-in-hand Forsyte! Not bad! Born too soon, Swithin had missed his vocation. Coming upon London twenty years later, he could not have failed to have become a stockbroker, but at the time when he was obliged to select, this great profession had not as yet became the chief glory of the upper-middle class. He had literally been forced into land agency.

Once in the driving seat, with the reins handed to him, and blinking over his pale old cheeks in the full sunlight, he took a slow look round—Adolf was already up behind; the cockaded groom at the horses' heads stood ready to let go; everything was prepared for the signal, and Swithin gave it. The equipage dashed forward, and before you could say Jack Robinson, with a rattle and flourish drew up at Soames' door.

Irene came out at once, and stepped in—he afterward described it at Timothy's—"as light as—er—Taglioni, no fuss about it, no wanting this or wanting that;" and above all, Swithin dwelt on this, staring at Mrs. Septimus in a way that disconcerted her a good deal, "no silly nervousness!" To Aunt Hester he portrayed Irene's hat. "Not one of your great flopping things, sprawling about, and catching the dust, that women are so fond of nowadays, but a neat little—" he made a circular motion of his hand, "white veil—capital taste."

"What was it made of?" inquired Aunt Hester, who manifested a languid but permanent excitement at any mention of dress.

"Made of?" returned Swithin; "now how should I know?"

He sank into silence so profound that Aunt Hester began to be afraid he had fallen into a trance. She did not try to rouse him herself, it not being her custom.

'I wish somebody would come,' she thought; 'I don't like the look of him!'

But suddenly Swithin returned to life. "Made of" he wheezed out slowly, "what should it be made of?"

They had not gone four miles before Swithin received the impression that Irene liked driving with him. Her face was so soft behind that white veil, and her dark eyes shone so in the spring light, and whenever he spoke she raised them to him and smiled.

On Saturday morning Soames had found her at her writing-table with a note written to Swithin, putting him off. Why did she want to put him off? he asked. She might put her own people off when she liked, he would not have her putting off his people!

She had looked at him intently, had torn up the note, and said: "Very well!"

And then she began writing another. He took a casual glance presently, and saw that it was addressed to Bosinney.

"What are you writing to him about?" he asked.

Irene, looking at him again with that intent look, said quietly: "Something he wanted me to do for him!"

"Humph!" said Soames,—"Commissions!"

"You'll have your work cut out if you begin that sort of thing!" He said no more.

Swithin opened his eyes at the mention of Robin Hill; it was a long way for his horses, and he always dined at half-past seven, before the rush at the Club began; the new chef took more trouble with an early dinner—a lazy rascal!

He would like to have a look at the house, however. A house appealed to any Forsyte, and especially to one who had been an auctioneer. After all he said the distance was nothing. When he was a younger man he had had rooms at Richmond for many years, kept his carriage and pair there, and drove them up and down to business every day of his life.

Four-in-hand Forsyte they called him! His T-cart, his horses had been known from Hyde Park Corner to the Star and Garter. The Duke of Z..... wanted to get hold of them, would have given him double the money, but he had kept them; know a good thing when you have it, eh? A look of solemn pride came portentously on his shaven square old face, he rolled his head in his stand-up collar, like a turkey-cock preening himself.

She was really—a charming woman! He enlarged upon her frock afterwards to Aunt Juley, who held up her hands at his way of putting it.

Fitted her like a skin—tight as a drum; that was how he liked 'em, all of a piece, none of your daverdy, scarecrow women! He gazed at Mrs. Septimus Small, who took after James—long and thin.

"There's style about her," he went on, "fit for a king! And she's so quiet with it too!"

"She seems to have made quite a conquest of you, any way," drawled Aunt Hester from her corner.

Swithin heard extremely well when anybody attacked him.

"What's that?" he said. "I know a—pretty—woman when I see one, and all I can say is, I don't see the young man about that's fit for her; but perhaps—you—do, come, perhaps—you-do!"

"Oh?" murmured Aunt Hester, "ask Juley!"

Long before they reached Robin Hill, however, the unaccustomed airing had made him terribly sleepy; he drove with his eyes closed, a life-time of deportment alone keeping his tall and bulky form from falling askew.

Bosinney, who was watching, came out to meet them, and all three entered the house together; Swithin in front making play with a stout gold-mounted Malacca cane, put into his hand by Adolf, for his knees were feeling the effects of their long stay in the same position. He had assumed his fur coat, to guard against the draughts of the unfinished house.

The staircase—he said—was handsome! the baronial style! They would want some statuary about! He came to a standstill between the columns of the doorway into the inner court, and held out his cane inquiringly.

What was this to be—this vestibule, or whatever they called it? But gazing at the skylight, inspiration came to him.

"Ah! the billiard-room!"

When told it was to be a tiled court with plants in the centre, he turned to Irene:

"Waste this on plants? You take my advice and have a billiard table here!"

Irene smiled. She had lifted her veil, banding it like a nun's coif across her forehead, and the smile of her dark eyes below this seemed to Swithin more charming than ever. He nodded. She would take his advice he saw.

He had little to say of the drawing or dining-rooms, which he described as "spacious"; but fell into such raptures as he permitted to a man of his dignity, in the wine-cellar, to which he descended by stone steps, Bosinney going first with a light.

"You'll have room here," he said, "for six or seven hundred dozen—a very pooty little cellar!"

Bosinney having expressed the wish to show them the house from the copse below, Swithin came to a stop.

"There's a fine view from here," he remarked; "you haven't such a thing as a chair?"

A chair was brought him from Bosinney's tent.

"You go down," he said blandly; "you two! I'll sit here and look at the view."

He sat down by the oak tree, in the sun; square and upright, with one hand stretched out, resting on the nob of his cane, the other planted on his knee; his fur coat thrown open, his hat, roofing with its flat top the pale square of his face; his stare, very blank, fixed on the landscape.

He nodded to them as they went off down through the fields. He was, indeed, not sorry to be left thus for a quiet moment of reflection. The air was balmy, not too much heat in the sun; the prospect a fine one, a remarka.... His head fell a little to one side; he jerked it up and thought: Odd! He—ah! They were waving to him from the bottom! He put up his hand, and moved it more than once. They were active—the prospect was remar.... His head fell to the left, he jerked it up at once; it fell to the right. It remained there; he was asleep.

And asleep, a sentinel on the—top of the rise, he appeared to rule over this prospect—remarkable—like some image blocked out by the special artist, of primeval Forsytes in pagan days, to record the domination of mind over matter!

And all the unnumbered generations of his yeoman ancestors, wont of a Sunday to stand akimbo surveying their little plots of land, their grey unmoving eyes hiding their instinct with its hidden roots of violence, their instinct for possession to the exclusion of all the world—all these unnumbered generations seemed to sit there with him on the top of the rise.

But from him, thus slumbering, his jealous Forsyte spirit travelled far, into God-knows-what jungle of fancies; with those two young people, to see what they were doing down there in the copse—in the copse where the spring was running riot with the scent of sap and bursting buds, the song of birds innumerable, a carpet of bluebells and sweet growing things, and the sun caught like gold in the tops of the trees; to see what they were doing, walking along there so close together on the path that was too narrow; walking along there so close that they were always touching; to watch Irene's eyes, like dark thieves, stealing the heart out of the spring. And a great unseen chaperon, his spirit was there, stopping with them to look at the little furry corpse of a mole, not dead an hour, with his mushroom-and-silver coat untouched by the rain or dew; watching over Irene's bent head, and the soft look of her pitying eyes; and over that young man's head, gazing at her so hard, so strangely. Walking on with them, too, across the open space where a wood-cutter had been at work, where the bluebells were trampled down, and a trunk had swayed and staggered down from its gashed stump. Climbing it with them, over, and on to the very edge of the copse, whence there stretched an undiscovered country, from far away in which came the sounds, 'Cuckoo-cuckoo!'

Silent, standing with them there, and uneasy at their silence! Very queer, very strange!

Then back again, as though guilty, through the wood—back to the cutting, still silent, amongst the songs of birds that never ceased, and the wild scent—hum! what was it—like that herb they put in—back to the log across the path....

And then unseen, uneasy, flapping above them, trying to make noises, his Forsyte spirit watched her balanced on the log, her pretty figure swaying, smiling down at that young man gazing up with such strange, shining eyes, slipping now—a—ah! falling, o—oh! sliding—down his breast; her soft, warm body clutched, her head bent back from his lips; his kiss; her recoil; his cry: "You must know—I love you!" Must know—indeed, a pretty...? Love! Hah!

Swithin awoke; virtue had gone out of him. He had a taste in his mouth. Where was he?

Damme! He had been asleep!

He had dreamed something about a new soup, with a taste of mint in it.

Those young people—where had they got to? His left leg had pins and needles.

"Adolf!" The rascal was not there; the rascal was asleep somewhere.

He stood up, tall, square, bulky in his fur, looking anxiously down over the fields, and presently he saw them coming.

Irene was in front; that young fellow—what had they nicknamed him—"The Buccaneer?" looked precious hangdog there behind her; had got a flea in his ear, he shouldn't wonder. Serve him right, taking her down all that way to look at the house! The proper place to look at a house from was the lawn.

They saw him. He extended his arm, and moved it spasmodically to encourage them. But they had stopped. What were they standing there for, talking—talking? They came on again. She had been, giving him a rub, he had not the least doubt of it, and no wonder, over a house like that—a great ugly thing, not the sort of house he was accustomed to.

He looked intently at their faces, with his pale, immovable stare. That young man looked very queer!

"You'll never make anything of this!" he said tartly, pointing at the mansion;—"too newfangled!"

Bosinney gazed at him as though he had not heard; and Swithin afterwards described him to Aunt Hester as "an extravagant sort of fellow very odd way of looking at you—a bumpy beggar!"

What gave rise to this sudden piece of psychology he did not state; possibly Bosinney's, prominent forehead and cheekbones and chin, or something hungry in his face, which quarrelled with Swithin's conception of the calm satiety that should characterize the perfect gentleman.

He brightened up at the mention of tea. He had a contempt for tea—his brother Jolyon had been in tea; made a lot of money by it—but he was so thirsty, and had such a taste in his mouth, that he was prepared to drink anything. He longed to inform Irene of the taste in his mouth—she was so sympathetic—but it would not be a distinguished thing to do; he rolled his tongue round, and faintly smacked it against his palate.

In a far corner of the tent Adolf was bending his cat-like moustaches over a kettle. He left it at once to draw the cork of a pint-bottle of champagne. Swithin smiled, and, nodding at Bosinney, said: "Why, you're quite a Monte Cristo!" This celebrated novel—one of the half-dozen he had read—had produced an extraordinary impression on his mind.

Taking his glass from the table, he held it away from him to scrutinize the colour; thirsty as he was, it was not likely that he was going to drink trash! Then, placing it to his lips, he took a sip.

"A very nice wine," he said at last, passing it before his nose; "not the equal of my Heidsieck!"

It was at this moment that the idea came to him which he afterwards imparted at Timothy's in this nutshell: "I shouldn't wonder a bit if that architect chap were sweet upon Mrs. Soames!"

And from this moment his pale, round eyes never ceased to bulge with the interest of his discovery.

"The fellow," he said to Mrs. Septimus, "follows her about with his eyes like a dog—the bumpy beggar! I don't wonder at it—she's a very charming woman, and, I should say, the pink of discretion!" A vague consciousness of perfume caging about Irene, like that from a flower with half-closed petals and a passionate heart, moved him to the creation of this image. "But I wasn't sure of it," he said, "till I saw him pick up her handkerchief."

Mrs. Small's eyes boiled with excitement.

"And did he give it her back?" she asked.

"Give it back?" said Swithin: "I saw him slobber on it when he thought I wasn't looking!"

Mrs. Small gasped—too interested to speak.

"But she gave him no encouragement," went on Swithin; he stopped, and stared for a minute or two in the way that alarmed Aunt Hester so—he had suddenly recollected that, as they were starting back in the phaeton, she had given Bosinney her hand a second time, and let it stay there too.... He had touched his horses smartly with the whip, anxious to get her all to himself. But she had looked back, and she had not answered his first question; neither had he been able to see her face—she had kept it hanging down.

There is somewhere a picture, which Swithin has not seen, of a man sitting on a rock, and by him, immersed in the still, green water, a sea-nymph lying on her back, with her hand on her naked breast. She has a half-smile on her face—a smile of hopeless surrender and of secret joy.

Seated by Swithin's side, Irene may have been smiling like that.

When, warmed by champagne, he had her all to himself, he unbosomed himself of his wrongs; of his smothered resentment against the new chef at the club; his worry over the house in Wigmore Street, where the rascally tenant had gone bankrupt through helping his brother-in-law as if charity did not begin at home; of his deafness, too, and that pain he sometimes got in his right side. She listened, her eyes swimming under their lids. He thought she was thinking deeply of his troubles, and pitied himself terribly. Yet in his fur coat, with frogs across the breast, his top hat aslant, driving this beautiful woman, he had never felt more distinguished.

A coster, however, taking his girl for a Sunday airing, seemed to have the same impression about himself. This person had flogged his donkey into a gallop alongside, and sat, upright as a waxwork, in his shallopy chariot, his chin settled pompously on a red handkerchief, like Swithin's on his full cravat; while his girl, with the ends of a fly-blown boa floating out behind, aped a woman of fashion. Her swain moved a stick with a ragged bit of string dangling from the end, reproducing with strange fidelity the circular flourish of Swithin's whip, and rolled his head at his lady with a leer that had a weird likeness to Swithin's primeval stare.

Though for a time unconscious of the lowly ruffian's presence, Swithin presently took it into his head that he was being guyed. He laid his whip-lash across the mares flank. The two chariots, however, by some unfortunate fatality continued abreast. Swithin's yellow, puffy face grew red; he raised his whip to lash the costermonger, but was saved from so far forgetting his dignity by a special intervention of Providence. A carriage driving out through a gate forced phaeton and donkey-cart into proximity; the wheels grated, the lighter vehicle skidded, and was overturned.

Swithin did not look round. On no account would he have pulled up to help the ruffian. Serve him right if he had broken his neck!

But he could not if he would. The greys had taken alarm. The phaeton swung from side to side, and people raised frightened faces as they went dashing past. Swithin's great arms, stretched at full length, tugged at the reins. His cheeks were puffed, his lips compressed, his swollen face was of a dull, angry red.

Irene had her hand on the rail, and at every lurch she gripped it tightly. Swithin heard her ask:

"Are we going to have an accident, Uncle Swithin?"

He gasped out between his pants: "It's nothing; a—little fresh!"

"I've never been in an accident."

"Don't you move!" He took a look at her. She was smiling, perfectly calm. "Sit still," he repeated. "Never fear, I'll get you home!"

And in the midst of all his terrible efforts, he was surprised to hear her answer in a voice not like her own:

"I don't care if I never get home!"

The carriage giving a terrific lurch, Swithin's exclamation was jerked back into his throat. The horses, winded by the rise of a hill, now steadied to a trot, and finally stopped of their own accord.

"When"—Swithin described it at Timothy's—"I pulled 'em up, there she was as cool as myself. God bless my soul! she behaved as if she didn't care whether she broke her neck or not! What was it she said: 'I don't care if I never get home?'" Leaning over the handle of his cane, he wheezed out, to Mrs. Small's terror: "And I'm not altogether surprised, with a finickin' feller like young Soames for a husband!"

It did not occur to him to wonder what Bosinney had done after they had left him there alone; whether he had gone wandering about like the dog to which Swithin had compared him; wandering down to that copse where the spring was still in riot, the cuckoo still calling from afar; gone down there with her handkerchief pressed to lips, its fragrance mingling with the scent of mint and thyme. Gone down there with such a wild, exquisite pain in his heart that he could have cried out among the trees. Or what, indeed, the fellow had done. In fact, till he came to Timothy's, Swithin had forgotten all about him.

CHAPTER IV—JAMES GOES TO SEE FOR HIMSELF

Those ignorant of Forsyte 'Change would not, perhaps, foresee all the stir made by Irene's visit to the house.

After Swithin had related at Timothy's the full story of his memorable drive, the same, with the least suspicion of curiosity, the merest touch of malice, and a real desire to do good, was passed on to June.

"And what a dreadful thing to say, my dear!" ended Aunt Juley; "that about not going home. What did she mean?"

It was a strange recital for the girl. She heard it flushing painfully, and, suddenly, with a curt handshake, took her departure.

"Almost rude!" Mrs. Small said to Aunt Hester, when June was gone.

The proper construction was put on her reception of the news. She was upset. Something was therefore very wrong. Odd! She and Irene had been such friends!

It all tallied too well with whispers and hints that had been going about for some time past. Recollections of Euphemia's account of the visit to the theatre—Mr. Bosinney always at Soames's? Oh, indeed! Yes, of course, he would be about the house! Nothing open. Only upon the greatest, the most important provocation was it necessary to say anything open on Forsyte 'Change. This machine was too nicely adjusted; a hint, the merest trifling expression of regret or doubt, sufficed to set the family soul so sympathetic—vibrating. No one desired that harm should come of these vibrations—far from it; they were set in motion with the best intentions, with the feeling, that each member of the family had a stake in the family soul.

And much kindness lay at the bottom of the gossip; it would frequently result in visits of condolence being made, in accordance with the customs of Society, thereby conferring a real benefit upon the sufferers, and affording consolation to the sound, who felt pleasantly that someone at all events was suffering from that from which they themselves were not suffering. In fact, it was simply a desire to keep things well-aired, the desire which animates the Public Press, that brought James, for instance, into communication with Mrs. Septimus, Mrs. Septimus, with the little Nicholases, the little Nicholases with who-knows-whom, and so on. That great class to which they had risen, and now belonged, demanded a certain candour, a still more certain reticence. This combination guaranteed their membership.

Many of the younger Forsytes felt, very naturally, and would openly declare, that they did not want their affairs pried into; but so powerful was the invisible, magnetic current of family gossip, that for the life of them they could not help knowing all about everything. It was felt to be hopeless.

One of them (young Roger) had made an heroic attempt to free the rising generation, by speaking of Timothy as an 'old cat.' The effort had justly recoiled upon himself; the words, coming round in the most delicate way to Aunt Juley's ears, were repeated by her in a shocked voice to Mrs. Roger, whence they returned again to young Roger.

And, after all, it was only the wrong-doers who suffered; as, for instance, George, when he lost all that money playing billiards; or young Roger himself, when he was so dreadfully near to marrying the girl to whom, it was whispered, he was already married by the laws of Nature; or again Irene, who was thought, rather than said, to be in danger.

All this was not only pleasant but salutary. And it made so many hours go lightly at Timothy's in the Bayswater Road; so many hours that must otherwise have been sterile and heavy to those three who lived there; and Timothy's was but one of hundreds of such homes in this City of London—the homes of neutral persons of the secure classes, who are out of the battle themselves, and must find their reason for existing, in the battles of others.

But for the sweetness of family gossip, it must indeed have been lonely there. Rumours and tales, reports, surmises—were they not the children of the house, as dear and precious as the prattling babes the brother and sisters had missed in their own journey? To talk about them was as near as they could get to the possession of all those children and grandchildren, after whom their soft hearts yearned. For though it is doubtful whether Timothy's heart yearned, it is indubitable that at the arrival of each fresh Forsyte child he was quite upset.

Useless for young Roger to say, "Old cat!" for Euphemia to hold up her hands and cry: "Oh! those three!" and break into her silent laugh with the squeak at the end. Useless, and not too kind.

The situation which at this stage might seem, and especially to Forsyte eyes, strange—not to say 'impossible'—was, in view of certain facts, not so strange after all. Some things had been lost sight of. And first, in the security bred of many harmless marriages, it had been forgotten that Love is no hot-house flower, but a wild plant, born of a wet night, born of an hour of sunshine; sprung from wild seed, blown along the road by a wild wind. A wild plant that, when it blooms by chance within the hedge of our gardens, we call a flower; and when it blooms outside we call a weed; but, flower or weed, whose scent and colour are always, wild! And further—the facts and figures of their own lives being against the perception of this truth—it was not generally recognised by Forsytes that, where, this wild plant springs, men and women are but moths around the pale, flame-like blossom.

It was long since young Jolyon's escapade—there was danger of a tradition again arising that people in their position never cross the hedge to pluck that flower; that one could reckon on having love, like measles, once in due season, and getting over it comfortably for all time—as with measles, on a soothing mixture of butter and honey—in the arms of wedlock.

Of all those whom this strange rumour about Bosinney and Mrs. Soames reached, James was the most affected. He had long forgotten how he had hovered, lanky and pale, in side whiskers of chestnut hue, round Emily, in the days of his own courtship. He had long forgotten the small house in the purlieus of Mayfair, where he had spent the early days of his married life, or rather, he had long forgotten the early days, not the small house,—a Forsyte never forgot a house—he had afterwards sold it at a clear profit of four hundred pounds.

He had long forgotten those days, with their hopes and fears and doubts about the prudence of the match (for Emily, though pretty, had nothing, and he himself at that time was making a bare thousand a year), and that strange, irresistible attraction which had drawn him on, till he felt he must die if he could not marry the girl with the fair hair, looped so neatly back, the fair arms emerging from a skin-tight bodice, the fair form decorously shielded by a cage of really stupendous circumference.

James had passed through the fire, but he had passed also through the river of years which washes out the fire; he had experienced the saddest experience of all—forgetfulness of what it was like to be in love.

Forgotten! Forgotten so long, that he had forgotten even that he had forgotten.

And now this rumour had come upon him, this rumour about his son's wife; very vague, a shadow dodging among the palpable, straightforward appearances of things, unreal, unintelligible as a ghost, but carrying with it, like a ghost, inexplicable terror.

He tried to bring it home to his mind, but it was no more use than trying to apply to himself one of those tragedies he read of daily in his evening paper. He simply could not. There could be nothing in it. It was all their nonsense. She didn't get on with Soames as well as she might, but she was a good little thing—a good little thing!

Like the not inconsiderable majority of men, James relished a nice little bit of scandal, and would say, in a matter-of-fact tone, licking his lips, "Yes, yes—she and young Dyson; they tell me they're living at Monte Carlo!"

But the significance of an affair of this sort—of its past, its present, or its future—had never struck him. What it meant, what torture and raptures had gone to its construction, what slow, overmastering fate had lurked within the facts, very naked, sometimes sordid, but generally spicy, presented to his gaze. He was not in the habit of blaming, praising, drawing deductions, or generalizing at all about such things; he simply listened rather greedily, and repeated what he was told, finding considerable benefit from the practice, as from the consumption of a sherry and bitters before a meal.

Now, however, that such a thing—or rather the rumour, the breath of it—had come near him personally, he felt as in a fog, which filled his mouth full of a bad, thick flavour, and made it difficult to draw breath.

A scandal! A possible scandal!

To repeat this word to himself thus was the only way in which he could focus or make it thinkable. He had forgotten the sensations necessary for understanding the progress, fate, or meaning of any such business; he simply could no longer grasp the possibilities of people running any risk for the sake of passion.

Amongst all those persons of his acquaintance, who went into the City day after day and did their business there, whatever it was, and in their leisure moments bought shares, and houses, and ate dinners, and played games, as he was told, it would have seemed to him ridiculous to suppose that there were any who would run risks for the sake of anything so recondite, so figurative, as passion.

Passion! He seemed, indeed, to have heard of it, and rules such as 'A young man and a young woman ought never to be trusted together' were fixed in his mind as the parallels of latitude are fixed on a map (for all Forsytes, when it comes to 'bed-rock' matters of fact, have quite a fine taste in realism); but as to anything else—well, he could only appreciate it at all through the catch-word 'scandal.'

Ah! but there was no truth in it—could not be. He was not afraid; she was really a good little thing. But there it was when you got a thing like that into your mind. And James was of a nervous temperament—one of those men whom things will not leave alone, who suffer tortures from anticipation and indecision. For fear of letting something slip that he might otherwise secure, he was physically unable to make up his mind until absolutely certain that, by not making it up, he would suffer loss.

In life, however, there were many occasions when the business of making up his mind did not even rest with himself, and this was one of them.

What could he do? Talk it over with Soames? That would only make matters worse. And, after all, there was nothing in it, he felt sure.

It was all that house. He had mistrusted the idea from the first. What did Soames want to go into the country for? And, if he must go spending a lot of money building himself a house, why not have a first-rate man, instead of this young Bosinney, whom nobody knew anything about? He had told them how it would be. And he had heard that the house was costing Soames a pretty penny beyond what he had reckoned on spending.

This fact, more than any other, brought home to James the real danger of the situation. It was always like this with these 'artistic' chaps; a sensible man should have nothing to say to them. He had warned Irene, too. And see what had come of it!

And it suddenly sprang into James's mind that he ought to go and see for himself. In the midst of that fog of uneasiness in which his mind was enveloped the notion that he could go and look at the house afforded him inexplicable satisfaction. It may have been simply the decision to do something—more possibly the fact that he was going to look at a house—that gave him relief. He felt that in staring at an edifice of bricks and mortar, of wood and stone, built by the suspected man himself, he would be looking into the heart of that rumour about Irene.

Without saying a word, therefore, to anyone, he took a hansom to the station and proceeded by train to Robin Hill; thence—there being no 'flies,' in accordance with the custom of the neighbourhood—he found himself obliged to walk.

He started slowly up the hill, his angular knees and high shoulders bent complainingly, his eyes fixed on his feet, yet, neat for all that, in his high hat and his frock-coat, on which was the speckless gloss imparted by perfect superintendence. Emily saw to that; that is, she did not, of course, see to it—people of good position not seeing to each other's buttons, and Emily was of good position—but she saw that the butler saw to it.

He had to ask his way three times; on each occasion he repeated the directions given him, got the man to repeat them, then repeated them a second time, for he was naturally of a talkative disposition, and one could not be too careful in a new neighbourhood.

He kept assuring them that it was a new house he was looking for; it was only, however, when he was shown the roof through the trees that he could feel really satisfied that he had not been directed entirely wrong.

A heavy sky seemed to cover the world with the grey whiteness of a whitewashed ceiling. There was no freshness or fragrance in the air. On such a day even British workmen scarcely cared to do more then they were obliged, and moved about their business without the drone of talk which whiles away the pangs of labour.

Through spaces of the unfinished house, shirt-sleeved figures worked slowly, and sounds arose—spasmodic knockings, the scraping of metal, the sawing of wood, with the rumble of wheelbarrows along boards; now and again the foreman's dog, tethered by a string to an oaken beam, whimpered feebly, with a sound like the singing of a kettle.

The fresh-fitted window-panes, daubed each with a white patch in the centre, stared out at James like the eyes of a blind dog.

And the building chorus went on, strident and mirthless under the grey-white sky. But the thrushes, hunting amongst the fresh-turned earth for worms, were silent quite.

James picked his way among the heaps of gravel—the drive was being laid—till he came opposite the porch. Here he stopped and raised his eyes. There was but little to see from this point of view, and that little he took in at once; but he stayed in this position many minutes, and who shall know of what he thought.

His china-blue eyes under white eyebrows that jutted out in little horns, never stirred; the long upper lip of his wide mouth, between the fine white whiskers, twitched once or twice; it was easy to see from that anxious rapt expression, whence Soames derived the handicapped look which sometimes came upon his face. James might have been saying to himself: 'I don't know—life's a tough job.'

In this position Bosinney surprised him.

James brought his eyes down from whatever bird's-nest they had been looking for in the sky to Bosinney's face, on which was a kind of humorous scorn.

"How do you do, Mr. Forsyte? Come down to see for yourself?"

It was exactly what James, as we know, had come for, and he was made correspondingly uneasy. He held out his hand, however, saying:

"How are you?" without looking at Bosinney.

The latter made way for him with an ironical smile.

James scented something suspicious in this courtesy. "I should like to walk round the outside first," he said, "and see what you've been doing!"

A flagged terrace of rounded stones with a list of two or three inches to port had been laid round the south-east and south-west sides of the house, and ran with a bevelled edge into mould, which was in preparation for being turfed; along this terrace James led the way.

"Now what did this cost?" he asked, when he saw the terrace extending round the corner.

"What should you think?" inquired Bosinney.

"How should I know?" replied James somewhat nonplussed; "two or three hundred, I dare say!"

"The exact sum!"

James gave him a sharp look, but the architect appeared unconscious, and he put the answer down to mishearing.

On arriving at the garden entrance, he stopped to look at the view.

"That ought to come down," he said, pointing to the oak-tree.

"You think so? You think that with the tree there you don't get enough view for your money."

Again James eyed him suspiciously—this young man had a peculiar way of putting things: "Well!" he said, with a perplexed, nervous, emphasis, "I don't see what you want with a tree."

"It shall come down to-morrow," said Bosinney.

James was alarmed. "Oh," he said, "don't go saying I said it was to come down! I know nothing about it!"

"No?"

James went on in a fluster: "Why, what should I know about it? It's nothing to do with me! You do it on your own responsibility."

"You'll allow me to mention your name?"

James grew more and more alarmed: "I don't know what you want mentioning my name for," he muttered; "you'd better leave the tree alone. It's not your tree!"

He took out a silk handkerchief and wiped his brow. They entered the house. Like Swithin, James was impressed by the inner court-yard.

"You must have spent a deuce of a lot of money here," he said, after staring at the columns and gallery for some time. "Now, what did it cost to put up those columns?"

"I can't tell you off-hand," thoughtfully answered Bosinney, "but I know it was a deuce of a lot!"

"I should think so," said James. "I should...." He caught the architect's eye, and broke off. And now, whenever he came to anything of which he desired to know the cost, he stifled that curiosity.

Bosinney appeared determined that he should see everything, and had not James been of too 'noticing' a nature, he would certainly have found himself going round the house a second time. He seemed so anxious to be asked questions, too, that James felt he must be on his guard. He began to suffer from his exertions, for, though wiry enough for a man of his long build, he was seventy-five years old.

He grew discouraged; he seemed no nearer to anything, had not obtained from his inspection any of the knowledge he had vaguely hoped for. He had merely increased his dislike and mistrust of this young man, who had tired him out with his politeness, and in whose manner he now certainly detected mockery.

The fellow was sharper than he had thought, and better-looking than he had hoped. He had a—a 'don't care' appearance that James, to whom risk was the most intolerable thing in life, did not appreciate; a peculiar smile, too, coming when least expected; and very queer eyes. He reminded James, as he said afterwards, of a hungry cat. This was as near as he could get, in conversation with Emily, to a description of the peculiar exasperation, velvetiness, and mockery, of which Bosinney's manner had been composed.

At last, having seen all that was to be seen, he came out again at the door where he had gone in; and now, feeling that he was wasting time and strength and money, all for nothing, he took the courage of a Forsyte in both hands, and, looking sharply at Bosinney, said:

"I dare say you see a good deal of my daughter-in-law; now, what does she think of the house? But she hasn't seen it, I suppose?"

This he said, knowing all about Irene's visit not, of course, that there was anything in the visit, except that extraordinary remark she had made about 'not caring to get home'—and the story of how June had taken the news!

He had determined, by this way of putting the question, to give Bosinney a chance, as he said to himself.

The latter was long in answering, but kept his eyes with uncomfortable steadiness on James.

"She has seen the house, but I can't tell you what she thinks of it."

Nervous and baffled, James was constitutionally prevented from letting the matter drop.

"Oh!" he said, "she has seen it? Soames brought her down, I suppose?"

Bosinney smilingly replied: "Oh, no!"

"What, did she come down alone?"

"Oh, no!"

"Then—who brought her?"

"I really don't know whether I ought to tell you who brought her."

To James, who knew that it was Swithin, this answer appeared incomprehensible.

"Why!" he stammered, "you know that...." but he stopped, suddenly perceiving his danger.

"Well," he said, "if you don't want to tell me I suppose you won't! Nobody tells me anything."

Somewhat to his surprise Bosinney asked him a question.

"By the by," he said, "could you tell me if there are likely to be any more of you coming down? I should like to be on the spot!"

"Any more?" said James bewildered, "who should there be more? I don't know of any more. Good-bye?"

Looking at the ground he held out his hand, crossed the palm of it with Bosinney's, and taking his umbrella just above the silk, walked away along the terrace.

Before he turned the corner he glanced back, and saw Bosinney following him slowly— 'slinking along the wall' as he put it to himself, 'like a great cat.' He paid no attention when the young fellow raised his hat.

Outside the drive, and out of sight, he slackened his pace still more. Very slowly, more bent than when he came, lean, hungry, and disheartened, he made his way back to the station.

The Buccaneer, watching him go so sadly home, felt sorry perhaps for his behaviour to the old man.

CHAPTER V—SOAMES AND BOSINNEY CORRESPOND

James said nothing to his son of this visit to the house; but, having occasion to go to Timothy's one morning on a matter connected with a drainage scheme which was being forced by the sanitary authorities on his brother, he mentioned it there.

It was not, he said, a bad house. He could see that a good deal could be made of it. The fellow was clever in his way, though what it was going to cost Soames before it was done with he didn't know.

Euphemia Forsyte, who happened to be in the room—she had come round to borrow the Rev. Mr. Scoles' last novel, 'Passion and Paregoric', which was having such a vogue—chimed in.

"I saw Irene yesterday at the Stores; she and Mr. Bosinney were having a nice little chat in the Groceries."

It was thus, simply, that she recorded a scene which had really made a deep and complicated impression on her. She had been hurrying to the silk department of the Church and Commercial Stores—that Institution than which, with its admirable system, admitting only guaranteed persons on a basis of payment before delivery, no emporium can be more highly recommended to Forsytes—to match a piece of prunella silk for her mother, who was waiting in the carriage outside.

Passing through the Groceries her eye was unpleasantly attracted by the back view of a very beautiful figure. It was so charmingly proportioned, so balanced, and so well clothed, that Euphemia's instinctive propriety was at once alarmed; such figures, she knew, by intuition rather than experience, were rarely connected with virtue—certainly never in her mind, for her own back was somewhat difficult to fit.

Her suspicions were fortunately confirmed. A young man coming from the Drugs had snatched off his hat, and was accosting the lady with the unknown back.

It was then that she saw with whom she had to deal; the lady was undoubtedly Mrs. Soames, the young man Mr. Bosinney. Concealing herself rapidly over the purchase of a box of Tunisian dates, for she was impatient of awkwardly meeting people with parcels in her hands, and at the busy time of the morning, she was quite unintentionally an interested observer of their little interview.

Mrs. Soames, usually somewhat pale, had a delightful colour in her cheeks; and Mr. Bosinney's manner was strange, though attractive (she thought him rather a distinguished-looking man, and George's name for him, 'The Buccaneer'—about which there was something romantic—quite charming). He seemed to be pleading. Indeed, they talked so earnestly—or, rather, he talked so earnestly, for Mrs. Soames did not say much—that they caused, inconsiderately, an eddy in the traffic. One nice old General, going towards Cigars, was obliged to step quite out of the way, and chancing to look up and see Mrs. Soames' face, he actually took off his hat, the old fool! So like a man!

But it was Mrs. Soames' eyes that worried Euphemia. She never once looked at Mr. Bosinney until he moved on, and then she looked after him. And, oh, that look!

On that look Euphemia had spent much anxious thought. It is not too much to say that it had hurt her with its dark, lingering softness, for all the world as though the woman wanted to drag him back, and unsay something she had been saying.

Ah, well, she had had no time to go deeply into the matter just then, with that prunella silk on her hands; but she was 'very intriguee'—very! She had just nodded to Mrs. Soames, to show her that she had seen; and, as she confided, in talking it over afterwards, to her chum Francie (Roger's daughter), "Didn't she look caught out just?..."

James, most averse at the first blush to accepting any news confirmatory of his own poignant suspicions, took her up at once.

"Oh" he said, "they'd be after wall-papers no doubt."

Euphemia smiled. "In the Groceries?" she said softly; and, taking 'Passion and Paregoric' from the table, added: "And so you'll lend me this, dear Auntie? Good-bye!" and went away.

James left almost immediately after; he was late as it was.

When he reached the office of Forsyte, Bustard and Forsyte, he found Soames, sitting in his revolving, chair, drawing up a defence. The latter greeted his father with a curt good-morning, and, taking an envelope from his pocket, said:

"It may interest you to look through this."

James read as follows:

'309D, SLOANE STREET, May 15,

'DEAR FORSYTE,

'The construction of your house being now completed, my duties as architect have come to an end. If I am to go on with the business of decoration, which at your request I undertook, I should like you to clearly understand that I must have a free hand.

'You never come down without suggesting something that goes counter to my scheme. I have here three letters from you, each of which recommends an article I should never dream of putting in. I had your father here yesterday afternoon, who made further valuable suggestions.

'Please make up your mind, therefore, whether you want me to decorate for you, or to retire which on the whole I should prefer to do.

'But understand that, if I decorate, I decorate alone, without interference of any sort.

If I do the thing, I will do it thoroughly, but I must have a free hand.

'Yours truly,

'PHILIP BOSINNEY.'

The exact and immediate cause of this letter cannot, of course, be told, though it is not improbable that Bosinney may have been moved by some sudden revolt against his position towards Soames—that eternal position of Art towards Property—which is so admirably summed up, on the back of the most indispensable of modern appliances, in a sentence comparable to the very finest in Tacitus:

THOS. T. SORROW, Inventor. BERT M. PADLAND, Proprietor.

"What are you going to say to him?" James asked.

Soames did not even turn his head. "I haven't made up my mind," he said, and went on with his defence.

A client of his, having put some buildings on a piece of ground that did not belong to him, had been suddenly and most irritatingly warned to take them off again. After carefully going into the facts, however, Soames had seen his way to advise that his client had what was known as a title by possession, and that, though undoubtedly the ground did not belong to him, he was entitled to keep it, and had better do so; and he was now following up this advice by taking steps to—as the sailors say—'make it so.'

He had a distinct reputation for sound advice; people saying of him: "Go to young Forsyte—a long-headed fellow!" and he prized this reputation highly.

His natural taciturnity was in his favour; nothing could be more calculated to give people, especially people with property (Soames had no other clients), the impression that he was a safe man. And he was safe. Tradition, habit, education, inherited aptitude, native caution, all joined to form a solid professional honesty, superior to temptation—from the very fact that it was built on an innate avoidance of risk. How could he fall, when his soul abhorred circumstances which render a fall possible—a man cannot fall off the floor!

And those countless Forsytes, who, in the course of innumerable transactions concerned with property of all sorts (from wives to water rights), had occasion for the services of a safe man, found it both reposeful and profitable to confide in Soames. That slight superciliousness of his, combined with an air of mousing amongst precedents, was in his favour too—a man would not be supercilious unless he knew!

He was really at the head of the business, for though James still came nearly every day to, see for himself, he did little now but sit in his chair, twist his legs, slightly confuse things already decided, and presently go away again, and the other partner, Bustard, was a poor thing, who did a great deal of work, but whose opinion was never taken.

So Soames went steadily on with his defence. Yet it would be idle to say that his mind was at ease. He was suffering from a sense of impending trouble, that had haunted him for some time past. He tried to think it physical—a condition of his liver—but knew that it was not.

He looked at his watch. In a quarter of an hour he was due at the General Meeting of the New Colliery Company—one of Uncle Jolyon's concerns; he should see Uncle Jolyon there, and say something to him about Bosinney—he had not made up his mind what, but something—in any case he should not answer this letter until he had seen Uncle Jolyon. He got up and methodically put away the draft of his defence. Going into a dark little cupboard, he turned up the light, washed his hands with a piece of brown Windsor soap, and dried them on a roller towel. Then he brushed his hair, paying strict attention to the parting, turned down the light, took his hat, and saying he would be back at half-past two, stepped into the Poultry.

It was not far to the Offices of the New Colliery Company in Ironmonger Lane, where, and not at the Cannon Street Hotel, in accordance with the more ambitious practice of other companies, the General Meeting was always held. Old Jolyon had from the first set his face against the Press. What business—he said—had the Public with his concerns!

Soames arrived on the stroke of time, and took his seat alongside the Board, who, in a row, each Director behind his own ink-pot, faced their Shareholders.

In the centre of this row old Jolyon, conspicuous in his black, tightly-buttoned frock-coat and his white moustaches, was leaning back with finger tips crossed on a copy of the Directors' report and accounts.

On his right hand, always a little larger than life, sat the Secretary, 'Down-by-the-starn' Hemmings; an all-too-sad sadness beaming in his fine eyes; his iron-grey beard, in mourning like the rest of him, giving the feeling of an all-too-black tie behind it.

The occasion indeed was a melancholy one, only six weeks having elapsed since that telegram had come from Scorrier, the mining expert, on a private mission to the Mines, informing them that Pippin, their Superintendent, had committed suicide in endeavouring, after his extraordinary two years' silence, to write a letter to his Board. That letter was on the table now; it would be read to the Shareholders, who would of course be put into possession of all the facts.

Hemmings had often said to Soames, standing with his coat-tails divided before the fireplace:

"What our Shareholders don't know about our affairs isn't worth knowing. You may take that from me, Mr. Soames."

On one occasion, old Jolyon being present, Soames recollected a little unpleasantness. His uncle had looked up sharply and said: "Don't talk nonsense, Hemmings! You mean that what they do know isn't worth knowing!" Old Jolyon detested humbug.

Hemmings, angry-eyed, and wearing a smile like that of a trained poodle, had replied in an outburst of artificial applause: "Come, now, that's good, sir—that's very good. Your uncle will have his joke!"

The next time he had seen Soames he had taken the opportunity of saying to him: "The chairman's getting very old!—I can't get him to understand things; and he's so wilful—but what can you expect, with a chin like his?"

Soames had nodded.

Everyone knew that Uncle Jolyon's chin was a caution. He was looking worried to-day, in spite of his General Meeting look; he (Soames) should certainly speak to him about Bosinney.

Beyond old Jolyon on the left was little Mr. Booker, and he, too, wore his General Meeting look, as though searching for some particularly tender shareholder. And next him was the deaf director, with a frown; and beyond the deaf director, again, was old Mr. Bleedham, very bland, and having an air of conscious virtue—as well he might, knowing that the brown-paper parcel he always brought to the Board-room was concealed behind his hat (one of that old-fashioned class, of flat-brimmed top-hats which go with very large bow ties, clean-shaven lips, fresh cheeks, and neat little, white whiskers).

Soames always attended the General Meeting; it was considered better that he should do so, in case 'anything should arise!' He glanced round with his close, supercilious air at the walls of the room, where hung plans of the mine and harbour, together with a large photograph of a shaft leading to a working which had proved quite remarkably unprofitable. This photograph—a witness to the eternal irony underlying commercial enterprise—still retained its position on the wall, an effigy of the directors' pet, but dead, lamb.

And now old Jolyon rose, to present the report and accounts.

Veiling under a Jove-like serenity that perpetual antagonism deep-seated in the bosom of a director towards his shareholders, he faced them calmly. Soames faced them too. He knew most of them by sight. There was old Scrubsole, a tar man, who always came, as Hemmings would say, 'to make himself nasty,' a cantankerous-looking old fellow with a red face, a jowl, and an enormous low-crowned hat reposing on his knee. And the Rev. Mr.

Boms, who always proposed a vote of thanks to the chairman, in which he invariably expressed the hope that the Board would not forget to elevate their employees, using the word with a double e, as being more vigorous and Anglo-Saxon (he had the strong Imperialistic tendencies of his cloth). It was his salutary custom to buttonhole a director afterwards, and ask him whether he thought the coming year would be good or bad; and, according to the trend of the answer, to buy or sell three shares within the ensuing fortnight.

And there was that military man, Major O'Bally, who could not help speaking, if only to second the re-election of the auditor, and who sometimes caused serious consternation by taking toasts—proposals rather—out of the hands of persons who had been flattered with little slips of paper, entrusting the said proposals to their care.

These made up the lot, together with four or five strong, silent shareholders, with whom Soames could sympathize—men of business, who liked to keep an eye on their affairs for themselves, without being fussy—good, solid men, who came to the City every day and went back in the evening to good, solid wives.

Good, solid wives! There was something in that thought which roused the nameless uneasiness in Soames again.

What should he say to his uncle? What answer should he make to this letter?

. . . . "If any shareholder has any question to put, I shall be glad to answer it." A soft thump. Old Jolyon had let the report and accounts fall, and stood twisting his tortoise-shell glasses between thumb and forefinger.

The ghost of a smile appeared on Soames' face. They had better hurry up with their questions! He well knew his uncle's method (the ideal one) of at once saying: "I propose, then, that the report and accounts be adopted!" Never let them get their wind—shareholders were notoriously wasteful of time!

A tall, white-bearded man, with a gaunt, dissatisfied face, arose:

"I believe I am in order, Mr. Chairman, in raising a question on this figure of L5000 in the accounts. 'To the widow and family'" (he looked sourly round), "'of our late superintendent,' who so—er—ill-advisedly (I say—ill-advisedly) committed suicide, at a time when his services were of the utmost value to this Company. You have stated that the agreement which he has so unfortunately cut short with his own hand was for a period of five years, of which one only had expired—I—"

Old Jolyon made a gesture of impatience.

"I believe I am in order, Mr. Chairman—I ask whether this amount paid, or proposed to be paid, by the Board to the er—deceased—is for services which might have been rendered to the Company—had he not committed suicide?"

"It is in recognition of past services, which we all know—you as well as any of us—to have been of vital value."

"Then, sir, all I have to say is that the services being past, the amount is too much."

The shareholder sat down.

Old Jolyon waited a second and said: "I now propose that the report and—"

The shareholder rose again: "May I ask if the Board realizes that it is not their money which—I don't hesitate to say that if it were their money...."

A second shareholder, with a round, dogged face, whom Soames recognised as the late superintendent's brother-in-law, got up and said warmly: "In my opinion, sir, the sum is not enough!"

The Rev. Mr. Boms now rose to his feet. "If I may venture to express myself," he said, "I should say that the fact of the—er—deceased having committed suicide should weigh very heavily—very heavily with our worthy chairman. I have no doubt it has weighed with him, for—I say this for myself and I think for everyone present (hear, hear)—he enjoys our confidence in a high degree. We all desire, I should hope, to be charitable. But I feel sure" (he-looked severely at the late superintendent's brother-in-law) "that he will in some way, by some written expression, or better perhaps by reducing the amount, record our grave disapproval that so promising and valuable a life should have been thus impiously removed from a sphere where both its own interests and—if I may say so—our interests so imperatively demanded its continuance. We should not—nay, we may not—countenance so grave a dereliction of all duty, both human and divine."

The reverend gentleman resumed his seat. The late superintendent's brother-in-law again rose: "What I have said I stick to," he said; "the amount is not enough!"

The first shareholder struck in: "I challenge the legality of the payment. In my opinion this payment is not legal. The Company's solicitor is present; I believe I am in order in asking him the question."

All eyes were now turned upon Soames. Something had arisen!

He stood up, close-lipped and cold; his nerves inwardly fluttered, his attention tweaked away at last from contemplation of that cloud looming on the horizon of his mind.

"The point," he said in a low, thin voice, "is by no means clear. As there is no possibility of future consideration being received, it is doubtful whether the payment is strictly legal. If it is desired, the opinion of the court could be taken."

The superintendent's brother-in-law frowned, and said in a meaning tone: "We have no doubt the opinion of the court could be taken. May I ask the name of the gentleman who has given us that striking piece of information? Mr. Soames Forsyte? Indeed!" He looked from Soames to old Jolyon in a pointed manner.

A flush coloured Soames' pale cheeks, but his superciliousness did not waver. Old Jolyon fixed his eyes on the speaker.

"If," he said, "the late superintendents brother-in-law has nothing more to say, I propose that the report and accounts...."

At this moment, however, there rose one of those five silent, stolid shareholders, who had excited Soames' sympathy. He said:

"I deprecate the proposal altogether. We are expected to give charity to this man's wife and children, who, you tell us, were dependent on him. They may have been; I do not care whether they were or not. I object to the whole thing on principle. It is high time a stand was made against this sentimental humanitarianism. The country is eaten up with it. I object to my money being paid to these people of whom I know nothing, who have done nothing to earn it. I object in toto; it is not business. I now move that the report and accounts be put back, and amended by striking out the grant altogether."

Old Jolyon had remained standing while the strong, silent man was speaking. The speech awoke an echo in all hearts, voicing, as it did, the worship of strong men, the movement against generosity, which had at that time already commenced among the saner members of the community.

The words 'it is not business' had moved even the Board; privately everyone felt that indeed it was not. But they knew also the chairman's domineering temper and tenacity. He, too, at heart must feel that it was not business; but he was committed to his own proposition. Would he go back upon it? It was thought to be unlikely.

All waited with interest. Old Jolyon held up his hand; dark-rimmed glasses depending between his finger and thumb quivered slightly with a suggestion of menace.

He addressed the strong, silent shareholder.

"Knowing, as you do, the efforts of our late superintendent upon the occasion of the explosion at the mines, do you seriously wish me to put that amendment, sir?"

"I do."

Old Jolyon put the amendment.

"Does anyone second this?" he asked, looking calmly round.

And it was then that Soames, looking at his uncle, felt the power of will that was in that old man. No one stirred. Looking straight into the eyes of the strong, silent shareholder, old Jolyon said:

"I now move, 'That the report and accounts for the year 1886 be received and adopted.' You second that? Those in favour signify the same in the usual way. Contrary—no. Carried. The next business, gentlemen...."

Soames smiled. Certainly Uncle Jolyon had a way with him!

But now his attention relapsed upon Bosinney.

Odd how that fellow haunted his thoughts, even in business hours.

Irene's visit to the house—but there was nothing in that, except that she might have told him; but then, again, she never did tell him anything. She was more silent, more touchy, every day. He wished to God the house were finished, and they were in it, away from London. Town did not suit her; her nerves were not strong enough. That nonsense of the separate room had cropped up again!

The meeting was breaking up now. Underneath the photograph of the lost shaft Hemmings was buttonholed by the Rev. Mr. Boms. Little Mr. Booker, his bristling eyebrows wreathed in angry smiles, was having a parting turn-up with old Scrubsole. The two hated each other like poison. There was some matter of a tar-contract between them, little Mr. Booker having secured it from the Board for a nephew of his, over old Scrubsole's head. Soames had heard that from Hemmings, who liked a gossip, more especially about his directors, except, indeed, old Jolyon, of whom he was afraid.

Soames awaited his opportunity. The last shareholder was vanishing through the door, when he approached his uncle, who was putting on his hat.

"Can I speak to you for a minute, Uncle Jolyon?"

It is uncertain what Soames expected to get out of this interview.

Apart from that somewhat mysterious awe in which Forsytes in general held old Jolyon, due to his philosophic twist, or perhaps—as Hemmings would doubtless have said—to his chin, there was, and always had been, a subtle antagonism between the younger man and the old. It had lurked under their dry manner of greeting, under their non-committal allusions to each other, and arose perhaps from old Jolyon's perception of the quiet tenacity ('obstinacy,' he rather naturally called it) of the young man, of a secret doubt whether he could get his own way with him.

Both these Forsytes, wide asunder as the poles in many respects, possessed in their different ways—to a greater degree than the rest of the family—that essential quality of tenacious and prudent insight into 'affairs,' which is the highwater mark of their great class. Either of them, with a little luck and opportunity, was equal to a lofty career; either of them would have made a good financier, a great contractor, a statesman, though old Jolyon, in certain of his moods when under the influence of a cigar or of Nature—would have been capable of, not perhaps despising, but certainly of questioning, his own high position, while Soames, who never smoked cigars, would not.

Then, too, in old Jolyon's mind there was always the secret ache, that the son of James—of James, whom he had always thought such a poor thing, should be pursuing the paths of success, while his own son...!

And last, not least—for he was no more outside the radiation of family gossip than any other Forsyte—he had now heard the sinister, indefinite, but none the less disturbing rumour about Bosinney, and his pride was wounded to the quick.

Characteristically, his irritation turned not against Irene but against Soames. The idea that his nephew's wife (why couldn't the fellow take better care of her—Oh! quaint injustice! as though Soames could possibly take more care!)—should be drawing to herself June's lover, was intolerably humiliating. And seeing the danger, he did not, like James, hide it away in sheer nervousness, but owned with the dispassion of his broader outlook, that it was not unlikely; there was something very attractive about Irene!

He had a presentiment on the subject of Soames' communication as they left the Board Room together, and went out into the noise and hurry of Cheapside. They walked together a good minute without speaking, Soames with his mousing, mincing step, and old Jolyon upright and using his umbrella languidly as a walking-stick.

They turned presently into comparative quiet, for old Jolyon's way to a second Board led him in the direction of Moorage Street.

Then Soames, without lifting his eyes, began: "I've had this letter from Bosinney. You see what he says; I thought I'd let you know. I've spent a lot more than I intended on this house, and I want the position to be clear."

Old Jolyon ran his eyes unwillingly over the letter: "What he says is clear enough," he said.

"He talks about 'a free hand,'" replied Soames.

Old Jolyon looked at him. The long-suppressed irritation and antagonism towards this young fellow, whose affairs were beginning to intrude upon his own, burst from him.

"Well, if you don't trust him, why do you employ him?"

Soames stole a sideway look: "It's much too late to go into that," he said, "I only want it to be quite understood that if I give him a free hand, he doesn't let me in. I thought if you were to speak to him, it would carry more weight!"

"No," said old Jolyon abruptly; "I'll have nothing to do with it!"

The words of both uncle and nephew gave the impression of unspoken meanings, far more important, behind. And the look they interchanged was like a revelation of this consciousness.

"Well," said Soames; "I thought, for June's sake, I'd tell you, that's all; I thought you'd better know I shan't stand any nonsense!"

"What is that to me?" old Jolyon took him up.

"Oh! I don't know," said Soames, and flurried by that sharp look he was unable to say more. "Don't say I didn't tell you," he added sulkily, recovering his composure.

"Tell me!" said old Jolyon; "I don't know what you mean. You come worrying me about a thing like this. I don't want to hear about your affairs; you must manage them yourself!"

"Very well," said Soames immovably, "I will!"

"Good-morning, then," said old Jolyon, and they parted.

Soames retraced his steps, and going into a celebrated eating-house, asked for a plate of smoked salmon and a glass of Chablis; he seldom ate much in the middle of the day, and generally ate standing, finding the position beneficial to his liver, which was very sound, but to which he desired to put down all his troubles.

When he had finished he went slowly back to his office, with bent head, taking no notice of the swarming thousands on the pavements, who in their turn took no notice of him.

The evening post carried the following reply to Bosinney:

'FORSYTE, BUSTARD AND FORSYTE,

'Commissioners for Oaths,

'92001, BRANCH LANE, POULTRY, E.C.,

'May 17, 1887.

'DEAR BOSINNEY,

'I have, received your letter, the terms of which not a little surprise me. I was under the impression that you had, and have had all along, a "free hand"; for I do not recollect that any suggestions I have been so unfortunate as to make have met with your approval. In giving you, in accordance with your request, this "free hand," I wish you to clearly understand that the total cost of the house as handed over to me completely decorated, inclusive of your fee (as arranged between us), must not exceed twelve thousand pounds— L12,000. This gives you an ample margin, and, as you know, is far more than I originally contemplated.

'I am,

'Yours truly,

'SOAMES FORSYTE.'

On the following day he received a note from Bosinney:

'PHILIP BAYNES BOSINNEY,

'Architect,

'309D, SLOANE STREET, S.W.,

'May 18.

'DEAR FORSYTE,

'If you think that in such a delicate matter as decoration I can bind myself to the exact pound, I am afraid you are mistaken. I can see that you are tired of the arrangement, and of me, and I had better, therefore, resign.

'Yours faithfully,

'PHILIP BAYNES BOSINNEY.'

Soames pondered long and painfully over his answer, and late at night in the dining-room, when Irene had gone to bed, he composed the following:

'62, MONTPELLIER SQUARE, S.W.,

'May 19, 1887.

'DEAR BOSINNEY,

'I think that in both our interests it would be extremely undesirable that matters should be so left at this stage. I did not mean to say that if you should exceed the sum named in my letter to you by ten or twenty or even fifty pounds, there would be any difficulty between us. This being so, I should like you to reconsider your answer. You have a "free hand" in the terms of this correspondence, and I hope you will see your way to completing the decorations, in the matter of which I know it is difficult to be absolutely exact.

'Yours truly,

'SOAMES FORSYTE.'

Bosinney's answer, which came in the course of the next day, was:

'May 20.

'DEAR FORSYTE,

'Very well.

'PH. BOSINNEY.'

CHAPTER VI—OLD JOLYON AT THE ZOO

Old Jolyon disposed of his second Meeting—an ordinary Board—summarily. He was so dictatorial that his fellow directors were left in cabal over the increasing domineeringness of old Forsyte, which they were far from intending to stand much longer, they said.

He went out by Underground to Portland Road Station, whence he took a cab and drove to the Zoo.

He had an assignation there, one of those assignations that had lately been growing more frequent, to which his increasing uneasiness about June and the 'change in her,' as he expressed it, was driving him.

She buried herself away, and was growing thin; if he spoke to her he got no answer, or had his head snapped off, or she looked as if she would burst into tears. She was as changed as she could be, all through this Bosinney. As for telling him about anything, not a bit of it!

And he would sit for long spells brooding, his paper unread before him, a cigar extinct between his lips. She had been such a companion to him ever since she was three years old! And he loved her so!

Forces regardless of family or class or custom were beating down his guard; impending events over which he had no control threw their shadows on his head. The irritation of one accustomed to have his way was roused against he knew not what.

Chafing at the slowness of his cab, he reached the Zoo door; but, with his sunny instinct for seizing the good of each moment, he forgot his vexation as he walked towards the tryst.

From the stone terrace above the bear-pit his son and his two grandchildren came hastening down when they saw old Jolyon coming, and led him away towards the lion-house. They supported him on either side, holding one to each of his hands,—whilst Jolly, perverse like his father, carried his grandfather's umbrella in such a way as to catch people's legs with the crutch of the handle.

Young Jolyon followed.

It was as good as a play to see his father with the children, but such a play as brings smiles with tears behind. An old man and two small children walking together can be seen at any hour of the day; but the sight of old Jolyon, with Jolly and Holly seemed to young Jolyon a special peep-show of the things that lie at the bottom of our hearts. The complete surrender of that erect old figure to those little figures on either hand was too poignantly tender, and, being a man of an habitual reflex action, young Jolyon swore softly under his breath. The show affected him in a way unbecoming to a Forsyte, who is nothing if not undemonstrative.

Thus they reached the lion-house.

There had been a morning fete at the Botanical Gardens, and a large number of Forsy...'— that is, of well-dressed people who kept carriages had brought them on to the Zoo, so as to have more, if possible, for their money, before going back to Rutland Gate or Bryanston Square.

"Let's go on to the Zoo," they had said to each other; "it'll be great fun!" It was a shilling day; and there would not be all those horrid common people.

In front of the long line of cages they were collected in rows, watching the tawny, ravenous beasts behind the bars await their only pleasure of the four-and-twenty hours. The hungrier the beast, the greater the fascination. But whether because the spectators envied his appetite, or, more humanely, because it was so soon to be satisfied, young Jolyon could not tell. Remarks kept falling on his ears: "That's a nasty-looking brute, that tiger!" "Oh, what a love! Look at his little mouth!" "Yes, he's rather nice! Don't go too near, mother."

And frequently, with little pats, one or another would clap their hands to their pockets behind and look round, as though expecting young Jolyon or some disinterested-looking person to relieve them of the contents.

A well-fed man in a white waistcoat said slowly through his teeth: "It's all greed; they can't be hungry. Why, they take no exercise." At these words a tiger snatched a piece of bleeding liver, and the fat man laughed. His wife, in a Paris model frock and gold nose-nippers, reproved him: "How can you laugh, Harry? Such a horrid sight!"

Young Jolyon frowned.

The circumstances of his life, though he had ceased to take a too personal view of them, had left him subject to an intermittent contempt; and the class to which he had belonged— the carriage class—especially excited his sarcasm.

To shut up a lion or tiger in confinement was surely a horrible barbarity. But no cultivated person would admit this.

The idea of its being barbarous to confine wild animals had probably never even occurred to his father for instance; he belonged to the old school, who considered it at once humanizing and educational to confine baboons and panthers, holding the view, no doubt, that in course of time they might induce these creatures not so unreasonably to die of misery and heart-sickness against the bars of their cages, and put the society to the expense of getting others! In his eyes, as in the eyes of all Forsytes, the pleasure of seeing these beautiful creatures in a state of captivity far outweighed the inconvenience of imprisonment to beasts whom God had so improvidently placed in a state of freedom! It was for the animals good, removing them at once from the countless dangers of open air and exercise, and enabling them to exercise their functions in the guaranteed seclusion of a private compartment! Indeed, it was doubtful what wild animals were made for but to be shut up in cages!

But as young Jolyon had in his constitution the elements of impartiality, he reflected that to stigmatize as barbarity that which was merely lack of imagination must be wrong; for none who held these views had been placed in a similar position to the animals they caged, and could not, therefore, be expected to enter into their sensations. It was not until they were leaving the gardens—Jolly and Holly in a state of blissful delirium—that old Jolyon found an opportunity of speaking to his son on the matter next his heart. "I don't know what to make of it," he said; "if she's to go on as she's going on now, I can't tell what's to come. I wanted her to see the doctor, but she won't. She's not a bit like me. She's your mother all over. Obstinate as a mule! If she doesn't want to do a thing, she won't, and there's an end of it!"

Young Jolyon smiled; his eyes had wandered to his father's chin. 'A pair of you,' he thought, but he said nothing.

"And then," went on old Jolyon, "there's this Bosinney. I should like to punch the fellow's head, but I can't, I suppose, though—I don't see why you shouldn't," he added doubtfully.

"What has he done? Far better that it should come to an end, if they don't hit it off!"

Old Jolyon looked at his son. Now they had actually come to discuss a subject connected with the relations between the sexes he felt distrustful. Jo would be sure to hold some loose view or other.

"Well, I don't know what you think," he said; "I dare say your sympathy's with him—shouldn't be surprised; but I think he's behaving precious badly, and if he comes my way I shall tell him so." He dropped the subject.

It was impossible to discuss with his son the true nature and meaning of Bosinney's defection. Had not his son done the very same thing (worse, if possible) fifteen years ago? There seemed no end to the consequences of that piece of folly.

Young Jolyon also was silent; he had quickly penetrated his father's thought, for, dethroned from the high seat of an obvious and uncomplicated view of things, he had become both perceptive and subtle.

The attitude he had adopted towards sexual matters fifteen years before, however, was too different from his father's. There was no bridging the gulf.

He said coolly: "I suppose he's fallen in love with some other woman?"

Old Jolyon gave him a dubious look: "I can't tell," he said; "they say so!"

"Then, it's probably true," remarked young Jolyon unexpectedly; "and I suppose they've told you who she is?"

"Yes," said old Jolyon, "Soames's wife!"

Young Jolyon did not whistle: The circumstances of his own life had rendered him incapable of whistling on such a subject, but he looked at his father, while the ghost of a smile hovered over his face.

If old Jolyon saw, he took no notice.

"She and June were bosom friends!" he muttered.

"Poor little June!" said young Jolyon softly. He thought of his daughter still as a babe of three.

Old Jolyon came to a sudden halt.

"I don't believe a word of it," he said, "it's some old woman's tale. Get me a cab, Jo, I'm tired to death!"

They stood at a corner to see if an empty cab would come along, while carriage after carriage drove past, bearing Forsytes of all descriptions from the Zoo. The harness, the liveries, the gloss on the horses' coats, shone and glittered in the May sunlight, and each equipage, landau, sociable, barouche, Victoria, or brougham, seemed to roll out proudly from its wheels:

'I and my horses and my men you know,' Indeed the whole turn-out have cost a pot. But we were worth it every penny. Look At Master and at Missis now, the dawgs! Ease with security—ah! that's the ticket!

And such, as everyone knows, is fit accompaniment for a perambulating Forsyte.

Amongst these carriages was a barouche coming at a greater pace than the others, drawn by a pair of bright bay horses. It swung on its high springs, and the four people who filled it seemed rocked as in a cradle.

This chariot attracted young Jolyon's attention; and suddenly, on the back seat, he recognised his Uncle James, unmistakable in spite of the increased whiteness of his whiskers; opposite, their backs defended by sunshades, Rachel Forsyte and her elder but married sister, Winifred Dartie, in irreproachable toilettes, had posed their heads haughtily, like two of the birds they had been seeing at the Zoo; while by James' side reclined Dartie, in a brand-new frock-coat buttoned tight and square, with a large expanse of carefully shot linen protruding below each wristband.

An extra, if subdued, sparkle, an added touch of the best gloss or varnish characterized this vehicle, and seemed to distinguish it from all the others, as though by some happy extravagance—like that which marks out the real 'work of art' from the ordinary 'picture'—it were designated as the typical car, the very throne of Forsytedom.

Old Jolyon did not see them pass; he was petting poor Holly who was tired, but those in the carriage had taken in the little group; the ladies' heads tilted suddenly, there was a spasmodic screening movement of parasols; James' face protruded naively, like the head of a long bird, his mouth slowly opening. The shield-like rounds of the parasols grew smaller and smaller, and vanished.

Young Jolyon saw that he had been recognised, even by Winifred, who could not have been more than fifteen when he had forfeited the right to be considered a Forsyte.

There was not much change in them! He remembered the exact look of their turn-out all that time ago: Horses, men, carriage—all different now, no doubt—but of the precise stamp of fifteen years before; the same neat display, the same nicely calculated arrogance ease with security! The swing exact, the pose of the sunshades exact, exact the spirit of the whole thing.

And in the sunlight, defended by the haughty shields of parasols, carriage after carriage went by.

"Uncle James has just passed, with his female folk," said young Jolyon.

His father looked black. "Did your uncle see us? Yes? Hmph! What's he want, coming down into these parts?"

An empty cab drove up at this moment, and old Jolyon stopped it.

"I shall see you again before long, my boy!" he said. "Don't you go paying any attention to what I've been saying about young Bosinney—I don't believe a word of it!"

Kissing the children, who tried to detain him, he stepped in and was borne away.

Young Jolyon, who had taken Holly up in his arms, stood motionless at the corner, looking after the cab.

CHAPTER VII—AFTERNOON AT TIMOTHY'S

If old Jolyon, as he got into his cab, had said: 'I won't believe a word of it!' he would more truthfully have expressed his sentiments.

The notion that James and his womankind had seen him in the company of his son had awakened in him not only the impatience he always felt when crossed, but that secret hostility natural between brothers, the roots of which—little nursery rivalries—sometimes toughen and deepen as life goes on, and, all hidden, support a plant capable of producing in season the bitterest fruits.

Hitherto there had been between these six brothers no more unfriendly feeling than that caused by the secret and natural doubt that the others might be richer than themselves; a feeling increased to the pitch of curiosity by the approach of death—that end of all handicaps—and the great 'closeness' of their man of business, who, with some sagacity, would profess to Nicholas ignorance of James' income, to James ignorance of old Jolyon's, to Jolyon ignorance of Roger's, to Roger ignorance of Swithin's, while to Swithin he would say most irritatingly that Nicholas must be a rich man. Timothy alone was exempt, being in gilt-edged securities.

But now, between two of them at least, had arisen a very different sense of injury. From the moment when James had the impertinence to pry into his affairs—as he put it—old Jolyon no longer chose to credit this story about Bosinney. His grand-daughter slighted through a member of 'that fellow's' family! He made up his mind that Bosinney was maligned. There must be some other reason for his defection.

June had flown out at him, or something; she was as touchy as she could be!

He would, however, let Timothy have a bit of his mind, and see if he would go on dropping hints! And he would not let the grass grow under his feet either, he would go there at once, and take very good care that he didn't have to go again on the same errand.

He saw James' carriage blocking the pavement in front of 'The Bower.' So they had got there before him—cackling about having seen him, he dared say! And further on, Swithin's greys were turning their noses towards the noses of James' bays, as though in conclave over the family, while their coachmen were in conclave above.

Old Jolyon, depositing his hat on the chair in the narrow hall, where that hat of Bosinney's had so long ago been mistaken for a cat, passed his thin hand grimly over his face with its great drooping white moustaches, as though to remove all traces of expression, and made his way upstairs.

He found the front drawing-room full. It was full enough at the best of times—without visitors—without any one in it—for Timothy and his sisters, following the tradition of their generation, considered that a room was not quite 'nice' unless it was 'properly' furnished. It held, therefore, eleven chairs, a sofa, three tables, two cabinets, innumerable knicknacks, and part of a large grand piano. And now, occupied by Mrs. Small, Aunt Hester, by Swithin, James, Rachel, Winifred, Euphemia, who had come in again to return 'Passion and Paregoric' which she had read at lunch, and her chum Frances, Roger's daughter (the musical Forsyte, the one who composed songs), there was only one chair left unoccupied, except, of course, the two that nobody ever sat on—and the only standing room was occupied by the cat, on whom old Jolyon promptly stepped.

In these days it was by no means unusual for Timothy to have so many visitors. The family had always, one and all, had a real respect for Aunt Ann, and now that she was gone, they were coming far more frequently to The Bower, and staying longer.

Swithin had been the first to arrive, and seated torpid in a red satin chair with a gilt back, he gave every appearance of lasting the others out. And symbolizing Bosinney's name 'the big one,' with his great stature and bulk, his thick white hair, his puffy immovable shaven face, he looked more primeval than ever in the highly upholstered room.

His conversation, as usual of late, had turned at once upon Irene, and he had lost no time in giving Aunts Juley and Hester his opinion with regard to this rumour he heard was going about. No—as he said—she might want a bit of flirtation—a pretty woman must have her fling; but more than that he did not believe. Nothing open; she had too much good sense, too much proper appreciation of what was due to her position, and to the family! No sc—, he was going to say 'scandal' but the very idea was so preposterous that he waved his hand as though to say—'but let that pass!'

Granted that Swithin took a bachelor's view of the situation—still what indeed was not due to that family in which so many had done so well for themselves, had attained a certain position? If he had heard in dark, pessimistic moments the words 'yeomen' and 'very small beer' used in connection with his origin, did he believe them?

No! he cherished, hugging it pathetically to his bosom the secret theory that there was something distinguished somewhere in his ancestry.

"Must be," he once said to young Jolyon, before the latter went to the bad. "Look at us, we've got on! There must be good blood in us somewhere."

He had been fond of young Jolyon: the boy had been in a good set at College, had known that old ruffian Sir Charles Fiste's sons—a pretty rascal one of them had turned out, too; and there was style about him—it was a thousand pities he had run off with that half-foreign governess! If he must go off like that why couldn't he have chosen someone who would have done them credit! And what was he now?—an underwriter at Lloyd's; they said he even painted pictures—pictures! Damme! he might have ended as Sir Jolyon Forsyte, Bart., with a seat in Parliament, and a place in the country!

It was Swithin who, following the impulse which sooner or later urges thereto some member of every great family, went to the Heralds' Office, where they assured him that he was undoubtedly of the same family as the well-known Forsites with an 'i,' whose arms were 'three dexter buckles on a sable ground gules,' hoping no doubt to get him to take them up.

Swithin, however, did not do this, but having ascertained that the crest was a 'pheasant proper,' and the motto 'For Forsite,' he had the pheasant proper placed upon his carriage and the buttons of his coachman, and both crest and motto on his writing-paper. The arms he hugged to himself, partly because, not having paid for them, he thought it would look ostentatious to put them on his carriage, and he hated ostentation, and partly because he, like any practical man all over the country, had a secret dislike and contempt for things he could not understand he found it hard, as anyone might, to swallow 'three dexter buckles on a sable ground gules.'

He never forgot, however, their having told him that if he paid for them he would be entitled to use them, and it strengthened his conviction that he was a gentleman. Imperceptibly the rest of the family absorbed the 'pheasant proper,' and some, more serious than others, adopted the motto; old Jolyon, however, refused to use the latter, saying that it was humbug meaning nothing, so far as he could see.

Among the older generation it was perhaps known at bottom from what great historical event they derived their crest; and if pressed on the subject, sooner than tell a lie—they did not like telling lies, having an impression that only Frenchmen and Russians told them—they would confess hurriedly that Swithin had got hold of it somehow.

Among the younger generation the matter was wrapped in a discretion proper. They did not want to hurt the feelings of their elders, nor to feel ridiculous themselves; they simply used the crest....

"No," said Swithin, "he had had an opportunity of seeing for himself, and what he should say was, that there was nothing in her manner to that young Buccaneer or Bosinney or whatever his name was, different from her manner to himself; in fact, he should rather say...." But here the entrance of Frances and Euphemia put an unfortunate stop to the conversation, for this was not a subject which could be discussed before young people.

And though Swithin was somewhat upset at being stopped like this on the point of saying something important, he soon recovered his affability. He was rather fond of Frances—Francie, as she was called in the family. She was so smart, and they told him she made a pretty little pot of pin-money by her songs; he called it very clever of her.

He rather prided himself indeed on a liberal attitude towards women, not seeing any reason why they shouldn't paint pictures, or write tunes, or books even, for the matter of that, especially if they could turn a useful penny by it; not at all—kept them out of mischief. It was not as if they were men!

'Little Francie,' as she was usually called with good-natured contempt, was an important personage, if only as a standing illustration of the attitude of Forsytes towards the Arts. She was not really 'little,' but rather tall, with dark hair for a Forsyte, which, together with a grey eye, gave her what was called 'a Celtic appearance.' She wrote songs with titles like 'Breathing Sighs,' or 'Kiss me, Mother, ere I die,' with a refrain like an anthem:

'Kiss me, Mother, ere I die;

Kiss me-kiss me, Mother, ah!

Kiss, ah! kiss me e-ere I—

Kiss me, Mother, ere I d-d-die!'

She wrote the words to them herself, and other poems. In lighter moments she wrote waltzes, one of which, the 'Kensington Coil,' was almost national to Kensington, having a sweet dip in it.

It was very original. Then there were her 'Songs for Little People,' at once educational and witty, especially 'Gran'ma's Porgie,' and that ditty, almost prophetically imbued with the coming Imperial spirit, entitled 'Black Him In His Little Eye.'

Any publisher would take these, and reviews like 'High Living,' and the 'Ladies' Genteel Guide' went into raptures over: 'Another of Miss Francie Forsyte's spirited ditties, sparkling and pathetic. We ourselves were moved to tears and laughter. Miss Forsyte should go far.'

With the true instinct of her breed, Francie had made a point of knowing the right people—people who would write about her, and talk about her, and people in Society, too—keeping a mental register of just where to exert her fascinations, and an eye on that steady scale of rising prices, which in her mind's eye represented the future. In this way she caused herself to be universally respected.

Once, at a time when her emotions were whipped by an attachment—for the tenor of Roger's life, with its whole-hearted collection of house property, had induced in his only daughter a tendency towards passion—she turned to great and sincere work, choosing the sonata form, for the violin. This was the only one of her productions that troubled the Forsytes. They felt at once that it would not sell.

Roger, who liked having a clever daughter well enough, and often alluded to the amount of pocket-money she made for herself, was upset by this violin sonata.

"Rubbish like that!" he called it. Francie had borrowed young Flageoletti from Euphemia, to play it in the drawing-room at Prince's Gardens.

As a matter of fact Roger was right. It was rubbish, but—annoying! the sort of rubbish that wouldn't sell. As every Forsyte knows, rubbish that sells is not rubbish at all—far from it.

And yet, in spite of the sound common sense which fixed the worth of art at what it would fetch, some of the Forsytes—Aunt Hester, for instance, who had always been musical—could not help regretting that Francie's music was not 'classical'; the same with her poems. But then, as Aunt Hester said, they didn't see any poetry nowadays, all the poems were 'little light things.'

There was nobody who could write a poem like 'Paradise Lost,' or 'Childe Harold'; either of which made you feel that you really had read something. Still, it was nice for Francie to have something to occupy her; while other girls were spending money shopping she was making it!

And both Aunt Hester and Aunt Juley were always ready to listen to the latest story of how Francie had got her price increased.

They listened now, together with Swithin, who sat pretending not to, for these young people talked so fast and mumbled so, he never could catch what they said.

"And I can't think," said Mrs. Septimus, "how you do it. I should never have the audacity!"

Francie smiled lightly. "I'd much rather deal with a man than a woman. Women are so sharp!"

"My dear," cried Mrs. Small, "I'm sure we're not."

Euphemia went off into her silent laugh, and, ending with the squeak, said, as though being strangled: "Oh, you'll kill me some day, auntie."

Swithin saw no necessity to laugh; he detested people laughing when he himself perceived no joke. Indeed, he detested Euphemia altogether, to whom he always alluded as 'Nick's daughter, what's she called—the pale one?' He had just missed being her god-father—indeed, would have been, had he not taken a firm stand against her outlandish name. He hated becoming a godfather. Swithin then said to Francie with dignity: "It's a fine day—er—for the time of year." But Euphemia, who knew perfectly well that he had refused to be her godfather, turned to Aunt Hester, and began telling her how she had seen Irene—Mrs. Soames—at the Church and Commercial Stores.

"And Soames was with her?" said Aunt Hester, to whom Mrs. Small had as yet had no opportunity of relating the incident.

"Soames with her? Of course not!"

"But was she all alone in London?"

"Oh, no; there was Mr. Bosinney with her. She was perfectly dressed."

But Swithin, hearing the name Irene, looked severely at Euphemia, who, it is true, never did look well in a dress, whatever she may have done on other occasions, and said:

"Dressed like a lady, I've no doubt. It's a pleasure to see her."

At this moment James and his daughters were announced. Dartie, feeling badly in want of a drink, had pleaded an appointment with his dentist, and, being put down at the Marble Arch, had got into a hansom, and was already seated in the window of his club in Piccadilly.

His wife, he told his cronies, had wanted to take him to pay some calls. It was not in his line—not exactly. Haw!

Hailing the waiter, he sent him out to the hall to see what had won the 4.30 race. He was dog-tired, he said, and that was a fact; had been drivin' about with his wife to 'shows' all the afternoon. Had put his foot down at last. A fellow must live his own life.

At this moment, glancing out of the bay window—for he loved this seat whence he could see everybody pass—his eye unfortunately, or perhaps fortunately, chanced to light on the figure of Soames, who was mousing across the road from the Green Park-side, with the evident intention of coming in, for he, too, belonged to 'The Iseeum.'

Dartie sprang to his feet; grasping his glass, he muttered something about 'that 4.30 race,' and swiftly withdrew to the card-room, where Soames never came. Here, in complete isolation and a dim light, he lived his own life till half past seven, by which hour he knew Soames must certainly have left the club.

It would not do, as he kept repeating to himself whenever he felt the impulse to join the gossips in the bay-window getting too strong for him—it absolutely would not do, with finances as low as his, and the 'old man' (James) rusty ever since that business over the oil shares, which was no fault of his, to risk a row with Winifred.

If Soames were to see him in the club it would be sure to come round to her that he wasn't at the dentist's at all. He never knew a family where things 'came round' so. Uneasily, amongst the green baize card-tables, a frown on his olive coloured face, his check trousers crossed, and patent-leather boots shining through the gloom, he sat biting his forefinger, and wondering where the deuce he was to get the money if Erotic failed to win the Lancashire Cup.

His thoughts turned gloomily to the Forsytes. What a set they were! There was no getting anything out of them—at least, it was a matter of extreme difficulty. They were so d——d particular about money matters; not a sportsman amongst the lot, unless it were George. That fellow Soames, for instance, would have a fit if you tried to borrow a tenner from him, or, if he didn't have a fit, he looked at you with his cursed supercilious smile, as if you were a lost soul because you were in want of money.

And that wife of his (Dartie's mouth watered involuntarily), he had tried to be on good terms with her, as one naturally would with any pretty sister-in-law, but he would be cursed if the (he mentally used a coarse word)—would have anything to say to him—she looked at him, indeed, as if he were dirt—and yet she could go far enough, he wouldn't mind betting. He knew women; they weren't made with soft eyes and figures like that for nothing, as that fellow Soames would jolly soon find out, if there were anything in what he had heard about this Buccaneer Johnny.

Rising from his chair, Dartie took a turn across the room, ending in front of the looking-glass over the marble chimney-piece; and there he stood for a long time contemplating in the glass the reflection of his face. It had that look, peculiar to some men, of having been steeped in linseed oil, with its waxed dark moustaches and the little distinguished commencements of side whiskers; and concernedly he felt the promise of a pimple on the side of his slightly curved and fattish nose.

In the meantime old Jolyon had found the remaining chair in Timothy's commodious drawing-room. His advent had obviously put a stop to the conversation, decided awkwardness having set in. Aunt Juley, with her well-known kindheartedness, hastened to set people at their ease again.

"Yes, Jolyon," she said, "we were just saying that you haven't been here for a long time; but we mustn't be surprised. You're busy, of course? James was just saying what a busy time of year...."

"Was he?" said old Jolyon, looking hard at James. "It wouldn't be half so busy if everybody minded their own business."

James, brooding in a small chair from which his knees ran uphill, shifted his feet uneasily, and put one of them down on the cat, which had unwisely taken refuge from old Jolyon beside him.

"Here, you've got a cat here," he said in an injured voice, withdrawing his foot nervously as he felt it squeezing into the soft, furry body.

"Several," said old Jolyon, looking at one face and another; "I trod on one just now."

A silence followed.

Then Mrs. Small, twisting her fingers and gazing round with 'pathetic calm', asked: "And how is dear June?"

A twinkle of humour shot through the sternness of old Jolyon's eyes. Extraordinary old woman, Juley! No one quite like her for saying the wrong thing!

"Bad!" he said; "London don't agree with her—too many people about, too much clatter and chatter by half." He laid emphasis on the words, and again looked James in the face.

Nobody spoke.

A feeling of its being too dangerous to take a step in any direction, or hazard any remark, had fallen on them all. Something of the sense of the impending, that comes over the spectator of a Greek tragedy, had entered that upholstered room, filled with those white-haired, frock-coated old men, and fashionably attired women, who were all of the same blood, between all of whom existed an unseizable resemblance.

Not that they were conscious of it—the visits of such fateful, bitter spirits are only felt.

Then Swithin rose. He would not sit there, feeling like that—he was not to be put down by anyone! And, manoeuvring round the room with added pomp, he shook hands with each separately.

"You tell Timothy from me," he said, "that he coddles himself too much!" Then, turning to Francie, whom he considered 'smart,' he added: "You come with me for a drive one of these days." But this conjured up the vision of that other eventful drive which had been so much talked about, and he stood quite still for a second, with glassy eyes, as though waiting to catch up with the significance of what he himself had said; then, suddenly recollecting that he didn't care a damn, he turned to old Jolyon: "Well, good-bye, Jolyon! You shouldn't go about without an overcoat; you'll be getting sciatica or something!" And, kicking the cat slightly with the pointed tip of his patent leather boot, he took his huge form away.

When he had gone everyone looked secretly at the others, to see how they had taken the mention of the word 'drive'—the word which had become famous, and acquired an overwhelming importance, as the only official—so to speak—news in connection with the vague and sinister rumour clinging to the family tongue.

Euphemia, yielding to an impulse, said with a short laugh: "I'm glad Uncle Swithin doesn't ask me to go for drives."

Mrs. Small, to reassure her and smooth over any little awkwardness the subject might have, replied: "My dear, he likes to take somebody well dressed, who will do him a little credit. I shall never forget the drive he took me. It was an experience!" And her chubby round old face was spread for a moment with a strange contentment; then broke into pouts, and tears came into her eyes. She was thinking of that long ago driving tour she had once taken with Septimus Small.

James, who had relapsed into his nervous brooding in the little chair, suddenly roused himself: "He's a funny fellow, Swithin," he said, but in a half-hearted way.

Old Jolyon's silence, his stern eyes, held them all in a kind of paralysis. He was disconcerted himself by the effect of his own words—an effect which seemed to deepen the importance of the very rumour he had come to scotch; but he was still angry.

He had not done with them yet—No, no—he would give them another rub or two.

He did not wish to rub his nieces, he had no quarrel with them—a young and presentable female always appealed to old Jolyon's clemency—but that fellow James, and, in a less degree perhaps, those others, deserved all they would get. And he, too, asked for Timothy.

As though feeling that some danger threatened her younger brother, Aunt Juley suddenly offered him tea: "There it is," she said, "all cold and nasty, waiting for you in the back drawing room, but Smither shall make you some fresh."

Old Jolyon rose: "Thank you," he said, looking straight at James, "but I've no time for tea, and—scandal, and the rest of it! It's time I was at home. Good-bye, Julia; good-bye, Hester; good-bye, Winifred."

Without more ceremonious adieux, he marched out.

Once again in his cab, his anger evaporated, for so it ever was with his wrath—when he had rapped out, it was gone. Sadness came over his spirit. He had stopped their mouths, maybe, but at what a cost! At the cost of certain knowledge that the rumour he had been resolved not to believe was true. June was abandoned, and for the wife of that fellow's son! He felt it was true, and hardened himself to treat it as if it were not; but the pain he hid beneath this resolution began slowly, surely, to vent itself in a blind resentment against James and his son.

The six women and one man left behind in the little drawing-room began talking as easily as might be after such an occurrence, for though each one of them knew for a fact that he or she never talked scandal, each one of them also knew that the other six did; all were therefore angry and at a loss. James only was silent, disturbed, to the bottom of his soul.

Presently Francie said: "Do you know, I think Uncle Jolyon is terribly changed this last year. What do you think, Aunt Hester?"

Aunt Hester made a little movement of recoil: "Oh, ask your Aunt Julia!" she said; "I know nothing about it."

No one else was afraid of assenting, and James muttered gloomily at the floor: "He's not half the man he was."

"I've noticed it a long time," went on Francie; "he's aged tremendously."

Aunt Juley shook her head; her face seemed suddenly to have become one immense pout.

"Poor dear Jolyon," she said, "somebody ought to see to it for him!"

There was again silence; then, as though in terror of being left solitarily behind, all five visitors rose simultaneously, and took their departure.

Mrs. Small, Aunt Hester, and their cat were left once more alone, the sound of a door closing in the distance announced the approach of Timothy.

That evening, when Aunt Hester had just got off to sleep in the back bedroom that used to be Aunt Juley's before Aunt Juley took Aunt Ann's, her door was opened, and Mrs. Small, in a pink night-cap, a candle in her hand, entered: "Hester!" she said. "Hester!"

Aunt Hester faintly rustled the sheet.

"Hester," repeated Aunt Juley, to make quite sure that she had awakened her, "I am quite troubled about poor dear Jolyon. What," Aunt Juley dwelt on the word, "do you think ought to be done?"

Aunt Hester again rustled the sheet, her voice was heard faintly pleading: "Done? How should I know?"

Aunt Juley turned away satisfied, and closing the door with extra gentleness so as not to disturb dear Hester, let it slip through her fingers and fall to with a 'crack.'

Back in her own room, she stood at the window gazing at the moon over the trees in the Park, through a chink in the muslin curtains, close drawn lest anyone should see. And there, with her face all round and pouting in its pink cap, and her eyes wet, she thought of 'dear Jolyon,' so old and so lonely, and how she could be of some use to him; and how he would come to love her, as she had never been loved since—since poor Septimus went away.

CHAPTER VIII—DANCE AT ROGER'S

Roger's house in Prince's Gardens was brilliantly alight. Large numbers of wax candles had been collected and placed in cut-glass chandeliers, and the parquet floor of the long, double drawing-room reflected these constellations. An appearance of real spaciousness had been secured by moving out all the furniture on to the upper landings, and enclosing the room with those strange appendages of civilization known as 'rout' seats. In a remote corner, embowered in palms, was a cottage piano, with a copy of the 'Kensington Coil' open on the music-stand.

Roger had objected to a band. He didn't see in the least what they wanted with a band; he wouldn't go to the expense, and there was an end of it. Francie (her mother, whom Roger had long since reduced to chronic dyspepsia, went to bed on such occasions), had been obliged to content herself with supplementing the piano by a young man who played the cornet, and she so arranged with palms that anyone who did not look into the heart of things might imagine there were several musicians secreted there. She made up her mind to tell them to play loud—there was a lot of music in a cornet, if the man would only put his soul into it.

In the more cultivated American tongue, she was 'through' at last—through that tortuous labyrinth of make-shifts, which must be traversed before fashionable display can be combined with the sound economy of a Forsyte. Thin but brilliant, in her maize-coloured frock with much tulle about the shoulders, she went from place to place, fitting on her gloves, and casting her eye over it all.

To the hired butler (for Roger only kept maids) she spoke about the wine. Did he quite understand that Mr. Forsyte wished a dozen bottles of the champagne from Whiteley's to be put out? But if that were finished (she did not suppose it would be, most of the ladies would drink water, no doubt), but if it were, there was the champagne cup, and he must do the best he could with that.

She hated having to say this sort of thing to a butler, it was so infra dig.; but what could you do with father? Roger, indeed, after making himself consistently disagreeable about the dance, would come down presently, with his fresh colour and bumpy forehead, as though he had been its promoter; and he would smile, and probably take the prettiest woman in to supper; and at two o'clock, just as they were getting into the swing, he would go up secretly to the musicians and tell them to play 'God Save the Queen,' and go away.

Francie devoutly hoped he might soon get tired, and slip off to bed.

The three or four devoted girl friends who were staying in the house for this dance had partaken with her, in a small, abandoned room upstairs, of tea and cold chicken-legs, hurriedly served; the men had been sent out to dine at Eustace's Club, it being felt that they must be fed up.

Punctually on the stroke of nine arrived Mrs. Small alone. She made elaborate apologies for the absence of Timothy, omitting all mention of Aunt Hester, who, at the last minute, had said she could not be bothered. Francie received her effusively, and placed her on a rout seat, where she left her, pouting and solitary in lavender-coloured satin—the first time she had worn colour since Aunt Ann's death.

The devoted maiden friends came now from their rooms, each by magic arrangement in a differently coloured frock, but all with the same liberal allowance of tulle on the shoulders and at the bosom—for they were, by some fatality, lean to a girl. They were all taken up to Mrs. Small. None stayed with her more than a few seconds, but clustering together talked and twisted their programmes, looking secretly at the door for the first appearance of a man.

Then arrived in a group a number of Nicholases, always punctual—the fashion up Ladbroke Grove way; and close behind them Eustace and his men, gloomy and smelling rather of smoke.

Three or four of Francie's lovers now appeared, one after the other; she had made each promise to come early. They were all clean-shaven and sprightly, with that peculiar kind of young-man sprightliness which had recently invaded Kensington; they did not seem to mind each other's presence in the least, and wore their ties bunching out at the ends, white waistcoats, and socks with clocks. All had handkerchiefs concealed in their cuffs. They moved buoyantly, each armoured in professional gaiety, as though he had come to do great deeds. Their faces when they danced, far from wearing the traditional solemn look of the dancing Englishman, were irresponsible, charming, suave; they bounded, twirling their partners at great pace, without pedantic attention to the rhythm of the music.

At other dancers they looked with a kind of airy scorn—they, the light brigade, the heroes of a hundred Kensington 'hops'—from whom alone could the right manner and smile and step be hoped.

After this the stream came fast; chaperones silting up along the wall facing the entrance, the volatile element swelling the eddy in the larger room.

Men were scarce, and wallflowers wore their peculiar, pathetic expression, a patient, sourish smile which seemed to say: "Oh, no! don't mistake me, I know you are not coming up to me. I can hardly expect that!" And Francie would plead with one of her lovers, or with some callow youth: "Now, to please me, do let me introduce you to Miss Pink; such a nice girl, really!" and she would bring him up, and say: "Miss Pink—Mr. Gathercole. Can you spare him a dance?" Then Miss Pink, smiling her forced smile, colouring a little, answered: "Oh! I think so!" and screening her empty card, wrote on it the name of Gathercole, spelling it passionately in the district that he proposed, about the second extra.

But when the youth had murmured that it was hot, and passed, she relapsed into her attitude of hopeless expectation, into her patient, sourish smile.

Mothers, slowly fanning their faces, watched their daughters, and in their eyes could be read all the story of those daughters' fortunes. As for themselves, to sit hour after hour, dead tired, silent, or talking spasmodically—what did it matter, so long as the girls were having a good time! But to see them neglected and passed by! Ah! they smiled, but their eyes stabbed like the eyes of an offended swan; they longed to pluck young Gathercole by the slack of his dandified breeches, and drag him to their daughters—the jackanapes!

And all the cruelties and hardness of life, its pathos and unequal chances, its conceit, self-forgetfulness, and patience, were presented on the battle-field of this Kensington ball-room.

Here and there, too, lovers—not lovers like Francie's, a peculiar breed, but simply lovers—trembling, blushing, silent, sought each other by flying glances, sought to meet and touch in the mazes of the dance, and now and again dancing together, struck some beholder by the light in their eyes.

Not a second before ten o'clock came the Jameses—Emily, Rachel, Winifred (Dartie had been left behind, having on a former occasion drunk too much of Roger's champagne), and Cicely, the youngest, making her debut; behind them, following in a hansom from the paternal mansion where they had dined, Soames and Irene.

All these ladies had shoulder-straps and no tulle—thus showing at once, by a bolder exposure of flesh, that they came from the more fashionable side of the Park.

Soames, sidling back from the contact of the dancers, took up a position against the wall. Guarding himself with his pale smile, he stood watching. Waltz after waltz began and ended, couple after couple brushed by with smiling lips, laughter, and snatches of talk; or with set lips, and eyes searching the throng; or again, with silent, parted lips, and eyes on each other. And the scent of festivity, the odour of flowers, and hair, of essences that women love, rose suffocatingly in the heat of the summer night.

Silent, with something of scorn in his smile, Soames seemed to notice nothing; but now and again his eyes, finding that which they sought, would fix themselves on a point in the shifting throng, and the smile die off his lips.

He danced with no one. Some fellows danced with their wives; his sense of 'form' had never permitted him to dance with Irene since their marriage, and the God of the Forsytes alone can tell whether this was a relief to him or not.

She passed, dancing with other men, her dress, iris-coloured, floating away from her feet. She danced well; he was tired of hearing women say with an acid smile: "How beautifully your wife dances, Mr. Forsyte—it's quite a pleasure to watch her!" Tired of answering them with his sidelong glance: "You think so?"

A young couple close by flirted a fan by turns, making an unpleasant draught. Francie and one of her lovers stood near. They were talking of love.

He heard Roger's voice behind, giving an order about supper to a servant. Everything was very second-class! He wished that he had not come! He had asked Irene whether she wanted him; she had answered with that maddening smile of hers "Oh, no!"

Why had he come? For the last quarter of an hour he had not even seen her. Here was George advancing with his Quilpish face; it was too late to get out of his way.

"Have you seen 'The Buccaneer'?" said this licensed wag; "he's on the warpath—hair cut and everything!"

Soames said he had not, and crossing the room, half-empty in an interval of the dance, he went out on the balcony, and looked down into the street.

A carriage had driven up with late arrivals, and round the door hung some of those patient watchers of the London streets who spring up to the call of light or music; their faces, pale and upturned above their black and rusty figures, had an air of stolid watching that annoyed Soames. Why were they allowed to hang about; why didn't the bobby move them on?

But the policeman took no notice of them; his feet were planted apart on the strip of crimson carpet stretched across the pavement; his face, under the helmet, wore the same stolid, watching look as theirs.

Across the road, through the railings, Soames could see the branches of trees shining, faintly stirring in the breeze, by the gleam of the street lamps; beyond, again, the upper lights of the houses on the other side, so many eyes looking down on the quiet blackness of the garden; and over all, the sky, that wonderful London sky, dusted with the innumerable reflection of countless lamps; a dome woven over between its stars with the refraction of human needs and human fancies—immense mirror of pomp and misery that night after night stretches its kindly mocking over miles of houses and gardens, mansions and squalor, over Forsytes, policemen, and patient watchers in the streets.

Soames turned away, and, hidden in the recess, gazed into the lighted room. It was cooler out there. He saw the new arrivals, June and her grandfather, enter. What had made them so late? They stood by the doorway. They looked fagged. Fancy Uncle Jolyon turning out at this time of night! Why hadn't June come to Irene, as she usually did, and it occurred to him suddenly that he had seen nothing of June for a long time now.

Watching her face with idle malice, he saw it change, grow so pale that he thought she would drop, then flame out crimson. Turning to see at what she was looking, he saw his wife on Bosinney's arm, coming from the conservatory at the end of the room. Her eyes were raised to his, as though answering some question he had asked, and he was gazing at her intently.

Soames looked again at June. Her hand rested on old Jolyon's arm; she seemed to be making a request. He saw a surprised look on his uncle's face; they turned and passed through the door out of his sight.

The music began again—a waltz—and, still as a statue in the recess of the window, his face unmoved, but no smile on his lips, Soames waited. Presently, within a yard of the dark balcony, his wife and Bosinney passed. He caught the perfume of the gardenias that she wore, saw the rise and fall of her bosom, the languor in her eyes, her parted lips, and a look on her face that he did not know. To the slow, swinging measure they danced by, and it seemed to him that they clung to each other; he saw her raise her eyes, soft and dark, to Bosinney's, and drop them again.

Very white, he turned back to the balcony, and leaning on it, gazed down on the Square; the figures were still there looking up at the light with dull persistency, the policeman's face, too, upturned, and staring, but he saw nothing of them. Below, a carriage drew up, two figures got in, and drove away....

That evening June and old Jolyon sat down to dinner at the usual hour. The girl was in her customary high-necked frock, old Jolyon had not dressed.

At breakfast she had spoken of the dance at Uncle Roger's, she wanted to go; she had been stupid enough, she said, not to think of asking anyone to take her. It was too late now.

Old Jolyon lifted his keen eyes. June was used to go to dances with Irene as a matter of course! and deliberately fixing his gaze on her, he asked: "Why don't you get Irene?"

No! June did not want to ask Irene; she would only go if—if her grandfather wouldn't mind just for once for a little time!

At her look, so eager and so worn, old Jolyon had grumblingly consented. He did not know what she wanted, he said, with going to a dance like this, a poor affair, he would wager; and she no more fit for it than a cat! What she wanted was sea air, and after his general meeting of the Globular Gold Concessions he was ready to take her. She didn't want to go away? Ah! she would knock herself up! Stealing a mournful look at her, he went on with his breakfast.

June went out early, and wandered restlessly about in the heat. Her little light figure that lately had moved so languidly about its business, was all on fire. She bought herself some flowers. She wanted—she meant to look her best. He would be there! She knew well enough that he had a card. She would show him that she did not care. But deep down in her heart she resolved that evening to win him back. She came in flushed, and talked brightly all lunch; old Jolyon was there, and he was deceived.

In the afternoon she was overtaken by a desperate fit of sobbing. She strangled the noise against the pillows of her bed, but when at last it ceased she saw in the glass a swollen face with reddened eyes, and violet circles round them. She stayed in the darkened room till dinner time.

All through that silent meal the struggle went on within her.

She looked so shadowy and exhausted that old Jolyon told 'Sankey' to countermand the carriage, he would not have her going out.... She was to go to bed! She made no resistance. She went up to her room, and sat in the dark. At ten o'clock she rang for her maid.

"Bring some hot water, and go down and tell Mr. Forsyte that I feel perfectly rested. Say that if he's too tired I can go to the dance by myself."

The maid looked askance, and June turned on her imperiously. "Go," she said, "bring the hot water at once!"

Her ball-dress still lay on the sofa, and with a sort of fierce care she arrayed herself, took the flowers in her hand, and went down, her small face carried high under its burden of hair. She could hear old Jolyon in his room as she passed.

Bewildered and vexed, he was dressing. It was past ten, they would not get there till eleven; the girl was mad. But he dared not cross her—the expression of her face at dinner haunted him.

With great ebony brushes he smoothed his hair till it shone like silver under the light; then he, too, came out on the gloomy staircase.

June met him below, and, without a word, they went to the carriage.

When, after that drive which seemed to last for ever, she entered Roger's drawing-room, she disguised under a mask of resolution a very torment of nervousness and emotion. The feeling of shame at what might be called 'running after him' was smothered by the dread that he might not be there, that she might not see him after all, and by that dogged resolve—somehow, she did not know how—to win him back.

The sight of the ballroom, with its gleaming floor, gave her a feeling of joy, of triumph, for she loved dancing, and when dancing she floated, so light was she, like a strenuous, eager little spirit. He would surely ask her to dance, and if he danced with her it would all be as it was before. She looked about her eagerly.

The sight of Bosinney coming with Irene from the conservatory, with that strange look of utter absorption on his face, struck her too suddenly. They had not seen—no one should see—her distress, not even her grandfather.

She put her hand on Jolyon's arm, and said very low:

"I must go home, Gran; I feel ill."

He hurried her away, grumbling to himself that he had known how it would be.

To her he said nothing; only when they were once more in the carriage, which by some fortunate chance had lingered near the door, he asked her: "What is it, my darling?"

Feeling her whole slender body shaken by sobs, he was terribly alarmed. She must have Blank to-morrow. He would insist upon it. He could not have her like this.... There, there!

June mastered her sobs, and squeezing his hand feverishly, she lay back in her corner, her face muffled in a shawl.

He could only see her eyes, fixed and staring in the dark, but he did not cease to stroke her hand with his thin fingers.

CHAPTER IX—EVENING AT RICHMOND

Other eyes besides the eyes of June and of Soames had seen 'those two' (as Euphemia had already begun to call them) coming from the conservatory; other eyes had noticed the look on Bosinney's face.

There are moments when Nature reveals the passion hidden beneath the careless calm of her ordinary moods—violent spring flashing white on almond-blossom through the purple clouds; a snowy, moonlit peak, with its single star, soaring up to the passionate blue; or against the flames of sunset, an old yew-tree standing dark guardian of some fiery secret.

There are moments, too, when in a picture-gallery, a work, noted by the casual spectator as '......Titian—remarkably fine,' breaks through the defences of some Forsyte better lunched perhaps than his fellows, and holds him spellbound in a kind of ecstasy. There are things, he feels—there are things here which—well, which are things. Something unreasoning, unreasonable, is upon him; when he tries to define it with the precision of a practical man, it eludes him, slips away, as the glow of the wine he has drunk is slipping away, leaving him cross, and conscious of his liver. He feels that he has been extravagant, prodigal of something; virtue has gone out of him. He did not desire this glimpse of what lay under the three stars of his catalogue. God forbid that he should know anything about the forces of Nature! God forbid that he should admit for a moment that there are such things! Once admit that, and where was he? One paid a shilling for entrance, and another for the programme.

The look which June had seen, which other Forsytes had seen, was like the sudden flashing of a candle through a hole in some imaginary canvas, behind which it was being moved— the sudden flaming-out of a vague, erratic glow, shadowy and enticing. It brought home to onlookers the consciousness that dangerous forces were at work. For a moment they noticed it with pleasure, with interest, then felt they must not notice it at all.

It supplied, however, the reason of June's coming so late and disappearing again without dancing, without even shaking hands with her lover. She was ill, it was said, and no wonder.

But here they looked at each other guiltily. They had no desire to spread scandal, no desire to be ill-natured. Who would have? And to outsiders no word was breathed, unwritten law keeping them silent.

Then came the news that June had gone to the seaside with old Jolyon.

He had carried her off to Broadstairs, for which place there was just then a feeling, Yarmouth having lost caste, in spite of Nicholas, and no Forsyte going to the sea without intending to have an air for his money such as would render him bilious in a week. That fatally aristocratic tendency of the first Forsyte to drink Madeira had left his descendants undoubtedly accessible.

So June went to the sea. The family awaited developments; there was nothing else to do.

But how far—how far had 'those two' gone? How far were they going to go? Could they really be going at all? Nothing could surely come of it, for neither of them had any money. At the most a flirtation, ending, as all such attachments should, at the proper time.

Soames' sister, Winifred Dartie, who had imbibed with the breezes of Mayfair—she lived in Green Street—more fashionable principles in regard to matrimonial behaviour than were current, for instance, in Ladbroke Grove, laughed at the idea of there being anything in it. The 'little thing'—Irene was taller than herself, and it was real testimony to the solid worth of a Forsyte that she should always thus be a 'little thing'—the little thing was bored. Why shouldn't she amuse herself? Soames was rather tiring; and as to Mr. Bosinney—only that buffoon George would have called him the Buccaneer—she maintained that he was very chic.

This dictum—that Bosinney was chic—caused quite a sensation. It failed to convince. That he was 'good-looking in a way' they were prepared to admit, but that anyone could call a man with his pronounced cheekbones, curious eyes, and soft felt hats chic was only another instance of Winifred's extravagant way of running after something new.

It was that famous summer when extravagance was fashionable, when the very earth was extravagant, chestnut-trees spread with blossom, and flowers drenched in perfume, as they had never been before; when roses blew in every garden; and for the swarming stars the nights had hardly space; when every day and all day long the sun, in full armour, swung his brazen shield above the Park, and people did strange things, lunching and dining in the open air. Unprecedented was the tale of cabs and carriages that streamed across the bridges of the shining river, bearing the upper-middle class in thousands to the green glories of Bushey, Richmond, Kew, and Hampton Court. Almost every family with any pretensions to be of the carriage-class paid one visit that year to the horse-chestnuts at Bushey, or took one drive amongst the Spanish chestnuts of Richmond Park. Bowling smoothly, if dustily, along, in a cloud of their own creation, they would stare fashionably at the antlered heads which the great slow deer raised out of a forest of bracken that promised to autumn lovers such cover as was never seen before. And now and again, as the amorous perfume of chestnut flowers and of fern was drifted too near, one would say to the other: "My dear! What a peculiar scent!"

And the lime-flowers that year were of rare prime, near honey-coloured. At the corners of London squares they gave out, as the sun went down, a perfume sweeter than the honey bees had taken—a perfume that stirred a yearning unnamable in the hearts of Forsytes and their peers, taking the cool after dinner in the precincts of those gardens to which they alone had keys.

And that yearning made them linger amidst the dim shapes of flower-beds in the failing daylight, made them turn, and turn, and turn again, as though lovers were waiting for them—waiting for the last light to die away under the shadow of the branches.

Some vague sympathy evoked by the scent of the limes, some sisterly desire to see for herself, some idea of demonstrating the soundness of her dictum that there was 'nothing in it'; or merely the craving to drive down to Richmond, irresistible that summer, moved the mother of the little Darties (of little Publius, of Imogen, Maud, and Benedict) to write the following note to her sister-in-law:

'DEAR IRENE, 'June 30.

'I hear that Soames is going to Henley tomorrow for the night. I thought it would be great fun if we made up a little party and drove down to, Richmond. Will you ask Mr. Bosinney, and I will get young Flippard.

'Emily (they called their mother Emily—it was so chic) will lend us the carriage. I will call for you and your young man at seven o'clock.

'Your affectionate sister,

'WINIFRED DARTIE.

'Montague believes the dinner at the Crown and Sceptre to be quite eatable.'

Montague was Dartie's second and better known name—his first being Moses; for he was nothing if not a man of the world.

Her plan met with more opposition from Providence than so benevolent a scheme deserved. In the first place young Flippard wrote:

'DEAR Mrs. DARTIE,

'Awfully sorry. Engaged two deep.

'Yours,

'AUGUSTUS FLIPPARD.'

It was late to send into the by-ways and hedges to remedy this misfortune. With the promptitude and conduct of a mother, Winifred fell back on her husband. She had, indeed, the decided but tolerant temperament that goes with a good deal of profile, fair hair, and greenish eyes. She was seldom or never at a loss; or if at a loss, was always able to convert it into a gain.

Dartie, too, was in good feather. Erotic had failed to win the Lancashire Cup. Indeed, that celebrated animal, owned as he was by a pillar of the turf, who had secretly laid many thousands against him, had not even started. The forty-eight hours that followed his scratching were among the darkest in Dartie's life.

Visions of James haunted him day and night. Black thoughts about Soames mingled with the faintest hopes. On the Friday night he got drunk, so greatly was he affected. But on Saturday morning the true Stock Exchange instinct triumphed within him. Owing some hundreds, which by no possibility could he pay, he went into town and put them all on Concertina for the Saltown Borough Handicap.

As he said to Major Scrotton, with whom he lunched at the Iseeum: "That little Jew boy, Nathans, had given him the tip. He didn't care a cursh. He wash in—a mucker. If it didn't come up—well then, damme, the old man would have to pay!"

A bottle of Pol Roger to his own cheek had given him a new contempt for James.

It came up. Concertina was squeezed home by her neck—a terrible squeak! But, as Dartie said: There was nothing like pluck!

He was by no means averse to the expedition to Richmond. He would 'stand' it himself! He cherished an admiration for Irene, and wished to be on more playful terms with her.

At half-past five the Park Lane footman came round to say: Mrs. Forsyte was very sorry, but one of the horses was coughing!

Undaunted by this further blow, Winifred at once despatched little Publius (now aged seven) with the nursery governess to Montpellier Square.

They would go down in hansoms and meet at the Crown and Sceptre at 7.45.

Dartie, on being told, was pleased enough. It was better than going down with your back to the horses! He had no objection to driving down with Irene. He supposed they would pick up the others at Montpellier Square, and swop hansoms there?

Informed that the meet was at the Crown and Sceptre, and that he would have to drive with his wife, he turned sulky, and said it was d——d slow!

At seven o'clock they started, Dartie offering to bet the driver half-a-crown he didn't do it in the three-quarters of an hour.

Twice only did husband and wife exchange remarks on the way.

Dartie said: "It'll put Master Soames's nose out of joint to hear his wife's been drivin' in a hansom with Master Bosinney!"

Winifred replied: "Don't talk such nonsense, Monty!"

"Nonsense!" repeated Dartie. "You don't know women, my fine lady!"

On the other occasion he merely asked: "How am I looking? A bit puffy about the gills? That fizz old George is so fond of is a windy wine!"

He had been lunching with George Forsyte at the Haversnake.

Bosinney and Irene had arrived before them. They were standing in one of the long French windows overlooking the river.

Windows that summer were open all day long, and all night too, and day and night the scents of flowers and trees came in, the hot scent of parching grass, and the cool scent of the heavy dews.

To the eye of the observant Dartie his two guests did not appear to be making much running, standing there close together, without a word. Bosinney was a hungry-looking creature—not much go about him.

He left them to Winifred, however, and busied himself to order the dinner.

A Forsyte will require good, if not delicate feeding, but a Dartie will tax the resources of a Crown and Sceptre. Living as he does, from hand to mouth, nothing is too good for him to eat; and he will eat it. His drink, too, will need to be carefully provided; there is much drink in this country 'not good enough' for a Dartie; he will have the best. Paying for things vicariously, there is no reason why he should stint himself. To stint yourself is the mark of a fool, not of a Dartie.

The best of everything! No sounder principle on which a man can base his life, whose father-in-law has a very considerable income, and a partiality for his grandchildren.

With his not unable eye Dartie had spotted this weakness in James the very first year after little Publius's arrival (an error); he had profited by his perspicacity. Four little Darties were now a sort of perpetual insurance.

The feature of the feast was unquestionably the red mullet. This delectable fish, brought from a considerable distance in a state of almost perfect preservation, was first fried, then boned, then served in ice, with Madeira punch in place of sauce, according to a recipe known to a few men of the world.

Nothing else calls for remark except the payment of the bill by Dartie.

He had made himself extremely agreeable throughout the meal; his bold, admiring stare seldom abandoning Irene's face and figure. As he was obliged to confess to himself, he got no change out of her—she was cool enough, as cool as her shoulders looked under their veil of creamy lace. He expected to have caught her out in some little game with Bosinney; but not a bit of it, she kept up her end remarkably well. As for that architect chap, he was as glum as a bear with a sore head—Winifred could barely get a word out of him; he ate nothing, but he certainly took his liquor, and his face kept getting whiter, and his eyes looked queer.

It was all very amusing.

For Dartie himself was in capital form, and talked freely, with a certain poignancy, being no fool. He told two or three stories verging on the improper, a concession to the company, for his stories were not used to verging. He proposed Irene's health in a mock speech. Nobody drank it, and Winifred said: "Don't be such a clown, Monty!"

At her suggestion they went after dinner to the public terrace overlooking the river.

"I should like to see the common people making love," she said, "it's such fun!"

There were numbers of them walking in the cool, after the day's heat, and the air was alive with the sound of voices, coarse and loud, or soft as though murmuring secrets.

It was not long before Winifred's better sense—she was the only Forsyte present—secured them an empty bench. They sat down in a row. A heavy tree spread a thick canopy above their heads, and the haze darkened slowly over the river.

Dartie sat at the end, next to him Irene, then Bosinney, then Winifred. There was hardly room for four, and the man of the world could feel Irene's arm crushed against his own; he knew that she could not withdraw it without seeming rude, and this amused him; he devised every now and again a movement that would bring her closer still. He thought: "That Buccaneer Johnny shan't have it all to himself! It's a pretty tight fit, certainly!"

From far down below on the dark river came drifting the tinkle of a mandoline, and voices singing the old round:

'A boat, a boat, unto the ferry, For we'll go over and be merry; And laugh, and quaff, and drink brown sherry!'

And suddenly the moon appeared, young and tender, floating up on her back from behind a tree; and as though she had breathed, the air was cooler, but down that cooler air came always the warm odour of the limes.

Over his cigar Dartie peered round at Bosinney, who was sitting with his arms crossed, staring straight in front of him, and on his face the look of a man being tortured.

And Dartie shot a glance at the face between, so veiled by the overhanging shadow that it was but like a darker piece of the darkness shaped and breathed on; soft, mysterious, enticing.

A hush had fallen on the noisy terrace, as if all the strollers were thinking secrets too precious to be spoken.

And Dartie thought: 'Women!'

The glow died above the river, the singing ceased; the young moon hid behind a tree, and all was dark. He pressed himself against Irene.

He was not alarmed at the shuddering that ran through the limbs he touched, or at the troubled, scornful look of her eyes. He felt her trying to draw herself away, and smiled.

It must be confessed that the man of the world had drunk quite as much as was good for him.

With thick lips parted under his well-curled moustaches, and his bold eyes aslant upon her, he had the malicious look of a satyr.

Along the pathway of sky between the hedges of the tree tops the stars clustered forth; like mortals beneath, they seemed to shift and swarm and whisper. Then on the terrace the buzz broke out once more, and Dartie thought: 'Ah! he's a poor, hungry-looking devil, that Bosinney!' and again he pressed himself against Irene.

The movement deserved a better success. She rose, and they all followed her.

The man of the world was more than ever determined to see what she was made of. Along the terrace he kept close at her elbow. He had within him much good wine. There was the long drive home, the long drive and the warm dark and the pleasant closeness of the hansom cab—with its insulation from the world devised by some great and good man. That hungry architect chap might drive with his wife—he wished him joy of her! And, conscious that his voice was not too steady, he was careful not to speak; but a smile had become fixed on his thick lips.

They strolled along toward the cabs awaiting them at the farther end. His plan had the merit of all great plans, an almost brutal simplicity— he would merely keep at her elbow till she got in, and get in quickly after her.

But when Irene reached the cab she did not get in; she slipped, instead, to the horse's head. Dartie was not at the moment sufficiently master of his legs to follow. She stood stroking the horse's nose, and, to his annoyance, Bosinney was at her side first. She turned and spoke to him rapidly, in a low voice; the words 'That man' reached Dartie. He stood stubbornly by the cab step, waiting for her to come back. He knew a trick worth two of that!

Here, in the lamp-light, his figure (no more than medium height), well squared in its white evening waistcoat, his light overcoat flung over his arm, a pink flower in his button-hole, and on his dark face that look of confident, good-humoured insolence, he was at his best—a thorough man of the world.

Winifred was already in her cab. Dartie reflected that Bosinney would have a poorish time in that cab if he didn't look sharp! Suddenly he received a push which nearly overturned him in the road. Bosinney's voice hissed in his ear: "I am taking Irene back; do you understand?" He saw a face white with passion, and eyes that glared at him like a wild cat's.

"Eh?" he stammered. "What? Not a bit. You take my wife!"

"Get away!" hissed Bosinney—"or I'll throw you into the road!"

Dartie recoiled; he saw as plainly as possible that the fellow meant it. In the space he made Irene had slipped by, her dress brushed his legs. Bosinney stepped in after her.

"Go on!" he heard the Buccaneer cry. The cabman flicked his horse. It sprang forward.

Dartie stood for a moment dumbfounded; then, dashing at the cab where his wife sat, he scrambled in.

"Drive on!" he shouted to the driver, "and don't you lose sight of that fellow in front!"

Seated by his wife's side, he burst into imprecations. Calming himself at last with a supreme effort, he added: "A pretty mess you've made of it, to let the Buccaneer drive home with her; why on earth couldn't you keep hold of him? He's mad with love; any fool can see that!"

He drowned Winifred's rejoinder with fresh calls to the Almighty; nor was it until they reached Barnes that he ceased a Jeremiad, in the course of which he had abused her, her father, her brother, Irene, Bosinney, the name of Forsyte, his own children, and cursed the day when he had ever married.

Winifred, a woman of strong character, let him have his say, at the end of which he lapsed into sulky silence. His angry eyes never deserted the back of that cab, which, like a lost chance, haunted the darkness in front of him.

Fortunately he could not hear Bosinney's passionate pleading—that pleading which the man of the world's conduct had let loose like a flood; he could not see Irene shivering, as though some garment had been torn from her, nor her eyes, black and mournful, like the eyes of a beaten child. He could not hear Bosinney entreating, entreating, always entreating; could not hear her sudden, soft weeping, nor see that poor, hungry-looking devil, awed and trembling, humbly touching her hand.

In Montpellier Square their cabman, following his instructions to the letter, faithfully drew up behind the cab in front. The Darties saw Bosinney spring out, and Irene follow, and hasten up the steps with bent head. She evidently had her key in her hand, for she disappeared at once. It was impossible to tell whether she had turned to speak to Bosinney.

The latter came walking past their cab; both husband and wife had an admirable view of his face in the light of a street lamp. It was working with violent emotion.

"Good-night, Mr. Bosinney!" called Winifred.

Bosinney started, clawed off his hat, and hurried on. He had obviously forgotten their existence.

"There!" said Dartie, "did you see the beast's face? What did I say? Fine games!" He improved the occasion.

There had so clearly been a crisis in the cab that Winifred was unable to defend her theory. She said: "I shall say nothing about it. I don't see any use in making a fuss!"

With that view Dartie at once concurred; looking upon James as a private preserve, he disapproved of his being disturbed by the troubles of others.

"Quite right," he said; "let Soames look after himself. He's jolly well able to!"

Thus speaking, the Darties entered their habitat in Green Street, the rent of which was paid by James, and sought a well-earned rest. The hour was midnight, and no Forsytes remained abroad in the streets to spy out Bosinney's wanderings; to see him return and stand against the rails of the Square garden, back from the glow of the street lamp; to see him stand there in the shadow of trees, watching the house where in the dark was hidden she whom he would have given the world to see for a single minute—she who was now to him the breath of the lime-trees, the meaning of the light and the darkness, the very beating of his own heart.

CHAPTER X—DIAGNOSIS OF A FORSYTE

It is in the nature of a Forsyte to be ignorant that he is a Forsyte; but young Jolyon was well aware of being one. He had not known it till after the decisive step which had made him an outcast; since then the knowledge had been with him continually. He felt it throughout his alliance, throughout all his dealings with his second wife, who was emphatically not a Forsyte.

He knew that if he had not possessed in great measure the eye for what he wanted, the tenacity to hold on to it, the sense of the folly of wasting that for which he had given so big a price—in other words, the 'sense of property' he could never have retained her (perhaps never would have desired to retain her) with him through all the financial troubles, slights, and misconstructions of those fifteen years; never have induced her to marry him on the death of his first wife; never have lived it all through, and come up, as it were, thin, but smiling.

He was one of those men who, seated cross-legged like miniature Chinese idols in the cages of their own hearts, are ever smiling at themselves a doubting smile. Not that this smile, so intimate and eternal, interfered with his actions, which, like his chin and his temperament, were quite a peculiar blend of softness and determination.

He was conscious, too, of being a Forsyte in his work, that painting of water-colours to which he devoted so much energy, always with an eye on himself, as though he could not take so unpractical a pursuit quite seriously, and always with a certain queer uneasiness that he did not make more money at it.

It was, then, this consciousness of what it meant to be a Forsyte, that made him receive the following letter from old Jolyon, with a mixture of sympathy and disgust:

'SHELDRAKE HOUSE, 'BROADSTAIRS,

'July 1. 'MY DEAR JO,'

(The Dad's handwriting had altered very little in the thirty odd years that he remembered it.)

'We have been here now a fortnight, and have had good weather on the whole. The air is bracing, but my liver is out of order, and I shall be glad enough to get back to town. I cannot say much for June, her health and spirits are very indifferent, and I don't see what is to come of it. She says nothing, but it is clear that she is harping on this engagement, which is an engagement and no engagement, and—goodness knows what. I have grave doubts whether she ought to be allowed to return to London in the present state of affairs, but she is so self-willed that she might take it into her head to come up at any moment. The fact is someone ought to speak to Bosinney and ascertain what he means. I'm afraid of this myself, for I should certainly rap him over the knuckles, but I thought that you, knowing him at the Club, might put in a word, and get to ascertain what the fellow is about. You will of course in no way commit June. I shall be glad to hear from you in the course of a few days whether you have succeeded in gaining any information. The situation is very distressing to me, I worry about it at night.

With my love to Jolly and Holly.

'I am,

'Your affect. father,

'JOLYON FORSYTE.'

Young Jolyon pondered this letter so long and seriously that his wife noticed his preoccupation, and asked him what was the matter. He replied: "Nothing."

It was a fixed principle with him never to allude to June. She might take alarm, he did not know what she might think; he hastened, therefore, to banish from his manner all traces of absorption, but in this he was about as successful as his father would have been, for he had inherited all old Jolyon's transparency in matters of domestic finesse; and young Mrs. Jolyon, busying herself over the affairs of the house, went about with tightened lips, stealing at him unfathomable looks.

He started for the Club in the afternoon with the letter in his pocket, and without having made up his mind.

To sound a man as to 'his intentions' was peculiarly unpleasant to him; nor did his own anomalous position diminish this unpleasantness. It was so like his family, so like all the people they knew and mixed with, to enforce what they called their rights over a man, to bring him up to the mark; so like them to carry their business principles into their private relations.

And how that phrase in the letter—'You will, of course, in no way commit June'—gave the whole thing away.

Yet the letter, with the personal grievance, the concern for June, the 'rap over the knuckles,' was all so natural. No wonder his father wanted to know what Bosinney meant, no wonder he was angry.

It was difficult to refuse! But why give the thing to him to do? That was surely quite unbecoming; but so long as a Forsyte got what he was after, he was not too particular about the means, provided appearances were saved.

How should he set about it, or how refuse? Both seemed impossible. So, young Jolyon!

He arrived at the Club at three o'clock, and the first person he saw was Bosinney himself, seated in a corner, staring out of the window.

Young Jolyon sat down not far off, and began nervously to reconsider his position. He looked covertly at Bosinney sitting there unconscious. He did not know him very well, and studied him attentively for perhaps the first time; an unusual looking man, unlike in dress, face, and manner to most of the other members of the Club—young Jolyon himself, however different he had become in mood and temper, had always retained the neat reticence of Forsyte appearance. He alone among Forsytes was ignorant of Bosinney's nickname. The man was unusual, not eccentric, but unusual; he looked worn, too, haggard, hollow in the cheeks beneath those broad, high cheekbones, though without any appearance of ill-health, for he was strongly built, with curly hair that seemed to show all the vitality of a fine constitution.

Something in his face and attitude touched young Jolyon. He knew what suffering was like, and this man looked as if he were suffering.

He got up and touched his arm.

Bosinney started, but exhibited no sign of embarrassment on seeing who it was.

Young Jolyon sat down.

"I haven't seen you for a long time," he said. "How are you getting on with my cousin's house?"

"It'll be finished in about a week."

"I congratulate you!"

"Thanks—I don't know that it's much of a subject for congratulation."

"No?" queried young Jolyon; "I should have thought you'd be glad to get a long job like that off your hands; but I suppose you feel it much as I do when I part with a picture—a sort of child?"

He looked kindly at Bosinney.

"Yes," said the latter more cordially, "it goes out from you and there's an end of it. I didn't know you painted."

"Only water-colours; I can't say I believe in my work."

"Don't believe in it? There—how can you do it? Work's no use unless you believe in it!"

"Good," said young Jolyon; "it's exactly what I've always said. By-the-bye, have you noticed that whenever one says 'Good,' one always adds 'it's exactly what I've always said'! But if you ask me how I do it, I answer, because I'm a Forsyte."

"A Forsyte! I never thought of you as one!"

"A Forsyte," replied young Jolyon, "is not an uncommon animal. There are hundreds among the members of this Club. Hundreds out there in the streets; you meet them wherever you go!"

"And how do you tell them, may I ask?" said Bosinney.

"By their sense of property. A Forsyte takes a practical—one might say a commonsense—view of things, and a practical view of things is based fundamentally on a sense of property. A Forsyte, you will notice, never gives himself away."

"Joking?"

Young Jolyon's eye twinkled.

"Not much. As a Forsyte myself, I have no business to talk. But I'm a kind of thoroughbred mongrel; now, there's no mistaking you: You're as different from me as I am from my Uncle James, who is the perfect specimen of a Forsyte. His sense of property is extreme, while you have practically none. Without me in between, you would seem like a different species. I'm the missing link. We are, of course, all of us the slaves of property, and I admit that it's a question of degree, but what I call a 'Forsyte' is a man who is decidedly more than less a slave of property. He knows a good thing, he knows a safe thing, and his grip on property—it doesn't matter whether it be wives, houses, money, or reputation—is his hall-mark."

"Ah!" murmured Bosinney. "You should patent the word."

"I should like," said young Jolyon, "to lecture on it:

"Properties and quality of a Forsyte: This little animal, disturbed by the ridicule of his own sort, is unaffected in his motions by the laughter of strange creatures (you or I). Hereditarily disposed to myopia, he recognises only the persons of his own species, amongst which he passes an existence of competitive tranquillity."

"You talk of them," said Bosinney, "as if they were half England."

"They are," repeated young Jolyon, "half England, and the better half, too, the safe half, the three per cent. half, the half that counts. It's their wealth and security that makes everything possible; makes your art possible, makes literature, science, even religion, possible. Without Forsytes, who believe in none of these things, and habitats but turn them all to use, where should we be? My dear sir, the Forsytes are the middlemen, the commercials, the pillars of society, the cornerstones of convention; everything that is admirable!"

"I don't know whether I catch your drift," said Bosinney, "but I fancy there are plenty of Forsytes, as you call them, in my profession."

"Certainly," replied young Jolyon. "The great majority of architects, painters, or writers have no principles, like any other Forsytes. Art, literature, religion, survive by virtue of the few cranks who really believe in such things, and the many Forsytes who make a commercial use of them. At a low estimate, three-fourths of our Royal Academicians are Forsytes, seven-eighths of our novelists, a large proportion of the press. Of science I can't speak; they are magnificently represented in religion; in the House of Commons perhaps more numerous than anywhere; the aristocracy speaks for itself. But I'm not laughing. It is dangerous to go against the majority and what a majority!" He fixed his eyes on Bosinney: "It's dangerous to let anything carry you away—a house, a picture, a—woman!"

They looked at each other.—And, as though he had done that which no Forsyte did— given himself away, young Jolyon drew into his shell. Bosinney broke the silence.

"Why do you take your own people as the type?" said he.

"My people," replied young Jolyon, "are not very extreme, and they have their own private peculiarities, like every other family, but they possess in a remarkable degree those two qualities which are the real tests of a Forsyte—the power of never being able to give yourself up to anything soul and body, and the 'sense of property'."

Bosinney smiled: "How about the big one, for instance?"

"Do you mean Swithin?" asked young Jolyon. "Ah! in Swithin there's something primeval still. The town and middle-class life haven't digested him yet. All the old centuries of farm work and brute force have settled in him, and there they've stuck, for all he's so distinguished."

Bosinney seemed to ponder. "Well, you've hit your cousin Soames off to the life," he said suddenly. "He'll never blow his brains out."

Young Jolyon shot at him a penetrating glance.

"No," he said; "he won't. That's why he's to be reckoned with. Look out for their grip! It's easy to laugh, but don't mistake me. It doesn't do to despise a Forsyte; it doesn't do to disregard them!"

"Yet you've done it yourself!"

Young Jolyon acknowledged the hit by losing his smile.

"You forget," he said with a queer pride, "I can hold on, too—I'm a Forsyte myself. We're all in the path of great forces. The man who leaves the shelter of the wall—well—you know what I mean. I don't," he ended very low, as though uttering a threat, "recommend every man to-go-my-way. It depends."

The colour rushed into Bosinney's face, but soon receded, leaving it sallow-brown as before. He gave a short laugh, that left his lips fixed in a queer, fierce smile; his eyes mocked young Jolyon.

"Thanks," he said. "It's deuced kind of you. But you're not the only chaps that can hold on." He rose.

Young Jolyon looked after him as he walked away, and, resting his head on his hand, sighed.

In the drowsy, almost empty room the only sounds were the rustle of newspapers, the scraping of matches being struck. He stayed a long time without moving, living over again those days when he, too, had sat long hours watching the clock, waiting for the minutes to pass—long hours full of the torments of uncertainty, and of a fierce, sweet aching; and the slow, delicious agony of that season came back to him with its old poignancy. The sight of Bosinney, with his haggard face, and his restless eyes always wandering to the clock, had roused in him a pity, with which was mingled strange, irresistible envy.

He knew the signs so well. Whither was he going—to what sort of fate? What kind of woman was it who was drawing him to her by that magnetic force which no consideration of honour, no principle, no interest could withstand; from which the only escape was flight.

Flight! But why should Bosinney fly? A man fled when he was in danger of destroying hearth and home, when there were children, when he felt himself trampling down ideals, breaking something. But here, so he had heard, it was all broken to his hand.

He himself had not fled, nor would he fly if it were all to come over again. Yet he had gone further than Bosinney, had broken up his own unhappy home, not someone else's: And the old saying came back to him: 'A man's fate lies in his own heart.'

In his own heart! The proof of the pudding was in the eating—Bosinney had still to eat his pudding.

His thoughts passed to the woman, the woman whom he did not know, but the outline of whose story he had heard.

An unhappy marriage! No ill-treatment—only that indefinable malaise, that terrible blight which killed all sweetness under Heaven; and so from day to day, from night to night, from week to week, from year to year, till death should end it.

But young Jolyon, the bitterness of whose own feelings time had assuaged, saw Soames' side of the question too. Whence should a man like his cousin, saturated with all the prejudices and beliefs of his class, draw the insight or inspiration necessary to break up this life? It was a question of imagination, of projecting himself into the future beyond the unpleasant gossip, sneers, and tattle that followed on such separations, beyond the passing pangs that the lack of the sight of her would cause, beyond the grave disapproval of the worthy. But few men, and especially few men of Soames' class, had imagination enough for that. A deal of mortals in this world, and not enough imagination to go round! And sweet Heaven, what a difference between theory and practice; many a man, perhaps even Soames, held chivalrous views on such matters, who when the shoe pinched found a distinguishing factor that made of himself an exception.

Then, too, he distrusted his judgment. He had been through the experience himself, had tasted too the dregs the bitterness of an unhappy marriage, and how could he take the wide and dispassionate view of those who had never been within sound of the battle? His evidence was too first-hand—like the evidence on military matters of a soldier who has been through much active service, against that of civilians who have not suffered the disadvantage of seeing things too close. Most people would consider such a marriage as that of Soames and Irene quite fairly successful; he had money, she had beauty; it was a case for compromise. There was no reason why they should not jog along, even if they hated each other. It would not matter if they went their own ways a little so long as the decencies were observed—the sanctity of the marriage tie, of the common home, respected. Half the marriages of the upper classes were conducted on these lines: Do not offend the susceptibilities of Society; do not offend the susceptibilities of the Church. To avoid offending these is worth the sacrifice of any private feelings. The advantages of the stable home are visible, tangible, so many pieces of property; there is no risk in the statu quo. To break up a home is at the best a dangerous experiment, and selfish into the bargain.

This was the case for the defence, and young Jolyon sighed.

'The core of it all,' he thought, 'is property, but there are many people who would not like it put that way. To them it is "the sanctity of the marriage tie"; but the sanctity of the marriage tie is dependent on the sanctity of the family, and the sanctity of the family is dependent on the sanctity of property. And yet I imagine all these people are followers of One who never owned anything. It is curious!

And again young Jolyon sighed.

'Am I going on my way home to ask any poor devils I meet to share my dinner, which will then be too little for myself, or, at all events, for my wife, who is necessary to my health and happiness? It may be that after all Soames does well to exercise his rights and support by his practice the sacred principle of property which benefits us all, with the exception of those who suffer by the process.'

And so he left his chair, threaded his way through the maze of seats, took his hat, and languidly up the hot streets crowded with carriages, reeking with dusty odours, wended his way home.

Before reaching Wistaria Avenue he removed old Jolyon's letter from his pocket, and tearing it carefully into tiny pieces, scattered them in the dust of the road.

He let himself in with his key, and called his wife's name. But she had gone out, taking Jolly and Holly, and the house was empty; alone in the garden the dog Balthasar lay in the shade snapping at flies.

Young Jolyon took his seat there, too, under the pear-tree that bore no fruit.

CHAPTER XI—BOSINNEY ON PAROLE

The day after the evening at Richmond Soames returned from Henley by a morning train. Not constitutionally interested in amphibious sports, his visit had been one of business rather than pleasure, a client of some importance having asked him down.

He went straight to the City, but finding things slack, he left at three o'clock, glad of this chance to get home quietly. Irene did not expect him. Not that he had any desire to spy on her actions, but there was no harm in thus unexpectedly surveying the scene.

After changing to Park clothes he went into the drawing-room. She was sitting idly in the corner of the sofa, her favourite seat; and there were circles under her eyes, as though she had not slept.

He asked: "How is it you're in? Are you expecting somebody?"

"Yes that is, not particularly."

"Who?"

"Mr. Bosinney said he might come."

"Bosinney. He ought to be at work."

To this she made no answer.

"Well," said Soames, "I want you to come out to the Stores with me, and after that we'll go to the Park."

"I don't want to go out; I have a headache."

Soames replied: "If ever I want you to do anything, you've always got a headache. It'll do you good to come and sit under the trees."

She did not answer.

Soames was silent for some minutes; at last he said: "I don't know what your idea of a wife's duty is. I never have known!"

He had not expected her to reply, but she did.

"I have tried to do what you want; it's not my fault that I haven't been able to put my heart into it."

"Whose fault is it, then?" He watched her askance.

"Before we were married you promised to let me go if our marriage was not a success. Is it a success?"

Soames frowned.

"Success," he stammered—"it would be a success if you behaved yourself properly!"

"I have tried," said Irene. "Will you let me go?"

Soames turned away. Secretly alarmed, he took refuge in bluster.

"Let you go? You don't know what you're talking about. Let you go? How can I let you go? We're married, aren't we? Then, what are you talking about? For God's sake, don't let's have any of this sort of nonsense! Get your hat on, and come and sit in the Park."

"Then, you won't let me go?"

He felt her eyes resting on him with a strange, touching look.

"Let you go!" he said; "and what on earth would you do with yourself if I did? You've got no money!"

"I could manage somehow."

He took a swift turn up and down the room; then came and stood before her.

"Understand," he said, "once and for all, I won't have you say this sort of thing. Go and get your hat on!"

She did not move.

"I suppose," said Soames, "you don't want to miss Bosinney if he comes!"

Irene got up slowly and left the room. She came down with her hat on.

They went out.

In the Park, the motley hour of mid-afternoon, when foreigners and other pathetic folk drive, thinking themselves to be in fashion, had passed; the right, the proper, hour had come, was nearly gone, before Soames and Irene seated themselves under the Achilles statue.

It was some time since he had enjoyed her company in the Park. That was one of the past delights of the first two seasons of his married life, when to feel himself the possessor of this gracious creature before all London had been his greatest, though secret, pride. How many afternoons had he not sat beside her, extremely neat, with light grey gloves and faint, supercilious smile, nodding to acquaintances, and now and again removing his hat.

His light grey gloves were still on his hands, and on his lips his smile sardonic, but where the feeling in his heart?

The seats were emptying fast, but still he kept her there, silent and pale, as though to work out a secret punishment. Once or twice he made some comment, and she bent her head, or answered "Yes" with a tired smile.

Along the rails a man was walking so fast that people stared after him when he passed.

"Look at that ass!" said Soames; "he must be mad to walk like that in this heat!"

He turned; Irene had made a rapid movement.

"Hallo!" he said: "it's our friend the Buccaneer!"

And he sat still, with his sneering smile, conscious that Irene was sitting still, and smiling too.

"Will she bow to him?" he thought.

But she made no sign.

Bosinney reached the end of the rails, and came walking back amongst the chairs, quartering his ground like a pointer. When he saw them he stopped dead, and raised his hat.

The smile never left Soames' face; he also took off his hat.

Bosinney came up, looking exhausted, like a man after hard physical exercise; the sweat stood in drops on his brow, and Soames' smile seemed to say: "You've had a trying time, my friend.... What are *you* doing in the Park?" he asked. "We thought you despised such frivolity!"

Bosinney did not seem to hear; he made his answer to Irene: "I've been round to your place; I hoped I should find you in."

Somebody tapped Soames on the back, and spoke to him; and in the exchange of those platitudes over his shoulder, he missed her answer, and took a resolution.

"We're just going in," he said to Bosinney; "you'd better come back to dinner with us." Into that invitation he put a strange bravado, a stranger pathos: "You, can't deceive me," his look and voice seemed saying, "but see—I trust you—I'm not afraid of you!"

They started back to Montpellier Square together, Irene between them. In the crowded streets Soames went on in front. He did not listen to their conversation; the strange resolution of trustfulness he had taken seemed to animate even his secret conduct. Like a gambler, he said to himself: 'It's a card I dare not throw away—I must play it for what it's worth. I have not too many chances.'

He dressed slowly, heard her leave her room and go downstairs, and, for full five minutes after, dawdled about in his dressing-room. Then he went down, purposely shutting the door loudly to show that he was coming. He found them standing by the hearth, perhaps talking, perhaps not; he could not say.

He played his part out in the farce, the long evening through—his manner to his guest more friendly than it had ever been before; and when at last Bosinney went, he said: "You must come again soon; Irene likes to have you to talk about the house!" Again his voice had the strange bravado and the stranger pathos; but his hand was cold as ice.

Loyal to his resolution, he turned away from their parting, turned away from his wife as she stood under the hanging lamp to say good-night—away from the sight of her golden head shining so under the light, of her smiling mournful lips; away from the sight of Bosinney's eyes looking at her, so like a dog's looking at its master.

And he went to bed with the certainty that Bosinney was in love with his wife.

The summer night was hot, so hot and still that through every opened window came in but hotter air. For long hours he lay listening to her breathing.

She could sleep, but he must lie awake. And, lying awake, he hardened himself to play the part of the serene and trusting husband.

In the small hours he slipped out of bed, and passing into his dressing-room, leaned by the open window.

He could hardly breathe.

A night four years ago came back to him—the night but one before his marriage; as hot and stifling as this.

He remembered how he had lain in a long cane chair in the window of his sitting-room off Victoria Street. Down below in a side street a man had banged at a door, a woman had cried out; he remembered, as though it were now, the sound of the scuffle, the slam of the door, the dead silence that followed. And then the early water-cart, cleansing the reek of the streets, had approached through the strange-seeming, useless lamp-light; he seemed to hear again its rumble, nearer and nearer, till it passed and slowly died away.

He leaned far out of the dressing-room window over the little court below, and saw the first light spread. The outlines of dark walls and roofs were blurred for a moment, then came out sharper than before.

He remembered how that other night he had watched the lamps paling all the length of Victoria Street; how he had hurried on his clothes and gone down into the street, down past houses and squares, to the street where she was staying, and there had stood and looked at the front of the little house, as still and grey as the face of a dead man.

And suddenly it shot through his mind; like a sick man's fancy: What's he doing?—that fellow who haunts me, who was here this evening, who's in love with my wife—prowling out there, perhaps, looking for her as I know he was looking for her this afternoon; watching my house now, for all I can tell!

He stole across the landing to the front of the house, stealthily drew aside a blind, and raised a window.

The grey light clung about the trees of the square, as though Night, like a great downy moth, had brushed them with her wings. The lamps were still alight, all pale, but not a soul stirred—no living thing in sight.

Yet suddenly, very faint, far off in the deathly stillness, he heard a cry writhing, like the voice of some wandering soul barred out of heaven, and crying for its happiness. There it was again—again! Soames shut the window, shuddering.

Then he thought: 'Ah! it's only the peacocks, across the water.'

CHAPTER XII—JUNE PAYS SOME CALLS

Jolyon stood in the narrow hall at Broadstairs, inhaling that odour of oilcloth and herrings which permeates all respectable seaside lodging-houses. On a chair—a shiny leather chair, displaying its horsehair through a hole in the top left-hand corner—stood a black despatch case. This he was filling with papers, with the Times, and a bottle of Eau-de Cologne. He had meetings that day of the 'Globular Gold Concessions' and the 'New Colliery Company, Limited,' to which he was going up, for he never missed a Board; to 'miss a Board' would be one more piece of evidence that he was growing old, and this his jealous Forsyte spirit could not bear.

His eyes, as he filled that black despatch case, looked as if at any moment they might blaze up with anger. So gleams the eye of a schoolboy, baited by a ring of his companions; but he controls himself, deterred by the fearful odds against him. And old Jolyon controlled himself, keeping down, with his masterful restraint now slowly wearing out, the irritation fostered in him by the conditions of his life.

He had received from his son an unpractical letter, in which by rambling generalities the boy seemed trying to get out of answering a plain question. 'I've seen Bosinney,' he said; 'he is not a criminal. The more I see of people the more I am convinced that they are never good or bad—merely comic, or pathetic. You probably don't agree with me!'

Old Jolyon did not; he considered it cynical to so express oneself; he had not yet reached that point of old age when even Forsytes, bereft of those illusions and principles which they have cherished carefully for practical purposes but never believed in, bereft of all corporeal enjoyment, stricken to the very heart by having nothing left to hope for—break through the barriers of reserve and say things they would never have believed themselves capable of saying.

Perhaps he did not believe in 'goodness' and 'badness' any more than his son; but as he would have said: He didn't know—couldn't tell; there might be something in it; and why, by an unnecessary expression of disbelief, deprive yourself of possible advantage?

131

Accustomed to spend his holidays among the mountains, though (like a true Forsyte) he had never attempted anything too adventurous or too foolhardy, he had been passionately fond of them. And when the wonderful view (mentioned in Baedeker—'fatiguing but repaying')—was disclosed to him after the effort of the climb, he had doubtless felt the existence of some great, dignified principle crowning the chaotic strivings, the petty precipices, and ironic little dark chasms of life. This was as near to religion, perhaps, as his practical spirit had ever gone.

But it was many years since he had been to the mountains. He had taken June there two seasons running, after his wife died, and had realized bitterly that his walking days were over.

To that old mountain—given confidence in a supreme order of things he had long been a stranger.

He knew himself to be old, yet he felt young; and this troubled him. It troubled and puzzled him, too, to think that he, who had always been so careful, should be father and grandfather to such as seemed born to disaster. He had nothing to say against Jo—who could say anything against the boy, an amiable chap?—but his position was deplorable, and this business of June's nearly as bad. It seemed like a fatality, and a fatality was one of those things no man of his character could either understand or put up with.

In writing to his son he did not really hope that anything would come of it. Since the ball at Roger's he had seen too clearly how the land lay—he could put two and two together quicker than most men—and, with the example of his own son before his eyes, knew better than any Forsyte of them all that the pale flame singes men's wings whether they will or no.

In the days before June's engagement, when she and Mrs. Soames were always together, he had seen enough of Irene to feel the spell she cast over men. She was not a flirt, not even a coquette—words dear to the heart of his generation, which loved to define things by a good, broad, inadequate word—but she was dangerous. He could not say why. Tell him of a quality innate in some women—a seductive power beyond their own control! He would but answer: 'Humbug!' She was dangerous, and there was an end of it. He wanted to close his eyes to that affair. If it was, it was; he did not want to hear any more about it—he only wanted to save June's position and her peace of mind. He still hoped she might once more become a comfort to himself.

And so he had written. He got little enough out of the answer. As to what young Jolyon had made of the interview, there was practically only the queer sentence: 'I gather that he's in the stream.' The stream! What stream? What was this new-fangled way of talking?

He sighed, and folded the last of the papers under the flap of the bag; he knew well enough what was meant.

June came out of the dining-room, and helped him on with his summer coat. From her costume, and the expression of her little resolute face, he saw at once what was coming.

"I'm going with you," she said.

"Nonsense, my dear; I go straight into the City. I can't have you racketting about!"

"I must see old Mrs. Smeech."

"Oh, your precious 'lame ducks!'" grumbled out old Jolyon. He did not believe her excuse, but ceased his opposition. There was no doing anything with that pertinacity of hers.

At Victoria he put her into the carriage which had been ordered for himself—a characteristic action, for he had no petty selfishnesses.

"Now, don't you go tiring yourself, my darling," he said, and took a cab on into the city.

June went first to a back-street in Paddington, where Mrs. Smeech, her 'lame duck,' lived— an aged person, connected with the charring interest; but after half an hour spent in hearing her habitually lamentable recital, and dragooning her into temporary comfort, she went on to Stanhope Gate. The great house was closed and dark.

She had decided to learn something at all costs. It was better to face the worst, and have it over. And this was her plan: To go first to Phil's aunt, Mrs. Baynes, and, failing information there, to Irene herself. She had no clear notion of what she would gain by these visits.

At three o'clock she was in Lowndes Square. With a woman's instinct when trouble is to be faced, she had put on her best frock, and went to the battle with a glance as courageous as old Jolyon's itself. Her tremors had passed into eagerness.

Mrs. Baynes, Bosinney's aunt (Louisa was her name), was in her kitchen when June was announced, organizing the cook, for she was an excellent housewife, and, as Baynes always said, there was 'a lot in a good dinner.' He did his best work after dinner. It was Baynes who built that remarkably fine row of tall crimson houses in Kensington which compete with so many others for the title of 'the ugliest in London.'

On hearing June's name, she went hurriedly to her bedroom, and, taking two large bracelets from a red morocco case in a locked drawer, put them on her white wrists—for she possessed in a remarkable degree that 'sense of property,' which, as we know, is the touchstone of Forsyteism, and the foundation of good morality.

Her figure, of medium height and broad build, with a tendency to embonpoint, was reflected by the mirror of her whitewood wardrobe, in a gown made under her own organization, of one of those half-tints, reminiscent of the distempered walls of corridors in large hotels. She raised her hands to her hair, which she wore a la Princesse de Galles, and touched it here and there, settling it more firmly on her head, and her eyes were full of an unconscious realism, as though she were looking in the face one of life's sordid facts, and making the best of it. In youth her cheeks had been of cream and roses, but they were mottled now by middle-age, and again that hard, ugly directness came into her eyes as she dabbed a powder-puff across her forehead. Putting the puff down, she stood quite still before the glass, arranging a smile over her high, important nose, her chin, (never large, and now growing smaller with the increase of her neck), her thin-lipped, down-drooping mouth. Quickly, not to lose the effect, she grasped her skirts strongly in both hands, and went downstairs.

She had been hoping for this visit for some time past. Whispers had reached her that things were not all right between her nephew and his fiancee. Neither of them had been near her for weeks. She had asked Phil to dinner many times; his invariable answer had been 'Too busy.'

Her instinct was alarmed, and the instinct in such matters of this excellent woman was keen. She ought to have been a Forsyte; in young Jolyon's sense of the word, she certainly had that privilege, and merits description as such.

She had married off her three daughters in a way that people said was beyond their deserts, for they had the professional plainness only to be found, as a rule, among the female kind of the more legal callings. Her name was upon the committees of numberless charities connected with the Church-dances, theatricals, or bazaars—and she never lent her name unless sure beforehand that everything had been thoroughly organized.

She believed, as she often said, in putting things on a commercial basis; the proper function of the Church, of charity, indeed, of everything, was to strengthen the fabric of 'Society.'

Individual action, therefore, she considered immoral. Organization was the only thing, for by organization alone could you feel sure that you were getting a return for your money. Organization—and again, organization! And there is no doubt that she was what old Jolyon called her—"a 'dab' at that"—he went further, he called her "a humbug."

The enterprises to which she lent her name were organized so admirably that by the time the takings were handed over, they were indeed skim milk divested of all cream of human kindness. But as she often justly remarked, sentiment was to be deprecated. She was, in fact, a little academic.

This great and good woman, so highly thought of in ecclesiastical circles, was one of the principal priestesses in the temple of Forsyteism, keeping alive day and night a sacred flame to the God of Property, whose altar is inscribed with those inspiring words: 'Nothing for nothing, and really remarkably little for sixpence.'

When she entered a room it was felt that something substantial had come in, which was probably the reason of her popularity as a patroness. People liked something substantial when they had paid money for it; and they would look at her—surrounded by her staff in charity ballrooms, with her high nose and her broad, square figure, attired in an uniform covered with sequins—as though she were a general.

The only thing against her was that she had not a double name. She was a power in upper middle-class society, with its hundred sets and circles, all intersecting on the common battlefield of charity functions, and on that battlefield brushing skirts so pleasantly with the skirts of Society with the capital 'S.' She was a power in society with the smaller 's,' that larger, more significant, and more powerful body, where the commercially Christian institutions, maxims, and 'principle,' which Mrs. Baynes embodied, were real life-blood, circulating freely, real business currency, not merely the sterilized imitation that flowed in the veins of smaller Society with the larger 'S.' People who knew her felt her to be sound— a sound woman, who never gave herself away, nor anything else, if she could possibly help it.

She had been on the worst sort of terms with Bosinney's father, who had not infrequently made her the object of an unpardonable ridicule. She alluded to him now that he was gone as her 'poor, dear, irreverend brother.'

She greeted June with the careful effusion of which she was a mistress, a little afraid of her as far as a woman of her eminence in the commercial and Christian world could be afraid—for so slight a girl June had a great dignity, the fearlessness of her eyes gave her that. And Mrs. Baynes, too, shrewdly recognized that behind the uncompromising frankness of June's manner there was much of the Forsyte. If the girl had been merely frank and courageous, Mrs. Baynes would have thought her 'cranky,' and despised her; if she had been merely a Forsyte, like Francie—let us say—she would have patronized her from sheer weight of metal; but June, small though she was—Mrs. Baynes habitually admired quantity—gave her an uneasy feeling; and she placed her in a chair opposite the light.

There was another reason for her respect which Mrs. Baynes, too good a churchwoman to be worldly, would have been the last to admit—she often heard her husband describe old Jolyon as extremely well off, and was biassed towards his granddaughter for the soundest of all reasons. To-day she felt the emotion with which we read a novel describing a hero and an inheritance, nervously anxious lest, by some frightful lapse of the novelist, the young man should be left without it at the end.

Her manner was warm; she had never seen so clearly before how distinguished and desirable a girl this was. She asked after old Jolyon's health. A wonderful man for his age;

so upright, and young looking, and how old was he? Eighty-one! She would never have thought it! They were at the sea! Very nice for them; she supposed June heard from Phil every day? Her light grey eyes became more prominent as she asked this question; but the girl met the glance without flinching.

"No," she said, "he never writes!"

Mrs. Baynes's eyes dropped; they had no intention of doing so, but they did. They recovered immediately.

"Of course not. That's Phil all over—he was always like that!"

"Was he?" said June.

The brevity of the answer caused Mrs. Baynes's bright smile a moment's hesitation; she disguised it by a quick movement, and spreading her skirts afresh, said: "Why, my dear—he's quite the most harum-scarum person; one never pays the slightest attention to what he does!"

The conviction came suddenly to June that she was wasting her time; even were she to put a question point-blank, she would never get anything out of this woman.

'Do you see him?' she asked, her face crimsoning.

The perspiration broke out on Mrs. Baynes' forehead beneath the powder.

"Oh, yes! I don't remember when he was here last—indeed, we haven't seen much of him lately. He's so busy with your cousin's house; I'm told it'll be finished directly. We must organize a little dinner to celebrate the event; do come and stay the night with us!"

"Thank you," said June. Again she thought: 'I'm only wasting my time. This woman will tell me nothing.'

She got up to go. A change came over Mrs. Baynes. She rose too; her lips twitched, she fidgeted her hands. Something was evidently very wrong, and she did not dare to ask this girl, who stood there, a slim, straight little figure, with her decided face, her set jaw, and resentful eyes. She was not accustomed to be afraid of asking questions—all organization was based on the asking of questions!

But the issue was so grave that her nerve, normally strong, was fairly shaken; only that morning her husband had said: "Old Mr. Forsyte must be worth well over a hundred thousand pounds!"

And this girl stood there, holding out her hand—holding out her hand!

The chance might be slipping away—she couldn't tell—the chance of keeping her in the family, and yet she dared not speak.

Her eyes followed June to the door.

It closed.

Then with an exclamation Mrs. Baynes ran forward, wobbling her bulky frame from side to side, and opened it again.

Too late! She heard the front door click, and stood still, an expression of real anger and mortification on her face.

June went along the Square with her bird-like quickness. She detested that woman now whom in happier days she had been accustomed to think so kind. Was she always to be put off thus, and forced to undergo this torturing suspense?

She would go to Phil himself, and ask him what he meant. She had the right to know. She hurried on down Sloane Street till she came to Bosinney's number. Passing the swing-door at the bottom, she ran up the stairs, her heart thumping painfully.

At the top of the third flight she paused for breath, and holding on to the bannisters, stood listening. No sound came from above.

With a very white face she mounted the last flight. She saw the door, with his name on the plate. And the resolution that had brought her so far evaporated.

The full meaning of her conduct came to her. She felt hot all over; the palms of her hands were moist beneath the thin silk covering of her gloves.

She drew back to the stairs, but did not descend. Leaning against the rail she tried to get rid of a feeling of being choked; and she gazed at the door with a sort of dreadful courage. No! she refused to go down. Did it matter what people thought of her? They would never know! No one would help her if she did not help herself! She would go through with it.

Forcing herself, therefore, to leave the support of the wall, she rang the bell. The door did not open, and all her shame and fear suddenly abandoned her; she rang again and again, as though in spite of its emptiness she could drag some response out of that closed room, some recompense for the shame and fear that visit had cost her. It did not open; she left off ringing, and, sitting down at the top of the stairs, buried her face in her hands.

Presently she stole down, out into the air. She felt as though she had passed through a bad illness, and had no desire now but to get home as quickly as she could. The people she met seemed to know where she had been, what she had been doing; and suddenly—over on the opposite side, going towards his rooms from the direction of Montpellier Square—she saw Bosinney himself.

She made a movement to cross into the traffic. Their eyes met, and he raised his hat. An omnibus passed, obscuring her view; then, from the edge of the pavement, through a gap in the traffic, she saw him walking on.

And June stood motionless, looking after him.

CHAPTER XIII—PERFECTION OF THE HOUSE

'One mockturtle, clear; one oxtail; two glasses of port.'

In the upper room at French's, where a Forsyte could still get heavy English food, James and his son were sitting down to lunch.

Of all eating-places James liked best to come here; there was something unpretentious, well-flavoured, and filling about it, and though he had been to a certain extent corrupted by the necessity for being fashionable, and the trend of habits keeping pace with an income that would increase, he still hankered in quiet City moments after the tasty fleshpots of his earlier days. Here you were served by hairy English waiters in aprons; there was sawdust on the floor, and three round gilt looking-glasses hung just above the line of sight. They had only recently done away with the cubicles, too, in which you could have your chop, prime chump, with a floury-potato, without seeing your neighbours, like a gentleman.

He tucked the top corner of his napkin behind the third button of his waistcoat, a practice he had been obliged to abandon years ago in the West End. He felt that he should relish his soup—the entire morning had been given to winding up the estate of an old friend.

After filling his mouth with household bread, stale, he at once began: "How are you going down to Robin Hill? You going to take Irene? You'd better take her. I should think there'll be a lot that'll want seeing to."

Without looking up, Soames answered: "She won't go."

"Won't go? What's the meaning of that? She's going to live in the house, isn't she?"

Soames made no reply.

"I don't know what's coming to women nowadays," mumbled James; "I never used to have any trouble with them. She's had too much liberty. She's spoiled...."

Soames lifted his eyes: "I won't have anything said against her," he said unexpectedly.

The silence was only broken now by the supping of James's soup.

The waiter brought the two glasses of port, but Soames stopped him.

"That's not the way to serve port," he said; "take them away, and bring the bottle."

Rousing himself from his reverie over the soup, James took one of his rapid shifting surveys of surrounding facts.

"Your mother's in bed," he said; "you can have the carriage to take you down. I should think Irene'd like the drive. This young Bosinney'll be there, I suppose, to show you over."

Soames nodded.

"I should like to go and see for myself what sort of a job he's made finishing off," pursued James. "I'll just drive round and pick you both up."

"I am going down by train," replied Soames. "If you like to drive round and see, Irene might go with you, I can't tell."

He signed to the waiter to bring the bill, which James paid.

They parted at St. Paul's, Soames branching off to the station, James taking his omnibus westwards.

He had secured the corner seat next the conductor, where his long legs made it difficult for anyone to get in, and at all who passed him he looked resentfully, as if they had no business to be using up his air.

He intended to take an opportunity this afternoon of speaking to Irene. A word in time saved nine; and now that she was going to live in the country there was a chance for her to turn over a new leaf! He could see that Soames wouldn't stand very much more of her goings on!

It did not occur to him to define what he meant by her 'goings on'; the expression was wide, vague, and suited to a Forsyte. And James had more than his common share of courage after lunch.

On reaching home, he ordered out the barouche, with special instructions that the groom was to go too. He wished to be kind to her, and to give her every chance.

When the door of No.62 was opened he could distinctly hear her singing, and said so at once, to prevent any chance of being denied entrance.

Yes, Mrs. Soames was in, but the maid did not know if she was seeing people.

James, moving with the rapidity that ever astonished the observers of his long figure and absorbed expression, went forthwith into the drawing-room without permitting this to be ascertained. He found Irene seated at the piano with her hands arrested on the keys, evidently listening to the voices in the hall. She greeted him without smiling.

"Your mother-in-law's in bed," he began, hoping at once to enlist her sympathy. "I've got the carriage here. Now, be a good girl, and put on your hat and come with me for a drive. It'll do you good!"

Irene looked at him as though about to refuse, but, seeming to change her mind, went upstairs, and came down again with her hat on.

"Where are you going to take me?" she asked.

"We'll just go down to Robin Hill," said James, spluttering out his words very quick; "the horses want exercise, and I should like to see what they've been doing down there."

Irene hung back, but again changed her mind, and went out to the carriage, James brooding over her closely, to make quite sure.

It was not before he had got her more than half way that he began: "Soames is very fond of you—he won't have anything said against you; why don't you show him more affection?"

Irene flushed, and said in a low voice: "I can't show what I haven't got."

James looked at her sharply; he felt that now he had her in his own carriage, with his own horses and servants, he was really in command of the situation. She could not put him off; nor would she make a scene in public.

"I can't think what you're about," he said. "He's a very good husband!"

Irene's answer was so low as to be almost inaudible among the sounds of traffic. He caught the words: "You are not married to him!"

"What's that got to do with it? He's given you everything you want. He's always ready to take you anywhere, and now he's built you this house in the country. It's not as if you had anything of your own."

"No."

Again James looked at her; he could not make out the expression on her face. She looked almost as if she were going to cry, and yet....

"I'm sure," he muttered hastily, "we've all tried to be kind to you."

Irene's lips quivered; to his dismay James saw a tear steal down her cheek. He felt a choke rise in his own throat.

"We're all fond of you," he said, "if you'd only"—he was going to say, "behave yourself," but changed it to—"if you'd only be more of a wife to him."

Irene did not answer, and James, too, ceased speaking. There was something in her silence which disconcerted him; it was not the silence of obstinacy, rather that of acquiescence in all that he could find to say. And yet he felt as if he had not had the last word. He could not understand this.

He was unable, however, to long keep silence.

"I suppose that young Bosinney," he said, "will be getting married to June now?"

Irene's face changed. "I don't know," she said; "you should ask her."

"Does she write to you?"No.

"No."

"How's that?" said James. "I thought you and she were such great friends."

Irene turned on him. "Again," she said, "you should ask her!"

"Well," flustered James, frightened by her look, "it's very odd that I can't get a plain answer to a plain question, but there it is."

He sat ruminating over his rebuff, and burst out at last:

"Well, I've warned you. You won't look ahead. Soames he doesn't say much, but I can see he won't stand a great deal more of this sort of thing. You'll have nobody but yourself to blame, and, what's more, you'll get no sympathy from anybody."

Irene bent her head with a little smiling bow. "I am very much obliged to you."

James did not know what on earth to answer.

The bright hot morning had changed slowly to a grey, oppressive afternoon; a heavy bank of clouds, with the yellow tinge of coming thunder, had risen in the south, and was creeping up.

The branches of the trees dropped motionless across the road without the smallest stir of foliage. A faint odour of glue from the heated horses clung in the thick air; the coachman and groom, rigid and unbending, exchanged stealthy murmurs on the box, without ever turning their heads.

To James' great relief they reached the house at last; the silence and impenetrability of this woman by his side, whom he had always thought so soft and mild, alarmed him.

The carriage put them down at the door, and they entered.

The hall was cool, and so still that it was like passing into a tomb; a shudder ran down James's spine. He quickly lifted the heavy leather curtains between the columns into the inner court.

He could not restrain an exclamation of approval.

The decoration was really in excellent taste. The dull ruby tiles that extended from the foot of the walls to the verge of a circular clump of tall iris plants, surrounding in turn a sunken basin of white marble filled with water, were obviously of the best quality. He admired extremely the purple leather curtains drawn along one entire side, framing a huge white-tiled stove. The central partitions of the skylight had been slid back, and the warm air from outside penetrated into the very heart of the house.

He stood, his hands behind him, his head bent back on his high, narrow shoulders, spying the tracery on the columns and the pattern of the frieze which ran round the ivory-coloured walls under the gallery. Evidently, no pains had been spared. It was quite the house of a gentleman. He went up to the curtains, and, having discovered how they were worked, drew them asunder and disclosed the picture-gallery, ending in a great window taking up the whole end of the room. It had a black oak floor, and its walls, again, were of ivory white. He went on throwing open doors, and peeping in. Everything was in apple-pie order, ready for immediate occupation.

He turned round at last to speak to Irene, and saw her standing over in the garden entrance, with her husband and Bosinney.

Though not remarkable for sensibility, James felt at once that something was wrong. He went up to them, and, vaguely alarmed, ignorant of the nature of the trouble, made an attempt to smooth things over.

"How are you, Mr. Bosinney?" he said, holding out his hand. "You've been spending money pretty freely down here, I should say!"

Soames turned his back, and walked away.

James looked from Bosinney's frowning face to Irene, and, in his agitation, spoke his thoughts aloud: "Well, I can't tell what's the matter. Nobody tells me anything!" And, making off after his son, he heard Bosinney's short laugh, and his "Well, thank God! You look so...." Most unfortunately he lost the rest.

What had happened? He glanced back. Irene was very close to the architect, and her face not like the face he knew of her. He hastened up to his son.

Soames was pacing the picture-gallery.

"What's the matter?" said James. "What's all this?"

Soames looked at him with his supercilious calm unbroken, but James knew well enough that he was violently angry.

"Our friend," he said, "has exceeded his instructions again, that's all. So much the worse for him this time."

He turned round and walked back towards the door. James followed hurriedly, edging himself in front. He saw Irene take her finger from before her lips, heard her say something in her ordinary voice, and began to speak before he reached them.

"There's a storm coming on. We'd better get home. We can't take you, I suppose, Mr. Bosinney? No, I suppose not. Then, good-bye!" He held out his hand. Bosinney did not take it, but, turning with a laugh, said:

"Good-bye, Mr. Forsyte. Don't get caught in the storm!" and walked away.

"Well," began James, "I don't know...."

But the sight of Irene's face stopped him. Taking hold of his daughter-in-law by the elbow, he escorted her towards the carriage. He felt certain, quite certain, they had been making some appointment or other....

Nothing in this world is more sure to upset a Forsyte than the discovery that something on which he has stipulated to spend a certain sum has cost more. And this is reasonable, for upon the accuracy of his estimates the whole policy of his life is ordered. If he cannot rely on definite values of property, his compass is amiss; he is adrift upon bitter waters without a helm.

After writing to Bosinney in the terms that have already been chronicled, Soames had dismissed the cost of the house from his mind. He believed that he had made the matter of the final cost so very plain that the possibility of its being again exceeded had really never entered his head. On hearing from Bosinney that his limit of twelve thousand pounds would be exceeded by something like four hundred, he had grown white with anger. His original estimate of the cost of the house completed had been ten thousand pounds, and he had often blamed himself severely for allowing himself to be led into repeated excesses. Over this last expenditure, however, Bosinney had put himself completely in the wrong. How on earth a fellow could make such an ass of himself Soames could not conceive; but he had done so, and all the rancour and hidden jealousy that had been burning against him for so long was now focussed in rage at this crowning piece of extravagance. The attitude of the confident and friendly husband was gone. To preserve property—his wife—he had assumed it, to preserve property of another kind he lost it now.

"Ah!" he had said to Bosinney when he could speak, "and I suppose you're perfectly contented with yourself. But I may as well tell you that you've altogether mistaken your man!"

What he meant by those words he did not quite know at the time, but after dinner he looked up the correspondence between himself and Bosinney to make quite sure. There could be no two opinions about it—the fellow had made himself liable for that extra four hundred, or, at all events, for three hundred and fifty of it, and he would have to make it good.

He was looking at his wife's face when he came to this conclusion. Seated in her usual seat on the sofa, she was altering the lace on a collar. She had not once spoken to him all the evening.

He went up to the mantelpiece, and contemplating his face in the mirror said: "Your friend the Buccaneer has made a fool of himself; he will have to pay for it!"

She looked at him scornfully, and answered: "I don't know what you are talking about!"

"You soon will. A mere trifle, quite beneath your contempt—four hundred pounds."

"Do you mean that you are going to make him pay that towards this hateful, house?"

"I do."

"And you know he's got nothing?"

"Yes."

"Then you are meaner than I thought you."

Soames turned from the mirror, and unconsciously taking a china cup from the mantelpiece, clasped his hands around it as though praying. He saw her bosom rise and fall, her eyes darkening with anger, and taking no notice of the taunt, he asked quietly:

"Are you carrying on a flirtation with Bosinney?"

"No, I am not!"

Her eyes met his, and he looked away. He neither believed nor disbelieved her, but he knew that he had made a mistake in asking; he never had known, never would know, what she was thinking. The sight of her inscrutable face, the thought of all the hundreds of evenings he had seen her sitting there like that soft and passive, but unreadable, unknown, enraged him beyond measure.

"I believe you are made of stone," he said, clenching his fingers so hard that he broke the fragile cup. The pieces fell into the grate. And Irene smiled.

"You seem to forget," she said, "that cup is not!"

Soames gripped her arm. "A good beating," he said, "is the only thing that would bring you to your senses," but turning on his heel, he left the room.

CHAPTER XIV—SOAMES SITS ON THE STAIRS

Soames went up-stairs that night with the feeling that he had gone too far. He was prepared to offer excuses for his words.

He turned out the gas still burning in the passage outside their room. Pausing, with his hand on the knob of the door, he tried to shape his apology, for he had no intention of letting her see that he was nervous.

But the door did not open, nor when he pulled it and turned the handle firmly. She must have locked it for some reason, and forgotten.

Entering his dressing-room, where the gas was also lighted and burning low, he went quickly to the other door. That too was locked. Then he noticed that the camp bed which he occasionally used was prepared, and his sleeping-suit laid out upon it. He put his hand up to his forehead, and brought it away wet. It dawned on him that he was barred out.

He went back to the door, and rattling the handle stealthily, called: "Unlock the door, do you hear? Unlock the door!"

There was a faint rustling, but no answer.

"Do you hear? Let me in at once—I insist on being let in!"

He could catch the sound of her breathing close to the door, like the breathing of a creature threatened by danger.

There was something terrifying in this inexorable silence, in the impossibility of getting at her. He went back to the other door, and putting his whole weight against it, tried to burst it open. The door was a new one—he had had them renewed himself, in readiness for their coming in after the honeymoon. In a rage he lifted his foot to kick in the panel; the thought of the servants restrained him, and he felt suddenly that he was beaten.

Flinging himself down in the dressing-room, he took up a book.

But instead of the print he seemed to see his wife—with her yellow hair flowing over her bare shoulders, and her great dark eyes—standing like an animal at bay. And the whole meaning of her act of revolt came to him. She meant it to be for good.

He could not sit still, and went to the door again. He could still hear her, and he called: "Irene! Irene!"

He did not mean to make his voice pathetic.

In ominous answer, the faint sounds ceased. He stood with clenched hands, thinking.

Presently he stole round on tiptoe, and running suddenly at the other door, made a supreme effort to break it open. It creaked, but did not yield. He sat down on the stairs and buried his face in his hands.

For a long time he sat there in the dark, the moon through the skylight above laying a pale smear which lengthened slowly towards him down the stairway. He tried to be philosophical.

Since she had locked her doors she had no further claim as a wife, and he would console himself with other women.

It was but a spectral journey he made among such delights—he had no appetite for these exploits. He had never had much, and he had lost the habit. He felt that he could never recover it. His hunger could only be appeased by his wife, inexorable and frightened, behind these shut doors. No other woman could help him.

This conviction came to him with terrible force out there in the dark.

His philosophy left him; and surly anger took its place. Her conduct was immoral, inexcusable, worthy of any punishment within his power. He desired no one but her, and she refused him!

She must really hate him, then! He had never believed it yet. He did not believe it now. It seemed to him incredible. He felt as though he had lost for ever his power of judgment. If she, so soft and yielding as he had always judged her, could take this decided step—what could not happen?

Then he asked himself again if she were carrying on an intrigue with Bosinney. He did not believe that she was; he could not afford to believe such a reason for her conduct—the thought was not to be faced.

It would be unbearable to contemplate the necessity of making his marital relations public property. Short of the most convincing proofs he must still refuse to believe, for he did not wish to punish himself. And all the time at heart—he did believe.

The moonlight cast a greyish tinge over his figure, hunched against the staircase wall.

Bosinney was in love with her! He hated the fellow, and would not spare him now. He could and would refuse to pay a penny piece over twelve thousand and fifty pounds—the extreme limit fixed in the correspondence; or rather he would pay, he would pay and sue him for damages. He would go to Jobling and Boulter and put the matter in their hands. He would ruin the impecunious beggar! And suddenly—though what connection between the thoughts?—he reflected that Irene had no money either. They were both beggars. This gave him a strange satisfaction.

The silence was broken by a faint creaking through the wall. She was going to bed at last. Ah! Joy and pleasant dreams! If she threw the door open wide he would not go in now!

But his lips, that were twisted in a bitter smile, twitched; he covered his eyes with his hands....

It was late the following afternoon when Soames stood in the dining-room window gazing gloomily into the Square.

The sunlight still showered on the plane-trees, and in the breeze their gay broad leaves shone and swung in rhyme to a barrel organ at the corner. It was playing a waltz, an old waltz that was out of fashion, with a fateful rhythm in the notes; and it went on and on, though nothing indeed but leaves danced to the tune.

The woman did not look too gay, for she was tired; and from the tall houses no one threw her down coppers. She moved the organ on, and three doors off began again.

It was the waltz they had played at Roger's when Irene had danced with Bosinney; and the perfume of the gardenias she had worn came back to Soames, drifted by the malicious music, as it had been drifted to him then, when she passed, her hair glistening, her eyes so soft, drawing Bosinney on and on down an endless ballroom.

The organ woman plied her handle slowly; she had been grinding her tune all day-grinding it in Sloane Street hard by, grinding it perhaps to Bosinney himself.

Soames turned, took a cigarette from the carven box, and walked back to the window. The tune had mesmerized him, and there came into his view Irene, her sunshade furled, hastening homewards down the Square, in a soft, rose-coloured blouse with drooping sleeves, that he did not know. She stopped before the organ, took out her purse, and gave the woman money.

Soames shrank back and stood where he could see into the hall.

She came in with her latch-key, put down her sunshade, and stood looking at herself in the glass. Her cheeks were flushed as if the sun had burned them; her lips were parted in a smile. She stretched her arms out as though to embrace herself, with a laugh that for all the world was like a sob.

Soames stepped forward.

"Very-pretty!" he said.

But as though shot she spun round, and would have passed him up the stairs. He barred the way.

"Why such a hurry?" he said, and his eyes fastened on a curl of hair fallen loose across her ear....

He hardly recognised her. She seemed on fire, so deep and rich the colour of her cheeks, her eyes, her lips, and of the unusual blouse she wore.

She put up her hand and smoothed back the curl. She was breathing fast and deep, as though she had been running, and with every breath perfume seemed to come from her hair, and from her body, like perfume from an opening flower.

"I don't like that blouse," he said slowly, "it's a soft, shapeless thing!"

He lifted his finger towards her breast, but she dashed his hand aside.

"Don't touch me!" she cried.

He caught her wrist; she wrenched it away.

"And where may you have been?" he asked.

"In heaven—out of this house!" With those words she fled upstairs.

Outside—in thanksgiving—at the very door, the organ-grinder was playing the waltz.

And Soames stood motionless. What prevented him from following her?

Was it that, with the eyes of faith, he saw Bosinney looking down from that high window in Sloane Street, straining his eyes for yet another glimpse of Irene's vanished figure, cooling his flushed face, dreaming of the moment when she flung herself on his breast—the scent of her still in the air around, and the sound of her laugh that was like a sob?

PART III

CHAPTER I—MRS. MACANDER'S EVIDENCE

Many people, no doubt, including the editor of the 'Ultra Vivisectionist,' then in the bloom of its first youth, would say that Soames was less than a man not to have removed the locks from his wife's doors, and, after beating her soundly, resumed wedded happiness.

Brutality is not so deplorably diluted by humaneness as it used to be, yet a sentimental segment of the population may still be relieved to learn that he did none of these things. For active brutality is not popular with Forsytes; they are too circumspect, and, on the whole, too softhearted. And in Soames there was some common pride, not sufficient to make him do a really generous action, but enough to prevent his indulging in an extremely mean one, except, perhaps, in very hot blood. Above all this a true Forsyte refused to feel himself ridiculous. Short of actually beating his wife, he perceived nothing to be done; he therefore accepted the situation without another word.

Throughout the summer and autumn he continued to go to the office, to sort his pictures, and ask his friends to dinner.

He did not leave town; Irene refused to go away. The house at Robin Hill, finished though it was, remained empty and ownerless. Soames had brought a suit against the Buccaneer, in which he claimed from him the sum of three hundred and fifty pounds.

A firm of solicitors, Messrs. Freak and Able, had put in a defence on Bosinney's behalf. Admitting the facts, they raised a point on the correspondence which, divested of legal phraseology, amounted to this: To speak of 'a free hand in the terms of this correspondence' is an Irish bull.

By a chance, fortuitous but not improbable in the close borough of legal circles, a good deal of information came to Soames' ear anent this line of policy, the working partner in his firm, Bustard, happening to sit next at dinner at Walmisley's, the Taxing Master, to young Chankery, of the Common Law Bar.

The necessity for talking what is known as 'shop,' which comes on all lawyers with the removal of the ladies, caused Chankery, a young and promising advocate, to propound an impersonal conundrum to his neighbour, whose name he did not know, for, seated as he permanently was in the background, Bustard had practically no name.

He had, said Chankery, a case coming on with a 'very nice point.' He then explained, preserving every professional discretion, the riddle in Soames' case. Everyone, he said, to whom he had spoken, thought it a nice point. The issue was small unfortunately, 'though d——d serious for his client he believed'—Walmisley's champagne was bad but plentiful. A Judge would make short work of it, he was afraid. He intended to make a big effort—the point was a nice one. What did his neighbour say?

Bustard, a model of secrecy, said nothing. He related the incident to Soames however with some malice, for this quiet man was capable of human feeling, ending with his own opinion that the point was 'a very nice one.'

In accordance with his resolve, our Forsyte had put his interests into the hands of Jobling and Boulter. From the moment of doing so he regretted that he had not acted for himself. On receiving a copy of Bosinney's defence he went over to their offices.

Boulter, who had the matter in hand, Jobling having died some years before, told him that in his opinion it was rather a nice point; he would like counsel's opinion on it.

Soames told him to go to a good man, and they went to Waterbuck, Q.C., marking him ten and one, who kept the papers six weeks and then wrote as follows:

'In my opinion the true interpretation of this correspondence depends very much on the intention of the parties, and will turn upon the evidence given at the trial. I am of opinion that an attempt should be made to secure from the architect an admission that he understood he was not to spend at the outside more than twelve thousand and fifty pounds. With regard to the expression, "a free hand in the terms of this correspondence," to which my attention is directed, the point is a nice one; but I am of opinion that upon the whole the ruling in "Boileau v. The Blasted Cement Co., Ltd.," will apply.'

Upon this opinion they acted, administering interrogatories, but to their annoyance Messrs. Freak and Able answered these in so masterly a fashion that nothing whatever was admitted and that without prejudice.

It was on October 1 that Soames read Waterbuck's opinion, in the dining-room before dinner.

It made him nervous; not so much because of the case of 'Boileau v. The Blasted Cement Co., Ltd.,' as that the point had lately begun to seem to him, too, a nice one; there was about it just that pleasant flavour of subtlety so attractive to the best legal appetites. To have his own impression confirmed by Waterbuck, Q.C., would have disturbed any man.

He sat thinking it over, and staring at the empty grate, for though autumn had come, the weather kept as gloriously fine that jubilee year as if it were still high August. It was not pleasant to be disturbed; he desired too passionately to set his foot on Bosinney's neck.

Though he had not seen the architect since the last afternoon at Robin Hill, he was never free from the sense of his presence—never free from the memory of his worn face with its high cheek bones and enthusiastic eyes. It would not be too much to say that he had never got rid of the feeling of that night when he heard the peacock's cry at dawn—the feeling that Bosinney haunted the house. And every man's shape that he saw in the dark evenings walking past, seemed that of him whom George had so appropriately named the Buccaneer.

Irene still met him, he was certain; where, or how, he neither knew, nor asked; deterred by a vague and secret dread of too much knowledge. It all seemed subterranean nowadays.

Sometimes when he questioned his wife as to where she had been, which he still made a point of doing, as every Forsyte should, she looked very strange. Her self-possession was wonderful, but there were moments when, behind the mask of her face, inscrutable as it had always been to him, lurked an expression he had never been used to see there.

She had taken to lunching out too; when he asked Bilson if her mistress had been in to lunch, as often as not she would answer: "No, sir."

He strongly disapproved of her gadding about by herself, and told her so. But she took no notice. There was something that angered, amazed, yet almost amused him about the calm way in which she disregarded his wishes. It was really as if she were hugging to herself the thought of a triumph over him.

He rose from the perusal of Waterbuck, Q.C.'s opinion, and, going upstairs, entered her room, for she did not lock her doors till bed-time—she had the decency, he found, to save the feelings of the servants. She was brushing her hair, and turned to him with strange fierceness.

"What do you want?" she said. "Please leave my room!"

He answered: "I want to know how long this state of things between us is to last? I have put up with it long enough."

"Will you please leave my room?"

"Will you treat me as your husband?"

"No."

"Then, I shall take steps to make you."

"Do!"

He stared, amazed at the calmness of her answer. Her lips were compressed in a thin line; her hair lay in fluffy masses on her bare shoulders, in all its strange golden contrast to her dark eyes—those eyes alive with the emotions of fear, hate, contempt, and odd, haunting triumph.

"Now, please, will you leave my room?" He turned round, and went sulkily out.

He knew very well that he had no intention of taking steps, and he saw that she knew too—knew that he was afraid to.

It was a habit with him to tell her the doings of his day: how such and such clients had called; how he had arranged a mortgage for Parkes; how that long-standing suit of Fryer v. Forsyte was getting on, which, arising in the preternaturally careful disposition of his property by his great uncle Nicholas, who had tied it up so that no one could get at it at all, seemed likely to remain a source of income for several solicitors till the Day of Judgment.

And how he had called in at Jobson's, and seen a Boucher sold, which he had just missed buying of Talleyrand and Sons in Pall Mall.

He had an admiration for Boucher, Watteau, and all that school. It was a habit with him to tell her all these matters, and he continued to do it even now, talking for long spells at dinner, as though by the volubility of words he could conceal from himself the ache in his heart.

Often, if they were alone, he made an attempt to kiss her when she said good-night. He may have had some vague notion that some night she would let him; or perhaps only the feeling that a husband ought to kiss his wife. Even if she hated him, he at all events ought not to put himself in the wrong by neglecting this ancient rite.

And why did she hate him? Even now he could not altogether believe it. It was strange to be hated!—the emotion was too extreme; yet he hated Bosinney, that Buccaneer, that prowling vagabond, that night-wanderer. For in his thoughts Soames always saw him lying in wait—wandering. Ah, but he must be in very low water! Young Burkitt, the architect, had seen him coming out of a third-rate restaurant, looking terribly down in the mouth!

During all the hours he lay awake, thinking over the situation, which seemed to have no end—unless she should suddenly come to her senses—never once did the thought of separating from his wife seriously enter his head....

And the Forsytes! What part did they play in this stage of Soames' subterranean tragedy?

Truth to say, little or none, for they were at the sea.

From hotels, hydropathics, or lodging-houses, they were bathing daily; laying in a stock of ozone to last them through the winter.

Each section, in the vineyard of its own choosing, grew and culled and pressed and bottled the grapes of a pet sea-air.

The end of September began to witness their several returns.

In rude health and small omnibuses, with considerable colour in their cheeks, they arrived daily from the various termini. The following morning saw them back at their vocations.

On the next Sunday Timothy's was thronged from lunch till dinner.

Amongst other gossip, too numerous and interesting to relate, Mrs. Septimus Small mentioned that Soames and Irene had not been away.

It remained for a comparative outsider to supply the next evidence of interest.

It chanced that one afternoon late in September, Mrs. MacAnder, Winifred Dartie's greatest friend, taking a constitutional, with young Augustus Flippard, on her bicycle in Richmond Park, passed Irene and Bosinney walking from the bracken towards the Sheen Gate.

Perhaps the poor little woman was thirsty, for she had ridden long on a hard, dry road, and, as all London knows, to ride a bicycle and talk to young Flippard will try the toughest constitution; or perhaps the sight of the cool bracken grove, whence 'those two' were coming down, excited her envy. The cool bracken grove on the top of the hill, with the oak boughs for roof, where the pigeons were raising an endless wedding hymn, and the autumn, humming, whispered to the ears of lovers in the fern, while the deer stole by. The bracken grove of irretrievable delights, of golden minutes in the long marriage of heaven and earth! The bracken grove, sacred to stags, to strange tree-stump fauns leaping around the silver whiteness of a birch-tree nymph at summer dusk.

This lady knew all the Forsytes, and having been at June's 'at home,' was not at a loss to see with whom she had to deal. Her own marriage, poor thing, had not been successful, but having had the good sense and ability to force her husband into pronounced error, she herself had passed through the necessary divorce proceedings without incurring censure.

She was therefore a judge of all that sort of thing, and lived in one of those large buildings, where in small sets of apartments, are gathered incredible quantities of Forsytes, whose chief recreation out of business hours is the discussion of each other's affairs.

Poor little woman, perhaps she was thirsty, certainly she was bored, for Flippard was a wit. To see 'those two' in so unlikely a spot was quite a merciful 'pick-me-up.'

At the MacAnder, like all London, Time pauses.

This small but remarkable woman merits attention; her all-seeing eye and shrewd tongue were inscrutably the means of furthering the ends of Providence.

With an air of being in at the death, she had an almost distressing power of taking care of herself. She had done more, perhaps, in her way than any woman about town to destroy the sense of chivalry which still clogs the wheel of civilization. So smart she was, and spoken of endearingly as 'the little MacAnder!'

Dressing tightly and well, she belonged to a Woman's Club, but was by no means the neurotic and dismal type of member who was always thinking of her rights. She took her rights unconsciously, they came natural to her, and she knew exactly how to make the most of them without exciting anything but admiration amongst that great class to whom she was affiliated, not precisely perhaps by manner, but by birth, breeding, and the true, the secret gauge, a sense of property.

The daughter of a Bedfordshire solicitor, by the daughter of a clergyman, she had never, through all the painful experience of being married to a very mild painter with a cranky love of Nature, who had deserted her for an actress, lost touch with the requirements, beliefs, and inner feeling of Society; and, on attaining her liberty, she placed herself without effort in the very van of Forsyteism.

Always in good spirits, and 'full of information,' she was universally welcomed. She excited neither surprise nor disapprobation when encountered on the Rhine or at Zermatt, either alone, or travelling with a lady and two gentlemen; it was felt that she was perfectly capable of taking care of herself; and the hearts of all Forsytes warmed to that wonderful instinct, which enabled her to enjoy everything without giving anything away. It was generally felt that to such women as Mrs. MacAnder should we look for the perpetuation and increase of our best type of woman. She had never had any children.

If there was one thing more than another that she could not stand it was one of those soft women with what men called 'charm' about them, and for Mrs. Soames she always had an especial dislike.

Obscurely, no doubt, she felt that if charm were once admitted as the criterion, smartness and capability must go to the wall; and she hated—with a hatred the deeper that at times this so-called charm seemed to disturb all calculations—the subtle seductiveness which she could not altogether overlook in Irene.

She said, however, that she could see nothing in the woman—there was no 'go' about her—she would never be able to stand up for herself—anyone could take advantage of her, that was plain—she could not see in fact what men found to admire!

She was not really ill-natured, but, in maintaining her position after the trying circumstances of her married life, she had found it so necessary to be 'full of information,' that the idea of holding her tongue about 'those two' in the Park never occurred to her.

And it so happened that she was dining that very evening at Timothy's, where she went sometimes to 'cheer the old things up,' as she was wont to put it. The same people were always asked to meet her: Winifred Dartie and her husband; Francie, because she belonged to the artistic circles, for Mrs. MacAnder was known to contribute articles on dress to 'The Ladies Kingdom Come'; and for her to flirt with, provided they could be obtained, two of the Hayman boys, who, though they never said anything, were believed to be fast and thoroughly intimate with all that was latest in smart Society.

At twenty-five minutes past seven she turned out the electric light in her little hall, and wrapped in her opera cloak with the chinchilla collar, came out into the corridor, pausing a moment to make sure she had her latch-key. These little self-contained flats were convenient; to be sure, she had no light and no air, but she could shut it up whenever she liked and go away. There was no bother with servants, and she never felt tied as she used to when poor, dear Fred was always about, in his mooney way. She retained no rancour against poor, dear Fred, he was such a fool; but the thought of that actress drew from her, even now, a little, bitter, derisive smile.

Firmly snapping the door to, she crossed the corridor, with its gloomy, yellow-ochre walls, and its infinite vista of brown, numbered doors. The lift was going down; and wrapped to the ears in the high cloak, with every one of her auburn hairs in its place, she waited motionless for it to stop at her floor. The iron gates clanked open; she entered. There were already three occupants, a man in a great white waistcoat, with a large, smooth face like a baby's, and two old ladies in black, with mittened hands.

Mrs. MacAnder smiled at them; she knew everybody; and all these three, who had been admirably silent before, began to talk at once. This was Mrs. MacAnder's successful secret. She provoked conversation.

Throughout a descent of five stories the conversation continued, the lift boy standing with his back turned, his cynical face protruding through the bars.

At the bottom they separated, the man in the white waistcoat sentimentally to the billiard room, the old ladies to dine and say to each other: "A dear little woman!" "Such a rattle!" and Mrs. MacAnder to her cab.

When Mrs. MacAnder dined at Timothy's, the conversation (although Timothy himself could never be induced to be present) took that wider, man-of-the-world tone current among Forsytes at large, and this, no doubt, was what put her at a premium there.

Mrs. Small and Aunt Hester found it an exhilarating change. "If only," they said, "Timothy would meet her!" It was felt that she would do him good. She could tell you, for instance, the latest story of Sir Charles Fiste's son at Monte Carlo; who was the real heroine of Tynemouth Eddy's fashionable novel that everyone was holding up their hands over, and what they were doing in Paris about wearing bloomers. She was so sensible, too, knowing all about that vexed question, whether to send young Nicholas' eldest into the navy as his mother wished, or make him an accountant as his father thought would be safer. She strongly deprecated the navy. If you were not exceptionally brilliant or exceptionally well connected, they passed you over so disgracefully, and what was it after all to look forward to, even if you became an admiral—a pittance! An accountant had many more chances, but let him be put with a good firm, where there was no risk at starting!

Sometimes she would give them a tip on the Stock Exchange; not that Mrs. Small or Aunt Hester ever took it. They had indeed no money to invest; but it seemed to bring them into such exciting touch with the realities of life. It was an event. They would ask Timothy, they said. But they never did, knowing in advance that it would upset him. Surreptitiously, however, for weeks after they would look in that paper, which they took with respect on account of its really fashionable proclivities, to see where 'Bright's Rubies' or 'The Woollen Mackintosh Company' were up or down. Sometimes they could not find the name of the company at all; and they would wait until James or Roger or even Swithin came in, and ask them in voices trembling with curiosity how that 'Bolivia Lime and Speltrate' was doing—they could not find it in the paper.

And Roger would answer: "What do you want to know for? Some trash! You'll go burning your fingers—investing your money in lime, and things you know nothing about! Who told you?" and ascertaining what they had been told, he would go away, and, making inquiries in the City, would perhaps invest some of his own money in the concern.

It was about the middle of dinner, just in fact as the saddle of mutton had been brought in by Smither, that Mrs. MacAnder, looking airily round, said: "Oh! and whom do you think I passed to-day in Richmond Park? You'll never guess—Mrs. Soames and—Mr. Bosinney. They must have been down to look at the house!"

Winifred Dartie coughed, and no one said a word. It was the piece of evidence they had all unconsciously been waiting for.

To do Mrs. MacAnder justice, she had been to Switzerland and the Italian lakes with a party of three, and had not heard of Soames' rupture with his architect. She could not tell, therefore, the profound impression her words would make.

Upright and a little flushed, she moved her small, shrewd eyes from face to face, trying to gauge the effect of her words. On either side of her a Hayman boy, his lean, taciturn, hungry face turned towards his plate, ate his mutton steadily.

These two, Giles and Jesse, were so alike and so inseparable that they were known as the Dromios. They never talked, and seemed always completely occupied in doing nothing. It was popularly supposed that they were cramming for an important examination. They walked without hats for long hours in the Gardens attached to their house, books in their hands, a fox-terrier at their heels, never saying a word, and smoking all the time. Every morning, about fifty yards apart, they trotted down Campden Hill on two lean hacks, with legs as long as their own, and every morning about an hour later, still fifty yards apart, they cantered up again. Every evening, wherever they had dined, they might be observed about half-past ten, leaning over the balustrade of the Alhambra promenade.

They were never seen otherwise than together; in this way passing their lives, apparently perfectly content.

Inspired by some dumb stirring within them of the feelings of gentlemen, they turned at this painful moment to Mrs. MacAnder, and said in precisely the same voice: "Have you seen the...?"

Such was her surprise at being thus addressed that she put down her fork; and Smither, who was passing, promptly removed her plate. Mrs. MacAnder, however, with presence of mind, said instantly: "I must have a little more of that nice mutton."

But afterwards in the drawing—room she sat down by Mrs. Small, determined to get to the bottom of the matter. And she began:

"What a charming woman, Mrs. Soames; such a sympathetic temperament! Soames is a really lucky man!"

Her anxiety for information had not made sufficient allowance for that inner Forsyte skin which refuses to share its troubles with outsiders.

Mrs. Septimus Small, drawing herself up with a creak and rustle of her whole person, said, shivering in her dignity:

"My dear, it is a subject we do not talk about!"

CHAPTER II—NIGHT IN THE PARK

Although with her infallible instinct Mrs. Small had said the very thing to make her guest 'more intriguee than ever,' it is difficult to see how else she could truthfully have spoken.

It was not a subject which the Forsytes could talk about even among themselves—to use the word Soames had invented to characterize to himself the situation, it was 'subterranean.'

Yet, within a week of Mrs. MacAnder's encounter in Richmond Park, to all of them—save Timothy, from whom it was carefully kept—to James on his domestic beat from the Poultry to Park Lane, to George the wild one, on his daily adventure from the bow window at the Haversnake to the billiard room at the 'Red Pottle,' was it known that 'those two' had gone to extremes.

George (it was he who invented many of those striking expressions still current in fashionable circles) voiced the sentiment more accurately than any one when he said to his brother Eustace that 'the Buccaneer' was 'going it'; he expected Soames was about 'fed up.'

It was felt that he must be, and yet, what could be done? He ought perhaps to take steps; but to take steps would be deplorable.

Without an open scandal which they could not see their way to recommending, it was difficult to see what steps could be taken. In this impasse, the only thing was to say nothing to Soames, and nothing to each other; in fact, to pass it over.

By displaying towards Irene a dignified coldness, some impression might be made upon her; but she was seldom now to be seen, and there seemed a slight difficulty in seeking her out on purpose to show her coldness. Sometimes in the privacy of his bedroom James would reveal to Emily the real suffering that his son's misfortune caused him.

"I can't tell," he would say; "it worries me out of my life. There'll be a scandal, and that'll do him no good. I shan't say anything to him. There might be nothing in it. What do you think? She's very artistic, they tell me. What? Oh, you're a 'regular Juley'! Well, I don't know;

I expect the worst. This is what comes of having no children. I knew how it would be from the first. They never told me they didn't mean to have any children—nobody tells me anything!"

On his knees by the side of the bed, his eyes open and fixed with worry, he would breathe into the counterpane. Clad in his nightshirt, his neck poked forward, his back rounded, he resembled some long white bird.

"Our Father-," he repeated, turning over and over again the thought of this possible scandal.

Like old Jolyon, he, too, at the bottom of his heart set the blame of the tragedy down to family interference. What business had that lot—he began to think of the Stanhope Gate branch, including young Jolyon and his daughter, as 'that lot'—to introduce a person like this Bosinney into the family? (He had heard George's soubriquet, 'The Buccaneer,' but he could make nothing of that—the young man was an architect.)

He began to feel that his brother Jolyon, to whom he had always looked up and on whose opinion he had relied, was not quite what he had expected.

Not having his eldest brother's force of character, he was more sad than angry. His great comfort was to go to Winifred's, and take the little Darties in his carriage over to Kensington Gardens, and there, by the Round Pond, he could often be seen walking with his eyes fixed anxiously on little Publius Dartie's sailing-boat, which he had himself freighted with a penny, as though convinced that it would never again come to shore; while little Publius—who, James delighted to say, was not a bit like his father skipping along under his lee, would try to get him to bet another that it never would, having found that it always did. And James would make the bet; he always paid—sometimes as many as three or four pennies in the afternoon, for the game seemed never to pall on little Publius—and always in paying he said: "Now, that's for your money-box. Why, you're getting quite a rich man!" The thought of his little grandson's growing wealth was a real pleasure to him. But little Publius knew a sweet-shop, and a trick worth two of that.

And they would walk home across the Park, James' figure, with high shoulders and absorbed and worried face, exercising its tall, lean protectorship, pathetically unregarded, over the robust child-figures of Imogen and little Publius.

But those Gardens and that Park were not sacred to James. Forsytes and tramps, children and lovers, rested and wandered day after day, night after night, seeking one and all some freedom from labour, from the reek and turmoil of the streets.

The leaves browned slowly, lingering with the sun and summer-like warmth of the nights.

On Saturday, October 5, the sky that had been blue all day deepened after sunset to the bloom of purple grapes. There was no moon, and a clear dark, like some velvety garment, was wrapped around the trees, whose thinned branches, resembling plumes, stirred not in the still, warm air. All London had poured into the Park, draining the cup of summer to its dregs.

Couple after couple, from every gate, they streamed along the paths and over the burnt grass, and one after another, silently out of the lighted spaces, stole into the shelter of the feathery trees, where, blotted against some trunk, or under the shadow of shrubs, they were lost to all but themselves in the heart of the soft darkness.

To fresh-comers along the paths, these forerunners formed but part of that passionate dusk, whence only a strange murmur, like the confused beating of hearts, came forth. But when that murmur reached each couple in the lamp-light their voices wavered, and ceased;

their arms enlaced, their eyes began seeking, searching, probing the blackness. Suddenly, as though drawn by invisible hands, they, too, stepped over the railing, and, silent as shadows, were gone from the light.

The stillness, enclosed in the far, inexorable roar of the town, was alive with the myriad passions, hopes, and loves of multitudes of struggling human atoms; for in spite of the disapproval of that great body of Forsytes, the Municipal Council—to whom Love had long been considered, next to the Sewage Question, the gravest danger to the community—a process was going on that night in the Park, and in a hundred other parks, without which the thousand factories, churches, shops, taxes, and drains, of which they were custodians, were as arteries without blood, a man without a heart.

The instincts of self-forgetfulness, of passion, and of love, hiding under the trees, away from the trustees of their remorseless enemy, the 'sense of property,' were holding a stealthy revel, and Soames, returning from Bayswater—for he had been alone to dine at Timothy's walking home along the water, with his mind upon that coming lawsuit, had the blood driven from his heart by a low laugh and the sound of kisses. He thought of writing to the Times the next morning, to draw the attention of the Editor to the condition of our parks. He did not, however, for he had a horror of seeing his name in print.

But starved as he was, the whispered sounds in the stillness, the half-seen forms in the dark, acted on him like some morbid stimulant. He left the path along the water and stole under the trees, along the deep shadow of little plantations, where the boughs of chestnut trees hung their great leaves low, and there was blacker refuge, shaping his course in circles which had for their object a stealthy inspection of chairs side by side, against tree-trunks, of enlaced lovers, who stirred at his approach.

Now he stood still on the rise overlooking the Serpentine, where, in full lamp-light, black against the silver water, sat a couple who never moved, the woman's face buried on the man's neck—a single form, like a carved emblem of passion, silent and unashamed.

And, stung by the sight, Soames hurried on deeper into the shadow of the trees.

In this search, who knows what he thought and what he sought? Bread for hunger—light in darkness? Who knows what he expected to find—impersonal knowledge of the human heart—the end of his private subterranean tragedy—for, again, who knew, but that each dark couple, unnamed, unnameable, might not be he and she?

But it could not be such knowledge as this that he was seeking—the wife of Soames Forsyte sitting in the Park like a common wench! Such thoughts were inconceivable; and from tree to tree, with his noiseless step, he passed.

Once he was sworn at; once the whisper, "If only it could always be like this!" sent the blood flying again from his heart, and he waited there, patient and dogged, for the two to move. But it was only a poor thin slip of a shop-girl in her draggled blouse who passed him, clinging to her lover's arm.

A hundred other lovers too whispered that hope in the stillness of the trees, a hundred other lovers clung to each other.

But shaking himself with sudden disgust, Soames returned to the path, and left that seeking for he knew not what.

CHAPTER III—MEETING AT THE BOTANICAL

Young Jolyon, whose circumstances were not those of a Forsyte, found at times a difficulty in sparing the money needful for those country jaunts and researches into Nature, without having prosecuted which no watercolour artist ever puts brush to paper.

He was frequently, in fact, obliged to take his colour-box into the Botanical Gardens, and there, on his stool, in the shade of a monkey-puzzler or in the lee of some India-rubber plant, he would spend long hours sketching.

An Art critic who had recently been looking at his work had delivered himself as follows:

"In a way your drawings are very good; tone and colour, in some of them certainly quite a feeling for Nature. But, you see, they're so scattered; you'll never get the public to look at them. Now, if you'd taken a definite subject, such as 'London by Night,' or 'The Crystal Palace in the Spring,' and made a regular series, the public would have known at once what they were looking at. I can't lay too much stress upon that. All the men who are making great names in Art, like Crum Stone or Bleeder, are making them by avoiding the unexpected; by specializing and putting their works all in the same pigeon-hole, so that the public know at once where to go. And this stands to reason, for if a man's a collector he doesn't want people to smell at the canvas to find out whom his pictures are by; he wants them to be able to say at once, 'A capital Forsyte!' It is all the more important for you to be careful to choose a subject that they can lay hold of on the spot, since there's no very marked originality in your style."

Young Jolyon, standing by the little piano, where a bowl of dried rose leaves, the only produce of the garden, was deposited on a bit of faded damask, listened with his dim smile.

Turning to his wife, who was looking at the speaker with an angry expression on her thin face, he said:

"You see, dear?"

"I do not," she answered in her staccato voice, that still had a little foreign accent; "your style has originality."

The critic looked at her, smiled' deferentially, and said no more. Like everyone else, he knew their history.

The words bore good fruit with young Jolyon; they were contrary to all that he believed in, to all that he theoretically held good in his Art, but some strange, deep instinct moved him against his will to turn them to profit.

He discovered therefore one morning that an idea had come to him for making a series of watercolour drawings of London. How the idea had arisen he could not tell; and it was not till the following year, when he had completed and sold them at a very fair price, that in one of his impersonal moods, he found himself able to recollect the Art critic, and to discover in his own achievement another proof that he was a Forsyte.

He decided to commence with the Botanical Gardens, where he had already made so many studies, and chose the little artificial pond, sprinkled now with an autumn shower of red and yellow leaves, for though the gardeners longed to sweep them off, they could not reach them with their brooms. The rest of the gardens they swept bare enough, removing every morning Nature's rain of leaves; piling them in heaps, whence from slow fires rose the sweet, acrid smoke that, like the cuckoo's note for spring, the scent of lime trees for the summer, is the true emblem of the fall. The gardeners' tidy souls could not abide the gold and green and russet pattern on the grass. The gravel paths must lie unstained, ordered, methodical, without knowledge of the realities of life, nor of that slow and beautiful decay which flings crowns underfoot to star the earth with fallen glories, whence, as the cycle rolls, will leap again wild spring.

Thus each leaf that fell was marked from the moment when it fluttered a good-bye and dropped, slow turning, from its twig.

But on that little pond the leaves floated in peace, and praised Heaven with their hues, the sunlight haunting over them.

And so young Jolyon found them.

Coming there one morning in the middle of October, he was disconcerted to find a bench about twenty paces from his stand occupied, for he had a proper horror of anyone seeing him at work.

A lady in a velvet jacket was sitting there, with her eyes fixed on the ground. A flowering laurel, however, stood between, and, taking shelter behind this, young Jolyon prepared his easel.

His preparations were leisurely; he caught, as every true artist should, at anything that might delay for a moment the effort of his work, and he found himself looking furtively at this unknown dame.

Like his father before him, he had an eye for a face. This face was charming!

He saw a rounded chin nestling in a cream ruffle, a delicate face with large dark eyes and soft lips. A black 'picture' hat concealed the hair; her figure was lightly poised against the back of the bench, her knees were crossed; the tip of a patent-leather shoe emerged beneath her skirt. There was something, indeed, inexpressibly dainty about the person of this lady, but young Jolyon's attention was chiefly riveted by the look on her face, which reminded him of his wife. It was as though its owner had come into contact with forces too strong for her. It troubled him, arousing vague feelings of attraction and chivalry. Who was she? And what doing there, alone?

Two young gentlemen of that peculiar breed, at once forward and shy, found in the Regent's Park, came by on their way to lawn tennis, and he noted with disapproval their furtive stares of admiration. A loitering gardener halted to do something unnecessary to a clump of pampas grass; he, too, wanted an excuse for peeping. A gentleman, old, and, by his hat, a professor of horticulture, passed three times to scrutinize her long and stealthily, a queer expression about his lips.

With all these men young Jolyon felt the same vague irritation. She looked at none of them, yet was he certain that every man who passed would look at her like that.

Her face was not the face of a sorceress, who in every look holds out to men the offer of pleasure; it had none of the 'devil's beauty' so highly prized among the first Forsytes of the land; neither was it of that type, no less adorable, associated with the box of chocolate; it was not of the spiritually passionate, or passionately spiritual order, peculiar to house-decoration and modern poetry; nor did it seem to promise to the playwright material for the production of the interesting and neurasthenic figure, who commits suicide in the last act.

In shape and colouring, in its soft persuasive passivity, its sensuous purity, this woman's face reminded him of Titian's 'Heavenly Love,' a reproduction of which hung over the sideboard in his dining-room. And her attraction seemed to be in this soft passivity, in the feeling she gave that to pressure she must yield.

For what or whom was she waiting, in the silence, with the trees dropping here and there a leaf, and the thrushes strutting close on grass, touched with the sparkle of the autumn rime? Then her charming face grew eager, and, glancing round, with almost a lover's jealousy, young Jolyon saw Bosinney striding across the grass.

Curiously he watched the meeting, the look in their eyes, the long clasp of their hands. They sat down close together, linked for all their outward discretion. He heard the rapid murmur of their talk; but what they said he could not catch.

He had rowed in the galley himself! He knew the long hours of waiting and the lean minutes of a half-public meeting; the tortures of suspense that haunt the unhallowed lover.

It required, however, but a glance at their two faces to see that this was none of those affairs of a season that distract men and women about town; none of those sudden appetites that wake up ravening, and are surfeited and asleep again in six weeks. This was the real thing! This was what had happened to himself! Out of this anything might come!

Bosinney was pleading, and she so quiet, so soft, yet immovable in her passivity, sat looking over the grass.

Was he the man to carry her off, that tender, passive being, who would never stir a step for herself? Who had given him all herself, and would die for him, but perhaps would never run away with him!

It seemed to young Jolyon that he could hear her saying: "But, darling, it would ruin you!" For he himself had experienced to the full the gnawing fear at the bottom of each woman's heart that she is a drag on the man she loves.

And he peeped at them no more; but their soft, rapid talk came to his ears, with the stuttering song of some bird who seemed trying to remember the notes of spring: Joy— tragedy? Which—which?

And gradually their talk ceased; long silence followed.

'And where does Soames come in?' young Jolyon thought. 'People think she is concerned about the sin of deceiving her husband! Little they know of women! She's eating, after starvation—taking her revenge! And Heaven help her—for he'll take his.'

He heard the swish of silk, and, spying round the laurel, saw them walking away, their hands stealthily joined....

At the end of July old Jolyon had taken his grand-daughter to the mountains; and on that visit (the last they ever paid) June recovered to a great extent her health and spirits. In the hotels, filled with British Forsytes—for old Jolyon could not bear a 'set of Germans,' as he called all foreigners—she was looked upon with respect—the only grand-daughter of that fine-looking, and evidently wealthy, old Mr. Forsyte. She did not mix freely with people— to mix freely with people was not June's habit—but she formed some friendships, and notably one in the Rhone Valley, with a French girl who was dying of consumption.

Determining at once that her friend should not die, she forgot, in the institution of a campaign against Death, much of her own trouble.

Old Jolyon watched the new intimacy with relief and disapproval; for this additional proof that her life was to be passed amongst 'lame ducks' worried him. Would she never make a friendship or take an interest in something that would be of real benefit to her?

'Taking up with a parcel of foreigners,' he called it. He often, however, brought home grapes or roses, and presented them to 'Mam'zelle' with an ingratiating twinkle.

Towards the end of September, in spite of June's disapproval, Mademoiselle Vigor breathed her last in the little hotel at St. Luc, to which they had moved her; and June took her defeat so deeply to heart that old Jolyon carried her away to Paris. Here, in contemplation of the 'Venus de Milo' and the 'Madeleine,' she shook off her depression, and when, towards the middle of October, they returned to town, her grandfather believed that he had effected a cure.

No sooner, however, had they established themselves in Stanhope Gate than he perceived to his dismay a return of her old absorbed and brooding manner. She would sit, staring in front of her, her chin on her hand, like a little Norse spirit, grim and intent, while all around in the electric light, then just installed, shone the great, drawing-room brocaded up to the frieze, full of furniture from Baple and Pullbred's. And in the huge gilt mirror were reflected those Dresden china groups of young men in tight knee breeches, at the feet of full-bosomed ladies nursing on their laps pet lambs, which old Jolyon had bought when he was a bachelor and thought so highly of in these days of degenerate taste. He was a man of most open mind, who, more than any Forsyte of them all, had moved with the times, but he could never forget that he had bought these groups at Jobson's, and given a lot of money for them. He often said to June, with a sort of disillusioned contempt:

"You don't care about them! They're not the gimcrack things you and your friends like, but they cost me seventy pounds!" He was not a man who allowed his taste to be warped when he knew for solid reasons that it was sound.

One of the first things that June did on getting home was to go round to Timothy's. She persuaded herself that it was her duty to call there, and cheer him with an account of all her travels; but in reality she went because she knew of no other place where, by some random speech, or roundabout question, she could glean news of Bosinney.

They received her most cordially: And how was her dear grandfather? He had not been to see them since May. Her Uncle Timothy was very poorly, he had had a lot of trouble with the chimney-sweep in his bedroom; the stupid man had let the soot down the chimney! It had quite upset her uncle.

June sat there a long time, dreading, yet passionately hoping, that they would speak of Bosinney.

But paralyzed by unaccountable discretion, Mrs. Septimus Small let fall no word, neither did she question June about him. In desperation the girl asked at last whether Soames and Irene were in town—she had not yet been to see anyone.

It was Aunt Hester who replied: Oh, yes, they were in town, they had not been away at all. There was some little difficulty about the house, she believed. June had heard, no doubt! She had better ask her Aunt Juley!

June turned to Mrs. Small, who sat upright in her chair, her hands clasped, her face covered with innumerable pouts. In answer to the girl's look she maintained a strange silence, and when she spoke it was to ask June whether she had worn night-socks up in those high hotels where it must be so cold of a night.

June answered that she had not, she hated the stuffy things; and rose to leave.

Mrs. Small's infallibly chosen silence was far more ominous to her than anything that could have been said.

Before half an hour was over she had dragged the truth from Mrs. Baynes in Lowndes Square, that Soames was bringing an action against Bosinney over the decoration of the house.

Instead of disturbing her, the news had a strangely calming effect; as though she saw in the prospect of this struggle new hope for herself. She learnt that the case was expected to come on in about a month, and there seemed little or no prospect of Bosinney's success.

"And whatever he'll do I can't think," said Mrs. Baynes; "it's very dreadful for him, you know—he's got no money—he's very hard up. And we can't help him, I'm sure. I'm told the money-lenders won't lend if you have no security, and he has none—none at all."

Her embonpoint had increased of late; she was in the full swing of autumn organization, her writing-table literally strewn with the menus of charity functions. She looked meaningly at June, with her round eyes of parrot-grey.

The sudden flush that rose on the girl's intent young face—she must have seen spring up before her a great hope—the sudden sweetness of her smile, often came back to Lady Baynes in after years (Baynes was knighted when he built that public Museum of Art which has given so much employment to officials, and so little pleasure to those working classes for whom it was designed).

The memory of that change, vivid and touching, like the breaking open of a flower, or the first sun after long winter, the memory, too, of all that came after, often intruded itself, unaccountably, inopportunely on Lady Baynes, when her mind was set upon the most important things.

This was the very afternoon of the day that young Jolyon witnessed the meeting in the Botanical Gardens, and on this day, too, old Jolyon paid a visit to his solicitors, Forsyte, Bustard, and Forsyte, in the Poultry. Soames was not in, he had gone down to Somerset House; Bustard was buried up to the hilt in papers and that inaccessible apartment, where he was judiciously placed, in order that he might do as much work as possible; but James was in the front office, biting a finger, and lugubriously turning over the pleadings in Forsyte v. Bosinney.

This sound lawyer had only a sort of luxurious dread of the 'nice point,' enough to set up a pleasurable feeling of fuss; for his good practical sense told him that if he himself were on the Bench he would not pay much attention to it. But he was afraid that this Bosinney would go bankrupt and Soames would have to find the money after all, and costs into the bargain. And behind this tangible dread there was always that intangible trouble, lurking in the background, intricate, dim, scandalous, like a bad dream, and of which this action was but an outward and visible sign.

He raised his head as old Jolyon came in, and muttered: "How are you, Jolyon? I haven't seen you for an age. You've been to Switzerland, they tell me. This young Bosinney, he's got himself into a mess. I knew how it would be!" He held out the papers, regarding his elder brother with nervous gloom.

Old Jolyon read them in silence, and while he read them James looked at the floor, biting his fingers the while.

Old Jolyon pitched them down at last, and they fell with a thump amongst a mass of affidavits in 're Buncombe, deceased,' one of the many branches of that parent and profitable tree, 'Fryer v. Forsyte.'

"I don't know what Soames is about," he said, "to make a fuss over a few hundred pounds. I thought he was a man of property."

James' long upper lip twitched angrily; he could not bear his son to be attacked in such a spot.

"It's not the money," he began, but meeting his brother's glance, direct, shrewd, judicial, he stopped.

There was a silence.

"I've come in for my Will," said old Jolyon at last, tugging at his moustache.

James' curiosity was roused at once. Perhaps nothing in this life was more stimulating to him than a Will; it was the supreme deal with property, the final inventory of a man's belongings, the last word on what he was worth. He sounded the bell.

"Bring in Mr. Jolyon's Will," he said to an anxious, dark-haired clerk.

"You going to make some alterations?" And through his mind there flashed the thought: 'Now, am I worth as much as he?'

Old Jolyon put the Will in his breast pocket, and James twisted his long legs regretfully.

"You've made some nice purchases lately, they tell me," he said.

"I don't know where you get your information from," answered old Jolyon sharply. "When's this action coming on? Next month? I can't tell what you've got in your minds. You must manage your own affairs; but if you take my advice, you'll settle it out of Court. Good-bye!" With a cold handshake he was gone.

James, his fixed grey-blue eye corkscrewing round some secret anxious image, began again to bite his finger.

Old Jolyon took his Will to the offices of the New Colliery Company, and sat down in the empty Board Room to read it through. He answered 'Down-by-the-starn' Hemmings so tartly when the latter, seeing his Chairman seated there, entered with the new Superintendent's first report, that the Secretary withdrew with regretful dignity; and sending for the transfer clerk, blew him up till the poor youth knew not where to look.

It was not—by George—as he (Down-by-the-starn) would have him know, for a whippersnapper of a young fellow like him, to come down to that office, and think that he was God Almighty. He (Down-by-the-starn) had been head of that office for more years than a boy like him could count, and if he thought that when he had finished all his work, he could sit there doing nothing, he did not know him, Hemmings (Down-by-the-starn), and so forth.

On the other side of the green baize door old Jolyon sat at the long, mahogany-and-leather board table, his thick, loose-jointed, tortoiseshell eye-glasses perched on the bridge of his nose, his gold pencil moving down the clauses of his Will.

It was a simple affair, for there were none of those vexatious little legacies and donations to charities, which fritter away a man's possessions, and damage the majestic effect of that little paragraph in the morning papers accorded to Forsytes who die with a hundred thousand pounds.

A simple affair. Just a bequest to his son of twenty thousand, and 'as to the residue of my property of whatsoever kind whether realty or personalty, or partaking of the nature of either—upon trust to pay the proceeds rents annual produce dividends or interest thereof and thereon to my said grand-daughter June Forsyte or her assigns during her life to be for her sole use and benefit and without, etc... and from and after her death or decease upon trust to convey assign transfer or make over the said last-mentioned lands hereditaments premises trust moneys stocks funds investments and securities or such as shall then stand for and represent the same unto such person or persons whether one or more for such intents purposes and uses and generally in such manner way and form in all respects as the said June Forsyte notwithstanding coverture shall by her last Will and Testament or any writing or writings in the nature of a Will testament or testamentary disposition to be by her duly made signed and published direct appoint or make over give and dispose of the same And in default etc.... Provided always...' and so on, in seven folios of brief and simple phraseology.

The Will had been drawn by James in his palmy days. He had foreseen almost every contingency.

Old Jolyon sat a long time reading this Will; at last he took half a sheet of paper from the rack, and made a prolonged pencil note; then buttoning up the Will, he caused a cab to be called and drove to the offices of Paramor and Herring, in Lincoln's Inn Fields. Jack Herring was dead, but his nephew was still in the firm, and old Jolyon was closeted with him for half an hour.

He had kept the hansom, and on coming out, gave the driver the address—3, Wistaria Avenue.

He felt a strange, slow satisfaction, as though he had scored a victory over James and the man of property. They should not poke their noses into his affairs any more; he had just cancelled their trusteeships of his Will; he would take the whole of his business out of their hands, and put it into the hands of young Herring, and he would move the business of his Companies too. If that young Soames were such a man of property, he would never miss a thousand a year or so; and under his great white moustache old Jolyon grimly smiled. He felt that what he was doing was in the nature of retributive justice, richly deserved.

Slowly, surely, with the secret inner process that works the destruction of an old tree, the poison of the wounds to his happiness, his will, his pride, had corroded the comely edifice of his philosophy. Life had worn him down on one side, till, like that family of which he was the head, he had lost balance.

To him, borne northwards towards his son's house, the thought of the new disposition of property, which he had just set in motion, appeared vaguely in the light of a stroke of punishment, levelled at that family and that Society, of which James and his son seemed to him the representatives. He had made a restitution to young Jolyon, and restitution to young Jolyon satisfied his secret craving for revenge-revenge against Time, sorrow, and interference, against all that incalculable sum of disapproval that had been bestowed by the world for fifteen years on his only son. It presented itself as the one possible way of asserting once more the domination of his will; of forcing James, and Soames, and the family, and all those hidden masses of Forsytes—a great stream rolling against the single dam of his obstinacy—to recognise once and for all that he would be master. It was sweet to think that at last he was going to make the boy a richer man by far than that son of James, that 'man of property.' And it was sweet to give to Jo, for he loved his son.

Neither young Jolyon nor his wife were in (young Jolyon indeed was not back from the Botanical), but the little maid told him that she expected the master at any moment:

"He's always at 'ome to tea, sir, to play with the children."

Old Jolyon said he would wait; and sat down patiently enough in the faded, shabby drawing room, where, now that the summer chintzes were removed, the old chairs and sofas revealed all their threadbare deficiencies. He longed to send for the children; to have them there beside him, their supple bodies against his knees; to hear Jolly's: "Hallo, Gran!" and see his rush; and feel Holly's soft little hand stealing up against his cheek. But he would not. There was solemnity in what he had come to do, and until it was over he would not play. He amused himself by thinking how with two strokes of his pen he was going to restore the look of caste so conspicuously absent from everything in that little house; how he could fill these rooms, or others in some larger mansion, with triumphs of art from Baple and Pullbred's; how he could send little Jolly to Harrow and Oxford (he no longer had faith in Eton and Cambridge, for his son had been there); how he could procure little Holly the best musical instruction, the child had a remarkable aptitude.

As these visions crowded before him, causing emotion to swell his heart, he rose, and stood at the window, looking down into the little walled strip of garden, where the pear-tree, bare of leaves before its time, stood with gaunt branches in the slow-gathering mist of the autumn afternoon. The dog Balthasar, his tail curled tightly over a piebald, furry back, was walking at the farther end, sniffing at the plants, and at intervals placing his leg for support against the wall.

And old Jolyon mused.

What pleasure was there left but to give? It was pleasant to give, when you could find one who would be thankful for what you gave—one of your own flesh and blood! There was no such satisfaction to be had out of giving to those who did not belong to you, to those who had no claim on you! Such giving as that was a betrayal of the individualistic convictions and actions of his life, of all his enterprise, his labour, and his moderation, of the great and proud fact that, like tens of thousands of Forsytes before him, tens of thousands in the present, tens of thousands in the future, he had always made his own, and held his own, in the world.

And, while he stood there looking down on the smut-covered foliage of the laurels, the black-stained grass-plot, the progress of the dog Balthasar, all the suffering of the fifteen years during which he had been baulked of legitimate enjoyment mingled its gall with the sweetness of the approaching moment.

Young Jolyon came at last, pleased with his work, and fresh from long hours in the open air. On hearing that his father was in the drawing room, he inquired hurriedly whether Mrs. Forsyte was at home, and being informed that she was not, heaved a sigh of relief. Then putting his painting materials carefully in the little coat-closet out of sight, he went in.

With characteristic decision old Jolyon came at once to the point. "I've been altering my arrangements, Jo," he said. "You can cut your coat a bit longer in the future—I'm settling a thousand a year on you at once. June will have fifty thousand at my death; and you the rest. That dog of yours is spoiling the garden. I shouldn't keep a dog, if I were you!"

The dog Balthasar, seated in the centre of the lawn, was examining his tail.

Young Jolyon looked at the animal, but saw him dimly, for his eyes were misty.

"Yours won't come short of a hundred thousand, my boy," said old Jolyon; "I thought you'd better know. I haven't much longer to live at my age. I shan't allude to it again. How's your wife? And—give her my love."

Young Jolyon put his hand on his father's shoulder, and, as neither spoke, the episode closed.

Having seen his father into a hansom, young Jolyon came back to the drawing-room and stood, where old Jolyon had stood, looking down on the little garden. He tried to realize all that this meant to him, and, Forsyte that he was, vistas of property were opened out in his brain; the years of half rations through which he had passed had not sapped his natural instincts. In extremely practical form, he thought of travel, of his wife's costume, the children's education, a pony for Jolly, a thousand things; but in the midst of all he thought, too, of Bosinney and his mistress, and the broken song of the thrush. Joy—tragedy! Which? Which?

The old past—the poignant, suffering, passionate, wonderful past, that no money could buy, that nothing could restore in all its burning sweetness—had come back before him.

When his wife came in he went straight up to her and took her in his arms; and for a long time he stood without speaking, his eyes closed, pressing her to him, while she looked at him with a wondering, adoring, doubting look in her eyes.

CHAPTER IV—VOYAGE INTO THE INFERNO

The morning after a certain night on which Soames at last asserted his rights and acted like a man, he breakfasted alone.

He breakfasted by gaslight, the fog of late November wrapping the town as in some monstrous blanket till the trees of the Square even were barely visible from the dining-room window.

He ate steadily, but at times a sensation as though he could not swallow attacked him. Had he been right to yield to his overmastering hunger of the night before, and break down the resistance which he had suffered now too long from this woman who was his lawful and solemnly constituted helpmate?

He was strangely haunted by the recollection of her face, from before which, to soothe her, he had tried to pull her hands—of her terrible smothered sobbing, the like of which he had never heard, and still seemed to hear; and he was still haunted by the odd, intolerable feeling of remorse and shame he had felt, as he stood looking at her by the flame of the single candle, before silently slinking away.

And somehow, now that he had acted like this, he was surprised at himself.

Two nights before, at Winifred Dartie's, he had taken Mrs. MacAnder into dinner. She had said to him, looking in his face with her sharp, greenish eyes: "And so your wife is a great friend of that Mr. Bosinney's?"

Not deigning to ask what she meant, he had brooded over her words.

They had roused in him a fierce jealousy, which, with the peculiar perversion of this instinct, had turned to fiercer desire.

Without the incentive of Mrs. MacAnder's words he might never have done what he had done. Without their incentive and the accident of finding his wife's door for once unlocked, which had enabled him to steal upon her asleep.

Slumber had removed his doubts, but the morning brought them again. One thought comforted him: No one would know—it was not the sort of thing that she would speak about.

And, indeed, when the vehicle of his daily business life, which needed so imperatively the grease of clear and practical thought, started rolling once more with the reading of his letters, those nightmare-like doubts began to assume less extravagant importance at the back of his mind. The incident was really not of great moment; women made a fuss about it in books; but in the cool judgment of right-thinking men, of men of the world, of such as he recollected often received praise in the Divorce Court, he had but done his best to sustain the sanctity of marriage, to prevent her from abandoning her duty, possibly, if she were still seeing Bosinney, from....

No, he did not regret it.

Now that the first step towards reconciliation had been taken, the rest would be comparatively—comparatively....

He, rose and walked to the window. His nerve had been shaken. The sound of smothered sobbing was in his ears again. He could not get rid of it.

He put on his fur coat, and went out into the fog; having to go into the City, he took the underground railway from Sloane Square station.

In his corner of the first-class compartment filled with City men the smothered sobbing still haunted him, so he opened the Times with the rich crackle that drowns all lesser sounds, and, barricaded behind it, set himself steadily to con the news.

He read that a Recorder had charged a grand jury on the previous day with a more than usually long list of offences. He read of three murders, five manslaughters, seven arsons, and as many as eleven rapes—a surprisingly high number—in addition to many less conspicuous crimes, to be tried during a coming Sessions; and from one piece of news he went on to another, keeping the paper well before his face.

And still, inseparable from his reading, was the memory of Irene's tear-stained face, and the sounds from her broken heart.

The day was a busy one, including, in addition to the ordinary affairs of his practice, a visit to his brokers, Messrs. Grin and Grinning, to give them instructions to sell his shares in the New Colliery Co., Ltd., whose business he suspected, rather than knew, was stagnating (this enterprise afterwards slowly declined, and was ultimately sold for a song to an American syndicate); and a long conference at Waterbuck, Q.C.'s chambers, attended by Boulter, by Fiske, the junior counsel, and Waterbuck, Q.C., himself.

The case of Forsyte v. Bosinney was expected to be reached on the morrow, before Mr. Justice Bentham.

Mr. Justice Bentham, a man of common-sense rather than too great legal knowledge, was considered to be about the best man they could have to try the action. He was a 'strong' Judge.

Waterbuck, Q.C., in pleasing conjunction with an almost rude neglect of Boulter and Fiske paid to Soames a good deal of attention, by instinct or the sounder evidence of rumour, feeling him to be a man of property.

He held with remarkable consistency to the opinion he had already expressed in writing, that the issue would depend to a great extent on the evidence given at the trial, and in a few well directed remarks he advised Soames not to be too careful in giving that evidence. "A little bluffness, Mr. Forsyte," he said, "a little bluffness," and after he had spoken he laughed firmly, closed his lips tight, and scratched his head just below where he had pushed his wig back, for all the world like the gentleman-farmer for whom he loved to be taken. He was considered perhaps the leading man in breach of promise cases.

Soames used the underground again in going home.

The fog was worse than ever at Sloane Square station. Through the still, thick blur, men groped in and out; women, very few, grasped their reticules to their bosoms and handkerchiefs to their mouths; crowned with the weird excrescence of the driver, haloed by a vague glow of lamp-light that seemed to drown in vapour before it reached the pavement, cabs loomed dim-shaped ever and again, and discharged citizens, bolting like rabbits to their burrows.

And these shadowy figures, wrapped each in his own little shroud of fog, took no notice of each other. In the great warren, each rabbit for himself, especially those clothed in the more expensive fur, who, afraid of carriages on foggy days, are driven underground.

One figure, however, not far from Soames, waited at the station door.

Some buccaneer or lover, of whom each Forsyte thought: 'Poor devil! looks as if he were having a bad time!' Their kind hearts beat a stroke faster for that poor, waiting, anxious lover in the fog; but they hurried by, well knowing that they had neither time nor money to spare for any suffering but their own.

Only a policeman, patrolling slowly and at intervals, took an interest in that waiting figure, the brim of whose slouch hat half hid a face reddened by the cold, all thin, and haggard, over which a hand stole now and again to smooth away anxiety, or renew the resolution that kept him waiting there. But the waiting lover (if lover he were) was used to policemen's scrutiny, or too absorbed in his anxiety, for he never flinched. A hardened case, accustomed to long trysts, to anxiety, and fog, and cold, if only his mistress came at last. Foolish lover! Fogs last until the spring; there is also snow and rain, no comfort anywhere; gnawing fear if you bring her out, gnawing fear if you bid her stay at home!

"Serve him right; he should arrange his affairs better!"

So any respectable Forsyte. Yet, if that sounder citizen could have listened at the waiting lover's heart, out there in the fog and the cold, he would have said again: "Yes, poor devil he's having a bad time!"

Soames got into his cab, and, with the glass down, crept along Sloane Street, and so along the Brompton Road, and home. He reached his house at five.

His wife was not in. She had gone out a quarter of an hour before. Out at such a time of night, into this terrible fog! What was the meaning of that?

He sat by the dining-room fire, with the door open, disturbed to the soul, trying to read the evening paper. A book was no good—in daily papers alone was any narcotic to such worry as his. From the customary events recorded in the journal he drew some comfort. 'Suicide of an actress'—'Grave indisposition of a Statesman' (that chronic sufferer)—'Divorce of an army officer'—'Fire in a colliery'—he read them all. They helped him a little—prescribed by the greatest of all doctors, our natural taste.

It was nearly seven when he heard her come in.

The incident of the night before had long lost its importance under stress of anxiety at her strange sortie into the fog. But now that Irene was home, the memory of her broken-hearted sobbing came back to him, and he felt nervous at the thought of facing her.

She was already on the stairs; her grey fur coat hung to her knees, its high collar almost hid her face, she wore a thick veil.

She neither turned to look at him nor spoke. No ghost or stranger could have passed more silently.

Bilson came to lay dinner, and told him that Mrs. Forsyte was not coming down; she was having the soup in her room.

For once Soames did not 'change'; it was, perhaps, the first time in his life that he had sat down to dinner with soiled cuffs, and, not even noticing them, he brooded long over his wine. He sent Bilson to light a fire in his picture-room, and presently went up there himself.

Turning on the gas, he heaved a deep sigh, as though amongst these treasures, the backs of which confronted him in stacks, around the little room, he had found at length his peace of mind. He went straight up to the greatest treasure of them all, an undoubted Turner, and, carrying it to the easel, turned its face to the light. There had been a movement in Turners, but he had not been able to make up his mind to part with it. He stood for a long time, his pale, clean-shaven face poked forward above his stand-up collar, looking at the picture as though he were adding it up; a wistful expression came into his eyes; he found, perhaps, that it came to too little. He took it down from the easel to put it back against the wall; but, in crossing the room, stopped, for he seemed to hear sobbing.

It was nothing—only the sort of thing that had been bothering him in the morning. And soon after, putting the high guard before the blazing fire, he stole downstairs.

Fresh for the morrow! was his thought. It was long before he went to sleep....

It is now to George Forsyte that the mind must turn for light on the events of that fog-engulfed afternoon.

The wittiest and most sportsmanlike of the Forsytes had passed the day reading a novel in the paternal mansion at Princes' Gardens. Since a recent crisis in his financial affairs he had been kept on parole by Roger, and compelled to reside 'at home.'

Towards five o'clock he went out, and took train at South Kensington Station (for everyone to-day went Underground). His intention was to dine, and pass the evening playing billiards at the Red Pottle—that unique hostel, neither club, hotel, nor good gilt restaurant.

He got out at Charing Cross, choosing it in preference to his more usual St. James's Park, that he might reach Jermyn Street by better lighted ways.

On the platform his eyes—for in combination with a composed and fashionable appearance, George had sharp eyes, and was always on the look-out for fillips to his sardonic humour—his eyes were attracted by a man, who, leaping from a first-class compartment, staggered rather than walked towards the exit.

'So ho, my bird!' said George to himself; 'why, it's "the Buccaneer!"' and he put his big figure on the trail. Nothing afforded him greater amusement than a drunken man.

Bosinney, who wore a slouch hat, stopped in front of him, spun around, and rushed back towards the carriage he had just left. He was too late. A porter caught him by the coat; the train was already moving on.

George's practised glance caught sight of the face of a lady clad in a grey fur coat at the carriage window. It was Mrs. Soames—and George felt that this was interesting!

And now he followed Bosinney more closely than ever—up the stairs, past the ticket collector into the street. In that progress, however, his feelings underwent a change; no longer merely curious and amused, he felt sorry for the poor fellow he was shadowing. 'The Buccaneer' was not drunk, but seemed to be acting under the stress of violent emotion; he was talking to himself, and all that George could catch were the words "Oh, God!" Nor did he appear to know what he was doing, or where going; but stared, hesitated, moved like a man out of his mind; and from being merely a joker in search of amusement, George felt that he must see the poor chap through.

He had 'taken the knock'—'taken the knock!' And he wondered what on earth Mrs. Soames had been saying, what on earth she had been telling him in the railway carriage. She had looked bad enough herself! It made George sorry to think of her travelling on with her trouble all alone.

He followed close behind Bosinney's elbow—tall, burly figure, saying nothing, dodging warily—and shadowed him out into the fog.

There was something here beyond a jest! He kept his head admirably, in spite of some excitement, for in addition to compassion, the instincts of the chase were roused within him.

Bosinney walked right out into the thoroughfare—a vast muffled blackness, where a man could not see six paces before him; where, all around, voices or whistles mocked the sense of direction; and sudden shapes came rolling slow upon them; and now and then a light showed like a dim island in an infinite dark sea.

And fast into this perilous gulf of night walked Bosinney, and fast after him walked George. If the fellow meant to put his 'twopenny' under a 'bus, he would stop it if he could! Across the street and back the hunted creature strode, not groping as other men were groping in that gloom, but driven forward as though the faithful George behind wielded a knout; and this chase after a haunted man began to have for George the strangest fascination.

But it was now that the affair developed in a way which ever afterwards caused it to remain green in his mind. Brought to a stand-still in the fog, he heard words which threw a sudden light on these proceedings. What Mrs. Soames had said to Bosinney in the train was now no longer dark. George understood from those mutterings that Soames had exercised his rights over an estranged and unwilling wife in the greatest—the supreme act of property.

His fancy wandered in the fields of this situation; it impressed him; he guessed something of the anguish, the sexual confusion and horror in Bosinney's heart. And he thought: 'Yes, it's a bit thick! I don't wonder the poor fellow is half-cracked!'

He had run his quarry to earth on a bench under one of the lions in Trafalgar Square, a monster sphynx astray like themselves in that gulf of darkness. Here, rigid and silent, sat Bosinney, and George, in whose patience was a touch of strange brotherliness, took his stand behind. He was not lacking in a certain delicacy—a sense of form—that did not permit him to intrude upon this tragedy, and he waited, quiet as the lion above, his fur collar hitched above his ears concealing the fleshy redness of his cheeks, concealing all but his eyes with their sardonic, compassionate stare. And men kept passing back from business on the way to their clubs—men whose figures shrouded in cocoons of fog came into view like spectres, and like spectres vanished. Then even in his compassion George's Quilpish humour broke forth in a sudden longing to pluck these spectres by the sleeve, and say:

"Hi, you Johnnies! You don't often see a show like this! Here's a poor devil whose mistress has just been telling him a pretty little story of her husband; walk up, walk up! He's taken the knock, you see."

In fancy he saw them gaping round the tortured lover; and grinned as he thought of some respectable, newly-married spectre enabled by the state of his own affections to catch an inkling of what was going on within Bosinney; he fancied he could see his mouth getting wider and wider, and the fog going down and down. For in George was all that contempt of the middle-class—especially of the married middle-class—peculiar to the wild and sportsmanlike spirits in its ranks.

But he began to be bored. Waiting was not what he had bargained for.

'After all,' he thought, 'the poor chap will get over it; not the first time such a thing has happened in this little city!' But now his quarry again began muttering words of violent hate and anger. And following a sudden impulse George touched him on the shoulder.

Bosinney spun round.

"Who are you? What do you want?"

George could have stood it well enough in the light of the gas lamps, in the light of that everyday world of which he was so hardy a connoisseur; but in this fog, where all was gloomy and unreal, where nothing had that matter-of-fact value associated by Forsytes with earth, he was a victim to strange qualms, and as he tried to stare back into the eyes of this maniac, he thought:

'If I see a bobby, I'll hand him over; he's not fit to be at large.'

But waiting for no answer, Bosinney strode off into the fog, and George followed, keeping perhaps a little further off, yet more than ever set on tracking him down.

'He can't go on long like this,' he thought. 'It's God's own miracle he's not been run over already.' He brooded no more on policemen, a sportsman's sacred fire alive again within him.

Into a denser gloom than ever Bosinney held on at a furious pace; but his pursuer perceived more method in his madness—he was clearly making his way westwards.

'He's really going for Soames!' thought George. The idea was attractive. It would be a sporting end to such a chase. He had always disliked his cousin.

The shaft of a passing cab brushed against his shoulder and made him leap aside. He did not intend to be killed for the Buccaneer, or anyone. Yet, with hereditary tenacity, he stuck to the trail through vapour that blotted out everything but the shadow of the hunted man and the dim moon of the nearest lamp.

Then suddenly, with the instinct of a town-stroller, George knew himself to be in Piccadilly. Here he could find his way blindfold; and freed from the strain of geographical uncertainty, his mind returned to Bosinney's trouble.

Down the long avenue of his man-about-town experience, bursting, as it were, through a smirch of doubtful amours, there stalked to him a memory of his youth. A memory, poignant still, that brought the scent of hay, the gleam of moonlight, a summer magic, into the reek and blackness of this London fog—the memory of a night when in the darkest shadow of a lawn he had overheard from a woman's lips that he was not her sole possessor. And for a moment George walked no longer in black Piccadilly, but lay again, with hell in his heart, and his face to the sweet-smelling, dewy grass, in the long shadow of poplars that hid the moon.

A longing seized him to throw his arm round the Buccaneer, and say, "Come, old boy. Time cures all. Let's go and drink it off!"

But a voice yelled at him, and he started back. A cab rolled out of blackness, and into blackness disappeared. And suddenly George perceived that he had lost Bosinney. He ran forward and back, felt his heart clutched by a sickening fear, the dark fear which lives in the wings of the fog. Perspiration started out on his brow. He stood quite still, listening with all his might.

"And then," as he confided to Dartie the same evening in the course of a game of billiards at the Red Pottle, "I lost him."

Dartie twirled complacently at his dark moustache. He had just put together a neat break of twenty-three,—failing at a 'Jenny.' "And who was she?" he asked.

George looked slowly at the 'man of the world's' fattish, sallow face, and a little grim smile lurked about the curves of his cheeks and his heavy-lidded eyes.

'No, no, my fine fellow,' he thought, 'I'm not going to tell you.' For though he mixed with Dartie a good deal, he thought him a bit of a cad.

"Oh, some little love-lady or other," he said, and chalked his cue.

"A love-lady!" exclaimed Dartie—he used a more figurative expression. "I made sure it was our friend Soa...."

"Did you?" said George curtly. "Then damme you've made an error."

He missed his shot. He was careful not to allude to the subject again till, towards eleven o'clock, having, in his poetic phraseology, 'looked upon the drink when it was yellow,' he drew aside the blind, and gazed out into the street. The murky blackness of the fog was but faintly broken by the lamps of the 'Red Pottle,' and no shape of mortal man or thing was in sight.

"I can't help thinking of that poor Buccaneer," he said. "He may be wandering out there now in that fog. If he's not a corpse," he added with strange dejection.

"Corpse!" said Dartie, in whom the recollection of his defeat at Richmond flared up. "He's all right. Ten to one if he wasn't tight!"

George turned on him, looking really formidable, with a sort of savage gloom on his big face.

"Dry up!" he said. "Don't I tell you he's 'taken the knock!'"

CHAPTER V—THE TRIAL

In the morning of his case, which was second in the list, Soames was again obliged to start without seeing Irene, and it was just as well, for he had not as yet made up his mind what attitude to adopt towards her.

He had been requested to be in court by half-past ten, to provide against the event of the first action (a breach of promise) collapsing, which however it did not, both sides showing a courage that afforded Waterbuck, Q.C., an opportunity for improving his already great reputation in this class of case. He was opposed by Ram, the other celebrated breach of promise man. It was a battle of giants.

The court delivered judgment just before the luncheon interval. The jury left the box for good, and Soames went out to get something to eat. He met James standing at the little luncheon-bar, like a pelican in the wilderness of the galleries, bent over a sandwich with a glass of sherry before him. The spacious emptiness of the great central hall, over which father and son brooded as they stood together, was marred now and then for a fleeting moment by barristers in wig and gown hurriedly bolting across, by an occasional old lady or rusty-coated man, looking up in a frightened way, and by two persons, bolder than their generation, seated in an embrasure arguing. The sound of their voices arose, together with a scent as of neglected wells, which, mingling with the odour of the galleries, combined to form the savour, like nothing but the emanation of a refined cheese, so indissolubly connected with the administration of British Justice.

It was not long before James addressed his son.

"When's your case coming on? I suppose it'll be on directly. I shouldn't wonder if this Bosinney'd say anything; I should think he'd have to. He'll go bankrupt if it goes against him." He took a large bite at his sandwich and a mouthful of sherry. "Your mother," he said, "wants you and Irene to come and dine to-night."

A chill smile played round Soames' lips; he looked back at his father. Anyone who had seen the look, cold and furtive, thus interchanged, might have been pardoned for not appreciating the real understanding between them. James finished his sherry at a draught.

"How much?" he asked.

On returning to the court Soames took at once his rightful seat on the front bench beside his solicitor. He ascertained where his father was seated with a glance so sidelong as to commit nobody.

James, sitting back with his hands clasped over the handle of his umbrella, was brooding on the end of the bench immediately behind counsel, whence he could get away at once when the case was over. He considered Bosinney's conduct in every way outrageous, but he did not wish to run up against him, feeling that the meeting would be awkward.

Next to the Divorce Court, this court was, perhaps, the favourite emporium of justice, libel, breach of promise, and other commercial actions being frequently decided there. Quite a sprinkling of persons unconnected with the law occupied the back benches, and the hat of a woman or two could be seen in the gallery.

The two rows of seats immediately in front of James were gradually filled by barristers in wigs, who sat down to make pencil notes, chat, and attend to their teeth; but his interest was soon diverted from these lesser lights of justice by the entrance of Waterbuck, Q.C., with the wings of his silk gown rustling, and his red, capable face supported by two short, brown whiskers. The famous Q.C. looked, as James freely admitted, the very picture of a man who could heckle a witness.

For all his experience, it so happened that he had never seen Waterbuck, Q.C., before, and, like many Forsytes in the lower branch of the profession, he had an extreme admiration for a good cross-examiner. The long, lugubrious folds in his cheeks relaxed somewhat after seeing him, especially as he now perceived that Soames alone was represented by silk.

Waterbuck, Q.C., had barely screwed round on his elbow to chat with his Junior before Mr. Justice Bentham himself appeared—a thin, rather hen-like man, with a little stoop, clean-shaven under his snowy wig. Like all the rest of the court, Waterbuck rose, and remained on his feet until the judge was seated. James rose but slightly; he was already comfortable, and had no opinion of Bentham, having sat next but one to him at dinner twice at the Bumley Tomms'. Bumley Tomm was rather a poor thing, though he had been so successful. James himself had given him his first brief. He was excited, too, for he had just found out that Bosinney was not in court.

'Now, what's he mean by that?' he kept on thinking.

The case having been called on, Waterbuck, Q.C., pushing back his papers, hitched his gown on his shoulder, and, with a semi-circular look around him, like a man who is going to bat, arose and addressed the Court.

The facts, he said, were not in dispute, and all that his Lordship would be asked was to interpret the correspondence which had taken place between his client and the defendant, an architect, with reference to the decoration of a house. He would, however, submit that this correspondence could only mean one very plain thing. After briefly reciting the history of the house at Robin Hill, which he described as a mansion, and the actual facts of expenditure, he went on as follows:

"My client, Mr. Soames Forsyte, is a gentleman, a man of property, who would be the last to dispute any legitimate claim that might be made against him, but he has met with such treatment from his architect in the matter of this house, over which he has, as your lordship has heard, already spent some twelve—some twelve thousand pounds, a sum considerably in advance of the amount he had originally contemplated, that as a matter of principle—and this I cannot too strongly emphasize—as a matter of principle, and in the interests of others, he has felt himself compelled to bring this action. The point put forward in defence by the architect I will suggest to your lordship is not worthy of a moment's serious consideration." He then read the correspondence.

His client, "a man of recognised position," was prepared to go into the box, and to swear that he never did authorize, that it was never in his mind to authorize, the expenditure of any money beyond the extreme limit of twelve thousand and fifty pounds, which he had clearly fixed; and not further to waste the time of the court, he would at once call Mr. Forsyte.

Soames then went into the box. His whole appearance was striking in its composure. His face, just supercilious enough, pale and clean-shaven, with a little line between the eyes, and compressed lips; his dress in unostentatious order, one hand neatly gloved, the other bare. He answered the questions put to him in a somewhat low, but distinct voice. His evidence under cross-examination savoured of taciturnity.

Had he not used the expression, "a free hand"? No.

"Come, come!"

The expression he had used was 'a free hand in the terms of this correspondence.'

"Would you tell the Court that that was English?"

"Yes!"

"What do you say it means?"

"What it says!"

"Are you prepared to deny that it is a contradiction in terms?"

"Yes."

"You are not an Irishman?"

"No."

"Are you a well-educated man?"

"Yes."

"And yet you persist in that statement?"

"Yes."

Throughout this and much more cross-examination, which turned again and again around the 'nice point,' James sat with his hand behind his ear, his eyes fixed upon his son.

He was proud of him! He could not but feel that in similar circumstances he himself would have been tempted to enlarge his replies, but his instinct told him that this taciturnity was the very thing. He sighed with relief, however, when Soames, slowly turning, and without any change of expression, descended from the box.

When it came to the turn of Bosinney's Counsel to address the Judge, James redoubled his attention, and he searched the Court again and again to see if Bosinney were not somewhere concealed.

Young Chankery began nervously; he was placed by Bosinney's absence in an awkward position. He therefore did his best to turn that absence to account.

He could not but fear—he said—that his client had met with an accident. He had fully expected him there to give evidence; they had sent round that morning both to Mr. Bosinney's office and to his rooms (though he knew they were one and the same, he thought it was as well not to say so), but it was not known where he was, and this he considered to be ominous, knowing how anxious Mr. Bosinney had been to give his evidence. He had not, however, been instructed to apply for an adjournment, and in default of such instruction he conceived it his duty to go on. The plea on which he somewhat confidently relied, and which his client, had he not unfortunately been prevented in some way from attending, would have supported by his evidence, was that such an expression as a 'free hand' could not be limited, fettered, and rendered unmeaning, by any verbiage which might follow it. He would go further and say that the correspondence showed that whatever he might have said in his evidence, Mr. Forsyte had in fact never contemplated repudiating liability on any of the work ordered or executed by his architect. The defendant had certainly never contemplated such a contingency, or, as was demonstrated by his letters, he would never have proceeded with the work—a work of extreme delicacy, carried out with great care and efficiency, to meet and satisfy the fastidious taste of a connoisseur, a rich man, a man of property. He felt strongly on this point, and feeling strongly he used, perhaps, rather strong words when he said that this action was of a most unjustifiable, unexpected, indeed—unprecedented character. If his Lordship had had the opportunity that he himself had made it his duty to take, to go over this very fine house and see the great delicacy and beauty of the decorations executed by his client—an artist in his most honourable profession—he felt convinced that not for one moment would his Lordship tolerate this, he would use no stronger word than daring attempt to evade legitimate responsibility.

Taking the text of Soames' letters, he lightly touched on 'Boileau v. The Blasted Cement Company, Limited.' "It is doubtful," he said, "what that authority has decided; in any case I would submit that it is just as much in my favour as in my friend's." He then argued the 'nice point' closely. With all due deference he submitted that Mr. Forsyte's expression nullified itself. His client not being a rich man, the matter was a serious one for him; he was a very talented architect, whose professional reputation was undoubtedly somewhat at stake. He concluded with a perhaps too personal appeal to the Judge, as a lover of the arts, to show himself the protector of artists, from what was occasionally—he said occasionally—the too iron hand of capital. "What," he said, "will be the position of the artistic professions, if men of property like this Mr. Forsyte refuse, and are allowed to refuse, to carry out the obligations of the commissions which they have given." He would now call his client, in case he should at the last moment have found himself able to be present.

The name Philip Baynes Bosinney was called three times by the Ushers, and the sound of the calling echoed with strange melancholy throughout the Court and Galleries.

The crying of this name, to which no answer was returned, had upon James a curious effect: it was like calling for your lost dog about the streets. And the creepy feeling that it gave him, of a man missing, grated on his sense of comfort and security-on his cosiness. Though he could not have said why, it made him feel uneasy.

He looked now at the clock—a quarter to three! It would be all over in a quarter of an hour. Where could the young fellow be?

It was only when Mr. Justice Bentham delivered judgment that he got over the turn he had received.

Behind the wooden erection, by which he was fenced from more ordinary mortals, the learned Judge leaned forward. The electric light, just turned on above his head, fell on his face, and mellowed it to an orange hue beneath the snowy crown of his wig; the amplitude of his robes grew before the eye; his whole figure, facing the comparative dusk of the Court, radiated like some majestic and sacred body. He cleared his throat, took a sip of water, broke the nib of a quill against the desk, and, folding his bony hands before him, began.

To James he suddenly loomed much larger than he had ever thought Bentham would loom. It was the majesty of the law; and a person endowed with a nature far less matter-of-fact than that of James might have been excused for failing to pierce this halo, and disinter therefrom the somewhat ordinary Forsyte, who walked and talked in every-day life under the name of Sir Walter Bentham.

He delivered judgment in the following words:

"The facts in this case are not in dispute. On May 15 last the defendant wrote to the plaintiff, requesting to be allowed to withdraw from his professional position in regard to the decoration of the plaintiff's house, unless he were given 'a free hand.' The plaintiff, on May 17, wrote back as follows: 'In giving you, in accordance with your request, this free hand, I wish you to clearly understand that the total cost of the house as handed over to me completely decorated, inclusive of your fee (as arranged between us) must not exceed twelve thousand pounds.' To this letter the defendant replied on May 18: 'If you think that in such a delicate matter as decoration I can bind myself to the exact pound, I am afraid you are mistaken.' On May 19 the plaintiff wrote as follows: 'I did not mean to say that if you should exceed the sum named in my letter to you by ten or twenty or even fifty pounds there would be any difficulty between us. You have a free hand in the terms of this correspondence, and I hope you will see your way to completing the decorations.' On May 20 the defendant replied thus shortly: 'Very well.'

"In completing these decorations, the defendant incurred liabilities and expenses which brought the total cost of this house up to the sum of twelve thousand four hundred pounds, all of which expenditure has been defrayed by the plaintiff. This action has been brought by the plaintiff to recover from the defendant the sum of three hundred and fifty pounds expended by him in excess of a sum of twelve thousand and fifty pounds, alleged by the plaintiff to have been fixed by this correspondence as the maximum sum that the defendant had authority to expend.

"The question for me to decide is whether or no the defendant is liable to refund to the plaintiff this sum. In my judgment he is so liable.

"What in effect the plaintiff has said is this 'I give you a free hand to complete these decorations, provided that you keep within a total cost to me of twelve thousand pounds. If you exceed that sum by as much as fifty pounds, I will not hold you responsible; beyond that point you are no agent of mine, and I shall repudiate liability.' It is not quite clear to me whether, had the plaintiff in fact repudiated liability under his agent's contracts, he would, under all the circumstances, have been successful in so doing; but he has not adopted this course. He has accepted liability, and fallen back upon his rights against the defendant under the terms of the latter's engagement.

"In my judgment the plaintiff is entitled to recover this sum from the defendant.

"It has been sought, on behalf of the defendant, to show that no limit of expenditure was fixed or intended to be fixed by this correspondence. If this were so, I can find no reason for the plaintiff's importation into the correspondence of the figures of twelve thousand pounds and subsequently of fifty pounds. The defendant's contention would render these figures meaningless. It is manifest to me that by his letter of May 20 he assented to a very clear proposition, by the terms of which he must be held to be bound.

"For these reasons there will be judgment for the plaintiff for the amount claimed with costs."

James sighed, and stooping, picked up his umbrella which had fallen with a rattle at the words 'importation into this correspondence.'

Untangling his legs, he rapidly left the Court; without waiting for his son, he snapped up a hansom cab (it was a clear, grey afternoon) and drove straight to Timothy's where he found Swithin; and to him, Mrs. Septimus Small, and Aunt Hester, he recounted the whole proceedings, eating two muffins not altogether in the intervals of speech.

"Soames did very well," he ended; "he's got his head screwed on the right way. This won't please Jolyon. It's a bad business for that young Bosinney; he'll go bankrupt, I shouldn't wonder," and then after a long pause, during which he had stared disquietly into the fire, he added:

"He wasn't there—now why?"

There was a sound of footsteps. The figure of a thick-set man, with the ruddy brown face of robust health, was seen in the back drawing-room. The forefinger of his upraised hand was outlined against the black of his frock coat. He spoke in a grudging voice.

"Well, James," he said, "I can't—I can't stop," and turning round, he walked out.

It was Timothy.

James rose from his chair. "There!" he said, "there! I knew there was something wro...." He checked himself, and was silent, staring before him, as though he had seen a portent.

CHAPTER VI—SOAMES BREAKS THE NEWS

In leaving the Court Soames did not go straight home. He felt disinclined for the City, and drawn by need for sympathy in his triumph, he, too, made his way, but slowly and on foot, to Timothy's in the Bayswater Road.

His father had just left; Mrs. Small and Aunt Hester, in possession of the whole story, greeted him warmly. They were sure he was hungry after all that evidence. Smither should toast him some more muffins, his dear father had eaten them all. He must put his legs up on the sofa; and he must have a glass of prune brandy too. It was so strengthening.

Swithin was still present, having lingered later than his wont, for he felt in want of exercise. On hearing this suggestion, he 'pished.' A pretty pass young men were coming to! His own liver was out of order, and he could not bear the thought of anyone else drinking prune brandy.

He went away almost immediately, saying to Soames: "And how's your wife? You tell her from me that if she's dull, and likes to come and dine with me quietly, I'll give her such a bottle of champagne as she doesn't get every day." Staring down from his height on Soames he contracted his thick, puffy, yellow hand as though squeezing within it all this small fry, and throwing out his chest he waddled slowly away.

Mrs. Small and Aunt Hester were left horrified. Swithin was so droll!

They themselves were longing to ask Soames how Irene would take the result, yet knew that they must not; he would perhaps say something of his own accord, to throw some light on this, the present burning question in their lives, the question that from necessity of silence tortured them almost beyond bearing; for even Timothy had now been told, and the effect on his health was little short of alarming. And what, too, would June do? This, also, was a most exciting, if dangerous speculation!

They had never forgotten old Jolyon's visit, since when he had not once been to see them; they had never forgotten the feeling it gave all who were present, that the family was no longer what it had been—that the family was breaking up.

But Soames gave them no help, sitting with his knees crossed, talking of the Barbizon school of painters, whom he had just discovered. These were the coming men, he said; he should not wonder if a lot of money were made over them; he had his eye on two pictures by a man called Corot, charming things; if he could get them at a reasonable price he was going to buy them—they would, he thought, fetch a big price some day.

Interested as they could not but be, neither Mrs. Septimus Small nor Aunt Hester could entirely acquiesce in being thus put off.

It was interesting—most interesting—and then Soames was so clever that they were sure he would do something with those pictures if anybody could; but what was his plan now that he had won his case; was he going to leave London at once, and live in the country, or what was he going to do?

Soames answered that he did not know, he thought they should be moving soon. He rose and kissed his aunts.

No sooner had Aunt Juley received this emblem of departure than a change came over her, as though she were being visited by dreadful courage; every little roll of flesh on her face seemed trying to escape from an invisible, confining mask.

She rose to the full extent of her more than medium height, and said: "It has been on my mind a long time, dear, and if nobody else will tell you, I have made up my mind that...."

Aunt Hester interrupted her: "Mind, Julia, you do it...." she gasped—"on your own responsibility!"

Mrs. Small went on as though she had not heard: "I think you ought to know, dear, that Mrs. MacAnder saw Irene walking in Richmond Park with Mr. Bosinney."

Aunt Hester, who had also risen, sank back in her chair, and turned her face away. Really Juley was too—she should not do such things when she—Aunt Hester, was in the room; and, breathless with anticipation, she waited for what Soames would answer.

He had flushed the peculiar flush which always centred between his eyes; lifting his hand, and, as it were, selecting a finger, he bit a nail delicately; then, drawling it out between set lips, he said: "Mrs. MacAnder is a cat!"

Without waiting for any reply, he left the room.

When he went into Timothy's he had made up his mind what course to pursue on getting home. He would go up to Irene and say:

"Well, I've won my case, and there's an end of it! I don't want to be hard on Bosinney; I'll see if we can't come to some arrangement; he shan't be pressed. And now let's turn over a new leaf! We'll let the house, and get out of these fogs. We'll go down to Robin Hill at once. I—I never meant to be rough with you! Let's shake hands—and—" Perhaps she would let him kiss her, and forget!

When he came out of Timothy's his intentions were no longer so simple. The smouldering jealousy and suspicion of months blazed up within him. He would put an end to that sort of thing once and for all; he would not have her drag his name in the dirt! If she could not or would not love him, as was her duty and his right—she should not play him tricks with anyone else! He would tax her with it; threaten to divorce her! That would make her behave; she would never face that. But—but—what if she did? He was staggered; this had not occurred to him.

What if she did? What if she made him a confession? How would he stand then? He would have to bring a divorce!

A divorce! Thus close, the word was paralyzing, so utterly at variance with all the principles that had hitherto guided his life. Its lack of compromise appalled him; he felt—like the captain of a ship, going to the side of his vessel, and, with his own hands throwing over the most precious of his bales. This jettisoning of his property with his own hand seemed uncanny to Soames. It would injure him in his profession: He would have to get rid of the house at Robin Hill, on which he had spent so much money, so much anticipation—and at a sacrifice. And she! She would no longer belong to him, not even in name! She would pass out of his life, and he—he should never see her again!

He traversed in the cab the length of a street without getting beyond the thought that he should never see her again!

But perhaps there was nothing to confess, even now very likely there was nothing to confess. Was it wise to push things so far? Was it wise to put himself into a position where he might have to eat his words? The result of this case would ruin Bosinney; a ruined man was desperate, but—what could he do? He might go abroad, ruined men always went abroad. What could they do—if indeed it was 'they'—without money? It would be better to wait and see how things turned out. If necessary, he could have her watched. The agony of his jealousy (for all the world like the crisis of an aching tooth) came on again; and he almost cried out. But he must decide, fix on some course of action before he got home. When the cab drew up at the door, he had decided nothing.

He entered, pale, his hands moist with perspiration, dreading to meet her, burning to meet her, ignorant of what he was to say or do.

The maid Bilson was in the hall, and in answer to his question: "Where is your mistress?" told him that Mrs. Forsyte had left the house about noon, taking with her a trunk and bag.

Snatching the sleeve of his fur coat away from her grasp, he confronted her:

"What?" he exclaimed; "what's that you said?" Suddenly recollecting that he must not betray emotion, he added: "What message did she leave?" and noticed with secret terror the startled look of the maid's eyes.

"Mrs. Forsyte left no message, sir."

"No message; very well, thank you, that will do. I shall be dining out."

The maid went downstairs, leaving him still in his fur coat, idly turning over the visiting cards in the porcelain bowl that stood on the carved oak rug chest in the hall.

Mr. and Mrs. Bareham Culcher. Mrs. Septimus Small. Mrs. Baynes. Mr. Solomon Thornworthy. Lady Bellis. Miss Hermione Bellis. Miss Winifred Bellis. Miss Ella Bellis.

Who the devil were all these people? He seemed to have forgotten all familiar things. The words 'no message—a trunk, and a bag,' played a hide-and-seek in his brain. It was incredible that she had left no message, and, still in his fur coat, he ran upstairs two steps at a time, as a young married man when he comes home will run up to his wife's room.

Everything was dainty, fresh, sweet-smelling; everything in perfect order. On the great bed with its lilac silk quilt, was the bag she had made and embroidered with her own hands to hold her sleeping things; her slippers ready at the foot; the sheets even turned over at the head as though expecting her.

On the table stood the silver-mounted brushes and bottles from her dressing bag, his own present. There must, then, be some mistake. What bag had she taken? He went to the bell to summon Bilson, but remembered in time that he must assume knowledge of where Irene had gone, take it all as a matter of course, and grope out the meaning for himself.

He locked the doors, and tried to think, but felt his brain going round; and suddenly tears forced themselves into his eyes.

Hurriedly pulling off his coat, he looked at himself in the mirror.

He was too pale, a greyish tinge all over his face; he poured out water, and began feverishly washing.

Her silver-mounted brushes smelt faintly of the perfumed lotion she used for her hair; and at this scent the burning sickness of his jealousy seized him again.

Struggling into his fur, he ran downstairs and out into the street.

He had not lost all command of himself, however, and as he went down Sloane Street he framed a story for use, in case he should not find her at Bosinney's. But if he should? His power of decision again failed; he reached the house without knowing what he should do if he did find her there.

It was after office hours, and the street door was closed; the woman who opened it could not say whether Mr. Bosinney were in or no; she had not seen him that day, not for two or three days; she did not attend to him now, nobody attended to him, he....

Soames interrupted her, he would go up and see for himself. He went up with a dogged, white face.

The top floor was unlighted, the door closed, no one answered his ringing, he could hear no sound. He was obliged to descend, shivering under his fur, a chill at his heart. Hailing a cab, he told the man to drive to Park Lane.

On the way he tried to recollect when he had last given her a cheque; she could not have more than three or four pounds, but there were her jewels; and with exquisite torture he remembered how much money she could raise on these; enough to take them abroad; enough for them to live on for months! He tried to calculate; the cab stopped, and he got out with the calculation unmade.

The butler asked whether Mrs. Soames was in the cab, the master had told him they were both expected to dinner.

Soames answered: "No. Mrs. Forsyte has a cold."

The butler was sorry.

Soames thought he was looking at him inquisitively, and remembering that he was not in dress clothes, asked: "Anybody here to dinner, Warmson?"

"Nobody but Mr. and Mrs. Dartie, sir."

Again it seemed to Soames that the butler was looking curiously at him. His composure gave way.

"What are you looking at?" he said. "What's the matter with me, eh?"

The butler blushed, hung up the fur coat, murmured something that sounded like: "Nothing, sir, I'm sure, sir," and stealthily withdrew.

Soames walked upstairs. Passing the drawing-room without a look, he went straight up to his mother's and father's bedroom.

James, standing sideways, the concave lines of his tall, lean figure displayed to advantage in shirt-sleeves and evening waistcoat, his head bent, the end of his white tie peeping askew from underneath one white Dundreary whisker, his eyes peering with intense concentration, his lips pouting, was hooking the top hooks of his wife's bodice. Soames stopped; he felt half-choked, whether because he had come upstairs too fast, or for some other reason. He—he himself had never—never been asked to....

He heard his father's voice, as though there were a pin in his mouth, saying: "Who's that? Who's there? What d'you want?" His mother's: "Here, Felice, come and hook this; your master'll never get done."

He put his hand up to his throat, and said hoarsely:

"It's I—Soames!"

He noticed gratefully the affectionate surprise in Emily's: "Well, my dear boy?" and James', as he dropped the hook: "What, Soames! What's brought you up? Aren't you well?"

He answered mechanically: "I'm all right," and looked at them, and it seemed impossible to bring out his news.

James, quick to take alarm, began: "You don't look well. I expect you've taken a chill—it's liver, I shouldn't wonder. Your mother'll give you...."

But Emily broke in quietly: "Have you brought Irene?"

Soames shook his head.

"No," he stammered, "she—she's left me!"

Emily deserted the mirror before which she was standing. Her tall, full figure lost its majesty and became very human as she came running over to Soames.

"My dear boy! My dear boy!"

She put her lips to his forehead, and stroked his hand.

James, too, had turned full towards his son; his face looked older.

"Left you?" he said. "What d'you mean—left you? You never told me she was going to leave you."

Soames answered surlily: "How could I tell? What's to be done?"

James began walking up and down; he looked strange and stork-like without a coat. "What's to be done!" he muttered. "How should I know what's to be done? What's the good of asking me? Nobody tells me anything, and then they come and ask me what's to be done; and I should like to know how I'm to tell them! Here's your mother, there she stands; she doesn't say anything. What I should say you've got to do is to follow her.."

Soames smiled; his peculiar, supercilious smile had never before looked pitiable.

"I don't know where she's gone," he said.

"Don't know where she's gone!" said James. "How d'you mean, don't know where she's gone? Where d'you suppose she's gone? She's gone after that young Bosinney, that's where she's gone. I knew how it would be."

Soames, in the long silence that followed, felt his mother pressing his hand. And all that passed seemed to pass as though his own power of thinking or doing had gone to sleep.

177

His father's face, dusky red, twitching as if he were going to cry, and words breaking out that seemed rent from him by some spasm in his soul.

"There'll be a scandal; I always said so." Then, no one saying anything: "And there you stand, you and your mother!"

And Emily's voice, calm, rather contemptuous: "Come, now, James! Soames will do all that he can."

And James, staring at the floor, a little brokenly: "Well, I can't help you; I'm getting old. Don't you be in too great a hurry, my boy."

And his mother's voice again: "Soames will do all he can to get her back. We won't talk of it. It'll all come right, I dare say."

And James: "Well, I can't see how it can come right. And if she hasn't gone off with that young Bosinney, my advice to you is not to listen to her, but to follow her and get her back."

Once more Soames felt his mother stroking his hand, in token of her approval, and as though repeating some form of sacred oath, he muttered between his teeth: "I will!"

All three went down to the drawing-room together. There, were gathered the three girls and Dartie; had Irene been present, the family circle would have been complete.

James sank into his armchair, and except for a word of cold greeting to Dartie, whom he both despised and dreaded, as a man likely to be always in want of money, he said nothing till dinner was announced. Soames, too, was silent; Emily alone, a woman of cool courage, maintained a conversation with Winifred on trivial subjects. She was never more composed in her manner and conversation than that evening.

A decision having been come to not to speak of Irene's flight, no view was expressed by any other member of the family as to the right course to be pursued; there can be little doubt, from the general tone adopted in relation to events as they afterwards turned out, that James's advice: "Don't you listen to her, follow her and get her back!" would, with here and there an exception, have been regarded as sound, not only in Park Lane, but amongst the Nicholases, the Rogers, and at Timothy's. Just as it would surely have been endorsed by that wider body of Forsytes all over London, who were merely excluded from judgment by ignorance of the story.

In spite then of Emily's efforts, the dinner was served by Warmson and the footman almost in silence. Dartie was sulky, and drank all he could get; the girls seldom talked to each other at any time. James asked once where June was, and what she was doing with herself in these days. No one could tell him. He sank back into gloom. Only when Winifred recounted how little Publius had given his bad penny to a beggar, did he brighten up.

"Ah!" he said, "that's a clever little chap. I don't know what'll become of him, if he goes on like this. An intelligent little chap, I call him!" But it was only a flash.

The courses succeeded one another solemnly, under the electric light, which glared down onto the table, but barely reached the principal ornament of the walls, a so-called 'Sea Piece by Turner,' almost entirely composed of cordage and drowning men.

Champagne was handed, and then a bottle of James' prehistoric port, but as by the chill hand of some skeleton.

At ten o'clock Soames left; twice in reply to questions, he had said that Irene was not well; he felt he could no longer trust himself. His mother kissed him with her large soft kiss, and he pressed her hand, a flush of warmth in his cheeks. He walked away in the cold wind, which whistled desolately round the corners of the streets, under a sky of clear steel-blue, alive with stars; he noticed neither their frosty greeting, nor the crackle of the curled-up plane-leaves, nor the night-women hurrying in their shabby furs, nor the pinched faces of vagabonds at street corners. Winter was come! But Soames hastened home, oblivious; his hands trembled as he took the late letters from the gilt wire cage into which they had been thrust through the slit in the door.'

None from Irene!

He went into the dining-room; the fire was bright there, his chair drawn up to it, slippers ready, spirit case, and carven cigarette box on the table; but after staring at it all for a minute or two, he turned out the light and went upstairs. There was a fire too in his dressing-room, but her room was dark and cold. It was into this room that Soames went.

He made a great illumination with candles, and for a long time continued pacing up and down between the bed and the door. He could not get used to the thought that she had really left him, and as though still searching for some message, some reason, some reading of all the mystery of his married life, he began opening every recess and drawer.

There were her dresses; he had always liked, indeed insisted, that she should be well-dressed—she had taken very few; two or three at most, and drawer after drawer; full of linen and silk things, was untouched.

Perhaps after all it was only a freak, and she had gone to the seaside for a few days' change. If only that were so, and she were really coming back, he would never again do as he had done that fatal night before last, never again run that risk—though it was her duty, her duty as a wife; though she did belong to him—he would never again run that risk; she was evidently not quite right in her head!

He stooped over the drawer where she kept her jewels; it was not locked, and came open as he pulled; the jewel box had the key in it. This surprised him until he remembered that it was sure to be empty. He opened it.

It was far from empty. Divided, in little green velvet compartments, were all the things he had given her, even her watch, and stuck into the recess that contained the watch was a three-cornered note addressed 'Soames Forsyte,' in Irene's handwriting:

'I think I have taken nothing that you or your people have given me.' And that was all.

He looked at the clasps and bracelets of diamonds and pearls, at the little flat gold watch with a great diamond set in sapphires, at the chains and rings, each in its nest, and the tears rushed up in his eyes and dropped upon them.

Nothing that she could have done, nothing that she had done, brought home to him like this the inner significance of her act. For the moment, perhaps, he understood nearly all there was to understand—understood that she loathed him, that she had loathed him for years, that for all intents and purposes they were like people living in different worlds, that there was no hope for him, never had been; even, that she had suffered—that she was to be pitied.

In that moment of emotion he betrayed the Forsyte in him—forgot himself, his interests, his property—was capable of almost anything; was lifted into the pure ether of the selfless and unpractical.

Such moments pass quickly.

And as though with the tears he had purged himself of weakness, he got up, locked the box, and slowly, almost trembling, carried it with him into the other room.

CHAPTER VII—JUNE'S VICTORY

June had waited for her chance, scanning the duller columns of the journals, morning and evening with an assiduity which at first puzzled old Jolyon; and when her chance came, she took it with all the promptitude and resolute tenacity of her character.

She will always remember best in her life that morning when at last she saw amongst the reliable Cause List of the Times newspaper, under the heading of Court XIII, Mr. Justice Bentham, the case of Forsyte v. Bosinney.

Like a gambler who stakes his last piece of money, she had prepared to hazard her all upon this throw; it was not her nature to contemplate defeat. How, unless with the instinct of a woman in love, she knew that Bosinney's discomfiture in this action was assured, cannot be told—on this assumption, however, she laid her plans, as upon a certainty.

Half past eleven found her at watch in the gallery of Court XIII., and there she remained till the case of Forsyte v. Bosinney was over. Bosinney's absence did not disquiet her; she had felt instinctively that he would not defend himself. At the end of the judgment she hastened down, and took a cab to his rooms.

She passed the open street-door and the offices on the three lower floors without attracting notice; not till she reached the top did her difficulties begin.

Her ring was not answered; she had now to make up her mind whether she would go down and ask the caretaker in the basement to let her in to await Mr. Bosinney's return, or remain patiently outside the door, trusting that no one would come up. She decided on the latter course.

A quarter of an hour had passed in freezing vigil on the landing, before it occurred to her that Bosinney had been used to leave the key of his rooms under the door-mat. She looked and found it there. For some minutes she could not decide to make use of it; at last she let herself in and left the door open that anyone who came might see she was there on business.

This was not the same June who had paid the trembling visit five months ago; those months of suffering and restraint had made her less sensitive; she had dwelt on this visit so long, with such minuteness, that its terrors were discounted beforehand. She was not there to fail this time, for if she failed no one could help her.

Like some mother beast on the watch over her young, her little quick figure never stood still in that room, but wandered from wall to wall, from window to door, fingering now one thing, now another. There was dust everywhere, the room could not have been cleaned for weeks, and June, quick to catch at anything that should buoy up her hope, saw in it a sign that he had been obliged, for economy's sake, to give up his servant.

She looked into the bedroom; the bed was roughly made, as though by the hand of man. Listening intently, she darted in, and peered into his cupboards. A few shirts and collars, a pair of muddy boots—the room was bare even of garments.

She stole back to the sitting-room, and now she noticed the absence of all the little things he had set store by. The clock that had been his mother's, the field-glasses that had hung over the sofa; two really valuable old prints of Harrow, where his father had been at school, and last, not least, the piece of Japanese pottery she herself had given him. All were gone;

and in spite of the rage roused within her championing soul at the thought that the world should treat him thus, their disappearance augured happily for the success of her plan.

It was while looking at the spot where the piece of Japanese pottery had stood that she felt a strange certainty of being watched, and, turning, saw Irene in the open doorway.

The two stood gazing at each other for a minute in silence; then June walked forward and held out her hand. Irene did not take it.

When her hand was refused, June put it behind her. Her eyes grew steady with anger; she waited for Irene to speak; and thus waiting, took in, with who-knows-what rage of jealousy, suspicion, and curiosity, every detail of her friend's face and dress and figure.

Irene was clothed in her long grey fur; the travelling cap on her head left a wave of gold hair visible above her forehead. The soft fullness of the coat made her face as small as a child's.

Unlike June's cheeks, her cheeks had no colour in them, but were ivory white and pinched as if with cold. Dark circles lay round her eyes. In one hand she held a bunch of violets.

She looked back at June, no smile on her lips; and with those great dark eyes fastened on her, the girl, for all her startled anger, felt something of the old spell.

She spoke first, after all.

"What have you come for?" But the feeling that she herself was being asked the same question, made her add: "This horrible case. I came to tell him—he has lost it."

Irene did not speak, her eyes never moved from June's face, and the girl cried:

"Don't stand there as if you were made of stone!"

Irene laughed: "I wish to God I were!"

But June turned away: "Stop!" she cried, "don't tell me! I don't want to hear! I don't want to hear what you've come for. I don't want to hear!" And like some uneasy spirit, she began swiftly walking to and fro. Suddenly she broke out:

"I was here first. We can't both stay here together!"

On Irene's face a smile wandered up, and died out like a flicker of firelight. She did not move. And then it was that June perceived under the softness and immobility of this figure something desperate and resolved; something not to be turned away, something dangerous. She tore off her hat, and, putting both hands to her brow, pressed back the bronze mass of her hair.

"You have no right here!" she cried defiantly.

Irene answered: "I have no right anywhere!

"What do you mean?"

"I have left Soames. You always wanted me to!"

June put her hands over her ears.

"Don't! I don't want to hear anything—I don't want to know anything. It's impossible to fight with you! What makes you stand like that? Why don't you go?"

Irene's lips moved; she seemed to be saying: "Where should I go?"

June turned to the window. She could see the face of a clock down in the street. It was nearly four. At any moment he might come! She looked back across her shoulder, and her face was distorted with anger.

181

But Irene had not moved; in her gloved hands she ceaselessly turned and twisted the little bunch of violets.

The tears of rage and disappointment rolled down June's cheeks.

"How could you come?" she said. "You have been a false friend to me!"

Again Irene laughed. June saw that she had played a wrong card, and broke down.

"Why have you come?" she sobbed. "You've ruined my life, and now you want to ruin his!"

Irene's mouth quivered; her eyes met June's with a look so mournful that the girl cried out in the midst of her sobbing, "No, no!"

But Irene's head bent till it touched her breast. She turned, and went quickly out, hiding her lips with the little bunch of violets.

June ran to the door. She heard the footsteps going down and down. She called out: "Come back, Irene! Come back!"

The footsteps died away....

Bewildered and torn, the girl stood at the top of the stairs. Why had Irene gone, leaving her mistress of the field? What did it mean? Had she really given him up to her? Or had she...? And she was the prey of a gnawing uncertainty.... Bosinney did not come....

About six o'clock that afternoon old Jolyon returned from Wistaria Avenue, where now almost every day he spent some hours, and asked if his grand-daughter were upstairs. On being told that she had just come in, he sent up to her room to request her to come down and speak to him.

He had made up his mind to tell her that he was reconciled with her father. In future bygones must be bygones. He would no longer live alone, or practically alone, in this great house; he was going to give it up, and take one in the country for his son, where they could all go and live together. If June did not like this, she could have an allowance and live by herself. It wouldn't make much difference to her, for it was a long time since she had shown him any affection.

But when June came down, her face was pinched and piteous; there was a strained, pathetic look in her eyes. She snuggled up in her old attitude on the arm of his chair, and what he said compared but poorly with the clear, authoritative, injured statement he had thought out with much care. His heart felt sore, as the great heart of a mother-bird feels sore when its youngling flies and bruises its wing. His words halted, as though he were apologizing for having at last deviated from the path of virtue, and succumbed, in defiance of sounder principles, to his more natural instincts.

He seemed nervous lest, in thus announcing his intentions, he should be setting his granddaughter a bad example; and now that he came to the point, his way of putting the suggestion that, if she didn't like it, she could live by herself and lump it, was delicate in the extreme.'

"And if, by any chance, my darling," he said, "you found you didn't get on—with them, why, I could make that all right. You could have what you liked. We could find a little flat in London where you could set up, and I could be running to continually. But the children," he added, "are dear little things!"

Then, in the midst of this grave, rather transparent, explanation of changed policy, his eyes twinkled. "This'll astonish Timothy's weak nerves. That precious young thing will have something to say about this, or I'm a Dutchman!"

June had not yet spoken. Perched thus on the arm of his chair, with her head above him, her face was invisible. But presently he felt her warm cheek against his own, and knew that, at all events, there was nothing very alarming in her attitude towards his news. He began to take courage.

"You'll like your father," he said—"an amiable chap. Never was much push about him, but easy to get on with. You'll find him artistic and all that."

And old Jolyon bethought him of the dozen or so water-colour drawings all carefully locked up in his bedroom; for now that his son was going to become a man of property he did not think them quite such poor things as heretofore.

"As to your—your stepmother," he said, using the word with some little difficulty, "I call her a refined woman—a bit of a Mrs. Gummidge, I shouldn't wonder—but very fond of Jo. And the children," he repeated—indeed, this sentence ran like music through all his solemn self-justification—"are sweet little things!"

If June had known, those words but reincarnated that tender love for little children, for the young and weak, which in the past had made him desert his son for her tiny self, and now, as the cycle rolled, was taking him from her.

But he began to get alarmed at her silence, and asked impatiently: "Well, what do you say?"

June slid down to his knee, and she in her turn began her tale. She thought it would all go splendidly; she did not see any difficulty, and she did not care a bit what people thought.

Old Jolyon wriggled. H'm! then people would think! He had thought that after all these years perhaps they wouldn't! Well, he couldn't help it! Nevertheless, he could not approve of his granddaughter's way of putting it—she ought to mind what people thought!

Yet he said nothing. His feelings were too mixed, too inconsistent for expression.

No—went on June—she did not care; what business was it of theirs? There was only one thing—and with her cheek pressing against his knee, old Jolyon knew at once that this something was no trifle: As he was going to buy a house in the country, would he not—to please her—buy that splendid house of Soames' at Robin Hill? It was finished, it was perfectly beautiful, and no one would live in it now. They would all be so happy there.

Old Jolyon was on the alert at once. Wasn't the 'man of property' going to live in his new house, then? He never alluded to Soames now but under this title.

"No"—June said—"he was not; she knew that he was not!"

How did she know?

She could not tell him, but she knew. She knew nearly for certain! It was most unlikely; circumstances had changed! Irene's words still rang in her head: "I have left Soames. Where should I go?"

But she kept silence about that.

If her grandfather would only buy it and settle that wretched claim that ought never to have been made on Phil! It would be the very best thing for everybody, and everything—everything might come straight.

And June put her lips to his forehead, and pressed them close.

But old Jolyon freed himself from her caress, his face wore the judicial look which came upon it when he dealt with affairs. He asked: What did she mean? There was something behind all this—had she been seeing Bosinney?

June answered: "No; but I have been to his rooms."

"Been to his rooms? Who took you there?"

June faced him steadily. "I went alone. He has lost that case. I don't care whether it was right or wrong. I want to help him; and I will!"

Old Jolyon asked again: "Have you seen him?" His glance seemed to pierce right through the girl's eyes into her soul.

Again June answered: "No; he was not there. I waited, but he did not come."

Old Jolyon made a movement of relief. She had risen and looked down at him; so slight, and light, and young, but so fixed, and so determined; and disturbed, vexed, as he was, he could not frown away that fixed look. The feeling of being beaten, of the reins having slipped, of being old and tired, mastered him.

"Ah!" he said at last, "you'll get yourself into a mess one of these days, I can see. You want your own way in everything."

Visited by one of his strange bursts of philosophy, he added: "Like that you were born; and like that you'll stay until you die!"

And he, who in his dealings with men of business, with Boards, with Forsytes of all descriptions, with such as were not Forsytes, had always had his own way, looked at his indomitable grandchild sadly—for he felt in her that quality which above all others he unconsciously admired.

"Do you know what they say is going on?" he said slowly.

June crimsoned.

"Yes—no! I know—and I don't know—I don't care!" and she stamped her foot.

"I believe," said old Jolyon, dropping his eyes, "that you'd have him if he were dead!"

There was a long silence before he spoke again.

"But as to buying this house—you don't know what you're talking about!"

June said that she did. She knew that he could get it if he wanted. He would only have to give what it cost.

"What it cost! You know nothing about it. I won't go to Soames—I'll have nothing more to do with that young man."

"But you needn't; you can go to Uncle James. If you can't buy the house, will you pay his lawsuit claim? I know he is terribly hard up—I've seen it. You can stop it out of my money!"

A twinkle came into old Jolyon's eyes.

"Stop it out of your money! A pretty way. And what will you do, pray, without your money?"

But secretly, the idea of wresting the house from James and his son had begun to take hold of him. He had heard on Forsyte 'Change much comment, much rather doubtful praise of this house. It was 'too artistic,' but a fine place. To take from the 'man of property' that on which he had set his heart, would be a crowning triumph over James, practical proof that he was going to make a man of property of Jo, to put him back in his proper position, and there to keep him secure. Justice once for all on those who had chosen to regard his son as a poor, penniless outcast.

He would see, he would see! It might be out of the question; he was not going to pay a fancy price, but if it could be done, why, perhaps he would do it!

And still more secretly he knew that he could not refuse her.

But he did not commit himself. He would think it over—he said to June.

CHAPTER VIII—BOSINNEY'S DEPARTURE

Old Jolyon was not given to hasty decisions; it is probable that he would have continued to think over the purchase of the house at Robin Hill, had not June's face told him that he would have no peace until he acted.

At breakfast next morning she asked him what time she should order the carriage.

"Carriage!" he said, with some appearance of innocence; "what for? I'm not going out!"

She answered: "If you don't go early, you won't catch Uncle James before he goes into the City."

"James! what about your Uncle James?"

"The house," she replied, in such a voice that he no longer pretended ignorance.

"I've not made up my mind," he said.

"You must! You must! Oh! Gran—think of me!"

Old Jolyon grumbled out: "Think of you—I'm always thinking of you, but you don't think of yourself; you don't think what you're letting yourself in for. Well, order the carriage at ten!"

At a quarter past he was placing his umbrella in the stand at Park Lane—he did not choose to relinquish his hat and coat; telling Warmson that he wanted to see his master, he went, without being announced, into the study, and sat down.

James was still in the dining-room talking to Soames, who had come round again before breakfast. On hearing who his visitor was, he muttered nervously: "Now, what's he want, I wonder?"

He then got up.

"Well," he said to Soames, "don't you go doing anything in a hurry. The first thing is to find out where she is—I should go to Stainer's about it; they're the best men, if they can't find her, nobody can." And suddenly moved to strange softness, he muttered to himself, "Poor little thing, I can't tell what she was thinking about!" and went out blowing his nose.

Old Jolyon did not rise on seeing his brother, but held out his hand, and exchanged with him the clasp of a Forsyte.

James took another chair by the table, and leaned his head on his hand.

"Well," he said, "how are you? We don't see much of you nowadays!"

Old Jolyon paid no attention to the remark.

"How's Emily?" he asked; and waiting for no reply, went on "I've come to see you about this affair of young Bosinney's. I'm told that new house of his is a white elephant."

"I don't know anything about a white elephant," said James, "I know he's lost his case, and I should say he'll go bankrupt."

Old Jolyon was not slow to seize the opportunity this gave him.

"I shouldn't wonder a bit!" he agreed; "and if he goes bankrupt, the 'man of property'— that is, Soames'll be out of pocket. Now, what I was thinking was this: If he's not going to live there...."

Seeing both surprise and suspicion in James' eye, he quickly went on: "I don't want to know anything; I suppose Irene's put her foot down—it's not material to me. But I'm thinking of a house in the country myself, not too far from London, and if it suited me I don't say that I mightn't look at it, at a price."

James listened to this statement with a strange mixture of doubt, suspicion, and relief, merging into a dread of something behind, and tinged with the remains of his old undoubted reliance upon his elder brother's good faith and judgment. There was anxiety, too, as to what old Jolyon could have heard and how he had heard it; and a sort of hopefulness arising from the thought that if June's connection with Bosinney were completely at an end, her grandfather would hardly seem anxious to help the young fellow. Altogether he was puzzled; as he did not like either to show this, or to commit himself in any way, he said:

"They tell me you're altering your Will in favour of your son."

He had not been told this; he had merely added the fact of having seen old Jolyon with his son and grandchildren to the fact that he had taken his Will away from Forsyte, Bustard and Forsyte. The shot went home.

"Who told you that?" asked old Jolyon.

"I'm sure I don't know," said James; "I can't remember names—I know somebody told me Soames spent a lot of money on this house; he's not likely to part with it except at a good price."

"Well," said old Jolyon, "if, he thinks I'm going to pay a fancy price, he's mistaken. I've not got the money to throw away that he seems to have. Let him try and sell it at a forced sale, and see what he'll get. It's not every man's house, I hear!"

James, who was secretly also of this opinion, answered: "It's a gentleman's house. Soames is here now if you'd like to see him."

"No," said old Jolyon, "I haven't got as far as that; and I'm not likely to, I can see that very well if I'm met in this manner!"

James was a little cowed; when it came to the actual figures of a commercial transaction he was sure of himself, for then he was dealing with facts, not with men; but preliminary negotiations such as these made him nervous—he never knew quite how far he could go.

"Well," he said, "I know nothing about it. Soames, he tells me nothing; I should think he'd entertain it—it's a question of price."

"Oh!" said old Jolyon, "don't let him make a favour of it!" He placed his hat on his head in dudgeon.

The door was opened and Soames came in.

"There's a policeman out here," he said with his half smile, "for Uncle Jolyon."

Old Jolyon looked at him angrily, and James said: "A policeman? I don't know anything about a policeman. But I suppose you know something about him," he added to old Jolyon with a look of suspicion: "I suppose you'd better see him!"

In the hall an Inspector of Police stood stolidly regarding with heavy-lidded pale-blue eyes the fine old English furniture picked up by James at the famous Mavrojano sale in Portman Square. "You'll find my brother in there," said James.

The Inspector raised his fingers respectfully to his peaked cap, and entered the study.

James saw him go in with a strange sensation.

"Well," he said to Soames, "I suppose we must wait and see what he wants. Your uncle's been here about the house!"

He returned with Soames into the dining-room, but could not rest.

"Now what does he want?" he murmured again.

"Who?" replied Soames: "the Inspector? They sent him round from Stanhope Gate, that's all I know. That 'nonconformist' of Uncle Jolyon's has been pilfering, I shouldn't wonder!"

But in spite of his calmness, he too was ill at ease.

At the end of ten minutes old Jolyon came in. He walked up to the table, and stood there perfectly silent pulling at his long white moustaches. James gazed up at him with opening mouth; he had never seen his brother look like this.

Old Jolyon raised his hand, and said slowly:

"Young Bosinney has been run over in the fog and killed."

Then standing above his brother and his nephew, and looking down at him with his deep eyes:

"There's—some—talk—of—suicide," he said.

James' jaw dropped. "Suicide! What should he do that for?"

Old Jolyon answered sternly: "God knows, if you and your son don't!"

But James did not reply.

For all men of great age, even for all Forsytes, life has had bitter experiences. The passer-by, who sees them wrapped in cloaks of custom, wealth, and comfort, would never suspect that such black shadows had fallen on their roads. To every man of great age—to Sir Walter Bentham himself—the idea of suicide has once at least been present in the ante-room of his soul; on the threshold, waiting to enter, held out from the inmost chamber by some chance reality, some vague fear, some painful hope. To Forsytes that final renunciation of property is hard. Oh! it is hard! Seldom—perhaps never—can they achieve, it; and yet, how near have they not sometimes been!

So even with James! Then in the medley of his thoughts, he broke out: "Why I saw it in the paper yesterday: 'Run over in the fog!' They didn't know his name!" He turned from one face to the other in his confusion of soul; but instinctively all the time he was rejecting that rumour of suicide. He dared not entertain this thought, so against his interest, against the interest of his son, of every Forsyte. He strove against it; and as his nature ever unconsciously rejected that which it could not with safety accept, so gradually he overcame this fear. It was an accident! It must have been!

Old Jolyon broke in on his reverie.

"Death was instantaneous. He lay all day yesterday at the hospital. There was nothing to tell them who he was. I am going there now; you and your son had better come too."

No one opposing this command he led the way from the room.

The day was still and clear and bright, and driving over to Park Lane from Stanhope Gate, old Jolyon had had the carriage open. Sitting back on the padded cushions, finishing his cigar, he had noticed with pleasure the keen crispness of the air, the bustle of the cabs and people; the strange, almost Parisian, alacrity that the first fine day will bring into London streets after a spell of fog or rain. And he had felt so happy; he had not felt like it for months. His confession to June was off his mind; he had the prospect of his son's, above all, of his grandchildren's company in the future—(he had appointed to meet young Jolyon at the Hotch Potch that very manning to—discuss it again); and there was the pleasurable excitement of a coming encounter, a coming victory, over James and the 'man of property' in the matter of the house.

He had the carriage closed now; he had no heart to look on gaiety; nor was it right that Forsytes should be seen driving with an Inspector of Police.

In that carriage the Inspector spoke again of the death:

"It was not so very thick—Just there. The driver says the gentleman must have had time to see what he was about, he seemed to walk right into it. It appears that he was very hard up, we found several pawn tickets at his rooms, his account at the bank is overdrawn, and there's this case in to-day's papers;" his cold blue eyes travelled from one to another of the three Forsytes in the carriage.

Old Jolyon watching from his corner saw his brother's face change, and the brooding, worried, look deepen on it. At the Inspector's words, indeed, all James' doubts and fears revived. Hard-up—pawn-tickets—an overdrawn account! These words that had all his life been a far-off nightmare to him, seemed to make uncannily real that suspicion of suicide which must on no account be entertained. He sought his son's eye; but lynx-eyed, taciturn, immovable, Soames gave no answering look. And to old Jolyon watching, divining the league of mutual defence between them, there came an overmastering desire to have his own son at his side, as though this visit to the dead man's body was a battle in which otherwise he must single-handed meet those two. And the thought of how to keep June's name out of the business kept whirring in his brain. James had his son to support him! Why should he not send for Jo?

Taking out his card-case, he pencilled the following message:

'Come round at once. I've sent the carriage for you.'

On getting out he gave this card to his coachman, telling him to drive—as fast as possible to the Hotch Potch Club, and if Mr. Jolyon Forsyte were there to give him the card and bring him at once. If not there yet, he was to wait till he came.

He followed the others slowly up the steps, leaning on his umbrella, and stood a moment to get his breath. The Inspector said: "This is the mortuary, sir. But take your time."

In the bare, white-walled room, empty of all but a streak of sunshine smeared along the dustless floor, lay a form covered by a sheet. With a huge steady hand the Inspector took the hem and turned it back. A sightless face gazed up at them, and on either side of that sightless defiant face the three Forsytes gazed down; in each one of them the secret emotions, fears, and pity of his own nature rose and fell like the rising, falling waves of life, whose wash those white walls barred out now for ever from Bosinney. And in each one of them the trend of his nature, the odd essential spring, which moved him in fashions minutely, unalterably different from those of every other human being, forced him to a different attitude of thought. Far from the others, yet inscrutably close, each stood thus, alone with death, silent, his eyes lowered.

The Inspector asked softly:

"You identify the gentleman, sir?"

Old Jolyon raised his head and nodded. He looked at his brother opposite, at that long lean figure brooding over the dead man, with face dusky red, and strained grey eyes; and at the figure of Soames white and still by his father's side. And all that he had felt against those two was gone like smoke in the long white presence of Death. Whence comes it, how comes it—Death? Sudden reverse of all that goes before; blind setting forth on a path that leads to where? Dark quenching of the fire! The heavy, brutal crushing—out that all men must go through, keeping their eyes clear and brave unto the end! Small and of no import, insects though they are! And across old Jolyon's face there flitted a gleam, for Soames, murmuring to the Inspector, crept noiselessly away.

Then suddenly James raised his eyes. There was a queer appeal in that suspicious troubled look: "I know I'm no match for you," it seemed to say. And, hunting for handkerchief he wiped his brow; then, bending sorrowful and lank over the dead man, he too turned and hurried out.

Old Jolyon stood, still as death, his eyes fixed on the body. Who shall tell of what he was thinking? Of himself, when his hair was brown like the hair of that young fellow dead before him? Of himself, with his battle just beginning, the long, long battle he had loved; the battle that was over for this young man almost before it had begun? Of his grand-daughter, with her broken hopes? Of that other woman? Of the strangeness, and the pity of it? And the irony, inscrutable, and bitter of that end? Justice! There was no justice for men, for they were ever in the dark!

Or perhaps in his philosophy he thought: Better to be out of, it all! Better to have done with it, like this poor youth....

Some one touched him on the arm.

A tear started up and wetted his eyelash. "Well," he said, "I'm no good here. I'd better be going. You'll come to me as soon as you can, Jo," and with his head bowed he went away.

It was young Jolyon's turn to take his stand beside the dead man, round whose fallen body he seemed to see all the Forsytes breathless, and prostrated. The stroke had fallen too swiftly.

The forces underlying every tragedy—forces that take no denial, working through cross currents to their ironical end, had met and fused with a thunder-clap, flung out the victim, and flattened to the ground all those that stood around.

Or so at all events young Jolyon seemed to see them, lying around Bosinney's body.

He asked the Inspector to tell him what had happened, and the latter, like a man who does not every day get such a chance, again detailed such facts as were known.

"There's more here, sir, however," he said, "than meets the eye. I don't believe in suicide, nor in pure accident, myself. It's more likely I think that he was suffering under great stress of mind, and took no notice of things about him. Perhaps you can throw some light on these."

He took from his pocket a little packet and laid it on the table. Carefully undoing it, he revealed a lady's handkerchief, pinned through the folds with a pin of discoloured Venetian gold, the stone of which had fallen from the socket. A scent of dried violets rose to young Jolyon's nostrils.

"Found in his breast pocket," said the Inspector; "the name has been cut away!"

Young Jolyon with difficulty answered: "I'm afraid I cannot help you!" But vividly there rose before him the face he had seen light up, so tremulous and glad, at Bosinney's coming! Of her he thought more than of his own daughter, more than of them all—of her with the dark, soft glance, the delicate passive face, waiting for the dead man, waiting even at that moment, perhaps, still and patient in the sunlight.

He walked sorrowfully away from the hospital towards his father's house, reflecting that this death would break up the Forsyte family. The stroke had indeed slipped past their defences into the very wood of their tree. They might flourish to all appearance as before, preserving a brave show before the eyes of London, but the trunk was dead, withered by the same flash that had stricken down Bosinney. And now the saplings would take its place, each one a new custodian of the sense of property.

Good forest of Forsytes! thought young Jolyon—soundest timber of our land!

Concerning the cause of this death—his family would doubtless reject with vigour the suspicion of suicide, which was so compromising! They would take it as an accident, a stroke of fate. In their hearts they would even feel it an intervention of Providence, a retribution—had not Bosinney endangered their two most priceless possessions, the pocket and the hearth? And they would talk of 'that unfortunate accident of young Bosinney's,' but perhaps they would not talk—silence might be better!

As for himself, he regarded the bus-driver's account of the accident as of very little value. For no one so madly in love committed suicide for want of money; nor was Bosinney the sort of fellow to set much store by a financial crisis. And so he too, rejected this theory of suicide, the dead man's face rose too clearly before him. Gone in the heyday of his summer—and to believe thus that an accident had cut Bosinney off in the full sweep of his passion was more than ever pitiful to young Jolyon.

Then came a vision of Soames' home as it now was, and must be hereafter. The streak of lightning had flashed its clear uncanny gleam on bare bones with grinning spaces between, the disguising flesh was gone....

In the dining-room at Stanhope Gate old Jolyon was sitting alone when his son came in. He looked very wan in his great armchair. And his eyes travelling round the walls with their pictures of still life, and the masterpiece 'Dutch fishing-boats at Sunset' seemed as though passing their gaze over his life with its hopes, its gains, its achievements.

"Ah! Jo!" he said, "is that you? I've told poor little June. But that's not all of it. Are you going to Soames'? She's brought it on herself, I suppose; but somehow I can't bear to think of her, shut up there—and all alone." And holding up his thin, veined hand, he clenched it.

CHAPTER IX—IRENE'S RETURN

After leaving James and old Jolyon in the mortuary of the hospital, Soames hurried aimlessly along the streets.

The tragic event of Bosinney's death altered the complexion of everything. There was no longer the same feeling that to lose a minute would be fatal, nor would he now risk communicating the fact of his wife's flight to anyone till the inquest was over.

That morning he had risen early, before the postman came, had taken the first-post letters from the box himself, and, though there had been none from Irene, he had made an opportunity of telling Bilson that her mistress was at the sea; he would probably, he said, be going down himself from Saturday to Monday. This had given him time to breathe, time to leave no stone unturned to find her.

But now, cut off from taking steps by Bosinney's death—that strange death, to think of which was like putting a hot iron to his heart, like lifting a great weight from it—he did not know how to pass his day; and he wandered here and there through the streets, looking at every face he met, devoured by a hundred anxieties.

And as he wandered, he thought of him who had finished his wandering, his prowling, and would never haunt his house again.

Already in the afternoon he passed posters announcing the identity of the dead man, and bought the papers to see what they said. He would stop their mouths if he could, and he went into the City, and was closeted with Boulter for a long time.

On his way home, passing the steps of Jobson's about half past four, he met George Forsyte, who held out an evening paper to Soames, saying:

"Here! Have you seen this about the poor Buccaneer?"

Soames answered stonily: "Yes."

George stared at him. He had never liked Soames; he now held him responsible for Bosinney's death. Soames had done for him—done for him by that act of property that had sent the Buccaneer to run amok that fatal afternoon.

'The poor fellow,' he was thinking, 'was so cracked with jealousy, so cracked for his vengeance, that he heard nothing of the omnibus in that infernal fog.'

Soames had done for him! And this judgment was in George's eyes.

"They talk of suicide here," he said at last. "That cat won't jump."

Soames shook his head. "An accident," he muttered.

Clenching his fist on the paper, George crammed it into his pocket. He could not resist a parting shot.

"H'mm! All flourishing at home? Any little Soameses yet?"

With a face as white as the steps of Jobson's, and a lip raised as if snarling, Soames brushed past him and was gone....

On reaching home, and entering the little lighted hall with his latchkey, the first thing that caught his eye was his wife's gold-mounted umbrella lying on the rug chest. Flinging off his fur coat, he hurried to the drawing-room.

The curtains were drawn for the night, a bright fire of cedar-logs burned in the grate, and by its light he saw Irene sitting in her usual corner on the sofa. He shut the door softly, and went towards her. She did not move, and did not seem to see him.

"So you've come back?" he said. "Why are you sitting here in the dark?"

Then he caught sight of her face, so white and motionless that it seemed as though the blood must have stopped flowing in her veins; and her eyes, that looked enormous, like the great, wide, startled brown eyes of an owl.

Huddled in her grey fur against the sofa cushions, she had a strange resemblance to a captive owl, bunched in its soft feathers against the wires of a cage. The supple erectness of her figure was gone, as though she had been broken by cruel exercise; as though there were no longer any reason for being beautiful, and supple, and erect.

"So you've come back," he repeated.

She never looked up, and never spoke, the firelight playing over her motionless figure.

Suddenly she tried to rise, but he prevented her; it was then that he understood.

She had come back like an animal wounded to death, not knowing where to turn, not knowing what she was doing. The sight of her figure, huddled in the fur, was enough.

He knew then for certain that Bosinney had been her lover; knew that she had seen the report of his death—perhaps, like himself, had bought a paper at the draughty corner of a street, and read it.

She had come back then of her own accord, to the cage she had pined to be free of—and taking in all the tremendous significance of this, he longed to cry: "Take your hated body, that I love, out of my house! Take away that pitiful white face, so cruel and soft—before I crush it. Get out of my sight; never let me see you again!"

And, at those unspoken words, he seemed to see her rise and move away, like a woman in a terrible dream, from which she was fighting to awake—rise and go out into the dark and cold, without a thought of him, without so much as the knowledge of his presence.

Then he cried, contradicting what he had not yet spoken, "No; stay there!" And turning away from her, he sat down in his accustomed chair on the other side of the hearth.

They sat in silence.

And Soames thought: 'Why is all this? Why should I suffer so? What have I done? It is not my fault!'

Again he looked at her, huddled like a bird that is shot and dying, whose poor breast you see panting as the air is taken from it, whose poor eyes look at you who have shot it, with a slow, soft, unseeing look, taking farewell of all that is good—of the sun, and the air, and its mate.

So they sat, by the firelight, in the silence, one on each side of the hearth.

And the fume of the burning cedar logs, that he loved so well, seemed to grip Soames by the throat till he could bear it no longer. And going out into the hall he flung the door wide, to gulp down the cold air that came in; then without hat or overcoat went out into the Square.

Along the garden rails a half-starved cat came rubbing her way towards him, and Soames thought: 'Suffering! when will it cease, my suffering?'

At a front door across the way was a man of his acquaintance named Rutter, scraping his boots, with an air of 'I am master here.' And Soames walked on.

From far in the clear air the bells of the church where he and Irene had been married were pealing in 'practice' for the advent of Christ, the chimes ringing out above the sound of traffic. He felt a craving for strong drink, to lull him to indifference, or rouse him to fury. If only he could burst out of himself, out of this web that for the first time in his life he felt around him. If only he could surrender to the thought: 'Divorce her—turn her out! She has forgotten you. Forget her!'

If only he could surrender to the thought: 'Let her go—she has suffered enough!'

If only he could surrender to the desire: 'Make a slave of her—she is in your power!'

If only even he could surrender to the sudden vision: 'What does it all matter?' Forget himself for a minute, forget that it mattered what he did, forget that whatever he did he must sacrifice something.

If only he could act on an impulse!

He could forget nothing; surrender to no thought, vision, or desire; it was all too serious; too close around him, an unbreakable cage.

On the far side of the Square newspaper boys were calling their evening wares, and the ghoulish cries mingled and jangled with the sound of those church bells.

Soames covered his ears. The thought flashed across him that but for a chance, he himself, and not Bosinney, might be lying dead, and she, instead of crouching there like a shot bird with those dying eyes....

Something soft touched his legs, the cat was rubbing herself against them. And a sob that shook him from head to foot burst from Soames' chest. Then all was still again in the dark, where the houses seemed to stare at him, each with a master and mistress of its own, and a secret story of happiness or sorrow.

And suddenly he saw that his own door was open, and black against the light from the hall a man standing with his back turned. Something slid too in his breast, and he stole up close behind.

He could see his own fur coat flung across the carved oak chair; the Persian rugs; the silver bowls, the rows of porcelain plates arranged along the walls, and this unknown man who was standing there.

And sharply he asked: "What is it you want, sir?"

The visitor turned. It was young Jolyon.

"The door was open," he said. "Might I see your wife for a minute, I have a message for her?"

Soames gave him a strange, sidelong stare.

"My wife can see no one," he muttered doggedly.

Young Jolyon answered gently: "I shouldn't keep her a minute."

Soames brushed by him and barred the way.

"She can see no one," he said again.

Young Jolyon's glance shot past him into the hall, and Soames turned. There in the drawing-room doorway stood Irene, her eyes were wild and eager, her lips were parted, her hands outstretched. In the sight of both men that light vanished from her face; her hands dropped to her sides; she stood like stone.

Soames spun round, and met his visitor's eyes, and at the look he saw in them, a sound like a snarl escaped him. He drew his lips back in the ghost of a smile.

"This is my house," he said; "I manage my own affairs. I've told you once—I tell you again; we are not at home."

And in young Jolyon's face he slammed the door.

THE FORSYTE SAGA

VOLUME II

INDIAN SUMMER OF A FORSYTE
IN CHANCERY

BY

JOHN GALSWORTHY

NEW YORK
CHARLES SCRIBNER'S SONS
MCMXXII

Wingstone. Manaton

THE FORSYTE SAGA—VOLUME II

By John Galsworthy

TO ANDRE CHEVRILLON

INTERLUDE. INDIAN SUMMER OF A FORSYTE

"And Summer's lease hath all

too short a date."

—Shakespeare

I

In the last day of May in the early 'nineties, about six o'clock of the evening, old Jolyon Forsyte sat under the oak tree below the terrace of his house at Robin Hill. He was waiting for the midges to bite him, before abandoning the glory of the afternoon. His thin brown hand, where blue veins stood out, held the end of a cigar in its tapering, long-nailed fingers—a pointed polished nail had survived with him from those earlier Victorian days when to touch nothing, even with the tips of the fingers, had been so distinguished. His domed forehead, great white moustache, lean cheeks, and long lean jaw were covered from the westering sunshine by an old brown Panama hat. His legs were crossed; in all his attitude was serenity and a kind of elegance, as of an old man who every morning put eau de Cologne upon his silk handkerchief. At his feet lay a woolly brown-and-white dog trying to be a Pomeranian—the dog Balthasar between whom and old Jolyon primal aversion had changed into attachment with the years. Close to his chair was a swing, and on the swing was seated one of Holly's dolls—called 'Duffer Alice'—with her body fallen over her legs and her doleful nose buried in a black petticoat. She was never out of disgrace, so it did not matter to her how she sat. Below the oak tree the lawn dipped down a bank, stretched to the fernery, and, beyond that refinement, became fields, dropping to the pond, the coppice, and the prospect—'Fine, remarkable'—at which Swithin Forsyte, from under this very tree, had stared five years ago when he drove down with Irene to look at the house. Old Jolyon had heard of his brother's exploit—that drive which had become quite celebrated on Forsyte 'Change. Swithin! And the fellow had gone and died, last November, at the age of only seventy-nine, renewing the doubt whether Forsytes could live for ever, which had first arisen when Aunt Ann passed away. Died! and left only Jolyon and James, Roger and Nicholas and Timothy, Julia, Hester, Susan! And old Jolyon thought: 'Eighty-five! I don't feel it—except when I get that pain.'

His memory went searching. He had not felt his age since he had bought his nephew Soames' ill-starred house and settled into it here at Robin Hill over three years ago. It was as if he had been getting younger every spring, living in the country with his son and his grandchildren—June, and the little ones of the second marriage, Jolly and Holly; living down here out of the racket of London and the cackle of Forsyte 'Change,' free of his boards, in a delicious atmosphere of no work and all play, with plenty of occupation in the perfecting and mellowing of the house and its twenty acres, and in ministering to the whims of Holly and Jolly. All the knots and crankiness, which had gathered in his heart during that long and tragic business of June, Soames, Irene his wife, and poor young Bosinney, had been smoothed out. Even June had thrown off her melancholy at last—witness this travel in Spain she was taking now with her father and her stepmother. Curiously perfect peace was left by their departure; blissful, yet blank, because his son was not there. Jo was never anything but a comfort and a pleasure to him nowadays—an amiable chap; but women, somehow—even the best—got a little on one's nerves, unless of course one admired them.

Far-off a cuckoo called; a wood-pigeon was cooing from the first elm-tree in the field, and how the daisies and buttercups had sprung up after the last mowing! The wind had got into the sou' west, too—a delicious air, sappy! He pushed his hat back and let the sun fall on his chin and cheek. Somehow, to-day, he wanted company—wanted a pretty face to look at. People treated the old as if they wanted nothing. And with the un-Forsytean philosophy which ever intruded on his soul, he thought: 'One's never had enough. With a foot in the grave one'll want something, I shouldn't be surprised!' Down here—away from the exigencies of affairs—his grandchildren, and the flowers, trees, birds of his little domain, to say nothing of sun and moon and stars above them, said, 'Open, sesame,' to him day and night. And sesame had opened—how much, perhaps, he did not know. He had always been responsive to what they had begun to call 'Nature,' genuinely, almost religiously responsive, though he had never lost his habit of calling a sunset a sunset and a view a view, however deeply they might move him. But nowadays Nature actually made him ache, he appreciated it so. Every one of these calm, bright, lengthening days, with Holly's hand in his, and the dog Balthasar in front looking studiously for what he never found, he would stroll, watching the roses open, fruit budding on the walls, sunlight brightening the oak leaves and saplings in the coppice, watching the water-lily leaves unfold and glisten, and the silvery young corn of the one wheat field; listening to the starlings and skylarks, and the Alderney cows chewing the cud, flicking slow their tufted tails; and every one of these fine days he ached a little from sheer love of it all, feeling perhaps, deep down, that he had not very much longer to enjoy it. The thought that some day—perhaps not ten years hence, perhaps not five—all this world would be taken away from him, before he had exhausted his powers of loving it, seemed to him in the nature of an injustice brooding over his horizon. If anything came after this life, it wouldn't be what he wanted; not Robin Hill, and flowers and birds and pretty faces—too few, even now, of those about him! With the years his dislike of humbug had increased; the orthodoxy he had worn in the 'sixties, as he had worn side-whiskers out of sheer exuberance, had long dropped off, leaving him reverent before three things alone—beauty, upright conduct, and the sense of property; and the greatest of these now was beauty. He had always had wide interests, and, indeed could still read The Times, but he was liable at any moment to put it down if he heard a blackbird sing. Upright conduct, property—somehow, they were tiring; the blackbirds and the sunsets never tired him, only gave him an uneasy feeling that he could not get enough of them. Staring into the stilly radiance of the early evening and at the little gold and white flowers on the lawn, a thought came to him: This weather was like the music of 'Orfeo,' which he had recently heard at Covent Garden. A beautiful opera, not like Meyerbeer, nor even quite Mozart, but, in its way, perhaps even more lovely; something classical and of the Golden Age about it, chaste and mellow, and the Ravogli 'almost worthy of the old days'—highest praise he could bestow. The yearning of Orpheus for the beauty he was losing, for his love going down to Hades, as in life love and beauty did go—the yearning which sang and throbbed through the golden music, stirred also in the lingering beauty of the world that evening. And with the tip of his cork-soled, elastic-sided boot he involuntarily stirred the ribs of the dog Balthasar, causing the animal to wake and attack his fleas; for though he was supposed to have none, nothing could persuade him of the fact. When he had finished he rubbed the place he had been scratching against his master's calf, and settled down again with his chin over the instep of the disturbing boot. And into old Jolyon's mind came a sudden recollection—a face he had seen at that opera three weeks ago—Irene, the wife of his precious nephew Soames, that man of property! Though he had not met her since the day of the 'At Home' in his old house at Stanhope Gate, which celebrated his granddaughter June's ill-starred engagement to young Bosinney, he had remembered her at once, for he had always admired her—a very pretty creature. After the death of young Bosinney, whose mistress she had so reprehensibly become, he had heard that she had left Soames at once. Goodness only knew what she had been doing since. That sight of her face—a side view—in the row in front, had been literally the only reminder these three years that she was still alive. No one ever spoke of her. And yet Jo had told him something once—something which had upset him completely. The boy had got it from George Forsyte, he believed, who had seen Bosinney in the fog the day he was run over—something which explained the young fellow's distress—an act of Soames towards his wife—a shocking act. Jo had seen her, too, that afternoon, after the news was out, seen her for a moment, and his description had always lingered in old Jolyon's mind—'wild and lost' he had called her. And next day June had gone there—bottled up her feelings and gone there, and the maid had cried and told her how her mistress had slipped out in the night and vanished. A tragic business altogether! One thing was certain—Soames had never been able to lay hands on her again. And he was living at Brighton, and journeying up and down—a fitting fate, the man of property! For when he once took a dislike to anyone—as he had to his nephew—old Jolyon never got over it. He remembered still the sense of relief with which he had heard the news of Irene's disappearance. It had been shocking to think of her a prisoner in that house to which she must have wandered back, when Jo saw her, wandered back for a moment—like a wounded animal to its hole after seeing that news, 'Tragic death of an Architect,' in the street. Her face had struck him very much the other night—more beautiful than he had remembered, but like a mask, with something going on beneath it. A young woman still—twenty-eight perhaps. Ah, well! Very likely she had another lover by now. But at this subversive thought—for married women should never love: once, even, had been too much—his instep rose, and with it the dog Balthasar's head. The sagacious animal stood up and looked into old Jolyon's face. 'Walk?' he seemed to say; and old Jolyon answered: "Come on, old chap!"

Slowly, as was their wont, they crossed among the constellations of buttercups and daisies, and entered the fernery. This feature, where very little grew as yet, had been judiciously dropped below the level of the lawn so that it might come up again on the level of the other lawn and give the impression of irregularity, so important in horticulture. Its rocks and earth were beloved of the dog Balthasar, who sometimes found a mole there. Old Jolyon made a point of passing through it because, though it was not beautiful, he intended that it should be, some day, and he would think: 'I must get Varr to come down and look at it; he's better than Beech.' For plants, like houses and human complaints, required the best expert consideration. It was inhabited by snails, and if accompanied by his grandchildren, he would point to one and tell them the story of the little boy who said: 'Have plummers got leggers, Mother?' 'No, sonny.' 'Then darned if I haven't been and swallowed a snileybob.' And when they skipped and clutched his hand, thinking of the snileybob going down the little boy's 'red lane,' his eyes would twinkle. Emerging from the fernery, he opened the wicket gate, which just there led into the first field, a large and park-like area, out of which, within brick walls, the vegetable garden had been carved. Old Jolyon avoided this, which did not suit his mood, and made down the hill towards the pond. Balthasar, who knew a water-rat or two, gambolled in front, at the gait which marks an oldish dog who takes the same walk every day. Arrived at the edge, old Jolyon stood, noting another water-lily opened since yesterday; he would show it to Holly to-morrow, when 'his little sweet' had got over the upset which had followed on her eating a tomato at lunch—her little arrangements were very delicate. Now that Jolly had gone to school—his first term—Holly was with him nearly all day long, and he missed her badly. He felt that pain too, which often bothered him now, a little dragging at his left side. He looked back up the hill. Really, poor young Bosinney had made an uncommonly good job of the house; he would have done very well for himself if he had lived! And where was he now? Perhaps, still haunting this, the site of his last work, of his tragic love affair. Or was Philip Bosinney's spirit diffused in the general? Who could say? That dog was getting his legs muddy! And he moved towards the coppice. There had been the most delightful lot of bluebells, and he knew where some still lingered like little patches of sky fallen in between the trees, away out of the sun. He passed the cow-houses and the hen-houses there installed, and pursued a path into the thick of the saplings, making for one of the bluebell plots. Balthasar, preceding him once more, uttered a low growl. Old Jolyon stirred him with his foot, but the dog remained motionless, just where there was no room to pass, and the hair rose slowly along the centre of his woolly back. Whether from the growl and the look of the dog's stivered hair, or from the sensation which a man feels in a wood, old Jolyon also felt something move along his spine. And then the path turned, and there was an old mossy log, and on it a woman sitting. Her face was turned away, and he had just time to think: 'She's trespassing—I must have a board put up!' before she turned. Powers above! The face he had seen at the opera—the very woman he had just been thinking of! In that confused moment he saw things blurred, as if a spirit—queer effect—the slant of sunlight perhaps on her violet-grey frock! And then she rose and stood smiling, her head a little to one side. Old Jolyon thought: 'How pretty she is!' She did not speak, neither did he; and he realized why with a certain admiration. She was here no doubt because of some memory, and did not mean to try and get out of it by vulgar explanation.

"Don't let that dog touch your frock," he said; "he's got wet feet. Come here, you!"

But the dog Balthasar went on towards the visitor, who put her hand down and stroked his head. Old Jolyon said quickly:

"I saw you at the opera the other night; you didn't notice me."

"Oh, yes! I did."

He felt a subtle flattery in that, as though she had added: 'Do you think one could miss seeing you?'

"They're all in Spain," he remarked abruptly. "I'm alone; I drove up for the opera. The Ravogli's good. Have you seen the cow-houses?"

In a situation so charged with mystery and something very like emotion he moved instinctively towards that bit of property, and she moved beside him. Her figure swayed faintly, like the best kind of French figures; her dress, too, was a sort of French grey. He noticed two or three silver threads in her amber-coloured hair, strange hair with those dark eyes of hers, and that creamy-pale face. A sudden sidelong look from the velvety brown eyes disturbed him. It seemed to come from deep and far, from another world almost, or at all events from some one not living very much in this. And he said mechanically:

"Where are you living now?"

"I have a little flat in Chelsea."

He did not want to hear what she was doing, did not want to hear anything; but the perverse word came out:

"Alone?"

She nodded. It was a relief to know that. And it came into his mind that, but for a twist of fate, she would have been mistress of this coppice, showing these cow-houses to him, a visitor.

"All Alderneys," he muttered; "they give the best milk. This one's a pretty creature. Woa, Myrtle!"

The fawn-coloured cow, with eyes as soft and brown as Irene's own, was standing absolutely still, not having long been milked. She looked round at them out of the corner of those lustrous, mild, cynical eyes, and from her grey lips a little dribble of saliva threaded its way towards the straw. The scent of hay and vanilla and ammonia rose in the dim light of the cool cow-house; and old Jolyon said:

"You must come up and have some dinner with me. I'll send you home in the carriage."

He perceived a struggle going on within her; natural, no doubt, with her memories. But he wanted her company; a pretty face, a charming figure, beauty! He had been alone all the afternoon. Perhaps his eyes were wistful, for she answered: "Thank you, Uncle Jolyon. I should like to."

He rubbed his hands, and said:

"Capital! Let's go up, then!" And, preceded by the dog Balthasar, they ascended through the field. The sun was almost level in their faces now, and he could see, not only those silver threads, but little lines, just deep enough to stamp her beauty with a coin-like fineness—the special look of life unshared with others. "I'll take her in by the terrace," he thought: "I won't make a common visitor of her."

"What do you do all day?" he said.

"Teach music; I have another interest, too."

"Work!" said old Jolyon, picking up the doll from off the swing, and smoothing its black petticoat. "Nothing like it, is there? I don't do any now. I'm getting on. What interest is that?"

"Trying to help women who've come to grief." Old Jolyon did not quite understand. "To grief?" he repeated; then realised with a shock that she meant exactly what he would have meant himself if he had used that expression. Assisting the Magdalenes of London! What a weird and terrifying interest! And, curiosity overcoming his natural shrinking, he asked:

"Why? What do you do for them?"

"Not much. I've no money to spare. I can only give sympathy and food sometimes."

Involuntarily old Jolyon's hand sought his purse. He said hastily: "How d'you get hold of them?"

"I go to a hospital."

"A hospital! Phew!"

"What hurts me most is that once they nearly all had some sort of beauty."

Old Jolyon straightened the doll. "Beauty!" he ejaculated: "Ha! Yes! A sad business!" and he moved towards the house. Through a French window, under sun-blinds not yet drawn up, he preceded her into the room where he was wont to study The Times and the sheets of an agricultural magazine, with huge illustrations of mangold wurzels, and the like, which provided Holly with material for her paint brush.

"Dinner's in half an hour. You'd like to wash your hands! I'll take you to June's room."

He saw her looking round eagerly; what changes since she had last visited this house with her husband, or her lover, or both perhaps—he did not know, could not say! All that was dark, and he wished to leave it so. But what changes! And in the hall he said:

"My boy Jo's a painter, you know. He's got a lot of taste. It isn't mine, of course, but I've let him have his way."

She was standing very still, her eyes roaming through the hall and music room, as it now was—all thrown into one, under the great skylight. Old Jolyon had an odd impression of her. Was she trying to conjure somebody from the shades of that space where the colouring was all pearl-grey and silver? He would have had gold himself; more lively and solid. But Jo had French tastes, and it had come out shadowy like that, with an effect as of the fume of cigarettes the chap was always smoking, broken here and there by a little blaze of blue or crimson colour. It was not his dream! Mentally he had hung this space with those gold-framed masterpieces of still and stiller life which he had bought in days when quantity was precious. And now where were they? Sold for a song! That something which made him, alone among Forsytes, move with the times had warned him against the struggle to retain them. But in his study he still had 'Dutch Fishing Boats at Sunset.'

He began to mount the stairs with her, slowly, for he felt his side.

"These are the bathrooms," he said, "and other arrangements. I've had them tiled. The nurseries are along there. And this is Jo's and his wife's. They all communicate. But you remember, I expect."

Irene nodded. They passed on, up the gallery and entered a large room with a small bed, and several windows.

"This is mine," he said. The walls were covered with the photographs of children and watercolour sketches, and he added doubtfully:

"These are Jo's. The view's first-rate. You can see the Grand Stand at Epsom in clear weather."

The sun was down now, behind the house, and over the 'prospect' a luminous haze had settled, emanation of the long and prosperous day. Few houses showed, but fields and trees faintly glistened, away to a loom of downs.

"The country's changing," he said abruptly, "but there it'll be when we're all gone. Look at those thrushes—the birds are sweet here in the mornings. I'm glad to have washed my hands of London."

Her face was close to the window pane, and he was struck by its mournful look. 'Wish I could make her look happy!' he thought. 'A pretty face, but sad!' And taking up his can of hot water he went out into the gallery.

"This is June's room," he said, opening the next door and putting the can down; "I think you'll find everything." And closing the door behind her he went back to his own room. Brushing his hair with his great ebony brushes, and dabbing his forehead with eau de Cologne, he mused. She had come so strangely—a sort of visitation; mysterious, even romantic, as if his desire for company, for beauty, had been fulfilled by whatever it was which fulfilled that sort of thing. And before the mirror he straightened his still upright figure, passed the brushes over his great white moustache, touched up his eyebrows with eau de Cologne, and rang the bell.

"I forgot to let them know that I have a lady to dinner with me. Let cook do something extra, and tell Beacon to have the landau and pair at half-past ten to drive her back to Town to-night. Is Miss Holly asleep?"

The maid thought not. And old Jolyon, passing down the gallery, stole on tiptoe towards the nursery, and opened the door whose hinges he kept specially oiled that he might slip in and out in the evenings without being heard.

But Holly was asleep, and lay like a miniature Madonna, of that type which the old painters could not tell from Venus, when they had completed her. Her long dark lashes clung to her cheeks; on her face was perfect peace—her little arrangements were evidently all right again. And old Jolyon, in the twilight of the room, stood adoring her! It was so charming, solemn, and loving—that little face. He had more than his share of the blessed capacity of living again in the young. They were to him his future life—all of a future life that his fundamental pagan sanity perhaps admitted. There she was with everything before her, and his blood—some of it—in her tiny veins. There she was, his little companion, to be made as happy as ever he could make her, so that she knew nothing but love. His heart swelled, and he went out, stilling the sound of his patent-leather boots. In the corridor an eccentric notion attacked him: To think that children should come to that which Irene had told him she was helping! Women who were all, once, little things like this one sleeping there! 'I must give her a cheque!' he mused; 'Can't bear to think of them!' They had never borne reflecting on, those poor outcasts; wounding too deeply the core of true refinement hidden under layers of conformity to the sense of property—wounding too grievously the deepest thing in him—a love of beauty which could give him, even now, a flutter of the heart, thinking of his evening in the society of a pretty woman. And he went downstairs, through the swinging doors, to the back regions. There, in the wine-cellar, was a hock worth at least two pounds a bottle, a Steinberg Cabinet, better than any Johannisberg that ever went down throat; a wine of perfect bouquet, sweet as a nectarine—nectar indeed! He got a bottle out, handling it like a baby, and holding it level to the light, to look. Enshrined in its coat of dust, that mellow coloured, slender-necked bottle gave him deep pleasure. Three years to settle down again since the move from Town—ought to be in prime condition! Thirty-five years ago he had bought it—thank God he had kept his palate, and earned the right to drink it. She would appreciate this; not a spice of acidity in a dozen. He wiped the bottle, drew the cork with his own hands, put his nose down, inhaled its perfume, and went back to the music room.

Irene was standing by the piano; she had taken off her hat and a lace scarf she had been wearing, so that her gold-coloured hair was visible, and the pallor of her neck. In her grey frock she made a pretty picture for old Jolyon, against the rosewood of the piano.

He gave her his arm, and solemnly they went. The room, which had been designed to enable twenty-four people to dine in comfort, held now but a little round table. In his present solitude the big dining-table oppressed old Jolyon; he had caused it to be removed till his son came back. Here in the company of two really good copies of Raphael Madonnas he was wont to dine alone. It was the only disconsolate hour of his day, this summer weather. He had never been a large eater, like that great chap Swithin, or Sylvanus Heythorp, or Anthony Thornworthy, those cronies of past times; and to dine alone, overlooked by the Madonnas, was to him but a sorrowful occupation, which he got through quickly, that he might come to the more spiritual enjoyment of his coffee and cigar. But this evening was a different matter! His eyes twinkled at her across the little table and he spoke of Italy and Switzerland, telling her stories of his travels there, and other experiences which he could no longer recount to his son and grand-daughter because they knew them. This fresh audience was precious to him; he had never become one of those old men who ramble round and round the fields of reminiscence. Himself quickly fatigued by the insensitive, he instinctively avoided fatiguing others, and his natural flirtatiousness towards beauty guarded him specially in his relations with a woman. He would have liked to draw her out, but though she murmured and smiled and seemed to be enjoying what he told her, he remained conscious of that mysterious remoteness which constituted half her fascination. He could not bear women who threw their shoulders and eyes at you, and chattered away; or hard-mouthed women who laid down the law and knew more than you did. There was only one quality in a woman that appealed to him—charm; and the quieter it was, the more he liked it. And this one had charm, shadowy as afternoon sunlight on those Italian hills and valleys he had loved. The feeling, too, that she was, as it were, apart, cloistered, made her seem nearer to himself, a strangely desirable companion. When a man is very old and quite out of the running, he loves to feel secure from the rivalries of youth, for he would still be first in the heart of beauty. And he drank his hock, and watched her lips, and felt nearly young. But the dog Balthasar lay watching her lips too, and despising in his heart the interruptions of their talk, and the tilting of those greenish glasses full of a golden fluid which was distasteful to him.

The light was just failing when they went back into the music-room. And, cigar in mouth, old Jolyon said:

"Play me some Chopin."

By the cigars they smoke, and the composers they love, ye shall know the texture of men's souls. Old Jolyon could not bear a strong cigar or Wagner's music. He loved Beethoven and Mozart, Handel and Gluck, and Schumann, and, for some occult reason, the operas of Meyerbeer; but of late years he had been seduced by Chopin, just as in painting he had succumbed to Botticelli. In yielding to these tastes he had been conscious of divergence from the standard of the Golden Age. Their poetry was not that of Milton and Byron and Tennyson; of Raphael and Titian; Mozart and Beethoven. It was, as it were, behind a veil; their poetry hit no one in the face, but slipped its fingers under the ribs and turned and twisted, and melted up the heart. And, never certain that this was healthy, he did not care a rap so long as he could see the pictures of the one or hear the music of the other.

Irene sat down at the piano under the electric lamp festooned with pearl-grey, and old Jolyon, in an armchair, whence he could see her, crossed his legs and drew slowly at his cigar. She sat a few moments with her hands on the keys, evidently searching her mind for what to give him. Then she began and within old Jolyon there arose a sorrowful pleasure, not quite like anything else in the world. He fell slowly into a trance, interrupted only by the movements of taking the cigar out of his mouth at long intervals, and replacing it. She was there, and the hock within him, and the scent of tobacco; but there, too, was a world of sunshine lingering into moonlight, and pools with storks upon them, and bluish trees above, glowing with blurs of wine-red roses, and fields of lavender where milk-white cows were grazing, and a woman all shadowy, with dark eyes and a white neck, smiled, holding out her arms; and through air which was like music a star dropped and was caught on a cow's horn. He opened his eyes. Beautiful piece; she played well—the touch of an angel! And he closed them again. He felt miraculously sad and happy, as one does, standing under a lime-tree in full honey flower. Not live one's own life again, but just stand there and bask in the smile of a woman's eyes, and enjoy the bouquet! And he jerked his hand; the dog Balthasar had reached up and licked it.

"Beautiful!" He said: "Go on—more Chopin!"

She began to play again. This time the resemblance between her and 'Chopin' struck him. The swaying he had noticed in her walk was in her playing too, and the Nocturne she had chosen and the soft darkness of her eyes, the light on her hair, as of moonlight from a golden moon. Seductive, yes; but nothing of Delilah in her or in that music. A long blue spiral from his cigar ascended and dispersed. 'So we go out!' he thought. 'No more beauty! Nothing?'

Again Irene stopped.

"Would you like some Gluck? He used to write his music in a sunlit garden, with a bottle of Rhine wine beside him."

"Ah! yes. Let's have 'Orfeo.'" Round about him now were fields of gold and silver flowers, white forms swaying in the sunlight, bright birds flying to and fro. All was summer. Lingering waves of sweetness and regret flooded his soul. Some cigar ash dropped, and taking out a silk handkerchief to brush it off, he inhaled a mingled scent as of snuff and eau de Cologne. 'Ah!' he thought, 'Indian summer—that's all!' and he said: "You haven't played me 'Che faro.'"

She did not answer; did not move. He was conscious of something—some strange upset. Suddenly he saw her rise and turn away, and a pang of remorse shot through him. What a clumsy chap! Like Orpheus, she of course—she too was looking for her lost one in the hall of memory! And disturbed to the heart, he got up from his chair. She had gone to the great window at the far end. Gingerly he followed. Her hands were folded over her breast; he could just see her cheek, very white. And, quite emotionalized, he said:

"There, there, my love!" The words had escaped him mechanically, for they were those he used to Holly when she had a pain, but their effect was instantaneously distressing. She raised her arms, covered her face with them, and wept.

Old Jolyon stood gazing at her with eyes very deep from age. The passionate shame she seemed feeling at her abandonment, so unlike the control and quietude of her whole presence was as if she had never before broken down in the presence of another being.

"There, there—there, there!" he murmured, and putting his hand out reverently, touched her. She turned, and leaned the arms which covered her face against him. Old Jolyon stood very still, keeping one thin hand on her shoulder. Let her cry her heart out—it would do her good.

And the dog Balthasar, puzzled, sat down on his stern to examine them.

The window was still open, the curtains had not been drawn, the last of daylight from without mingled with faint intrusion from the lamp within; there was a scent of new-mown grass. With the wisdom of a long life old Jolyon did not speak. Even grief sobbed itself out in time; only Time was good for sorrow—Time who saw the passing of each mood, each emotion in turn; Time the layer-to-rest. There came into his mind the words: 'As panteth the hart after cooling streams'—but they were of no use to him. Then, conscious of a scent of violets, he knew she was drying her eyes. He put his chin forward, pressed his moustache against her forehead, and felt her shake with a quivering of her whole body, as of a tree which shakes itself free of raindrops. She put his hand to her lips, as if saying: "All over now! Forgive me!"

The kiss filled him with a strange comfort; he led her back to where she had been so upset. And the dog Balthasar, following, laid the bone of one of the cutlets they had eaten at their feet.

Anxious to obliterate the memory of that emotion, he could think of nothing better than china; and moving with her slowly from cabinet to cabinet, he kept taking up bits of Dresden and Lowestoft and Chelsea, turning them round and round with his thin, veined hands, whose skin, faintly freckled, had such an aged look.

"I bought this at Jobson's," he would say; "cost me thirty pounds. It's very old. That dog leaves his bones all over the place. This old 'ship-bowl' I picked up at the sale when that precious rip, the Marquis, came to grief. But you don't remember. Here's a nice piece of

Chelsea. Now, what would you say this was?" And he was comforted, feeling that, with her taste, she was taking a real interest in these things; for, after all, nothing better composes the nerves than a doubtful piece of china.

When the crunch of the carriage wheels was heard at last, he said:

"You must come again; you must come to lunch, then I can show you these by daylight, and my little sweet—she's a dear little thing. This dog seems to have taken a fancy to you."

For Balthasar, feeling that she was about to leave, was rubbing his side against her leg. Going out under the porch with her, he said:

"He'll get you up in an hour and a quarter. Take this for your protegees," and he slipped a cheque for fifty pounds into her hand. He saw her brightened eyes, and heard her murmur: "Oh! Uncle Jolyon!" and a real throb of pleasure went through him. That meant one or two poor creatures helped a little, and it meant that she would come again. He put his hand in at the window and grasped hers once more. The carriage rolled away. He stood looking at the moon and the shadows of the trees, and thought: 'A sweet night! She...!'

II

Two days of rain, and summer set in bland and sunny. Old Jolyon walked and talked with Holly. At first he felt taller and full of a new vigour; then he felt restless. Almost every afternoon they would enter the coppice, and walk as far as the log. 'Well, she's not there!' he would think, 'of course not!' And he would feel a little shorter, and drag his feet walking up the hill home, with his hand clapped to his left side. Now and then the thought would move in him: 'Did she come—or did I dream it?' and he would stare at space, while the dog Balthasar stared at him. Of course she would not come again! He opened the letters from Spain with less excitement. They were not returning till July; he felt, oddly, that he could bear it. Every day at dinner he screwed up his eyes and looked at where she had sat. She was not there, so he unscrewed his eyes again.

On the seventh afternoon he thought: 'I must go up and get some boots.' He ordered Beacon, and set out. Passing from Putney towards Hyde Park he reflected: 'I might as well go to Chelsea and see her.' And he called out: "Just drive me to where you took that lady the other night." The coachman turned his broad red face, and his juicy lips answered: "The lady in grey, sir?"

"Yes, the lady in grey." What other ladies were there! Stodgy chap!

The carriage stopped before a small three-storied block of flats, standing a little back from the river. With a practised eye old Jolyon saw that they were cheap. 'I should think about sixty pound a year,' he mused; and entering, he looked at the name-board. The name 'Forsyte' was not on it, but against 'First Floor, Flat C' were the words: 'Mrs. Irene Heron.' Ah! She had taken her maiden name again! And somehow this pleased him. He went upstairs slowly, feeling his side a little. He stood a moment, before ringing, to lose the feeling of drag and fluttering there. She would not be in! And then—Boots! The thought was black. What did he want with boots at his age? He could not wear out all those he had.

"Your mistress at home?"

"Yes, sir."

"Say Mr. Jolyon Forsyte."

"Yes, sir, will you come this way?"

Old Jolyon followed a very little maid—not more than sixteen one would say—into a very small drawing-room where the sun-blinds were drawn. It held a cottage piano and little else save a vague fragrance and good taste. He stood in the middle, with his top hat in his hand, and thought: 'I expect she's very badly off!' There was a mirror above the fireplace, and he saw himself reflected. An old-looking chap! He heard a rustle, and turned round. She was so close that his moustache almost brushed her forehead, just under her hair.

"I was driving up," he said. "Thought I'd look in on you, and ask you how you got up the other night."

And, seeing her smile, he felt suddenly relieved. She was really glad to see him, perhaps.

"Would you like to put on your hat and come for a drive in the Park?"

But while she was gone to put her hat on, he frowned. The Park! James and Emily! Mrs. Nicholas, or some other member of his precious family would be there very likely, prancing up and down. And they would go and wag their tongues about having seen him with her, afterwards. Better not! He did not wish to revive the echoes of the past on Forsyte 'Change. He removed a white hair from the lapel of his closely-buttoned-up frock coat, and passed his hand over his cheeks, moustache, and square chin. It felt very hollow there under the cheekbones. He had not been eating much lately—he had better get that little whippersnapper who attended Holly to give him a tonic. But she had come back and when they were in the carriage, he said:

"Suppose we go and sit in Kensington Gardens instead?" and added with a twinkle: "No prancing up and down there," as if she had been in the secret of his thoughts.

Leaving the carriage, they entered those select precincts, and strolled towards the water.

"You've gone back to your maiden name, I see," he said: "I'm not sorry."

She slipped her hand under his arm: "Has June forgiven me, Uncle Jolyon?"

He answered gently: "Yes—yes; of course, why not?"

"And have you?"

"I? I forgave you as soon as I saw how the land really lay." And perhaps he had; his instinct had always been to forgive the beautiful.

She drew a deep breath. "I never regretted—I couldn't. Did you ever love very deeply, Uncle Jolyon?"

At that strange question old Jolyon stared before him. Had he? He did not seem to remember that he ever had. But he did not like to say this to the young woman whose hand was touching his arm, whose life was suspended, as it were, by memory of a tragic love. And he thought: 'If I had met you when I was young I—I might have made a fool of myself, perhaps.' And a longing to escape in generalities beset him.

"Love's a queer thing," he said, "fatal thing often. It was the Greeks—wasn't it?—made love into a goddess; they were right, I dare say, but then they lived in the Golden Age."

"Phil adored them."

Phil! The word jarred him, for suddenly—with his power to see all round a thing, he perceived why she was putting up with him like this. She wanted to talk about her lover! Well! If it was any pleasure to her! And he said: "Ah! There was a bit of the sculptor in him, I fancy."

"Yes. He loved balance and symmetry; he loved the whole-hearted way the Greeks gave themselves to art."

Balance! The chap had no balance at all, if he remembered; as for symmetry—clean-built enough he was, no doubt; but those queer eyes of his, and high cheek-bones—Symmetry?

"You're of the Golden Age, too, Uncle Jolyon."

Old Jolyon looked round at her. Was she chaffing him? No, her eyes were soft as velvet. Was she flattering him? But if so, why? There was nothing to be had out of an old chap like him.

"Phil thought so. He used to say: 'But I can never tell him that I admire him.'"

Ah! There it was again. Her dead lover; her desire to talk of him! And he pressed her arm, half resentful of those memories, half grateful, as if he recognised what a link they were between herself and him.

"He was a very talented young fellow," he murmured. "It's hot; I feel the heat nowadays. Let's sit down."

They took two chairs beneath a chestnut tree whose broad leaves covered them from the peaceful glory of the afternoon. A pleasure to sit there and watch her, and feel that she liked to be with him. And the wish to increase that liking, if he could, made him go on:

"I expect he showed you a side of him I never saw. He'd be at his best with you. His ideas of art were a little new—to me "—he had stiffed the word 'fangled.'

"Yes: but he used to say you had a real sense of beauty." Old Jolyon thought: "The devil he did!' but answered with a twinkle: "Well, I have, or I shouldn't be sitting here with you." She was fascinating when she smiled with her eyes, like that!

"He thought you had one of those hearts that never grow old. Phil had real insight."

He was not taken in by this flattery spoken out of the past, out of a longing to talk of her dead lover—not a bit; and yet it was precious to hear, because she pleased his eyes and heart which—quite true!—had never grown old. Was that because—unlike her and her dead lover, he had never loved to desperation, had always kept his balance, his sense of symmetry. Well! It had left him power, at eighty-four, to admire beauty. And he thought, 'If I were a painter or a sculptor! But I'm an old chap. Make hay while the sun shines.'

A couple with arms entwined crossed on the grass before them, at the edge of the shadow from their tree. The sunlight fell cruelly on their pale, squashed, unkempt young faces. "We're an ugly lot!" said old Jolyon suddenly. "It amazes me to see how—love triumphs over that."

"Love triumphs over everything!"

"The young think so," he muttered.

"Love has no age, no limit, and no death."

With that glow in her pale face, her breast heaving, her eyes so large and dark and soft, she looked like Venus come to life! But this extravagance brought instant reaction, and, twinkling, he said: "Well, if it had limits, we shouldn't be born; for by George! it's got a lot to put up with."

Then, removing his top hat, he brushed it round with a cuff. The great clumsy thing heated his forehead; in these days he often got a rush of blood to the head—his circulation was not what it had been.

She still sat gazing straight before her, and suddenly she murmured:

"It's strange enough that I'm alive."

Those words of Jo's 'Wild and lost' came back to him.

"Ah!" he said: "my son saw you for a moment—that day."

"Was it your son? I heard a voice in the hall; I thought for a second it was—Phil."

Old Jolyon saw her lips tremble. She put her hand over them, took it away again, and went on calmly: "That night I went to the Embankment; a woman caught me by the dress. She told me about herself. When one knows that others suffer, one's ashamed."

"One of those?"

She nodded, and horror stirred within old Jolyon, the horror of one who has never known a struggle with desperation. Almost against his will he muttered: "Tell me, won't you?"

"I didn't care whether I lived or died. When you're like that, Fate ceases to want to kill you. She took care of me three days—she never left me. I had no money. That's why I do what I can for them, now."

But old Jolyon was thinking: 'No money!' What fate could compare with that? Every other was involved in it.

"I wish you had come to me," he said. "Why didn't you?" But Irene did not answer.

"Because my name was Forsyte, I suppose? Or was it June who kept you away? How are you getting on now?" His eyes involuntarily swept her body. Perhaps even now she was—! And yet she wasn't thin—not really!

"Oh! with my fifty pounds a year, I make just enough." The answer did not reassure him; he had lost confidence. And that fellow Soames! But his sense of justice stifled condemnation. No, she would certainly have died rather than take another penny from him. Soft as she looked, there must be strength in her somewhere—strength and fidelity. But what business had young Bosinney to have got run over and left her stranded like this!

"Well, you must come to me now," he said, "for anything you want, or I shall be quite cut up." And putting on his hat, he rose. "Let's go and get some tea. I told that lazy chap to put the horses up for an hour, and come for me at your place. We'll take a cab presently; I can't walk as I used to."

He enjoyed that stroll to the Kensington end of the gardens—the sound of her voice, the glancing of her eyes, the subtle beauty of a charming form moving beside him. He enjoyed their tea at Ruffel's in the High Street, and came out thence with a great box of chocolates swung on his little finger. He enjoyed the drive back to Chelsea in a hansom, smoking his cigar. She had promised to come down next Sunday and play to him again, and already in thought he was plucking carnations and early roses for her to carry back to town. It was a pleasure to give her a little pleasure, if it WERE pleasure from an old chap like him! The carriage was already there when they arrived. Just like that fellow, who was always late when he was wanted! Old Jolyon went in for a minute to say good-bye. The little dark hall of the flat was impregnated with a disagreeable odour of patchouli, and on a bench against the wall—its only furniture—he saw a figure sitting. He heard Irene say softly: "Just one minute." In the little drawing-room when the door was shut, he asked gravely: "One of your protegees?"

"Yes. Now thanks to you, I can do something for her."

He stood, staring, and stroking that chin whose strength had frightened so many in its time. The idea of her thus actually in contact with this outcast grieved and frightened him. What could she do for them? Nothing. Only soil and make trouble for herself, perhaps. And he said: "Take care, my dear! The world puts the worst construction on everything."

"I know that."

He was abashed by her quiet smile. "Well then—Sunday," he murmured: "Good-bye."

She put her cheek forward for him to kiss.

"Good-bye," he said again; "take care of yourself." And he went out, not looking towards the figure on the bench. He drove home by way of Hammersmith; that he might stop at a place he knew of and tell them to send her in two dozen of their best Burgundy. She must want picking-up sometimes! Only in Richmond Park did he remember that he had gone up to order himself some boots, and was surprised that he could have had so paltry an idea.

III

The little spirits of the past which throng an old man's days had never pushed their faces up to his so seldom as in the seventy hours elapsing before Sunday came. The spirit of the future, with the charm of the unknown, put up her lips instead. Old Jolyon was not restless now, and paid no visits to the log, because she was coming to lunch. There is wonderful finality about a meal; it removes a world of doubts, for no one misses meals except for reasons beyond control. He played many games with Holly on the lawn, pitching them up to her who was batting so as to be ready to bowl to Jolly in the holidays. For she was not a Forsyte, but Jolly was—and Forsytes always bat, until they have resigned and reached the age of eighty-five. The dog Balthasar, in attendance, lay on the ball as often as he could, and the page-boy fielded, till his face was like the harvest moon. And because the time was getting shorter, each day was longer and more golden than the last. On Friday night he took a liver pill, his side hurt him rather, and though it was not the liver side, there is no remedy like that. Anyone telling him that he had found a new excitement in life and that excitement was not good for him, would have been met by one of those steady and rather defiant looks of his deep-set iron-grey eyes, which seemed to say: 'I know my own business best.' He always had and always would.

On Sunday morning, when Holly had gone with her governess to church, he visited the strawberry beds. There, accompanied by the dog Balthasar, he examined the plants narrowly and succeeded in finding at least two dozen berries which were really ripe. Stooping was not good for him, and he became very dizzy and red in the forehead. Having placed the strawberries in a dish on the dining-table, he washed his hands and bathed his forehead with eau de Cologne. There, before the mirror, it occurred to him that he was thinner. What a 'threadpaper' he had been when he was young! It was nice to be slim—he could not bear a fat chap; and yet perhaps his cheeks were too thin! She was to arrive by train at half-past twelve and walk up, entering from the road past Drage's farm at the far end of the coppice. And, having looked into June's room to see that there was hot water ready, he set forth to meet her, leisurely, for his heart was beating. The air smelled sweet, larks sang, and the Grand Stand at Epsom was visible. A perfect day! On just such a one, no doubt, six years ago, Soames had brought young Bosinney down with him to look at the site before they began to build. It was Bosinney who had pitched on the exact spot for the house—as June had often told him. In these days he was thinking much about that young fellow, as if his spirit were really haunting the field of his last work, on the chance of seeing—her. Bosinney—the one man who had possessed her heart, to whom she had given her whole self with rapture! At his age one could not, of course, imagine such things, but there stirred in him a queer vague aching—as it were the ghost of an impersonal jealousy; and a feeling, too, more generous, of pity for that love so early lost. All over in a few poor months! Well, well! He looked at his watch before entering the coppice—only a quarter past, twenty-five minutes to wait! And then, turning the corner of the path, he saw her exactly where he had seen her the first time, on the log; and realised that she must have come by the earlier train to sit there alone for a couple of hours at least. Two hours of her society missed! What memory could make that log so dear to her? His face showed what he was thinking, for she said at once:

"Forgive me, Uncle Jolyon; it was here that I first knew."

"Yes, yes; there it is for you whenever you like. You're looking a little Londony; you're giving too many lessons."

That she should have to give lessons worried him. Lessons to a parcel of young girls thumping out scales with their thick fingers.

"Where do you go to give them?" he asked.

"They're mostly Jewish families, luckily."

Old Jolyon stared; to all Forsytes Jews seem strange and doubtful.

"They love music, and they're very kind."

"They had better be, by George!" He took her arm—his side always hurt him a little going uphill—and said:

"Did you ever see anything like those buttercups? They came like that in a night."

Her eyes seemed really to fly over the field, like bees after the flowers and the honey. "I wanted you to see them—wouldn't let them turn the cows in yet." Then, remembering that she had come to talk about Bosinney, he pointed to the clock-tower over the stables:

"I expect he wouldn't have let me put that there—had no notion of time, if I remember."

But, pressing his arm to her, she talked of flowers instead, and he knew it was done that he might not feel she came because of her dead lover.

"The best flower I can show you," he said, with a sort of triumph, "is my little sweet. She'll be back from Church directly. There's something about her which reminds me a little of you," and it did not seem to him peculiar that he had put it thus, instead of saying: "There's something about you which reminds me a little of her." Ah! And here she was!

Holly, followed closely by her elderly French governess, whose digestion had been ruined twenty-two years ago in the siege of Strasbourg, came rushing towards them from under the oak tree. She stopped about a dozen yards away, to pat Balthasar and pretend that this was all she had in her mind. Old Jolyon, who knew better, said:

"Well, my darling, here's the lady in grey I promised you."

Holly raised herself and looked up. He watched the two of them with a twinkle, Irene smiling, Holly beginning with grave inquiry, passing into a shy smile too, and then to something deeper. She had a sense of beauty, that child—knew what was what! He enjoyed the sight of the kiss between them.

"Mrs. Heron, Mam'zelle Beauce. Well, Mam'zelle—good sermon?"

For, now that he had not much more time before him, the only part of the service connected with this world absorbed what interest in church remained to him. Mam'zelle Beauce stretched out a spidery hand clad in a black kid glove—she had been in the best families—and the rather sad eyes of her lean yellowish face seemed to ask: "Are you well-brrred?" Whenever Holly or Jolly did anything unpleasing to her—a not uncommon occurrence—she would say to them: "The little Tayleurs never did that—they were such well-brrred little children." Jolly hated the little Tayleurs; Holly wondered dreadfully how it was she fell so short of them. 'A thin rum little soul,' old Jolyon thought her—Mam'zelle Beauce.

Luncheon was a successful meal, the mushrooms which he himself had picked in the mushroom house, his chosen strawberries, and another bottle of the Steinberg cabinet filled him with a certain aromatic spirituality, and a conviction that he would have a touch of eczema to-morrow.

After lunch they sat under the oak tree drinking Turkish coffee. It was no matter of grief to him when Mademoiselle Beauce withdrew to write her Sunday letter to her sister, whose future had been endangered in the past by swallowing a pin—an event held up daily in warning to the children to eat slowly and digest what they had eaten. At the foot of the bank, on a carriage rug, Holly and the dog Balthasar teased and loved each other, and in the shade old Jolyon with his legs crossed and his cigar luxuriously savoured, gazed at Irene sitting in the swing. A light, vaguely swaying, grey figure with a fleck of sunlight here and there upon it, lips just opened, eyes dark and soft under lids a little drooped. She looked content; surely it did her good to come and see him! The selfishness of age had not set its proper grip on him, for he could still feel pleasure in the pleasure of others, realising that what he wanted, though much, was not quite all that mattered.

"It's quiet here," he said; "you mustn't come down if you find it dull. But it's a pleasure to see you. My little sweet is the only face which gives me any pleasure, except yours."

From her smile he knew that she was not beyond liking to be appreciated, and this reassured him. "That's not humbug," he said. "I never told a woman I admired her when I didn't. In fact I don't know when I've told a woman I admired her, except my wife in the old days; and wives are funny." He was silent, but resumed abruptly:

"She used to expect me to say it more often than I felt it, and there we were." Her face looked mysteriously troubled, and, afraid that he had said something painful, he hurried on: "When my little sweet marries, I hope she'll find someone who knows what women feel. I shan't be here to see it, but there's too much topsy-turvydom in marriage; I don't want her to pitch up against that." And, aware that he had made bad worse, he added: "That dog will scratch."

A silence followed. Of what was she thinking, this pretty creature whose life was spoiled; who had done with love, and yet was made for love? Some day when he was gone, perhaps, she would find another mate—not so disorderly as that young fellow who had got himself run over. Ah! but her husband?

"Does Soames never trouble you?" he asked.

She shook her head. Her face had closed up suddenly. For all her softness there was something irreconcilable about her. And a glimpse of light on the inexorable nature of sex antipathies strayed into a brain which, belonging to early Victorian civilisation—so much older than this of his old age—had never thought about such primitive things.

"That's a comfort," he said. "You can see the Grand Stand to-day. Shall we take a turn round?"

Through the flower and fruit garden, against whose high outer walls peach trees and nectarines were trained to the sun, through the stables, the vinery, the mushroom house, the asparagus beds, the rosery, the summer-house, he conducted her—even into the kitchen garden to see the tiny green peas which Holly loved to scoop out of their pods with her finger, and lick up from the palm of her little brown hand. Many delightful things he showed her, while Holly and the dog Balthasar danced ahead, or came to them at intervals for attention. It was one of the happiest afternoons he had ever spent, but it tired him and he was glad to sit down in the music room and let her give him tea. A special little friend of Holly's had come in—a fair child with short hair like a boy's. And the two sported in the distance, under the stairs, on the stairs, and up in the gallery. Old Jolyon begged for Chopin. She played studies, mazurkas, waltzes, till the two children, creeping near, stood at the foot of the piano their dark and golden heads bent forward, listening. Old Jolyon watched.

"Let's see you dance, you two!"

Shyly, with a false start, they began. Bobbing and circling, earnest, not very adroit, they went past and past his chair to the strains of that waltz. He watched them and the face of her who was playing turned smiling towards those little dancers thinking:

'Sweetest picture I've seen for ages.'

A voice said:

"Hollee! Mais enfin—qu'est-ce que tu fais la—danser, le dimanche! Viens, donc!"

But the children came close to old Jolyon, knowing that he would save them, and gazed into a face which was decidedly 'caught out.'

"Better the day, better the deed, Mam'zelle. It's all my doing. Trot along, chicks, and have your tea."

And, when they were gone, followed by the dog Balthasar, who took every meal, he looked at Irene with a twinkle and said:

"Well, there we are! Aren't they sweet? Have you any little ones among your pupils?"

"Yes, three—two of them darlings."

"Pretty?"

"Lovely!"

Old Jolyon sighed; he had an insatiable appetite for the very young. "My little sweet," he said, "is devoted to music; she'll be a musician some day. You wouldn't give me your opinion of her playing, I suppose?"

"Of course I will."

"You wouldn't like—" but he stifled the words "to give her lessons." The idea that she gave lessons was unpleasant to him; yet it would mean that he would see her regularly. She left the piano and came over to his chair.

"I would like, very much; but there is—June. When are they coming back?"

Old Jolyon frowned. "Not till the middle of next month. What does that matter?"

"You said June had forgiven me; but she could never forget, Uncle Jolyon."

Forget! She must forget, if he wanted her to.

But as if answering, Irene shook her head. "You know she couldn't; one doesn't forget."

211

Always that wretched past! And he said with a sort of vexed finality:

"Well, we shall see."

He talked to her an hour or more, of the children, and a hundred little things, till the carriage came round to take her home. And when she had gone he went back to his chair, and sat there smoothing his face and chin, dreaming over the day.

That evening after dinner he went to his study and took a sheet of paper. He stayed for some minutes without writing, then rose and stood under the masterpiece 'Dutch Fishing Boats at Sunset.' He was not thinking of that picture, but of his life. He was going to leave her something in his Will; nothing could so have stirred the stilly deeps of thought and memory. He was going to leave her a portion of his wealth, of his aspirations, deeds, qualities, work—all that had made that wealth; going to leave her, too, a part of all he had missed in life, by his sane and steady pursuit of wealth. All! What had he missed? 'Dutch Fishing Boats' responded blankly; he crossed to the French window, and drawing the curtain aside, opened it. A wind had got up, and one of last year's oak leaves which had somehow survived the gardener's brooms, was dragging itself with a tiny clicking rustle along the stone terrace in the twilight. Except for that it was very quiet out there, and he could smell the heliotrope watered not long since. A bat went by. A bird uttered its last 'cheep.' And right above the oak tree the first star shone. Faust in the opera had bartered his soul for some fresh years of youth. Morbid notion! No such bargain was possible, that was real tragedy! No making oneself new again for love or life or anything. Nothing left to do but enjoy beauty from afar off while you could, and leave it something in your Will. But how much? And, as if he could not make that calculation looking out into the mild freedom of the country night, he turned back and went up to the chimney-piece. There were his pet bronzes—a Cleopatra with the asp at her breast; a Socrates; a greyhound playing with her puppy; a strong man reining in some horses. 'They last!' he thought, and a pang went through his heart. They had a thousand years of life before them!

'How much?' Well! enough at all events to save her getting old before her time, to keep the lines out of her face as long as possible, and grey from soiling that bright hair. He might live another five years. She would be well over thirty by then. 'How much?' She had none of his blood in her! In loyalty to the tenor of his life for forty years and more, ever since he married and founded that mysterious thing, a family, came this warning thought—None of his blood, no right to anything! It was a luxury then, this notion. An extravagance, a petting of an old man's whim, one of those things done in dotage. His real future was vested in those who had his blood, in whom he would live on when he was gone. He turned away from the bronzes and stood looking at the old leather chair in which he had sat and smoked so many hundreds of cigars. And suddenly he seemed to see her sitting there in her grey dress, fragrant, soft, dark-eyed, graceful, looking up at him. Why! She cared nothing for him, really; all she cared for was that lost lover of hers. But she was there, whether she would or no, giving him pleasure with her beauty and grace. One had no right to inflict an old man's company, no right to ask her down to play to him and let him look at her—for no reward! Pleasure must be paid for in this world. 'How much?' After all, there was plenty; his son and his three grandchildren would never miss that little lump. He had made it himself, nearly every penny; he could leave it where he liked, allow himself this little pleasure. He went back to the bureau. 'Well, I'm going to,' he thought, 'let them think what they like. I'm going to!' And he sat down.

'How much?' Ten thousand, twenty thousand—how much? If only with his money he could buy one year, one month of youth. And startled by that thought, he wrote quickly:

'DEAR HERRING,—Draw me a codicil to this effect: "I leave to my niece Irene Forsyte, born Irene Heron, by which name she now goes, fifteen thousand pounds free of legacy duty." 'Yours faithfully, 'JOLYON FORSYTE.'

When he had sealed and stamped the envelope, he went back to the window and drew in a long breath. It was dark, but many stars shone now.

IV

He woke at half-past two, an hour which long experience had taught him brings panic intensity to all awkward thoughts. Experience had also taught him that a further waking at the proper hour of eight showed the folly of such panic. On this particular morning the thought which gathered rapid momentum was that if he became ill, at his age not improbable, he would not see her. From this it was but a step to realisation that he would be cut off, too, when his son and June returned from Spain. How could he justify desire for the company of one who had stolen—early morning does not mince words—June's lover? That lover was dead; but June was a stubborn little thing; warm-hearted, but stubborn as wood, and—quite true—not one who forgot! By the middle of next month they would be back. He had barely five weeks left to enjoy the new interest which had come into what remained of his life. Darkness showed up to him absurdly clear the nature of his feeling. Admiration for beauty—a craving to see that which delighted his eyes.

Preposterous, at his age! And yet—what other reason was there for asking June to undergo such painful reminder, and how prevent his son and his son's wife from thinking him very queer? He would be reduced to sneaking up to London, which tired him; and the least indisposition would cut him off even from that. He lay with eyes open, setting his jaw against the prospect, and calling himself an old fool, while his heart beat loudly, and then seemed to stop beating altogether. He had seen the dawn lighting the window chinks, heard the birds chirp and twitter, and the cocks crow, before he fell asleep again, and awoke tired but sane. Five weeks before he need bother, at his age an eternity! But that early morning panic had left its mark, had slightly fevered the will of one who had always had his own way. He would see her as often as he wished! Why not go up to town and make that codicil at his solicitor's instead of writing about it; she might like to go to the opera! But, by train, for he would not have that fat chap Beacon grinning behind his back. Servants were such fools; and, as likely as not, they had known all the past history of Irene and young Bosinney—servants knew everything, and suspected the rest. He wrote to her that morning:

"MY DEAR IRENE,—I have to be up in town to-morrow. If you would like to have a look in at the opera, come and dine with me quietly ...."

But where? It was decades since he had dined anywhere in London save at his Club or at a private house. Ah! that new-fangled place close to Covent Garden....

"Let me have a line to-morrow morning to the Piedmont Hotel whether to expect you there at 7 o'clock.

"Yours affectionately,

"JOLYON FORSYTE."

She would understand that he just wanted to give her a little pleasure; for the idea that she should guess he had this itch to see her was instinctively unpleasant to him; it was not seemly that one so old should go out of his way to see beauty, especially in a woman.

The journey next day, short though it was, and the visit to his lawyer's, tired him. It was hot too, and after dressing for dinner he lay down on the sofa in his bedroom to rest a little. He must have had a sort of fainting fit, for he came to himself feeling very queer; and with some difficulty rose and rang the bell. Why! it was past seven! And there he was and she would be waiting. But suddenly the dizziness came on again, and he was obliged to relapse on the sofa. He heard the maid's voice say:

"Did you ring, sir?"

"Yes, come here"; he could not see her clearly, for the cloud in front of his eyes. "I'm not well, I want some sal volatile."

"Yes, sir." Her voice sounded frightened.

Old Jolyon made an effort.

"Don't go. Take this message to my niece—a lady waiting in the hall—a lady in grey. Say Mr. Forsyte is not well—the heat. He is very sorry; if he is not down directly, she is not to wait dinner."

When she was gone, he thought feebly: 'Why did I say a lady in grey—she may be in anything. Sal volatile!' He did not go off again, yet was not conscious of how Irene came to be standing beside him, holding smelling salts to his nose, and pushing a pillow up behind his head. He heard her say anxiously: "Dear Uncle Jolyon, what is it?" was dimly conscious of the soft pressure of her lips on his hand; then drew a long breath of smelling salts, suddenly discovered strength in them, and sneezed.

"Ha!" he said, "it's nothing. How did you get here? Go down and dine—the tickets are on the dressing-table. I shall be all right in a minute."

He felt her cool hand on his forehead, smelled violets, and sat divided between a sort of pleasure and a determination to be all right.

"Why! You are in grey!" he said. "Help me up." Once on his feet he gave himself a shake.

"What business had I to go off like that!" And he moved very slowly to the glass. What a cadaverous chap! Her voice, behind him, murmured:

"You mustn't come down, Uncle; you must rest."

"Fiddlesticks! A glass of champagne'll soon set me to rights. I can't have you missing the opera."

But the journey down the corridor was troublesome. What carpets they had in these newfangled places, so thick that you tripped up in them at every step! In the lift he noticed how concerned she looked, and said with the ghost of a twinkle:

"I'm a pretty host."

When the lift stopped he had to hold firmly to the seat to prevent its slipping under him; but after soup and a glass of champagne he felt much better, and began to enjoy an infirmity which had brought such solicitude into her manner towards him.

"I should have liked you for a daughter," he said suddenly; and watching the smile in her eyes, went on:

"You mustn't get wrapped up in the past at your time of life; plenty of that when you get to my age. That's a nice dress—I like the style."

"I made it myself."

Ah! A woman who could make herself a pretty frock had not lost her interest in life.

"Make hay while the sun shines," he said; "and drink that up. I want to see some colour in your cheeks. We mustn't waste life; it doesn't do. There's a new Marguerite to-night; let's hope she won't be fat. And Mephisto—anything more dreadful than a fat chap playing the Devil I can't imagine."

But they did not go to the opera after all, for in getting up from dinner the dizziness came over him again, and she insisted on his staying quiet and going to bed early. When he parted from her at the door of the hotel, having paid the cabman to drive her to Chelsea, he sat down again for a moment to enjoy the memory of her words: "You are such a darling to me, Uncle Jolyon!" Why! Who wouldn't be! He would have liked to stay up another day and take her to the Zoo, but two days running of him would bore her to death. No, he must wait till next Sunday; she had promised to come then. They would settle those lessons for Holly, if only for a month. It would be something. That little Mam'zelle Beauce wouldn't like it, but she would have to lump it. And crushing his old opera hat against his chest he sought the lift.

He drove to Waterloo next morning, struggling with a desire to say: 'Drive me to Chelsea.' But his sense of proportion was too strong. Besides, he still felt shaky, and did not want to risk another aberration like that of last night, away from home. Holly, too, was expecting him, and what he had in his bag for her. Not that there was any cupboard love in his little sweet—she was a bundle of affection. Then, with the rather bitter cynicism of the old, he wondered for a second whether it was not cupboard love which made Irene put up with him. No, she was not that sort either. She had, if anything, too little notion of how to butter her bread, no sense of property, poor thing! Besides, he had not breathed a word about that codicil, nor should he—sufficient unto the day was the good thereof.

In the victoria which met him at the station Holly was restraining the dog Balthasar, and their caresses made 'jubey' his drive home. All the rest of that fine hot day and most of the next he was content and peaceful, reposing in the shade, while the long lingering sunshine showered gold on the lawns and the flowers. But on Thursday evening at his lonely dinner he began to count the hours; sixty-five till he would go down to meet her again in the little coppice, and walk up through the fields at her side. He had intended to consult the doctor about his fainting fit, but the fellow would be sure to insist on quiet, no excitement and all that; and he did not mean to be tied by the leg, did not want to be told of an infirmity—if there were one, could not afford to hear of it at his time of life, now that this new interest had come. And he carefully avoided making any mention of it in a letter to his son. It would only bring them back with a run! How far this silence was due to consideration for their pleasure, how far to regard for his own, he did not pause to consider.

That night in his study he had just finished his cigar and was dozing off, when he heard the rustle of a gown, and was conscious of a scent of violets. Opening his eyes he saw her, dressed in grey, standing by the fireplace, holding out her arms. The odd thing was that, though those arms seemed to hold nothing, they were curved as if round someone's neck, and her own neck was bent back, her lips open, her eyes closed. She vanished at once, and there were the mantelpiece and his bronzes. But those bronzes and the mantelpiece had not been there when she was, only the fireplace and the wall! Shaken and troubled, he got up. 'I must take medicine,' he thought; 'I can't be well.' His heart beat too fast, he had an asthmatic feeling in the chest; and going to the window, he opened it to get some air. A

215

dog was barking far away, one of the dogs at Gage's farm no doubt, beyond the coppice. A beautiful still night, but dark. 'I dropped off,' he mused, 'that's it! And yet I'll swear my eyes were open!' A sound like a sigh seemed to answer.

"What's that?" he said sharply, "who's there?"

Putting his hand to his side to still the beating of his heart, he stepped out on the terrace. Something soft scurried by in the dark. "Shoo!" It was that great grey cat. 'Young Bosinney was like a great cat!' he thought. 'It was him in there, that she—that she was—He's got her still!' He walked to the edge of the terrace, and looked down into the darkness; he could just see the powdering of the daisies on the unmown lawn. Here to-day and gone to-morrow! And there came the moon, who saw all, young and old, alive and dead, and didn't care a dump! His own turn soon. For a single day of youth he would give what was left! And he turned again towards the house. He could see the windows of the night nursery up there. His little sweet would be asleep. 'Hope that dog won't wake her!' he thought. 'What is it makes us love, and makes us die! I must go to bed.'

And across the terrace stones, growing grey in the moonlight, he passed back within.

How should an old man live his days if not in dreaming of his well-spent past? In that, at all events, there is no agitating warmth, only pale winter sunshine. The shell can withstand the gentle beating of the dynamos of memory. The present he should distrust; the future shun. From beneath thick shade he should watch the sunlight creeping at his toes. If there be sun of summer, let him not go out into it, mistaking it for the Indian-summer sun! Thus peradventure he shall decline softly, slowly, imperceptibly, until impatient Nature clutches his wind-pipe and he gasps away to death some early morning before the world is aired, and they put on his tombstone: 'In the fulness of years!' yea! If he preserve his principles in perfect order, a Forsyte may live on long after he is dead.

Old Jolyon was conscious of all this, and yet there was in him that which transcended Forsyteism. For it is written that a Forsyte shall not love beauty more than reason; nor his own way more than his own health. And something beat within him in these days that with each throb fretted at the thinning shell. His sagacity knew this, but it knew too that he could not stop that beating, nor would if he could. And yet, if you had told him he was living on his capital, he would have stared you down. No, no; a man did not live on his capital; it was not done! The shibboleths of the past are ever more real than the actualities of the present. And he, to whom living on one's capital had always been anathema, could not have borne to have applied so gross a phrase to his own case. Pleasure is healthful; beauty good to see; to live again in the youth of the young—and what else on earth was he doing!

Methodically, as had been the way of his whole life, he now arranged his time. On Tuesdays he journeyed up to town by train; Irene came and dined with him. And they went to the opera. On Thursdays he drove to town, and, putting that fat chap and his horses up, met her in Kensington Gardens, picking up the carriage after he had left her, and driving home again in time for dinner. He threw out the casual formula that he had business in London on those two days. On Wednesdays and Saturdays she came down to give Holly music lessons. The greater the pleasure he took in her society, the more scrupulously fastidious he became, just a matter-of-fact and friendly uncle. Not even in feeling, really, was he more—for, after all, there was his age. And yet, if she were late he fidgeted himself to death. If she missed coming, which happened twice, his eyes grew sad as an old dog's, and he failed to sleep.

And so a month went by—a month of summer in the fields, and in his heart, with summer's heat and the fatigue thereof. Who could have believed a few weeks back that he would have looked forward to his son's and his grand-daughter's return with something like dread! There was such a delicious freedom, such recovery of that independence a man enjoys before he founds a family, about these weeks of lovely weather, and this new companionship with one who demanded nothing, and remained always a little unknown, retaining the fascination of mystery. It was like a draught of wine to him who has been drinking water for so long that he has almost forgotten the stir wine brings to his blood, the narcotic to his brain. The flowers were coloured brighter, scents and music and the sunlight had a living value—were no longer mere reminders of past enjoyment. There was something now to live for which stirred him continually to anticipation. He lived in that, not in retrospection; the difference is considerable to any so old as he. The pleasures of the table, never of much consequence to one naturally abstemious, had lost all value. He ate little, without knowing what he ate; and every day grew thinner and more worn to look at. He was again a 'threadpaper'; and to this thinned form his massive forehead, with hollows at the temples, gave more dignity than ever. He was very well aware that he ought to see the doctor, but liberty was too sweet. He could not afford to pet his frequent shortness of breath and the pain in his side at the expense of liberty. Return to the vegetable existence he had led among the agricultural journals with the life-size mangold wurzels, before this new attraction came into his life—no! He exceeded his allowance of cigars. Two a day had always been his rule. Now he smoked three and sometimes four—a man will when he is filled with the creative spirit. But very often he thought: 'I must give up smoking, and coffee; I must give up rattling up to town.' But he did not; there was no one in any sort of authority to notice him, and this was a priceless boon.

The servants perhaps wondered, but they were, naturally, dumb. Mam'zelle Beauce was too concerned with her own digestion, and too 'wellbrrred' to make personal allusions. Holly had not as yet an eye for the relative appearance of him who was her plaything and her god. It was left for Irene herself to beg him to eat more, to rest in the hot part of the day, to take a tonic, and so forth. But she did not tell him that she was the cause of his thinness— for one cannot see the havoc oneself is working. A man of eighty-five has no passions, but the Beauty which produces passion works on in the old way, till death closes the eyes which crave the sight of Her.

On the first day of the second week in July he received a letter from his son in Paris to say that they would all be back on Friday. This had always been more sure than Fate; but, with the pathetic improvidence given to the old, that they may endure to the end, he had never quite admitted it. Now he did, and something would have to be done. He had ceased to be able to imagine life without this new interest, but that which is not imagined sometimes exists, as Forsytes are perpetually finding to their cost. He sat in his old leather chair, doubling up the letter, and mumbling with his lips the end of an unlighted cigar. After to-morrow his Tuesday expeditions to town would have to be abandoned. He could still drive up, perhaps, once a week, on the pretext of seeing his man of business. But even that would be dependent on his health, for now they would begin to fuss about him. The lessons! The lessons must go on! She must swallow down her scruples, and June must put her feelings in her pocket. She had done so once, on the day after the news of Bosinney's death; what she had done then, she could surely do again now. Four years since that injury was inflicted on her—not Christian to keep the memory of old sores alive. June's will was strong, but his was stronger, for his sands were running out. Irene was soft, surely she would do this for him, subdue her natural shrinking, sooner than give him pain! The lessons must continue; for if they did, he was secure. And lighting his cigar at last, he began trying to shape out how to put it to them all, and explain this strange intimacy; how to veil and wrap it away from the naked truth—that he could not bear to be deprived of the sight of beauty. Ah! Holly! Holly was fond of her, Holly liked her lessons. She would save him—

his little sweet! And with that happy thought he became serene, and wondered what he had been worrying about so fearfully. He must not worry, it left him always curiously weak, and as if but half present in his own body.

That evening after dinner he had a return of the dizziness, though he did not faint. He would not ring the bell, because he knew it would mean a fuss, and make his going up on the morrow more conspicuous. When one grew old, the whole world was in conspiracy to limit freedom, and for what reason?—just to keep the breath in him a little longer. He did not want it at such cost. Only the dog Balthasar saw his lonely recovery from that weakness; anxiously watched his master go to the sideboard and drink some brandy, instead of giving him a biscuit. When at last old Jolyon felt able to tackle the stairs he went up to bed. And, though still shaky next morning, the thought of the evening sustained and strengthened him. It was always such a pleasure to give her a good dinner—he suspected her of undereating when she was alone; and, at the opera to watch her eyes glow and brighten, the unconscious smiling of her lips. She hadn't much pleasure, and this was the last time he would be able to give her that treat. But when he was packing his bag he caught himself wishing that he had not the fatigue of dressing for dinner before him, and the exertion, too, of telling her about June's return.

The opera that evening was 'Carmen,' and he chose the last entr'acte to break the news, instinctively putting it off till the latest moment.

She took it quietly, queerly; in fact, he did not know how she had taken it before the wayward music lifted up again and silence became necessary. The mask was down over her face, that mask behind which so much went on that he could not see. She wanted time to think it over, no doubt! He would not press her, for she would be coming to give her lesson to-morrow afternoon, and he should see her then when she had got used to the idea. In the cab he talked only of the Carmen; he had seen better in the old days, but this one was not bad at all. When he took her hand to say good-night, she bent quickly forward and kissed his forehead.

"Good-bye, dear Uncle Jolyon, you have been so sweet to me."

"To-morrow then," he said. "Good-night. Sleep well." She echoed softly: "Sleep well" and from the cab window, already moving away, he saw her face screwed round towards him, and her hand put out in a gesture which seemed to linger.

He sought his room slowly. They never gave him the same, and he could not get used to these 'spick-and-spandy' bedrooms with new furniture and grey-green carpets sprinkled all over with pink roses. He was wakeful and that wretched Habanera kept throbbing in his head.

His French had never been equal to its words, but its sense he knew, if it had any sense, a gipsy thing—wild and unaccountable. Well, there was in life something which upset all your care and plans—something which made men and women dance to its pipes. And he lay staring from deep-sunk eyes into the darkness where the unaccountable held sway. You thought you had hold of life, but it slipped away behind you, took you by the scruff of the neck, forced you here and forced you there, and then, likely as not, squeezed life out of you! It took the very stars like that, he shouldn't wonder, rubbed their noses together and flung them apart; it had never done playing its pranks. Five million people in this great blunderbuss of a town, and all of them at the mercy of that Life-Force, like a lot of little dried peas hopping about on a board when you struck your fist on it. Ah, well! Himself would not hop much longer—a good long sleep would do him good!

How hot it was up here!—how noisy! His forehead burned; she had kissed it just where he always worried; just there—as if she had known the very place and wanted to kiss it all away for him. But, instead, her lips left a patch of grievous uneasiness. She had never spoken in quite that voice, had never before made that lingering gesture or looked back at him as she drove away.

He got out of bed and pulled the curtains aside; his room faced down over the river. There was little air, but the sight of that breadth of water flowing by, calm, eternal, soothed him. 'The great thing,' he thought 'is not to make myself a nuisance. I'll think of my little sweet, and go to sleep.' But it was long before the heat and throbbing of the London night died out into the short slumber of the summer morning. And old Jolyon had but forty winks.

When he reached home next day he went out to the flower garden, and with the help of Holly, who was very delicate with flowers, gathered a great bunch of carnations. They were, he told her, for 'the lady in grey'—a name still bandied between them; and he put them in a bowl in his study where he meant to tackle Irene the moment she came, on the subject of June and future lessons. Their fragrance and colour would help. After lunch he lay down, for he felt very tired, and the carriage would not bring her from the station till four o'clock. But as the hour approached he grew restless, and sought the schoolroom, which overlooked the drive. The sun-blinds were down, and Holly was there with Mademoiselle Beauce, sheltered from the heat of a stifling July day, attending to their silkworms. Old Jolyon had a natural antipathy to these methodical creatures, whose heads and colour reminded him of elephants; who nibbled such quantities of holes in nice green leaves; and smelled, as he thought, horrid. He sat down on a chintz-covered windowseat whence he could see the drive, and get what air there was; and the dog Balthasar who appreciated chintz on hot days, jumped up beside him. Over the cottage piano a violet dust-sheet, faded almost to grey, was spread, and on it the first lavender, whose scent filled the room. In spite of the coolness here, perhaps because of that coolness the beat of life vehemently impressed his ebbed-down senses. Each sunbeam which came through the chinks had annoying brilliance; that dog smelled very strong; the lavender perfume was overpowering; those silkworms heaving up their grey-green backs seemed horribly alive; and Holly's dark head bent over them had a wonderfully silky sheen. A marvellous cruelly strong thing was life when you were old and weak; it seemed to mock you with its multitude of forms and its beating vitality. He had never, till those last few weeks, had this curious feeling of being with one half of him eagerly borne along in the stream of life, and with the other half left on the bank, watching that helpless progress. Only when Irene was with him did he lose this double consciousness.

Holly turned her head, pointed with her little brown fist to the piano—for to point with a finger was not 'well-brrred'—and said slyly:

"Look at the 'lady in grey,' Gran; isn't she pretty to-day?"

Old Jolyon's heart gave a flutter, and for a second the room was clouded; then it cleared, and he said with a twinkle:

"Who's been dressing her up?"

"Mam'zelle."

"Hollee! Don't be foolish!"

That prim little Frenchwoman! She hadn't yet got over the music lessons being taken away from her. That wouldn't help. His little sweet was the only friend they had. Well, they were her lessons. And he shouldn't budge shouldn't budge for anything. He stroked the warm wool on Balthasar's head, and heard Holly say: "When mother's home, there won't be any changes, will there? She doesn't like strangers, you know."

The child's words seemed to bring the chilly atmosphere of opposition about old Jolyon, and disclose all the menace to his new-found freedom. Ah! He would have to resign himself to being an old man at the mercy of care and love, or fight to keep this new and prized companionship; and to fight tired him to death. But his thin, worn face hardened into resolution till it appeared all jaw. This was his house, and his affair; he should not budge! He looked at his watch, old and thin like himself; he had owned it fifty years. Past four already! And kissing the top of Holly's head in passing, he went down to the hall. He wanted to get hold of her before she went up to give her lesson. At the first sound of wheels he stepped out into the porch, and saw at once that the victoria was empty.

"The train's in, sir; but the lady 'asn't come."

Old Jolyon gave him a sharp upward look, his eyes seemed to push away that fat chap's curiosity, and defy him to see the bitter disappointment he was feeling.

"Very well," he said, and turned back into the house. He went to his study and sat down, quivering like a leaf. What did this mean? She might have lost her train, but he knew well enough she hadn't. 'Good-bye, dear Uncle Jolyon.' Why 'Good-bye' and not 'Good-night'? And that hand of hers lingering in the air. And her kiss. What did it mean? Vehement alarm and irritation took possession of him. He got up and began to pace the Turkey carpet, between window and wall. She was going to give him up! He felt it for certain—and he defenceless. An old man wanting to look on beauty! It was ridiculous! Age closed his mouth, paralysed his power to fight. He had no right to what was warm and living, no right to anything but memories and sorrow. He could not plead with her; even an old man has his dignity. Defenceless! For an hour, lost to bodily fatigue, he paced up and down, past the bowl of carnations he had plucked, which mocked him with its scent. Of all things hard to bear, the prostration of will-power is hardest, for one who has always had his way. Nature had got him in its net, and like an unhappy fish he turned and swam at the meshes, here and there, found no hole, no breaking point. They brought him tea at five o'clock, and a letter. For a moment hope beat up in him. He cut the envelope with the butter knife, and read:

"DEAREST UNCLE JOLYON,—I can't bear to write anything that may disappoint you, but I was too cowardly to tell you last night. I feel I can't come down and give Holly any more lessons, now that June is coming back. Some things go too deep to be forgotten. It has been such a joy to see you and Holly. Perhaps I shall still see you sometimes when you come up, though I'm sure it's not good for you; I can see you are tiring yourself too much. I believe you ought to rest quite quietly all this hot weather, and now you have your son and June coming back you will be so happy. Thank you a million times for all your sweetness to me.

"Lovingly your IRENE."

So, there it was! Not good for him to have pleasure and what he chiefly cared about; to try and put off feeling the inevitable end of all things, the approach of death with its stealthy, rustling footsteps. Not good for him! Not even she could see how she was his new lease of interest in life, the incarnation of all the beauty he felt slipping from him.

His tea grew cold, his cigar remained unlit; and up and down he paced, torn between his dignity and his hold on life. Intolerable to be squeezed out slowly, without a say of your own, to live on when your will was in the hands of others bent on weighing you to the ground with care and love. Intolerable! He would see what telling her the truth would do— the truth that he wanted the sight of her more than just a lingering on. He sat down at his old bureau and took a pen. But he could not write. There was something revolting in having to plead like this; plead that she should warm his eyes with her beauty. It was tantamount to confessing dotage. He simply could not. And instead, he wrote:

"I had hoped that the memory of old sores would not be allowed to stand in the way of what is a pleasure and a profit to me and my little grand-daughter. But old men learn to forego their whims; they are obliged to, even the whim to live must be foregone sooner or later; and perhaps the sooner the better.

"My love to you,

"JOLYON FORSYTE."

'Bitter,' he thought, 'but I can't help it. I'm tired.' He sealed and dropped it into the box for the evening post, and hearing it fall to the bottom, thought: "There goes all I've looked forward to!'

That evening after dinner which he scarcely touched, after his cigar which he left half-smoked for it made him feel faint, he went very slowly upstairs and stole into the night-nursery. He sat down on the window-seat. A night-light was burning, and he could just see Holly's face, with one hand underneath the cheek. An early cockchafer buzzed in the Japanese paper with which they had filled the grate, and one of the horses in the stable stamped restlessly. To sleep like that child! He pressed apart two rungs of the venetian blind and looked out. The moon was rising, blood-red. He had never seen so red a moon. The woods and fields out there were dropping to sleep too, in the last glimmer of the summer light. And beauty, like a spirit, walked. 'I've had a long life,' he thought, 'the best of nearly everything. I'm an ungrateful chap; I've seen a lot of beauty in my time. Poor young Bosinney said I had a sense of beauty. There's a man in the moon to-night!' A moth went by, another, another. 'Ladies in grey!' He closed his eyes. A feeling that he would never open them again beset him; he let it grow, let himself sink; then, with a shiver, dragged the lids up. There was something wrong with him, no doubt, deeply wrong; he would have to have the doctor after all. It didn't much matter now! Into that coppice the moon-light would have crept; there would be shadows, and those shadows would be the only things awake. No birds, beasts, flowers, insects; Just the shadows —moving; 'Ladies in grey!' Over that log they would climb; would whisper together. She and Bosinney! Funny thought! And the frogs and little things would whisper too! How the clock ticked, in here! It was all eerie—out there in the light of that red moon; in here with the little steady night-light and, the ticking clock and the nurse's dressing-gown hanging from the edge of the screen, tall, like a woman's figure. 'Lady in grey!' And a very odd thought beset him: Did she exist? Had she ever come at all? Or was she but the emanation of all the beauty he had loved and must leave so soon? The violet-grey spirit with the dark eyes and the crown of amber hair, who walks the dawn and the moonlight, and at blue-bell time? What was she, who was she, did she exist? He rose and stood a moment clutching the window-sill, to give him a sense of reality again; then began tiptoeing towards the door. He stopped at the foot of the bed; and Holly, as if conscious of his eyes fixed on her, stirred, sighed, and curled up closer in defence. He tiptoed on and passed out into the dark passage; reached his room, undressed at once, and stood before a mirror in his night-shirt. What a scarecrow—with temples fallen in, and thin legs! His eyes resisted his own image, and a look of pride came on his face. All was in league to pull him down, even his reflection in the glass, but he was not down—yet! He got into bed, and lay a long time without sleeping, trying to reach resignation, only too well aware that fretting and disappointment were very bad for him.

He woke in the morning so unrefreshed and strengthless that he sent for the doctor. After sounding him, the fellow pulled a face as long as your arm, and ordered him to stay in bed and give up smoking. That was no hardship; there was nothing to get up for, and when he felt ill, tobacco always lost its savour. He spent the morning languidly with the sun-blinds down, turning and re-turning The Times, not reading much, the dog Balthasar lying beside his bed. With his lunch they brought him a telegram, running thus:

'Your letter received coming down this afternoon will be with you at four-thirty. Irene.'

Coming down! After all! Then she did exist—and he was not deserted. Coming down! A glow ran through his limbs; his cheeks and forehead felt hot. He drank his soup, and pushed the tray-table away, lying very quiet until they had removed lunch and left him alone; but every now and then his eyes twinkled. Coming down! His heart beat fast, and then did not seem to beat at all. At three o'clock he got up and dressed deliberately, noiselessly. Holly and Mam'zelle would be in the schoolroom, and the servants asleep after their dinner, he shouldn't wonder. He opened his door cautiously, and went downstairs. In the hall the dog Balthasar lay solitary, and, followed by him, old Jolyon passed into his study and out into the burning afternoon. He meant to go down and meet her in the coppice, but felt at once he could not manage that in this heat. He sat down instead under the oak tree by the swing, and the dog Balthasar, who also felt the heat, lay down beside him. He sat there smiling. What a revel of bright minutes! What a hum of insects, and cooing of pigeons! It was the quintessence of a summer day. Lovely! And he was happy—happy as a sand-boy, whatever that might be. She was coming; she had not given him up! He had everything in life he wanted—except a little more breath, and less weight—just here! He would see her when she emerged from the fernery, come swaying just a little, a violet-grey figure passing over the daisies and dandelions and 'soldiers' on the lawn—the soldiers with their flowery crowns. He would not move, but she would come up to him and say: 'Dear Uncle Jolyon, I am sorry!' and sit in the swing and let him look at her and tell her that he had not been very well but was all right now; and that dog would lick her hand. That dog knew his master was fond of her; that dog was a good dog.

It was quite shady under the tree; the sun could not get at him, only make the rest of the world bright so that he could see the Grand Stand at Epsom away out there, very far, and the cows cropping the clover in the field and swishing at the flies with their tails. He smelled the scent of limes, and lavender. Ah! that was why there was such a racket of bees. They were excited—busy, as his heart was busy and excited. Drowsy, too, drowsy and drugged on honey and happiness; as his heart was drugged and drowsy. Summer—summer—they seemed saying; great bees and little bees, and the flies too!

The stable clock struck four; in half an hour she would be here. He would have just one tiny nap, because he had had so little sleep of late; and then he would be fresh for her, fresh for youth and beauty, coming towards him across the sunlit lawn—lady in grey! And settling back in his chair he closed his eyes. Some thistle-down came on what little air there was, and pitched on his moustache more white than itself. He did not know; but his breathing stirred it, caught there. A ray of sunlight struck through and lodged on his boot. A bumble-bee alighted and strolled on the crown of his Panama hat. And the delicious surge of slumber reached the brain beneath that hat, and the head swayed forward and rested on his breast. Summer—summer! So went the hum.

The stable clock struck the quarter past. The dog Balthasar stretched and looked up at his master. The thistledown no longer moved. The dog placed his chin over the sunlit foot. It did not stir. The dog withdrew his chin quickly, rose, and leaped on old Jolyon's lap, looked in his face, whined; then, leaping down, sat on his haunches, gazing up. And suddenly he uttered a long, long howl.

But the thistledown was still as death, and the face of his old master.

Summer—summer—summer! The soundless footsteps on the grass! 1917

VOLUME II. IN CHANCERY

Two households both alike in dignity,

From ancient grudge, break into new mutiny.

—Romeo and Juliet

TO JESSIE AND JOSEPH CONRAD

PART 1

CHAPTER I—AT TIMOTHY'S

The possessive instinct never stands still. Through florescence and feud, frosts and fires, it followed the laws of progression even in the Forsyte family which had believed it fixed for ever. Nor can it be dissociated from environment any more than the quality of potato from the soil.

The historian of the English eighties and nineties will, in his good time, depict the somewhat rapid progression from self-contented and contained provincialism to still more self-contented if less contained imperialism—in other words, the 'possessive' instinct of the nation on the move. And so, as if in conformity, was it with the Forsyte family. They were spreading not merely on the surface, but within.

When, in 1895, Susan Hayman, the married Forsyte sister, followed her husband at the ludicrously low age of seventy-four, and was cremated, it made strangely little stir among the six old Forsytes left. For this apathy there were three causes. First: the almost surreptitious burial of old Jolyon in 1892 down at Robin Hill—first of the Forsytes to desert the family grave at Highgate. That burial, coming a year after Swithin's entirely proper funeral, had occasioned a great deal of talk on Forsyte 'Change, the abode of Timothy Forsyte on the Bayswater Road, London, which still collected and radiated family gossip. Opinions ranged from the lamentation of Aunt Juley to the outspoken assertion of Francie that it was 'a jolly good thing to stop all that stuffy Highgate business.' Uncle Jolyon in his later years—indeed, ever since the strange and lamentable affair between his granddaughter June's lover, young Bosinney, and Irene, his nephew Soames Forsyte's wife—had noticeably rapped the family's knuckles; and that way of his own which he had always taken had begun to seem to them a little wayward. The philosophic vein in him, of course, had always been too liable to crop out of the strata of pure Forsyteism, so they were in a way prepared for his interment in a strange spot. But the whole thing was an odd business, and when the contents of his Will became current coin on Forsyte 'Change, a shiver had gone round the clan. Out of his estate (L.145,304 gross, with liabilities L.35 7s. 4d.) he had actually left L.15,000 to "whomever do you think, my dear? To Irene!" that runaway wife of his nephew Soames; Irene, a woman who had almost disgraced the family, and—still more amazing was to him no blood relation. Not out and out, of course; only a life interest—only the income from it! Still, there it was; and old Jolyon's claim to be the perfect Forsyte was ended once for all. That, then, was the first reason why the burial of Susan Hayman—at Woking—made little stir.

The second reason was altogether more expansive and imperial. Besides the house on Campden Hill, Susan had a place (left her by Hayman when he died) just over the border in Hants, where the Hayman boys had learned to be such good shots and riders, as it was believed, which was of course nice for them, and creditable to everybody; and the fact of owning something really countrified seemed somehow to excuse the dispersion of her remains—though what could have put cremation into her head they could not think! The usual invitations, however, had been issued, and Soames had gone down and young Nicholas, and the Will had been quite satisfactory so far as it went, for she had only had a life interest; and everything had gone quite smoothly to the children in equal shares.

The third reason why Susan's burial made little stir was the most expansive of all. It was summed up daringly by Euphemia, the pale, the thin: "Well, I think people have a right to their own bodies, even when they're dead." Coming from a daughter of Nicholas, a Liberal of the old school and most tyrannical, it was a startling remark—showing in a flash what a lot of water had run under bridges since the death of Aunt Ann in '86, just when the proprietorship of Soames over his wife's body was acquiring the uncertainty which had led to such disaster. Euphemia, of course, spoke like a child, and had no experience; for though well over thirty by now, her name was still Forsyte. But, making all allowances, her remark did undoubtedly show expansion of the principle of liberty, decentralisation and shift in the central point of possession from others to oneself. When Nicholas heard his daughter's remark from Aunt Hester he had rapped out: "Wives and daughters! There's no end to their liberty in these days. I knew that 'Jackson' case would lead to things—lugging in Habeas Corpus like that!" He had, of course, never really forgiven the Married Woman's Property Act, which would so have interfered with him if he had not mercifully married before it was passed. But, in truth, there was no denying the revolt among the younger Forsytes against being owned by others; that, as it were, Colonial disposition to own oneself, which is the paradoxical forerunner of Imperialism, was making progress all the time. They were all now married, except George, confirmed to the Turf and the Iseeum Club; Francie, pursuing her musical career in a studio off the King's Road, Chelsea, and still taking 'lovers' to dances; Euphemia, living at home and complaining of Nicholas; and those two Dromios, Giles and Jesse Hayman. Of the third generation there were not very many—young Jolyon had three, Winifred Dartie four, young Nicholas six already, young Roger had one, Marian Tweetyman one; St. John Hayman two. But the rest of the sixteen married—Soames, Rachel and Cicely of James' family; Eustace and Thomas of Roger's; Ernest, Archibald and Florence of Nicholas'; Augustus and Annabel Spender of the Hayman's—were going down the years unreproduced.

Thus, of the ten old Forsytes twenty-one young Forsytes had been born; but of the twenty-one young Forsytes there were as yet only seventeen descendants; and it already seemed unlikely that there would be more than a further unconsidered trifle or so. A student of statistics must have noticed that the birth rate had varied in accordance with the rate of interest for your money. Grandfather 'Superior Dosset' Forsyte in the early nineteenth century had been getting ten per cent. for his, hence ten children. Those ten, leaving out the four who had not married, and Juley, whose husband Septimus Small had, of course, died almost at once, had averaged from four to five per cent. for theirs, and produced accordingly. The twenty-one whom they produced were now getting barely three per cent. in the Consols to which their father had mostly tied the Settlements they made to avoid death duties, and the six of them who had been reproduced had seventeen children, or just the proper two and five-sixths per stem.

There were other reasons, too, for this mild reproduction. A distrust of their earning powers, natural where a sufficiency is guaranteed, together with the knowledge that their fathers did not die, kept them cautious. If one had children and not much income, the standard of taste and comfort must of necessity go down; what was enough for two was not enough for four, and so on—it would be better to wait and see what Father did. Besides, it was nice to be able to take holidays unhampered. Sooner in fact than own children, they preferred to concentrate on the ownership of themselves, conforming to the growing tendency fin de siecle, as it was called. In this way, little risk was run, and one would be able to have a motor-car. Indeed, Eustace already had one, but it had shaken him horribly, and broken one of his eye teeth; so that it would be better to wait till they were a little safer. In the meantime, no more children! Even young Nicholas was drawing in his horns, and had made no addition to his six for quite three years.

The corporate decay, however, of the Forsytes, their dispersion rather, of which all this was symptomatic, had not advanced so far as to prevent a rally when Roger Forsyte died in 1899. It had been a glorious summer, and after holidays abroad and at the sea they were practically all back in London, when Roger with a touch of his old originality had suddenly breathed his last at his own house in Princes Gardens. At Timothy's it was whispered sadly that poor Roger had always been eccentric about his digestion—had he not, for instance, preferred German mutton to all the other brands?

Be that as it may, his funeral at Highgate had been perfect, and coming away from it Soames Forsyte made almost mechanically for his Uncle Timothy's in the Bayswater Road. The 'Old Things'—Aunt Juley and Aunt Hester—would like to hear about it. His father— James—at eighty-eight had not felt up to the fatigue of the funeral; and Timothy himself, of course, had not gone; so that Nicholas had been the only brother present. Still, there had been a fair gathering; and it would cheer Aunts Juley and Hester up to know. The kindly thought was not unmixed with the inevitable longing to get something out of everything you do, which is the chief characteristic of Forsytes, and indeed the saner elements in every nation. In this practice of taking family matters to Timothy's in the Bayswater Road, Soames was but following in the footsteps of his father, who had been in the habit of going at least once a week to see his sisters at Timothy's, and had only given it up when he lost his nerve at eighty-six, and could not go out without Emily. To go with Emily was of no use, for who could really talk to anyone in the presence of his own wife? Like James in the old days, Soames found time to go there nearly every Sunday, and sit in the little drawing-room into which, with his undoubted taste, he had introduced a good deal of change and china not quite up to his own fastidious mark, and at least two rather doubtful Barbizon pictures, at Christmastides. He himself, who had done extremely well with the Barbizons, had for some years past moved towards the Marises, Israels, and Mauve, and was hoping to do better. In the riverside house which he now inhabited near Mapledurham he had a gallery, beautifully hung and lighted, to which few London dealers were strangers. It served, too, as a Sunday afternoon attraction in those week-end parties which his sisters, Winifred or Rachel, occasionally organised for him. For though he was but a taciturn showman, his quiet collected determinism seldom failed to influence his guests, who knew that his reputation was grounded not on mere aesthetic fancy, but on his power of gauging the future of market values. When he went to Timothy's he almost always had some little tale of triumph over a dealer to unfold, and dearly he loved that coo of pride with which his aunts would greet it. This afternoon, however, he was differently animated, coming from Roger's funeral in his neat dark clothes—not quite black, for after all an uncle was but an uncle, and his soul abhorred excessive display of feeling. Leaning back in a marqueterie chair and gazing down his uplifted nose at the sky-blue walls plastered with gold frames, he was noticeably silent. Whether because he had been to a funeral or not, the peculiar Forsyte build of his face was seen to the best advantage this afternoon—a face concave and long, with a jaw which divested of flesh would have seemed extravagant: altogether a chinny face though not at all ill-looking. He was feeling more strongly than ever that Timothy's was hopelessly 'rum-ti-too' and the souls of his aunts dismally mid-Victorian. The subject on which alone he wanted to talk—his own undivorced position—was unspeakable. And yet it occupied his mind to the exclusion of all else. It was only since the Spring that this had been so and a new feeling grown up which was egging him on towards what he knew might well be folly in a Forsyte of forty-five. More and more of late he had been conscious that he was 'getting on.' The fortune already considerable when he conceived the house at Robin Hill which had finally wrecked his marriage with Irene, had mounted with surprising vigour in the twelve lonely years during which he had devoted himself to little else. He was worth to-day well over a hundred thousand pounds, and had no one to leave it to—no real object for going on with what was his religion. Even if he were to relax his efforts, money made money, and he felt that he would have a hundred and fifty thousand before he knew where he was. There had always been a strongly domestic, philoprogenitive side to Soames; baulked and frustrated, it had hidden itself away, but now had crept out again in this his 'prime of life.' Concreted and focussed of late by the attraction of a girl's undoubted beauty, it had become a veritable prepossession.

And this girl was French, not likely to lose her head, or accept any unlegalised position. Moreover, Soames himself disliked the thought of that. He had tasted of the sordid side of sex during those long years of forced celibacy, secretively, and always with disgust, for he was fastidious, and his sense of law and order innate. He wanted no hole and corner liaison. A marriage at the Embassy in Paris, a few months' travel, and he could bring Annette back quite separated from a past which in truth was not too distinguished, for she only kept the accounts in her mother's Soho Restaurant; he could bring her back as something very new and chic with her French taste and self-possession, to reign at 'The Shelter' near Mapledurham. On Forsyte 'Change and among his riverside friends it would be current that he had met a charming French girl on his travels and married her. There would be the flavour of romance, and a certain cachet about a French wife. No! He was not at all afraid of that. It was only this cursed undivorced condition of his, and—and the question whether Annette would take him, which he dared not put to the touch until he had a clear and even dazzling future to offer her.

In his aunts' drawing-room he heard with but muffled ears those usual questions: How was his dear father? Not going out, of course, now that the weather was turning chilly? Would Soames be sure to tell him that Hester had found boiled holly leaves most comforting for that pain in her side; a poultice every three hours, with red flannel afterwards. And could he relish just a little pot of their very best prune preserve—it was so delicious this year, and had such a wonderful effect. Oh! and about the Darties—had Soames heard that dear Winifred was having a most distressing time with Montague? Timothy thought she really ought to have protection It was said—but Soames mustn't take this for certain—that he had given some of Winifred's jewellery to a dreadful dancer. It was such a bad example for dear Val just as he was going to college. Soames had not heard? Oh, but he must go and see his sister and look into it at once! And did he think these Boers were really going to resist? Timothy was in quite a stew about it. The price of Consols was so high, and he had such a lot of money in them. Did Soames think they must go down if there was a war? Soames nodded. But it would be over very quickly. It would be so bad for Timothy if it wasn't. And of course Soames' dear father would feel it very much at his age. Luckily poor dear Roger had been spared this dreadful anxiety. And Aunt Juley with a little handkerchief wiped away the large tear trying to climb the permanent pout on her now quite withered left cheek; she was remembering dear Roger, and all his originality, and how he used to stick pins into her when they were little together. Aunt Hester, with her instinct for avoiding the unpleasant, here chimed in: Did Soames think they would make Mr. Chamberlain Prime Minister at once? He would settle it all so quickly. She would like to see that old Kruger sent to St. Helena. She could remember so well the news of Napoleon's death, and what a relief it had been to his grandfather. Of course she and Juley—"We were in pantalettes then, my dear"—had not felt it much at the time.

Soames took a cup of tea from her, drank it quickly, and ate three of those macaroons for which Timothy's was famous. His faint, pale, supercilious smile had deepened just a little. Really, his family remained hopelessly provincial, however much of London they might possess between them. In these go-ahead days their provincialism stared out even more than it used to. Why, old Nicholas was still a Free Trader, and a member of that antediluvian home of Liberalism, the Remove Club—though, to be sure, the members were pretty well all Conservatives now, or he himself could not have joined; and Timothy, they said, still wore a nightcap. Aunt Juley spoke again. Dear Soames was looking so well, hardly a day older than he did when dear Ann died, and they were all there together, dear Jolyon, and dear Swithin, and dear Roger. She paused and caught the tear which had climbed the pout on her right cheek. Did he—did he ever hear anything of Irene nowadays? Aunt Hester visibly interposed her shoulder. Really, Juley was always saying something! The smile left Soames' face, and he put his cup down. Here was his subject broached for him, and for all his desire to expand, he could not take advantage.

Aunt Juley went on rather hastily:

"They say dear Jolyon first left her that fifteen thousand out and out; then of course he saw it would not be right, and made it for her life only."

Had Soames heard that?

Soames nodded.

"Your cousin Jolyon is a widower now. He is her trustee; you knew that, of course?"

Soames shook his head. He did know, but wished to show no interest. Young Jolyon and he had not met since the day of Bosinney's death.

"He must be quite middle-aged by now," went on Aunt Juley dreamily. "Let me see, he was born when your dear uncle lived in Mount Street; long before they went to Stanhope Gate in December. Just before that dreadful Commune. Over fifty! Fancy that! Such a pretty baby, and we were all so proud of him; the very first of you all." Aunt Juley sighed, and a lock of not quite her own hair came loose and straggled, so that Aunt Hester gave a little shiver. Soames rose, he was experiencing a curious piece of self-discovery. That old wound to his pride and self-esteem was not yet closed. He had come thinking he could talk of it, even wanting to talk of his fettered condition, and—behold! he was shrinking away from this reminder by Aunt Juley, renowned for her Malapropisms.

Oh, Soames was not going already!

Soames smiled a little vindictively, and said:

"Yes. Good-bye. Remember me to Uncle Timothy!" And, leaving a cold kiss on each forehead, whose wrinkles seemed to try and cling to his lips as if longing to be kissed away, he left them looking brightly after him—dear Soames, it had been so good of him to come to-day, when they were not feeling very...!

With compunction tweaking at his chest Soames descended the stairs, where was always that rather pleasant smell of camphor and port wine, and house where draughts are not permitted. The poor old things—he had not meant to be unkind! And in the street he instantly forgot them, repossessed by the image of Annette and the thought of the cursed coil around him. Why had he not pushed the thing through and obtained divorce when that wretched Bosinney was run over, and there was evidence galore for the asking! And he turned towards his sister Winifred Dartie's residence in Green Street, Mayfair.

CHAPTER II—EXIT A MAN OF THE WORLD

That a man of the world so subject to the vicissitudes of fortunes as Montague Dartie should still be living in a house he had inhabited twenty years at least would have been more noticeable if the rent, rates, taxes, and repairs of that house had not been defrayed by his father-in-law. By that simple if wholesale device James Forsyte had secured a certain stability in the lives of his daughter and his grandchildren. After all, there is something invaluable about a safe roof over the head of a sportsman so dashing as Dartie. Until the events of the last few days he had been almost-supernaturally steady all this year. The fact was he had acquired a half share in a filly of George Forsyte's, who had gone irreparably on the turf, to the horror of Roger, now stilled by the grave. Sleeve-links, by Martyr, out of Shirt-on-fire, by Suspender, was a bay filly, three years old, who for a variety of reasons had never shown her true form. With half ownership of this hopeful animal, all the idealism latent somewhere in Dartie, as in every other man, had put up its head, and kept him quietly ardent for months past. When a man has some thing good to live for it is astonishing how sober he becomes; and what Dartie had was really good—a three to one chance for an autumn handicap, publicly assessed at twenty-five to one. The old-fashioned heaven was a poor thing beside it, and his shirt was on the daughter of Shirt-on-fire. But how much more than his shirt depended on this granddaughter of Suspender! At that roving age of forty-five, trying to Forsytes—and, though perhaps less distinguishable from any other age, trying even to Darties—Montague had fixed his current fancy on a dancer. It was no mean passion, but without money, and a good deal of it, likely to remain a love as airy as her skirts; and Dartie never had any money, subsisting miserably on what he could beg or borrow from Winifred—a woman of character, who kept him because he was the father of her children, and from a lingering admiration for those now-dying Wardour Street good looks which in their youth had fascinated her. She, together with anyone else who would lend him anything, and his losses at cards and on the turf (extraordinary how some men make a good thing out of losses!) were his whole means of subsistence; for James was now too old and nervous to approach, and Soames too formidably adamant. It is not too much to say that Dartie had been living on hope for months. He had never been fond of money for itself, had always despised the Forsytes with their investing habits, though careful to make such use of them as he could. What he liked about money was what it bought—personal sensation.

"No real sportsman cares for money," he would say, borrowing a 'pony' if it was no use trying for a 'monkey.' There was something delicious about Montague Dartie. He was, as George Forsyte said, a 'daisy.'

The morning of the Handicap dawned clear and bright, the last day of September, and Dartie who had travelled to Newmarket the night before, arrayed himself in spotless checks and walked to an eminence to see his half of the filly take her final canter: If she won he would be a cool three thou. in pocket—a poor enough recompense for the sobriety and patience of these weeks of hope, while they had been nursing her for this race. But he had not been able to afford more. Should he 'lay it off' at the eight to one to which she had advanced? This was his single thought while the larks sang above him, and the grassy downs smelled sweet, and the pretty filly passed, tossing her head and glowing like satin.

After all, if he lost it would not be he who paid, and to 'lay it off' would reduce his winnings to some fifteen hundred—hardly enough to purchase a dancer out and out. Even more potent was the itch in the blood of all the Darties for a real flutter. And turning to George he said: "She's a clipper. She'll win hands down; I shall go the whole hog." George, who had laid off every penny, and a few besides, and stood to win, however it came out, grinned down on him from his bulky height, with the words: "So ho, my wild one!" for after a chequered apprenticeship weathered with the money of a deeply complaining Roger, his Forsyte blood was beginning to stand him in good stead in the profession of owner.

There are moments of disillusionment in the lives of men from which the sensitive recorder shrinks. Suffice it to say that the good thing fell down. Sleeve-links finished in the ruck. Dartie's shirt was lost.

Between the passing of these things and the day when Soames turned his face towards Green Street, what had not happened!

When a man with the constitution of Montague Dartie has exercised self-control for months from religious motives, and remains unrewarded, he does not curse God and die, he curses God and lives, to the distress of his family.

Winifred—a plucky woman, if a little too fashionable—who had borne the brunt of him for exactly twenty-one years, had never really believed that he would do what he now did. Like so many wives, she thought she knew the worst, but she had not yet known him in his forty-fifth year, when he, like other men, felt that it was now or never. Paying on the 2nd of October a visit of inspection to her jewel case, she was horrified to observe that her woman's crown and glory was gone—the pearls which Montague had given her in '86, when Benedict was born, and which James had been compelled to pay for in the spring of '87, to save scandal. She consulted her husband at once. He 'pooh-poohed' the matter. They would turn up! Nor till she said sharply: "Very well, then, Monty, I shall go down to Scotland Yard myself," did he consent to take the matter in hand. Alas! that the steady and resolved continuity of design necessary to the accomplishment of sweeping operations should be liable to interruption by drink. That night Dartie returned home without a care in the world or a particle of reticence. Under normal conditions Winifred would merely have locked her door and let him sleep it off, but torturing suspense about her pearls had caused her to wait up for him. Taking a small revolver from his pocket and holding on to the dining table, he told her at once that he did not care a cursh whether she lived s'long as she was quiet; but he himself wash tired o' life. Winifred, holding onto the other side of the dining table, answered:

"Don't be a clown, Monty. Have you been to Scotland Yard?"

Placing the revolver against his chest, Dartie had pulled the trigger several times. It was not loaded. Dropping it with an imprecation, he had muttered: "For shake o' the children," and sank into a chair. Winifred, having picked up the revolver, gave him some soda water. The liquor had a magical effect. Life had illused him; Winifred had never 'unshtood'm.' If he hadn't the right to take the pearls he had given her himself, who had? That Spanish filly had got'm. If Winifred had any 'jection he w'd cut—her—throat. What was the matter with that? (Probably the first use of that celebrated phrase—so obscure are the origins of even the most classical language!)

Winifred, who had learned self-containment in a hard school, looked up at him, and said: "Spanish filly! Do you mean that girl we saw dancing in the Pandemonium Ballet? Well, you are a thief and a blackguard." It had been the last straw on a sorely loaded consciousness; reaching up from his chair Dartie seized his wife's arm, and recalling the achievements of his boyhood, twisted it. Winifred endured the agony with tears in her eyes, but no murmur. Watching for a moment of weakness, she wrenched it free; then placing the dining table between them, said between her teeth: "You are the limit, Monty." (Undoubtedly the inception of that phrase—so is English formed under the stress of circumstances.) Leaving Dartie with foam on his dark moustache she went upstairs, and, after locking her door and bathing her arm in hot water, lay awake all night, thinking of her pearls adorning the neck of another, and of the consideration her husband had presumably received therefor.

The man of the world awoke with a sense of being lost to that world, and a dim recollection of having been called a 'limit.' He sat for half an hour in the dawn and the armchair where he had slept—perhaps the unhappiest half-hour he had ever spent, for even to a Dartie there is something tragic about an end. And he knew that he had reached it. Never again would he sleep in his dining-room and wake with the light filtering through those curtains bought by Winifred at Nickens and Jarveys with the money of James. Never again eat a devilled kidney at that rose-wood table, after a roll in the sheets and a hot bath. He took his note case from his dress coat pocket. Four hundred pounds, in fives and tens—the remainder of the proceeds of his half of Sleeve-links, sold last night, cash down, to George Forsyte, who, having won over the race, had not conceived the sudden dislike to the animal which he himself now felt. The ballet was going to Buenos Aires the day after to-morrow, and he was going too. Full value for the pearls had not yet been received; he was only at the soup.

He stole upstairs. Not daring to have a bath, or shave (besides, the water would be cold), he changed his clothes and packed stealthily all he could. It was hard to leave so many shining boots, but one must sacrifice something. Then, carrying a valise in either hand, he stepped out onto the landing. The house was very quiet—that house where he had begotten his four children. It was a curious moment, this, outside the room of his wife, once admired, if not perhaps loved, who had called him 'the limit.' He steeled himself with that phrase, and tiptoed on; but the next door was harder to pass. It was the room his daughters slept in. Maud was at school, but Imogen would be lying there; and moisture came into Dartie's early morning eyes. She was the most like him of the four, with her dark hair, and her luscious brown glance. Just coming out, a pretty thing! He set down the two valises. This almost formal abdication of fatherhood hurt him. The morning light fell on a face which worked with real emotion. Nothing so false as penitence moved him; but genuine paternal feeling, and that melancholy of 'never again.' He moistened his lips; and complete irresolution for a moment paralysed his legs in their check trousers. It was hard— hard to be thus compelled to leave his home! "D——nit!" he muttered, "I never thought it would come to this." Noises above warned him that the maids were beginning to get up. And grasping the two valises, he tiptoed on downstairs. His cheeks were wet, and the knowledge of that was comforting, as though it guaranteed the genuineness of his sacrifice. He lingered a little to pack all the cigars he had, some papers, a crush hat, a silver cigarette box, a Ruff's Guide. Then, mixing himself a stiff whisky and soda, and lighting a cigarette, he stood hesitating before a photograph of his two girls, in a silver frame. It belonged to Winifred. 'Never mind,' he thought; 'she can get another taken, and I can't!' He slipped it into the valise. Then, putting on his hat and overcoat, he took two others, his best malacca cane, an umbrella, and opened the front door. Closing it softly behind him, he walked out, burdened as he had never been in all his life, and made his way round the corner to wait there for an early cab to come by.

Thus had passed Montague Dartie in the forty-fifth year of his age from the house which he had called his own.

When Winifred came down, and realised that he was not in the house, her first feeling was one of dull anger that he should thus elude the reproaches she had carefully prepared in those long wakeful hours. He had gone off to Newmarket or Brighton, with that woman as likely as not. Disgusting! Forced to a complete reticence before Imogen and the servants, and aware that her father's nerves would never stand the disclosure, she had been unable to refrain from going to Timothy's that afternoon, and pouring out the story of the pearls to Aunts Juley and Hester in utter confidence. It was only on the following morning that she noticed the disappearance of that photograph. What did it mean? Careful examination of her husband's relics prompted the thought that he had gone for good. As that conclusion hardened she stood quite still in the middle of his dressing-room, with all the drawers pulled out, to try and realise what she was feeling. By no means easy! Though he was 'the limit' he was yet her property, and for the life of her she could not but feel the poorer. To be widowed yet not widowed at forty-two; with four children; made conspicuous, an object of commiseration! Gone to the arms of a Spanish Jade! Memories, feelings, which she had thought quite dead, revived within her, painful, sullen, tenacious. Mechanically she closed drawer after drawer, went to her bed, lay on it, and buried her face in the pillows. She did not cry. What was the use of that? When she got off her bed to go down to lunch she felt as if only one thing could do her good, and that was to have Val home. He—her eldest boy—who was to go to Oxford next month at James' expense, was at Littlehampton taking his final gallops with his trainer for Smalls, as he would have phrased it following his father's diction. She caused a telegram to be sent to him.

"I must see about his clothes," she said to Imogen; "I can't have him going up to Oxford all anyhow. Those boys are so particular."

"Val's got heaps of things," Imogen answered.

"I know; but they want overhauling. I hope he'll come."

"He'll come like a shot, Mother. But he'll probably skew his Exam."

"I can't help that," said Winifred. "I want him."

With an innocent shrewd look at her mother's face, Imogen kept silence. It was father, of course! Val did come 'like a shot' at six o'clock.

Imagine a cross between a pickle and a Forsyte and you have young Publius Valerius Dartie. A youth so named could hardly turn out otherwise. When he was born, Winifred, in the heyday of spirits, and the craving for distinction, had determined that her children should have names such as no others had ever had. (It was a mercy—she felt now—that she had just not named Imogen Thisbe.) But it was to George Forsyte, always a wag, that Val's christening was due. It so happened that Dartie, dining with him a week after the birth of his son and heir, had mentioned this aspiration of Winifred's.

"Call him Cato," said George, "it'll be damned piquant!" He had just won a tenner on a horse of that name.

"Cato!" Dartie had replied—they were a little 'on' as the phrase was even in those days—"it's not a Christian name."

"Halo you!" George called to a waiter in knee breeches. "Bring me the Encyc'pedia Brit. from the Library, letter C."

The waiter brought it.

"Here you are!" said George, pointing with his cigar: "Cato Publius Valerius by Virgil out of Lydia. That's what you want. Publius Valerius is Christian enough."

Dartie, on arriving home, had informed Winifred. She had been charmed. It was so 'chic.' And Publius Valerius became the baby's name, though it afterwards transpired that they had got hold of the inferior Cato. In 1890, however, when little Publius was nearly ten, the word 'chic' went out of fashion, and sobriety came in; Winifred began to have doubts. They were confirmed by little Publius himself who returned from his first term at school complaining that life was a burden to him—they called him Pubby. Winifred—a woman of real decision—promptly changed his school and his name to Val, the Publius being dropped even as an initial.

At nineteen he was a limber, freckled youth with a wide mouth, light eyes, long dark lashes; a rather charming smile, considerable knowledge of what he should not know, and no experience of what he ought to do. Few boys had more narrowly escaped being expelled— the engaging rascal. After kissing his mother and pinching Imogen, he ran upstairs three at a time, and came down four, dressed for dinner. He was awfully sorry, but his 'trainer,' who had come up too, had asked him to dine at the Oxford and Cambridge; it wouldn't do to miss—the old chap would be hurt. Winifred let him go with an unhappy pride. She had wanted him at home, but it was very nice to know that his tutor was so fond of him. He went out with a wink at Imogen, saying: "I say, Mother, could I have two plover's eggs when I come in?—cook's got some. They top up so jolly well. Oh! and look here—have you any money?—I had to borrow a fiver from old Snobby."

Winifred, looking at him with fond shrewdness, answered:

"My dear, you are naughty about money. But you shouldn't pay him to-night, anyway; you're his guest. How nice and slim he looked in his white waistcoat, and his dark thick lashes!"

"Oh, but we may go to the theatre, you see, Mother; and I think I ought to stand the tickets; he's always hard up, you know."

Winifred produced a five-pound note, saying:

"Well, perhaps you'd better pay him, but you mustn't stand the tickets too."

Val pocketed the fiver.

"If I do, I can't," he said. "Good-night, Mum!"

He went out with his head up and his hat cocked joyously, sniffing the air of Piccadilly like a young hound loosed into covert. Jolly good biz! After that mouldy old slow hole down there!

He found his 'tutor,' not indeed at the Oxford and Cambridge, but at the Goat's Club. This 'tutor' was a year older than himself, a good-looking youth, with fine brown eyes, and smooth dark hair, a small mouth, an oval face, languid, immaculate, cool to a degree, one of those young men who without effort establish moral ascendancy over their companions. He had missed being expelled from school a year before Val, had spent that year at Oxford, and Val could almost see a halo round his head. His name was Crum, and no one could get through money quicker. It seemed to be his only aim in life—dazzling to young Val, in whom, however, the Forsyte would stand apart, now and then, wondering where the value for that money was.

They dined quietly, in style and taste; left the Club smoking cigars, with just two bottles inside them, and dropped into stalls at the Liberty. For Val the sound of comic songs, the sight of lovely legs were fogged and interrupted by haunting fears that he would never equal Crum's quiet dandyism. His idealism was roused; and when that is so, one is never quite at ease. Surely he had too wide a mouth, not the best cut of waistcoat, no braid on his trousers, and his lavender gloves had no thin black stitchings down the back. Besides, he laughed too much—Crum never laughed, he only smiled, with his regular dark brows raised a little so that they formed a gable over his just drooped lids. No! he would never be

Crum's equal. All the same it was a jolly good show, and Cynthia Dark simply ripping. Between the acts Crum regaled him with particulars of Cynthia's private life, and the awful knowledge became Val's that, if he liked, Crum could go behind. He simply longed to say: "I say, take me!" but dared not, because of his deficiencies; and this made the last act or two almost miserable. On coming out Crum said: "It's half an hour before they close; let's go on to the Pandemonium." They took a hansom to travel the hundred yards, and seats costing seven-and-six apiece because they were going to stand, and walked into the Promenade. It was in these little things, this utter negligence of money that Crum had such engaging polish. The ballet was on its last legs and night, and the traffic of the Promenade was suffering for the moment. Men and women were crowded in three rows against the barrier. The whirl and dazzle on the stage, the half dark, the mingled tobacco fumes and women's scent, all that curious lure to promiscuity which belongs to Promenades, began to free young Val from his idealism. He looked admiringly in a young woman's face, saw she was not young, and quickly looked away. Shades of Cynthia Dark! The young woman's arm touched his unconsciously; there was a scent of musk and mignonette. Val looked round the corner of his lashes. Perhaps she was young, after all. Her foot trod on his; she begged his pardon. He said:

"Not at all; jolly good ballet, isn't it?"

"Oh, I'm tired of it; aren't you?"

Young Val smiled—his wide, rather charming smile. Beyond that he did not go—not yet convinced. The Forsyte in him stood out for greater certainty. And on the stage the ballet whirled its kaleidoscope of snow-white, salmon-pink, and emerald-green and violet and seemed suddenly to freeze into a stilly spangled pyramid. Applause broke out, and it was over! Maroon curtains had cut it off. The semi-circle of men and women round the barrier broke up, the young woman's arm pressed his. A little way off disturbance seemed centring round a man with a pink carnation; Val stole another glance at the young woman, who was looking towards it. Three men, unsteady, emerged, walking arm in arm. The one in the centre wore the pink carnation, a white waistcoat, a dark moustache; he reeled a little as he walked. Crum's voice said slow and level: "Look at that bounder, he's screwed!" Val turned to look. The 'bounder' had disengaged his arm, and was pointing straight at them. Crum's voice, level as ever, said:

"He seems to know you!" The 'bounder' spoke:

"H'llo!" he said. "You f'llows, look! There's my young rascal of a son!"

Val saw. It was his father! He could have sunk into the crimson carpet. It was not the meeting in this place, not even that his father was 'screwed'; it was Crum's word 'bounder,' which, as by heavenly revelation, he perceived at that moment to be true. Yes, his father looked a bounder with his dark good looks, and his pink carnation, and his square, self-assertive walk. And without a word he ducked behind the young woman and slipped out of the Promenade. He heard the word, "Val!" behind him, and ran down deep-carpeted steps past the 'chuckersout,' into the Square.

To be ashamed of his own father is perhaps the bitterest experience a young man can go through. It seemed to Val, hurrying away, that his career had ended before it had begun. How could he go up to Oxford now amongst all those chaps, those splendid friends of Crum's, who would know that his father was a 'bounder'! And suddenly he hated Crum. Who the devil was Crum, to say that? If Crum had been beside him at that moment, he would certainly have been jostled off the pavement. His own father—his own! A choke came up in his throat, and he dashed his hands down deep into his overcoat pockets. Damn Crum! He conceived the wild idea of running back and fending his father, taking him by the arm and walking about with him in front of Crum; but gave it up at once and pursued his way down Piccadilly. A young woman planted herself before him. "Not so angry, darling!" He shied, dodged her, and suddenly became quite cool. If Crum ever said a word, he would jolly well punch his head, and there would be an end of it. He walked a hundred yards or more, contented with that thought, then lost its comfort utterly. It wasn't simple like that! He remembered how, at school, when some parent came down who did not pass the standard, it just clung to the fellow afterwards. It was one of those things nothing could remove. Why had his mother married his father, if he was a 'bounder'? It was bitterly unfair—jolly low-down on a fellow to give him a 'bounder' for father. The worst of it was that now Crum had spoken the word, he realised that he had long known subconsciously that his father was not 'the clean potato.' It was the beastliest thing that had ever happened to him—beastliest thing that had ever happened to any fellow! And, down-hearted as he had never yet been, he came to Green Street, and let himself in with a smuggled latch-key. In the dining-room his plover's eggs were set invitingly, with some cut bread and butter, and a little whisky at the bottom of a decanter—just enough, as Winifred had thought, for him to feel himself a man. It made him sick to look at them, and he went upstairs.

Winifred heard him pass, and thought: 'The dear boy's in. Thank goodness! If he takes after his father I don't know what I shall do! But he won't he's like me. Dear Val!'

CHAPTER III—SOAMES PREPARES TO TAKE STEPS

When Soames entered his sister's little Louis Quinze drawing-room, with its small balcony, always flowered with hanging geraniums in the summer, and now with pots of Lilium Auratum, he was struck by the immutability of human affairs. It looked just the same as on his first visit to the newly married Darties twenty-one years ago. He had chosen the furniture himself, and so completely that no subsequent purchase had ever been able to change the room's atmosphere. Yes, he had founded his sister well, and she had wanted it. Indeed, it said a great deal for Winifred that after all this time with Dartie she remained well-founded. From the first Soames had nosed out Dartie's nature from underneath the plausibility, savoir faire, and good looks which had dazzled Winifred, her mother, and even James, to the extent of permitting the fellow to marry his daughter without bringing anything but shares of no value into settlement.

Winifred, whom he noticed next to the furniture, was sitting at her Buhl bureau with a letter in her hand. She rose and came towards him. Tall as himself, strong in the cheekbones, well tailored, something in her face disturbed Soames. She crumpled the letter in her hand, but seemed to change her mind and held it out to him. He was her lawyer as well as her brother.

Soames read, on Iseeum Club paper, these words:

'You will not get chance to insult in my own again. I am leaving country to-morrow. It's played out. I'm tired of being insulted by you. You've brought on yourself. No self-respecting man can stand it. I shall not ask you for anything again. Good-bye. I took the photograph of the two girls. Give them my love. I don't care what your family say. It's all their doing. I'm going to live new life. 'M.D.'

This after-dinner note had a splotch on it not yet quite dry. He looked at Winifred—the splotch had clearly come from her; and he checked the words: 'Good riddance!' Then it occurred to him that with this letter she was entering that very state which he himself so earnestly desired to quit—the state of a Forsyte who was not divorced.

Winifred had turned away, and was taking a long sniff from a little gold-topped bottle. A dull commiseration, together with a vague sense of injury, crept about Soames' heart. He had come to her to talk of his own position, and get sympathy, and here was she in the same position, wanting of course to talk of it, and get sympathy from him. It was always like that! Nobody ever seemed to think that he had troubles and interests of his own. He folded up the letter with the splotch inside, and said:

"What's it all about, now?"

Winifred recited the story of the pearls calmly.

"Do you think he's really gone, Soames? You see the state he was in when he wrote that."

Soames who, when he desired a thing, placated Providence by pretending that he did not think it likely to happen, answered:

"I shouldn't think so. I might find out at his Club."

"If George is there," said Winifred, "he would know."

"George?" said Soames; "I saw him at his father's funeral."

"Then he's sure to be there."

Soames, whose good sense applauded his sister's acumen, said grudgingly: "Well, I'll go round. Have you said anything in Park Lane?"

"I've told Emily," returned Winifred, who retained that 'chic' way of describing her mother. "Father would have a fit."

Indeed, anything untoward was now sedulously kept from James. With another look round at the furniture, as if to gauge his sister's exact position, Soames went out towards Piccadilly. The evening was drawing in—a touch of chill in the October haze. He walked quickly, with his close and concentrated air. He must get through, for he wished to dine in Soho. On hearing from the hall porter at the Iseeum that Mr. Dartie had not been in to-day, he looked at the trusty fellow and decided only to ask if Mr. George Forsyte was in the Club. He was. Soames, who always looked askance at his cousin George, as one inclined to jest at his expense, followed the pageboy, slightly reassured by the thought that George had just lost his father. He must have come in for about thirty thousand, besides what he had under that settlement of Roger's, which had avoided death duty. He found George in a bow-window, staring out across a half-eaten plate of muffins. His tall, bulky, black-clothed figure loomed almost threatening, though preserving still the supernatural neatness of the racing man. With a faint grin on his fleshy face, he said:

"Hallo, Soames! Have a muffin?"

"No, thanks," murmured Soames; and, nursing his hat, with the desire to say something suitable and sympathetic, added:

"How's your mother?"

"Thanks," said George; "so-so. Haven't seen you for ages. You never go racing. How's the City?"

Soames, scenting the approach of a jest, closed up, and answered:

"I wanted to ask you about Dartie. I hear he's...."

"Flitted, made a bolt to Buenos Aires with the fair Lola. Good for Winifred and the little Darties. He's a treat."

Soames nodded. Naturally inimical as these cousins were, Dartie made them kin.

"Uncle James'll sleep in his bed now," resumed George; "I suppose he's had a lot off you, too."

Soames smiled.

"Ah! You saw him further," said George amicably. "He's a real rouser. Young Val will want a bit of looking after. I was always sorry for Winifred. She's a plucky woman."

Again Soames nodded. "I must be getting back to her," he said; "she just wanted to know for certain. We may have to take steps. I suppose there's no mistake?"

"It's quite O.K.," said George—it was he who invented so many of those quaint sayings which have been assigned to other sources. "He was drunk as a lord last night; but he went off all right this morning. His ship's the Tuscarora;" and, fishing out a card, he read mockingly:

"'Mr. Montague Dartie, Poste Restante, Buenos Aires.' I should hurry up with the steps, if I were you. He fairly fed me up last night."

"Yes," said Soames; "but it's not always easy." Then, conscious from George's eyes that he had roused reminiscence of his own affair, he got up, and held out his hand. George rose too.

"Remember me to Winifred.... You'll enter her for the Divorce Stakes straight off if you ask me."

Soames took a sidelong look back at him from the doorway. George had seated himself again and was staring before him; he looked big and lonely in those black clothes. Soames had never known him so subdued. 'I suppose he feels it in a way,' he thought. 'They must have about fifty thousand each, all told. They ought to keep the estate together. If there's a war, house property will go down. Uncle Roger was a good judge, though.' And the face of Annette rose before him in the darkening street; her brown hair and her blue eyes with their dark lashes, her fresh lips and cheeks, dewy and blooming in spite of London, her perfect French figure. 'Take steps!' he thought. Re-entering Winifred's house he encountered Val, and they went in together. An idea had occurred to Soames. His cousin Jolyon was Irene's trustee, the first step would be to go down and see him at Robin Hill. Robin Hill! The odd—the very odd feeling those words brought back! Robin Hill—the house Bosinney had built for him and Irene—the house they had never lived in—the fatal house! And Jolyon lived there now! H'm! And suddenly he thought: 'They say he's got a boy at Oxford! Why not take young Val down and introduce them! It's an excuse! Less bald—very much less bald!' So, as they went upstairs, he said to Val:

"You've got a cousin at Oxford; you've never met him. I should like to take you down with me to-morrow to where he lives and introduce you. You'll find it useful."

Val, receiving the idea with but moderate transports, Soames clinched it.

"I'll call for you after lunch. It's in the country—not far; you'll enjoy it."

On the threshold of the drawing-room he recalled with an effort that the steps he contemplated concerned Winifred at the moment, not himself.

Winifred was still sitting at her Buhl bureau.

"It's quite true," he said; "he's gone to Buenos Aires, started this morning—we'd better have him shadowed when he lands. I'll cable at once. Otherwise we may have a lot of expense. The sooner these things are done the better. I'm always regretting that I didn't..." he stopped, and looked sidelong at the silent Winifred. "By the way," he went on, "can you prove cruelty?"

Winifred said in a dull voice:

"I don't know. What is cruelty?"

"Well, has he struck you, or anything?"

Winifred shook herself, and her jaw grew square.

"He twisted my arm. Or would pointing a pistol count? Or being too drunk to undress himself, or—No—I can't bring in the children."

"No," said Soames; "no! I wonder! Of course, there's legal separation—we can get that. But separation! Um!"

"What does it mean?" asked Winifred desolately.

"That he can't touch you, or you him; you're both of you married and unmarried." And again he grunted. What was it, in fact, but his own accursed position, legalised! No, he would not put her into that!

"It must be divorce," he said decisively; "failing cruelty, there's desertion. There's a way of shortening the two years, now. We get the Court to give us restitution of conjugal rights. Then if he doesn't obey, we can bring a suit for divorce in six months' time. Of course you don't want him back. But they won't know that. Still, there's the risk that he might come. I'd rather try cruelty."

Winifred shook her head. "It's so beastly."

"Well," Soames murmured, "perhaps there isn't much risk so long as he's infatuated and got money. Don't say anything to anybody, and don't pay any of his debts."

Winifred sighed. In spite of all she had been through, the sense of loss was heavy on her. And this idea of not paying his debts any more brought it home to her as nothing else yet had. Some richness seemed to have gone out of life. Without her husband, without her pearls, without that intimate sense that she made a brave show above the domestic whirlpool, she would now have to face the world. She felt bereaved indeed.

And into the chilly kiss he placed on her forehead, Soames put more than his usual warmth.

"I have to go down to Robin Hill to-morrow," he said, "to see young Jolyon on business. He's got a boy at Oxford. I'd like to take Val with me and introduce him. Come down to 'The Shelter' for the week-end and bring the children. Oh! by the way, no, that won't do; I've got some other people coming." So saying, he left her and turned towards Soho.

CHAPTER IV—SOHO

Of all quarters in the queer adventurous amalgam called London, Soho is perhaps least suited to the Forsyte spirit. 'So-ho, my wild one!' George would have said if he had seen his cousin going there. Untidy, full of Greeks, Ishmaelites, cats, Italians, tomatoes, restaurants, organs, coloured stuffs, queer names, people looking out of upper windows, it dwells remote from the British Body Politic. Yet has it haphazard proprietary instincts of its own, and a certain possessive prosperity which keeps its rents up when those of other quarters go down. For long years Soames' acquaintanceship with Soho had been confined to its Western bastion, Wardour Street. Many bargains had he picked up there. Even during those seven years at Brighton after Bosinney's death and Irene's flight, he had bought treasures there sometimes, though he had no place to put them; for when the conviction that his wife had gone for good at last became firm within him, he had caused a board to be put up in Montpellier Square:

FOR SALE

THE LEASE OF THIS DESIRABLE RESIDENCE

Enquire of Messrs. Lesson and Tukes,

Court Street, Belgravia.

It had sold within a week—that desirable residence, in the shadow of whose perfection a man and a woman had eaten their hearts out.

Of a misty January evening, just before the board was taken down, Soames had gone there once more, and stood against the Square railings, looking at its unlighted windows, chewing the cud of possessive memories which had turned so bitter in the mouth. Why had she never loved him? Why? She had been given all she had wanted, and in return had given him, for three long years, all he had wanted—except, indeed, her heart. He had uttered a little involuntary groan, and a passing policeman had glanced suspiciously at him who no longer possessed the right to enter that green door with the carved brass knocker beneath the board 'For Sale!' A choking sensation had attacked his throat, and he had hurried away into the mist. That evening he had gone to Brighton to live....

Approaching Malta Street, Soho, and the Restaurant Bretagne, where Annette would be drooping her pretty shoulders over her accounts, Soames thought with wonder of those seven years at Brighton. How had he managed to go on so long in that town devoid of the scent of sweetpeas, where he had not even space to put his treasures? True, those had been years with no time at all for looking at them—years of almost passionate money-making, during which Forsyte, Bustard and Forsyte had become solicitors to more limited Companies than they could properly attend to. Up to the City of a morning in a Pullman car, down from the City of an evening in a Pullman car. Law papers again after dinner, then the sleep of the tired, and up again next morning. Saturday to Monday was spent at his Club in town—curious reversal of customary procedure, based on the deep and careful instinct that while working so hard he needed sea air to and from the station twice a day, and while resting must indulge his domestic affections. The Sunday visit to his family in Park Lane, to Timothy's, and to Green Street; the occasional visits elsewhere had seemed to him as necessary to health as sea air on weekdays. Even since his migration to Mapledurham he had maintained those habits until—he had known Annette.

Whether Annette had produced the revolution in his outlook, or that outlook had produced Annette, he knew no more than we know where a circle begins. It was intricate and deeply involved with the growing consciousness that property without anyone to leave it to is the negation of true Forsyteism. To have an heir, some continuance of self, who would begin where he left off—ensure, in fact, that he would not leave off—had quite obsessed him for the last year and more. After buying a bit of Wedgwood one evening in April, he had dropped into Malta Street to look at a house of his father's which had been turned into a restaurant—a risky proceeding, and one not quite in accordance with the terms of the lease. He had stared for a little at the outside painted a good cream colour, with two peacock-blue tubs containing little bay-trees in a recessed doorway—and at the words 'Restaurant Bretagne' above them in gold letters, rather favourably impressed. Entering, he had noticed that several people were already seated at little round green tables with little pots of fresh flowers on them and Brittany-ware plates, and had asked of a trim waitress to see the proprietor. They had shown him into a back room, where a girl was sitting at a simple bureau covered with papers, and a small round, table was laid for two. The impression of cleanliness, order, and good taste was confirmed when the girl got up, saying, "You wish to see Maman, Monsieur?" in a broken accent.

"Yes," Soames had answered, "I represent your landlord; in fact, I'm his son."

"Won't you sit down, sir, please? Tell Maman to come to this gentleman."

He was pleased that the girl seemed impressed, because it showed business instinct; and suddenly he noticed that she was remarkably pretty—so remarkably pretty that his eyes found a difficulty in leaving her face. When she moved to put a chair for him, she swayed in a curious subtle way, as if she had been put together by someone with a special secret skill; and her face and neck, which was a little bared, looked as fresh as if they had been sprayed with dew. Probably at this moment Soames decided that the lease had not been violated; though to himself and his father he based the decision on the efficiency of those illicit adaptations in the building, on the signs of prosperity, and the obvious business capacity of Madame Lamotte. He did not, however, neglect to leave certain matters to future consideration, which had necessitated further visits, so that the little back room had become quite accustomed to his spare, not unsolid, but unobtrusive figure, and his pale, chinny face with clipped moustache and dark hair not yet grizzling at the sides.

"Un Monsieur tres distingue," Madame Lamotte found him; and presently, "Tres amical, tres gentil," watching his eyes upon her daughter.

She was one of those generously built, fine-faced, dark-haired Frenchwomen, whose every action and tone of voice inspire perfect confidence in the thoroughness of their domestic tastes, their knowledge of cooking, and the careful increase of their bank balances.

After those visits to the Restaurant Bretagne began, other visits ceased—without, indeed, any definite decision, for Soames, like all Forsytes, and the great majority of their countrymen, was a born empiricist. But it was this change in his mode of life which had gradually made him so definitely conscious that he desired to alter his condition from that of the unmarried married man to that of the married man remarried.

Turning into Malta Street on this evening of early October, 1899, he bought a paper to see if there were any after-development of the Dreyfus case—a question which he had always found useful in making closer acquaintanceship with Madame Lamotte and her daughter, who were Catholic and anti-Dreyfusard.

Scanning those columns, Soames found nothing French, but noticed a general fall on the Stock Exchange and an ominous leader about the Transvaal. He entered, thinking: 'War's a certainty. I shall sell my consols.' Not that he had many, personally, the rate of interest was too wretched; but he should advise his Companies—consols would assuredly go down. A look, as he passed the doorways of the restaurant, assured him that business was good as ever, and this, which in April would have pleased him, now gave him a certain uneasiness. If the steps which he had to take ended in his marrying Annette, he would rather see her mother safely back in France, a move to which the prosperity of the Restaurant Bretagne might become an obstacle. He would have to buy them out, of course, for French people only came to England to make money; and it would mean a higher price. And then that peculiar sweet sensation at the back of his throat, and a slight thumping about the heart, which he always experienced at the door of the little room, prevented his thinking how much it would cost.

Going in, he was conscious of an abundant black skirt vanishing through the door into the restaurant, and of Annette with her hands up to her hair. It was the attitude in which of all others he admired her—so beautifully straight and rounded and supple. And he said:

"I just came in to talk to your mother about pulling down that partition. No, don't call her."

"Monsieur will have supper with us? It will be ready in ten minutes." Soames, who still held her hand, was overcome by an impulse which surprised him.

"You look so pretty to-night," he said, "so very pretty. Do you know how pretty you look, Annette?"

Annette withdrew her hand, and blushed. "Monsieur is very good."

"Not a bit good," said Soames, and sat down gloomily.

Annette made a little expressive gesture with her hands; a smile was crinkling her red lips untouched by salve.

And, looking at those lips, Soames said:

"Are you happy over here, or do you want to go back to France?"

"Oh, I like London. Paris, of course. But London is better than Orleans, and the English country is so beautiful. I have been to Richmond last Sunday."

Soames went through a moment of calculating struggle. Mapledurham! Dared he? After all, dared he go so far as that, and show her what there was to look forward to! Still! Down there one could say things. In this room it was impossible.

"I want you and your mother," he said suddenly, "to come for the afternoon next Sunday. My house is on the river, it's not too late in this weather; and I can show you some good pictures. What do you say?"

Annette clasped her hands.

"It will be lovelee. The river is so beautiful"

"That's understood, then. I'll ask Madame."

He need say no more to her this evening, and risk giving himself away. But had he not already said too much? Did one ask restaurant proprietors with pretty daughters down to one's country house without design? Madame Lamotte would see, if Annette didn't. Well! there was not much that Madame did not see. Besides, this was the second time he had stayed to supper with them; he owed them hospitality.

Walking home towards Park Lane—for he was staying at his father's—with the impression of Annette's soft clever hand within his own, his thoughts were pleasant, slightly sensual, rather puzzled. Take steps! What steps? How? Dirty linen washed in public? Pah! With his reputation for sagacity, for far-sightedness and the clever extrication of others, he, who stood for proprietary interests, to become the plaything of that Law of which he was a pillar! There was something revolting in the thought! Winifred's affair was bad enough! To have a double dose of publicity in the family! Would not a liaison be better than that—a liaison, and a son he could adopt? But dark, solid, watchful, Madame Lamotte blocked the avenue of that vision. No! that would not work. It was not as if Annette could have a real passion for him; one could not expect that at his age. If her mother wished, if the worldly advantage were manifestly great—perhaps! If not, refusal would be certain. Besides, he thought: 'I'm not a villain. I don't want to hurt her; and I don't want anything underhand. But I do want her, and I want a son! There's nothing for it but divorce—somehow—anyhow—divorce!' Under the shadow of the plane-trees, in the lamplight, he passed slowly along the railings of the Green Park. Mist clung there among the bluish tree shapes, beyond range of the lamps. How many hundred times he had walked past those trees from his father's house in Park Lane, when he was quite a young man; or from his own house in Montpellier Square in those four years of married life! And, to-night, making up his mind to free himself if he could of that long useless marriage tie, he took a fancy to walk on, in at Hyde Park Corner, out at Knightsbridge Gate, just as he used to when going home to Irene in the old days. What could she be like now?—how had she passed the years since he last saw her, twelve years in all, seven already since Uncle Jolyon left her that money? Was she still beautiful? Would he know her if he saw her? 'I've not changed much,' he thought; 'I expect she has. She made me suffer.' He remembered suddenly one night, the first on which he went out to dinner alone—an old Malburian dinner—the first year of their marriage. With what eagerness he had hurried back; and, entering softly as a cat, had heard her playing. Opening the drawing-room door noiselessly, he had stood watching the expression on her face, different from any he knew, so much more open, so confiding, as though to her music she was giving a heart he had never seen. And he remembered how she stopped and looked round, how her face changed back to that which he did know, and what an icy shiver had gone through him, for all that the next moment he was fondling her shoulders. Yes, she had made him suffer! Divorce! It seemed ridiculous, after all these years of utter separation! But it would have to be. No other way! 'The question,' he thought with sudden realism, 'is—which of us? She or me? She deserted me. She ought to pay for it. There'll be someone, I suppose.' Involuntarily he uttered a little snarling sound, and, turning, made his way back to Park Lane.

CHAPTER V—JAMES SEES VISIONS

The butler himself opened the door, and closing it softly, detained Soames on the inner mat.

"The master's poorly, sir," he murmured. "He wouldn't go to bed till you came in. He's still in the diningroom."

Soames responded in the hushed tone to which the house was now accustomed.

"What's the matter with him, Warmson?"

"Nervous, sir, I think. Might be the funeral; might be Mrs. Dartie's comin' round this afternoon. I think he overheard something. I've took him in a negus. The mistress has just gone up."

Soames hung his hat on a mahogany stag's-horn.

"All right, Warmson, you can go to bed; I'll take him up myself." And he passed into the dining-room.

James was sitting before the fire, in a big armchair, with a camel-hair shawl, very light and warm, over his frock-coated shoulders, on to which his long white whiskers drooped. His white hair, still fairly thick, glistened in the lamplight; a little moisture from his fixed, light-grey eyes stained the cheeks, still quite well coloured, and the long deep furrows running to the corners of the clean-shaven lips, which moved as if mumbling thoughts. His long legs, thin as a crow's, in shepherd's plaid trousers, were bent at less than a right angle, and on one knee a spindly hand moved continually, with fingers wide apart and glistening tapered nails. Beside him, on a low stool, stood a half-finished glass of negus, bedewed with beads of heat. There he had been sitting, with intervals for meals, all day. At eighty-eight he was still organically sound, but suffering terribly from the thought that no one ever told him anything. It is, indeed, doubtful how he had become aware that Roger was being buried that day, for Emily had kept it from him. She was always keeping things from him. Emily was only seventy! James had a grudge against his wife's youth. He felt sometimes that he would never have married her if he had known that she would have so many years before her, when he had so few. It was not natural. She would live fifteen or twenty years after he was gone, and might spend a lot of money; she had always had extravagant tastes. For all he knew she might want to buy one of these motor-cars. Cicely and Rachel and Imogen and all the young people—they all rode those bicycles now and went off Goodness knew where. And now Roger was gone. He didn't know—couldn't tell! The family was breaking up. Soames would know how much his uncle had left. Curiously he thought of Roger as Soames' uncle not as his own brother. Soames! It was more and more the one solid spot in a vanishing world. Soames was careful; he was a warm man; but he had no one to leave his money to. There it was! He didn't know! And there was that fellow Chamberlain! For James' political principles had been fixed between '70 and '85 when 'that rascally Radical' had been the chief thorn in the side of property and he distrusted him to this day in spite of his conversion; he would get the country into a mess and make money go down before he had done with it. A stormy petrel of a chap! Where was Soames? He had gone to the funeral of course which they had tried to keep from him. He knew that perfectly well; he had seen his son's trousers. Roger! Roger in his coffin! He remembered how, when they came up from school together from the West, on the box seat of the old Slowflyer in 1824, Roger had got into the 'boot' and gone to sleep. James uttered a thin cackle. A funny fellow—Roger—an original! He didn't know! Younger than himself, and in his coffin! The family was breaking up. There was Val going to the university; he never came to see him now. He would cost a pretty penny up there. It was an extravagant age. And all the pretty pennies that his four grandchildren would cost him danced before James' eyes. He did not grudge them the money, but he grudged terribly the risk which the spending of that money might bring on them; he grudged the diminution of security. And now that Cicely had married, she might be having children too. He didn't know—couldn't tell! Nobody thought of anything but spending money in these days, and racing about, and having what they called 'a good time.' A motor-car went past the window. Ugly great lumbering thing, making all that racket! But there it was, the country rattling to the dogs! People in such a hurry that they couldn't even care for style—a neat turnout like his barouche and bays was worth all those new-fangled things. And consols at 116! There must be a lot of money in the country. And now there was this old Kruger! They had tried to keep old Kruger from him. But he knew better; there would be a pretty kettle of fish out there! He had known how it would be when that fellow Gladstone—dead now, thank God!—made such a mess of it after that dreadful business at Majuba. He shouldn't wonder if the Empire split up and went to pot. And this vision of the Empire going to pot filled a full quarter of an hour with qualms of the most serious character. He had eaten a poor lunch because of them. But it was after lunch that the real disaster to his nerves occurred. He had been dozing when he became aware of voices—low voices. Ah! they never told him anything! Winifred's and her mother's. "Monty!" That fellow Dartie—always that fellow Dartie! The voices had receded; and James had been left alone, with his ears standing up like a hare's, and fear creeping about his inwards. Why did they leave him alone? Why didn't they come and tell him? And an awful thought, which through long years had haunted him, concreted again swiftly in his brain. Dartie had gone bankrupt—fraudulently bankrupt, and to save Winifred and the children, he—James—would have to pay! Could he—could Soames turn him into a limited company? No, he couldn't! There it was! With every minute before Emily came back the spectre fiercened. Why, it might be forgery! With eyes fixed on the doubted Turner in the centre of the wall, James suffered tortures. He saw Dartie in the dock, his grandchildren in the gutter, and himself in bed. He saw the doubted Turner being sold at Jobson's, and all the majestic edifice of property in rags. He saw in fancy Winifred unfashionably dressed, and heard in fancy Emily's voice saying: "Now, don't fuss, James!" She was always saying: "Don't fuss!" She had no nerves; he ought never to have married a woman eighteen years younger than himself. Then Emily's real voice said:

"Have you had a nice nap, James?"

Nap! He was in torment, and she asked him that!

"What's this about Dartie?" he said, and his eyes glared at her.

Emily's self-possession never deserted her.

"What have you been hearing?" she asked blandly.

"What's this about Dartie?" repeated James. "He's gone bankrupt."

"Fiddle!"

James made a great effort, and rose to the full height of his stork-like figure.

"You never tell me anything," he said; "he's gone bankrupt."

The destruction of that fixed idea seemed to Emily all that mattered at the moment.

"He has not," she answered firmly. "He's gone to Buenos Aires."

If she had said "He's gone to Mars" she could not have dealt James a more stunning blow; his imagination, invested entirely in British securities, could as little grasp one place as the other.

"What's he gone there for?" he said. "He's got no money. What did he take?"

Agitated within by Winifred's news, and goaded by the constant reiteration of this jeremiad, Emily said calmly:

"He took Winifred's pearls and a dancer."

"What!" said James, and sat down.

His sudden collapse alarmed her, and smoothing his forehead, she said:

"Now, don't fuss, James!"

A dusky red had spread over James' cheeks and forehead.

"I paid for them," he said tremblingly; "he's a thief! I——I knew how it would be. He'll be the death of me; he ...." Words failed him and he sat quite still. Emily, who thought she knew him so well, was alarmed, and went towards the sideboard where she kept some sal volatile. She could not see the tenacious Forsyte spirit working in that thin, tremulous shape against the extravagance of the emotion called up by this outrage on Forsyte principles—the Forsyte spirit deep in there, saying: 'You mustn't get into a fantod, it'll never do. You won't digest your lunch. You'll have a fit!' All unseen by her, it was doing better work in James than sal volatile.

"Drink this," she said.

James waved it aside.

243

"What was Winifred about," he said, "to let him take her pearls?" Emily perceived the crisis past.

"She can have mine," she said comfortably. "I never wear them. She'd better get a divorce."

"There you go!" said James. "Divorce! We've never had a divorce in the family. Where's Soames?"

"He'll be in directly."

"No, he won't," said James, almost fiercely; "he's at the funeral. You think I know nothing."

"Well," said Emily with calm, "you shouldn't get into such fusses when we tell you things." And plumping up his cushions, and putting the sal volatile beside him, she left the room.

But James sat there seeing visions—of Winifred in the Divorce Court, and the family name in the papers; of the earth falling on Roger's coffin; of Val taking after his father; of the pearls he had paid for and would never see again; of money back at four per cent., and the country going to the dogs; and, as the afternoon wore into evening, and tea-time passed, and dinnertime, those visions became more and more mixed and menacing—of being told nothing, till he had nothing left of all his wealth, and they told him nothing of it. Where was Soames? Why didn't he come in?... His hand grasped the glass of negus, he raised it to drink, and saw his son standing there looking at him. A little sigh of relief escaped his lips, and putting the glass down, he said:

"There you are! Dartie's gone to Buenos Aires."

Soames nodded. "That's all right," he said; "good riddance."

A wave of assuagement passed over James' brain. Soames knew. Soames was the only one of them all who had sense. Why couldn't he come and live at home? He had no son of his own. And he said plaintively:

"At my age I get nervous. I wish you were more at home, my boy."

Again Soames nodded; the mask of his countenance betrayed no understanding, but he went closer, and as if by accident touched his father's shoulder.

"They sent their love to you at Timothy's," he said. "It went off all right. I've been to see Winifred. I'm going to take steps." And he thought: 'Yes, and you mustn't hear of them.'

James looked up; his long white whiskers quivered, his thin throat between the points of his collar looked very gristly and naked.

"I've been very poorly all day," he said; "they never tell me anything."

Soames' heart twitched.

"Well, it's all right. There's nothing to worry about. Will you come up now?" and he put his hand under his father's arm.

James obediently and tremulously raised himself, and together they went slowly across the room, which had a rich look in the firelight, and out to the stairs. Very slowly they ascended.

"Good-night, my boy," said James at his bedroom door.

"Good-night, father," answered Soames. His hand stroked down the sleeve beneath the shawl; it seemed to have almost nothing in it, so thin was the arm. And, turning away from the light in the opening doorway, he went up the extra flight to his own bedroom.

'I want a son,' he thought, sitting on the edge of his bed; 'I want a son.'

CHAPTER VI—NO-LONGER-YOUNG JOLYON AT HOME

Trees take little account of time, and the old oak on the upper lawn at Robin Hill looked no day older than when Bosinney sprawled under it and said to Soames: "Forsyte, I've found the very place for your house." Since then Swithin had dreamed, and old Jolyon died, beneath its branches. And now, close to the swing, no-longer-young Jolyon often painted there. Of all spots in the world it was perhaps the most sacred to him, for he had loved his father.

Contemplating its great girth—crinkled and a little mossed, but not yet hollow—he would speculate on the passage of time. That tree had seen, perhaps, all real English history; it dated, he shouldn't wonder, from the days of Elizabeth at least. His own fifty years were as nothing to its wood. When the house behind it, which he now owned, was three hundred years of age instead of twelve, that tree might still be standing there, vast and hollow—for who would commit such sacrilege as to cut it down? A Forsyte might perhaps still be living in that house, to guard it jealously. And Jolyon would wonder what the house would look like coated with such age. Wistaria was already about its walls—the new look had gone. Would it hold its own and keep the dignity Bosinney had bestowed on it, or would the giant London have lapped it round and made it into an asylum in the midst of a jerry-built wilderness? Often, within and without of it, he was persuaded that Bosinney had been moved by the spirit when he built. He had put his heart into that house, indeed! It might even become one of the 'homes of England'—a rare achievement for a house in these degenerate days of building. And the aesthetic spirit, moving hand in hand with his Forsyte sense of possessive continuity, dwelt with pride and pleasure on his ownership thereof. There was the smack of reverence and ancestor-worship (if only for one ancestor) in his desire to hand this house down to his son and his son's son. His father had loved the house, had loved the view, the grounds, that tree; his last years had been happy there, and no one had lived there before him. These last eleven years at Robin Hill had formed in Jolyon's life as a painter, the important period of success. He was now in the very van of water-colour art, hanging on the line everywhere. His drawings fetched high prices. Specialising in that one medium with the tenacity of his breed, he had 'arrived'—rather late, but not too late for a member of the family which made a point of living for ever. His art had really deepened and improved. In conformity with his position he had grown a short fair beard, which was just beginning to grizzle, and hid his Forsyte chin; his brown face had lost the warped expression of his ostracised period—he looked, if anything, younger. The loss of his wife in 1894 had been one of those domestic tragedies which turn out in the end for the good of all. He had, indeed, loved her to the last, for his was an affectionate spirit, but she had become increasingly difficult: jealous of her step-daughter June, jealous even of her own little daughter Holly, and making ceaseless plaint that he could not love her, ill as she was, and 'useless to everyone, and better dead.' He had mourned her sincerely, but his face had looked younger since she died. If she could only have believed that she made him happy, how much happier would the twenty years of their companionship have been!

June had never really got on well with her who had reprehensibly taken her own mother's place; and ever since old Jolyon died she had been established in a sort of studio in London. But she had come back to Robin Hill on her stepmother's death, and gathered the reins there into her small decided hands. Jolly was then at Harrow; Holly still learning from

Mademoiselle Beauce. There had been nothing to keep Jolyon at home, and he had removed his grief and his paint-box abroad. There he had wandered, for the most part in Brittany, and at last had fetched up in Paris. He had stayed there several months, and come back with the younger face and the short fair beard. Essentially a man who merely lodged in any house, it had suited him perfectly that June should reign at Robin Hill, so that he was free to go off with his easel where and when he liked. She was inclined, it is true, to regard the house rather as an asylum for her proteges! but his own outcast days had filled Jolyon for ever with sympathy towards an outcast, and June's 'lame ducks' about the place did not annoy him. By all means let her have them down—and feed them up; and though his slightly cynical humour perceived that they ministered to his daughter's love of domination as well as moved her warm heart, he never ceased to admire her for having so many ducks. He fell, indeed, year by year into a more and more detached and brotherly attitude towards his own son and daughters, treating them with a sort of whimsical equality. When he went down to Harrow to see Jolly, he never quite knew which of them was the elder, and would sit eating cherries with him out of one paper bag, with an affectionate and ironical smile twisting up an eyebrow and curling his lips a little. And he was always careful to have money in his pocket, and to be modish in his dress, so that his son need not blush for him. They were perfect friends, but never seemed to have occasion for verbal confidences, both having the competitive self-consciousness of Forsytes. They knew they would stand by each other in scrapes, but there was no need to talk about it. Jolyon had a striking horror—partly original sin, but partly the result of his early immorality—of the moral attitude. The most he could ever have said to his son would have been:

"Look here, old man; don't forget you're a gentleman," and then have wondered whimsically whether that was not a snobbish sentiment. The great cricket match was perhaps the most searching and awkward time they annually went through together, for Jolyon had been at Eton. They would be particularly careful during that match, continually saying: "Hooray! Oh! hard luck, old man!" or "Hooray! Oh! bad luck, Dad!" to each other, when some disaster at which their hearts bounded happened to the opposing school. And Jolyon would wear a grey top hat, instead of his usual soft one, to save his son's feelings, for a black top hat he could not stomach. When Jolly went up to Oxford, Jolyon went up with him, amused, humble, and a little anxious not to discredit his boy amongst all these youths who seemed so much more assured and old than himself. He often thought, 'Glad I'm a painter' for he had long dropped under-writing at Lloyds—'it's so innocuous. You can't look down on a painter—you can't take him seriously enough.' For Jolly, who had a sort of natural lordliness, had passed at once into a very small set, who secretly amused his father. The boy had fair hair which curled a little, and his grandfather's deepset iron-grey eyes. He was well-built and very upright, and always pleased Jolyon's aesthetic sense, so that he was a tiny bit afraid of him, as artists ever are of those of their own sex whom they admire physically. On that occasion, however, he actually did screw up his courage to give his son advice, and this was it:

"Look here, old man, you're bound to get into debt; mind you come to me at once. Of course, I'll always pay them. But you might remember that one respects oneself more afterwards if one pays one's own way. And don't ever borrow, except from me, will you?"

And Jolly had said:

"All right, Dad, I won't," and he never had.

"And there's just one other thing. I don't know much about morality and that, but there is this: It's always worth while before you do anything to consider whether it's going to hurt another person more than is absolutely necessary."

Jolly had looked thoughtful, and nodded, and presently had squeezed his father's hand. And Jolyon had thought: 'I wonder if I had the right to say that?' He always had a sort of dread of losing the dumb confidence they had in each other; remembering how for long years he had lost his own father's, so that there had been nothing between them but love at a great distance. He under-estimated, no doubt, the change in the spirit of the age since he himself went up to Cambridge in '65; and perhaps he underestimated, too, his boy's power of understanding that he was tolerant to the very bone. It was that tolerance of his, and possibly his scepticism, which ever made his relations towards June so queerly defensive. She was such a decided mortal; knew her own mind so terribly well; wanted things so inexorably until she got them—and then, indeed, often dropped them like a hot potato. Her mother had been like that, whence had come all those tears. Not that his incompatibility with his daughter was anything like what it had been with the first Mrs. Young Jolyon. One could be amused where a daughter was concerned; in a wife's case one could not be amused. To see June set her heart and jaw on a thing until she got it was all right, because it was never anything which interfered fundamentally with Jolyon's liberty— the one thing on which his jaw was also absolutely rigid, a considerable jaw, under that short grizzling beard. Nor was there ever any necessity for real heart-to-heart encounters. One could break away into irony—as indeed he often had to. But the real trouble with June was that she had never appealed to his aesthetic sense, though she might well have, with her red-gold hair and her viking-coloured eyes, and that touch of the Berserker in her spirit. It was very different with Holly, soft and quiet, shy and affectionate, with a playful imp in her somewhere. He watched this younger daughter of his through the duckling stage with extraordinary interest. Would she come out a swan? With her sallow oval face and her grey wistful eyes and those long dark lashes, she might, or she might not. Only this last year had he been able to guess. Yes, she would be a swan—rather a dark one, always a shy one, but an authentic swan. She was eighteen now, and Mademoiselle Beauce was gone—the excellent lady had removed, after eleven years haunted by her continuous reminiscences of the 'well-brrred little Tayleurs,' to another family whose bosom would now be agitated by her reminiscences of the 'well-brrred little Forsytes.' She had taught Holly to speak French like herself.

Portraiture was not Jolyon's forte, but he had already drawn his younger daughter three times, and was drawing her a fourth, on the afternoon of October 4th, 1899, when a card was brought to him which caused his eyebrows to go up:

MR. SOAMES FORSYTE

THE SHELTER, CONNOISSEURS CLUB,

MAPLEDURHAM. ST. JAMES'S.

But here the Forsyte Saga must digress again....

To return from a long travel in Spain to a darkened house, to a little daughter bewildered with tears, to the sight of a loved father lying peaceful in his last sleep, had never been, was never likely to be, forgotten by so impressionable and warm-hearted a man as Jolyon. A sense as of mystery, too, clung to that sad day, and about the end of one whose life had been so well-ordered, balanced, and above-board. It seemed incredible that his father could thus have vanished without, as it were, announcing his intention, without last words to his son, and due farewells. And those incoherent allusions of little Holly to 'the lady in grey,' of Mademoiselle Beauce to a Madame Errant (as it sounded) involved all things in a mist, lifted a little when he read his father's will and the codicil thereto. It had been his duty as executor of that will and codicil to inform Irene, wife of his cousin Soames, of her life interest in fifteen thousand pounds. He had called on her to explain that the existing investment in India Stock, ear-marked to meet the charge, would produce for her the interesting net sum of L430 odd a year, clear of income tax. This was but the third time he had seen his cousin Soames' wife—if indeed she was still his wife, of which he was not quite sure. He remembered having seen her sitting in the Botanical Gardens waiting for Bosinney—a passive, fascinating figure, reminding him of Titian's 'Heavenly Love,' and again, when, charged by his father, he had gone to Montpellier Square on the afternoon when Bosinney's death was known. He still recalled vividly her sudden appearance in the drawing-room doorway on that occasion—her beautiful face, passing from wild eagerness of hope to stony despair; remembered the compassion he had felt, Soames' snarling smile, his words, "We are not at home!" and the slam of the front door.

This third time he saw a face and form more beautiful—freed from that warp of wild hope and despair. Looking at her, he thought: 'Yes, you are just what the Dad would have admired!' And the strange story of his father's Indian summer became slowly clear to him. She spoke of old Jolyon with reverence and tears in her eyes. "He was so wonderfully kind to me; I don't know why. He looked so beautiful and peaceful sitting in that chair under the tree; it was I who first came on him sitting there, you know. Such a lovely day. I don't think an end could have been happier. We should all like to go out like that."

'Quite right!' he had thought. 'We should all like to go out in full summer with beauty stepping towards us across a lawn.' And looking round the little, almost empty drawing-room, he had asked her what she was going to do now. "I am going to live again a little, Cousin Jolyon. It's wonderful to have money of one's own. I've never had any. I shall keep this flat, I think; I'm used to it; but I shall be able to go to Italy."

"Exactly!" Jolyon had murmured, looking at her faintly smiling lips; and he had gone away thinking: 'A fascinating woman! What a waste! I'm glad the Dad left her that money.' He had not seen her again, but every quarter he had signed her cheque, forwarding it to her bank, with a note to the Chelsea flat to say that he had done so; and always he had received a note in acknowledgment, generally from the flat, but sometimes from Italy; so that her personality had become embodied in slightly scented grey paper, an upright fine handwriting, and the words, 'Dear Cousin Jolyon.' Man of property that he now was, the slender cheque he signed often gave rise to the thought: 'Well, I suppose she just manages'; sliding into a vague wonder how she was faring otherwise in a world of men not wont to let beauty go unpossessed. At first Holly had spoken of her sometimes, but 'ladies in grey' soon fade from children's memories; and the tightening of June's lips in those first weeks after her grandfather's death whenever her former friend's name was mentioned, had discouraged allusion. Only once, indeed, had June spoken definitely: "I've forgiven her. I'm frightfully glad she's independent now...."

On receiving Soames' card, Jolyon said to the maid—for he could not abide butlers— "Show him into the study, please, and say I'll be there in a minute"; and then he looked at Holly and asked:

"Do you remember 'the lady in grey,' who used to give you music-lessons?"

"Oh yes, why? Has she come?"

Jolyon shook his head, and, changing his holland blouse for a coat, was silent, perceiving suddenly that such history was not for those young ears. His face, in fact, became whimsical perplexity incarnate while he journeyed towards the study.

Standing by the french-window, looking out across the terrace at the oak tree, were two figures, middle-aged and young, and he thought: 'Who's that boy? Surely they never had a child.'

The elder figure turned. The meeting of those two Forsytes of the second generation, so much more sophisticated than the first, in the house built for the one and owned and occupied by the other, was marked by subtle defensiveness beneath distinct attempt at cordiality. 'Has he come about his wife?' Jolyon was thinking; and Soames, 'How shall I begin?' while Val, brought to break the ice, stood negligently scrutinising this 'bearded pard' from under his dark, thick eyelashes.

"This is Val Dartie," said Soames, "my sister's son. He's just going up to Oxford. I thought I'd like him to know your boy."

"Ah! I'm sorry Jolly's away. What college?"

"B.N.C.," replied Val.

"Jolly's at the 'House,' but he'll be delighted to look you up."

"Thanks awfully."

"Holly's in—if you could put up with a female relation, she'd show you round. You'll find her in the hall if you go through the curtains. I was just painting her."

With another "Thanks, awfully!" Val vanished, leaving the two cousins with the ice unbroken.

"I see you've some drawings at the 'Water Colours,'" said Soames.

Jolyon winced. He had been out of touch with the Forsyte family at large for twenty-six years, but they were connected in his mind with Frith's 'Derby Day' and Landseer prints. He had heard from June that Soames was a connoisseur, which made it worse. He had become aware, too, of a curious sensation of repugnance.

"I haven't seen you for a long time," he said.

"No," answered Soames between close lips, "not since—as a matter of fact, it's about that I've come. You're her trustee, I'm told."

Jolyon nodded.

"Twelve years is a long time," said Soames rapidly: "I—I'm tired of it."

Jolyon found no more appropriate answer than:

"Won't you smoke?"

"No, thanks."

Jolyon himself lit a cigarette.

"I wish to be free," said Soames abruptly.

"I don't see her," murmured Jolyon through the fume of his cigarette.

"But you know where she lives, I suppose?"

Jolyon nodded. He did not mean to give her address without permission. Soames seemed to divine his thought.

"I don't want her address," he said; "I know it."

"What exactly do you want?"

"She deserted me. I want a divorce."

"Rather late in the day, isn't it?"

"Yes," said Soames. And there was a silence.

"I don't know much about these things—at least, I've forgotten," said Jolyon with a wry smile. He himself had had to wait for death to grant him a divorce from the first Mrs. Jolyon. "Do you wish me to see her about it?"

Soames raised his eyes to his cousin's face. "I suppose there's someone," he said.

A shrug moved Jolyon's shoulders.

"I don't know at all. I imagine you may have both lived as if the other were dead. It's usual in these cases."

Soames turned to the window. A few early fallen oak-leaves strewed the terrace already, and were rolling round in the wind. Jolyon saw the figures of Holly and Val Dartie moving across the lawn towards the stables. 'I'm not going to run with the hare and hunt with the hounds,' he thought. 'I must act for her. The Dad would have wished that.' And for a swift moment he seemed to see his father's figure in the old armchair, just beyond Soames, sitting with knees crossed, The Times in his hand. It vanished.

"My father was fond of her," he said quietly.

"Why he should have been I don't know," Soames answered without looking round. "She brought trouble to your daughter June; she brought trouble to everyone. I gave her all she wanted. I would have given her even—forgiveness—but she chose to leave me."

In Jolyon compassion was checked by the tone of that close voice. What was there in the fellow that made it so difficult to be sorry for him?

"I can go and see her, if you like," he said. "I suppose she might be glad of a divorce, but I know nothing."

Soames nodded.

"Yes, please go. As I say, I know her address; but I've no wish to see her." His tongue was busy with his lips, as if they were very dry.

"You'll have some tea?" said Jolyon, stifling the words: 'And see the house.' And he led the way into the hall. When he had rung the bell and ordered tea, he went to his easel to turn his drawing to the wall. He could not bear, somehow, that his work should be seen by Soames, who was standing there in the middle of the great room which had been designed expressly to afford wall space for his own pictures. In his cousin's face, with its unseizable family likeness to himself, and its chinny, narrow, concentrated look, Jolyon saw that which moved him to the thought: 'That chap could never forget anything—nor ever give himself away. He's pathetic!'

CHAPTER VII—THE COLT AND THE FILLY

When young Val left the presence of the last generation he was thinking: 'This is jolly dull! Uncle Soames does take the bun. I wonder what this filly's like?' He anticipated no pleasure from her society; and suddenly he saw her standing there looking at him. Why, she was pretty! What luck!

"I'm afraid you don't know me," he said. "My name's Val Dartie—I'm once removed, second cousin, something like that, you know. My mother's name was Forsyte."

Holly, whose slim brown hand remained in his because she was too shy to withdraw it, said:

"I don't know any of my relations. Are there many?"

"Tons. They're awful—most of them. At least, I don't know—some of them. One's relations always are, aren't they?"

"I expect they think one awful too," said Holly.

"I don't know why they should. No one could think you awful, of course."

Holly looked at him—the wistful candour in those grey eyes gave young Val a sudden feeling that he must protect her.

"I mean there are people and people," he added astutely. "Your dad looks awfully decent, for instance."

"Oh yes!" said Holly fervently; "he is."

A flush mounted in Val's cheeks—that scene in the Pandemonium promenade—the dark man with the pink carnation developing into his own father! "But you know what the Forsytes are," he said almost viciously. "Oh! I forgot; you don't."

"What are they?"

"Oh! fearfully careful; not sportsmen a bit. Look at Uncle Soames!"

"I'd like to," said Holly.

Val resisted a desire to run his arm through hers. "Oh! no," he said, "let's go out. You'll see him quite soon enough. What's your brother like?"

Holly led the way on to the terrace and down to the lawn without answering. How describe Jolly, who, ever since she remembered anything, had been her lord, master, and ideal?

"Does he sit on you?" said Val shrewdly. "I shall be knowing him at Oxford. Have you got any horses?"

Holly nodded. "Would you like to see the stables?"

"Rather!"

They passed under the oak tree, through a thin shrubbery, into the stable-yard. There under a clock-tower lay a fluffy brown-and-white dog, so old that he did not get up, but faintly waved the tail curled over his back.

"That's Balthasar," said Holly; "he's so old—awfully old, nearly as old as I am. Poor old boy! He's devoted to Dad."

"Balthasar! That's a rum name. He isn't purebred you know."

"No! but he's a darling," and she bent down to stroke the dog. Gentle and supple, with dark covered head and slim browned neck and hands, she seemed to Val strange and sweet, like a thing slipped between him and all previous knowledge.

"When grandfather died," she said, "he wouldn't eat for two days. He saw him die, you know."

"Was that old Uncle Jolyon? Mother always says he was a topper."

"He was," said Holly simply, and opened the stable door.

In a loose-box stood a silver roan of about fifteen hands, with a long black tail and mane. "This is mine—Fairy."

"Ah!" said Val, "she's a jolly palfrey. But you ought to bang her tail. She'd look much smarter." Then catching her wondering look, he thought suddenly: 'I don't know—

anything she likes!' And he took a long sniff of the stable air. "Horses are ripping, aren't they? My Dad..." he stopped.

"Yes?" said Holly.

An impulse to unbosom himself almost overcame him—but not quite. "Oh! I don't know he's often gone a mucker over them. I'm jolly keen on them too—riding and hunting. I like racing awfully, as well; I should like to be a gentleman rider." And oblivious of the fact that he had but one more day in town, with two engagements, he plumped out:

"I say, if I hire a gee to-morrow, will you come a ride in Richmond Park?"

Holly clasped her hands.

"Oh yes! I simply love riding. But there's Jolly's horse; why don't you ride him? Here he is. We could go after tea."

Val looked doubtfully at his trousered legs.

He had imagined them immaculate before her eyes in high brown boots and Bedford cords.

"I don't much like riding his horse," he said. "He mightn't like it. Besides, Uncle Soames wants to get back, I expect. Not that I believe in buckling under to him, you know. You haven't got an uncle, have you? This is rather a good beast," he added, scrutinising Jolly's horse, a dark brown, which was showing the whites of its eyes. "You haven't got any hunting here, I suppose?"

"No; I don't know that I want to hunt. It must be awfully exciting, of course; but it's cruel, isn't it? June says so."

"Cruel?" ejaculated Val. "Oh! that's all rot. Who's June?"

"My sister—my half-sister, you know—much older than me." She had put her hands up to both cheeks of Jolly's horse, and was rubbing her nose against its nose with a gentle snuffling noise which seemed to have an hypnotic effect on the animal. Val contemplated her cheek resting against the horse's nose, and her eyes gleaming round at him. 'She's really a duck,' he thought.

They returned to the house less talkative, followed this time by the dog Balthasar, walking more slowly than anything on earth, and clearly expecting them not to exceed his speed limit.

"This is a ripping place," said Val from under the oak tree, where they had paused to allow the dog Balthasar to come up.

"Yes," said Holly, and sighed. "Of course I want to go everywhere. I wish I were a gipsy."

"Yes, gipsies are jolly," replied Val, with a conviction which had just come to him; "you're rather like one, you know."

Holly's face shone suddenly and deeply, like dark leaves gilded by the sun.

"To go mad-rabbiting everywhere and see everything, and live in the open—oh! wouldn't it be fun?"

"Let's do it!" said Val.

"Oh yes, let's!"

"It'd be grand sport, just you and I."

Then Holly perceived the quaintness and gushed.

"Well, we've got to do it," said Val obstinately, but reddening too.

"I believe in doing things you want to do. What's down there?"

"The kitchen-garden, and the pond and the coppice, and the farm."

"Let's go down!"

Holly glanced back at the house.

"It's tea-time, I expect; there's Dad beckoning."

Val, uttering a growly sound, followed her towards the house.

When they re-entered the hall gallery the sight of two middle-aged Forsytes drinking tea together had its magical effect, and they became quite silent. It was, indeed, an impressive spectacle. The two were seated side by side on an arrangement in marqueterie which looked like three silvery pink chairs made one, with a low tea-table in front of them. They seemed to have taken up that position, as far apart as the seat would permit, so that they need not look at each other too much; and they were eating and drinking rather than talking—Soames with his air of despising the tea-cake as it disappeared, Jolyon of finding himself slightly amusing. To the casual eye neither would have seemed greedy, but both were getting through a good deal of sustenance. The two young ones having been supplied with food, the process went on silent and absorbative, till, with the advent of cigarettes, Jolyon said to Soames:

"And how's Uncle James?"

"Thanks, very shaky."

"We're a wonderful family, aren't we? The other day I was calculating the average age of the ten old Forsytes from my father's family Bible. I make it eighty-four already, and five still living. They ought to beat the record;" and looking whimsically at Soames, he added:

"We aren't the men they were, you know."

Soames smiled. 'Do you really think I shall admit that I'm not their equal'; he seemed to be saying, 'or that I've got to give up anything, especially life?'

"We may live to their age, perhaps," pursued Jolyon, "but self-consciousness is a handicap, you know, and that's the difference between us. We've lost conviction. How and when self-consciousness was born I never can make out. My father had a little, but I don't believe any other of the old Forsytes ever had a scrap. Never to see yourself as others see you, it's a wonderful preservative. The whole history of the last century is in the difference between us. And between us and you," he added, gazing through a ring of smoke at Val and Holly, uncomfortable under his quizzical regard, "there'll be—another difference. I wonder what."

Soames took out his watch.

"We must go," he said, "if we're to catch our train."

"Uncle Soames never misses a train," muttered Val, with his mouth full.

"Why should I?" Soames answered simply.

"Oh! I don't know," grumbled Val, "other people do."

At the front door he gave Holly's slim brown hand a long and surreptitious squeeze.

"Look out for me to-morrow," he whispered; "three o'clock. I'll wait for you in the road; it'll save time. We'll have a ripping ride." He gazed back at her from the lodge gate, and, but for the principles of a man about town, would have waved his hand. He felt in no mood to tolerate his uncle's conversation. But he was not in danger. Soames preserved a perfect muteness, busy with far-away thoughts.

The yellow leaves came down about those two walking the mile and a half which Soames had traversed so often in those long-ago days when he came down to watch with secret pride the building of the house—that house which was to have been the home of him and her from whom he was now going to seek release. He looked back once, up that endless vista of autumn lane between the yellowing hedges. What an age ago! "I don't want to see her," he had said to Jolyon. Was that true? 'I may have to,' he thought; and he shivered, seized by one of those queer shudderings that they say mean footsteps on one's grave. A chilly world! A queer world! And glancing sidelong at his nephew, he thought: 'Wish I were his age! I wonder what she's like now!'

CHAPTER VIII—JOLYON PROSECUTES TRUSTEESHIP

When those two were gone Jolyon did not return to his painting, for daylight was failing, but went to the study, craving unconsciously a revival of that momentary vision of his father sitting in the old leather chair with his knees crossed and his straight eyes gazing up from under the dome of his massive brow. Often in this little room, cosiest in the house, Jolyon would catch a moment of communion with his father. Not, indeed, that he had definitely any faith in the persistence of the human spirit—the feeling was not so logical—it was, rather, an atmospheric impact, like a scent, or one of those strong animistic impressions from forms, or effects of light, to which those with the artist's eye are especially prone. Here only—in this little unchanged room where his father had spent the most of his waking hours—could be retrieved the feeling that he was not quite gone, that the steady counsel of that old spirit and the warmth of his masterful lovability endured.

What would his father be advising now, in this sudden recrudescence of an old tragedy—what would he say to this menace against her to whom he had taken such a fancy in the last weeks of his life? 'I must do my best for her,' thought Jolyon; 'he left her to me in his will. But what is the best?'

And as if seeking to regain the sapience, the balance and shrewd common sense of that old Forsyte, he sat down in the ancient chair and crossed his knees. But he felt a mere shadow sitting there; nor did any inspiration come, while the fingers of the wind tapped on the darkening panes of the french-window.

'Go and see her?' he thought, 'or ask her to come down here? What's her life been? What is it now, I wonder? Beastly to rake up things at this time of day.' Again the figure of his cousin standing with a hand on a front door of a fine olive-green leaped out, vivid, like one of those figures from old-fashioned clocks when the hour strikes; and his words sounded in Jolyon's ears clearer than any chime: "I manage my own affairs. I've told you once, I tell you again: We are not at home." The repugnance he had then felt for Soames—for his flat-cheeked, shaven face full of spiritual bull-doggedness; for his spare, square, sleek figure slightly crouched as it were over the bone he could not digest—came now again, fresh as ever, nay, with an odd increase. 'I dislike him,' he thought, 'I dislike him to the very roots of me. And that's lucky; it'll make it easier for me to back his wife.' Half-artist, and half-Forsyte, Jolyon was constitutionally averse from what he termed 'ructions'; unless angered, he conformed deeply to that classic description of the she-dog, 'Er'd ruther run than fight.' A little smile became settled in his beard. Ironical that Soames should come down here—to this house, built for himself! How he had gazed and gaped at this ruin of his past intention; furtively nosing at the walls and stairway, appraising everything! And intuitively Jolyon thought: 'I believe the fellow even now would like to be living here. He could never leave off longing for what he once owned! Well, I must act, somehow or other; but it's a bore—a great bore.'

Late that evening he wrote to the Chelsea flat, asking if Irene would see him.

The old century which had seen the plant of individualism flower so wonderfully was setting in a sky orange with coming storms. Rumours of war added to the briskness of a London turbulent at the close of the summer holidays. And the streets to Jolyon, who was not often up in town, had a feverish look, due to these new motorcars and cabs, of which he disapproved aesthetically. He counted these vehicles from his hansom, and made the proportion of them one in twenty. 'They were one in thirty about a year ago,' he thought; 'they've come to stay. Just so much more rattling round of wheels and general stink'—for he was one of those rather rare Liberals who object to anything new when it takes a material form; and he instructed his driver to get down to the river quickly, out of the traffic, desiring to look at the water through the mellowing screen of plane-trees. At the little block of flats which stood back some fifty yards from the Embankment, he told the cabman to wait, and went up to the first floor.

Yes, Mrs. Heron was at home!

The effect of a settled if very modest income was at once apparent to him remembering the threadbare refinement in that tiny flat eight years ago when he announced her good fortune. Everything was now fresh, dainty, and smelled of flowers. The general effect was silvery with touches of black, hydrangea colour, and gold. 'A woman of great taste,' he thought. Time had dealt gently with Jolyon, for he was a Forsyte. But with Irene Time hardly seemed to deal at all, or such was his impression. She appeared to him not a day older, standing there in mole-coloured velvet corduroy, with soft dark eyes and dark gold hair, with outstretched hand and a little smile.

"Won't you sit down?"

He had probably never occupied a chair with a fuller sense of embarrassment.

"You look absolutely unchanged," he said.

"And you look younger, Cousin Jolyon."

Jolyon ran his hands through his hair, whose thickness was still a comfort to him.

"I'm ancient, but I don't feel it. That's one thing about painting, it keeps you young. Titian lived to ninety-nine, and had to have plague to kill him off. Do you know, the first time I ever saw you I thought of a picture by him?"

"When did you see me for the first time?"

"In the Botanical Gardens."

"How did you know me, if you'd never seen me before?"

"By someone who came up to you." He was looking at her hardily, but her face did not change; and she said quietly:

"Yes; many lives ago."

"What is your recipe for youth, Irene?"

"People who don't live are wonderfully preserved."

H'm! a bitter little saying! People who don't live! But an opening, and he took it. "You remember my Cousin Soames?"

He saw her smile faintly at that whimsicality, and at once went on:

"He came to see me the day before yesterday! He wants a divorce. Do you?"

"I?" The word seemed startled out of her. "After twelve years? It's rather late. Won't it be difficult?"

Jolyon looked hard into her face. "Unless...." he said.

"Unless I have a lover now. But I have never had one since."

What did he feel at the simplicity and candour of those words? Relief, surprise, pity! Venus for twelve years without a lover!

"And yet," he said, "I suppose you would give a good deal to be free, too?"

"I don't know. What does it matter, now?"

"But if you were to love again?"

"I should love." In that simple answer she seemed to sum up the whole philosophy of one on whom the world had turned its back.

"Well! Is there anything you would like me to say to him?"

"Only that I'm sorry he's not free. He had his chance once. I don't know why he didn't take it."

"Because he was a Forsyte; we never part with things, you know, unless we want something in their place; and not always then."

Irene smiled. "Don't you, Cousin Jolyon?—I think you do."

"Of course, I'm a bit of a mongrel—not quite a pure Forsyte. I never take the halfpennies off my cheques, I put them on," said Jolyon uneasily.

"Well, what does Soames want in place of me now?"

"I don't know; perhaps children."

She was silent for a little, looking down.

"Yes," she murmured; "it's hard. I would help him to be free if I could."

Jolyon gazed into his hat, his embarrassment was increasing fast; so was his admiration, his wonder, and his pity. She was so lovely, and so lonely; and altogether it was such a coil!

"Well," he said, "I shall have to see Soames. If there's anything I can do for you I'm always at your service. You must think of me as a wretched substitute for my father. At all events I'll let you know what happens when I speak to Soames. He may supply the material himself."

She shook her head.

"You see, he has a lot to lose; and I have nothing. I should like him to be free; but I don't see what I can do."

"Nor I at the moment," said Jolyon, and soon after took his leave. He went down to his hansom. Half-past three! Soames would be at his office still.

"To the Poultry," he called through the trap. In front of the Houses of Parliament and in Whitehall, newsvendors were calling, "Grave situation in the Transvaal!" but the cries hardly roused him, absorbed in recollection of that very beautiful figure, of her soft dark glance, and the words: "I have never had one since." What on earth did such a woman do with her life, back-watered like this? Solitary, unprotected, with every man's hand against her or rather—reaching out to grasp her at the least sign. And year after year she went on like that!

The word 'Poultry' above the passing citizens brought him back to reality.

'Forsyte, Bustard and Forsyte,' in black letters on a ground the colour of peasoup, spurred him to a sort of vigour, and he went up the stone stairs muttering: "Fusty musty ownerships! Well, we couldn't do without them!"

"I want Mr. Soames Forsyte," he said to the boy who opened the door.

"What name?"

"Mr. Jolyon Forsyte."

The youth looked at him curiously, never having seen a Forsyte with a beard, and vanished.

The offices of 'Forsyte, Bustard and Forsyte' had slowly absorbed the offices of 'Tooting and Bowles,' and occupied the whole of the first floor.

The firm consisted now of nothing but Soames and a number of managing and articled clerks. The complete retirement of James some six years ago had accelerated business, to which the final touch of speed had been imparted when Bustard dropped off, worn out, as many believed, by the suit of 'Fryer versus Forsyte,' more in Chancery than ever and less likely to benefit its beneficiaries. Soames, with his saner grasp of actualities, had never permitted it to worry him; on the contrary, he had long perceived that Providence had presented him therein with L200 a year net in perpetuity, and—why not?

When Jolyon entered, his cousin was drawing out a list of holdings in Consols, which in view of the rumours of war he was going to advise his companies to put on the market at once, before other companies did the same. He looked round, sidelong, and said:

"How are you? Just one minute. Sit down, won't you?" And having entered three amounts, and set a ruler to keep his place, he turned towards Jolyon, biting the side of his flat forefinger....

"Yes?" he said.

"I have seen her."

Soames frowned.

"Well?"

"She has remained faithful to memory."

Having said that, Jolyon was ashamed. His cousin had flushed a dusky yellowish red. What had made him tease the poor brute!

"I was to tell you she is sorry you are not free. Twelve years is a long time. You know your law, and what chance it gives you." Soames uttered a curious little grunt, and the two remained a full minute without speaking. 'Like wax!' thought Jolyon, watching that close face, where the flush was fast subsiding. 'He'll never give me a sign of what he's thinking, or going to do. Like wax!' And he transferred his gaze to a plan of that flourishing town, 'By-Street on Sea,' the future existence of which lay exposed on the wall to the possessive instincts of the firm's clients. The whimsical thought flashed through him: 'I wonder if I shall get a bill of costs for this—"To attending Mr. Jolyon Forsyte in the matter of my divorce, to receiving his account of his visit to my wife, and to advising him to go and see her again, sixteen and eightpence."'

Suddenly Soames said: "I can't go on like this. I tell you, I can't go on like this." His eyes were shifting from side to side, like an animal's when it looks for way of escape. 'He really suffers,' thought Jolyon; 'I've no business to forget that, just because I don't like him.'

"Surely," he said gently, "it lies with yourself. A man can always put these things through if he'll take it on himself."

Soames turned square to him, with a sound which seemed to come from somewhere very deep.

"Why should I suffer more than I've suffered already? Why should I?"

Jolyon could only shrug his shoulders. His reason agreed, his instinct rebelled; he could not have said why.

"Your father," went on Soames, "took an interest in her—why, goodness knows! And I suppose you do too?" he gave Jolyon a sharp look. "It seems to me that one only has to do another person a wrong to get all the sympathy. I don't know in what way I was to blame—I've never known. I always treated her well. I gave her everything she could wish for. I wanted her."

Again Jolyon's reason nodded; again his instinct shook its head. 'What is it?' he thought; 'there must be something wrong in me. Yet if there is, I'd rather be wrong than right.'

"After all," said Soames with a sort of glum fierceness, "she was my wife."

In a flash the thought went through his listener: 'There it is! Ownerships! Well, we all own things. But—human beings! Pah!'

"You have to look at facts," he said drily, "or rather the want of them."

Soames gave him another quick suspicious look.

"The want of them?" he said. "Yes, but I am not so sure."

"I beg your pardon," replied Jolyon; "I've told you what she said. It was explicit."

"My experience has not been one to promote blind confidence in her word. We shall see."

Jolyon got up.

"Good-bye," he said curtly.

"Good-bye," returned Soames; and Jolyon went out trying to understand the look, half-startled, half-menacing, on his cousin's face. He sought Waterloo Station in a disturbed frame of mind, as though the skin of his moral being had been scraped; and all the way down in the train he thought of Irene in her lonely flat, and of Soames in his lonely office, and of the strange paralysis of life that lay on them both. 'In chancery!' he thought. 'Both their necks in chancery—and her's so pretty!'

CHAPTER IX—VAL HEARS THE NEWS

The keeping of engagements had not as yet been a conspicuous feature in the life of young Val Dartie, so that when he broke two and kept one, it was the latter event which caused him, if anything, the greater surprise, while jogging back to town from Robin Hill after his ride with Holly. She had been even prettier than he had thought her yesterday, on her silver-roan, long-tailed 'palfrey'; and it seemed to him, self-critical in the brumous October gloaming and the outskirts of London, that only his boots had shone throughout their two-hour companionship. He took out his new gold 'hunter'—present from James—and looked not at the time, but at sections of his face in the glittering back of its opened case. He had a temporary spot over one eyebrow, and it displeased him, for it must have displeased her. Crum never had any spots. Together with Crum rose the scene in the promenade of the Pandemonium. To-day he had not had the faintest desire to unbosom himself to Holly about his father. His father lacked poetry, the stirrings of which he was feeling for the first time in his nineteen years. The Liberty, with Cynthia Dark, that almost mythical embodiment of rapture; the Pandemonium, with the woman of uncertain age— both seemed to Val completely 'off,' fresh from communion with this new, shy, dark-haired young cousin of his. She rode 'jolly well,' too, so that it had been all the more flattering that she had let him lead her where he would in the long gallops of Richmond Park, though she knew them so much better than he did. Looking back on it all, he was mystified by the barrenness of his speech; he felt that he could say 'an awful lot of fetching things' if he had but the chance again, and the thought that he must go back to Littlehampton on the morrow, and to Oxford on the twelfth—'to that beastly exam,' too— without the faintest chance of first seeing her again, caused darkness to settle on his spirit even more quickly than on the evening. He should write to her, however, and she had promised to answer. Perhaps, too, she would come up to Oxford to see her brother. That thought was like the first star, which came out as he rode into Padwick's livery stables in the purlieus of Sloane Square. He got off and stretched himself luxuriously, for he had ridden some twenty-five good miles. The Dartie within him made him chaffer for five minutes with young Padwick concerning the favourite for the Cambridgeshire; then with the words, "Put the gee down to my account," he walked away, a little wide at the knees, and flipping his boots with his knotty little cane. 'I don't feel a bit inclined to go out,' he thought. 'I wonder if mother will stand fizz for my last night!' With 'fizz' and recollection, he could well pass a domestic evening.

When he came down, speckless after his bath, he found his mother scrupulous in a low evening dress, and, to his annoyance, his Uncle Soames. They stopped talking when he came in; then his uncle said:

"He'd better be told."

At those words, which meant something about his father, of course, Val's first thought was of Holly. Was it anything beastly? His mother began speaking.

"Your father," she said in her fashionably appointed voice, while her fingers plucked rather pitifully at sea-green brocade, "your father, my dear boy, has—is not at Newmarket; he's on his way to South America. He—he's left us."

Val looked from her to Soames. Left them! Was he sorry? Was he fond of his father? It seemed to him that he did not know. Then, suddenly—as at a whiff of gardenias and cigars—his heart twitched within him, and he was sorry. One's father belonged to one, could not go off in this fashion—it was not done! Nor had he always been the 'bounder' of the Pandemonium promenade. There were precious memories of tailors' shops and horses, tips at school, and general lavish kindness, when in luck.

"But why?" he said. Then, as a sportsman himself, was sorry he had asked. The mask of his mother's face was all disturbed; and he burst out:

"All right, Mother, don't tell me! Only, what does it mean?"

"A divorce, Val, I'm afraid."

Val uttered a queer little grunt, and looked quickly at his uncle—that uncle whom he had been taught to look on as a guarantee against the consequences of having a father, even against the Dartie blood in his own veins. The flat-checked visage seemed to wince, and this upset him.

"It won't be public, will it?"

So vividly before him had come recollection of his own eyes glued to the unsavoury details of many a divorce suit in the Public Press.

"Can't it be done quietly somehow? It's so disgusting for—for mother, and—and everybody."

"Everything will be done as quietly as it can, you may be sure."

"Yes—but, why is it necessary at all? Mother doesn't want to marry again."

Himself, the girls, their name tarnished in the sight of his schoolfellows and of Crum, of the men at Oxford, of—Holly! Unbearable! What was to be gained by it?

"Do you, Mother?" he said sharply.

Thus brought face to face with so much of her own feeling by the one she loved best in the world, Winifred rose from the Empire chair in which she had been sitting. She saw that her son would be against her unless he was told everything; and, yet, how could she tell him? Thus, still plucking at the green brocade, she stared at Soames. Val, too, stared at Soames. Surely this embodiment of respectability and the sense of property could not wish to bring such a slur on his own sister!

Soames slowly passed a little inlaid paperknife over the smooth surface of a marqueterie table; then, without looking at his nephew, he began:

"You don't understand what your mother has had to put up with these twenty years. This is only the last straw, Val." And glancing up sideways at Winifred, he added:

"Shall I tell him?"

Winifred was silent. If he were not told, he would be against her! Yet, how dreadful to be told such things of his own father! Clenching her lips, she nodded.

Soames spoke in a rapid, even voice:

"He has always been a burden round your mother's neck. She has paid his debts over and over again; he has often been drunk, abused and threatened her; and now he is gone to Buenos Aires with a dancer." And, as if distrusting the efficacy of those words on the boy, he went on quickly:

"He took your mother's pearls to give to her."

Val jerked up his hand, then. At that signal of distress Winifred cried out:

"That'll do, Soames—stop!"

In the boy, the Dartie and the Forsyte were struggling. For debts, drink, dancers, he had a certain sympathy; but the pearls—no! That was too much! And suddenly he found his mother's hand squeezing his.

"You see," he heard Soames say, "we can't have it all begin over again. There's a limit; we must strike while the iron's hot."

Val freed his hand.

"But—you're—never going to bring out that about the pearls! I couldn't stand that—I simply couldn't!"

Winifred cried out:

"No, no, Val—oh no! That's only to show you how impossible your father is!" And his uncle nodded. Somewhat assuaged, Val took out a cigarette. His father had bought him that thin curved case. Oh! it was unbearable—just as he was going up to Oxford!

"Can't mother be protected without?" he said. "I could look after her. It could always be done later if it was really necessary."

A smile played for a moment round Soames' lips, and became bitter.

"You don't know what you're talking of; nothing's so fatal as delay in such matters."

"Why?"

"I tell you, boy, nothing's so fatal. I know from experience."

His voice had the ring of exasperation. Val regarded him round-eyed, never having known his uncle express any sort of feeling. Oh! Yes—he remembered now—there had been an Aunt Irene, and something had happened—something which people kept dark; he had heard his father once use an unmentionable word of her.

"I don't want to speak ill of your father," Soames went on doggedly, "but I know him well enough to be sure that he'll be back on your mother's hands before a year's over. You can imagine what that will mean to her and to all of you after this. The only thing is to cut the knot for good."

In spite of himself, Val was impressed; and, happening to look at his mother's face, he got what was perhaps his first real insight into the fact that his own feelings were not always what mattered most.

"All right, mother," he said; "we'll back you up. Only I'd like to know when it'll be. It's my first term, you know. I don't want to be up there when it comes off."

"Oh! my dear boy," murmured Winifred, "it is a bore for you." So, by habit, she phrased what, from the expression of her face, was the most poignant regret. "When will it be, Soames?"

"Can't tell—not for months. We must get restitution first."

'What the deuce is that?' thought Val. 'What silly brutes lawyers are! Not for months! I know one thing: I'm not going to dine in!' And he said:

"Awfully sorry, mother, I've got to go out to dinner now."

Though it was his last night, Winifred nodded almost gratefully; they both felt that they had gone quite far enough in the expression of feeling.

Val sought the misty freedom of Green Street, reckless and depressed. And not till he reached Piccadilly did he discover that he had only eighteen-pence. One couldn't dine off eighteen-pence, and he was very hungry. He looked longingly at the windows of the Iseeum Club, where he had often eaten of the best with his father! Those pearls! There was no getting over them! But the more he brooded and the further he walked the hungrier he naturally became. Short of trailing home, there were only two places where he could go— his grandfather's in Park Lane, and Timothy's in the Bayswater Road. Which was the less deplorable? At his grandfather's he would probably get a better dinner on the spur of the moment. At Timothy's they gave you a jolly good feed when they expected you, not otherwise. He decided on Park Lane, not unmoved by the thought that to go up to Oxford

261

without affording his grandfather a chance to tip him was hardly fair to either of them. His mother would hear he had been there, of course, and might think it funny; but he couldn't help that. He rang the bell.

"Hullo, Warmson, any dinner for me, d'you think?"

"They're just going in, Master Val. Mr. Forsyte will be very glad to see you. He was saying at lunch that he never saw you nowadays."

Val grinned.

"Well, here I am. Kill the fatted calf, Warmson, let's have fizz."

Warmson smiled faintly—in his opinion Val was a young limb.

"I will ask Mrs. Forsyte, Master Val."

"I say," Val grumbled, taking off his overcoat, "I'm not at school any more, you know."

Warmson, not without a sense of humour, opened the door beyond the stag's-horn coat stand, with the words:

"Mr. Valerus, ma'am."

"Confound him!" thought Val, entering.

A warm embrace, a "Well, Val!" from Emily, and a rather quavery "So there you are at last!" from James, restored his sense of dignity.

"Why didn't you let us know? There's only saddle of mutton. Champagne, Warmson," said Emily. And they went in.

At the great dining-table, shortened to its utmost, under which so many fashionable legs had rested, James sat at one end, Emily at the other, Val half-way between them; and something of the loneliness of his grandparents, now that all their four children were flown, reached the boy's spirit. 'I hope I shall kick the bucket long before I'm as old as grandfather,' he thought. 'Poor old chap, he's as thin as a rail!' And lowering his voice while his grandfather and Warmson were in discussion about sugar in the soup, he said to Emily:

"It's pretty brutal at home, Granny. I suppose you know."

"Yes, dear boy."

"Uncle Soames was there when I left. I say, isn't there anything to be done to prevent a divorce? Why is he so beastly keen on it?"

"Hush, my dear!" murmured Emily; "we're keeping it from your grandfather."

James' voice sounded from the other end.

"What's that? What are you talking about?"

"About Val's college," returned Emily. "Young Pariser was there, James; you remember—he nearly broke the Bank at Monte Carlo afterwards."

James muttered that he did not know—Val must look after himself up there, or he'd get into bad ways. And he looked at his grandson with gloom, out of which affection distrustfully glimmered.

"What I'm afraid of," said Val to his plate, "is of being hard up, you know."

By instinct he knew that the weak spot in that old man was fear of insecurity for his grandchildren.

"Well," said James, and the soup in his spoon dribbled over, "you'll have a good allowance; but you must keep within it."

"Of course," murmured Val; "if it is good. How much will it be, Grandfather?"

"Three hundred and fifty; it's too much. I had next to nothing at your age."

Val sighed. He had hoped for four, and been afraid of three. "I don't know what your young cousin has," said James; "he's up there. His father's a rich man."

"Aren't you?" asked Val hardily.

"I?" replied James, flustered. "I've got so many expenses. Your father...." and he was silent.

"Cousin Jolyon's got an awfully jolly place. I went down there with Uncle Soames—ripping stables."

"Ah!" murmured James profoundly. "That house—I knew how it would be!" And he lapsed into gloomy meditation over his fish-bones. His son's tragedy, and the deep cleavage it had caused in the Forsyte family, had still the power to draw him down into a whirlpool of doubts and misgivings. Val, who hankered to talk of Robin Hill, because Robin Hill meant Holly, turned to Emily and said:

"Was that the house built for Uncle Soames?" And, receiving her nod, went on: "I wish you'd tell me about him, Granny. What became of Aunt Irene? Is she still going? He seems awfully worked-up about something to-night."

Emily laid her finger on her lips, but the word Irene had caught James' ear.

"What's that?" he said, staying a piece of mutton close to his lips. "Who's been seeing her? I knew we hadn't heard the last of that."

"Now, James," said Emily, "eat your dinner. Nobody's been seeing anybody."

James put down his fork.

"There you go," he said. "I might die before you'd tell me of it. Is Soames getting a divorce?"

"Nonsense," said Emily with incomparable aplomb; "Soames is much too sensible."

James had sought his own throat, gathering the long white whiskers together on the skin and bone of it.

"She—she was always...." he said, and with that enigmatic remark the conversation lapsed, for Warmson had returned. But later, when the saddle of mutton had been succeeded by sweet, savoury, and dessert, and Val had received a cheque for twenty pounds and his grandfather's kiss—like no other kiss in the world, from lips pushed out with a sort of fearful suddenness, as if yielding to weakness—he returned to the charge in the hall.

"Tell us about Uncle Soames, Granny. Why is he so keen on mother's getting a divorce?"

"Your Uncle Soames," said Emily, and her voice had in it an exaggerated assurance, "is a lawyer, my dear boy. He's sure to know best."

"Is he?" muttered Val. "But what did become of Aunt Irene? I remember she was jolly good-looking."

"She—er...." said Emily, "behaved very badly. We don't talk about it."

"Well, I don't want everybody at Oxford to know about our affairs," ejaculated Val; "it's a brutal idea. Why couldn't father be prevented without its being made public?"

Emily sighed. She had always lived rather in an atmosphere of divorce, owing to her fashionable proclivities—so many of those whose legs had been under her table having gained a certain notoriety. When, however, it touched her own family, she liked it no better than other people. But she was eminently practical, and a woman of courage, who never pursued a shadow in preference to its substance.

"Your mother," she said, "will be happier if she's quite free, Val. Good-night, my dear boy; and don't wear loud waistcoats up at Oxford, they're not the thing just now. Here's a little present."

With another five pounds in his hand, and a little warmth in his heart, for he was fond of his grandmother, he went out into Park Lane. A wind had cleared the mist, the autumn leaves were rustling, and the stars were shining. With all that money in his pocket an impulse to 'see life' beset him; but he had not gone forty yards in the direction of Piccadilly when Holly's shy face, and her eyes with an imp dancing in their gravity, came up before him, and his hand seemed to be tingling again from the pressure of her warm gloved hand. 'No, dash it!' he thought, 'I'm going home!'

CHAPTER X—SOAMES ENTERTAINS THE FUTURE

It was full late for the river, but the weather was lovely, and summer lingered below the yellowing leaves. Soames took many looks at the day from his riverside garden near Mapledurham that Sunday morning.

With his own hands he put flowers about his little house-boat, and equipped the punt, in which, after lunch, he proposed to take them on the river. Placing those Chinese-looking cushions, he could not tell whether or no he wished to take Annette alone. She was so very pretty—could he trust himself not to say irrevocable words, passing beyond the limits of discretion? Roses on the veranda were still in bloom, and the hedges ever-green, so that there was almost nothing of middle-aged autumn to chill the mood; yet was he nervous, fidgety, strangely distrustful of his powers to steer just the right course. This visit had been planned to produce in Annette and her mother a due sense of his possessions, so that they should be ready to receive with respect any overture he might later be disposed to make. He dressed with great care, making himself neither too young nor too old, very thankful that his hair was still thick and smooth and had no grey in it. Three times he went up to his picture-gallery. If they had any knowledge at all, they must see at once that his collection alone was worth at least thirty thousand pounds. He minutely inspected, too, the pretty bedroom overlooking the river where they would take off their hats. It would be her bedroom if—if the matter went through, and she became his wife. Going up to the dressing-table he passed his hand over the lilac-coloured pincushion, into which were stuck all kinds of pins; a bowl of pot-pourri exhaled a scent that made his head turn just a little. His wife! If only the whole thing could be settled out of hand, and there was not the nightmare of this divorce to be gone through first; and with gloom puckered on his forehead, he looked out at the river shining beyond the roses and the lawn. Madame Lamotte would never resist this prospect for her child; Annette would never resist her mother. If only he were free! He drove to the station to meet them. What taste Frenchwomen had! Madame Lamotte was in black with touches of lilac colour, Annette in greyish lilac linen, with cream coloured gloves and hat. Rather pale she looked and Londony; and her blue eyes were demure. Waiting for them to come down to lunch,

Soames stood in the open french-window of the diningroom moved by that sensuous delight in sunshine and flowers and trees which only came to the full when youth and beauty were there to share it with one. He had ordered the lunch with intense consideration; the wine was a very special Sauterne, the whole appointments of the meal perfect, the coffee served on the veranda super-excellent. Madame Lamotte accepted creme de menthe; Annette refused. Her manners were charming, with just a suspicion of 'the conscious beauty' creeping into them. 'Yes,' thought Soames, 'another year of London and that sort of life, and she'll be spoiled.'

Madame was in sedate French raptures. "Adorable! Le soleil est si bon! How everything is chic, is it not, Annette? Monsieur is a real Monte Cristo." Annette murmured assent, with a look up at Soames which he could not read. He proposed a turn on the river. But to punt two persons when one of them looked so ravishing on those Chinese cushions was merely to suffer from a sense of lost opportunity; so they went but a short way towards Pangbourne, drifting slowly back, with every now and then an autumn leaf dropping on Annette or on her mother's black amplitude. And Soames was not happy, worried by the thought: 'How—when—where—can I say—what?' They did not yet even know that he was married. To tell them he was married might jeopardise his every chance; yet, if he did not definitely make them understand that he wished for Annette's hand, it would be dropping into some other clutch before he was free to claim it.

At tea, which they both took with lemon, Soames spoke of the Transvaal.

"There'll be war," he said.

Madame Lamotte lamented.

"Ces pauvres gens bergers!" Could they not be left to themselves?

Soames smiled—the question seemed to him absurd.

Surely as a woman of business she understood that the British could not abandon their legitimate commercial interests.

"Ah! that!" But Madame Lamotte found that the English were a little hypocrite. They were talking of justice and the Uitlanders, not of business. Monsieur was the first who had spoken to her of that.

"The Boers are only half-civilised," remarked Soames; "they stand in the way of progress. It will never do to let our suzerainty go."

"What does that mean to say? Suzerainty!"

"What a strange word!" Soames became eloquent, roused by these threats to the principle of possession, and stimulated by Annette's eyes fixed on him. He was delighted when presently she said:

"I think Monsieur is right. They should be taught a lesson." She was sensible!

"Of course," he said, "we must act with moderation. I'm no jingo. We must be firm without bullying. Will you come up and see my pictures?" Moving from one to another of these treasures, he soon perceived that they knew nothing. They passed his last Mauve, that remarkable study of a 'Hay-cart going Home,' as if it were a lithograph. He waited almost with awe to see how they would view the jewel of his collection—an Israels whose price he had watched ascending till he was now almost certain it had reached top value, and would be better on the market again. They did not view it at all. This was a shock; and yet to have in Annette a virgin taste to form would be better than to have the silly, half-baked predilections of the English middle-class to deal with. At the end of the gallery was a

Meissonier of which he was rather ashamed—Meissonier was so steadily going down. Madame Lamotte stopped before it.

"Meissonier! Ah! What a jewel!" Soames took advantage of that moment. Very gently touching Annette's arm, he said:

"How do you like my place, Annette?"

She did not shrink, did not respond; she looked at him full, looked down, and murmured:

"Who would not like it? It is so beautiful!"

"Perhaps some day—" Soames said, and stopped.

So pretty she was, so self-possessed—she frightened him. Those cornflower-blue eyes, the turn of that creamy neck, her delicate curves—she was a standing temptation to indiscretion! No! No! One must be sure of one's ground—much surer! 'If I hold off,' he thought, 'it will tantalise her.' And he crossed over to Madame Lamotte, who was still in front of the Meissonier.

"Yes, that's quite a good example of his later work. You must come again, Madame, and see them lighted up. You must both come and spend a night."

Enchanted, would it not be beautiful to see them lighted? By moonlight too, the river must be ravishing!

Annette murmured:

"Thou art sentimental, Maman!"

Sentimental! That black-robed, comely, substantial Frenchwoman of the world! And suddenly he was certain as he could be that there was no sentiment in either of them. All the better. Of what use sentiment? And yet...!

He drove to the station with them, and saw them into the train. To the tightened pressure of his hand it seemed that Annette's fingers responded just a little; her face smiled at him through the dark.

He went back to the carriage, brooding. "Go on home, Jordan," he said to the coachman; "I'll walk." And he strode out into the darkening lanes, caution and the desire of possession playing see-saw within him. 'Bon soir, monsieur!' How softly she had said it. To know what was in her mind! The French—they were like cats—one could tell nothing! But—how pretty! What a perfect young thing to hold in one's arms! What a mother for his heir! And he thought, with a smile, of his family and their surprise at a French wife, and their curiosity, and of the way he would play with it and buffet it confound them!

The poplars sighed in the darkness; an owl hooted. Shadows deepened in the water. 'I will and must be free,' he thought. 'I won't hang about any longer. I'll go and see Irene. If you want things done, do them yourself. I must live again—live and move and have my being.' And in echo to that queer biblicality church-bells chimed the call to evening prayer.

CHAPTER XI—AND VISITS THE PAST

On a Tuesday evening after dining at his club Soames set out to do what required more courage and perhaps less delicacy than anything he had yet undertaken in his life—save perhaps his birth, and one other action. He chose the evening, indeed, partly because Irene was more likely to be in, but mainly because he had failed to find sufficient resolution by daylight, had needed wine to give him extra daring.

He left his hansom on the Embankment, and walked up to the Old Church, uncertain of the block of flats where he knew she lived. He found it hiding behind a much larger mansion; and having read the name, 'Mrs. Irene Heron'—Heron, forsooth! Her maiden name: so she used that again, did she?—he stepped back into the road to look up at the windows of the first floor. Light was coming through in the corner flat, and he could hear a piano being played. He had never had a love of music, had secretly borne it a grudge in the old days when so often she had turned to her piano, making of it a refuge place into which she knew he could not enter. Repulse! The long repulse, at first restrained and secret, at last open! Bitter memory came with that sound. It must be she playing, and thus almost assured of seeing her, he stood more undecided than ever. Shivers of anticipation ran through him; his tongue felt dry, his heart beat fast. 'I have no cause to be afraid,' he thought. And then the lawyer stirred within him. Was he doing a foolish thing? Ought he not to have arranged a formal meeting in the presence of her trustee? No! Not before that fellow Jolyon, who sympathised with her! Never! He crossed back into the doorway, and, slowly, to keep down the beating of his heart, mounted the single flight of stairs and rang the bell. When the door was opened to him his sensations were regulated by the scent which came—that perfume—from away back in the past, bringing muffled remembrance: fragrance of a drawing-room he used to enter, of a house he used to own—perfume of dried rose-leaves and honey!

"Say, Mr. Forsyte," he said, "your mistress will see me, I know." He had thought this out; she would think it was Jolyon!

When the maid was gone and he was alone in the tiny hall, where the light was dim from one pearly-shaded sconce, and walls, carpet, everything was silvery, making the walled-in space all ghostly, he could only think ridiculously: 'Shall I go in with my overcoat on, or take it off?' The music ceased; the maid said from the doorway:

"Will you walk in, sir?"

Soames walked in. He noted mechanically that all was still silvery, and that the upright piano was of satinwood. She had risen and stood recoiled against it; her hand, placed on the keys as if groping for support, had struck a sudden discord, held for a moment, and released. The light from the shaded piano-candle fell on her neck, leaving her face rather in shadow. She was in a black evening dress, with a sort of mantilla over her shoulders—he did not remember ever having seen her in black, and the thought passed through him: 'She dresses even when she's alone.'

"You!" he heard her whisper.

Many times Soames had rehearsed this scene in fancy. Rehearsal served him not at all. He simply could not speak. He had never thought that the sight of this woman whom he had once so passionately desired, so completely owned, and whom he had not seen for twelve years, could affect him in this way. He had imagined himself speaking and acting, half as man of business, half as judge. And now it was as if he were in the presence not of a mere woman and erring wife, but of some force, subtle and elusive as atmosphere itself within him and outside. A kind of defensive irony welled up in him.

"Yes, it's a queer visit! I hope you're well."

"Thank you. Will you sit down?"

She had moved away from the piano, and gone over to a window-seat, sinking on to it, with her hands clasped in her lap. Light fell on her there, so that Soames could see her face, eyes, hair, strangely as he remembered them, strangely beautiful.

He sat down on the edge of a satinwood chair, upholstered with silver-coloured stuff, close to where he was standing.

"You have not changed," he said.

"No? What have you come for?"

"To discuss things."

"I have heard what you want from your cousin."

"Well?"

"I am willing. I have always been."

The sound of her voice, reserved and close, the sight of her figure watchfully poised, defensive, was helping him now. A thousand memories of her, ever on the watch against him, stirred, and....

"Perhaps you will be good enough, then, to give me information on which I can act. The law must be complied with."

"I have none to give you that you don't know of."

"Twelve years! Do you suppose I can believe that?"

"I don't suppose you will believe anything I say; but it's the truth."

Soames looked at her hard. He had said that she had not changed; now he perceived that she had. Not in face, except that it was more beautiful; not in form, except that it was a little fuller—no! She had changed spiritually. There was more of her, as it were, something of activity and daring, where there had been sheer passive resistance. 'Ah!' he thought, 'that's her independent income! Confound Uncle Jolyon!'

"I suppose you're comfortably off now?" he said.

"Thank you, yes."

"Why didn't you let me provide for you? I would have, in spite of everything."

A faint smile came on her lips; but she did not answer.

"You are still my wife," said Soames. Why he said that, what he meant by it, he knew neither when he spoke nor after. It was a truism almost preposterous, but its effect was startling. She rose from the window-seat, and stood for a moment perfectly still, looking at him. He could see her bosom heaving. Then she turned to the window and threw it open.

"Why do that?" he said sharply. "You'll catch cold in that dress. I'm not dangerous." And he uttered a little sad laugh.

She echoed it—faintly, bitterly.

"It was—habit."

"Rather odd habit," said Soames as bitterly. "Shut the window!"

She shut it and sat down again. She had developed power, this woman—this—wife of his! He felt it issuing from her as she sat there, in a sort of armour. And almost unconsciously he rose and moved nearer; he wanted to see the expression on her face. Her eyes met his unflinching. Heavens! how clear they were, and what a dark brown against that white skin, and that burnt-amber hair! And how white her shoulders.

Funny sensation this! He ought to hate her.

"You had better tell me," he said; "it's to your advantage to be free as well as to mine. That old matter is too old."

"I have told you."

"Do you mean to tell me there has been nothing—nobody?"

"Nobody. You must go to your own life."

Stung by that retort, Soames moved towards the piano and back to the hearth, to and fro, as he had been wont in the old days in their drawing-room when his feelings were too much for him.

"That won't do," he said. "You deserted me. In common justice it's for you...."

He saw her shrug those white shoulders, heard her murmur:

"Yes. Why didn't you divorce me then? Should I have cared?"

He stopped, and looked at her intently with a sort of curiosity. What on earth did she do with herself, if she really lived quite alone? And why had he not divorced her? The old feeling that she had never understood him, never done him justice, bit him while he stared at her.

"Why couldn't you have made me a good wife?" he said.

"Yes; it was a crime to marry you. I have paid for it. You will find some way perhaps. You needn't mind my name, I have none to lose. Now I think you had better go."

A sense of defeat—of being defrauded of his self-justification, and of something else beyond power of explanation to himself, beset Soames like the breath of a cold fog. Mechanically he reached up, took from the mantel-shelf a little china bowl, reversed it, and said:

"Lowestoft. Where did you get this? I bought its fellow at Jobson's." And, visited by the sudden memory of how, those many years ago, he and she had bought china together, he remained staring at the little bowl, as if it contained all the past. Her voice roused him.

"Take it. I don't want it."

Soames put it back on the shelf.

"Will you shake hands?" he said.

A faint smile curved her lips. She held out her hand. It was cold to his rather feverish touch. 'She's made of ice,' he thought—'she was always made of ice!' But even as that thought darted through him, his senses were assailed by the perfume of her dress and body, as though the warmth within her, which had never been for him, were struggling to show its presence. And he turned on his heel. He walked out and away, as if someone with a whip were after him, not even looking for a cab, glad of the empty Embankment and the cold river, and the thick-strewn shadows of the plane-tree leaves—confused, flurried, sore at heart, and vaguely disturbed, as though he had made some deep mistake whose consequences he could not foresee. And the fantastic thought suddenly assailed him if instead of, 'I think you had better go,' she had said, 'I think you had better stay!' What should he have felt, what would he have done? That cursed attraction of her was there for him even now, after all these years of estrangement and bitter thoughts. It was there, ready to mount to his head at a sign, a touch. 'I was a fool to go!' he muttered. 'I've advanced nothing. Who could imagine? I never thought!' Memory, flown back to the first years of his marriage, played him torturing tricks. She had not deserved to keep her beauty—the beauty he had owned and known so well. And a kind of bitterness at the tenacity of his own admiration welled up in him. Most men would have hated the sight of her, as she had deserved. She had spoiled his life, wounded his pride to death, defrauded him of a son. And yet the mere sight of her, cold and resisting as ever, had this power to upset him utterly! It was some damned magnetism she had! And no wonder if, as she asserted; she had lived untouched these last twelve years. So Bosinney—cursed be his memory!—had lived on all this time with her! Soames could not tell whether he was glad of that knowledge or no.

Nearing his Club at last he stopped to buy a paper. A headline ran: 'Boers reported to repudiate suzerainty!' Suzerainty! 'Just like her!' he thought: 'she always did. Suzerainty! I still have it by rights. She must be awfully lonely in that wretched little flat!'

CHAPTER XII—ON FORSYTE 'CHANGE

Soames belonged to two clubs, 'The Connoisseurs,' which he put on his cards and seldom visited, and 'The Remove,' which he did not put on his cards and frequented. He had joined this Liberal institution five years ago, having made sure that its members were now nearly all sound Conservatives in heart and pocket, if not in principle. Uncle Nicholas had put him up. The fine reading-room was decorated in the Adam style.

On entering that evening he glanced at the tape for any news about the Transvaal, and noted that Consols were down seven-sixteenths since the morning. He was turning away to seek the reading-room when a voice behind him said:

"Well, Soames, that went off all right."

It was Uncle Nicholas, in a frock-coat and his special cut-away collar, with a black tie passed through a ring. Heavens! How young and dapper he looked at eighty-two!

"I think Roger'd have been pleased," his uncle went on. "The thing was very well done. Blackley's? I'll make a note of them. Buxton's done me no good. These Boers are upsetting me—that fellow Chamberlain's driving the country into war. What do you think?"

"Bound to come," murmured Soames.

Nicholas passed his hand over his thin, clean-shaven cheeks, very rosy after his summer cure; a slight pout had gathered on his lips. This business had revived all his Liberal principles.

"I mistrust that chap; he's a stormy petrel. House-property will go down if there's war. You'll have trouble with Roger's estate. I often told him he ought to get out of some of his houses. He was an opinionated beggar."

'There was a pair of you!' thought Soames. But he never argued with an uncle, in that way preserving their opinion of him as 'a long-headed chap,' and the legal care of their property.

"They tell me at Timothy's," said Nicholas, lowering his voice, "that Dartie has gone off at last. That'll be a relief to your father. He was a rotten egg."

Again Soames nodded. If there was a subject on which the Forsytes really agreed, it was the character of Montague Dartie.

"You take care," said Nicholas, "or he'll turn up again. Winifred had better have the tooth out, I should say. No use preserving what's gone bad."

Soames looked at him sideways. His nerves, exacerbated by the interview he had just come through, disposed him to see a personal allusion in those words.

"I'm advising her," he said shortly.

"Well," said Nicholas, "the brougham's waiting; I must get home. I'm very poorly. Remember me to your father."

And having thus reconsecrated the ties of blood, he passed down the steps at his youthful gait and was wrapped into his fur coat by the junior porter.

'I've never known Uncle Nicholas other than "very poorly,"' mused Soames, 'or seen him look other than everlasting. What a family! Judging by him, I've got thirty-eight years of health before me. Well, I'm not going to waste them.' And going over to a mirror he stood looking at his face. Except for a line or two, and three or four grey hairs in his little dark moustache, had he aged any more than Irene? The prime of life—he and she in the very prime of life! And a fantastic thought shot into his mind. Absurd! Idiotic! But again it came. And genuinely alarmed by the recurrence, as one is by the second fit of shivering which presages a feverish cold, he sat down on the weighing machine. Eleven stone! He had not varied two pounds in twenty years. What age was she? Nearly thirty-seven—not too old to have a child—not at all! Thirty-seven on the ninth of next month. He remembered her birthday well—he had always observed it religiously, even that last birthday so soon before she left him, when he was almost certain she was faithless. Four birthdays in his house. He had looked forward to them, because his gifts had meant a semblance of gratitude, a certain attempt at warmth. Except, indeed, that last birthday—which had tempted him to be too religious! And he shied away in thought. Memory heaps dead leaves on corpse-like deeds, from under which they do but vaguely offend the sense. And then he thought suddenly: 'I could send her a present for her birthday. After all, we're Christians! Couldn't!—couldn't we join up again!' And he uttered a deep sigh sitting there. Annette! Ah! but between him and Annette was the need for that wretched divorce suit! And how?

"A man can always work these things, if he'll take it on himself," Jolyon had said.

But why should he take the scandal on himself with his whole career as a pillar of the law at stake? It was not fair! It was quixotic! Twelve years' separation in which he had taken no steps to free himself put out of court the possibility of using her conduct with Bosinney as a ground for divorcing her. By doing nothing to secure relief he had acquiesced, even if the evidence could now be gathered, which was more than doubtful. Besides, his own pride would never let him use that old incident, he had suffered from it too much. No! Nothing but fresh misconduct on her part—but she had denied it; and—almost—he had believed her. Hung up! Utterly hung up!

He rose from the scooped-out red velvet seat with a feeling of constriction about his vitals. He would never sleep with this going on in him! And, taking coat and hat again, he went out, moving eastward. In Trafalgar Square he became aware of some special commotion travelling towards him out of the mouth of the Strand. It materialised in newspaper men calling out so loudly that no words whatever could be heard. He stopped to listen, and one came by.

"Payper! Special! Ultimatium by Krooger! Declaration of war!" Soames bought the paper. There it was in the stop press...! His first thought was: 'The Boers are committing suicide.' His second: 'Is there anything still I ought to sell?' If so he had missed the chance—there would certainly be a slump in the city to-morrow. He swallowed this thought with a nod of defiance. That ultimatum was insolent—sooner than let it pass he was prepared to lose money. They wanted a lesson, and they would get it; but it would take three months at least to bring them to heel. There weren't the troops out there; always behind time, the Government! Confound those newspaper rats! What was the use of waking everybody up? Breakfast to-morrow was quite soon enough. And he thought with alarm of his father. They would cry it down Park Lane. Hailing a hansom, he got in and told the man to drive there.

James and Emily had just gone up to bed, and after communicating the news to Warmson, Soames prepared to follow. He paused by after-thought to say:

"What do you think of it, Warmson?"

The butler ceased passing a hat brush over the silk hat Soames had taken off, and, inclining his face a little forward, said in a low voice: "Well, sir, they 'aven't a chance, of course; but I'm told they're very good shots. I've got a son in the Inniskillings."

"You, Warmson? Why, I didn't know you were married."

"No, sir. I don't talk of it. I expect he'll be going out."

The slighter shock Soames had felt on discovering that he knew so little of one whom he thought he knew so well was lost in the slight shock of discovering that the war might touch one personally. Born in the year of the Crimean War, he had only come to consciousness by the time the Indian Mutiny was over; since then the many little wars of the British Empire had been entirely professional, quite unconnected with the Forsytes and all they stood for in the body politic. This war would surely be no exception. But his mind ran hastily over his family. Two of the Haymans, he had heard, were in some Yeomanry or other—it had always been a pleasant thought, there was a certain distinction about the Yeomanry; they wore, or used to wear, a blue uniform with silver about it, and rode horses. And Archibald, he remembered, had once on a time joined the Militia, but had given it up because his father, Nicholas, had made such a fuss about his 'wasting his time peacocking about in a uniform.' Recently he had heard somewhere that young Nicholas' eldest, very young Nicholas, had become a Volunteer. 'No,' thought Soames, mounting the stairs slowly, 'there's nothing in that!'

He stood on the landing outside his parents' bed and dressing rooms, debating whether or not to put his nose in and say a reassuring word. Opening the landing window, he listened. The rumble from Piccadilly was all the sound he heard, and with the thought, 'If these motor-cars increase, it'll affect house property,' he was about to pass on up to the room always kept ready for him when he heard, distant as yet, the hoarse rushing call of a newsvendor. There it was, and coming past the house! He knocked on his mother's door and went in.

His father was sitting up in bed, with his ears pricked under the white hair which Emily kept so beautifully cut. He looked pink, and extraordinarily clean, in his setting of white sheet and pillow, out of which the points of his high, thin, nightgowned shoulders emerged in small peaks. His eyes alone, grey and distrustful under their withered lids, were moving from the window to Emily, who in a wrapper was walking up and down, squeezing a rubber ball attached to a scent bottle. The room reeked faintly of the eau-de-Cologne she was spraying.

"All right!" said Soames, "it's not a fire. The Boers have declared war—that's all."

Emily stopped her spraying.

"Oh!" was all she said, and looked at James.

Soames, too, looked at his father. He was taking it differently from their expectation, as if some thought, strange to them, were working in him.

"I'm!" he muttered suddenly, "I shan't live to see the end of this."

"Nonsense, James! It'll be over by Christmas."

"What do you know about it?" James answered her with asperity. "It's a pretty mess at this time of night, too!" He lapsed into silence, and his wife and son, as if hypnotised, waited for him to say: 'I can't tell—I don't know; I knew how it would be!' But he did not. The grey eyes shifted, evidently seeing nothing in the room; then movement occurred under the bedclothes, and the knees were drawn up suddenly to a great height.

"They ought to send out Roberts. It all comes from that fellow Gladstone and his Majuba."

The two listeners noted something beyond the usual in his voice, something of real anxiety. It was as if he had said: 'I shall never see the old country peaceful and safe again. I shall have to die before I know she's won.' And in spite of the feeling that James must not be encouraged to be fussy, they were touched. Soames went up to the bedside and stroked his father's hand which had emerged from under the bedclothes, long and wrinkled with veins.

"Mark my words!" said James, "consols will go to par. For all I know, Val may go and enlist."

"Oh, come, James!" cried Emily, "you talk as if there were danger."

Her comfortable voice seemed to soothe James for once.

"Well," he muttered, "I told you how it would be. I don't know, I'm sure—nobody tells me anything. Are you sleeping here, my boy?"

The crisis was past, he would now compose himself to his normal degree of anxiety; and, assuring his father that he was sleeping in the house, Soames pressed his hand, and went up to his room.

The following afternoon witnessed the greatest crowd Timothy's had known for many a year. On national occasions, such as this, it was, indeed, almost impossible to avoid going there. Not that there was any danger or rather only just enough to make it necessary to assure each other that there was none.

Nicholas was there early. He had seen Soames the night before—Soames had said it was bound to come. This old Kruger was in his dotage—why, he must be seventy-five if he was a day!

(Nicholas was eighty-two.) What had Timothy said? He had had a fit after Majuba. These Boers were a grasping lot! The dark-haired Francie, who had arrived on his heels, with the contradictious touch which became the free spirit of a daughter of Roger, chimed in:

"Kettle and pot, Uncle Nicholas. What price the Uitlanders?" What price, indeed! A new expression, and believed to be due to her brother George.

Aunt Juley thought Francie ought not to say such a thing. Dear Mrs. MacAnder's boy, Charlie MacAnder, was one, and no one could call him grasping. At this Francie uttered one of her mots, scandalising, and so frequently repeated:

"Well, his father's a Scotchman, and his mother's a cat."

Aunt Juley covered her ears, too late, but Aunt Hester smiled; as for Nicholas, he pouted—witticism of which he was not the author was hardly to his taste. Just then Marian Tweetyman arrived, followed almost immediately by young Nicholas. On seeing his son, Nicholas rose.

"Well, I must be going," he said, "Nick here will tell you what'll win the race." And with this hit at his eldest, who, as a pillar of accountancy, and director of an insurance company, was no more addicted to sport than his father had ever been, he departed. Dear Nicholas! What race was that? Or was it only one of his jokes? He was a wonderful man for his age! How many lumps would dear Marian take? And how were Giles and Jesse? Aunt Juley supposed their Yeomanry would be very busy now, guarding the coast, though of course the Boers had no ships. But one never knew what the French might do if they had the chance, especially since that dreadful Fashoda scare, which had upset Timothy so terribly that he had made no investments for months afterwards. It was the ingratitude of the Boers that was so dreadful, after everything had been done for them—Dr. Jameson imprisoned, and he was so nice, Mrs. MacAnder had always said. And Sir Alfred Milner sent out to talk to them—such a clever man! She didn't know what they wanted.

But at this moment occurred one of those sensations—so precious at Timothy's—which great occasions sometimes bring forth:

"Miss June Forsyte."

Aunts Juley and Hester were on their feet at once, trembling from smothered resentment, and old affection bubbling up, and pride at the return of a prodigal June! Well, this was a surprise! Dear June—after all these years! And how well she was looking! Not changed at all! It was almost on their lips to add, 'And how is your dear grandfather?' forgetting in that giddy moment that poor dear Jolyon had been in his grave for seven years now.

Ever the most courageous and downright of all the Forsytes, June, with her decided chin and her spirited eyes and her hair like flame, sat down, slight and short, on a gilt chair with a bead-worked seat, for all the world as if ten years had not elapsed since she had been to see them—ten years of travel and independence and devotion to lame ducks. Those ducks of late had been all definitely painters, etchers, or sculptors, so that her impatience with the Forsytes and their hopelessly inartistic outlook had become intense. Indeed, she had almost ceased to believe that her family existed, and looked round her now with a sort of challenging directness which brought exquisite discomfort to the roomful. She had not expected to meet any of them but 'the poor old things'; and why she had come to see them she hardly knew, except that, while on her way from Oxford Street to a studio in Latimer Road, she had suddenly remembered them with compunction as two long-neglected old lame ducks.

Aunt Juley broke the hush again. "We've just been saying, dear, how dreadful it is about these Boers! And what an impudent thing of that old Kruger!"

"Impudent!" said June. "I think he's quite right. What business have we to meddle with them? If he turned out all those wretched Uitlanders it would serve them right. They're only after money."

The silence of sensation was broken by Francie saying:

"What? Are you a pro-Boer?" (undoubtedly the first use of that expression).

"Well! Why can't we leave them alone?" said June, just as, in the open doorway, the maid said "Mr. Soames Forsyte." Sensation on sensation! Greeting was almost held up by curiosity to see how June and he would take this encounter, for it was shrewdly suspected, if not quite known, that they had not met since that old and lamentable affair of her fiancé Bosinney with Soames' wife. They were seen to just touch each other's hands, and look each at the other's left eye only. Aunt Juley came at once to the rescue:

"Dear June is so original. Fancy, Soames, she thinks the Boers are not to blame."

"They only want their independence," said June; "and why shouldn't they have it?"

"Because," answered Soames, with his smile a little on one side, "they happen to have agreed to our suzerainty."

"Suzerainty!" repeated June scornfully; "we shouldn't like anyone's suzerainty over us."

"They got advantages in payment," replied Soames; "a contract is a contract."

"Contracts are not always just," fumed out June, "and when they're not, they ought to be broken. The Boers are much the weaker. We could afford to be generous."

Soames sniffed. "That's mere sentiment," he said.

Aunt Hester, to whom nothing was more awful than any kind of disagreement, here leaned forward and remarked decisively:

"What lovely weather it has been for the time of year?"

But June was not to be diverted.

"I don't know why sentiment should be sneered at. It's the best thing in the world." She looked defiantly round, and Aunt Juley had to intervene again:

"Have you bought any pictures lately, Soames?"

Her incomparable instinct for the wrong subject had not failed her. Soames flushed. To disclose the name of his latest purchases would be like walking into the jaws of disdain. For somehow they all knew of June's predilection for 'genius' not yet on its legs, and her contempt for 'success' unless she had had a finger in securing it.

"One or two," he muttered.

But June's face had changed; the Forsyte within her was seeing its chance. Why should not Soames buy some of the pictures of Eric Cobbley—her last lame duck? And she promptly opened her attack: Did Soames know his work? It was so wonderful. He was the coming man.

Oh, yes, Soames knew his work. It was in his view 'splashy,' and would never get hold of the public.

June blazed up.

"Of course it won't; that's the last thing one would wish for. I thought you were a connoisseur, not a picture-dealer."

"Of course Soames is a connoisseur," Aunt Juley said hastily; "he has wonderful taste—he can always tell beforehand what's going to be successful."

"Oh!" gasped June, and sprang up from the bead-covered chair, "I hate that standard of success. Why can't people buy things because they like them?"

"You mean," said Francie, "because you like them."

And in the slight pause young Nicholas was heard saying gently that Violet (his fourth) was taking lessons in pastel, he didn't know if they were any use.

"Well, good-bye, Auntie," said June; "I must get on," and kissing her aunts, she looked defiantly round the room, said "Good-bye" again, and went. A breeze seemed to pass out with her, as if everyone had sighed.

The third sensation came before anyone had time to speak:

"Mr. James Forsyte."

James came in using a stick slightly and wrapped in a fur coat which gave him a fictitious bulk.

Everyone stood up. James was so old; and he had not been at Timothy's for nearly two years.

"It's hot in here," he said.

Soames divested him of his coat, and as he did so could not help admiring the glossy way his father was turned out. James sat down, all knees, elbows, frock-coat, and long white whiskers.

"What's the meaning of that?" he said.

Though there was no apparent sense in his words, they all knew that he was referring to June. His eyes searched his son's face.

"I thought I'd come and see for myself. What have they answered Kruger?"

Soames took out an evening paper, and read the headline.

"'Instant action by our Government—state of war existing!'"

"Ah!" said James, and sighed. "I was afraid they'd cut and run like old Gladstone. We shall finish with them this time."

All stared at him. James! Always fussy, nervous, anxious! James with his continual, 'I told you how it would be!' and his pessimism, and his cautious investments. There was something uncanny about such resolution in this the oldest living Forsyte.

"Where's Timothy?" said James. "He ought to pay attention to this."

Aunt Juley said she didn't know; Timothy had not said much at lunch to-day. Aunt Hester rose and threaded her way out of the room, and Francie said rather maliciously:

"The Boers are a hard nut to crack, Uncle James."

"H'm!" muttered James. "Where do you get your information? Nobody tells me."

Young Nicholas remarked in his mild voice that Nick (his eldest) was now going to drill regularly.

"Ah!" muttered James, and stared before him—his thoughts were on Val. "He's got to look after his mother," he said, "he's got no time for drilling and that, with that father of his." This cryptic saying produced silence, until he spoke again.

"What did June want here?" And his eyes rested with suspicion on all of them in turn. "Her father's a rich man now." The conversation turned on Jolyon, and when he had been seen last. It was supposed that he went abroad and saw all sorts of people now that his wife was dead; his water-colours were on the line, and he was a successful man. Francie went so far as to say:

"I should like to see him again; he was rather a dear."

Aunt Juley recalled how he had gone to sleep on the sofa one day, where James was sitting. He had always been very amiable; what did Soames think?

Knowing that Jolyon was Irene's trustee, all felt the delicacy of this question, and looked at Soames with interest. A faint pink had come up in his cheeks.

"He's going grey," he said.

Indeed! Had Soames seen him? Soames nodded, and the pink vanished.

James said suddenly: "Well—I don't know, I can't tell."

It so exactly expressed the sentiment of everybody present that there was something behind everything, that nobody responded. But at this moment Aunt Hester returned.

"Timothy," she said in a low voice, "Timothy has bought a map, and he's put in—he's put in three flags."

Timothy had...! A sigh went round the company.

If Timothy had indeed put in three flags already, well!—it showed what the nation could do when it was roused. The war was as good as over.

CHAPTER XIII—JOLYON FINDS OUT WHERE HE IS

Jolyon stood at the window in Holly's old night nursery, converted into a studio, not because it had a north light, but for its view over the prospect away to the Grand Stand at Epsom. He shifted to the side window which overlooked the stableyard, and whistled down to the dog Balthasar who lay for ever under the clock tower. The old dog looked up and wagged his tail. 'Poor old boy!' thought Jolyon, shifting back to the other window.

He had been restless all this week, since his attempt to prosecute trusteeship, uneasy in his conscience which was ever acute, disturbed in his sense of compassion which was easily excited, and with a queer sensation as if his feeling for beauty had received some definite embodiment. Autumn was getting hold of the old oak-tree, its leaves were browning. Sunshine had been plentiful and hot this summer. As with trees, so with men's lives! 'I ought to live long,' thought Jolyon; 'I'm getting mildewed for want of heat. If I can't work, I shall be off to Paris.' But memory of Paris gave him no pleasure. Besides, how could he go? He must stay and see what Soames was going to do. 'I'm her trustee. I can't leave her unprotected,' he thought. It had been striking him as curious how very clearly he could still see Irene in her little drawing-room which he had only twice entered. Her beauty must have a sort of poignant harmony! No literal portrait would ever do her justice; the essence of her was—ah I what?... The noise of hoofs called him back to the other window. Holly was riding into the yard on her long-tailed 'palfrey.' She looked up and he waved to her. She had been rather silent lately; getting old, he supposed, beginning to want her future, as they all did—youngsters!

Time was certainly the devil! And with the feeling that to waste this swift-travelling commodity was unforgivable folly, he took up his brush. But it was no use; he could not concentrate his eye—besides, the light was going. 'I'll go up to town,' he thought. In the hall a servant met him.

"A lady to see you, sir; Mrs. Heron."

Extraordinary coincidence! Passing into the picture-gallery, as it was still called, he saw Irene standing over by the window.

She came towards him saying:

"I've been trespassing; I came up through the coppice and garden. I always used to come that way to see Uncle Jolyon."

"You couldn't trespass here," replied Jolyon; "history makes that impossible. I was just thinking of you."

Irene smiled. And it was as if something shone through; not mere spirituality—serener, completer, more alluring.

"History!" she answered; "I once told Uncle Jolyon that love was for ever. Well, it isn't. Only aversion lasts."

Jolyon stared at her. Had she got over Bosinney at last?

"Yes!" he said, "aversion's deeper than love or hate because it's a natural product of the nerves, and we don't change them."

"I came to tell you that Soames has been to see me. He said a thing that frightened me. He said: 'You are still my wife!'"

"What!" ejaculated Jolyon. "You ought not to live alone." And he continued to stare at her, afflicted by the thought that where Beauty was, nothing ever ran quite straight, which, no doubt, was why so many people looked on it as immoral.

"What more?"

"He asked me to shake hands.

"Did you?"

"Yes. When he came in I'm sure he didn't want to; he changed while he was there."

"Ah! you certainly ought not to go on living there alone."

"I know no woman I could ask; and I can't take a lover to order, Cousin Jolyon."

"Heaven forbid!" said Jolyon. "What a damnable position! Will you stay to dinner? No? Well, let me see you back to town; I wanted to go up this evening."

"Truly?"

"Truly. I'll be ready in five minutes."

On that walk to the station they talked of pictures and music, contrasting the English and French characters and the difference in their attitude to Art. But to Jolyon the colours in the hedges of the long straight lane, the twittering of chaffinches who kept pace with them, the perfume of weeds being already burned, the turn of her neck, the fascination of those dark eyes bent on him now and then, the lure of her whole figure, made a deeper impression than the remarks they exchanged. Unconsciously he held himself straighter, walked with a more elastic step.

In the train he put her through a sort of catechism as to what she did with her days.

Made her dresses, shopped, visited a hospital, played her piano, translated from the French.

She had regular work from a publisher, it seemed, which supplemented her income a little. She seldom went out in the evening. "I've been living alone so long, you see, that I don't mind it a bit. I believe I'm naturally solitary."

"I don't believe that," said Jolyon. "Do you know many people?"

"Very few."

At Waterloo they took a hansom, and he drove with her to the door of her mansions. Squeezing her hand at parting, he said:

"You know, you could always come to us at Robin Hill; you must let me know everything that happens. Good-bye, Irene."

"Good-bye," she answered softly.

Jolyon climbed back into his cab, wondering why he had not asked her to dine and go to the theatre with him. Solitary, starved, hung-up life that she had! "Hotch Potch Club," he said through the trap-door. As his hansom debouched on to the Embankment, a man in top-hat and overcoat passed, walking quickly, so close to the wall that he seemed to be scraping it.

'By Jove!' thought Jolyon; 'Soames himself! What's he up to now?' And, stopping the cab round the corner, he got out and retraced his steps to where he could see the entrance to the mansions. Soames had halted in front of them, and was looking up at the light in her windows. 'If he goes in,' thought Jolyon, 'what shall I do? What have I the right to do?' What the fellow had said was true. She was still his wife, absolutely without protection from annoyance! 'Well, if he goes in,' he thought, 'I follow.' And he began moving towards the mansions. Again Soames advanced; he was in the very entrance now. But suddenly he stopped, spun round on his heel, and came back towards the river. 'What now?' thought Jolyon. 'In a dozen steps he'll recognise me.' And he turned tail. His cousin's footsteps kept pace with his own. But he reached his cab, and got in before Soames had turned the corner. "Go on!" he said through the trap. Soames' figure ranged up alongside.

"Hansom!" he said. "Engaged? Hallo!"

"Hallo!" answered Jolyon. "You?"

The quick suspicion on his cousin's face, white in the lamplight, decided him.

"I can give you a lift," he said, "if you're going West."

"Thanks," answered Soames, and got in.

"I've been seeing Irene," said Jolyon when the cab had started.

"Indeed!"

"You went to see her yesterday yourself, I understand."

"I did," said Soames; "she's my wife, you know."

The tone, the half-lifted sneering lip, roused sudden anger in Jolyon; but he subdued it.

"You ought to know best," he said, "but if you want a divorce it's not very wise to go seeing her, is it? One can't run with the hare and hunt with the hounds?"

"You're very good to warn me," said Soames, "but I have not made up my mind."

"She has," said Jolyon, looking straight before him; "you can't take things up, you know, as they were twelve years ago."

"That remains to be seen."

"Look here!" said Jolyon, "she's in a damnable position, and I am the only person with any legal say in her affairs."

"Except myself," retorted Soames, "who am also in a damnable position. Hers is what she made for herself; mine what she made for me. I am not at all sure that in her own interests I shan't require her to return to me."

"What!" exclaimed Jolyon; and a shiver went through his whole body.

"I don't know what you may mean by 'what,'" answered Soames coldly; "your say in her affairs is confined to paying out her income; please bear that in mind. In choosing not to disgrace her by a divorce, I retained my rights, and, as I say, I am not at all sure that I shan't require to exercise them."

"My God!" ejaculated Jolyon, and he uttered a short laugh.

"Yes," said Soames, and there was a deadly quality in his voice. "I've not forgotten the nickname your father gave me, 'The man of property'! I'm not called names for nothing."

"This is fantastic," murmured Jolyon. Well, the fellow couldn't force his wife to live with him. Those days were past, anyway! And he looked around at Soames with the thought: 'Is he real, this man?' But Soames looked very real, sitting square yet almost elegant with the clipped moustache on his pale face, and a tooth showing where a lip was lifted in a fixed smile. There was a long silence, while Jolyon thought: 'Instead of helping her, I've made things worse.' Suddenly Soames said:

"It would be the best thing that could happen to her in many ways."

At those words such a turmoil began taking place in Jolyon that he could barely sit still in the cab. It was as if he were boxed up with hundreds of thousands of his countrymen, boxed up with that something in the national character which had always been to him revolting, something which he knew to be extremely natural and yet which seemed to him inexplicable—their intense belief in contracts and vested rights, their complacent sense of virtue in the exaction of those rights. Here beside him in the cab was the very embodiment, the corporeal sum as it were, of the possessive instinct—his own kinsman, too! It was uncanny and intolerable! 'But there's something more in it than that!' he thought with a sick feeling. 'The dog, they say, returns to his vomit! The sight of her has reawakened something. Beauty! The devil's in it!'

"As I say," said Soames, "I have not made up my mind. I shall be obliged if you will kindly leave her quite alone."

Jolyon bit his lips; he who had always hated rows almost welcomed the thought of one now.

"I can give you no such promise," he said shortly.

"Very well," said Soames, "then we know where we are. I'll get down here." And stopping the cab he got out without word or sign of farewell. Jolyon travelled on to his Club.

The first news of the war was being called in the streets, but he paid no attention. What could he do to help her? If only his father were alive! He could have done so much! But why could he not do all that his father could have done? Was he not old enough?—turned fifty and twice married, with grown-up daughters and a son. 'Queer,' he thought. 'If she were plain I shouldn't be thinking twice about it. Beauty is the devil, when you're sensitive to it!' And into the Club reading-room he went with a disturbed heart. In that very room he and Bosinney had talked one summer afternoon; he well remembered even now the disguised and secret lecture he had given that young man in the interests of June, the diagnosis of the Forsytes he had hazarded; and how he had wondered what sort of woman it was he was warning him against. And now! He was almost in want of a warning himself. 'It's deuced funny!' he thought, 'really deuced funny!'

CHAPTER XIV—SOAMES DISCOVERS WHAT HE WANTS

It is so much easier to say, "Then we know where we are," than to mean anything particular by the words. And in saying them Soames did but vent the jealous rankling of his instincts.

He got out of the cab in a state of wary anger—with himself for not having seen Irene, with Jolyon for having seen her; and now with his inability to tell exactly what he wanted.

He had abandoned the cab because he could not bear to remain seated beside his cousin, and walking briskly eastwards he thought: 'I wouldn't trust that fellow Jolyon a yard. Once outcast, always outcast!' The chap had a natural sympathy with—with—laxity (he had shied at the word sin, because it was too melodramatic for use by a Forsyte).

Indecision in desire was to him a new feeling. He was like a child between a promised toy and an old one which had been taken away from him; and he was astonished at himself. Only last Sunday desire had seemed simple—just his freedom and Annette. 'I'll go and dine there,' he thought. To see her might bring back his singleness of intention, calm his exasperation, clear his mind.

The restaurant was fairly full—a good many foreigners and folk whom, from their appearance, he took to be literary or artistic. Scraps of conversation came his way through the clatter of plates and glasses. He distinctly heard the Boers sympathised with, the British Government blamed. 'Don't think much of their clientele,' he thought. He went stolidly through his dinner and special coffee without making his presence known, and when at last he had finished, was careful not to be seen going towards the sanctum of Madame Lamotte. They were, as he entered, having supper—such a much nicer-looking supper than the dinner he had eaten that he felt a kind of grief—and they greeted him with a surprise so seemingly genuine that he thought with sudden suspicion: 'I believe they knew I was here all the time.' He gave Annette a look furtive and searching. So pretty, seemingly so candid; could she be angling for him? He turned to Madame Lamotte and said:

"I've been dining here."

Really! If she had only known! There were dishes she could have recommended; what a pity! Soames was confirmed in his suspicion. 'I must look out what I'm doing!' he thought sharply.

"Another little cup of very special coffee, monsieur; a liqueur, Grand Marnier?" and Madame Lamotte rose to order these delicacies.

Alone with Annette Soames said, "Well, Annette?" with a defensive little smile about his lips.

The girl blushed. This, which last Sunday would have set his nerves tingling, now gave him much the same feeling a man has when a dog that he owns wriggles and looks at him. He had a curious sense of power, as if he could have said to her, 'Come and kiss me,' and she would have come. And yet—it was strange—but there seemed another face and form in the room too; and the itch in his nerves, was it for that—or for this? He jerked his head towards the restaurant and said: "You have some queer customers. Do you like this life?"

Annette looked up at him for a moment, looked down, and played with her fork.

"No," she said, "I do not like it."

'I've got her,' thought Soames, 'if I want her. But do I want her?' She was graceful, she was pretty—very pretty; she was fresh, she had taste of a kind. His eyes travelled round the little room; but the eyes of his mind went another journey—a half-light, and silvery walls, a satinwood piano, a woman standing against it, reined back as it were from him—a woman with white shoulders that he knew, and dark eyes that he had sought to know, and hair like dull dark amber. And as in an artist who strives for the unrealisable and is ever thirsty, so there rose in him at that moment the thirst of the old passion he had never satisfied.

"Well," he said calmly, "you're young. There's everything before you."

Annette shook her head.

"I think sometimes there is nothing before me but hard work. I am not so in love with work as mother."

"Your mother is a wonder," said Soames, faintly mocking; "she will never let failure lodge in her house."

Annette sighed. "It must be wonderful to be rich."

"Oh! You'll be rich some day," answered Soames, still with that faint mockery; "don't be afraid."

Annette shrugged her shoulders. "Monsieur is very kind." And between her pouting lips she put a chocolate.

'Yes, my dear,' thought Soames, 'they're very pretty.'

Madame Lamotte, with coffee and liqueur, put an end to that colloquy. Soames did not stay long.

Outside in the streets of Soho, which always gave him such a feeling of property improperly owned, he mused. If only Irene had given him a son, he wouldn't now be squirming after women! The thought had jumped out of its little dark sentry-box in his inner consciousness. A son—something to look forward to, something to make the rest of life worth while, something to leave himself to, some perpetuity of self. 'If I had a son,' he thought bitterly, 'a proper legal son, I could make shift to go on as I used. One woman's much the same as another, after all.' But as he walked he shook his head. No! One woman was not the same as another. Many a time had he tried to think that in the old days of his thwarted married life; and he had always failed. He was failing now. He was trying to think Annette the same as that other. But she was not, she had not the lure of that old passion. 'And Irene's my wife,' he thought, 'my legal wife. I have done nothing to put her away from me. Why shouldn't she come back to me? It's the right thing, the lawful thing. It makes no scandal, no disturbance. If it's disagreeable to her—but why should it be? I'm not a leper, and she—she's no longer in love!' Why should he be put to the shifts and the sordid disgraces and the lurking defeats of the Divorce Court, when there she was like an empty house only waiting to be retaken into use and possession by him who legally owned her? To one so secretive as Soames the thought of reentry into quiet possession of his own property with nothing given away to the world was intensely alluring. 'No,' he mused, 'I'm glad I went to see that girl. I know now what I want most. If only Irene will come back I'll be as considerate as she wishes; she could live her own life; but perhaps—perhaps she would come round to me.' There was a lump in his throat. And doggedly along by the railings of the Green Park, towards his father's house, he went, trying to tread on his shadow walking before him in the brilliant moonlight.

PART II

CHAPTER I—THE THIRD GENERATION

Jolly Forsyte was strolling down High Street, Oxford, on a November afternoon; Val Dartie was strolling up. Jolly had just changed out of boating flannels and was on his way to the 'Frying-pan,' to which he had recently been elected. Val had just changed out of riding clothes and was on his way to the fire—a bookmaker's in Cornmarket.

"Hallo!" said Jolly.

"Hallo!" replied Val.

The cousins had met but twice, Jolly, the second-year man, having invited the freshman to breakfast; and last evening they had seen each other again under somewhat exotic circumstances.

Over a tailor's in the Cornmarket resided one of those privileged young beings called minors, whose inheritances are large, whose parents are dead, whose guardians are remote, and whose instincts are vicious. At nineteen he had commenced one of those careers attractive and inexplicable to ordinary mortals for whom a single bankruptcy is good as a feast. Already famous for having the only roulette table then to be found in Oxford, he was anticipating his expectations at a dazzling rate. He out-crummed Crum, though of a sanguine and rather beefy type which lacked the latter's fascinating languor. For Val it had been in the nature of baptism to be taken there to play roulette; in the nature of confirmation to get back into college, after hours, through a window whose bars were deceptive. Once, during that evening of delight, glancing up from the seductive green before him, he had caught sight, through a cloud of smoke, of his cousin standing opposite. 'Rouge gagne, impair, et manque!' He had not seen him again.

"Come in to the Frying-pan and have tea," said Jolly, and they went in.

A stranger, seeing them together, would have noticed an unseizable resemblance between these second cousins of the third generations of Forsytes; the same bone formation in face, though Jolly's eyes were darker grey, his hair lighter and more wavy.

"Tea and buttered buns, waiter, please," said Jolly.

"Have one of my cigarettes?" said Val. "I saw you last night. How did you do?"

"I didn't play."

"I won fifteen quid."

Though desirous of repeating a whimsical comment on gambling he had once heard his father make—'When you're fleeced you're sick, and when you fleece you're sorry—Jolly contented himself with:

"Rotten game, I think; I was at school with that chap. He's an awful fool."

"Oh! I don't know," said Val, as one might speak in defence of a disparaged god; "he's a pretty good sport."

They exchanged whiffs in silence.

"You met my people, didn't you?" said Jolly. "They're coming up to-morrow."

Val grew a little red.

"Really! I can give you a rare good tip for the Manchester November handicap."

"Thanks, I only take interest in the classic races."

"You can't make any money over them," said Val.

"I hate the ring," said Jolly; "there's such a row and stink. I like the paddock."

"I like to back my judgment,'" answered Val.

Jolly smiled; his smile was like his father's.

"I haven't got any. I always lose money if I bet."

"You have to buy experience, of course."

"Yes, but it's all messed-up with doing people in the eye."

"Of course, or they'll do you—that's the excitement."

Jolly looked a little scornful.

"What do you do with yourself? Row?"

"No—ride, and drive about. I'm going to play polo next term, if I can get my granddad to stump up."

"That's old Uncle James, isn't it? What's he like?"

"Older than forty hills," said Val, "and always thinking he's going to be ruined."

"I suppose my granddad and he were brothers."

"I don't believe any of that old lot were sportsmen," said Val; "they must have worshipped money."

"Mine didn't!" said Jolly warmly.

Val flipped the ash off his cigarette.

"Money's only fit to spend," he said; "I wish the deuce I had more."

Jolly gave him that direct upward look of judgment which he had inherited from old Jolyon: One didn't talk about money! And again there was silence, while they drank tea and ate the buttered buns.

"Where are your people going to stay?" asked Val, elaborately casual.

"'Rainbow.' What do you think of the war?"

"Rotten, so far. The Boers aren't sports a bit. Why don't they come out into the open?"

"Why should they? They've got everything against them except their way of fighting. I rather admire them."

"They can ride and shoot," admitted Val, "but they're a lousy lot. Do you know Crum?"

"Of Merton? Only by sight. He's in that fast set too, isn't he? Rather La-di-da and Brummagem."

Val said fixedly: "He's a friend of mine."

"Oh! Sorry!" And they sat awkwardly staring past each other, having pitched on their pet points of snobbery. For Jolly was forming himself unconsciously on a set whose motto was:

'We defy you to bore us. Life isn't half long enough, and we're going to talk faster and more crisply, do more and know more, and dwell less on any subject than you can possibly imagine. We are "the best"—made of wire and whipcord.' And Val was unconsciously forming himself on a set whose motto was: 'We defy you to interest or excite us. We have had every sensation, or if we haven't, we pretend we have. We are so exhausted with living that no hours are too small for us. We will lose our shirts with equanimity. We have flown fast and are past everything. All is cigarette smoke. Bismillah!' Competitive spirit, bone-deep in the English, was obliging those two young Forsytes to have ideals; and at the close of a century ideals are mixed. The aristocracy had already in the main adopted the 'jumping-Jesus' principle; though here and there one like Crum—who was an 'honourable'—stood starkly languid for that gambler's Nirvana which had been the summum bonum of the old 'dandies' and of 'the mashers' in the eighties. And round Crum were still gathered a forlorn hope of blue-bloods with a plutocratic following.

But there was between the cousins another far less obvious antipathy—coming from the unseizable family resemblance, which each perhaps resented; or from some half-consciousness of that old feud persisting still between their branches of the clan, formed within them by odd words or half-hints dropped by their elders. And Jolly, tinkling his teaspoon, was musing: 'His tie-pin and his waistcoat and his drawl and his betting—good Lord!'

And Val, finishing his bun, was thinking: 'He's rather a young beast!'

"I suppose you'll be meeting your people?" he said, getting up. "I wish you'd tell them I should like to show them over B.N.C.—not that there's anything much there—if they'd care to come."

"Thanks, I'll ask them."

"Would they lunch? I've got rather a decent scout."

Jolly doubted if they would have time.

"You'll ask them, though?"

"Very good of you," said Jolly, fully meaning that they should not go; but, instinctively polite, he added: "You'd better come and have dinner with us to-morrow."

"Rather. What time?"

"Seven-thirty."

"Dress?"

"No." And they parted, a subtle antagonism alive within them.

Holly and her father arrived by a midday train. It was her first visit to the city of spires and dreams, and she was very silent, looking almost shyly at the brother who was part of this wonderful place. After lunch she wandered, examining his household gods with intense curiosity. Jolly's sitting-room was panelled, and Art represented by a set of Bartolozzi prints which had belonged to old Jolyon, and by college photographs—of young men, live young men, a little heroic, and to be compared with her memories of Val. Jolyon also scrutinised with care that evidence of his boy's character and tastes.

Jolly was anxious that they should see him rowing, so they set forth to the river. Holly, between her brother and her father, felt elated when heads were turned and eyes rested on her. That they might see him to the best advantage they left him at the Barge and crossed the river to the towing-path. Slight in build—for of all the Forsytes only old Swithin and George were beefy—Jolly was rowing 'Two' in a trial eight. He looked very earnest and strenuous. With pride Jolyon thought him the best-looking boy of the lot; Holly, as became a sister, was more struck by one or two of the others, but would not have said so for the world. The river was bright that afternoon, the meadows lush, the trees still beautiful with colour. Distinguished peace clung around the old city; Jolyon promised himself a day's sketching if the weather held. The Eight passed a second time, spurting home along the Barges—Jolly's face was very set, so as not to show that he was blown. They returned across the river and waited for him.

"Oh!" said Jolly in the Christ Church meadows, "I had to ask that chap Val Dartie to dine with us to-night. He wanted to give you lunch and show you B.N.C., so I thought I'd better; then you needn't go. I don't like him much."

Holly's rather sallow face had become suffused with pink.

"Why not?"

"Oh! I don't know. He seems to me rather showy and bad form. What are his people like, Dad? He's only a second cousin, isn't he?"

Jolyon took refuge in a smile.

"Ask Holly," he said; "she saw his uncle."

"I liked Val," Holly answered, staring at the ground before her; "his uncle looked—awfully different." She stole a glance at Jolly from under her lashes.

"Did you ever," said Jolyon with whimsical intention, "hear our family history, my dears? It's quite a fairy tale. The first Jolyon Forsyte—at all events the first we know anything of, and that would be your great-great-grandfather—dwelt in the land of Dorset on the edge of the sea, being by profession an 'agriculturalist,' as your great-aunt put it, and the son of an agriculturist—farmers, in fact; your grandfather used to call them, 'Very small beer.'" He looked at Jolly to see how his lordliness was standing it, and with the other eye noted Holly's malicious pleasure in the slight drop of her brother's face.

"We may suppose him thick and sturdy, standing for England as it was before the Industrial Era began. The second Jolyon Forsyte—your great-grandfather, Jolly; better known as Superior Dosset Forsyte—built houses, so the chronicle runs, begat ten children, and migrated to London town. It is known that he drank sherry. We may suppose him representing the England of Napoleon's wars, and general unrest. The eldest of his six sons was the third Jolyon, your grandfather, my dears—tea merchant and chairman of companies, one of the soundest Englishmen who ever lived—and to me the dearest." Jolyon's voice had lost its irony, and his son and daughter gazed at him solemnly, "He was just and tenacious, tender and young at heart. You remember him, and I remember him. Pass to the others! Your great-uncle James, that's young Val's grandfather, had a son called Soames—whereby hangs a tale of no love lost, and I don't think I'll tell it you. James and the other eight children of 'Superior Dosset,' of whom there are still five alive, may be said to have represented Victorian England, with its principles of trade and individualism at five per cent. and your money back—if you know what that means. At all events they've turned thirty thousand pounds into a cool million between them in the course of their long lives. They never did a wild thing—unless it was your great-uncle Swithin, who I believe was once swindled at thimble-rig, and was called 'Four-in-hand Forsyte' because he drove a pair. Their day is passing, and their type, not altogether for the advantage of the country. They were pedestrian, but they too were sound. I am the fourth Jolyon Forsyte—a poor holder of the name—"

"No, Dad," said Jolly, and Holly squeezed his hand.

"Yes," repeated Jolyon, "a poor specimen, representing, I'm afraid, nothing but the end of the century, unearned income, amateurism, and individual liberty—a different thing from individualism, Jolly. You are the fifth Jolyon Forsyte, old man, and you open the ball of the new century."

As he spoke they turned in through the college gates, and Holly said: "It's fascinating, Dad."

None of them quite knew what she meant. Jolly was grave.

The Rainbow, distinguished, as only an Oxford hostel can be, for lack of modernity, provided one small oak-panelled private sitting-room, in which Holly sat to receive, white-frocked, shy, and alone, when the only guest arrived. Rather as one would touch a moth,

Val took her hand. And wouldn't she wear this 'measly flower'? It would look ripping in her hair. He removed a gardenia from his coat.

"Oh! No, thank you—I couldn't!" But she took it and pinned it at her neck, having suddenly remembered that word 'showy'! Val's buttonhole would give offence; and she so much wanted Jolly to like him. Did she realise that Val was at his best and quietest in her presence, and was that, perhaps, half the secret of his attraction for her?

"I never said anything about our ride, Val."

"Rather not! It's just between us."

By the uneasiness of his hands and the fidgeting of his feet he was giving her a sense of power very delicious; a soft feeling too—the wish to make him happy.

"Do tell me about Oxford. It must be ever so lovely."

Val admitted that it was frightfully decent to do what you liked; the lectures were nothing; and there were some very good chaps. "Only," he added, "of course I wish I was in town, and could come down and see you."

Holly moved one hand shyly on her knee, and her glance dropped.

"You haven't forgotten," he said, suddenly gathering courage, "that we're going mad-rabbiting together?"

Holly smiled.

"Oh! That was only make-believe. One can't do that sort of thing after one's grown up, you know."

"Dash it! cousins can," said Val. "Next Long Vac.—it begins in June, you know, and goes on for ever—we'll watch our chance."

But, though the thrill of conspiracy ran through her veins, Holly shook her head. "It won't come off," she murmured.

"Won't it!" said Val fervently; "who's going to stop it? Not your father or your brother."

At this moment Jolyon and Jolly came in; and romance fled into Val's patent leather and Holly's white satin toes, where it itched and tingled during an evening not conspicuous for open-heartedness.

Sensitive to atmosphere, Jolyon soon felt the latent antagonism between the boys, and was puzzled by Holly; so he became unconsciously ironical, which is fatal to the expansiveness of youth. A letter, handed to him after dinner, reduced him to a silence hardly broken till Jolly and Val rose to go. He went out with them, smoking his cigar, and walked with his son to the gates of Christ Church. Turning back, he took out the letter and read it again beneath a lamp.

"DEAR JOLYON,

"Soames came again to-night—my thirty-seventh birthday. You were right, I mustn't stay here. I'm going to-morrow to the Piedmont Hotel, but I won't go abroad without seeing you. I feel lonely and down-hearted.

"Yours affectionately,

"IRENE."

He folded the letter back into his pocket and walked on, astonished at the violence of his feelings. What had the fellow said or done?

He turned into High Street, down the Turf, and on among a maze of spires and domes and long college fronts and walls, bright or dark-shadowed in the strong moonlight. In this very heart of England's gentility it was difficult to realise that a lonely woman could be importuned or hunted, but what else could her letter mean? Soames must have been pressing her to go back to him again, with public opinion and the Law on his side, too! 'Eighteen-ninety-nine!,' he thought, gazing at the broken glass shining on the top of a villa garden wall; 'but when it comes to property we're still a heathen people! I'll go up to-morrow morning. I dare say it'll be best for her to go abroad.' Yet the thought displeased him. Why should Soames hunt her out of England! Besides, he might follow, and out there she would be still more helpless against the attentions of her own husband! 'I must tread warily,' he thought; 'that fellow could make himself very nasty. I didn't like his manner in the cab the other night.' His thoughts turned to his daughter June. Could she help? Once on a time Irene had been her greatest friend, and now she was a 'lame duck,' such as must appeal to June's nature! He determined to wire to his daughter to meet him at Paddington Station. Retracing his steps towards the Rainbow he questioned his own sensations. Would he be upsetting himself over every woman in like case? No! he would not. The candour of this conclusion discomfited him; and, finding that Holly had gone up to bed, he sought his own room. But he could not sleep, and sat for a long time at his window, huddled in an overcoat, watching the moonlight on the roofs.

Next door Holly too was awake, thinking of the lashes above and below Val's eyes, especially below; and of what she could do to make Jolly like him better. The scent of the gardenia was strong in her little bedroom, and pleasant to her.

And Val, leaning out of his first-floor window in B.N.C., was gazing at a moonlit quadrangle without seeing it at all, seeing instead Holly, slim and white-frocked, as she sat beside the fire when he first went in.

But Jolly, in his bedroom narrow as a ghost, lay with a hand beneath his cheek and dreamed he was with Val in one boat, rowing a race against him, while his father was calling from the towpath: 'Two! Get your hands away there, bless you!'

CHAPTER II—SOAMES PUTS IT TO THE TOUCH

Of all those radiant firms which emblazon with their windows the West End of London, Gaves and Cortegal were considered by Soames the most 'attractive' word just coming into fashion. He had never had his Uncle Swithin's taste in precious stones, and the abandonment by Irene when she left his house in 1887 of all the glittering things he had given her had disgusted him with this form of investment. But he still knew a diamond when he saw one, and during the week before her birthday he had taken occasion, on his way into the Poultry or his way out therefrom, to dally a little before the greater jewellers where one got, if not one's money's worth, at least a certain cachet with the goods.

Constant cogitation since his drive with Jolyon had convinced him more and more of the supreme importance of this moment in his life, the supreme need for taking steps and those not wrong. And, alongside the dry and reasoned sense that it was now or never with his self-preservation, now or never if he were to range himself and found a family, went the secret urge of his senses roused by the sight of her who had once been a passionately desired wife, and the conviction that it was a sin against common sense and the decent secrecy of Forsytes to waste the wife he had.

In an opinion on Winifred's case, Dreamer, Q.C.—he would much have preferred Waterbuck, but they had made him a judge (so late in the day as to rouse the usual suspicion of a political job)—had advised that they should go forward and obtain restitution of conjugal rights, a point which to Soames had never been in doubt. When they had obtained a decree to that effect they must wait to see if it was obeyed. If not, it would constitute legal desertion, and they should obtain evidence of misconduct and file their petition for divorce. All of which Soames knew perfectly well. They had marked him ten and one. This simplicity in his sister's case only made him the more desperate about the difficulty in his own. Everything, in fact, was driving him towards the simple solution of Irene's return. If it were still against the grain with her, had he not feelings to subdue, injury to forgive, pain to forget? He at least had never injured her, and this was a world of compromise! He could offer her so much more than she had now. He would be prepared to make a liberal settlement on her which could not be upset. He often scrutinised his image in these days. He had never been a peacock like that fellow Dartie, or fancied himself a woman's man, but he had a certain belief in his own appearance—not unjustly, for it was well-coupled and preserved, neat, healthy, pale, unblemished by drink or excess of any kind. The Forsyte jaw and the concentration of his face were, in his eyes, virtues. So far as he could tell there was no feature of him which need inspire dislike.

Thoughts and yearnings, with which one lives daily, become natural, even if far-fetched in their inception. If he could only give tangible proof enough of his determination to let bygones be bygones, and to do all in his power to please her, why should she not come back to him?

He entered Gaves and Cortegal's therefore, on the morning of November the 9th, to buy a certain diamond brooch. "Four twenty-five and dirt cheap, sir, at the money. It's a lady's brooch." There was that in his mood which made him accept without demur. And he went on into the Poultry with the flat green morocco case in his breast pocket. Several times that day he opened it to look at the seven soft shining stones in their velvet oval nest.

"If the lady doesn't like it, sir, happy to exchange it any time. But there's no fear of that." If only there were not! He got through a vast amount of work, only soother of the nerves he knew. A cablegram came while he was in the office with details from the agent in Buenos Aires, and the name and address of a stewardess who would be prepared to swear to what was necessary. It was a timely spur to Soames, with his rooted distaste for the washing of dirty linen in public. And when he set forth by Underground to Victoria Station he received a fresh impetus towards the renewal of his married life from the account in his evening paper of a fashionable divorce suit. The homing instinct of all true Forsytes in anxiety and trouble, the corporate tendency which kept them strong and solid, made him choose to dine at Park Lane. He neither could nor would breath a word to his people of his intention—too reticent and proud—but the thought that at least they would be glad if they knew, and wish him luck, was heartening.

James was in lugubrious mood, for the fire which the impudence of Kruger's ultimatum had lit in him had been cold-watered by the poor success of the last month, and the exhortations to effort in The Times. He didn't know where it would end. Soames sought to cheer him by the continual use of the word Buller. But James couldn't tell! There was Colley—and he got stuck on that hill, and this Ladysmith was down in a hollow, and altogether it looked to him a 'pretty kettle of fish'; he thought they ought to be sending the sailors—they were the chaps, they did a lot of good in the Crimea. Soames shifted the ground of consolation. Winifred had heard from Val that there had been a 'rag' and a bonfire on Guy Fawkes Day at Oxford, and that he had escaped detection by blacking his face.

"Ah!" James muttered, "he's a clever little chap." But he shook his head shortly afterwards and remarked that he didn't know what would become of him, and looking wistfully at his son, murmured on that Soames had never had a boy. He would have liked a grandson of his own name. And now—well, there it was!

Soames flinched. He had not expected such a challenge to disclose the secret in his heart. And Emily, who saw him wince, said:

"Nonsense, James; don't talk like that!"

But James, not looking anyone in the face, muttered on. There were Roger and Nicholas and Jolyon; they all had grandsons. And Swithin and Timothy had never married. He had done his best; but he would soon be gone now. And, as though he had uttered words of profound consolation, he was silent, eating brains with a fork and a piece of bread, and swallowing the bread.

Soames excused himself directly after dinner. It was not really cold, but he put on his fur coat, which served to fortify him against the fits of nervous shivering to which he had been subject all day. Subconsciously, he knew that he looked better thus than in an ordinary black overcoat. Then, feeling the morocco case flat against his heart, he sallied forth. He was no smoker, but he lit a cigarette, and smoked it gingerly as he walked along. He moved slowly down the Row towards Knightsbridge, timing himself to get to Chelsea at nine-fifteen. What did she do with herself evening after evening in that little hole? How mysterious women were! One lived alongside and knew nothing of them. What could she have seen in that fellow Bosinney to send her mad? For there was madness after all in what she had done—crazy moonstruck madness, in which all sense of values had been lost, and her life and his life ruined! And for a moment he was filled with a sort of exaltation, as though he were a man read of in a story who, possessed by the Christian spirit, would restore to her all the prizes of existence, forgiving and forgetting, and becoming the godfather of her future. Under a tree opposite Knightsbridge Barracks, where the moon-light struck down clear and white, he took out once more the morocco case, and let the beams draw colour from those stones. Yes, they were of the first water! But, at the hard closing snap of the case, another cold shiver ran through his nerves; and he walked on faster, clenching his gloved hands in the pockets of his coat, almost hoping she would not be in. The thought of how mysterious she was again beset him. Dining alone there night after night—in an evening dress, too, as if she were making believe to be in society! Playing the piano—to herself! Not even a dog or cat, so far as he had seen. And that reminded him suddenly of the mare he kept for station work at Mapledurham. If ever he went to the stable, there she was quite alone, half asleep, and yet, on her home journeys going more freely than on her way out, as if longing to be back and lonely in her stable! 'I would treat her well,' he thought incoherently. 'I would be very careful.' And all that capacity for home life of which a mocking Fate seemed for ever to have deprived him swelled suddenly in Soames, so that he dreamed dreams opposite South Kensington Station. In the King's Road a man came slithering out of a public house playing a concertina. Soames watched him for a moment dance crazily on the pavement to his own drawling jagged sounds, then crossed over to avoid contact with this piece of drunken foolery. A night in the lock-up! What asses people were! But the man had noticed his movement of avoidance, and streams of genial blasphemy followed him across the street. 'I hope they'll run him in,' thought Soames viciously. 'To have ruffians like that about, with women out alone!' A woman's figure in front had induced this thought. Her walk seemed oddly familiar, and when she turned the corner for which he was bound, his heart began to beat. He hastened on to the corner to make certain. Yes! It was Irene; he could not mistake her walk in that little drab street. She threaded two more turnings, and from the last corner he saw her enter her block of flats. To make sure of her now, he ran those few paces, hurried up the stairs, and caught her standing at her door. He heard the latchkey in the lock, and reached her side just as she turned round, startled, in the open doorway.

"Don't be alarmed," he said, breathless. "I happened to see you. Let me come in a minute."

She had put her hand up to her breast, her face was colourless, her eyes widened by alarm. Then seeming to master herself, she inclined her head, and said: "Very well."

Soames closed the door. He, too, had need to recover, and when she had passed into the sitting-room, waited a full minute, taking deep breaths to still the beating of his heart. At this moment, so fraught with the future, to take out that morocco case seemed crude. Yet, not to take it out left him there before her with no preliminary excuse for coming. And in this dilemma he was seized with impatience at all this paraphernalia of excuse and justification. This was a scene—it could be nothing else, and he must face it. He heard her voice, uncomfortably, pathetically soft:

"Why have you come again? Didn't you understand that I would rather you did not?"

He noticed her clothes—a dark brown velvet corduroy, a sable boa, a small round toque of the same. They suited her admirably. She had money to spare for dress, evidently! He said abruptly:

"It's your birthday. I brought you this," and he held out to her the green morocco case.

"Oh! No-no!"

Soames pressed the clasp; the seven stones gleamed out on the pale grey velvet.

"Why not?" he said. "Just as a sign that you don't bear me ill-feeling any longer."

"I couldn't."

Soames took it out of the case.

"Let me just see how it looks."

She shrank back.

He followed, thrusting his hand with the brooch in it against the front of her dress. She shrank again.

Soames dropped his hand.

"Irene," he said, "let bygones be bygones. If I can, surely you might. Let's begin again, as if nothing had been. Won't you?" His voice was wistful, and his eyes, resting on her face, had in them a sort of supplication.

She, who was standing literally with her back against the wall, gave a little gulp, and that was all her answer. Soames went on:

"Can you really want to live all your days half-dead in this little hole? Come back to me, and I'll give you all you want. You shall live your own life; I swear it."

He saw her face quiver ironically.

"Yes," he repeated, "but I mean it this time. I'll only ask one thing. I just want—I just want a son. Don't look like that! I want one. It's hard." His voice had grown hurried, so that he hardly knew it for his own, and twice he jerked his head back as if struggling for breath. It was the sight of her eyes fixed on him, dark with a sort of fascinated fright, which pulled him together and changed that painful incoherence to anger.

"Is it so very unnatural?" he said between his teeth, "Is it unnatural to want a child from one's own wife? You wrecked our life and put this blight on everything. We go on only half

291

alive, and without any future. Is it so very unflattering to you that in spite of everything I—I still want you for my wife? Speak, for Goodness' sake! do speak."

Irene seemed to try, but did not succeed.

"I don't want to frighten you," said Soames more gently. "Heaven knows. I only want you to see that I can't go on like this. I want you back. I want you."

Irene raised one hand and covered the lower part of her face, but her eyes never moved from his, as though she trusted in them to keep him at bay. And all those years, barren and bitter, since—ah! when?—almost since he had first known her, surged up in one great wave of recollection in Soames; and a spasm that for his life he could not control constricted his face.

"It's not too late," he said; "it's not—if you'll only believe it."

Irene uncovered her lips, and both her hands made a writhing gesture in front of her breast. Soames seized them.

"Don't!" she said under her breath. But he stood holding on to them, trying to stare into her eyes which did not waver. Then she said quietly:

"I am alone here. You won't behave again as you once behaved."

Dropping her hands as though they had been hot irons, he turned away. Was it possible that there could be such relentless unforgiveness! Could that one act of violent possession be still alive within her? Did it bar him thus utterly? And doggedly he said, without looking up:

"I am not going till you've answered me. I am offering what few men would bring themselves to offer, I want a—a reasonable answer."

And almost with surprise he heard her say:

"You can't have a reasonable answer. Reason has nothing to do with it. You can only have the brutal truth: I would rather die."

Soames stared at her.

"Oh!" he said. And there intervened in him a sort of paralysis of speech and movement, the kind of quivering which comes when a man has received a deadly insult, and does not yet know how he is going to take it, or rather what it is going to do with him.

"Oh!" he said again, "as bad as that? Indeed! You would rather die. That's pretty!"

"I am sorry. You wanted me to answer. I can't help the truth, can I?"

At that queer spiritual appeal Soames turned for relief to actuality. He snapped the brooch back into its case and put it in his pocket.

"The truth!" he said; "there's no such thing with women. It's nerves-nerves."

He heard the whisper:

"Yes; nerves don't lie. Haven't you discovered that?" He was silent, obsessed by the thought: 'I will hate this woman. I will hate her.' That was the trouble! If only he could! He shot a glance at her who stood unmoving against the wall with her head up and her hands clasped, for all the world as if she were going to be shot. And he said quickly:

"I don't believe a word of it. You have a lover. If you hadn't, you wouldn't be such a—such a little idiot." He was conscious, before the expression in her eyes, that he had uttered something of a non-sequitur, and dropped back too abruptly into the verbal freedom of his connubial days. He turned away to the door. But he could not go out. Something within him—that most deep and secret Forsyte quality, the impossibility of letting go, the impossibility of seeing the fantastic and forlorn nature of his own tenacity—prevented him. He turned about again, and there stood, with his back against the door, as hers was against the wall opposite, quite unconscious of anything ridiculous in this separation by the whole width of the room.

"Do you ever think of anybody but yourself?" he said.

Irene's lips quivered; then she answered slowly:

"Do you ever think that I found out my mistake—my hopeless, terrible mistake—the very first week of our marriage; that I went on trying three years—you know I went on trying? Was it for myself?"

Soames gritted his teeth. "God knows what it was. I've never understood you; I shall never understand you. You had everything you wanted; and you can have it again, and more. What's the matter with me? I ask you a plain question: What is it?" Unconscious of the pathos in that enquiry, he went on passionately: "I'm not lame, I'm not loathsome, I'm not a boor, I'm not a fool. What is it? What's the mystery about me?"

Her answer was a long sigh.

He clasped his hands with a gesture that for him was strangely full of expression. "When I came here to-night I was—I hoped—I meant everything that I could to do away with the past, and start fair again. And you meet me with 'nerves,' and silence, and sighs. There's nothing tangible. It's like—it's like a spider's web."

"Yes."

That whisper from across the room maddened Soames afresh.

"Well, I don't choose to be in a spider's web. I'll cut it." He walked straight up to her. "Now!" What he had gone up to her to do he really did not know. But when he was close, the old familiar scent of her clothes suddenly affected him. He put his hands on her shoulders and bent forward to kiss her. He kissed not her lips, but a little hard line where the lips had been drawn in; then his face was pressed away by her hands; he heard her say: "Oh! No!" Shame, compunction, sense of futility flooded his whole being, he turned on his heel and went straight out.

CHAPTER III—VISIT TO IRENE

Jolyon found June waiting on the platform at Paddington. She had received his telegram while at breakfast. Her abode—a studio and two bedrooms in a St. John's Wood garden—had been selected by her for the complete independence which it guaranteed. Unwatched by Mrs. Grundy, unhindered by permanent domestics, she could receive lame ducks at any hour of day or night, and not seldom had a duck without studio of its own made use of June's. She enjoyed her freedom, and possessed herself with a sort of virginal passion; the warmth which she would have lavished on Bosinney, and of which—given her Forsyte tenacity—he must surely have tired, she now expended in championship of the underdogs and budding 'geniuses' of the artistic world. She lived, in fact, to turn ducks into the swans she believed they were. The very fervour of her protection warped her judgments. But she was loyal and liberal; her small eager hand was ever against the oppressions of academic and commercial opinion, and though her income was considerable, her bank balance was often a minus quantity.

She had come to Paddington Station heated in her soul by a visit to Eric Cobbley. A miserable Gallery had refused to let that straight-haired genius have his one-man show after all. Its impudent manager, after visiting his studio, had expressed the opinion that it would only be a 'one-horse show from the selling point of view.' This crowning example of commercial cowardice towards her favourite lame duck—and he so hard up, with a wife and two children, that he had caused her account to be overdrawn—was still making the blood glow in her small, resolute face, and her red-gold hair to shine more than ever. She gave her father a hug, and got into a cab with him, having as many fish to fry with him as he with her. It became at once a question which would fry them first.

Jolyon had reached the words: "My dear, I want you to come with me," when, glancing at her face, he perceived by her blue eyes moving from side to side—like the tail of a preoccupied cat—that she was not attending. "Dad, is it true that I absolutely can't get at any of my money?"

"Only the income, fortunately, my love."

"How perfectly beastly! Can't it be done somehow? There must be a way. I know I could buy a small Gallery for ten thousand pounds."

"A small Gallery," murmured Jolyon, "seems a modest desire. But your grandfather foresaw it."

"I think," cried June vigorously, "that all this care about money is awful, when there's so much genius in the world simply crushed out for want of a little. I shall never marry and have children; why shouldn't I be able to do some good instead of having it all tied up in case of things which will never come off?"

"Our name is Forsyte, my dear," replied Jolyon in the ironical voice to which his impetuous daughter had never quite grown accustomed; "and Forsytes, you know, are people who so settle their property that their grandchildren, in case they should die before their parents, have to make wills leaving the property that will only come to themselves when their parents die. Do you follow that? Nor do I, but it's a fact, anyway; we live by the principle that so long as there is a possibility of keeping wealth in the family it must not go out; if you die unmarried, your money goes to Jolly and Holly and their children if they marry. Isn't it pleasant to know that whatever you do you can none of you be destitute?"

"But can't I borrow the money?"

Jolyon shook his head. "You could rent a Gallery, no doubt, if you could manage it out of your income."

June uttered a contemptuous sound.

"Yes; and have no income left to help anybody with."

"My dear child," murmured Jolyon, "wouldn't it come to the same thing?"

"No," said June shrewdly, "I could buy for ten thousand; that would only be four hundred a year. But I should have to pay a thousand a year rent, and that would only leave me five hundred. If I had the Gallery, Dad, think what I could do. I could make Eric Cobbley's name in no time, and ever so many others."

"Names worth making make themselves in time."

"When they're dead."

"Did you ever know anybody living, my dear, improved by having his name made?"

"Yes, you," said June, pressing his arm.

Jolyon started. 'I?' he thought. 'Oh! Ah! Now she's going to ask me to do something. We take it out, we Forsytes, each in our different ways.'

June came closer to him in the cab.

"Darling," she said, "you buy the Gallery, and I'll pay you four hundred a year for it. Then neither of us will be any the worse off. Besides, it's a splendid investment."

Jolyon wriggled. "Don't you think," he said, "that for an artist to buy a Gallery is a bit dubious? Besides, ten thousand pounds is a lump, and I'm not a commercial character."

June looked at him with admiring appraisement.

"Of course you're not, but you're awfully businesslike. And I'm sure we could make it pay. It'll be a perfect way of scoring off those wretched dealers and people." And again she squeezed her father's arm.

Jolyon's face expressed quizzical despair.

"Where is this desirable Gallery? Splendidly situated, I suppose?"

"Just off Cork Street."

'Ah!' thought Jolyon, 'I knew it was just off somewhere. Now for what I want out of her!'

"Well, I'll think of it, but not just now. You remember Irene? I want you to come with me and see her. Soames is after her again. She might be safer if we could give her asylum somewhere."

The word asylum, which he had used by chance, was of all most calculated to rouse June's interest.

"Irene! I haven't seen her since! Of course! I'd love to help her."

It was Jolyon's turn to squeeze her arm, in warm admiration for this spirited, generous-hearted little creature of his begetting.

"Irene is proud," he said, with a sidelong glance, in sudden doubt of June's discretion; "she's difficult to help. We must tread gently. This is the place. I wired her to expect us. Let's send up our cards."

"I can't bear Soames," said June as she got out; "he sneers at everything that isn't successful."

Irene was in what was called the 'Ladies' drawing-room' of the Piedmont Hotel.

Nothing if not morally courageous, June walked straight up to her former friend, kissed her cheek, and the two settled down on a sofa never sat on since the hotel's foundation. Jolyon could see that Irene was deeply affected by this simple forgiveness.

"So Soames has been worrying you?" he said.

"I had a visit from him last night; he wants me to go back to him."

"You're not going, of course?" cried June.

Irene smiled faintly and shook her head. "But his position is horrible," she murmured.

"It's his own fault; he ought to have divorced you when he could."

Jolyon remembered how fervently in the old days June had hoped that no divorce would smirch her dead and faithless lover's name.

"Let us hear what Irene is going to do," he said.

Irene's lips quivered, but she spoke calmly.

"I'd better give him fresh excuse to get rid of me."

"How horrible!" cried June.

"What else can I do?"

"Out of the question," said Jolyon very quietly, "sans amour."

He thought she was going to cry; but, getting up quickly, she half turned her back on them, and stood regaining control of herself.

June said suddenly:

"Well, I shall go to Soames and tell him he must leave you alone. What does he want at his age?"

"A child. It's not unnatural"

"A child!" cried June scornfully. "Of course! To leave his money to. If he wants one badly enough let him take somebody and have one; then you can divorce him, and he can marry her."

Jolyon perceived suddenly that he had made a mistake to bring June—her violent partizanship was fighting Soames' battle.

"It would be best for Irene to come quietly to us at Robin Hill, and see how things shape."

"Of course," said June; "only...."

Irene looked full at Jolyon—in all his many attempts afterwards to analyze that glance he never could succeed.

"No! I should only bring trouble on you all. I will go abroad."

He knew from her voice that this was final. The irrelevant thought flashed through him: 'Well, I could see her there.' But he said:

"Don't you think you would be more helpless abroad, in case he followed?"

"I don't know. I can but try."

June sprang up and paced the room. "It's all horrible," she said. "Why should people be tortured and kept miserable and helpless year after year by this disgusting sanctimonious law?" But someone had come into the room, and June came to a standstill. Jolyon went up to Irene:

"Do you want money?"

"No."

"And would you like me to let your flat?"

"Yes, Jolyon, please."

"When shall you be going?"

"To-morrow."

"You won't go back there in the meantime, will you?" This he said with an anxiety strange to himself.

"No; I've got all I want here."

"You'll send me your address?"

She put out her hand to him. "I feel you're a rock."

"Built on sand," answered Jolyon, pressing her hand hard; "but it's a pleasure to do anything, at any time, remember that. And if you change your mind...! Come along, June; say good-bye."

June came from the window and flung her arms round Irene.

"Don't think of him," she said under her breath; "enjoy yourself, and bless you!"

With a memory of tears in Irene's eyes, and of a smile on her lips, they went away extremely silent, passing the lady who had interrupted the interview and was turning over the papers on the table.

Opposite the National Gallery June exclaimed:

"Of all undignified beasts and horrible laws!"

But Jolyon did not respond. He had something of his father's balance, and could see things impartially even when his emotions were roused. Irene was right; Soames' position was as bad or worse than her own. As for the law—it catered for a human nature of which it took a naturally low view. And, feeling that if he stayed in his daughter's company he would in one way or another commit an indiscretion, he told her he must catch his train back to Oxford; and hailing a cab, left her to Turner's water-colours, with the promise that he would think over that Gallery.

But he thought over Irene instead. Pity, they said, was akin to love! If so he was certainly in danger of loving her, for he pitied her profoundly. To think of her drifting about Europe so handicapped and lonely! 'I hope to goodness she'll keep her head!' he thought; 'she might easily grow desperate.' In fact, now that she had cut loose from her poor threads of occupation, he couldn't imagine how she would go on—so beautiful a creature, hopeless, and fair game for anyone! In his exasperation was more than a little fear and jealousy. Women did strange things when they were driven into corners. 'I wonder what Soames will do now!' he thought. 'A rotten, idiotic state of things! And I suppose they would say it was her own fault.' Very preoccupied and sore at heart, he got into his train, mislaid his ticket, and on the platform at Oxford took his hat off to a lady whose face he seemed to remember without being able to put a name to her, not even when he saw her having tea at the Rainbow.

CHAPTER IV—WHERE FORSYTES FEAR TO TREAD

Quivering from the defeat of his hopes, with the green morocco case still flat against his heart, Soames revolved thoughts bitter as death. A spider's web! Walking fast, and noting nothing in the moonlight, he brooded over the scene he had been through, over the memory of her figure rigid in his grasp. And the more he brooded, the more certain he became that she had a lover—her words, 'I would sooner die!' were ridiculous if she had not. Even if she had never loved him, she had made no fuss until Bosinney came on the scene. No; she was in love again, or she would not have made that melodramatic answer to his proposal, which in all the circumstances was reasonable! Very well! That simplified matters.

'I'll take steps to know where I am,' he thought; 'I'll go to Polteed's the first thing tomorrow morning.'

But even in forming that resolution he knew he would have trouble with himself. He had employed Polteed's agency several times in the routine of his profession, even quite lately over Dartie's case, but he had never thought it possible to employ them to watch his own wife.

It was too insulting to himself!

He slept over that project and his wounded pride—or rather, kept vigil. Only while shaving did he suddenly remember that she called herself by her maiden name of Heron. Polteed would not know, at first at all events, whose wife she was, would not look at him obsequiously and leer behind his back. She would just be the wife of one of his clients. And that would be true—for was he not his own solicitor?

He was literally afraid not to put his design into execution at the first possible moment, lest, after all, he might fail himself. And making Warmson bring him an early cup of coffee; he stole out of the house before the hour of breakfast. He walked rapidly to one of those small West End streets where Polteed's and other firms ministered to the virtues of the wealthier classes. Hitherto he had always had Polteed to see him in the Poultry; but he well knew their address, and reached it at the opening hour. In the outer office, a room furnished so cosily that it might have been a money-lender's, he was attended by a lady who might have been a schoolmistress.

"I wish to see Mr. Claud Polteed. He knows me—never mind my name."

To keep everybody from knowing that he, Soames Forsyte, was reduced to having his wife spied on, was the overpowering consideration.

Mr. Claud Polteed—so different from Mr. Lewis Polteed—was one of those men with dark hair, slightly curved noses, and quick brown eyes, who might be taken for Jews but are really Phoenicians; he received Soames in a room hushed by thickness of carpet and curtains. It was, in fact, confidentially furnished, without trace of document anywhere to be seen.

Greeting Soames deferentially, he turned the key in the only door with a certain ostentation.

"If a client sends for me," he was in the habit of saying, "he takes what precaution he likes. If he comes here, we convince him that we have no leakages. I may safely say we lead in security, if in nothing else....Now, sir, what can I do for you?"

Soames' gorge had risen so that he could hardly speak. It was absolutely necessary to hide from this man that he had any but professional interest in the matter; and, mechanically, his face assumed its sideway smile.

"I've come to you early like this because there's not an hour to lose"—if he lost an hour he might fail himself yet! "Have you a really trustworthy woman free?"

Mr. Polteed unlocked a drawer, produced a memorandum, ran his eyes over it, and locked the drawer up again.

"Yes," he said; "the very woman."

Soames had seated himself and crossed his legs—nothing but a faint flush, which might have been his normal complexion, betrayed him.

"Send her off at once, then, to watch a Mrs. Irene Heron of Flat C, Truro Mansions, Chelsea, till further notice."

"Precisely," said Mr. Polteed; "divorce, I presume?" and he blew into a speaking-tube. "Mrs. Blanch in? I shall want to speak to her in ten minutes."

"Deal with any reports yourself," resumed Soames, "and send them to me personally, marked confidential, sealed and registered. My client exacts the utmost secrecy."

Mr. Polteed smiled, as though saying, 'You are teaching your grandmother, my dear sir;' and his eyes slid over Soames' face for one unprofessional instant.

"Make his mind perfectly easy," he said. "Do you smoke?"

"No," said Soames. "Understand me: Nothing may come of this. If a name gets out, or the watching is suspected, it may have very serious consequences."

Mr. Polteed nodded. "I can put it into the cipher category. Under that system a name is never mentioned; we work by numbers."

He unlocked another drawer and took out two slips of paper, wrote on them, and handed one to Soames.

"Keep that, sir; it's your key. I retain this duplicate. The case we'll call 7x. The party watched will be 17; the watcher 19; the Mansions 25; yourself—I should say, your firm— 31; my firm 32, myself 2. In case you should have to mention your client in writing I have called him 43; any person we suspect will be 47; a second person 51. Any special hint or instruction while we're about it?"

"No," said Soames; "that is—every consideration compatible."

Again Mr. Polteed nodded. "Expense?"

Soames shrugged. "In reason," he answered curtly, and got up. "Keep it entirely in your own hands."

"Entirely," said Mr. Polteed, appearing suddenly between him and the door. "I shall be seeing you in that other case before long. Good morning, sir." His eyes slid unprofessionally over Soames once more, and he unlocked the door.

"Good morning," said Soames, looking neither to right nor left.

Out in the street he swore deeply, quietly, to himself. A spider's web, and to cut it he must use this spidery, secret, unclean method, so utterly repugnant to one who regarded his private life as his most sacred piece of property. But the die was cast, he could not go back. And he went on into the Poultry, and locked away the green morocco case and the key to that cipher destined to make crystal-clear his domestic bankruptcy.

Odd that one whose life was spent in bringing to the public eye all the private coils of property, the domestic disagreements of others, should dread so utterly the public eye turned on his own; and yet not odd, for who should know so well as he the whole unfeeling process of legal regulation.

He worked hard all day. Winifred was due at four o'clock; he was to take her down to a conference in the Temple with Dreamer Q.C., and waiting for her he re-read the letter he had caused her to write the day of Dartie's departure, requiring him to return.

"DEAR MONTAGUE,

"I have received your letter with the news that you have left me for ever and are on your way to Buenos Aires. It has naturally been a great shock. I am taking this earliest opportunity of writing to tell you that I am prepared to let bygones be bygones if you will return to me at once. I beg you to do so. I am very much upset, and will not say any more now. I am sending this letter registered to the address you left at your Club. Please cable to me.

"Your still affectionate wife,

"WINIFRED DARTIE."

Ugh! What bitter humbug! He remembered leaning over Winifred while she copied what he had pencilled, and how she had said, laying down her pen, "Suppose he comes, Soames!" in such a strange tone of voice, as if she did not know her own mind. "He won't come," he had answered, "till he's spent his money. That's why we must act at once." Annexed to the copy of that letter was the original of Dartie's drunken scrawl from the Iseeum Club. Soames could have wished it had not been so manifestly penned in liquor. Just the sort of thing the Court would pitch on. He seemed to hear the Judge's voice say: "You took this seriously! Seriously enough to write him as you did? Do you think he meant it?" Never mind! The fact was clear that Dartie had sailed and had not returned. Annexed also was his cabled answer: "Impossible return. Dartie." Soames shook his head. If the whole thing were not disposed of within the next few months the fellow would turn up again like a bad penny. It saved a thousand a year at least to get rid of him, besides all the worry to Winifred and his father. 'I must stiffen Dreamer's back,' he thought; 'we must push it on.'

Winifred, who had adopted a kind of half-mourning which became her fair hair and tall figure very well, arrived in James' barouche drawn by James' pair. Soames had not seen it in the City since his father retired from business five years ago, and its incongruity gave him a shock. 'Times are changing,' he thought; 'one doesn't know what'll go next!' Top hats even were scarcer. He enquired after Val. Val, said Winifred, wrote that he was going to play polo next term. She thought he was in a very good set. She added with fashionably disguised anxiety: "Will there be much publicity about my affair, Soames? Must it be in the papers? It's so bad for him, and the girls."

With his own calamity all raw within him, Soames answered:

"The papers are a pushing lot; it's very difficult to keep things out. They pretend to be guarding the public's morals, and they corrupt them with their beastly reports. But we haven't got to that yet. We're only seeing Dreamer to-day on the restitution question. Of course he understands that it's to lead to a divorce; but you must seem genuinely anxious to get Dartie back—you might practice that attitude to-day."

Winifred sighed.

"Oh! What a clown Monty's been!" she said.

Soames gave her a sharp look. It was clear to him that she could not take her Dartie seriously, and would go back on the whole thing if given half a chance. His own instinct had been firm in this matter from the first. To save a little scandal now would only bring on his sister and her children real disgrace and perhaps ruin later on if Dartie were allowed to hang on to them, going down-hill and spending the money James would leave his daughter. Though it was all tied up, that fellow would milk the settlements somehow, and make his family pay through the nose to keep him out of bankruptcy or even perhaps gaol! They left the shining carriage, with the shining horses and the shining-hatted servants on the Embankment, and walked up to Dreamer Q.C.'s Chambers in Crown Office Row.

"Mr. Bellby is here, sir," said the clerk; "Mr. Dreamer will be ten minutes."

Mr. Bellby, the junior—not as junior as he might have been, for Soames only employed barristers of established reputation; it was, indeed, something of a mystery to him how barristers ever managed to establish that which made him employ them—Mr. Bellby was seated, taking a final glance through his papers. He had come from Court, and was in wig and gown, which suited a nose jutting out like the handle of a tiny pump, his small shrewd blue eyes, and rather protruding lower lip—no better man to supplement and stiffen Dreamer.

The introduction to Winifred accomplished, they leaped the weather and spoke of the war. Soames interrupted suddenly:

"If he doesn't comply we can't bring proceedings for six months. I want to get on with the matter, Bellby."

Mr. Bellby, who had the ghost of an Irish brogue, smiled at Winifred and murmured: "The Law's delays, Mrs. Dartie."

"Six months!" repeated Soames; "it'll drive it up to June! We shan't get the suit on till after the long vacation. We must put the screw on, Bellby"—he would have all his work cut out to keep Winifred up to the scratch.

"Mr. Dreamer will see you now, sir."

They filed in, Mr. Bellby going first, and Soames escorting Winifred after an interval of one minute by his watch.

Dreamer Q.C., in a gown but divested of wig, was standing before the fire, as if this conference were in the nature of a treat; he had the leathery, rather oily complexion which goes with great learning, a considerable nose with glasses perched on it, and little greyish whiskers; he luxuriated in the perpetual cocking of one eye, and the concealment of his lower with his upper lip, which gave a smothered turn to his speech. He had a way, too, of coming suddenly round the corner on the person he was talking to; this, with a disconcerting tone of voice, and a habit of growling before he began to speak—had secured a reputation second in Probate and Divorce to very few. Having listened, eye cocked, to Mr. Bellby's breezy recapitulation of the facts, he growled, and said:

"I know all that;" and coming round the corner at Winifred, smothered the words:

"We want to get him back, don't we, Mrs. Dartie?"

Soames interposed sharply:

"My sister's position, of course, is intolerable."

Dreamer growled. "Exactly. Now, can we rely on the cabled refusal, or must we wait till after Christmas to give him a chance to have written—that's the point, isn't it?"

"The sooner...." Soames began.

"What do you say, Bellby?" said Dreamer, coming round his corner.

Mr. Bellby seemed to sniff the air like a hound.

"We won't be on till the middle of December. We've no need to give um more rope than that."

"No," said Soames, "why should my sister be incommoded by his choosing to go..."

"To Jericho!" said Dreamer, again coming round his corner; "quite so. People oughtn't to go to Jericho, ought they, Mrs. Dartie?" And he raised his gown into a sort of fantail. "I agree. We can go forward. Is there anything more?"

"Nothing at present," said Soames meaningly; "I wanted you to see my sister."

Dreamer growled softly: "Delighted. Good evening!" And let fall the protection of his gown.

They filed out. Winifred went down the stairs. Soames lingered. In spite of himself he was impressed by Dreamer.

"The evidence is all right, I think," he said to Bellby. "Between ourselves, if we don't get the thing through quick, we never may. D'you think he understands that?"

"I'll make um," said Bellby. "Good man though—good man."

Soames nodded and hastened after his sister. He found her in a draught, biting her lips behind her veil, and at once said:

"The evidence of the stewardess will be very complete."

Winifred's face hardened; she drew herself up, and they walked to the carriage. And, all through that silent drive back to Green Street, the souls of both of them revolved a single thought: 'Why, oh! why should I have to expose my misfortune to the public like this? Why have to employ spies to peer into my private troubles? They were not of my making.'

CHAPTER V—JOLLY SITS IN JUDGMENT

The possessive instinct, which, so determinedly balked, was animating two members of the Forsyte family towards riddance of what they could no longer possess, was hardening daily in the British body politic. Nicholas, originally so doubtful concerning a war which must affect property, had been heard to say that these Boers were a pig-headed lot; they were causing a lot of expense, and the sooner they had their lesson the better. He would send out Wolseley! Seeing always a little further than other people—whence the most considerable fortune of all the Forsytes—he had perceived already that Buller was not the man—'a bull of a chap, who just went butting, and if they didn't look out Ladysmith would fall.' This was early in December, so that when Black Week came, he was enabled to say to everybody: 'I told you so.' During that week of gloom such as no Forsyte could remember, very young Nicholas attended so many drills in his corps, 'The Devil's Own,' that young Nicholas consulted the family physician about his son's health and was alarmed to find that he was perfectly sound. The boy had only just eaten his dinners and been called to the bar, at some expense, and it was in a way a nightmare to his father and mother that he should be playing with military efficiency at a time when military efficiency in the civilian population might conceivably be wanted. His grandfather, of course, pooh-poohed the notion, too thoroughly educated in the feeling that no British war could be other than little and professional, and profoundly distrustful of Imperial commitments, by which, moreover, he stood to lose, for he owned De Beers, now going down fast, more than a sufficient sacrifice on the part of his grandson.

At Oxford, however, rather different sentiments prevailed. The inherent effervescence of conglomerate youth had, during the two months of the term before Black Week, been gradually crystallising out into vivid oppositions. Normal adolescence, ever in England of a conservative tendency though not taking things too seriously, was vehement for a fight to a finish and a good licking for the Boers. Of this larger faction Val Dartie was naturally a member. Radical youth, on the other hand, a small but perhaps more vocal body, was for stopping the war and giving the Boers autonomy. Until Black Week, however, the groups were amorphous, without sharp edges, and argument remained but academic. Jolly was one of those who knew not where he stood. A streak of his grandfather old Jolyon's love of justice prevented, him from seeing one side only. Moreover, in his set of 'the best' there was a 'jumping-Jesus' of extremely advanced opinions and some personal magnetism. Jolly wavered. His father, too, seemed doubtful in his views. And though, as was proper at the age of twenty, he kept a sharp eye on his father, watchful for defects which might still be remedied, still that father had an 'air' which gave a sort of glamour to his creed of ironic tolerance. Artists of course; were notoriously Hamlet-like, and to this extent one must discount for one's father, even if one loved him. But Jolyon's original view, that to 'put your nose in where you aren't wanted' (as the Uitlanders had done) 'and then work the oracle till you get on top is not being quite the clean potato,' had, whether founded in fact or no, a certain attraction for his son, who thought a deal about gentility. On the other hand Jolly could not abide such as his set called 'cranks,' and Val's set called 'smugs,' so that he was still balancing when the clock of Black Week struck. One—two—three, came those ominous repulses at Stormberg, Magersfontein, Colenso. The sturdy English soul reacting after the first cried, 'Ah! but Methuen!' after the second: 'Ah! but Buller!' then, in inspissated gloom, hardened. And Jolly said to himself: 'No, damn it! We've got to lick the beggars now; I don't care whether we're right or wrong.' And, if he had known it, his father was thinking the same thought.

That next Sunday, last of the term, Jolly was bidden to wine with 'one of the best.' After the second toast, 'Buller and damnation to the Boers,' drunk—no heel taps—in the college Burgundy, he noticed that Val Dartie, also a guest, was looking at him with a grin and saying something to his neighbour. He was sure it was disparaging. The last boy in the world to make himself conspicuous or cause public disturbance, Jolly grew rather red and shut his lips. The queer hostility he had always felt towards his second-cousin was strongly and suddenly reinforced. 'All right!' he thought, 'you wait, my friend!' More wine than was good for him, as the custom was, helped him to remember, when they all trooped forth to a secluded spot, to touch Val on the arm.

"What did you say about me in there?"

"Mayn't I say what I like?"

"No."

"Well, I said you were a pro-Boer—and so you are!"

"You're a liar!"

"D'you want a row?"

"Of course, but not here; in the garden."

"All right. Come on."

They went, eyeing each other askance, unsteady, and unflinching; they climbed the garden railings. The spikes on the top slightly ripped Val's sleeve, and occupied his mind. Jolly's mind was occupied by the thought that they were going to fight in the precincts of a college foreign to them both. It was not the thing, but never mind—the young beast!

They passed over the grass into very nearly darkness, and took off their coats.

"You're not screwed, are you?" said Jolly suddenly. "I can't fight you if you're screwed."

"No more than you."

"All right then."

Without shaking hands, they put themselves at once into postures of defence. They had drunk too much for science, and so were especially careful to assume correct attitudes, until

Jolly smote Val almost accidentally on the nose. After that it was all a dark and ugly scrimmage in the deep shadow of the old trees, with no one to call 'time,' till, battered and blown, they unclinched and staggered back from each other, as a voice said:

"Your names, young gentlemen?"

At this bland query spoken from under the lamp at the garden gate, like some demand of a god, their nerves gave way, and snatching up their coats, they ran at the railings, shinned up them, and made for the secluded spot whence they had issued to the fight. Here, in dim light, they mopped their faces, and without a word walked, ten paces apart, to the college gate. They went out silently, Val going towards the Broad along the Brewery, Jolly down the lane towards the High. His head, still fumed, was busy with regret that he had not displayed more science, passing in review the counters and knockout blows which he had not delivered. His mind strayed on to an imagined combat, infinitely unlike that which he had just been through, infinitely gallant, with sash and sword, with thrust and parry, as if he were in the pages of his beloved Dumas. He fancied himself La Mole, and Aramis, Bussy, Chicot, and D'Artagnan rolled into one, but he quite failed to envisage Val as Coconnas, Brissac, or Rochefort. The fellow was just a confounded cousin who didn't come up to Cocker. Never mind! He had given him one or two. 'Pro-Boer!' The word still rankled, and thoughts of enlisting jostled his aching head; of riding over the veldt, firing gallantly, while the Boers rolled over like rabbits. And, turning up his smarting eyes, he saw the stars shining between the housetops of the High, and himself lying out on the Karoo (whatever that was) rolled in a blanket, with his rifle ready and his gaze fixed on a glittering heaven.

He had a fearful 'head' next morning, which he doctored, as became one of 'the best,' by soaking it in cold water, brewing strong coffee which he could not drink, and only sipping a little Hock at lunch. The legend that 'some fool' had run into him round a corner accounted for a bruise on his cheek. He would on no account have mentioned the fight, for, on second thoughts, it fell far short of his standards.

The next day he went 'down,' and travelled through to Robin Hill. Nobody was there but June and Holly, for his father had gone to Paris. He spent a restless and unsettled Vacation, quite out of touch with either of his sisters. June, indeed, was occupied with lame ducks, whom, as a rule, Jolly could not stand, especially that Eric Cobbley and his family, 'hopeless outsiders,' who were always littering up the house in the Vacation. And between Holly and himself there was a strange division, as if she were beginning to have opinions of her own, which was so—unnecessary. He punched viciously at a ball, rode furiously but alone in Richmond Park, making a point of jumping the stiff, high hurdles put up to close certain worn avenues of grass—keeping his nerve in, he called it. Jolly was more afraid of being afraid than most boys are. He bought a rifle, too, and put a range up in the home field, shooting across the pond into the kitchen-garden wall, to the peril of gardeners, with the thought that some day, perhaps, he would enlist and save South Africa for his country. In fact, now that they were appealing for Yeomanry recruits the boy was thoroughly upset. Ought he to go? None of 'the best,' so far as he knew—and he was in correspondence with several—were thinking of joining. If they had been making a move he would have gone at once—very competitive, and with a strong sense of form, he could not bear to be left behind in anything—but to do it off his own bat might look like 'swagger'; because of course it wasn't really necessary. Besides, he did not want to go, for the other side of this young Forsyte recoiled from leaping before he looked. It was altogether mixed pickles within him, hot and sickly pickles, and he became quite unlike his serene and rather lordly self.

And then one day he saw that which moved him to uneasy wrath—two riders, in a glade of the Park close to the Ham Gate, of whom she on the left-hand was most assuredly Holly on her silver roan, and he on the right-hand as assuredly that 'squirt' Val Dartie. His first impulse was to urge on his own horse and demand the meaning of this portent, tell the fellow to 'bunk,' and take Holly home. His second—to feel that he would look a fool if they refused. He reined his horse in behind a tree, then perceived that it was equally impossible to spy on them. Nothing for it but to go home and await her coming! Sneaking out with that young bounder! He could not consult with June, because she had gone up that morning in the train of Eric Cobbley and his lot. And his father was still in 'that rotten Paris.' He felt that this was emphatically one of those moments for which he had trained himself, assiduously, at school, where he and a boy called Brent had frequently set fire to newspapers and placed them in the centre of their studies to accustom them to coolness in moments of danger. He did not feel at all cool waiting in the stable-yard, idly stroking the dog Balthasar, who queasy as an old fat monk, and sad in the absence of his master, turned up his face, panting with gratitude for this attention. It was half an hour before Holly came, flushed and ever so much prettier than she had any right to look. He saw her look at him quickly—guiltily of course—then followed her in, and, taking her arm, conducted her into what had been their grandfather's study. The room, not much used now, was still vaguely haunted for them both by a presence with which they associated tenderness, large drooping white moustaches, the scent of cigar smoke, and laughter. Here Jolly, in the prime of his youth, before he went to school at all, had been wont to wrestle with his grandfather, who even at eighty had an irresistible habit of crooking his leg. Here Holly, perched on the arm of the great leather chair, had stroked hair curving silvery over an ear into which she would whisper secrets. Through that window they had all three sallied times without number to cricket on the lawn, and a mysterious game called 'Wopsy-doozle,' not to be understood by outsiders, which made old Jolyon very hot. Here once on a warm night Holly had appeared in her 'nighty,' having had a bad dream, to have the clutch of it released. And here Jolly, having begun the day badly by introducing fizzy magnesia into Mademoiselle Beauce's new-laid egg, and gone on to worse, had been sent down (in the absence of his father) to the ensuing dialogue:

"Now, my boy, you mustn't go on like this."

"Well, she boxed my ears, Gran, so I only boxed hers, and then she boxed mine again."

"Strike a lady? That'll never do! Have you begged her pardon?"

"Not yet."

"Then you must go and do it at once. Come along."

"But she began it, Gran; and she had two to my one."

"My dear, it was an outrageous thing to do."

"Well, she lost her temper; and I didn't lose mine."

"Come along."

"You come too, then, Gran."

"Well—this time only."

And they had gone hand in hand.

Here—where the Waverley novels and Byron's works and Gibbon's Roman Empire and Humboldt's Cosmos, and the bronzes on the mantelpiece, and that masterpiece of the oily school, 'Dutch Fishing-Boats at Sunset,' were fixed as fate, and for all sign of change old Jolyon might have been sitting there still, with legs crossed, in the arm chair, and domed forehead and deep eyes grave above The Times—here they came, those two grandchildren. And Jolly said:

"I saw you and that fellow in the Park."

The sight of blood rushing into her cheeks gave him some satisfaction; she ought to be ashamed!

"Well?" she said.

Jolly was surprised; he had expected more, or less.

"Do you know," he said weightily, "that he called me a pro-Boer last term? And I had to fight him."

"Who won?"

Jolly wished to answer: 'I should have,' but it seemed beneath him.

"Look here!" he said, "what's the meaning of it? Without telling anybody!"

"Why should I? Dad isn't here; why shouldn't I ride with him?"

"You've got me to ride with. I think he's an awful young rotter."

Holly went pale with anger.

"He isn't. It's your own fault for not liking him."

And slipping past her brother she went out, leaving him staring at the bronze Venus sitting on a tortoise, which had been shielded from him so far by his sister's dark head under her soft felt riding hat. He felt queerly disturbed, shaken to his young foundations. A lifelong domination lay shattered round his feet. He went up to the Venus and mechanically inspected the tortoise.

Why didn't he like Val Dartie? He could not tell. Ignorant of family history, barely aware of that vague feud which had started thirteen years before with Bosinney's defection from June in favour of Soames' wife, knowing really almost nothing about Val he was at sea. He just did dislike him. The question, however, was: What should he do? Val Dartie, it was true, was a second-cousin, but it was not the thing for Holly to go about with him. And yet to 'tell' of what he had chanced on was against his creed. In this dilemma he went and sat in the old leather chair and crossed his legs. It grew dark while he sat there staring out through the long window at the old oak-tree, ample yet bare of leaves, becoming slowly just a shape of deeper dark printed on the dusk.

'Grandfather!' he thought without sequence, and took out his watch. He could not see the hands, but he set the repeater going. 'Five o'clock!' His grandfather's first gold hunter watch, butter-smooth with age—all the milling worn from it, and dented with the mark of many a fall. The chime was like a little voice from out of that golden age, when they first came from St. John's Wood, London, to this house—came driving with grandfather in his carriage, and almost instantly took to the trees. Trees to climb, and grandfather watering the geranium-beds below! What was to be done? Tell Dad he must come home? Confide in June?—only she was so—so sudden! Do nothing and trust to luck? After all, the Vac. would soon be over. Go up and see Val and warn him off? But how get his address? Holly wouldn't give it him! A maze of paths, a cloud of possibilities! He lit a cigarette. When he had smoked it halfway through his brow relaxed, almost as if some thin old hand had been passed gently over it; and in his ear something seemed to whisper: 'Do nothing; be nice to Holly, be nice to her, my dear!' And Jolly heaved a sigh of contentment, blowing smoke through his nostrils....

But up in her room, divested of her habit, Holly was still frowning. 'He is not—he is not!' were the words which kept forming on her lips.

CHAPTER VI—JOLYON IN TWO MINDS

A little private hotel over a well-known restaurant near the Gare St. Lazare was Jolyon's haunt in Paris. He hated his fellow Forsytes abroad—vapid as fish out of water in their well-trodden runs, the Opera, Rue de Rivoli, and Moulin Rouge. Their air of having come because they wanted to be somewhere else as soon as possible annoyed him. But no other Forsyte came near this haunt, where he had a wood fire in his bedroom and the coffee was excellent. Paris was always to him more attractive in winter. The acrid savour from woodsmoke and chestnut-roasting braziers, the sharpness of the wintry sunshine on bright rays, the open cafes defying keen-aired winter, the self-contained brisk boulevard crowds, all informed him that in winter Paris possessed a soul which, like a migrant bird, in high summer flew away.

He spoke French well, had some friends, knew little places where pleasant dishes could be met with, queer types observed. He felt philosophic in Paris, the edge of irony sharpened; life took on a subtle, purposeless meaning, became a bunch of flavours tasted, a darkness shot with shifting gleams of light.

When in the first week of December he decided to go to Paris, he was far from admitting that Irene's presence was influencing him. He had not been there two days before he owned that the wish to see her had been more than half the reason. In England one did not admit what was natural. He had thought it might be well to speak to her about the letting of her flat and other matters, but in Paris he at once knew better. There was a glamour over the city. On the third day he wrote to her, and received an answer which procured him a pleasurable shiver of the nerves:

"MY DEAR JOLYON,

"It will be a happiness for me to see you.

"IRENE."

He took his way to her hotel on a bright day with a feeling such as he had often had going to visit an adored picture. No woman, so far as he remembered, had ever inspired in him this special sensuous and yet impersonal sensation. He was going to sit and feast his eyes, and come away knowing her no better, but ready to go and feast his eyes again to-morrow. Such was his feeling, when in the tarnished and ornate little lounge of a quiet hotel near the river she came to him preceded by a small page-boy who uttered the word, "Madame," and vanished. Her face, her smile, the poise of her figure, were just as he had pictured, and the expression of her face said plainly: 'A friend!'

"Well," he said, "what news, poor exile?"

"None."

"Nothing from Soames?"

"Nothing."

"I have let the flat for you, and like a good steward I bring you some money. How do you like Paris?"

While he put her through this catechism, it seemed to him that he had never seen lips so fine and sensitive, the lower lip curving just a little upwards, the upper touched at one corner by the least conceivable dimple. It was like discovering a woman in what had hitherto been a sort of soft and breathed-on statue, almost impersonally admired. She owned that to be alone in Paris was a little difficult; and yet, Paris was so full of its own life that it was often, she confessed, as innocuous as a desert. Besides, the English were not liked just now!

"That will hardly be your case," said Jolyon; "you should appeal to the French."

"It has its disadvantages."

Jolyon nodded.

"Well, you must let me take you about while I'm here. We'll start to-morrow. Come and dine at my pet restaurant; and we'll go to the Opera-Comique."

It was the beginning of daily meetings.

Jolyon soon found that for those who desired a static condition of the affections, Paris was at once the first and last place in which to be friendly with a pretty woman. Revelation was alighting like a bird in his heart, singing: 'Elle est ton reve! Elle est ton reve! Sometimes this seemed natural, sometimes ludicrous—a bad case of elderly rapture. Having once been ostracised by Society, he had never since had any real regard for conventional morality; but the idea of a love which she could never return—and how could she at his age?—hardly mounted beyond his subconscious mind. He was full, too, of resentment, at the waste and loneliness of her life. Aware of being some comfort to her, and of the pleasure she clearly took in their many little outings, he was amiably desirous of doing and saying nothing to destroy that pleasure. It was like watching a starved plant draw up water, to see her drink in his companionship. So far as they could tell, no one knew her address except himself; she was unknown in Paris, and he but little known, so that discretion seemed unnecessary in those walks, talks, visits to concerts, picture-galleries, theatres, little dinners, expeditions to Versailles, St. Cloud, even Fontainebleau. And time fled—one of those full months without past to it or future. What in his youth would certainly have been headlong passion, was now perhaps as deep a feeling, but far gentler, tempered to protective companionship by admiration, hopelessness, and a sense of chivalry—arrested in his veins at least so long as she was there, smiling and happy in their friendship, and always to him more beautiful and spiritually responsive: for her philosophy of life seemed to march in admirable step with his own, conditioned by emotion more than by reason, ironically mistrustful, susceptible to beauty, almost passionately humane and tolerant, yet subject to instinctive rigidities of which as a mere man he was less capable. And during all this companionable month he never quite lost that feeling with which he had set out on the first day as if to visit an adored work of art, a well-nigh impersonal desire. The future—inexorable pendant to the present he took care not to face, for fear of breaking up his untroubled manner; but he made plans to renew this time in places still more delightful, where the sun was hot and there were strange things to see and paint. The end came swiftly on the 20th of January with a telegram:

"Have enlisted in Imperial Yeomanry. JOLLY."

Jolyon received it just as he was setting out to meet her at the Louvre. It brought him up with a round turn. While he was lotus-eating here, his boy, whose philosopher and guide he ought to be, had taken this great step towards danger, hardship, perhaps even death. He felt disturbed to the soul, realising suddenly how Irene had twined herself round the roots of his being. Thus threatened with severance, the tie between them—for it had become a kind of tie—no longer had impersonal quality. The tranquil enjoyment of things in common, Jolyon perceived, was gone for ever. He saw his feeling as it was, in the nature of an infatuation. Ridiculous, perhaps, but so real that sooner or later it must disclose itself. And now, as it seemed to him, he could not, must not, make any such disclosure. The news of Jolly stood inexorably in the way. He was proud of this enlistment; proud of his boy for going off to fight for the country; for on Jolyon's pro-Boerism, too, Black Week had left its mark. And so the end was reached before the beginning! Well, luckily he had never made a sign!

When he came into the Gallery she was standing before the 'Virgin of the Rocks,' graceful, absorbed, smiling and unconscious. 'Have I to give up seeing that?' he thought. 'It's unnatural, so long as she's willing that I should see her.' He stood, unnoticed, watching her, storing up the image of her figure, envying the picture on which she was bending that long scrutiny. Twice she turned her head towards the entrance, and he thought: "That's for me!' At last he went forward.

"Look!" he said.

She read the telegram, and he heard her sigh.

That sigh, too, was for him! His position was really cruel! To be loyal to his son he must just shake her hand and go. To be loyal to the feeling in his heart he must at least tell her what that feeling was. Could she, would she understand the silence in which he was gazing at that picture?

"I'm afraid I must go home at once," he said at last. "I shall miss all this awfully."

"So shall I; but, of course, you must go."

"Well!" said Jolyon holding out his hand.

Meeting her eyes, a flood of feeling nearly mastered him.

"Such is life!" he said. "Take care of yourself, my dear!"

He had a stumbling sensation in his legs and feet, as if his brain refused to steer him away from her. From the doorway, he saw her lift her hand and touch its fingers with her lips. He raised his hat solemnly, and did not look back again.

CHAPTER VII—DARTIE VERSUS DARTIE

The suit—Dartie versus Dartie—for restitution of those conjugal rights concerning which Winifred was at heart so deeply undecided, followed the laws of subtraction towards day of judgment. This was not reached before the Courts rose for Christmas, but the case was third on the list when they sat again. Winifred spent the Christmas holidays a thought more fashionably than usual, with the matter locked up in her low-cut bosom. James was particularly liberal to her that Christmas, expressing thereby his sympathy, and relief, at the approaching dissolution of her marriage with that 'precious rascal,' which his old heart felt but his old lips could not utter.

The disappearance of Dartie made the fall in Consols a comparatively small matter; and as to the scandal—the real animus he felt against that fellow, and the increasing lead which property was attaining over reputation in a true Forsyte about to leave this world, served to drug a mind from which all allusions to the matter (except his own) were studiously kept. What worried him as a lawyer and a parent was the fear that Dartie might suddenly turn up and obey the Order of the Court when made. That would be a pretty how-de-do! The fear preyed on him in fact so much that, in presenting Winifred with a large Christmas cheque, he said: "It's chiefly for that chap out there; to keep him from coming back." It was, of course, to pitch away good money, but all in the nature of insurance against that bankruptcy which would no longer hang over him if only the divorce went through; and he questioned Winifred rigorously until she could assure him that the money had been sent. Poor woman!—it cost her many a pang to send what must find its way into the vanity-bag of 'that creature!' Soames, hearing of it, shook his head. They were not dealing with a Forsyte, reasonably tenacious of his purpose. It was very risky without knowing how the land lay out there. Still, it would look well with the Court; and he would see that Dreamer brought it out. "I wonder," he said suddenly, "where that ballet goes after the Argentine"; never omitting a chance of reminder; for he knew that Winifred still had a weakness, if not for Dartie, at least for not laundering him in public. Though not good at showing admiration, he admitted that she was behaving extremely well, with all her children at home gaping like young birds for news of their father—Imogen just on the point of coming out, and Val very restive about the whole thing. He felt that Val was the real heart of the matter to Winifred, who certainly loved him beyond her other children. The boy could spoke the wheel of this divorce yet if he set his mind to it. And Soames was very careful to keep the proximity of the preliminary proceedings from his nephew's ears. He did more. He asked him to dine at the Remove, and over Val's cigar introduced the subject which he knew to be nearest to his heart.

"I hear," he said, "that you want to play polo up at Oxford."

Val became less recumbent in his chair.

"Rather!" he said.

"Well," continued Soames, "that's a very expensive business. Your grandfather isn't likely to consent to it unless he can make sure that he's not got any other drain on him." And he paused to see whether the boy understood his meaning.

Val's thick dark lashes concealed his eyes, but a slight grimace appeared on his wide mouth, and he muttered:

"I suppose you mean my Dad!"

"Yes," said Soames; "I'm afraid it depends on whether he continues to be a drag or not;" and said no more, letting the boy dream it over.

But Val was also dreaming in those days of a silver-roan palfrey and a girl riding it. Though Crum was in town and an introduction to Cynthia Dark to be had for the asking, Val did not ask; indeed, he shunned Crum and lived a life strange even to himself, except in so far as accounts with tailor and livery stable were concerned. To his mother, his sisters, his young brother, he seemed to spend this Vacation in 'seeing fellows,' and his evenings sleepily at home. They could not propose anything in daylight that did not meet with the one response: "Sorry; I've got to see a fellow"; and he was put to extraordinary shifts to get in and out of the house unobserved in riding clothes; until, being made a member of the Goat's Club, he was able to transport them there, where he could change unregarded and slip off on his hack to Richmond Park. He kept his growing sentiment religiously to himself. Not for a world would he breathe to the 'fellows,' whom he was not 'seeing,' anything so ridiculous from the point of view of their creed and his. But he could not help its destroying his other appetites. It was coming between him and the legitimate pleasures of youth at last on its own in a way which must, he knew, make him a milksop in the eyes of Crum. All he cared for was to dress in his last-created riding togs, and steal away to the Robin Hill Gate, where presently the silver roan would come demurely sidling with its slim and dark-haired rider, and in the glades bare of leaves they would go off side by side, not talking very much, riding races sometimes, and sometimes holding hands. More than once of an evening, in a moment of expansion, he had been tempted to tell his mother how this shy sweet cousin had stolen in upon him and wrecked his 'life.' But bitter experience, that all persons above thirty-five were spoil-sports, prevented him. After all, he supposed he would have to go through with College, and she would have to 'come out,' before they could be married; so why complicate things, so long as he could see her? Sisters were teasing and unsympathetic beings, a brother worse, so there was no one to confide in. Ah! And this beastly divorce business! What a misfortune to have a name which other people hadn't! If only he had been called Gordon or Scott or Howard or something fairly common! But Dartie—there wasn't another in the directory! One might as well have been named Morkin for all the covert it afforded! So matters went on, till one day in the middle of January the silver-roan palfrey and its rider were missing at the tryst. Lingering in the cold, he debated whether he should ride on to the house: But Jolly might be there, and the memory of their dark encounter was still fresh within him. One could not be always fighting with her brother! So he returned dismally to town and spent an evening plunged in gloom. At breakfast next day he noticed that his mother had on an unfamiliar dress and was wearing her hat. The dress was black with a glimpse of peacock blue, the hat black and large—she looked exceptionally well. But when after breakfast she said to him, "Come in here, Val," and led the way to the drawing-room, he was at once beset by qualms. Winifred carefully shut the door and passed her handkerchief over her lips; inhaling the violette de Parme with which it had been soaked, Val thought: 'Has she found out about Holly?'

Her voice interrupted

"Are you going to be nice to me, dear boy?"

Val grinned doubtfully.

"Will you come with me this morning...."

"I've got to see...." began Val, but something in her face stopped him. "I say," he said, "you don't mean...."

"Yes, I have to go to the Court this morning." Already!—that d——d business which he had almost succeeded in forgetting, since nobody ever mentioned it. In self-commiseration he stood picking little bits of skin off his fingers. Then noticing that his mother's lips were all awry, he said impulsively: "All right, mother; I'll come. The brutes!" What brutes he did not know, but the expression exactly summed up their joint feeling, and restored a measure of equanimity.

"I suppose I'd better change into a 'shooter,'" he muttered, escaping to his room. He put on the 'shooter,' a higher collar, a pearl pin, and his neatest grey spats, to a somewhat blasphemous accompaniment. Looking at himself in the glass, he said, "Well, I'm damned if I'm going to show anything!" and went down. He found his grandfather's carriage at the door, and his mother in furs, with the appearance of one going to a Mansion House Assembly. They seated themselves side by side in the closed barouche, and all the way to the Courts of Justice Val made but one allusion to the business in hand. "There'll be nothing about those pearls, will there?"

The little tufted white tails of Winifred's muff began to shiver.

"Oh, no," she said, "it'll be quite harmless to-day. Your grandmother wanted to come too, but I wouldn't let her. I thought you could take care of me. You look so nice, Val. Just pull your coat collar up a little more at the back—that's right."

"If they bully you...." began Val.

"Oh! they won't. I shall be very cool. It's the only way."

"They won't want me to give evidence or anything?"

"No, dear; it's all arranged." And she patted his hand. The determined front she was putting on it stayed the turmoil in Val's chest, and he busied himself in drawing his gloves off and on. He had taken what he now saw was the wrong pair to go with his spats; they should have been grey, but were deerskin of a dark tan; whether to keep them on or not he could not decide. They arrived soon after ten. It was his first visit to the Law Courts, and the building struck him at once.

"By Jove!" he said as they passed into the hall, "this'd make four or five jolly good racket courts."

Soames was awaiting them at the foot of some stairs.

"Here you are!" he said, without shaking hands, as if the event had made them too familiar for such formalities. "It's Happerly Browne, Court I. We shall be on first."

A sensation such as he had known when going in to bat was playing now in the top of Val's chest, but he followed his mother and uncle doggedly, looking at no more than he could help, and thinking that the place smelled 'fuggy.' People seemed to be lurking everywhere, and he plucked Soames by the sleeve.

"I say, Uncle, you're not going to let those beastly papers in, are you?"

Soames gave him the sideway look which had reduced many to silence in its time.

"In here," he said. "You needn't take off your furs, Winifred."

Val entered behind them, nettled and with his head up. In this confounded hole everybody—and there were a good many of them—seemed sitting on everybody else's knee, though really divided from each other by pews; and Val had a feeling that they might all slip down together into the well. This, however, was but a momentary vision—of mahogany, and black gowns, and white blobs of wigs and faces and papers, all rather secret and whispery—before he was sitting next his mother in the front row, with his back to it all, glad of her violette de Parme, and taking off his gloves for the last time. His mother was looking at him; he was suddenly conscious that she had really wanted him there next to her, and that he counted for something in this business.

All right! He would show them! Squaring his shoulders, he crossed his legs and gazed inscrutably at his spats. But just then an 'old Johnny' in a gown and long wig, looking awfully like a funny raddled woman, came through a door into the high pew opposite, and he had to uncross his legs hastily, and stand up with everybody else.

'Dartie versus Dartie!'

It seemed to Val unspeakably disgusting to have one's name called out like this in public! And, suddenly conscious that someone nearly behind him had begun talking about his family, he screwed his face round to see an old be-wigged buffer, who spoke as if he were eating his own words—queer-looking old cuss, the sort of man he had seen once or twice dining at Park Lane and punishing the port; he knew now where they 'dug them up.' All the same he found the old buffer quite fascinating, and would have continued to stare if his mother had not touched his arm. Reduced to gazing before him, he fixed his eyes on the Judge's face instead. Why should that old 'sportsman' with his sarcastic mouth and his quick-moving eyes have the power to meddle with their private affairs—hadn't he affairs of his own, just as many, and probably just as nasty? And there moved in Val, like an illness, all the deep-seated individualism of his breed. The voice behind him droned along: "Differences about money matters—extravagance of the respondent" (What a word! Was that his father?)—"strained situation—frequent absences on the part of Mr. Dartie. My client, very rightly, your Ludship will agree, was anxious to check a course—but lead to ruin—remonstrated—gambling at cards and on the racecourse—" ('That's right!' thought Val, 'pile it on!') "Crisis early in October, when the respondent wrote her this letter from his Club." Val sat up and his ears burned. "I propose to read it with the emendations necessary to the epistle of a gentleman who has been—shall we say dining, me Lud?"

'Old brute!' thought Val, flushing deeper; 'you're not paid to make jokes!'

"'You will not get the chance to insult me again in my own house. I am leaving the country to-morrow. It's played out'—an expression, your Ludship, not unknown in the mouths of those who have not met with conspicuous success."

'Sniggering owls!' thought Val, and his flush deepened.

"'I am tired of being insulted by you.' My client will tell your Ludship that these so-called insults consisted in her calling him 'the limit',—a very mild expression, I venture to suggest, in all the circumstances."

Val glanced sideways at his mother's impassive face, it had a hunted look in the eyes. 'Poor mother,' he thought, and touched her arm with his own. The voice behind droned on.

"'I am going to live a new life. M. D.'"

"And next day, me Lud, the respondent left by the steamship Tuscarora for Buenos Aires. Since then we have nothing from him but a cabled refusal in answer to the letter which my client wrote the following day in great distress, begging him to return to her. With your Ludship's permission, I shall now put Mrs. Dartie in the box."

When his mother rose, Val had a tremendous impulse to rise too and say: 'Look here! I'm going to see you jolly well treat her decently.' He subdued it, however; heard her saying, 'the truth, the whole truth, and nothing but the truth,' and looked up. She made a rich figure of it, in her furs and large hat, with a slight flush on her cheek-bones, calm, matter-of-fact; and he felt proud of her thus confronting all these 'confounded lawyers.' The examination began. Knowing that this was only the preliminary to divorce, Val followed with a certain glee the questions framed so as to give the impression that she really wanted his father back. It seemed to him that they were 'foxing Old Bagwigs finely.'

And he received a most unpleasant jar when the Judge said suddenly:

"Now, why did your husband leave you—not because you called him 'the limit,' you know?"

Val saw his uncle lift his eyes to the witness box, without moving his face; heard a shuffle of papers behind him; and instinct told him that the issue was in peril. Had Uncle Soames and the old buffer behind made a mess of it? His mother was speaking with a slight drawl.

"No, my Lord, but it had gone on a long time."

"What had gone on?"

"Our differences about money."

"But you supplied the money. Do you suggest that he left you to better his position?"

'The brute! The old brute, and nothing but the brute!' thought Val suddenly. 'He smells a rat he's trying to get at the pastry!' And his heart stood still. If—if he did, then, of course, he would know that his mother didn't really want his father back. His mother spoke again, a thought more fashionably.

"No, my Lord, but you see I had refused to give him any more money. It took him a long time to believe that, but he did at last—and when he did...."

"I see, you had refused. But you've sent him some since."

"My Lord, I wanted him back."

"And you thought that would bring him?"

"I don't know, my Lord, I acted on my father's advice."

Something in the Judge's face, in the sound of the papers behind him, in the sudden crossing of his uncle's legs, told Val that she had made just the right answer. 'Crafty!' he thought; 'by Jove, what humbug it all is!'

The Judge was speaking:

"Just one more question, Mrs. Dartie. Are you still fond of your husband?"

Val's hands, slack behind him, became fists. What business had that Judge to make things human suddenly? To make his mother speak out of her heart, and say what, perhaps, she didn't know herself, before all these people! It wasn't decent. His mother answered, rather low: "Yes, my Lord." Val saw the Judge nod. 'Wish I could take a cock-shy at your head!' he thought irreverently, as his mother came back to her seat beside him. Witnesses to his father's departure and continued absence followed—one of their own maids even, which struck Val as particularly beastly; there was more talking, all humbug; and then the Judge pronounced the decree for restitution, and they got up to go. Val walked out behind his mother, chin squared, eyelids drooped, doing his level best to despise everybody. His mother's voice in the corridor roused him from an angry trance.

"You behaved beautifully, dear. It was such a comfort to have you. Your uncle and I are going to lunch."

"All right," said Val; "I shall have time to go and see that fellow." And, parting from them abruptly, he ran down the stairs and out into the air. He bolted into a hansom, and drove to the Goat's Club. His thoughts were on Holly and what he must do before her brother showed her this thing in to-morrow's paper.

When Val had left them Soames and Winifred made their way to the Cheshire Cheese. He had suggested it as a meeting place with Mr. Bellby. At that early hour of noon they would have it to themselves, and Winifred had thought it would be 'amusing' to see this far-famed hostelry. Having ordered a light repast, to the consternation of the waiter, they awaited its arrival together with that of Mr. Bellby, in silent reaction after the hour and a half's suspense on the tenterhooks of publicity. Mr. Bellby entered presently, preceded by his nose, as cheerful as they were glum. Well! they had got the decree of restitution, and what was the matter with that!

"Quite," said Soames in a suitably low voice, "but we shall have to begin again to get evidence. He'll probably try the divorce—it will look fishy if it comes out that we knew of misconduct from the start. His questions showed well enough that he doesn't like this restitution dodge."

"Pho!" said Mr. Bellby cheerily, "he'll forget! Why, man, he'll have tried a hundred cases between now and then. Besides, he's bound by precedent to give ye your divorce, if the evidence is satisfactory. We won't let um know that Mrs. Dartie had knowledge of the facts. Dreamer did it very nicely—he's got a fatherly touch about um!"

Soames nodded.

"And I compliment ye, Mrs. Dartie," went on Mr. Bellby; "ye've a natural gift for giving evidence. Steady as a rock."

Here the waiter arrived with three plates balanced on one arm, and the remark: "I 'urried up the pudden, sir. You'll find plenty o' lark in it to-day."

Mr. Bellby applauded his forethought with a dip of his nose. But Soames and Winifred looked with dismay at their light lunch of gravified brown masses, touching them gingerly with their forks in the hope of distinguishing the bodies of the tasty little song-givers. Having begun, however, they found they were hungrier than they thought, and finished the lot, with a glass of port apiece. Conversation turned on the war. Soames thought Ladysmith would fall, and it might last a year. Bellby thought it would be over by the summer. Both agreed that they wanted more men. There was nothing for it but complete victory, since it was now a question of prestige. Winifred brought things back to more solid ground by saying that she did not want the divorce suit to come on till after the summer holidays had begun at Oxford, then the boys would have forgotten about it before Val had to go up again; the London season too would be over. The lawyers reassured her, an interval of six months was necessary—after that the earlier the better. People were now beginning to come in, and they parted—Soames to the city, Bellby to his chambers, Winifred in a hansom to Park Lane to let her mother know how she had fared. The issue had been so satisfactory on the whole that it was considered advisable to tell James, who never failed to say day after day that he didn't know about Winifred's affair, he couldn't tell. As his sands ran out; the importance of mundane matters became increasingly grave to him, as if he were feeling: 'I must make the most of it, and worry well; I shall soon have nothing to worry about.'

He received the report grudgingly. It was a new-fangled way of going about things, and he didn't know! But he gave Winifred a cheque, saying:

"I expect you'll have a lot of expense. That's a new hat you've got on. Why doesn't Val come and see us?"

Winifred promised to bring him to dinner soon. And, going home, she sought her bedroom where she could be alone. Now that her husband had been ordered back into her custody with a view to putting him away from her for ever, she would try once more to find out from her sore and lonely heart what she really wanted.

CHAPTER VIII—THE CHALLENGE

The morning had been misty, verging on frost, but the sun came out while Val was jogging towards the Roehampton Gate, whence he would canter on to the usual tryst. His spirits were rising rapidly. There had been nothing so very terrible in the morning's proceedings beyond the general disgrace of violated privacy. 'If we were engaged!' he thought, 'what happens wouldn't matter.' He felt, indeed, like human society, which kicks and clamours at the results of matrimony, and hastens to get married. And he galloped over the winter-dried grass of Richmond Park, fearing to be late. But again he was alone at the trysting spot, and this second defection on the part of Holly upset him dreadfully. He could not go back without seeing her to-day! Emerging from the Park, he proceeded towards Robin Hill. He could not make up his mind for whom to ask. Suppose her father were back, or her sister or brother were in! He decided to gamble, and ask for them all first, so that if he were in luck and they were not there, it would be quite natural in the end to ask for Holly; while if any of them were in—an 'excuse for a ride' must be his saving grace.

"Only Miss Holly is in, sir."

"Oh! thanks. Might I take my horse round to the stables? And would you say—her cousin, Mr. Val Dartie."

When he returned she was in the hall, very flushed and shy. She led him to the far end, and they sat down on a wide window-seat.

"I've been awfully anxious," said Val in a low voice. "What's the matter?"

"Jolly knows about our riding."

"Is he in?"

"No; but I expect he will be soon."

"Then!" cried Val, and diving forward, he seized her hand. She tried to withdraw it, failed, gave up the attempt, and looked at him wistfully.

"First of all," he said, "I want to tell you something about my family. My Dad, you know, isn't altogether—I mean, he's left my mother and they're trying to divorce him; so they've ordered him to come back, you see. You'll see that in the paper to-morrow."

Her eyes deepened in colour and fearful interest; her hand squeezed his. But the gambler in Val was roused now, and he hurried on:

"Of course there's nothing very much at present, but there will be, I expect, before it's over; divorce suits are beastly, you know. I wanted to tell you, because—because—you ought to know—if—" and he began to stammer, gazing at her troubled eyes, "if—if you're going to be a darling and love me, Holly. I love you—ever so; and I want to be engaged." He had done it in a manner so inadequate that he could have punched his own head; and dropping on his knees, he tried to get nearer to that soft, troubled face. "You do love me—don't you? If you don't I...." There was a moment of silence and suspense, so awful that he could hear the sound of a mowing-machine far out on the lawn pretending there was grass to cut. Then she swayed forward; her free hand touched his hair, and he gasped: "Oh, Holly!"

Her answer was very soft: "Oh, Val!"

He had dreamed of this moment, but always in an imperative mood, as the masterful young lover, and now he felt humble, touched, trembly. He was afraid to stir off his knees lest he should break the spell; lest, if he did, she should shrink and deny her own surrender—so tremulous was she in his grasp, with her eyelids closed and his lips nearing them. Her eyes opened, seemed to swim a little; he pressed his lips to hers. Suddenly he sprang up; there had been footsteps, a sort of startled grunt. He looked round. No one! But the long curtains which barred off the outer hall were quivering.

"My God! Who was that?"

Holly too was on her feet.

"Jolly, I expect," she whispered.

Val clenched fists and resolution.

"All right!" he said, "I don't care a bit now we're engaged," and striding towards the curtains, he drew them aside. There at the fireplace in the hall stood Jolly, with his back elaborately turned. Val went forward. Jolly faced round on him.

"I beg your pardon for hearing," he said.

With the best intentions in the world, Val could not help admiring him at that moment; his face was clear, his voice quiet, he looked somehow distinguished, as if acting up to principle.

"Well!" Val said abruptly, "it's nothing to you."

"Oh!" said Jolly; "you come this way," and he crossed the hall. Val followed. At the study door he felt a touch on his arm; Holly's voice said:

"I'm coming too."

"No," said Jolly.

"Yes," said Holly.

Jolly opened the door, and they all three went in. Once in the little room, they stood in a sort of triangle on three corners of the worn Turkey carpet; awkwardly upright, not looking at each other, quite incapable of seeing any humour in the situation.

Val broke the silence.

"Holly and I are engaged."

Jolly stepped back and leaned against the lintel of the window.

"This is our house," he said; "I'm not going to insult you in it. But my father's away. I'm in charge of my sister. You've taken advantage of me.

"I didn't mean to," said Val hotly.

"I think you did," said Jolly. "If you hadn't meant to, you'd have spoken to me, or waited for my father to come back."

"There were reasons," said Val.

"What reasons?"

"About my family—I've just told her. I wanted her to know before things happen."

Jolly suddenly became less distinguished.

"You're kids," he said, "and you know you are.

"I am not a kid," said Val.

"You are—you're not twenty."

"Well, what are you?"

"I am twenty," said Jolly.

"Only just; anyway, I'm as good a man as you."

Jolly's face crimsoned, then clouded. Some struggle was evidently taking place in him; and Val and Holly stared at him, so clearly was that struggle marked; they could even hear him breathing. Then his face cleared up and became oddly resolute.

"We'll see that," he said. "I dare you to do what I'm going to do."

"Dare me?"

Jolly smiled. "Yes," he said, "dare you; and I know very well you won't."

A stab of misgiving shot through Val; this was riding very blind.

"I haven't forgotten that you're a fire-eater," said Jolly slowly, "and I think that's about all you are; or that you called me a pro-Boer."

Val heard a gasp above the sound of his own hard breathing, and saw Holly's face poked a little forward, very pale, with big eyes.

"Yes," went on Jolly with a sort of smile, "we shall soon see. I'm going to join the Imperial Yeomanry, and I dare you to do the same, Mr. Val Dartie."

Val's head jerked on its stem. It was like a blow between the eyes, so utterly unthought of, so extreme and ugly in the midst of his dreaming; and he looked at Holly with eyes grown suddenly, touchingly haggard.

"Sit down!" said Jolly. "Take your time! Think it over well." And he himself sat down on the arm of his grandfather's chair.

Val did not sit down; he stood with hands thrust deep into his breeches' pockets-hands clenched and quivering. The full awfulness of this decision one way or the other knocked at his mind with double knocks as of an angry postman. If he did not take that 'dare' he was disgraced in Holly's eyes, and in the eyes of that young enemy, her brute of a brother. Yet if he took it, ah! then all would vanish—her face, her eyes, her hair, her kisses just begun!

"Take your time," said Jolly again; "I don't want to be unfair."

And they both looked at Holly. She had recoiled against the bookshelves reaching to the ceiling; her dark head leaned against Gibbon's Roman Empire, her eyes in a sort of soft grey agony were fixed on Val. And he, who had not much gift of insight, had suddenly a gleam of vision. She would be proud of her brother—that enemy! She would be ashamed of him! His hands came out of his pockets as if lifted by a spring.

"All right!" he said. "Done!"

Holly's face—oh! it was queer! He saw her flush, start forward. He had done the right thing—her face was shining with wistful admiration. Jolly stood up and made a little bow as who should say: 'You've passed.'

"To-morrow, then," he said, "we'll go together."

Recovering from the impetus which had carried him to that decision, Val looked at him maliciously from under his lashes. 'All right,' he thought, 'one to you. I shall have to join—but I'll get back on you somehow.' And he said with dignity: "I shall be ready."

"We'll meet at the main Recruiting Office, then," said Jolly, "at twelve o'clock." And, opening the window, he went out on to the terrace, conforming to the creed which had made him retire when he surprised them in the hall.

The confusion in the mind of Val thus left alone with her for whom he had paid this sudden price was extreme. The mood of 'showing-off' was still, however, uppermost. One must do the wretched thing with an air.

"We shall get plenty of riding and shooting, anyway," he said; "that's one comfort." And it gave him a sort of grim pleasure to hear the sigh which seemed to come from the bottom of her heart.

"Oh! the war'll soon be over," he said; "perhaps we shan't even have to go out. I don't care, except for you." He would be out of the way of that beastly divorce. It was an ill-wind! He felt her warm hand slip into his. Jolly thought he had stopped their loving each other, did he? He held her tightly round the waist, looking at her softly through his lashes, smiling to cheer her up, promising to come down and see her soon, feeling somehow six inches taller and much more in command of her than he had ever dared feel before. Many times he kissed her before he mounted and rode back to town. So, swiftly, on the least provocation, does the possessive instinct flourish and grow.

CHAPTER IX—DINNER AT JAMES'

Dinner parties were not now given at James' in Park Lane—to every house the moment comes when Master or Mistress is no longer 'up to it'; no more can nine courses be served to twenty mouths above twenty fine white expanses; nor does the household cat any longer wonder why she is suddenly shut up.

So with something like excitement Emily—who at seventy would still have liked a little feast and fashion now and then—ordered dinner for six instead of two, herself wrote a number of foreign words on cards, and arranged the flowers—mimosa from the Riviera, and white Roman hyacinths not from Rome. There would only be, of course, James and herself, Soames, Winifred, Val, and Imogen—but she liked to pretend a little and dally in imagination with the glory of the past. She so dressed herself that James remarked:

"What are you putting on that thing for? You'll catch cold."

But Emily knew that the necks of women are protected by love of shining, unto fourscore years, and she only answered:

"Let me put you on one of those dickies I got you, James; then you'll only have to change your trousers, and put on your velvet coat, and there you'll be. Val likes you to look nice."

"Dicky!" said James. "You're always wasting your money on something."

But he suffered the change to be made till his neck also shone, murmuring vaguely:

"He's an extravagant chap, I'm afraid."

A little brighter in the eye, with rather more colour than usual in his cheeks, he took his seat in the drawing-room to wait for the sound of the front-door bell.

"I've made it a proper dinner party," Emily said comfortably; "I thought it would be good practice for Imogen—she must get used to it now she's coming out."

James uttered an indeterminate sound, thinking of Imogen as she used to climb about his knee or pull Christmas crackers with him.

"She'll be pretty," he muttered, "I shouldn't wonder."

"She is pretty," said Emily; "she ought to make a good match."

"There you go," murmured James; "she'd much better stay at home and look after her mother." A second Dartie carrying off his pretty granddaughter would finish him! He had never quite forgiven Emily for having been as much taken in by Montague Dartie as he himself had been.

"Where's Warmson?" he said suddenly. "I should like a glass of Madeira to-night."

"There's champagne, James."

James shook his head. "No body," he said; "I can't get any good out of it."

Emily reached forward on her side of the fire and rang the bell.

"Your master would like a bottle of Madeira opened, Warmson."

"No, no!" said James, the tips of his ears quivering with vehemence, and his eyes fixed on an object seen by him alone. "Look here, Warmson, you go to the inner cellar, and on the middle shelf of the end bin on the left you'll see seven bottles; take the one in the centre, and don't shake it. It's the last of the Madeira I had from Mr. Jolyon when we came in here—never been moved; it ought to be in prime condition still; but I don't know, I can't tell."

"Very good, sir," responded the withdrawing Warmson.

"I was keeping it for our golden wedding," said James suddenly, "but I shan't live three years at my age."

"Nonsense, James," said Emily, "don't talk like that."

"I ought to have got it up myself," murmured James, "he'll shake it as likely as not." And he sank into silent recollection of long moments among the open gas-jets, the cobwebs and the good smell of wine-soaked corks, which had been appetiser to so many feasts. In the wine from that cellar was written the history of the forty odd years since he had come to the Park Lane house with his young bride, and of the many generations of friends and acquaintances who had passed into the unknown; its depleted bins preserved the record of family festivity—all the marriages, births, deaths of his kith and kin. And when he was gone there it would be, and he didn't know what would become of it. It'd be drunk or spoiled, he shouldn't wonder!

From that deep reverie the entrance of his son dragged him, followed very soon by that of Winifred and her two eldest.

They went down arm-in-arm—James with Imogen, the debutante, because his pretty grandchild cheered him; Soames with Winifred; Emily with Val, whose eyes lighting on the oysters brightened. This was to be a proper full 'blowout' with 'fizz' and port! And he felt in need of it, after what he had done that day, as yet undivulged. After the first glass or two it became pleasant to have this bombshell up his sleeve, this piece of sensational patriotism, or example, rather, of personal daring, to display—for his pleasure in what he had done for his Queen and Country was so far entirely personal. He was now a 'blood,' indissolubly connected with guns and horses; he had a right to swagger—not, of course, that he was going to. He should just announce it quietly, when there was a pause. And, glancing down the menu, he determined on 'Bombe aux fraises' as the proper moment; there would be a certain solemnity while they were eating that. Once or twice before they reached that rosy summit of the dinner he was attacked by remembrance that his grandfather was never told anything! Still, the old boy was drinking Madeira, and looking jolly fit! Besides, he ought to be pleased at this set-off to the disgrace of the divorce. The sight of his uncle opposite, too, was a sharp incentive. He was so far from being a sportsman that it would be worth a lot to see his face. Besides, better to tell his mother in this way than privately, which might upset them both! He was sorry for her, but after all one couldn't be expected to feel much for others when one had to part from Holly.

His grandfather's voice travelled to him thinly. "Val, try a little of the Madeira with your ice. You won't get that up at college."

Val watched the slow liquid filling his glass, the essential oil of the old wine glazing the surface; inhaled its aroma, and thought: 'Now for it!' It was a rich moment. He sipped, and a gentle glow spread in his veins, already heated. With a rapid look round, he said, "I joined the Imperial Yeomanry to-day, Granny," and emptied his glass as though drinking the health of his own act.

"What!" It was his mother's desolate little word.

"Young Jolly Forsyte and I went down there together."

"You didn't sign?" from Uncle Soames.

"Rather! We go into camp on Monday."

"I say!" cried Imogen.

All looked at James. He was leaning forward with his hand behind his ear.

"What's that?" he said. "What's he saying? I can't hear."

Emily reached forward to pat Val's hand.

"It's only that Val has joined the Yeomanry, James; it's very nice for him. He'll look his best in uniform."

"Joined the—rubbish!" came from James, tremulously loud. "You can't see two yards before your nose. He—he'll have to go out there. Why! he'll be fighting before he knows where he is."

Val saw Imogen's eyes admiring him, and his mother still and fashionable with her handkerchief before her lips.

Suddenly his uncle spoke.

"You're under age."

"I thought of that," smiled Val; "I gave my age as twenty-one."

He heard his grandmother's admiring, "Well, Val, that was plucky of you;" was conscious of Warmson deferentially filling his champagne glass; and of his grandfather's voice moaning: "I don't know what'll become of you if you go on like this."

Imogen was patting his shoulder, his uncle looking at him sidelong; only his mother sat unmoving, till, affected by her stillness, Val said:

"It's all right, you know; we shall soon have them on the run. I only hope I shall come in for something."

He felt elated, sorry, tremendously important all at once. This would show Uncle Soames, and all the Forsytes, how to be sportsmen. He had certainly done something heroic and exceptional in giving his age as twenty-one.

Emily's voice brought him back to earth.

"You mustn't have a second glass, James. Warmson!"

"Won't they be astonished at Timothy's!" burst out Imogen. "I'd give anything to see their faces. Do you have a sword, Val, or only a popgun?"

"What made you?"

His uncle's voice produced a slight chill in the pit of Val's stomach. Made him? How answer that? He was grateful for his grandmother's comfortable:

"Well, I think it's very plucky of Val. I'm sure he'll make a splendid soldier; he's just the figure for it. We shall all be proud of him."

"What had young Jolly Forsyte to do with it? Why did you go together?" pursued Soames, uncannily relentless. "I thought you weren't friendly with him?"

"I'm not," mumbled Val, "but I wasn't going to be beaten by him." He saw his uncle look at him quite differently, as if approving. His grandfather was nodding too, his grandmother tossing her head. They all approved of his not being beaten by that cousin of his. There must be a reason! Val was dimly conscious of some disturbing point outside his range of vision; as it might be, the unlocated centre of a cyclone. And, staring at his uncle's face, he had a quite unaccountable vision of a woman with dark eyes, gold hair, and a white neck, who smelt nice, and had pretty silken clothes which he had liked feeling when he was quite small. By Jove, yes! Aunt Irene! She used to kiss him, and he had bitten her arm once, playfully, because he liked it—so soft. His grandfather was speaking:

"What's his father doing?"

"He's away in Paris," Val said, staring at the very queer expression on his uncle's face, like—like that of a snarling dog.

"Artists!" said James. The word coming from the very bottom of his soul, broke up the dinner.

Opposite his mother in the cab going home, Val tasted the after-fruits of heroism, like medlars over-ripe.

She only said, indeed, that he must go to his tailor's at once and have his uniform properly made, and not just put up with what they gave him. But he could feel that she was very much upset. It was on his lips to console her with the spoken thought that he would be out of the way of that beastly divorce, but the presence of Imogen, and the knowledge that his mother would not be out of the way, restrained him. He felt aggrieved that she did not seem more proud of him. When Imogen had gone to bed, he risked the emotional.

"I'm awfully sorry to have to leave you, Mother."

"Well, I must make the best of it. We must try and get you a commission as soon as we can; then you won't have to rough it so. Do you know any drill, Val?"

"Not a scrap."

"I hope they won't worry you much. I must take you about to get the things to-morrow. Good-night; kiss me."

With that kiss, soft and hot, between his eyes, and those words, 'I hope they won't worry you much,' in his ears, he sat down to a cigarette, before a dying fire. The heat was out of him—the glow of cutting a dash. It was all a damned heart-aching bore. 'I'll be even with that chap Jolly,' he thought, trailing up the stairs, past the room where his mother was biting her pillow to smother a sense of desolation which was trying to make her sob.

And soon only one of the diners at James' was awake—Soames, in his bedroom above his father's.

So that fellow Jolyon was in Paris—what was he doing there? Hanging round Irene! The last report from Polteed had hinted that there might be something soon. Could it be this? That fellow, with his beard and his cursed amused way of speaking—son of the old man who had given him the nickname 'Man of Property,' and bought the fatal house from him. Soames had ever resented having had to sell the house at Robin Hill; never forgiven his uncle for having bought it, or his cousin for living in it.

Reckless of the cold, he threw his window up and gazed out across the Park. Bleak and dark the January night; little sound of traffic; a frost coming; bare trees; a star or two. 'I'll see Polteed to-morrow,' he thought. 'By God! I'm mad, I think, to want her still. That fellow! If...? Um! No!'

CHAPTER X—DEATH OF THE DOG BALTHASAR

Jolyon, who had crossed from Calais by night, arrived at Robin Hill on Sunday morning. He had sent no word beforehand, so walked up from the station, entering his domain by the coppice gate. Coming to the log seat fashioned out of an old fallen trunk, he sat down, first laying his overcoat on it.

'Lumbago!' he thought; 'that's what love ends in at my time of life!' And suddenly Irene seemed very near, just as she had been that day of rambling at Fontainebleau when they had sat on a log to eat their lunch. Hauntingly near! Odour drawn out of fallen leaves by the pale-filtering sunlight soaked his nostrils. 'I'm glad it isn't spring,' he thought. With the scent of sap, and the song of birds, and the bursting of the blossoms, it would have been unbearable! 'I hope I shall be over it by then, old fool that I am!' and picking up his coat, he walked on into the field. He passed the pond and mounted the hill slowly.

Near the top a hoarse barking greeted him. Up on the lawn above the fernery he could see his old dog Balthasar. The animal, whose dim eyes took his master for a stranger, was warning the world against him. Jolyon gave his special whistle. Even at that distance of a hundred yards and more he could see the dawning recognition in the obese brown-white body. The old dog got off his haunches, and his tail, close-curled over his back, began a feeble, excited fluttering; he came waddling forward, gathered momentum, and disappeared over the edge of the fernery. Jolyon expected to meet him at the wicket gate, but Balthasar was not there, and, rather alarmed, he turned into the fernery. On his fat side, looking up with eyes already glazing, the old dog lay.

"What is it, my poor old man?" cried Jolyon. Balthasar's curled and fluffy tail just moved; his filming eyes seemed saying: "I can't get up, master, but I'm glad to see you."

Jolyon knelt down; his eyes, very dimmed, could hardly see the slowly ceasing heave of the dog's side. He raised the head a little—very heavy.

"What is it, dear man? Where are you hurt?" The tail fluttered once; the eyes lost the look of life. Jolyon passed his hands all over the inert warm bulk. There was nothing—the heart had simply failed in that obese body from the emotion of his master's return. Jolyon could feel the muzzle, where a few whitish bristles grew, cooling already against his lips. He stayed for some minutes kneeling; with his hand beneath the stiffening head. The body was very heavy when he bore it to the top of the field; leaves had drifted there, and he strewed it with a covering of them; there was no wind, and they would keep him from curious eyes until the afternoon. 'I'll bury him myself,' he thought. Eighteen years had gone since he first went into the St. John's Wood house with that tiny puppy in his pocket. Strange that the old dog should die just now! Was it an omen? He turned at the gate to look back at that russet mound, then went slowly towards the house, very choky in the throat.

June was at home; she had come down hotfoot on hearing the news of Jolly's enlistment. His patriotism had conquered her feeling for the Boers. The atmosphere of his house was strange and pocketty when Jolyon came in and told them of the dog Balthasar's death. The news had a unifying effect. A link with the past had snapped—the dog Balthasar! Two of them could remember nothing before his day; to June he represented the last years of her grandfather; to Jolyon that life of domestic stress and aesthetic struggle before he came again into the kingdom of his father's love and wealth! And he was gone!

In the afternoon he and Jolly took picks and spades and went out to the field. They chose a spot close to the russet mound, so that they need not carry him far, and, carefully cutting off the surface turf, began to dig. They dug in silence for ten minutes, and then rested.

"Well, old man," said Jolyon, "so you thought you ought?"

"Yes," answered Jolly; "I don't want to a bit, of course."

How exactly those words represented Jolyon's own state of mind

"I admire you for it, old boy. I don't believe I should have done it at your age—too much of a Forsyte, I'm afraid. But I suppose the type gets thinner with each generation. Your son, if you have one, may be a pure altruist; who knows?"

"He won't be like me, then, Dad; I'm beastly selfish."

"No, my dear, that you clearly are not." Jolly shook his head, and they dug again.

"Strange life a dog's," said Jolyon suddenly: "The only four-footer with rudiments of altruism and a sense of God!"

Jolly looked at his father.

"Do you believe in God, Dad? I've never known."

At so searching a question from one to whom it was impossible to make a light reply, Jolyon stood for a moment feeling his back tried by the digging.

"What do you mean by God?" he said; "there are two irreconcilable ideas of God. There's the Unknowable Creative Principle—one believes in That. And there's the Sum of altruism in man—naturally one believes in That."

"I see. That leaves out Christ, doesn't it?"

Jolyon stared. Christ, the link between those two ideas! Out of the mouth of babes! Here was orthodoxy scientifically explained at last! The sublime poem of the Christ life was man's attempt to join those two irreconcilable conceptions of God. And since the Sum of human altruism was as much a part of the Unknowable Creative Principle as anything else in Nature and the Universe, a worse link might have been chosen after all! Funny—how one went through life without seeing it in that sort of way!

"What do you think, old man?" he said.

Jolly frowned. "Of course, my first year we talked a good bit about that sort of thing. But in the second year one gives it up; I don't know why—it's awfully interesting."

Jolyon remembered that he also had talked a good deal about it his first year at Cambridge, and given it up in his second.

"I suppose," said Jolly, "it's the second God, you mean, that old Balthasar had a sense of."

"Yes, or he would never have burst his poor old heart because of something outside himself."

"But wasn't that just selfish emotion, really?"

Jolyon shook his head. "No, dogs are not pure Forsytes, they love something outside themselves."

Jolly smiled.

"Well, I think I'm one," he said. "You know, I only enlisted because I dared Val Dartie to."

"But why?"

"We bar each other," said Jolly shortly.

"Ah!" muttered Jolyon. So the feud went on, unto the third generation—this modern feud which had no overt expression?

'Shall I tell the boy about it?' he thought. But to what end—if he had to stop short of his own part?

And Jolly thought: 'It's for Holly to let him know about that chap. If she doesn't, it means she doesn't want him told, and I should be sneaking. Anyway, I've stopped it. I'd better leave well alone!'

So they dug on in silence, till Jolyon said:

"Now, old man, I think it's big enough." And, resting on their spades, they gazed down into the hole where a few leaves had drifted already on a sunset wind.

"I can't bear this part of it," said Jolyon suddenly.

"Let me do it, Dad. He never cared much for me."

Jolyon shook his head.

"We'll lift him very gently, leaves and all. I'd rather not see him again. I'll take his head. Now!"

With extreme care they raised the old dog's body, whose faded tan and white showed here and there under the leaves stirred by the wind. They laid it, heavy, cold, and unresponsive, in the grave, and Jolly spread more leaves over it, while Jolyon, deeply afraid to show emotion before his son, began quickly shovelling the earth on to that still shape. There went the past! If only there were a joyful future to look forward to! It was like stamping down earth on one's own life. They replaced the turf carefully on the smooth little mound, and, grateful that they had spared each other's feelings, returned to the house arm-in-arm.

CHAPTER XI—TIMOTHY STAYS THE ROT

On Forsyte 'Change news of the enlistment spread fast, together with the report that June, not to be outdone, was going to become a Red Cross nurse. These events were so extreme, so subversive of pure Forsyteism, as to have a binding effect upon the family, and Timothy's was thronged next Sunday afternoon by members trying to find out what they thought about it all, and exchange with each other a sense of family credit. Giles and Jesse Hayman would no longer defend the coast but go to South Africa quite soon; Jolly and Val would be following in April; as to June—well, you never knew what she would really do.

The retirement from Spion Kop and the absence of any good news from the seat of war imparted an air of reality to all this, clinched in startling fashion by Timothy. The youngest of the old Forsytes—scarcely eighty, in fact popularly supposed to resemble their father, 'Superior Dosset,' even in his best-known characteristic of drinking Sherry—had been invisible for so many years that he was almost mythical. A long generation had elapsed since the risks of a publisher's business had worked on his nerves at the age of forty, so that he had got out with a mere thirty-five thousand pounds in the world, and started to make his living by careful investment. Putting by every year, at compound interest, he had doubled his capital in forty years without having once known what it was like to shake in his shoes over money matters. He was now putting aside some two thousand a year, and, with the care he was taking of himself, expected, so Aunt Hester said, to double his capital again before he died. What he would do with it then, with his sisters dead and himself dead, was often mockingly queried by free spirits such as Francie, Euphemia, or young Nicholas' second, Christopher, whose spirit was so free that he had actually said he was going on the stage. All admitted, however, that this was best known to Timothy himself, and possibly to Soames, who never divulged a secret.

Those few Forsytes who had seen him reported a man of thick and robust appearance, not very tall, with a brown-red complexion, grey hair, and little of the refinement of feature with which most of the Forsytes had been endowed by 'Superior Dosset's' wife, a woman of some beauty and a gentle temperament. It was known that he had taken surprising interest in the war, sticking flags into a map ever since it began, and there was uneasiness as to what would happen if the English were driven into the sea, when it would be almost impossible for him to put the flags in the right places. As to his knowledge of family movements or his views about them, little was known, save that Aunt Hester was always declaring that he was very upset. It was, then, in the nature of a portent when Forsytes, arriving on the Sunday after the evacuation of Spion Kop, became conscious, one after the other, of a presence seated in the only really comfortable armchair, back to the light, concealing the lower part of his face with a large hand, and were greeted by the awed voice of Aunt Hester:

"Your Uncle Timothy, my dear."

Timothy's greeting to them all was somewhat identical; and rather, as it were, passed over by him than expressed:

"How de do? How de do? 'Xcuse me gettin' up!"

Francie was present, and Eustace had come in his car; Winifred had brought Imogen, breaking the ice of the restitution proceedings with the warmth of family appreciation at Val's enlistment; and Marian Tweetyman with the last news of Giles and Jesse. These with Aunt Juley and Hester, young Nicholas, Euphemia, and—of all people!—George, who had come with Eustace in the car, constituted an assembly worthy of the family's palmiest days. There was not one chair vacant in the whole of the little drawing-room, and anxiety was felt lest someone else should arrive.

The constraint caused by Timothy's presence having worn off a little, conversation took a military turn. George asked Aunt Juley when she was going out with the Red Cross, almost reducing her to a state of gaiety; whereon he turned to Nicholas and said:

"Young Nick's a warrior bold, isn't he? When's he going to don the wild khaki?"

Young Nicholas, smiling with a sort of sweet deprecation, intimated that of course his mother was very anxious.

"The Dromios are off, I hear," said George, turning to Marian Tweetyman; "we shall all be there soon. En avant, the Forsytes! Roll, bowl, or pitch! Who's for a cooler?"

Aunt Juley gurgled, George was so droll! Should Hester get Timothy's map? Then he could show them all where they were.

At a sound from Timothy, interpreted as assent, Aunt Hester left the room.

George pursued his image of the Forsyte advance, addressing Timothy as Field Marshal; and Imogen, whom he had noted at once for 'a pretty filly,'—as Vivandiere; and holding his top hat between his knees, he began to beat it with imaginary drumsticks. The reception accorded to his fantasy was mixed. All laughed—George was licensed; but all felt that the family was being 'rotted'; and this seemed to them unnatural, now that it was going to give five of its members to the service of the Queen. George might go too far; and there was relief when he got up, offered his arm to Aunt Juley, marched up to Timothy, saluted him, kissed his aunt with mock passion, said, "Oh! what a treat, dear papa! Come on, Eustace!" and walked out, followed by the grave and fastidious Eustace, who had never smiled.

Aunt Juley's bewildered, "Fancy not waiting for the map! You mustn't mind him, Timothy. He's so droll!" broke the hush, and Timothy removed the hand from his mouth.

"I don't know what things are comin' to," he was heard to say. "What's all this about goin' out there? That's not the way to beat those Boers."

Francie alone had the hardihood to observe: "What is, then, Uncle Timothy?"

"All this new-fangled volunteerin' and expense—lettin' money out of the country."

Just then Aunt Hester brought in the map, handling it like a baby with eruptions. With the assistance of Euphemia it was laid on the piano, a small Colwood grand, last played on, it was believed, the summer before Aunt Ann died, thirteen years ago. Timothy rose. He walked over to the piano, and stood looking at his map while they all gathered round.

"There you are," he said; "that's the position up to date; and very poor it is. H'm!"

"Yes," said Francie, greatly daring, "but how are you going to alter it, Uncle Timothy, without more men?"

"Men!" said Timothy; "you don't want men—wastin' the country's money. You want a Napoleon, he'd settle it in a month."

"But if you haven't got him, Uncle Timothy?"

"That's their business," replied Timothy. "What have we kept the Army up for—to eat their heads off in time of peace! They ought to be ashamed of themselves, comin' on the country to help them like this! Let every man stick to his business, and we shall get on."

And looking round him, he added almost angrily:

"Volunteerin', indeed! Throwin' good money after bad! We must save! Conserve energy that's the only way." And with a prolonged sound, not quite a sniff and not quite a snort, he trod on Euphemia's toe, and went out, leaving a sensation and a faint scent of barley-sugar behind him.

The effect of something said with conviction by one who has evidently made a sacrifice to say it is ever considerable. And the eight Forsytes left behind, all women except young Nicholas, were silent for a moment round the map. Then Francie said:

"Really, I think he's right, you know. After all, what is the Army for? They ought to have known. It's only encouraging them."

"My dear!" cried Aunt Juley, "but they've been so progressive. Think of their giving up their scarlet. They were always so proud of it. And now they all look like convicts. Hester and I were saying only yesterday we were sure they must feel it very much. Fancy what the Iron Duke would have said!"

"The new colour's very smart," said Winifred; "Val looks quite nice in his."

Aunt Juley sighed.

"I do so wonder what Jolyon's boy is like. To think we've never seen him! His father must be so proud of him."

"His father's in Paris," said Winifred.

Aunt Hester's shoulder was seen to mount suddenly, as if to ward off her sister's next remark, for Juley's crumpled cheeks had gushed.

"We had dear little Mrs. MacAnder here yesterday, just back from Paris. And whom d'you think she saw there in the street? You'll never guess."

"We shan't try, Auntie," said Euphemia.

"Irene! Imagine! After all this time; walking with a fair beard...."

"Auntie! you'll kill me! A fair beard...."

"I was going to say," said Aunt Juley severely, "a fair-bearded gentleman. And not a day older; she was always so pretty," she added, with a sort of lingering apology.

"Oh! tell us about her, Auntie," cried Imogen; "I can just remember her. She's the skeleton in the family cupboard, isn't she? And they're such fun."

Aunt Hester sat down. Really, Juley had done it now!

"She wasn't much of a skeleton as I remember her," murmured Euphemia, "extremely well-covered."

"My dear!" said Aunt Juley, "what a peculiar way of putting it—not very nice."

"No, but what was she like?" persisted Imogen.

"I'll tell you, my child," said Francie; "a kind of modern Venus, very well-dressed."

Euphemia said sharply: "Venus was never dressed, and she had blue eyes of melting sapphire."

At this juncture Nicholas took his leave.

"Mrs. Nick is awfully strict," said Francie with a laugh.

"She has six children," said Aunt Juley; "it's very proper she should be careful."

"Was Uncle Soames awfully fond of her?" pursued the inexorable Imogen, moving her dark luscious eyes from face to face.

Aunt Hester made a gesture of despair, just as Aunt Juley answered:

"Yes, your Uncle Soames was very much attached to her."

"I suppose she ran off with someone?"

"No, certainly not; that is—not precisely.'

"What did she do, then, Auntie?"

"Come along, Imogen," said Winifred, "we must be getting back."

But Aunt Juley interjected resolutely: "She—she didn't behave at all well."

"Oh, bother!" cried Imogen; "that's as far as I ever get."

"Well, my dear," said Francie, "she had a love affair which ended with the young man's death; and then she left your uncle. I always rather liked her."

"She used to give me chocolates," murmured Imogen, "and smell nice."

"Of course!" remarked Euphemia.

"Not of course at all!" replied Francie, who used a particularly expensive essence of gillyflower herself.

"I can't think what we are about," said Aunt Juley, raising her hands, "talking of such things!"

"Was she divorced?" asked Imogen from the door.

"Certainly not," cried Aunt Juley; "that is—certainly not."

A sound was heard over by the far door. Timothy had re-entered the back drawing-room. "I've come for my map," he said. "Who's been divorced?"

"No one, Uncle," replied Francie with perfect truth.

Timothy took his map off the piano.

"Don't let's have anything of that sort in the family," he said. "All this enlistin's bad enough. The country's breakin' up; I don't know what we're comin' to." He shook a thick finger at the room: "Too many women nowadays, and they don't know what they want."

So saying, he grasped the map firmly with both hands, and went out as if afraid of being answered.

The seven women whom he had addressed broke into a subdued murmur, out of which emerged Francie's, "Really, the Forsytes!" and Aunt Juley's: "He must have his feet in mustard and hot water to-night, Hester; will you tell Jane? The blood has gone to his head again, I'm afraid...."

That evening, when she and Hester were sitting alone after dinner, she dropped a stitch in her crochet, and looked up:

"Hester, I can't think where I've heard that dear Soames wants Irene to come back to him again. Who was it told us that George had made a funny drawing of him with the words, 'He won't be happy till he gets it'?"

"Eustace," answered Aunt Hester from behind The Times; "he had it in his pocket, but he wouldn't show it us."

Aunt Juley was silent, ruminating. The clock ticked, The Times crackled, the fire sent forth its rustling purr. Aunt Juley dropped another stitch.

"Hester," she said, "I have had such a dreadful thought."

"Then don't tell me," said Aunt Hester quickly.

"Oh! but I must. You can't think how dreadful!" Her voice sank to a whisper:

"Jolyon—Jolyon, they say, has a—has a fair beard, now."

CHAPTER XII—PROGRESS OF THE CHASE

Two days after the dinner at James', Mr. Polteed provided Soames with food for thought.

"A gentleman," he said, consulting the key concealed in his left hand, "47 as we say, has been paying marked attention to 17 during the last month in Paris. But at present there seems to have been nothing very conclusive. The meetings have all been in public places, without concealment—restaurants, the Opera, the Comique, the Louvre, Luxembourg Gardens, lounge of the hotel, and so forth. She has not yet been traced to his rooms, nor vice versa. They went to Fontainebleau—but nothing of value. In short, the situation is promising, but requires patience." And, looking up suddenly, he added:

"One rather curious point—47 has the same name as—er—31!"

'The fellow knows I'm her husband,' thought Soames.

"Christian name—an odd one—Jolyon," continued Mr. Polteed. "We know his address in Paris and his residence here. We don't wish, of course, to be running a wrong hare."

"Go on with it, but be careful," said Soames doggedly.

Instinctive certainty that this detective fellow had fathomed his secret made him all the more reticent.

"Excuse me," said Mr. Polteed, "I'll just see if there's anything fresh in."

He returned with some letters. Relocking the door, he glanced at the envelopes.

"Yes, here's a personal one from 19 to myself."

"Well?" said Soames.

"Um!" said Mr. Polteed, "she says: '47 left for England to-day. Address on his baggage: Robin Hill. Parted from 17 in Louvre Gallery at 3.30; nothing very striking. Thought it best to stay and continue observation of 17. You will deal with 47 in England if you think desirable, no doubt.'" And Mr. Polteed lifted an unprofessional glance on Soames, as though he might be storing material for a book on human nature after he had gone out of business. "Very intelligent woman, 19, and a wonderful make-up. Not cheap, but earns her money well. There's no suspicion of being shadowed so far. But after a time, as you know, sensitive people are liable to get the feeling of it, without anything definite to go on. I should rather advise letting-up on 17, and keeping an eye on 47. We can't get at correspondence without great risk. I hardly advise that at this stage. But you can tell your client that it's looking up very well." And again his narrowed eyes gleamed at his taciturn customer.

"No," said Soames suddenly, "I prefer that you should keep the watch going discreetly in Paris, and not concern yourself with this end."

"Very well," replied Mr. Polteed, "we can do it."

"What—what is the manner between them?"

"I'll read you what she says," said Mr. Polteed, unlocking a bureau drawer and taking out a file of papers; "she sums it up somewhere confidentially. Yes, here it is! '17 very attractive—conclude 47, longer in the tooth' (slang for age, you know)—'distinctly gone—waiting his time—17 perhaps holding off for terms, impossible to say without knowing more. But inclined to think on the whole—doesn't know her mind—likely to act on impulse some day. Both have style.'"

"What does that mean?" said Soames between close lips.

"Well," murmured Mr. Polteed with a smile, showing many white teeth, "an expression we use. In other words, it's not likely to be a weekend business—they'll come together seriously or not at all."

"H'm!" muttered Soames, "that's all, is it?"

"Yes," said Mr. Polteed, "but quite promising."

'Spider!' thought Soames. "Good-day!"

He walked into the Green Park that he might cross to Victoria Station and take the Underground into the City. For so late in January it was warm; sunlight, through the haze, sparkled on the frosty grass—an illumined cobweb of a day.

Little spiders—and great spiders! And the greatest spinner of all, his own tenacity, for ever wrapping its cocoon of threads round any clear way out. What was that fellow hanging round Irene for? Was it really as Polteed suggested? Or was Jolyon but taking compassion on her loneliness, as he would call it—sentimental radical chap that he had always been? If it were, indeed, as Polteed hinted! Soames stood still. It could not be! The fellow was seven years older than himself, no better looking! No richer! What attraction had he?

'Besides, he's come back,' he thought; 'that doesn't look——I'll go and see him!' and, taking out a card, he wrote:

"If you can spare half an hour some afternoon this week, I shall be at the Connoisseurs any day between 5.30 and 6, or I could come to the Hotch Potch if you prefer it. I want to see you.—S. F."

He walked up St. James's Street and confided it to the porter at the Hotch Potch.

"Give Mr. Jolyon Forsyte this as soon as he comes in," he said, and took one of the new motor cabs into the City....

Jolyon received that card the same afternoon, and turned his face towards the Connoisseurs. What did Soames want now? Had he got wind of Paris? And stepping across St. James's Street, he determined to make no secret of his visit. 'But it won't do,' he thought, 'to let him know she's there, unless he knows already.' In this complicated state of mind he was conducted to where Soames was drinking tea in a small bay-window.

"No tea, thanks," said Jolyon, "but I'll go on smoking if I may."

The curtains were not yet drawn, though the lamps outside were lighted; the two cousins sat waiting on each other.

"You've been in Paris, I hear," said Soames at last.

"Yes; just back."

"Young Val told me; he and your boy are going off, then?" Jolyon nodded.

"You didn't happen to see Irene, I suppose. It appears she's abroad somewhere."

Jolyon wreathed himself in smoke before he answered: "Yes, I saw her."

"How was she?"

"Very well."

There was another silence; then Soames roused himself in his chair.

"When I saw you last," he said, "I was in two minds. We talked, and you expressed your opinion. I don't wish to reopen that discussion. I only wanted to say this: My position with her is extremely difficult. I don't want you to go using your influence against me. What happened is a very long time ago. I'm going to ask her to let bygones be bygones."

"You have asked her, you know," murmured Jolyon.

"The idea was new to her then; it came as a shock. But the more she thinks of it, the more she must see that it's the only way out for both of us."

"That's not my impression of her state of mind," said Jolyon with particular calm. "And, forgive my saying, you misconceive the matter if you think reason comes into it at all."

He saw his cousin's pale face grow paler—he had used, without knowing it, Irene's own words.

"Thanks," muttered Soames, "but I see things perhaps more plainly than you think. I only want to be sure that you won't try to influence her against me."

"I don't know what makes you think I have any influence," said Jolyon; "but if I have I'm bound to use it in the direction of what I think is her happiness. I am what they call a 'feminist,' I believe."

"Feminist!" repeated Soames, as if seeking to gain time. "Does that mean that you're against me?"

"Bluntly," said Jolyon, "I'm against any woman living with any man whom she definitely dislikes. It appears to me rotten."

"And I suppose each time you see her you put your opinions into her mind."

"I am not likely to be seeing her."

"Not going back to Paris?"

"Not so far as I know," said Jolyon, conscious of the intent watchfulness in Soames' face.

"Well, that's all I had to say. Anyone who comes between man and wife, you know, incurs heavy responsibility."

Jolyon rose and made him a slight bow.

"Good-bye," he said, and, without offering to shake hands, moved away, leaving Soames staring after him. 'We Forsytes,' thought Jolyon, hailing a cab, 'are very civilised. With simpler folk that might have come to a row. If it weren't for my boy going to the war....' The war! A gust of his old doubt swept over him. A precious war! Domination of peoples or of women! Attempts to master and possess those who did not want you! The negation of gentle decency! Possession, vested rights; and anyone 'agin' 'em—outcast! 'Thank Heaven!' he thought, 'I always felt "agin" 'em, anyway!' Yes! Even before his first disastrous marriage he could remember fuming over the bludgeoning of Ireland, or the matrimonial suits of women trying to be free of men they loathed. Parsons would have it that freedom of soul and body were quite different things! Pernicious doctrine! Body and soul could not thus be separated. Free will was the strength of any tie, and not its weakness. 'I ought to have told Soames,' he thought, 'that I think him comic. Ah! but he's tragic, too!' Was there anything, indeed, more tragic in the world than a man enslaved by his own possessive instinct, who couldn't see the sky for it, or even enter fully into what another person felt! 'I must write and warn her,' he thought; 'he's going to have another try.' And all the way home to Robin Hill he rebelled at the strength of that duty to his son which prevented him from posting back to Paris....

But Soames sat long in his chair, the prey of a no less gnawing ache—a jealous ache, as if it had been revealed to him that this fellow held precedence of himself, and had spun fresh threads of resistance to his way out. 'Does that mean that you're against me?' he had got nothing out of that disingenuous question. Feminist! Phrasey fellow! 'I mustn't rush things,' he thought. 'I have some breathing space; he's not going back to Paris, unless he was lying. I'll let the spring come!' Though how the spring could serve him, save by adding to his ache, he could not tell. And gazing down into the street, where figures were passing from pool to pool of the light from the high lamps, he thought: 'Nothing seems any good— nothing seems worth while. I'm loney—that's the trouble.'

He closed his eyes; and at once he seemed to see Irene, in a dark street below a church— passing, turning her neck so that he caught the gleam of her eyes and her white forehead under a little dark hat, which had gold spangles on it and a veil hanging down behind. He opened his eyes—so vividly he had seen her! A woman was passing below, but not she! Oh no, there was nothing there!

CHAPTER XIII—'HERE WE ARE AGAIN!'

Imogen's frocks for her first season exercised the judgment of her mother and the purse of her grandfather all through the month of March. With Forsyte tenacity Winifred quested for perfection. It took her mind off the slowly approaching rite which would give her a freedom but doubtfully desired; took her mind, too, off her boy and his fast approaching departure for a war from which the news remained disquieting. Like bees busy on summer flowers, or bright gadflies hovering and darting over spiky autumn blossoms, she and her 'little daughter,' tall nearly as herself and with a bust measurement not far inferior, hovered in the shops of Regent Street, the establishments of Hanover Square and of Bond Street, lost in consideration and the feel of fabrics. Dozens of young women of striking deportment and peculiar gait paraded before Winifred and Imogen, draped in 'creations.' The models—'Very new, modom; quite the latest thing—' which those two reluctantly turned down, would have filled a museum; the models which they were obliged to have nearly emptied James' bank. It was no good doing things by halves, Winifred felt, in view of the need for making this first and sole untarnished season a conspicuous success. Their patience in trying the patience of those impersonal creatures who swam about before them could alone have been displayed by such as were moved by faith. It was for Winifred a long prostration before her dear goddess Fashion, fervent as a Catholic might make before the Virgin; for Imogen an experience by no means too unpleasant—she often looked so nice, and flattery was implicit everywhere: in a word it was 'amusing.'

On the afternoon of the 20th of March, having, as it were, gutted Skywards, they had sought refreshment over the way at Caramel and Baker's, and, stored with chocolate frothed at the top with cream, turned homewards through Berkeley Square of an evening touched with spring. Opening the door—freshly painted a light olive-green; nothing neglected that year to give Imogen a good send-off—Winifred passed towards the silver basket to see if anyone had called, and suddenly her nostrils twitched. What was that scent?

Imogen had taken up a novel sent from the library, and stood absorbed. Rather sharply, because of the queer feeling in her breast, Winifred said:

"Take that up, dear, and have a rest before dinner."

Imogen, still reading, passed up the stairs. Winifred heard the door of her room slammed to, and drew a long savouring breath. Was it spring tickling her senses—whipping up nostalgia for her 'clown,' against all wisdom and outraged virtue? A male scent! A faint reek of cigars and lavender-water not smelt since that early autumn night six months ago, when she had called him 'the limit.' Whence came it, or was it ghost of scent—sheer emanation from memory? She looked round her. Nothing—not a thing, no tiniest disturbance of her hall, nor of the diningroom. A little day-dream of a scent—illusory, saddening, silly! In the silver basket were new cards, two with 'Mr. and Mrs. Polegate Thom,' and one with 'Mr. Polegate Thom' thereon; she sniffed them, but they smelled severe. 'I must be tired,' she thought, 'I'll go and lie down.' Upstairs the drawing-room was darkened, waiting for some hand to give it evening light; and she passed on up to her bedroom. This, too, was half-curtained and dim, for it was six o'clock. Winifred threw off her coat—that scent again!—then stood, as if shot, transfixed against the bed-rail. Something dark had risen from the sofa in the far corner. A word of horror—in her family—escaped her: "God!"

"It's I—Monty," said a voice.

Clutching the bed-rail, Winifred reached up and turned the switch of the light hanging above her dressing-table. He appeared just on the rim of the light's circumference, emblazoned from the absence of his watch-chain down to boots neat and sooty brown, but—yes!—split at the toecap. His chest and face were shadowy. Surely he was thin—or was it a trick of the light? He advanced, lighted now from toe-cap to the top of his dark head—surely a little grizzled! His complexion had darkened, sallowed; his black moustache had lost boldness, become sardonic; there were lines which she did not know about his face. There was no pin in his tie. His suit—ah!—she knew that—but how unpressed, unglossy! She stared again at the toe-cap of his boot. Something big and relentless had been 'at him,' had turned and twisted, raked and scraped him. And she stayed, not speaking, motionless, staring at that crack across the toe.

"Well!" he said, "I got the order. I'm back."

Winifred's bosom began to heave. The nostalgia for her husband which had rushed up with that scent was struggling with a deeper jealousy than any she had felt yet. There he was—a dark, and as if harried, shadow of his sleek and brazen self! What force had done this to him—squeezed him like an orange to its dry rind! That woman!

"I'm back," he said again. "I've had a beastly time. By God! I came steerage. I've got nothing but what I stand up in, and that bag."

"And who has the rest?" cried Winifred, suddenly alive. "How dared you come? You knew it was just for divorce that you got that order to come back. Don't touch me!"

They held each to the rail of the big bed where they had spent so many years of nights together. Many times, yes—many times she had wanted him back. But now that he had come she was filled with this cold and deadly resentment. He put his hand up to his moustache; but did not frizz and twist it in the old familiar way, he just pulled it downwards.

"Gad!" he said: "If you knew the time I've had!"

"I'm glad I don't!"

"Are the kids all right?"

Winifred nodded. "How did you get in?"

"With my key."

"Then the maids don't know. You can't stay here, Monty."

He uttered a little sardonic laugh.

"Where then?"

"Anywhere."

"Well, look at me! That—that damned...."

"If you mention her," cried Winifred, "I go straight out to Park Lane and I don't come back."

Suddenly he did a simple thing, but so uncharacteristic that it moved her. He shut his eyes. It was as if he had said: 'All right! I'm dead to the world!'

"You can have a room for the night," she said; "your things are still here. Only Imogen is at home."

He leaned back against the bed-rail. "Well, it's in your hands," and his own made a writhing movement. "I've been through it. You needn't hit too hard—it isn't worth while. I've been frightened; I've been frightened, Freddie."

That old pet name, disused for years and years, sent a shiver through Winifred.

'What am I to do with him?' she thought. 'What in God's name am I to do with him?'

"Got a cigarette?"

She gave him one from a little box she kept up there for when she couldn't sleep at night, and lighted it. With that action the matter-of-fact side of her nature came to life again.

"Go and have a hot bath. I'll put some clothes out for you in the dressing-room. We can talk later."

He nodded, and fixed his eyes on her—they looked half-dead, or was it that the folds in the lids had become heavier?

'He's not the same,' she thought. He would never be quite the same again! But what would he be?

"All right!" he said, and went towards the door. He even moved differently, like a man who has lost illusion and doubts whether it is worth while to move at all.

When he was gone, and she heard the water in the bath running, she put out a complete set of garments on the bed in his dressing-room, then went downstairs and fetched up the biscuit box and whisky. Putting on her coat again, and listening a moment at the bathroom door, she went down and out. In the street she hesitated. Past seven o'clock! Would Soames be at his Club or at Park Lane? She turned towards the latter. Back!

Soames had always feared it—she had sometimes hoped it.... Back! So like him—clown that he was—with this: 'Here we are again!' to make fools of them all—of the Law, of Soames, of herself!

Yet to have done with the Law, not to have that murky cloud hanging over her and the children! What a relief! Ah! but how to accept his return? That 'woman' had ravaged him, taken from him passion such as he had never bestowed on herself, such as she had not thought him capable of. There was the sting! That selfish, blatant 'clown' of hers, whom she herself had never really stirred, had been swept and ungarnished by another woman! Insulting! Too insulting! Not right, not decent to take him back! And yet she had asked for him; the Law perhaps would make her now! He was as much her husband as ever—she had put herself out of court! And all he wanted, no doubt, was money—to keep him in cigars and lavender-water! That scent! 'After all, I'm not old,' she thought, 'not old yet!' But that woman who had reduced him to those words: 'I've been through it. I've been frightened—frightened, Freddie!' She neared her father's house, driven this way and that, while all the time the Forsyte undertow was drawing her to deep conclusion that after all he was her property, to be held against a robbing world. And so she came to James'.

"Mr. Soames? In his room? I'll go up; don't say I'm here."

Her brother was dressing. She found him before a mirror, tying a black bow with an air of despising its ends.

"Hullo!" he said, contemplating her in the glass; "what's wrong?"

"Monty!" said Winifred stonily.

Soames spun round. "What!"

"Back!"

"Hoist," muttered Soames, "with our own petard. Why the deuce didn't you let me try cruelty? I always knew it was too much risk this way."

"Oh! Don't talk about that! What shall I do?"

Soames answered, with a deep, deep sound.

"Well?" said Winifred impatiently.

"What has he to say for himself?"

"Nothing. One of his boots is split across the toe."

Soames stared at her.

"Ah!" he said, "of course! On his beam ends. So—it begins again! This'll about finish father."

"Can't we keep it from him?"

"Impossible. He has an uncanny flair for anything that's worrying."

And he brooded, with fingers hooked into his blue silk braces. "There ought to be some way in law," he muttered, "to make him safe."

"No," cried Winifred, "I won't be made a fool of again; I'd sooner put up with him."

The two stared at each other. Their hearts were full of feeling, but they could give it no expression—Forsytes that they were.

"Where did you leave him?"

"In the bath," and Winifred gave a little bitter laugh. "The only thing he's brought back is lavender-water."

"Steady!" said Soames, "you're thoroughly upset. I'll go back with you."

"What's the use?"

"We ought to make terms with him."

"Terms! It'll always be the same. When he recovers—cards and betting, drink and...!" She was silent, remembering the look on her husband's face. The burnt child—the burnt child. Perhaps...!

"Recovers?" replied Soames: "Is he ill?"

"No; burnt out; that's all."

Soames took his waistcoat from a chair and put it on, he took his coat and got into it, he scented his handkerchief with eau-de-Cologne, threaded his watch-chain, and said: "We haven't any luck."

And in the midst of her own trouble Winifred was sorry for him, as if in that little saying he had revealed deep trouble of his own.

"I'd like to see mother," she said.

"She'll be with father in their room. Come down quietly to the study. I'll get her."

Winifred stole down to the little dark study, chiefly remarkable for a Canaletto too doubtful to be placed elsewhere, and a fine collection of Law Reports unopened for many years. Here she stood, with her back to maroon-coloured curtains close-drawn, staring at the empty grate, till her mother came in followed by Soames.

"Oh! my poor dear!" said Emily: "How miserable you look in here! This is too bad of him, really!"

As a family they had so guarded themselves from the expression of all unfashionable emotion that it was impossible to go up and give her daughter a good hug. But there was comfort in her cushioned voice, and her still dimpled shoulders under some rare black lace. Summoning pride and the desire not to distress her mother, Winifred said in her most off-hand voice:

"It's all right, Mother; no good fussing."

"I don't see," said Emily, looking at Soames, "why Winifred shouldn't tell him that she'll prosecute him if he doesn't keep off the premises. He took her pearls; and if he's not brought them back, that's quite enough."

Winifred smiled. They would all plunge about with suggestions of this and that, but she knew already what she would be doing, and that was—nothing. The feeling that, after all, she had won a sort of victory, retained her property, was every moment gaining ground in her. No! if she wanted to punish him, she could do it at home without the world knowing.

"Well," said Emily, "come into the dining-room comfortably—you must stay and have dinner with us. Leave it to me to tell your father." And, as Winifred moved towards the door, she turned out the light. Not till then did they see the disaster in the corridor.

There, attracted by light from a room never lighted, James was standing with his duncoloured camel-hair shawl folded about him, so that his arms were not free and his silvered head looked cut off from his fashionably trousered legs as if by an expanse of desert. He stood, inimitably stork-like, with an expression as if he saw before him a frog too large to swallow.

"What's all this?" he said. "Tell your father? You never tell me anything."

The moment found Emily without reply. It was Winifred who went up to him, and, laying one hand on each of his swathed, helpless arms, said:

"Monty's not gone bankrupt, Father. He's only come back."

They all three expected something serious to happen, and were glad she had kept that grip of his arms, but they did not know the depth of root in that shadowy old Forsyte. Something wry occurred about his shaven mouth and chin, something scratchy between those long silvery whiskers. Then he said with a sort of dignity: "He'll be the death of me. I knew how it would be."

"You mustn't worry, Father," said Winifred calmly. "I mean to make him behave."

"Ah!" said James. "Here, take this thing off, I'm hot." They unwound the shawl. He turned, and walked firmly to the dining-room.

"I don't want any soup," he said to Warmson, and sat down in his chair. They all sat down too, Winifred still in her hat, while Warmson laid the fourth place. When he left the room, James said: "What's he brought back?"

"Nothing, Father."

James concentrated his eyes on his own image in a tablespoon. "Divorce!" he muttered; "rubbish! What was I about? I ought to have paid him an allowance to stay out of England. Soames you go and propose it to him."

It seemed so right and simple a suggestion that even Winifred was surprised when she said: "No, I'll keep him now he's back; he must just behave—that's all."

They all looked at her. It had always been known that Winifred had pluck.

"Out there!" said James elliptically, "who knows what cut-throats! You look for his revolver! Don't go to bed without. You ought to have Warmson to sleep in the house. I'll see him myself tomorrow."

They were touched by this declaration, and Emily said comfortably: "That's right, James, we won't have any nonsense."

"Ah!" muttered James darkly, "I can't tell."

The advent of Warmson with fish diverted conversation.

When, directly after dinner, Winifred went over to kiss her father good-night, he looked up with eyes so full of question and distress that she put all the comfort she could into her voice.

"It's all right, Daddy, dear; don't worry. I shan't need anyone—he's quite bland. I shall only be upset if you worry. Good-night, bless you!"

James repeated the words, "Bless you!" as if he did not quite know what they meant, and his eyes followed her to the door.

She reached home before nine, and went straight upstairs.

Dartie was lying on the bed in his dressing-room, fully redressed in a blue serge suit and pumps; his arms were crossed behind his head, and an extinct cigarette drooped from his mouth.

Winifred remembered ridiculously the flowers in her window-boxes after a blazing summer day; the way they lay, or rather stood—parched, yet rested by the sun's retreat. It was as if a little dew had come already on her burnt-up husband.

He said apathetically: "I suppose you've been to Park Lane. How's the old man?"

Winifred could not help the bitter answer: "Not dead."

He winced, actually he winced.

"Understand, Monty," she said, "I will not have him worried. If you aren't going to behave yourself, you may go back, you may go anywhere. Have you had dinner?"

No.

"Would you like some?"

He shrugged his shoulders.

"Imogen offered me some. I didn't want any."

Imogen! In the plenitude of emotion Winifred had forgotten her.

"So you've seen her? What did she say?"

"She gave me a kiss."

With mortification Winifred saw his dark sardonic face relaxed. 'Yes!' she thought, 'he cares for her, not for me a bit.'

Dartie's eyes were moving from side to side.

"Does she know about me?" he said.

It flashed through Winifred that here was the weapon she needed. He minded their knowing!

"No. Val knows. The others don't; they only know you went away."

She heard him sigh with relief.

"But they shall know," she said firmly, "if you give me cause."

"All right!" he muttered, "hit me! I'm down!"

Winifred went up to the bed. "Look here, Monty! I don't want to hit you. I don't want to hurt you. I shan't allude to anything. I'm not going to worry. What's the use?" She was silent a moment. "I can't stand any more, though, and I won't! You'd better know. You've made me suffer. But I used to be fond of you. For the sake of that...." She met the heavy-lidded gaze of his brown eyes with the downward stare of her green-grey eyes; touched his hand suddenly, turned her back, and went into her room.

She sat there a long time before her glass, fingering her rings, thinking of this subdued dark man, almost a stranger to her, on the bed in the other room; resolutely not 'worrying,' but gnawed by jealousy of what he had been through, and now and again just visited by pity.

CHAPTER XIV—OUTLANDISH NIGHT

Soames doggedly let the spring come—no easy task for one conscious that time was flying, his birds in the bush no nearer the hand, no issue from the web anywhere visible. Mr. Polteed reported nothing, except that his watch went on—costing a lot of money. Val and his cousin were gone to the war, whence came news more favourable; Dartie was behaving himself so far; James had retained his health; business prospered almost terribly—there was nothing to worry Soames except that he was 'held up,' could make no step in any direction.

He did not exactly avoid Soho, for he could not afford to let them think that he had 'piped off,' as James would have put it—he might want to 'pipe on' again at any minute. But he had to be so restrained and cautious that he would often pass the door of the Restaurant Bretagne without going in, and wander out of the purlieus of that region which always gave him the feeling of having been possessively irregular.

He wandered thus one May night into Regent Street and the most amazing crowd he had ever seen; a shrieking, whistling, dancing, jostling, grotesque and formidably jovial crowd, with false noses and mouth-organs, penny whistles and long feathers, every appanage of idiocy, as it seemed to him. Mafeking! Of course, it had been relieved! Good! But was that an excuse? Who were these people, what were they, where had they come from into the West End? His face was tickled, his ears whistled into. Girls cried: 'Keep your hair on, stucco!' A youth so knocked off his top-hat that he recovered it with difficulty. Crackers were exploding beneath his nose, between his feet. He was bewildered, exasperated, offended. This stream of people came from every quarter, as if impulse had unlocked flood-gates, let flow waters of whose existence he had heard, perhaps, but believed in never. This, then, was the populace, the innumerable living negation of gentility and Forsyteism. This was—egad!—Democracy! It stank, yelled, was hideous! In the East End, or even Soho, perhaps—but here in Regent Street, in Piccadilly! What were the police about! In 1900, Soames, with his Forsyte thousands, had never seen the cauldron with the lid off; and now looking into it, could hardly believe his scorching eyes. The whole thing was unspeakable! These people had no restraint, they seemed to think him funny; such swarms of them, rude, coarse, laughing—and what laughter!

Nothing sacred to them! He shouldn't be surprised if they began to break windows. In Pall Mall, past those august dwellings, to enter which people paid sixty pounds, this shrieking, whistling, dancing dervish of a crowd was swarming. From the Club windows his own kind were looking out on them with regulated amusement. They didn't realise! Why, this was serious—might come to anything! The crowd was cheerful, but some day they would come in different mood! He remembered there had been a mob in the late eighties, when he was at Brighton; they had smashed things and made speeches. But more than dread, he felt a deep surprise. They were hysterical—it wasn't English! And all about the relief of a little town as big as—Watford, six thousand miles away. Restraint, reserve! Those qualities to him more dear almost than life, those indispensable attributes of property and culture, where were they? It wasn't English! No, it wasn't English! So Soames brooded, threading his way on. It was as if he had suddenly caught sight of someone cutting the covenant 'for quiet possession' out of his legal documents; or of a monster lurking and stalking out in the future, casting its shadow before. Their want of stolidity, their want of reverence! It was like discovering that nine-tenths of the people of England were foreigners. And if that were so—then, anything might happen!

At Hyde Park Corner he ran into George Forsyte, very sunburnt from racing, holding a false nose in his hand.

"Hallo, Soames!" he said, "have a nose!"

Soames responded with a pale smile.

"Got this from one of these sportsmen," went on George, who had evidently been dining; "had to lay him out—for trying to bash my hat. I say, one of these days we shall have to fight these chaps, they're getting so damned cheeky—all radicals and socialists. They want our goods. You tell Uncle James that, it'll make him sleep."

'In vino veritas,' thought Soames, but he only nodded, and passed on up Hamilton Place. There was but a trickle of roysterers in Park Lane, not very noisy. And looking up at the houses he thought: 'After all, we're the backbone of the country. They won't upset us easily. Possession's nine points of the law.'

But, as he closed the door of his father's house behind him, all that queer outlandish nightmare in the streets passed out of his mind almost as completely as if, having dreamed it, he had awakened in the warm clean morning comfort of his spring-mattressed bed.

Walking into the centre of the great empty drawing-room, he stood still.

A wife! Somebody to talk things over with. One had a right! Damn it! One had a right!

PART III

CHAPTER I—SOAMES IN PARIS

Soames had travelled little. Aged nineteen he had made the 'petty tour' with his father, mother, and Winifred—Brussels, the Rhine, Switzerland, and home by way of Paris. Aged twenty-seven, just when he began to take interest in pictures, he had spent five hot weeks in Italy, looking into the Renaissance—not so much in it as he had been led to expect—and a fortnight in Paris on his way back, looking into himself, as became a Forsyte surrounded by people so strongly self-centred and 'foreign' as the French. His knowledge of their language being derived from his public school, he did not understand them when they spoke. Silence he had found better for all parties; one did not make a fool of oneself. He had disliked the look of the men's clothes, the closed-in cabs, the theatres which looked like bee-hives, the Galleries which smelled of beeswax. He was too cautious and too shy to explore that side of Paris supposed by Forsytes to constitute its attraction under the rose;

and as for a collector's bargain—not one to be had! As Nicholas might have put it—they were a grasping lot. He had come back uneasy, saying Paris was overrated.

When, therefore, in June of 1900 he went to Paris, it was but his third attempt on the centre of civilisation. This time, however, the mountain was going to Mahomet; for he felt by now more deeply civilised than Paris, and perhaps he really was. Moreover, he had a definite objective. This was no mere genuflexion to a shrine of taste and immorality, but the prosecution of his own legitimate affairs. He went, indeed, because things were getting past a joke. The watch went on and on, and—nothing—nothing! Jolyon had never returned to Paris, and no one else was 'suspect!' Busy with new and very confidential matters, Soames was realising more than ever how essential reputation is to a solicitor. But at night and in his leisure moments he was ravaged by the thought that time was always flying and money flowing in, and his own future as much 'in irons' as ever. Since Mafeking night he had become aware that a 'young fool of a doctor' was hanging round Annette. Twice he had come across him—a cheerful young fool, not more than thirty.

Nothing annoyed Soames so much as cheerfulness—an indecent, extravagant sort of quality, which had no relation to facts. The mixture of his desires and hopes was, in a word, becoming torture; and lately the thought had come to him that perhaps Irene knew she was being shadowed: It was this which finally decided him to go and see for himself; to go and once more try to break down her repugnance, her refusal to make her own and his path comparatively smooth once more. If he failed again—well, he would see what she did with herself, anyway!

He went to an hotel in the Rue Caumartin, highly recommended to Forsytes, where practically nobody spoke French. He had formed no plan. He did not want to startle her; yet must contrive that she had no chance to evade him by flight. And next morning he set out in bright weather.

Paris had an air of gaiety, a sparkle over its star-shape which almost annoyed Soames. He stepped gravely, his nose lifted a little sideways in real curiosity. He desired now to understand things French. Was not Annette French? There was much to be got out of his visit, if he could only get it. In this laudable mood and the Place de la Concorde he was nearly run down three times. He came on the 'Cours la Reine,' where Irene's hotel was situated, almost too suddenly, for he had not yet fixed on his procedure. Crossing over to the river side, he noted the building, white and cheerful-looking, with green sunblinds, seen through a screen of plane-tree leaves. And, conscious that it would be far better to meet her casually in some open place than to risk a call, he sat down on a bench whence he could watch the entrance. It was not quite eleven o'clock, and improbable that she had yet gone out. Some pigeons were strutting and preening their feathers in the pools of sunlight between the shadows of the plane-trees. A workman in a blue blouse passed, and threw them crumbs from the paper which contained his dinner. A 'bonne' coiffed with ribbon shepherded two little girls with pig-tails and frilled drawers. A cab meandered by, whose cocher wore a blue coat and a black-glazed hat. To Soames a kind of affectation seemed to cling about it all, a sort of picturesqueness which was out of date. A theatrical people, the French! He lit one of his rare cigarettes, with a sense of injury that Fate should be casting his life into outlandish waters. He shouldn't wonder if Irene quite enjoyed this foreign life; she had never been properly English—even to look at! And he began considering which of those windows could be hers under the green sunblinds. How could he word what he had come to say so that it might pierce the defence of her proud obstinacy? He threw the fag-end of his cigarette at a pigeon, with the thought: 'I can't stay here for ever twiddling my thumbs. Better give it up and call on her in the late afternoon.' But he still sat on, heard twelve strike, and then half-past. 'I'll wait till one,' he thought, 'while I'm about it.' But just then he started up, and shrinkingly sat down again. A woman had come out in a cream-coloured frock, and was moving away under a fawn-coloured parasol. Irene herself! He waited till she was too far away to recognise him, then set out after her. She was strolling as though she had no particular objective; moving, if he remembered rightly, toward the Bois de Boulogne. For half an hour at least he kept his distance on the far side of the way till she had passed into the Bois itself. Was she going to meet someone after all? Some confounded Frenchman—one of those 'Bel Ami' chaps, perhaps, who had nothing to do but hang about women—for he had read that book with difficulty and a sort of disgusted fascination. He followed doggedly along a shady alley, losing sight of her now and then when the path curved. And it came back to him how, long ago, one night in Hyde Park he had slid and sneaked from tree to tree, from seat to seat, hunting blindly, ridiculously, in burning jealousy for her and young Bosinney. The path bent sharply, and, hurrying, he came on her sitting in front of a small fountain—a little green-bronze Niobe veiled in hair to her slender hips, gazing at the pool she had wept: He came on her so suddenly that he was past before he could turn and take off his hat. She did not start up. She had always had great self-command—it was one of the things he most admired in her, one of his greatest grievances against her, because he had never been able to tell what she was thinking. Had she realised that he was following? Her self-possession made him angry; and, disdaining to explain his presence, he pointed to the mournful little Niobe, and said:

"That's rather a good thing."

He could see, then, that she was struggling to preserve her composure.

"I didn't want to startle you; is this one of your haunts?"

"Yes."

"A little lonely." As he spoke, a lady, strolling by, paused to look at the fountain and passed on.

Irene's eyes followed her.

"No," she said, prodding the ground with her parasol, "never lonely. One has always one's shadow."

Soames understood; and, looking at her hard, he exclaimed:

"Well, it's your own fault. You can be free of it at any moment. Irene, come back to me, and be free."

Irene laughed.

"Don't!" cried Soames, stamping his foot; "it's inhuman. Listen! Is there any condition I can make which will bring you back to me? If I promise you a separate house—and just a visit now and then?"

Irene rose, something wild suddenly in her face and figure.

"None! None! None! You may hunt me to the grave. I will not come."

Outraged and on edge, Soames recoiled.

"Don't make a scene!" he said sharply. And they both stood motionless, staring at the little Niobe, whose greenish flesh the sunlight was burnishing.

"That's your last word, then," muttered Soames, clenching his hands; "you condemn us both."

Irene bent her head. "I can't come back. Good-bye!"

A feeling of monstrous injustice flared up in Soames.

"Stop!" he said, "and listen to me a moment. You gave me a sacred vow—you came to me without a penny. You had all I could give you. You broke that vow without cause, you made me a by-word; you refused me a child; you've left me in prison; you—you still move me so that I want you—I want you. Well, what do you think of yourself?"

Irene turned, her face was deadly pale, her eyes burning dark.

"God made me as I am," she said; "wicked if you like—but not so wicked that I'll give myself again to a man I hate."

The sunlight gleamed on her hair as she moved away, and seemed to lay a caress all down her clinging cream-coloured frock.

Soames could neither speak nor move. That word 'hate'—so extreme, so primitive—made all the Forsyte in him tremble. With a deep imprecation he strode away from where she had vanished, and ran almost into the arms of the lady sauntering back—the fool, the shadowing fool!

He was soon dripping with perspiration, in the depths of the Bois.

'Well,' he thought, 'I need have no consideration for her now; she has not a grain of it for me. I'll show her this very day that she's my wife still.'

But on the way home to his hotel, he was forced to the conclusion that he did not know what he meant. One could not make scenes in public, and short of scenes in public what was there he could do? He almost cursed his own thin-skinnedness. She might deserve no consideration; but he—alas! deserved some at his own hands. And sitting lunchless in the hall of his hotel, with tourists passing every moment, Baedeker in hand, he was visited by black dejection. In irons! His whole life, with every natural instinct and every decent yearning gagged and fettered, and all because Fate had driven him seventeen years ago to set his heart upon this woman—so utterly, that even now he had no real heart to set on any other! Cursed was the day he had met her, and his eyes for seeing in her anything but the cruel Venus she was! And yet, still seeing her with the sunlight on the clinging China crepe of her gown, he uttered a little groan, so that a tourist who was passing, thought: 'Man in pain! Let's see! what did I have for lunch?'

Later, in front of a cafe near the Opera, over a glass of cold tea with lemon and a straw in it, he took the malicious resolution to go and dine at her hotel. If she were there, he would speak to her; if she were not, he would leave a note. He dressed carefully, and wrote as follows:

"Your idyll with that fellow Jolyon Forsyte is known to me at all events. If you pursue it, understand that I will leave no stone unturned to make things unbearable for him. 'S. F.'"

He sealed this note but did not address it, refusing to write the maiden name which she had impudently resumed, or to put the word Forsyte on the envelope lest she should tear it up unread. Then he went out, and made his way through the glowing streets, abandoned to evening pleasure-seekers. Entering her hotel, he took his seat in a far corner of the dining-room whence he could see all entrances and exits. She was not there. He ate little, quickly, watchfully. She did not come. He lingered in the lounge over his coffee, drank two liqueurs of brandy. But still she did not come. He went over to the keyboard and examined the names. Number twelve, on the first floor! And he determined to take the note up himself. He mounted red-carpeted stairs, past a little salon; eight-ten-twelve! Should he knock, push the note under, or...? He looked furtively round and turned the handle. The door opened, but into a little space leading to another door; he knocked on that—no answer. The door was locked. It fitted very closely to the floor; the note would not go under. He thrust it back into his pocket, and stood a moment listening. He felt somehow certain that she was not there. And suddenly he came away, passing the little salon down the stairs. He stopped at the bureau and said:

"Will you kindly see that Mrs. Heron has this note?"

"Madame Heron left to-day, Monsieur—suddenly, about three o'clock. There was illness in her family."

Soames compressed his lips. "Oh!" he said; "do you know her address?"

"Non, Monsieur. England, I think."

Soames put the note back into his pocket and went out. He hailed an open horse-cab which was passing.

"Drive me anywhere!"

The man, who, obviously, did not understand, smiled, and waved his whip. And Soames was borne along in that little yellow-wheeled Victoria all over star-shaped Paris, with here and there a pause, and the question, "C'est par ici, Monsieur?" "No, go on," till the man gave it up in despair, and the yellow-wheeled chariot continued to roll between the tall, flat-fronted shuttered houses and plane-tree avenues—a little Flying Dutchman of a cab.

'Like my life,' thought Soames, 'without object, on and on!'

CHAPTER II—IN THE WEB

Soames returned to England the following day, and on the third morning received a visit from Mr. Polteed, who wore a flower and carried a brown billycock hat. Soames motioned him to a seat.

"The news from the war is not so bad, is it?" said Mr. Polteed. "I hope I see you well, sir."

"Thanks! quite."

Mr. Polteed leaned forward, smiled, opened his hand, looked into it, and said softly:

"I think we've done your business for you at last."

"What?" ejaculated Soames.

"Nineteen reports quite suddenly what I think we shall be justified in calling conclusive evidence," and Mr. Polteed paused.

"Well?"

"On the 10th instant, after witnessing an interview between 17 and a party, earlier in the day, 19 can swear to having seen him coming out of her bedroom in the hotel about ten o'clock in the evening. With a little care in the giving of the evidence that will be enough, especially as 17 has left Paris—no doubt with the party in question. In fact, they both slipped off, and we haven't got on to them again, yet; but we shall—we shall. She's worked hard under very difficult circumstances, and I'm glad she's brought it off at last." Mr. Polteed took out a cigarette, tapped its end against the table, looked at Soames, and put it back. The expression on his client's face was not encouraging.

"Who is this new person?" said Soames abruptly.

"That we don't know. She'll swear to the fact, and she's got his appearance pat."

Mr. Polteed took out a letter, and began reading:

"'Middle-aged, medium height, blue dittoes in afternoon, evening dress at night, pale, dark hair, small dark moustache, flat cheeks, good chin, grey eyes, small feet, guilty look....'"

Soames rose and went to the window. He stood there in sardonic fury. Congenital idiot—spidery congenital idiot! Seven months at fifteen pounds a week—to be tracked down as his own wife's lover! Guilty look! He threw the window open.

"It's hot," he said, and came back to his seat.

Crossing his knees, he bent a supercilious glance on Mr. Polteed.

"I doubt if that's quite good enough," he said, drawling the words, "with no name or address. I think you may let that lady have a rest, and take up our friend 47 at this end." Whether Polteed had spotted him he could not tell; but he had a mental vision of him in the midst of his cronies dissolved in inextinguishable laughter. 'Guilty look!' Damnation!

Mr. Polteed said in a tone of urgency, almost of pathos: "I assure you we have put it through sometimes on less than that. It's Paris, you know. Attractive woman living alone. Why not risk it, sir? We might screw it up a peg."

Soames had sudden insight. The fellow's professional zeal was stirred: 'Greatest triumph of my career; got a man his divorce through a visit to his own wife's bedroom! Something to talk of there, when I retire!' And for one wild moment he thought: 'Why not?' After all, hundreds of men of medium height had small feet and a guilty look!

"I'm not authorised to take any risk!" he said shortly.

Mr. Polteed looked up.

"Pity," he said, "quite a pity! That other affair seemed very costive."

Soames rose.

"Never mind that. Please watch 47, and take care not to find a mare's nest. Good-morning!"

Mr. Polteed's eye glinted at the words 'mare's nest!'

"Very good. You shall be kept informed."

And Soames was alone again. The spidery, dirty, ridiculous business! Laying his arms on the table, he leaned his forehead on them. Full ten minutes he rested thus, till a managing clerk roused him with the draft prospectus of a new issue of shares, very desirable, in Manifold and Topping's. That afternoon he left work early and made his way to the Restaurant Bretagne. Only Madame Lamotte was in. Would Monsieur have tea with her?

Soames bowed.

When they were seated at right angles to each other in the little room, he said abruptly:

"I want a talk with you, Madame."

The quick lift of her clear brown eyes told him that she had long expected such words.

"I have to ask you something first: That young doctor—what's his name? Is there anything between him and Annette?"

Her whole personality had become, as it were, like jet—clear-cut, black, hard, shining.

"Annette is young," she said; "so is monsieur le docteur. Between young people things move quickly; but Annette is a good daughter. Ah! what a jewel of a nature!"

The least little smile twisted Soames' lips.

"Nothing definite, then?"

"But definite—no, indeed! The young man is veree nice, but—what would you? There is no money at present."

She raised her willow-patterned tea-cup; Soames did the same. Their eyes met.

"I am a married man," he said, "living apart from my wife for many years. I am seeking to divorce her."

Madame Lamotte put down her cup. Indeed! What tragic things there were! The entire absence of sentiment in her inspired a queer species of contempt in Soames.

"I am a rich man," he added, fully conscious that the remark was not in good taste. "It is useless to say more at present, but I think you understand."

Madame's eyes, so open that the whites showed above them, looked at him very straight.

"Ah! ca—mais nous avons le temps!" was all she said. "Another little cup?" Soames refused, and, taking his leave, walked westward.

He had got that off his mind; she would not let Annette commit herself with that cheerful young ass until...! But what chance of his ever being able to say: 'I'm free.' What chance? The future had lost all semblance of reality. He felt like a fly, entangled in cobweb filaments, watching the desirable freedom of the air with pitiful eyes.

He was short of exercise, and wandered on to Kensington Gardens, and down Queen's Gate towards Chelsea. Perhaps she had gone back to her flat. That at all events he could find out. For since that last and most ignominious repulse his wounded self-respect had taken refuge again in the feeling that she must have a lover. He arrived before the little Mansions at the dinner-hour. No need to enquire! A grey-haired lady was watering the flower-boxes in her window. It was evidently let. And he walked slowly past again, along the river—an evening of clear, quiet beauty, all harmony and comfort, except within his heart.

CHAPTER III—RICHMOND PARK

On the afternoon that Soames crossed to France a cablegram was received by Jolyon at Robin Hill:

"Your son down with enteric no immediate danger will cable again."

It reached a household already agitated by the imminent departure of June, whose berth was booked for the following day. She was, indeed, in the act of confiding Eric Cobbley and his family to her father's care when the message arrived.

The resolution to become a Red Cross nurse, taken under stimulus of Jolly's enlistment, had been loyally fulfilled with the irritation and regret which all Forsytes feel at what curtails their individual liberties. Enthusiastic at first about the 'wonderfulness' of the work, she had begun after a month to feel that she could train herself so much better than others could train her. And if Holly had not insisted on following her example, and being trained too, she must inevitably have 'cried off.' The departure of Jolly and Val with their troop in April had further stiffened her failing resolve. But now, on the point of departure, the thought of leaving Eric Cobbley, with a wife and two children, adrift in the cold waters of an unappreciative world weighed on her so that she was still in danger of backing out. The reading of that cablegram, with its disquieting reality, clinched the matter. She saw herself already nursing Jolly—for of course they would let her nurse her own brother! Jolyon—ever wide and doubtful—had no such hope. Poor June!

Could any Forsyte of her generation grasp how rude and brutal life was? Ever since he knew of his boy's arrival at Cape Town the thought of him had been a kind of recurrent sickness in Jolyon. He could not get reconciled to the feeling that Jolly was in danger all the time. The cablegram, grave though it was, was almost a relief. He was now safe from bullets, anyway. And yet—this enteric was a virulent disease! The Times was full of deaths therefrom. Why could he not be lying out there in that up-country hospital, and his boy safe at home? The un-Forsytean self-sacrifice of his three children, indeed, had quite bewildered Jolyon. He would eagerly change places with Jolly, because he loved his boy; but no such personal motive was influencing them. He could only think that it marked the decline of the Forsyte type.

Late that afternoon Holly came out to him under the old oak-tree. She had grown up very much during these last months of hospital training away from home. And, seeing her approach, he thought: 'She has more sense than June, child though she is; more wisdom. Thank God she isn't going out.' She had seated herself in the swing, very silent and still. 'She feels this,' thought Jolyon, 'as much as I' and, seeing her eyes fixed on him, he said: "Don't take it to heart too much, my child. If he weren't ill, he might be in much greater danger."

Holly got out of the swing.

"I want to tell you something, Dad. It was through me that Jolly enlisted and went out."

"How's that?"

"When you were away in Paris, Val Dartie and I fell in love. We used to ride in Richmond Park; we got engaged. Jolly found it out, and thought he ought to stop it; so he dared Val to enlist. It was all my fault, Dad; and I want to go out too. Because if anything happens to either of them I should feel awful. Besides, I'm just as much trained as June."

Jolyon gazed at her in a stupefaction that was tinged with irony. So this was the answer to the riddle he had been asking himself; and his three children were Forsytes after all. Surely Holly might have told him all this before! But he smothered the sarcastic sayings on his lips. Tenderness to the young was perhaps the most sacred article of his belief. He had got, no doubt, what he deserved. Engaged! So this was why he had so lost touch with her! And to young Val Dartie—nephew of Soames—in the other camp! It was all terribly distasteful. He closed his easel, and set his drawing against the tree.

"Have you told June?"

"Yes; she says she'll get me into her cabin somehow. It's a single cabin; but one of us could sleep on the floor. If you consent, she'll go up now and get permission."

'Consent?' thought Jolyon. 'Rather late in the day to ask for that!' But again he checked himself.

"You're too young, my dear; they won't let you."

"June knows some people that she helped to go to Cape Town. If they won't let me nurse yet, I could stay with them and go on training there. Let me go, Dad!"

Jolyon smiled because he could have cried.

"I never stop anyone from doing anything," he said.

Holly flung her arms round his neck.

"Oh! Dad, you are the best in the world."

'That means the worst,' thought Jolyon. If he had ever doubted his creed of tolerance he did so then.

"I'm not friendly with Val's family," he said, "and I don't know Val, but Jolly didn't like him."

Holly looked at the distance and said:

"I love him."

"That settles it," said Jolyon dryly, then catching the expression on her face, he kissed her, with the thought: 'Is anything more pathetic than the faith of the young?' Unless he actually forbade her going it was obvious that he must make the best of it, so he went up to town with June. Whether due to her persistence, or the fact that the official they saw was an old school friend of Jolyon's, they obtained permission for Holly to share the single cabin. He took them to Surbiton station the following evening, and they duly slid away from him, provided with money, invalid foods, and those letters of credit without which Forsytes do not travel.

He drove back to Robin Hill under a brilliant sky to his late dinner, served with an added care by servants trying to show him that they sympathised, eaten with an added scrupulousness to show them that he appreciated their sympathy. But it was a real relief to get to his cigar on the terrace of flag-stones—cunningly chosen by young Bosinney for shape and colour—with night closing in around him, so beautiful a night, hardly whispering in the trees, and smelling so sweet that it made him ache. The grass was drenched with dew, and he kept to those flagstones, up and down, till presently it began to seem to him that he was one of three, not wheeling, but turning right about at each end, so that his father was always nearest to the house, and his son always nearest to the terrace edge. Each had an arm lightly within his arm; he dared not lift his hand to his cigar lest he should disturb them, and it burned away, dripping ash on him, till it dropped from his lips, at last, which were getting hot. They left him then, and his arms felt chilly. Three Jolyons in one Jolyon they had walked.

He stood still, counting the sounds—a carriage passing on the highroad, a distant train, the dog at Gage's farm, the whispering trees, the groom playing on his penny whistle. A multitude of stars up there—bright and silent, so far off! No moon as yet! Just enough light to show him the dark flags and swords of the iris flowers along the terrace edge—his favourite flower that had the night's own colour on its curving crumpled petals. He turned round to the house. Big, unlighted, not a soul beside himself to live in all that part of it. Stark loneliness! He could not go on living here alone. And yet, so long as there was beauty, why should a man feel lonely? The answer—as to some idiot's riddle—was: Because he did. The greater the beauty, the greater the loneliness, for at the back of beauty was harmony, and at the back of harmony was—union. Beauty could not comfort if the soul were out of it. The night, maddeningly lovely, with bloom of grapes on it in starshine, and the breath of grass and honey coming from it, he could not enjoy, while she who was to him the life of beauty, its embodiment and essence, was cut off from him, utterly cut off now, he felt, by honourable decency.

He made a poor fist of sleeping, striving too hard after that resignation which Forsytes find difficult to reach, bred to their own way and left so comfortably off by their fathers. But after dawn he dozed off, and soon was dreaming a strange dream.

He was on a stage with immensely high rich curtains—high as the very stars—stretching in a semi-circle from footlights to footlights. He himself was very small, a little black restless figure roaming up and down; and the odd thing was that he was not altogether himself, but Soames as well, so that he was not only experiencing but watching. This figure of himself and Soames was trying to find a way out through the curtains, which, heavy and dark, kept him in. Several times he had crossed in front of them before he saw with delight a sudden narrow rift—a tall chink of beauty the colour of iris flowers, like a glimpse of Paradise, remote, ineffable. Stepping quickly forward to pass into it, he found the curtains closing before him. Bitterly disappointed he—or was it Soames?—moved on, and there was the chink again through the parted curtains, which again closed too soon. This went on and on and he never got through till he woke with the word "Irene" on his lips. The dream disturbed him badly, especially that identification of himself with Soames.

Next morning, finding it impossible to work, he spent hours riding Jolly's horse in search of fatigue. And on the second day he made up his mind to move to London and see if he could not get permission to follow his daughters to South Africa. He had just begun to pack the following morning when he received this letter:

"GREEN HOTEL,

"June 13.

"RICHMOND. "MY DEAR JOLYON,

"You will be surprised to see how near I am to you. Paris became impossible—and I have come here to be within reach of your advice. I would so love to see you again. Since you left Paris I don't think I have met anyone I could really talk to. Is all well with you and with your boy? No one knows, I think, that I am here at present.

"Always your friend,

"IRENE."

Irene within three miles of him!—and again in flight! He stood with a very queer smile on his lips. This was more than he had bargained for!

About noon he set out on foot across Richmond Park, and as he went along, he thought: 'Richmond Park! By Jove, it suits us Forsytes!' Not that Forsytes lived there—nobody lived there save royalty, rangers, and the deer—but in Richmond Park Nature was allowed to go so far and no further, putting up a brave show of being natural, seeming to say: 'Look at my instincts—they are almost passions, very nearly out of hand, but not quite, of course; the very hub of possession is to possess oneself.' Yes! Richmond Park possessed itself, even on that bright day of June, with arrowy cuckoos shifting the tree-points of their calls, and the wood doves announcing high summer.

The Green Hotel, which Jolyon entered at one o'clock, stood nearly opposite that more famous hostelry, the Crown and Sceptre; it was modest, highly respectable, never out of cold beef, gooseberry tart, and a dowager or two, so that a carriage and pair was almost always standing before the door.

In a room draped in chintz so slippery as to forbid all emotion, Irene was sitting on a piano stool covered with crewel work, playing 'Hansel and Gretel' out of an old score. Above her on a wall, not yet Morris-papered, was a print of the Queen on a pony, amongst deer-hounds, Scotch caps, and slain stags; beside her in a pot on the window-sill was a white and rosy fuchsia. The Victorianism of the room almost talked; and in her clinging frock Irene seemed to Jolyon like Venus emerging from the shell of the past century.

"If the proprietor had eyes," he said, "he would show you the door; you have broken through his decorations." Thus lightly he smothered up an emotional moment. Having eaten cold beef, pickled walnut, gooseberry tart, and drunk stone-bottle ginger-beer, they walked into the Park, and light talk was succeeded by the silence Jolyon had dreaded.

"You haven't told me about Paris," he said at last.

"No. I've been shadowed for a long time; one gets used to that. But then Soames came. By the little Niobe—the same story; would I go back to him?"

"Incredible!"

She had spoken without raising her eyes, but she looked up now. Those dark eyes clinging to his said as no words could have: 'I have come to an end; if you want me, here I am.'

For sheer emotional intensity had he ever—old as he was—passed through such a moment?

The words: 'Irene, I adore you!' almost escaped him. Then, with a clearness of which he would not have believed mental vision capable, he saw Jolly lying with a white face turned to a white wall.

"My boy is very ill out there," he said quietly.

Irene slipped her arm through his.

"Let's walk on; I understand."

No miserable explanation to attempt! She had understood! And they walked on among the bracken, knee-high already, between the rabbit-holes and the oak-trees, talking of Jolly. He left her two hours later at the Richmond Hill Gate, and turned towards home.

'She knows of my feeling for her, then,' he thought. Of course! One could not keep knowledge of that from such a woman!

CHAPTER IV—OVER THE RIVER

Jolly was tired to death of dreams. They had left him now too wan and weak to dream again; left him to lie torpid, faintly remembering far-off things; just able to turn his eyes and gaze through the window near his cot at the trickle of river running by in the sands, at the straggling milk-bush of the Karoo beyond. He knew what the Karoo was now, even if he had not seen a Boer roll over like a rabbit, or heard the whine of flying bullets. This pestilence had sneaked on him before he had smelled powder. A thirsty day and a rash drink, or perhaps a tainted fruit—who knew? Not he, who had not even strength left to grudge the evil thing its victory—just enough to know that there were many lying here with him, that he was sore with frenzied dreaming; just enough to watch that thread of river and be able to remember faintly those far-away things....

The sun was nearly down. It would be cooler soon. He would have liked to know the time—to feel his old watch, so butter-smooth, to hear the repeater strike. It would have been friendly, home-like. He had not even strength to remember that the old watch was last wound the day he began to lie here. The pulse of his brain beat so feebly that faces which came and went, nurse's, doctor's, orderly's, were indistinguishable, just one indifferent face; and the words spoken about him meant all the same thing, and that almost nothing. Those things he used to do, though far and faint, were more distinct—walking past the foot of the old steps at Harrow 'bill'—'Here, sir! Here, sir!'—wrapping boots in the Westminster Gazette, greenish paper, shining boots—grandfather coming from somewhere dark—a smell of earth—the mushroom house! Robin Hill! Burying poor old Balthasar in the leaves! Dad! Home....

Consciousness came again with noticing that the river had no water in it—someone was speaking too. Want anything? No. What could one want? Too weak to want—only to hear his watch strike....

Holly! She wouldn't bowl properly. Oh! Pitch them up! Not sneaks!... 'Back her, Two and Bow!' He was Two!... Consciousness came once more with a sense of the violet dusk outside, and a rising blood-red crescent moon. His eyes rested on it fascinated; in the long minutes of brain-nothingness it went moving up and up....

"He's going, doctor!" Not pack boots again? Never? 'Mind your form, Two!' Don't cry! Go quietly—over the river—sleep!... Dark? If somebody would—strike—his—watch!...

CHAPTER V—SOAMES ACTS

A sealed letter in the handwriting of Mr. Polteed remained unopened in Soames' pocket throughout two hours of sustained attention to the affairs of the 'New Colliery Company,' which, declining almost from the moment of old Jolyon's retirement from the Chairmanship, had lately run down so fast that there was now nothing for it but a 'winding-up.' He took the letter out to lunch at his City Club, sacred to him for the meals he had eaten there with his father in the early seventies, when James used to like him to come and see for himself the nature of his future life.

Here in a remote corner before a plate of roast mutton and mashed potato, he read:

"DEAR SIR,

"In accordance with your suggestion we have duly taken the matter up at the other end with gratifying results. Observation of 47 has enabled us to locate 17 at the Green Hotel, Richmond. The two have been observed to meet daily during the past week in Richmond Park. Nothing absolutely crucial has so far been notified. But in conjunction with what we had from Paris at the beginning of the year, I am confident we could now satisfy the Court. We shall, of course, continue to watch the matter until we hear from you.

"Very faithfully yours,

"CLAUD POLTEED."

Soames read it through twice and beckoned to the waiter:

"Take this away; it's cold."

"Shall I bring you some more, sir?"

"No. Get me some coffee in the other room."

And, paying for what he had not eaten, he went out, passing two acquaintances without sign of recognition.

'Satisfy the Court!' he thought, sitting at a little round marble table with the coffee before him. That fellow Jolyon! He poured out his coffee, sweetened and drank it. He would disgrace him in the eyes of his own children! And rising, with that resolution hot within him, he found for the first time the inconvenience of being his own solicitor. He could not treat this scandalous matter in his own office. He must commit the soul of his private dignity to a stranger, some other professional dealer in family dishonour. Who was there he could go to? Linkman and Laver in Budge Row, perhaps—reliable, not too conspicuous, only nodding acquaintances. But before he saw them he must see Polteed again. But at this thought Soames had a moment of sheer weakness. To part with his secret? How find the words? How subject himself to contempt and secret laughter? Yet, after all, the fellow knew already—oh yes, he knew! And, feeling that he must finish with it now, he took a cab into the West End.

In this hot weather the window of Mr. Polteed's room was positively open, and the only precaution was a wire gauze, preventing the intrusion of flies. Two or three had tried to come in, and been caught, so that they seemed to be clinging there with the intention of being devoured presently. Mr. Polteed, following the direction of his client's eye, rose apologetically and closed the window.

'Posing ass!' thought Soames. Like all who fundamentally believe in themselves he was rising to the occasion, and, with his little sideway smile, he said: "I've had your letter. I'm going to act. I suppose you know who the lady you've been watching really is?" Mr. Polteed's expression at that moment was a masterpiece. It so clearly said: 'Well, what do you think? But mere professional knowledge, I assure you—pray forgive it!' He made a little half airy movement with his hand, as who should say: 'Such things—such things will happen to us all!'

"Very well, then," said Soames, moistening his lips: "there's no need to say more. I'm instructing Linkman and Laver of Budge Row to act for me. I don't want to hear your evidence, but kindly make your report to them at five o'clock, and continue to observe the utmost secrecy."

Mr. Polteed half closed his eyes, as if to comply at once. "My dear sir," he said.

"Are you convinced," asked Soames with sudden energy, "that there is enough?"

The faintest movement occurred to Mr. Polteed's shoulders.

"You can risk it," he murmured; "with what we have, and human nature, you can risk it."

Soames rose. "You will ask for Mr. Linkman. Thanks; don't get up." He could not bear Mr. Polteed to slide as usual between him and the door. In the sunlight of Piccadilly he wiped his forehead. This had been the worst of it—he could stand the strangers better. And he went back into the City to do what still lay before him.

That evening in Park Lane, watching his father dine, he was overwhelmed by his old longing for a son—a son, to watch him eat as he went down the years, to be taken on his knee as James on a time had been wont to take him; a son of his own begetting, who could understand him because he was the same flesh and blood—understand, and comfort him, and become more rich and cultured than himself because he would start even better off. To get old—like that thin, grey wiry-frail figure sitting there—and be quite alone with possessions heaping up around him; to take no interest in anything because it had no future and must pass away from him to hands and mouths and eyes for whom he cared no jot! No! He would force it through now, and be free to marry, and have a son to care for him before he grew to be like the old old man his father, wistfully watching now his sweetbread, now his son.

In that mood he went up to bed. But, lying warm between those fine linen sheets of Emily's providing, he was visited by memories and torture. Visions of Irene, almost the solid feeling of her body, beset him. Why had he ever been fool enough to see her again, and let this flood back on him so that it was pain to think of her with that fellow—that stealing fellow.

CHAPTER VI—A SUMMER DAY

His boy was seldom absent from Jolyon's mind in the days which followed the first walk with Irene in Richmond Park. No further news had come; enquiries at the War Office elicited nothing; nor could he expect to hear from June and Holly for three weeks at least. In these days he felt how insufficient were his memories of Jolly, and what an amateur of a father he had been. There was not a single memory in which anger played a part; not one reconciliation, because there had never been a rupture; nor one heart-to-heart confidence, not even when Jolly's mother died. Nothing but half-ironical affection. He had been too afraid of committing himself in any direction, for fear of losing his liberty, or interfering with that of his boy.

Only in Irene's presence had he relief, highly complicated by the ever-growing perception of how divided he was between her and his son. With Jolly was bound up all that sense of continuity and social creed of which he had drunk deeply in his youth and again during his boy's public school and varsity life—all that sense of not going back on what father and son expected of each other. With Irene was bound up all his delight in beauty and in Nature. And he seemed to know less and less which was the stronger within him. From such sentimental paralysis he was rudely awakened, however, one afternoon, just as he was starting off to Richmond, by a young man with a bicycle and a face oddly familiar, who came forward faintly smiling.

"Mr. Jolyon Forsyte? Thank you!" Placing an envelope in Jolyon's hand he wheeled off the path and rode away. Bewildered, Jolyon opened it.

"Admiralty Probate and Divorce, Forsyte v. Forsyte and Forsyte!"

A sensation of shame and disgust was followed by the instant reaction 'Why, here's the very thing you want, and you don't like it!' But she must have had one too; and he must go to her at once. He turned things over as he went along. It was an ironical business. For, whatever the Scriptures said about the heart, it took more than mere longings to satisfy the law. They could perfectly well defend this suit, or at least in good faith try to. But the idea of doing so revolted Jolyon. If not her lover in deed he was in desire, and he knew that she was ready to come to him. Her face had told him so. Not that he exaggerated her feeling for him. She had had her grand passion, and he could not expect another from her at his age. But she had trust in him, affection for him, and must feel that he would be a refuge. Surely she would not ask him to defend the suit, knowing that he adored her! Thank Heaven she had not that maddening British conscientiousness which refused happiness for the sake of refusing! She must rejoice at this chance of being free after seventeen years of death in life! As to publicity, the fat was in the fire! To defend the suit would not take away the slur. Jolyon had all the proper feeling of a Forsyte whose privacy is threatened: If he was to be hung by the Law, by all means let it be for a sheep! Moreover the notion of standing in a witness box and swearing to the truth that no gesture, not even a word of love had passed between them seemed to him more degrading than to take the tacit stigma of being an adulterer—more truly degrading, considering the feeling in his heart, and just as bad and painful for his children. The thought of explaining away, if he could, before a judge and twelve average Englishmen, their meetings in Paris, and the walks in Richmond Park, horrified him. The brutality and hypocritical censoriousness of the whole process; the probability that they would not be believed—the mere vision of her, whom he looked on as the embodiment of Nature and of Beauty, standing there before all those suspicious, gloating eyes was hideous to him. No, no! To defend a suit only made a London holiday, and sold the newspapers. A thousand times better accept what Soames and the gods had sent!

'Besides,' he thought honestly, 'who knows whether, even for my boy's sake, I could have stood this state of things much longer? Anyway, her neck will be out of chancery at last!' Thus absorbed, he was hardly conscious of the heavy heat. The sky had become overcast, purplish with little streaks of white. A heavy heat-drop plashed a little star pattern in the dust of the road as he entered the Park. 'Phew!' he thought, 'thunder! I hope she's not come to meet me; there's a ducking up there!' But at that very minute he saw Irene coming towards the Gate. 'We must scuttle back to Robin Hill,' he thought.

The storm had passed over the Poultry at four o'clock, bringing welcome distraction to the clerks in every office. Soames was drinking a cup of tea when a note was brought in to him:

"DEAR SIR,

"Forsyte v. Forsyte and Forsyte

"In accordance with your instructions, we beg to inform you that we personally served the respondent and co-respondent in this suit to-day, at Richmond, and Robin Hill, respectively.

"Faithfully yours,

"LINKMAN AND LAVER."

For some minutes Soames stared at that note. Ever since he had given those instructions he had been tempted to annul them. It was so scandalous, such a general disgrace! The evidence, too, what he had heard of it, had never seemed to him conclusive; somehow, he believed less and less that those two had gone all lengths. But this, of course, would drive them to it; and he suffered from the thought. That fellow to have her love, where he had failed! Was it too late? Now that they had been brought up sharp by service of this petition, had he not a lever with which he could force them apart? 'But if I don't act at once,' he thought, 'it will be too late, now they've had this thing. I'll go and see him; I'll go down!'

And, sick with nervous anxiety, he sent out for one of the 'new-fangled' motor-cabs. It might take a long time to run that fellow to ground, and Goodness knew what decision they might come to after such a shock! 'If I were a theatrical ass,' he thought, 'I suppose I should be taking a horse-whip or a pistol or something!' He took instead a bundle of papers in the case of 'Magentie versus Wake,' intending to read them on the way down. He did not even open them, but sat quite still, jolted and jarred, unconscious of the draught down the back of his neck, or the smell of petrol. He must be guided by the fellow's attitude; the great thing was to keep his head!

London had already begun to disgorge its workers as he neared Putney Bridge; the ant-heap was on the move outwards. What a lot of ants, all with a living to get, holding on by their eyelids in the great scramble! Perhaps for the first time in his life Soames thought: 'I could let go if I liked! Nothing could touch me; I could snap my fingers, live as I wished—enjoy myself!' No! One could not live as he had and just drop it all—settle down in Capua, to spend the money and reputation he had made. A man's life was what he possessed and sought to possess. Only fools thought otherwise—fools, and socialists, and libertines!

The cab was passing villas now, going a great pace. 'Fifteen miles an hour, I should think!' he mused; 'this'll take people out of town to live!' and he thought of its bearing on the portions of London owned by his father—he himself had never taken to that form of investment, the gambler in him having all the outlet needed in his pictures. And the cab sped on, down the hill past Wimbledon Common. This interview! Surely a man of fifty-two with grown-up children, and hung on the line, would not be reckless. 'He won't want to disgrace the family,' he thought; 'he was as fond of his father as I am of mine, and they were brothers. That woman brings destruction—what is it in her? I've never known.' The cab branched off, along the side of a wood, and he heard a late cuckoo calling, almost the first he had heard that year. He was now almost opposite the site he had originally chosen for his house, and which had been so unceremoniously rejected by Bosinney in favour of his own choice. He began passing his handkerchief over his face and hands, taking deep breaths to give him steadiness. 'Keep one's head,' he thought, 'keep one's head!'

The cab turned in at the drive which might have been his own, and the sound of music met him. He had forgotten the fellow's daughters.

"I may be out again directly," he said to the driver, "or I may be kept some time"; and he rang the bell.

Following the maid through the curtains into the inner hall, he felt relieved that the impact of this meeting would be broken by June or Holly, whichever was playing in there, so that with complete surprise he saw Irene at the piano, and Jolyon sitting in an armchair listening. They both stood up. Blood surged into Soames' brain, and all his resolution to be guided by this or that left him utterly. The look of his farmer forbears—dogged Forsytes down by the sea, from 'Superior Dosset' back—grinned out of his face.

"Very pretty!" he said.

He heard the fellow murmur:

"This is hardly the place—we'll go to the study, if you don't mind." And they both passed him through the curtain opening. In the little room to which he followed them, Irene stood by the open window, and the 'fellow' close to her by a big chair. Soames pulled the door to behind him with a slam; the sound carried him back all those years to the day when he had shut out Jolyon—shut him out for meddling with his affairs.

"Well," he said, "what have you to say for yourselves?"

The fellow had the effrontery to smile.

"What we have received to-day has taken away your right to ask. I should imagine you will be glad to have your neck out of chancery."

"Oh!" said Soames; "you think so! I came to tell you that I'll divorce her with every circumstance of disgrace to you both, unless you swear to keep clear of each other from now on."

He was astonished at his fluency, because his mind was stammering and his hands twitching. Neither of them answered; but their faces seemed to him as if contemptuous.

"Well," he said; "you—Irene?"

Her lips moved, but Jolyon laid his hand on her arm.

"Let her alone!" said Soames furiously. "Irene, will you swear it?"

"No."

"Oh! and you?"

"Still less."

"So then you're guilty, are you?"

"Yes, guilty." It was Irene speaking in that serene voice, with that unreached air which had maddened him so often; and, carried beyond himself, he cried:

355

"You are a devil"

"Go out! Leave this house, or I'll do you an injury."

That fellow to talk of injuries! Did he know how near his throat was to being scragged?

"A trustee," he said, "embezzling trust property! A thief, stealing his cousin's wife."

"Call me what you like. You have chosen your part, we have chosen ours. Go out!"

If he had brought a weapon Soames might have used it at that moment.

"I'll make you pay!" he said.

"I shall be very happy."

At that deadly turning of the meaning of his speech by the son of him who had nicknamed him 'the man of property,' Soames stood glaring. It was ridiculous!

There they were, kept from violence by some secret force. No blow possible, no words to meet the case. But he could not, did not know how to turn and go away. His eyes fastened on Irene's face—the last time he would ever see that fatal face—the last time, no doubt!

"You," he said suddenly, "I hope you'll treat him as you treated me—that's all."

He saw her wince, and with a sensation not quite triumph, not quite relief, he wrenched open the door, passed out through the hall, and got into his cab. He lolled against the cushion with his eyes shut. Never in his life had he been so near to murderous violence, never so thrown away the restraint which was his second nature. He had a stripped and naked feeling, as if all virtue had gone out of him—life meaningless, mind-striking work. Sunlight streamed in on him, but he felt cold. The scene he had passed through had gone from him already, what was before him would not materialise, he could catch on to nothing; and he felt frightened, as if he had been hanging over the edge of a precipice, as if with another turn of the screw sanity would have failed him. 'I'm not fit for it,' he thought; 'I mustn't—I'm not fit for it.' The cab sped on, and in mechanical procession trees, houses, people passed, but had no significance. 'I feel very queer,' he thought; 'I'll take a Turkish bath.—I've been very near to something. It won't do.' The cab whirred its way back over the bridge, up the Fulham Road, along the Park.

"To the Hammam," said Soames.

Curious that on so warm a summer day, heat should be so comforting! Crossing into the hot room he met George Forsyte coming out, red and glistening.

"Hallo!" said George; "what are you training for? You've not got much superfluous."

Buffoon! Soames passed him with his sideway smile. Lying back, rubbing his skin uneasily for the first signs of perspiration, he thought: 'Let them laugh! I won't feel anything! I can't stand violence! It's not good for me!'

CHAPTER VII—A SUMMER NIGHT

Soames left dead silence in the little study. "Thank you for that good lie," said Jolyon suddenly. "Come out—the air in here is not what it was!"

In front of a long high southerly wall on which were trained peach-trees the two walked up and down in silence. Old Jolyon had planted some cupressus-trees, at intervals, between this grassy terrace and the dipping meadow full of buttercups and ox-eyed daisies; for twelve years they had flourished, till their dark spiral shapes had quite a look of Italy. Birds fluttered softly in the wet shrubbery; the swallows swooped past, with a steel-blue sheen on their swift little bodies; the grass felt springy beneath the feet, its green refreshed; butterflies chased each other. After that painful scene the quiet of Nature was wonderfully poignant. Under the sun-soaked wall ran a narrow strip of garden-bed full of mignonette and pansies, and from the bees came a low hum in which all other sounds were set—the mooing of a cow deprived of her calf, the calling of a cuckoo from an elm-tree at the bottom of the meadow. Who would have thought that behind them, within ten miles, London began—that London of the Forsytes, with its wealth, its misery; its dirt and noise; its jumbled stone isles of beauty, its grey sea of hideous brick and stucco? That London which had seen Irene's early tragedy, and Jolyon's own hard days; that web; that princely workhouse of the possessive instinct!

And while they walked Jolyon pondered those words: 'I hope you'll treat him as you treated me.' That would depend on himself. Could he trust himself? Did Nature permit a Forsyte not to make a slave of what he adored? Could beauty be confided to him? Or should she not be just a visitor, coming when she would, possessed for moments which passed, to return only at her own choosing? 'We are a breed of spoilers!' thought Jolyon, 'close and greedy; the bloom of life is not safe with us. Let her come to me as she will, when she will, not at all if she will not. Let me be just her stand-by, her perching-place; never-never her cage!'

She was the chink of beauty in his dream. Was he to pass through the curtains now and reach her? Was the rich stuff of many possessions, the close encircling fabric of the possessive instinct walling in that little black figure of himself, and Soames—was it to be rent so that he could pass through into his vision, find there something not of the senses only? 'Let me,' he thought, 'ah! let me only know how not to grasp and destroy!'

But at dinner there were plans to be made. To-night she would go back to the hotel, but tomorrow he would take her up to London. He must instruct his solicitor—Jack Herring. Not a finger must be raised to hinder the process of the Law. Damages exemplary, judicial strictures, costs, what they liked—let it go through at the first moment, so that her neck might be out of chancery at last! To-morrow he would see Herring—they would go and see him together. And then—abroad, leaving no doubt, no difficulty about evidence, making the lie she had told into the truth. He looked round at her; and it seemed to his adoring eyes that more than a woman was sitting there. The spirit of universal beauty, deep, mysterious, which the old painters, Titian, Giorgione, Botticelli, had known how to capture and transfer to the faces of their women—this flying beauty seemed to him imprinted on her brow, her hair, her lips, and in her eyes.

'And this is to be mine!' he thought. 'It frightens me!'

After dinner they went out on to the terrace to have coffee. They sat there long, the evening was so lovely, watching the summer night come very slowly on. It was still warm and the air smelled of lime blossom—early this summer. Two bats were flighting with the faint mysterious little noise they make. He had placed the chairs in front of the study window, and moths flew past to visit the discreet light in there. There was no wind, and not a whisper in the old oak-tree twenty yards away! The moon rose from behind the copse, nearly full; and the two lights struggled, till moonlight conquered, changing the colour and quality of all the garden, stealing along the flagstones, reaching their feet, climbing up, changing their faces.

"Well," said Jolyon at last, "you'll be tired, dear; we'd better start. The maid will show you Holly's room," and he rang the study bell. The maid who came handed him a telegram. Watching her take Irene away, he thought: "This must have come an hour or more ago, and she didn't bring it out to us! That shows! Well, we'll be hung for a sheep soon!' And, opening the telegram, he read:

"JOLYON FORSYTE, Robin Hill.—Your son passed painlessly away on June 20th. Deep sympathy"—some name unknown to him.

He dropped it, spun round, stood motionless. The moon shone in on him; a moth flew in his face. The first day of all that he had not thought almost ceaselessly of Jolly. He went blindly towards the window, struck against the old armchair—his father's—and sank down on to the arm of it. He sat there huddled' forward, staring into the night. Gone out like a candle flame; far from home, from love, all by himself, in the dark! His boy! From a little chap always so good to him—so friendly! Twenty years old, and cut down like grass—to have no life at all! 'I didn't really know him,' he thought, 'and he didn't know me; but we loved each other. It's only love that matters.'

To die out there—lonely—wanting them—wanting home! This seemed to his Forsyte heart more painful, more pitiful than death itself. No shelter, no protection, no love at the last! And all the deeply rooted clanship in him, the family feeling and essential clinging to his own flesh and blood which had been so strong in old Jolyon was so strong in all the Forsytes—felt outraged, cut, and torn by his boy's lonely passing. Better far if he had died in battle, without time to long for them to come to him, to call out for them, perhaps, in his delirium!

The moon had passed behind the oak-tree now, endowing it with uncanny life, so that it seemed watching him—the oak-tree his boy had been so fond of climbing, out of which he had once fallen and hurt himself, and hadn't cried!

The door creaked. He saw Irene come in, pick up the telegram and read it. He heard the faint rustle of her dress. She sank on her knees close to him, and he forced himself to smile at her. She stretched up her arms and drew his head down on her shoulder. The perfume and warmth of her encircled him; her presence gained slowly his whole being.

CHAPTER VIII—JAMES IN WAITING

Sweated to serenity, Soames dined at the Remove and turned his face toward Park Lane. His father had been unwell lately. This would have to be kept from him! Never till that moment had he realised how much the dread of bringing James' grey hairs down with sorrow to the grave had counted with him; how intimately it was bound up with his own shrinking from scandal. His affection for his father, always deep, had increased of late years with the knowledge that James looked on him as the real prop of his decline. It seemed pitiful that one who had been so careful all his life and done so much for the family name—so that it was almost a byword for solid, wealthy respectability—should at his last gasp have to see it in all the newspapers. This was like lending a hand to Death, that final enemy of Forsytes. 'I must tell mother,' he thought, 'and when it comes on, we must keep the papers from him somehow. He sees hardly anyone.' Letting himself in with his latchkey, he was beginning to ascend he stairs when he became conscious of commotion on the second-floor landing. His mother's voice was saying:

"Now, James, you'll catch cold. Why can't you wait quietly?"

His father's answering

"Wait? I'm always waiting. Why doesn't he come in?"

"You can speak to him to-morrow morning, instead of making a guy of yourself on the landing."

"He'll go up to bed, I shouldn't wonder. I shan't sleep."

"Now come back to bed, James."

"Um! I might die before to-morrow morning for all you can tell."

"You shan't have to wait till to-morrow morning; I'll go down and bring him up. Don't fuss!"

"There you go—always so cock-a-hoop. He mayn't come in at all."

"Well, if he doesn't come in you won't catch him by standing out here in your dressing-gown."

Soames rounded the last bend and came in sight of his father's tall figure wrapped in a brown silk quilted gown, stooping over the balustrade above. Light fell on his silvery hair and whiskers, investing his head with, a sort of halo.

"Here he is!" he heard him say in a voice which sounded injured, and his mother's comfortable answer from the bedroom door:

"That's all right. Come in, and I'll brush your hair." James extended a thin, crooked finger, oddly like the beckoning of a skeleton, and passed through the doorway of his bedroom.

'What is it?' thought Soames. 'What has he got hold of now?'

His father was sitting before the dressing-table sideways to the mirror, while Emily slowly passed two silver-backed brushes through and through his hair. She would do this several times a day, for it had on him something of the effect produced on a cat by scratching between its ears.

"There you are!" he said. "I've been waiting."

Soames stroked his shoulder, and, taking up a silver button-hook, examined the mark on it.

"Well," he said, "you're looking better."

James shook his head.

"I want to say something. Your mother hasn't heard." He announced Emily's ignorance of what he hadn't told her, as if it were a grievance.

"Your father's been in a great state all the evening. I'm sure I don't know what about."

The faint 'whisk-whisk' of the brushes continued the soothing of her voice.

"No! you know nothing," said James. "Soames can tell me." And, fixing his grey eyes, in which there was a look of strain, uncomfortable to watch, on his son, he muttered:

"I'm getting on, Soames. At my age I can't tell. I might die any time. There'll be a lot of money. There's Rachel and Cicely got no children; and Val's out there—that chap his father will get hold of all he can. And somebody'll pick up Imogen, I shouldn't wonder."

Soames listened vaguely—he had heard all this before. Whish-whish! went the brushes.

"If that's all!" said Emily.

"All!" cried James; "it's nothing. I'm coming to that." And again his eyes strained pitifully at Soames.

"It's you, my boy," he said suddenly; "you ought to get a divorce."

That word, from those of all lips, was almost too much for Soames' composure. His eyes reconcentrated themselves quickly on the buttonhook, and as if in apology James hurried on:

"I don't know what's become of her—they say she's abroad. Your Uncle Swithin used to admire her—he was a funny fellow." (So he always alluded to his dead twin-'The Stout and the Lean of it,' they had been called.) "She wouldn't be alone, I should say." And with that summing-up of the effect of beauty on human nature, he was silent, watching his son with eyes doubting as a bird's. Soames, too, was silent. Whish-whish went the brushes.

"Come, James! Soames knows best. It's his 'business."

"Ah!" said James, and the word came from deep down; "but there's all my money, and there's his—who's it to go to? And when he dies the name goes out."

Soames replaced the button-hook on the lace and pink silk of the dressing-table coverlet.

"The name?" said Emily, "there are all the other Forsytes."

"As if that helped me," muttered James. "I shall be in my grave, and there'll be nobody, unless he marries again."

"You're quite right," said Soames quietly; "I'm getting a divorce."

James' eyes almost started from his head.

"What?" he cried. "There! nobody tells me anything."

"Well," said Emily, "who would have imagined you wanted it? My dear boy, that is a surprise, after all these years."

"It'll be a scandal," muttered James, as if to himself; "but I can't help that. Don't brush so hard. When'll it come on?"

"Before the Long Vacation; it's not defended."

James' lips moved in secret calculation. "I shan't live to see my grandson," he muttered.

Emily ceased brushing. "Of course you will, James. Soames will be as quick as he can."

There was a long silence, till James reached out his arm.

"Here! let's have the eau-de-Cologne," and, putting it to his nose, he moved his forehead in the direction of his son. Soames bent over and kissed that brow just where the hair began. A relaxing quiver passed over James' face, as though the wheels of anxiety within were running down.

"I'll get to bed," he said; "I shan't want to see the papers when that comes. They're a morbid lot; I can't pay attention to them, I'm too old."

Queerly affected, Soames went to the door; he heard his father say:

"Here, I'm tired. I'll say a prayer in bed."

And his mother answering

"That's right, James; it'll be ever so much more comfy."

CHAPTER IX—OUT OF THE WEB

On Forsyte 'Change the announcement of Jolly's death, among a batch of troopers, caused mixed sensation. Strange to read that Jolyon Forsyte (fifth of the name in direct descent) had died of disease in the service of his country, and not be able to feel it personally. It revived the old grudge against his father for having estranged himself. For such was still the prestige of old Jolyon that the other Forsytes could never quite feel, as might have been expected, that it was they who had cut off his descendants for irregularity. The news increased, of course, the interest and anxiety about Val; but then Val's name was Dartie, and even if he were killed in battle or got the Victoria Cross, it would not be at all the same as if his name were Forsyte. Not even casualty or glory to the Haymans would be really satisfactory. Family pride felt defrauded.

How the rumour arose, then, that 'something very dreadful, my dear,' was pending, no one, least of all Soames, could tell, secret as he kept everything. Possibly some eye had seen 'Forsyte v. Forsyte and Forsyte,' in the cause list; and had added it to 'Irene in Paris with a fair beard.' Possibly some wall at Park Lane had ears. The fact remained that it was known—whispered among the old, discussed among the young—that family pride must soon receive a blow.

Soames, paying one, of his Sunday visits to Timothy's—paying it with the feeling that after the suit came on he would be paying no more—felt knowledge in the air as he came in. Nobody, of course, dared speak of it before him, but each of the four other Forsytes present held their breath, aware that nothing could prevent Aunt Juley from making them all uncomfortable. She looked so piteously at Soames, she checked herself on the point of speech so often, that Aunt Hester excused herself and said she must go and bathe Timothy's eye—he had a sty coming. Soames, impassive, slightly supercilious, did not stay long. He went out with a curse stifled behind his pale, just smiling lips.

Fortunately for the peace of his mind, cruelly tortured by the coming scandal, he was kept busy day and night with plans for his retirement—for he had come to that grim conclusion. To go on seeing all those people who had known him as a 'long-headed chap,' an astute adviser—after that—no! The fastidiousness and pride which was so strangely, so inextricably blended in him with possessive obtuseness, revolted against the thought. He would retire, live privately, go on buying pictures, make a great name as a collector—after all, his heart was more in that than it had ever been in Law. In pursuance of this now fixed resolve, he had to get ready to amalgamate his business with another firm without letting people know, for that would excite curiosity and make humiliation cast its shadow before. He had pitched on the firm of Cuthcott, Holliday and Kingson, two of whom were dead. The full name after the amalgamation would therefore be Cuthcott, Holliday, Kingson, Forsyte, Bustard and Forsyte. But after debate as to which of the dead still had any influence with the living, it was decided to reduce the title to Cuthcott, Kingson and Forsyte, of whom Kingson would be the active and Soames the sleeping partner. For leaving his name, prestige, and clients behind him, Soames would receive considerable value.

One night, as befitted a man who had arrived at so important a stage of his career, he made a calculation of what he was worth, and after writing off liberally for depreciation by the war, found his value to be some hundred and thirty thousand pounds. At his father's death, which could not, alas, be delayed much longer, he must come into at least another fifty thousand, and his yearly expenditure at present just reached two. Standing among his pictures, he saw before him a future full of bargains earned by the trained faculty of knowing better than other people. Selling what was about to decline, keeping what was still going up, and exercising judicious insight into future taste, he would make a unique collection, which at his death would pass to the nation under the title 'Forsyte Bequest.'

If the divorce went through, he had determined on his line with Madame Lamotte. She had, he knew, but one real ambition—to live on her 'renter' in Paris near her grandchildren. He would buy the goodwill of the Restaurant Bretagne at a fancy price. Madame would live like a Queen-Mother in Paris on the interest, invested as she would know how. (Incidentally Soames meant to put a capable manager in her place, and make the restaurant pay good interest on his money. There were great possibilities in Soho.) On Annette he would promise to settle fifteen thousand pounds (whether designedly or not), precisely the sum old Jolyon had settled on 'that woman.'

A letter from Jolyon's solicitor to his own had disclosed the fact that 'those two' were in Italy. And an opportunity had been duly given for noting that they had first stayed at an hotel in London. The matter was clear as daylight, and would be disposed of in half an hour or so; but during that half-hour he, Soames, would go down to hell; and after that half-hour all bearers of the Forsyte name would feel the bloom was off the rose. He had no illusions like Shakespeare that roses by any other name would smell as sweet. The name was a possession, a concrete, unstained piece of property, the value of which would be reduced some twenty per cent. at least. Unless it were Roger, who had once refused to stand for Parliament, and—oh, irony!—Jolyon, hung on the line, there had never been a distinguished Forsyte. But that very lack of distinction was the name's greatest asset. It was a private name, intensely individual, and his own property; it had never been exploited for good or evil by intrusive report. He and each member of his family owned it wholly, sanely, secretly, without any more interference from the public than had been necessitated by their births, their marriages, their deaths. And during these weeks of waiting and preparing to drop the Law, he conceived for that Law a bitter distaste, so deeply did he resent its coming violation of his name, forced on him by the need he felt to perpetuate that name in a lawful manner. The monstrous injustice of the whole thing excited in him a perpetual suppressed fury. He had asked no better than to live in spotless domesticity, and now he must go into the witness box, after all these futile, barren years, and proclaim his failure to keep his wife—incur the pity, the amusement, the contempt of his kind. It was all upside down. She and that fellow ought to be the sufferers, and they—were in Italy! In these weeks the Law he had served so faithfully, looked on so reverently as the guardian of all property, seemed to him quite pitiful. What could be more insane than to tell a man that he owned his wife, and punish him when someone unlawfully took her away from him? Did the Law not know that a man's name was to him the apple of his eye, that it was far harder to be regarded as cuckold than as seducer? He actually envied Jolyon the reputation of succeeding where he, Soames, had failed. The question of damages worried him, too. He wanted to make that fellow suffer, but he remembered his cousin's words, "I shall be very happy," with the uneasy feeling that to claim damages would make not Jolyon but himself suffer; he felt uncannily that Jolyon would rather like to pay them—the chap was so loose. Besides, to claim damages was not the thing to do. The claim, indeed, had been made almost mechanically; and as the hour drew near Soames saw in it just another dodge of this insensitive and topsy-turvy Law to make him ridiculous; so that people might sneer and say: "Oh, yes, he got quite a good price for her!" And he gave instructions that his Counsel should state that the money would be given to a Home for Fallen Women. He was a long time hitting off exactly the right charity; but, having pitched on it, he used to wake up in the night and think: 'It won't do, too lurid; it'll draw attention. Something quieter—better taste.' He did not care for dogs, or he would have named them; and it was in desperation at last—for his knowledge of charities was limited—that he decided on the blind. That could not be inappropriate, and it would make the Jury assess the damages high.

A good many suits were dropping out of the list, which happened to be exceptionally thin that summer, so that his case would be reached before August. As the day grew nearer,

Winifred was his only comfort. She showed the fellow-feeling of one who had been through the mill, and was the 'femme-sole' in whom he confided, well knowing that she would not let Dartie into her confidence. That ruffian would be only too rejoiced! At the end of July, on the afternoon before the case, he went in to see her. They had not yet been able to leave town, because Dartie had already spent their summer holiday, and Winifred dared not go to her father for more money while he was waiting not to be told anything about this affair of Soames.

Soames found her with a letter in her hand.

"That from Val," he asked gloomily. "What does he say?"

"He says he's married," said Winifred.

"Whom to, for Goodness' sake?"

Winifred looked up at him.

"To Holly Forsyte, Jolyon's daughter."

"What?"

"He got leave and did it. I didn't even know he knew her. Awkward, isn't it?"

Soames uttered a short laugh at that characteristic minimisation.

"Awkward! Well, I don't suppose they'll hear about this till they come back. They'd better stay out there. That fellow will give her money."

"But I want Val back," said Winifred almost piteously; "I miss him, he helps me to get on."

"I know," murmured Soames. "How's Dartie behaving now?"

"It might be worse; but it's always money. Would you like me to come down to the Court to-morrow, Soames?"

Soames stretched out his hand for hers. The gesture so betrayed the loneliness in him that she pressed it between her two.

"Never mind, old boy. You'll feel ever so much better when it's all over."

"I don't know what I've done," said Soames huskily; "I never have. It's all upside down. I was fond of her; I've always been."

Winifred saw a drop of blood ooze out of his lip, and the sight stirred her profoundly.

"Of course," she said, "it's been too bad of her all along! But what shall I do about this marriage of Val's, Soames? I don't know how to write to him, with this coming on. You've seen that child. Is she pretty?"

"Yes, she's pretty," said Soames. "Dark—lady-like enough."

'That doesn't sound so bad,' thought Winifred. 'Jolyon had style.'

"It is a coil," she said. "What will father say?

"Mustn't be told," said Soames. "The war'll soon be over now, you'd better let Val take to farming out there."

It was tantamount to saying that his nephew was lost.

"I haven't told Monty," Winifred murmured desolately.

The case was reached before noon next day, and was over in little more than half an hour. Soames—pale, spruce, sad-eyed in the witness-box—had suffered so much beforehand that he took it all like one dead. The moment the decree nisi was pronounced he left the Courts of Justice.

Four hours until he became public property! 'Solicitor's divorce suit!' A surly, dogged anger replaced that dead feeling within him. 'Damn them all!' he thought; 'I won't run away. I'll act as if nothing had happened.' And in the sweltering heat of Fleet Street and Ludgate Hill he walked all the way to his City Club, lunched, and went back to his office. He worked there stolidly throughout the afternoon.

On his way out he saw that his clerks knew, and answered their involuntary glances with a look so sardonic that they were immediately withdrawn. In front of St. Paul's, he stopped to buy the most gentlemanly of the evening papers. Yes! there he was! 'Well-known solicitor's divorce. Cousin co-respondent. Damages given to the blind'—so, they had got that in! At every other face, he thought: 'I wonder if you know!' And suddenly he felt queer, as if something were racing round in his head.

What was this? He was letting it get hold of him! He mustn't! He would be ill. He mustn't think! He would get down to the river and row about, and fish. 'I'm not going to be laid up,' he thought.

It flashed across him that he had something of importance to do before he went out of town. Madame Lamotte! He must explain the Law. Another six months before he was really free! Only he did not want to see Annette! And he passed his hand over the top of his head—it was very hot.

He branched off through Covent Garden. On this sultry day of late July the garbage-tainted air of the old market offended him, and Soho seemed more than ever the disenchanted home of rapscallionism. Alone, the Restaurant Bretagne, neat, daintily painted, with its blue tubs and the dwarf trees therein, retained an aloof and Frenchified self-respect. It was the slack hour, and pale trim waitresses were preparing the little tables for dinner. Soames went through into the private part. To his discomfiture Annette answered his knock. She, too, looked pale and dragged down by the heat.

"You are quite a stranger," she said languidly.

Soames smiled.

"I haven't wished to be; I've been busy."

"Where's your mother, Annette? I've got some news for her."

"Mother is not in."

It seemed to Soames that she looked at him in a queer way. What did she know? How much had her mother told her? The worry of trying to make that out gave him an alarming feeling in the head. He gripped the edge of the table, and dizzily saw Annette come forward, her eyes clear with surprise. He shut his own and said:

"It's all right. I've had a touch of the sun, I think." The sun! What he had was a touch of 'darkness'! Annette's voice, French and composed, said:

"Sit down, it will pass, then." Her hand pressed his shoulder, and Soames sank into a chair. When the dark feeling dispersed, and he opened his eyes, she was looking down at him. What an inscrutable and odd expression for a girl of twenty!

"Do you feel better?"

"It's nothing," said Soames. Instinct told him that to be feeble before her was not helping him—age was enough handicap without that. Will-power was his fortune with Annette, he had lost ground these latter months from indecision—he could not afford to lose any more. He got up, and said:

"I'll write to your mother. I'm going down to my river house for a long holiday. I want you both to come there presently and stay. It's just at its best. You will, won't you?"

"It will be veree nice." A pretty little roll of that 'r' but no enthusiasm. And rather sadly he added:

"You're feeling the heat; too, aren't you, Annette? It'll do you good to be on the river. Good-night." Annette swayed forward. There was a sort of compunction in the movement.

"Are you fit to go? Shall I give you some coffee?"

"No," said Soames firmly. "Give me your hand."

She held out her hand, and Soames raised it to his lips. When he looked up, her face wore again that strange expression. 'I can't tell,' he thought, as he went out; 'but I mustn't think—I mustn't worry:

But worry he did, walking toward Pall Mall. English, not of her religion, middle-aged, scarred as it were by domestic tragedy, what had he to give her? Only wealth, social position, leisure, admiration! It was much, but was it enough for a beautiful girl of twenty? He felt so ignorant about Annette. He had, too, a curious fear of the French nature of her mother and herself. They knew so well what they wanted. They were almost Forsytes. They would never grasp a shadow and miss a substance.

The tremendous effort it was to write a simple note to Madame Lamotte when he reached his Club warned him still further that he was at the end of his tether.

"MY DEAR MADAME (he said),

"You will see by the enclosed newspaper cutting that I obtained my decree of divorce to-day. By the English Law I shall not, however, be free to marry again till the decree is confirmed six months hence. In the meanwhile I have the honor to ask to be considered a formal suitor for the hand of your daughter. I shall write again in a few days and beg you both to come and stay at my river house.

"I am, dear Madame,

"Sincerely yours,

"SOAMES FORSYTE."

Having sealed and posted this letter, he went into the dining-room. Three mouthfuls of soup convinced him that he could not eat; and, causing a cab to be summoned, he drove to Paddington Station and took the first train to Reading. He reached his house just as the sun went down, and wandered out on to the lawn. The air was drenched with the scent of pinks and picotees in his flower-borders. A stealing coolness came off the river.

Rest-peace! Let a poor fellow rest! Let not worry and shame and anger chase like evil night-birds in his head! Like those doves perched half-sleeping on their dovecot, like the furry creatures in the woods on the far side, and the simple folk in their cottages, like the trees and the river itself, whitening fast in twilight, like the darkening cornflower-blue sky where stars were coming up—let him cease from himself, and rest!

CHAPTER X—PASSING OF AN AGE

The marriage of Soames with Annette took place in Paris on the last day of January, 1901, with such privacy that not even Emily was told until it was accomplished.

The day after the wedding he brought her to one of those quiet hotels in London where greater expense can be incurred for less result than anywhere else under heaven. Her beauty in the best Parisian frocks was giving him more satisfaction than if he had collected a perfect bit of china, or a jewel of a picture; he looked forward to the moment when he would exhibit her in Park Lane, in Green Street, and at Timothy's.

If some one had asked him in those days, "In confidence—are you in love with this girl?" he would have replied: "In love? What is love? If you mean do I feel to her as I did towards Irene in those old days when I first met her and she would not have me; when I sighed and starved after her and couldn't rest a minute until she yielded—no! If you mean do I admire her youth and prettiness, do my senses ache a little when I see her moving about—yes! Do I think she will keep me straight, make me a creditable wife and a good mother for my children?—again, yes!"

"What more do I need? and what more do three-quarters of the women who are married get from the men who marry them?" And if the enquirer had pursued his query, "And do you think it was fair to have tempted this girl to give herself to you for life unless you have really touched her heart?" he would have answered: "The French see these things differently from us. They look at marriage from the point of view of establishments and children; and, from my own experience, I am not at all sure that theirs is not the sensible view. I shall not expect this time more than I can get, or she can give. Years hence I shouldn't be surprised if I have trouble with her; but I shall be getting old, I shall have children by then. I shall shut my eyes. I have had my great passion; hers is perhaps to come—I don't suppose it will be for me. I offer her a great deal, and I don't expect much in return, except children, or at least a son. But one thing I am sure of—she has very good sense!"

And if, insatiate, the enquirer had gone on, "You do not look, then, for spiritual union in this marriage?" Soames would have lifted his sideway smile, and rejoined: "That's as it may be. If I get satisfaction for my senses, perpetuation of myself; good taste and good humour in the house; it is all I can expect at my age. I am not likely to be going out of my way towards any far-fetched sentimentalism." Whereon, the enquirer must in good taste have ceased enquiry.

The Queen was dead, and the air of the greatest city upon earth grey with unshed tears. Fur-coated and top-hatted, with Annette beside him in dark furs, Soames crossed Park Lane on the morning of the funeral procession, to the rails in Hyde Park. Little moved though he ever was by public matters, this event, supremely symbolical, this summing-up of a long rich period, impressed his fancy. In '37, when she came to the throne, 'Superior Dosset' was still building houses to make London hideous; and James, a stripling of twenty-six, just laying the foundations of his practice in the Law. Coaches still ran; men wore stocks, shaved their upper lips, ate oysters out of barrels; 'tigers' swung behind cabriolets; women said, 'La!' and owned no property; there were manners in the land, and pigsties for the poor; unhappy devils were hanged for little crimes, and Dickens had but just begun to write. Well-nigh two generations had slipped by—of steamboats, railways, telegraphs, bicycles, electric light, telephones, and now these motorcars—of such accumulated wealth, that eight per cent. had become three, and Forsytes were numbered by the thousand! Morals had changed, manners had changed, men had become monkeys twice-removed, God had become Mammon—Mammon so respectable as to deceive himself. Sixty-four years that favoured property, and had made the upper middle class; buttressed, chiselled, polished it, till it was almost indistinguishable in manners, morals, speech, appearance, habit, and soul from the nobility. An epoch which had gilded individual liberty so that if a man had money, he was free in law and fact, and if he had not money he was free in law and not in fact. An era which had canonised hypocrisy, so that to seem to be respectable was to be. A great Age, whose transmuting influence nothing had escaped save the nature of man and the nature of the Universe.

And to witness the passing of this Age, London—its pet and fancy—was pouring forth her citizens through every gate into Hyde Park, hub of Victorianism, happy hunting-ground of Forsytes. Under the grey heavens, whose drizzle just kept off, the dark concourse gathered to see the show. The 'good old' Queen, full of years and virtue, had emerged from her seclusion for the last time to make a London holiday. From Houndsditch, Acton, Ealing, Hampstead, Islington, and Bethnal Green; from Hackney, Hornsey, Leytonstone, Battersea, and Fulham; and from those green pastures where Forsytes flourish—Mayfair and Kensington, St. James' and Belgravia, Bayswater and Chelsea and the Regent's Park, the people swarmed down on to the roads where death would presently pass with dusky pomp and pageantry. Never again would a Queen reign so long, or people have a chance to see so much history buried for their money. A pity the war dragged on, and that the Wreath of Victory could not be laid upon her coffin! All else would be there to follow and commemorate—soldiers, sailors, foreign princes, half-masted bunting, tolling bells, and above all the surging, great, dark-coated crowd, with perhaps a simple sadness here and there deep in hearts beneath black clothes put on by regulation. After all, more than a Queen was going to her rest, a woman who had braved sorrow, lived well and wisely according to her lights.

Out in the crowd against the railings, with his arm hooked in Annette's, Soames waited. Yes! the Age was passing! What with this Trade Unionism, and Labour fellows in the House of Commons, with continental fiction, and something in the general feel of everything, not to be expressed in words, things were very different; he recalled the crowd on Mafeking night, and George Forsyte saying: "They're all socialists, they want our goods." Like James, Soames didn't know, he couldn't tell—with Edward on the throne! Things would never be as safe again as under good old Viccy! Convulsively he pressed his young wife's arm. There, at any rate, was something substantially his own, domestically certain again at last; something which made property worth while—a real thing once more. Pressed close against her and trying to ward others off, Soames was content. The crowd swayed round them, ate sandwiches and dropped crumbs; boys who had climbed the plane-trees chattered above like monkeys, threw twigs and orange-peel. It was past time; they should be coming soon! And, suddenly, a little behind them to the left, he saw a tallish man with a soft hat and short grizzling beard, and a tallish woman in a little round fur cap and veil. Jolyon and Irene talking, smiling at each other, close together like Annette and himself! They had not seen him; and stealthily, with a very queer feeling in his heart, Soames watched those two. They looked happy! What had they come here for—inherently illicit creatures, rebels from the Victorian ideal? What business had they in this crowd? Each of them twice exiled by morality—making a boast, as it were, of love and laxity! He watched them fascinated; admitting grudgingly even with his arm thrust through Annette's that—that she—Irene—No! he would not admit it; and he turned his eyes away. He would not see them, and let the old bitterness, the old longing rise up within him! And then Annette turned to him and said: "Those two people, Soames; they know you, I am sure. Who are they?"

Soames nosed sideways.

"What people?"

"There, you see them; just turning away. They know you."

"No," Soames answered; "a mistake, my dear."

"A lovely face! And how she walk! Elle est tres distinguee!"

Soames looked then. Into his life, out of his life she had walked like that swaying and erect, remote, unseizable; ever eluding the contact of his soul! He turned abruptly from that receding vision of the past.

"You'd better attend," he said, "they're coming now!"

But while he stood, grasping her arm, seemingly intent on the head of the procession, he was quivering with the sense of always missing something, with instinctive regret that he had not got them both.

Slow came the music and the march, till, in silence, the long line wound in through the Park gate. He heard Annette whisper, "How sad it is and beautiful!" felt the clutch of her hand as she stood up on tiptoe; and the crowd's emotion gripped him. There it was—the bier of the Queen, coffin of the Age slow passing! And as it went by there came a murmuring groan from all the long line of those who watched, a sound such as Soames had never heard, so unconscious, primitive, deep and wild, that neither he nor any knew whether they had joined in uttering it. Strange sound, indeed! Tribute of an Age to its own death.... Ah! Ah!... The hold on life had slipped. That which had seemed eternal was gone! The Queen—God bless her!

It moved on with the bier, that travelling groan, as a fire moves on over grass in a thin line; it kept step, and marched alongside down the dense crowds mile after mile. It was a human sound, and yet inhuman, pushed out by animal subconsciousness, by intimate knowledge of universal death and change. None of us—none of us can hold on for ever!

It left silence for a little—a very little time, till tongues began, eager to retrieve interest in the show. Soames lingered just long enough to gratify Annette, then took her out of the Park to lunch at his father's in Park Lane....

James had spent the morning gazing out of his bedroom window. The last show he would see, last of so many! So she was gone! Well, she was getting an old woman. Swithin and he had seen her crowned—slim slip of a girl, not so old as Imogen! She had got very stout of late. Jolyon and he had seen her married to that German chap, her husband—he had turned out all right before he died, and left her with that son of his. And he remembered the many evenings he and his brothers and their cronies had wagged their heads over their wine and walnuts and that fellow in his salad days. And now he had come to the throne. They said he had steadied down—he didn't know—couldn't tell! He'd make the money fly still, he shouldn't wonder. What a lot of people out there! It didn't seem so very long since he and Swithin stood in the crowd outside Westminster Abbey when she was crowned, and Swithin had taken him to Cremorne afterwards—racketty chap, Swithin; no, it didn't seem much longer ago than Jubilee Year, when he had joined with Roger in renting a balcony in Piccadilly.

Jolyon, Swithin, Roger all gone, and he would be ninety in August! And there was Soames married again to a French girl. The French were a queer lot, but they made good mothers, he had heard. Things changed! They said this German Emperor was here for the funeral, his telegram to old Kruger had been in shocking taste. He should not be surprised if that chap made trouble some day. Change! H'm! Well, they must look after themselves when he was gone: he didn't know where he'd be! And now Emily had asked Dartie to lunch, with Winifred and Imogen, to meet Soames' wife—she was always doing something. And there was Irene living with that fellow Jolyon, they said. He'd marry her now, he supposed.

'My brother Jolyon,' he thought, 'what would he have said to it all?' And somehow the utter impossibility of knowing what his elder brother, once so looked up to, would have said, so worried James that he got up from his chair by the window, and began slowly, feebly to pace the room.

'She was a pretty thing, too,' he thought; 'I was fond of her. Perhaps Soames didn't suit her—I don't know—I can't tell. We never had any trouble with our wives.' Women had changed everything had changed! And now the Queen was dead—well, there it was! A movement in the crowd brought him to a standstill at the window, his nose touching the pane and whitening from the chill of it. They had got her as far as Hyde Park Corner—they were passing now! Why didn't Emily come up here where she could see, instead of fussing about lunch. He missed her at that moment—missed her! Through the bare branches of the plane-trees he could just see the procession, could see the hats coming off the people's heads—a lot of them would catch colds, he shouldn't wonder! A voice behind him said:

"You've got a capital view here, James!"

"There you are!" muttered James; "why didn't you come before? You might have missed it!"

And he was silent, staring with all his might.

"What's the noise?" he asked suddenly.

"There's no noise," returned Emily; "what are you thinking of?—they wouldn't cheer."

"I can hear it."

"Nonsense, James!"

No sound came through those double panes; what James heard was the groaning in his own heart at sight of his Age passing.

"Don't you ever tell me where I'm buried," he said suddenly. "I shan't want to know." And he turned from the window. There she went, the old Queen; she'd had a lot of anxiety— she'd be glad to be out of it, he should think!

Emily took up the hair-brushes.

"There'll be just time to brush your head," she said, "before they come. You must look your best, James."

"Ah!" muttered James; "they say she's pretty."

The meeting with his new daughter-in-law took place in the dining-room. James was seated by the fire when she was brought in. He placed, his hands on the arms of the chair and slowly raised himself. Stooping and immaculate in his frock-coat, thin as a line in Euclid, he received Annette's hand in his; and the anxious eyes of his furrowed face, which had lost its colour now, doubted above her. A little warmth came into them and into his cheeks, refracted from her bloom.

"How are you?" he said. "You've been to see the Queen, I suppose? Did you have a good crossing?"

In this way he greeted her from whom he hoped for a grandson of his name.

Gazing at him, so old, thin, white, and spotless, Annette murmured something in French which James did not understand.

"Yes, yes," he said, "you want your lunch, I expect. Soames, ring the bell; we won't wait for that chap Dartie." But just then they arrived. Dartie had refused to go out of his way to see

369

'the old girl.' With an early cocktail beside him, he had taken a 'squint' from the smoking-room of the Iseeum, so that Winifred and Imogen had been obliged to come back from the Park to fetch him thence. His brown eyes rested on Annette with a stare of almost startled satisfaction. The second beauty that fellow Soames had picked up! What women could see in him! Well, she would play him the same trick as the other, no doubt; but in the meantime he was a lucky devil! And he brushed up his moustache, having in nine months of Green Street domesticity regained almost all his flesh and his assurance. Despite the comfortable efforts of Emily, Winifred's composure, Imogen's enquiring friendliness, Dartie's showing-off, and James' solicitude about her food, it was not, Soames felt, a successful lunch for his bride. He took her away very soon.

"That Monsieur Dartie," said Annette in the cab, "je n'aime pas ce type-la!"

"No, by George!" said Soames.

"Your sister is veree amiable, and the girl is pretty. Your father is veree old. I think your mother has trouble with him; I should not like to be her."

Soames nodded at the shrewdness, the clear hard judgment in his young wife; but it disquieted him a little. The thought may have just flashed through him, too: 'When I'm eighty she'll be fifty-five, having trouble with me!'

"There's just one other house of my relations I must take you to," he said; "you'll find it funny, but we must get it over; and then we'll dine and go to the theatre."

In this way he prepared her for Timothy's. But Timothy's was different. They were delighted to see dear Soames after this long long time; and so this was Annette!

"You are so pretty, my dear; almost too young and pretty for dear Soames, aren't you? But he's very attentive and careful—such a good husb...." Aunt Juley checked herself, and placed her lips just under each of Annette's eyes—she afterwards described them to Francie, who dropped in, as: "Cornflower-blue, so pretty, I quite wanted to kiss them. I must say dear Soames is a perfect connoisseur. In her French way, and not so very French either, I think she's as pretty—though not so distinguished, not so alluring—as Irene. Because she was alluring, wasn't she? with that white skin and those dark eyes, and that hair, couleur de—what was it? I always forget."

"Feuille morte," Francie prompted.

"Of course, dead leaves—so strange. I remember when I was a girl, before we came to London, we had a foxhound puppy—to 'walk' it was called then; it had a tan top to its head and a white chest, and beautiful dark brown eyes, and it was a lady."

"Yes, auntie," said Francie, "but I don't see the connection."

"Oh!" replied Aunt Juley, rather flustered, "it was so alluring, and her eyes and hair, you know...." She was silent, as if surprised in some indelicacy. "Feuille morte," she added suddenly; "Hester—do remember that!"....

Considerable debate took place between the two sisters whether Timothy should or should not be summoned to see Annette.

"Oh, don't bother!" said Soames.

"But it's no trouble, only of course Annette's being French might upset him a little. He was so scared about Fashoda. I think perhaps we had better not run the risk, Hester. It's nice to have her all to ourselves, isn't it? And how are you, Soames? Have you quite got over your...."

Hester interposed hurriedly:

"What do you think of London, Annette?"

Soames, disquieted, awaited the reply. It came, sensible, composed: "Oh! I know London. I have visited before."

He had never ventured to speak to her on the subject of the restaurant. The French had different notions about gentility, and to shrink from connection with it might seem to her ridiculous; he had waited to be married before mentioning it; and now he wished he hadn't.

"And what part do you know best?" said Aunt Juley.

"Soho," said Annette simply.

Soames snapped his jaw.

"Soho?" repeated Aunt Juley; "Soho?"

'That'll go round the family,' thought Soames.

"It's very French, and interesting," he said.

"Yes," murmured Aunt Juley, "your Uncle Roger had some houses there once; he was always having to turn the tenants out, I remember."

Soames changed the subject to Mapledurham.

"Of course," said Aunt Juley, "you will be going down there soon to settle in. We are all so looking forward to the time when Annette has a dear little...."

"Juley!" cried Aunt Hester desperately, "ring tea!"

Soames dared not wait for tea, and took Annette away.

"I shouldn't mention Soho if I were you," he said in the cab. "It's rather a shady part of London; and you're altogether above that restaurant business now; I mean," he added, "I want you to know nice people, and the English are fearful snobs."

Annette's clear eyes opened; a little smile came on her lips.

"Yes?" she said.

'H'm!' thought Soames, 'that's meant for me!' and he looked at her hard. 'She's got good business instincts,' he thought. 'I must make her grasp it once for all!'

"Look here, Annette! it's very simple, only it wants understanding. Our professional and leisured classes still think themselves a cut above our business classes, except of course the very rich. It may be stupid, but there it is, you see. It isn't advisable in England to let people know that you ran a restaurant or kept a shop or were in any kind of trade. It may have been extremely creditable, but it puts a sort of label on you; you don't have such a good time, or meet such nice people—that's all."

"I see," said Annette; "it is the same in France."

"Oh!" murmured Soames, at once relieved and taken aback. "Of course, class is everything, really."

"Yes," said Annette; "comme vous etes sage."

'That's all right,' thought Soames, watching her lips, 'only she's pretty cynical.' His knowledge of French was not yet such as to make him grieve that she had not said 'tu.' He slipped his arm round her, and murmured with an effort:

"Et vous etes ma belle femme."

Annette went off into a little fit of laughter.

371

"Oh, non!" she said. "Oh, non! ne parlez pas Francais, Soames. What is that old lady, your aunt, looking forward to?"

Soames bit his lip. "God knows!" he said; "she's always saying something;" but he knew better than God.

CHAPTER XI—SUSPENDED ANIMATION

The war dragged on. Nicholas had been heard to say that it would cost three hundred millions if it cost a penny before they'd done with it! The income-tax was seriously threatened. Still, there would be South Africa for their money, once for all. And though the possessive instinct felt badly shaken at three o'clock in the morning, it recovered by breakfast-time with the recollection that one gets nothing in this world without paying for it. So, on the whole, people went about their business much as if there were no war, no concentration camps, no slippery de Wet, no feeling on the Continent, no anything unpleasant. Indeed, the attitude of the nation was typified by Timothy's map, whose animation was suspended—for Timothy no longer moved the flags, and they could not move themselves, not even backwards and forwards as they should have done.

Suspended animation went further; it invaded Forsyte 'Change, and produced a general uncertainty as to what was going to happen next. The announcement in the marriage column of The Times, 'Jolyon Forsyte to Irene, only daughter of the late Professor Heron,' had occasioned doubt whether Irene had been justly described. And yet, on the whole, relief was felt that she had not been entered as 'Irene, late the wife,' or 'the divorced wife,' 'of Soames Forsyte.' Altogether, there had been a kind of sublimity from the first about the way the family had taken that 'affair.' As James had phrased it, 'There it was!' No use to fuss! Nothing to be had out of admitting that it had been a 'nasty jar'—in the phraseology of the day.

But what would happen now that both Soames and Jolyon were married again? That was very intriguing. George was known to have laid Eustace six to four on a little Jolyon before a little Soames. George was so droll! It was rumoured, too, that he and Dartie had a bet as to whether James would attain the age of ninety, though which of them had backed James no one knew.

Early in May, Winifred came round to say that Val had been wounded in the leg by a spent bullet, and was to be discharged. His wife was nursing him. He would have a little limp—nothing to speak of. He wanted his grandfather to buy him a farm out there where he could breed horses. Her father was giving Holly eight hundred a year, so they could be quite comfortable, because his grandfather would give Val five, he had said; but as to the farm, he didn't know—couldn't tell: he didn't want Val to go throwing away his money.

"But you know," said Winifred, "he must do something."

Aunt Hester thought that perhaps his dear grandfather was wise, because if he didn't buy a farm it couldn't turn out badly.

"But Val loves horses," said Winifred. "It'd be such an occupation for him."

Aunt Juley thought that horses were very uncertain, had not Montague found them so?

"Val's different," said Winifred; "he takes after me."

Aunt Juley was sure that dear Val was very clever. "I always remember," she added, "how he gave his bad penny to a beggar. His dear grandfather was so pleased. He thought it showed such presence of mind. I remember his saying that he ought to go into the Navy."

Aunt Hester chimed in: Did not Winifred think that it was much better for the young people to be secure and not run any risk at their age?

"Well," said Winifred, "if they were in London, perhaps; in London it's amusing to do nothing. But out there, of course, he'll simply get bored to death."

Aunt Hester thought that it would be nice for him to work, if he were quite sure not to lose by it. It was not as if they had no money. Timothy, of course, had done so well by retiring. Aunt Juley wanted to know what Montague had said.

Winifred did not tell her, for Montague had merely remarked: "Wait till the old man dies."

At this moment Francie was announced. Her eyes were brimming with a smile.

"Well," she said, "what do you think of it?"

"Of what, dear?"

"In The Times this morning."

"We haven't seen it, we always read it after dinner; Timothy has it till then."

Francie rolled her eyes.

"Do you think you ought to tell us?" said Aunt Juley. "What was it?"

"Irene's had a son at Robin Hill."

Aunt Juley drew in her breath. "But," she said, "they were only married in March!"

"Yes, Auntie; isn't it interesting?"

"Well," said Winifred, "I'm glad. I was sorry for Jolyon losing his boy. It might have been Val."

Aunt Juley seemed to go into a sort of dream. "I wonder," she murmured, "what dear Soames will think? He has so wanted to have a son himself. A little bird has always told me that."

"Well," said Winifred, "he's going to—bar accidents."

Gladness trickled out of Aunt Juley's eyes.

"How delightful!" she said. "When?"

"November."

Such a lucky month! But she did wish it could be sooner. It was a long time for James to wait, at his age!

To wait! They dreaded it for James, but they were used to it themselves. Indeed, it was their great distraction. To wait! For The Times to read; for one or other of their nieces or nephews to come in and cheer them up; for news of Nicholas' health; for that decision of Christopher's about going on the stage; for information concerning the mine of Mrs. MacAnder's nephew; for the doctor to come about Hester's inclination to wake up early in the morning; for books from the library which were always out; for Timothy to have a cold; for a nice quiet warm day, not too hot, when they could take a turn in Kensington Gardens. To wait, one on each side of the hearth in the drawing-room, for the clock between them to strike; their thin, veined, knuckled hands plying knitting-needles and crochet-hooks, their hair ordered to stop—like Canute's waves—from any further advance in colour. To wait in their black silks or satins for the Court to say that Hester might wear her dark green, and Juley her darker maroon. To wait, slowly turning over and over, in their old minds the little joys and sorrows, events and expectancies, of their little family world, as cows chew patient cuds in a familiar field. And this new event was so well worth waiting for. Soames had always been their pet, with his tendency to give them pictures, and his almost weekly visits which they missed so much, and his need for their sympathy evoked by the wreck of his first marriage. This new event—the birth of an heir to Soames—was so important for him, and for his dear father, too, that James might not have to die without some certainty about things. James did so dislike uncertainty; and with Montague, of course, he could not feel really satisfied to leave no grand-children but the young Darties. After all, one's own name did count! And as James' ninetieth birthday neared they wondered what precautions he was taking. He would be the first of the Forsytes to reach that age, and set, as it were, a new standard in holding on to life. That was so important, they felt, at their ages eighty-seven and eighty-five; though they did not want to think of themselves when they had Timothy, who was not yet eighty-two, to think of. There was, of course, a better world. 'In my Father's house are many mansions' was one of Aunt Juley's favourite sayings—it always comforted her, with its suggestion of house property, which had made the fortune of dear Roger. The Bible was, indeed, a great resource, and on very fine Sundays there was church in the morning; and sometimes Juley would steal into Timothy's study when she was sure he was out, and just put an open New Testament casually among the books on his little table—he was a great reader, of course, having been a publisher. But she had noticed that Timothy was always cross at dinner afterwards. And Smither had told her more than once that she had picked books off the floor in doing the room. Still, with all that, they did feel that heaven could not be quite so cosy as the rooms in which they and Timothy had been waiting so long. Aunt Hester, especially, could not bear the thought of the exertion. Any change, or rather the thought of a change—for there never was any—always upset her very much. Aunt Juley, who had more spirit, sometimes thought it would be quite exciting; she had so enjoyed that visit to Brighton the year dear Susan died. But then Brighton one knew was nice, and it was so difficult to tell what heaven would be like, so on the whole she was more than content to wait.

On the morning of James' birthday, August the 5th, they felt extraordinary animation, and little notes passed between them by the hand of Smither while they were having breakfast in their beds. Smither must go round and take their love and little presents and find out how Mr. James was, and whether he had passed a good night with all the excitement. And on the way back would Smither call in at Green Street—it was a little out of her way, but she could take the bus up Bond Street afterwards; it would be a nice little change for her—and ask dear Mrs. Dartie to be sure and look in before she went out of town.

All this Smither did—an undeniable servant trained many years ago under Aunt Ann to a perfection not now procurable. Mr. James, so Mrs. James said, had passed an excellent night, he sent his love; Mrs. James had said he was very funny and had complained that he didn't know what all the fuss was about. Oh! and Mrs. Dartie sent her love, and she would come to tea.

Aunts Juley and Hester, rather hurt that their presents had not received special mention—they forgot every year that James could not bear to receive presents, 'throwing away their money on him,' as he always called it—were 'delighted'; it showed that James was in good spirits, and that was so important for him. And they began to wait for Winifred. She came at four, bringing Imogen, and Maud, just back from school, and 'getting such a pretty girl, too,' so that it was extremely difficult to ask for news about Annette. Aunt Juley, however, summoned courage to enquire whether Winifred had heard anything, and if Soames was anxious.

"Uncle Soames is always anxious, Auntie," interrupted Imogen; "he can't be happy now he's got it."

The words struck familiarly on Aunt Juley's ears. Ah! yes; that funny drawing of George's, which had not been shown them! But what did Imogen mean? That her uncle always wanted more than he could have? It was not at all nice to think like that.

Imogen's voice rose clear and clipped:

"Imagine! Annette's only two years older than me; it must be awful for her, married to Uncle Soames."

Aunt Juley lifted her hands in horror.

"My dear," she said, "you don't know what you're talking about. Your Uncle Soames is a match for anybody. He's a very clever man, and good-looking and wealthy, and most considerate and careful, and not at all old, considering everything."

Imogen, turning her luscious glance from one to the other of the 'old dears,' only smiled.

"I hope," said Aunt Juley quite severely, "that you will marry as good a man."

"I shan't marry a good man, Auntie," murmured Imogen; "they're dull."

"If you go on like this," replied Aunt Juley, still very much upset, "you won't marry anybody. We'd better not pursue the subject;" and turning to Winifred, she said: "How is Montague?"

That evening, while they were waiting for dinner, she murmured:

"I've told Smither to get up half a bottle of the sweet champagne, Hester. I think we ought to drink dear James' health, and—and the health of Soames' wife; only, let's keep that quite secret. I'll just say like this, 'And you know, Hester!' and then we'll drink. It might upset Timothy."

"It's more likely to upset us," said Aunt Nester. "But we must, I suppose; for such an occasion."

"Yes," said Aunt Juley rapturously, "it is an occasion! Only fancy if he has a dear little boy, to carry the family on! I do feel it so important, now that Irene has had a son. Winifred says George is calling Jolyon 'The Three-Decker,' because of his three families, you know! George is droll. And fancy! Irene is living after all in the house Soames had built for them both. It does seem hard on dear Soames; and he's always been so regular."

That night in bed, excited and a little flushed still by her glass of wine and the secrecy of the second toast, she lay with her prayer-book opened flat, and her eyes fixed on a ceiling yellowed by the light from her reading-lamp. Young things! It was so nice for them all! And she would be so happy if she could see dear Soames happy. But, of course, he must be now, in spite of what Imogen had said. He would have all that he wanted: property, and wife, and children! And he would live to a green old age, like his dear father, and forget all about Irene and that dreadful case. If only she herself could be here to buy his children their first rocking-horse! Smither should choose it for her at the stores, nice and dappled. Ah! how Roger used to rock her until she fell off! Oh dear! that was a long time ago! It was! 'In my Father's house are many mansions—'A little scrattling noise caught her ear—'but no mice!' she thought mechanically. The noise increased. There! it was a mouse! How naughty of Smither to say there wasn't! It would be eating through the wainscot before they knew where they were, and they would have to have the builders in. They were such destructive things! And she lay, with her eyes just moving, following in her mind that little scrattling sound, and waiting for sleep to release her from it.

CHAPTER XII—BIRTH OF A FORSYTE

Soames walked out of the garden door, crossed the lawn, stood on the path above the river, turned round and walked back to the garden door, without having realised that he had moved. The sound of wheels crunching the drive convinced him that time had passed, and the doctor gone. What, exactly, had he said?

"This is the position, Mr. Forsyte. I can make pretty certain of her life if I operate, but the baby will be born dead. If I don't operate, the baby will most probably be born alive, but it's a great risk for the mother—a great risk. In either case I don't think she can ever have another child. In her state she obviously can't decide for herself, and we can't wait for her mother. It's for you to make the decision, while I'm getting what's necessary. I shall be back within the hour."

The decision! What a decision! No time to get a specialist down! No time for anything!

The sound of wheels died away, but Soames still stood intent; then, suddenly covering his ears, he walked back to the river. To come before its time like this, with no chance to foresee anything, not even to get her mother here! It was for her mother to make that decision, and she couldn't arrive from Paris till to-night! If only he could have understood the doctor's jargon, the medical niceties, so as to be sure he was weighing the chances properly; but they were Greek to him—like a legal problem to a layman. And yet he must decide! He brought his hand away from his brow wet, though the air was chilly. These sounds which came from her room! To go back there would only make it more difficult. He must be calm, clear. On the one hand life, nearly certain, of his young wife, death quite certain, of his child; and—no more children afterwards! On the other, death perhaps of his wife, nearly certain life for the child; and—no more children afterwards! Which to choose?.... It had rained this last fortnight—the river was very full, and in the water, collected round the little house-boat moored by his landing-stage, were many leaves from the woods above, brought off by a frost. Leaves fell, lives drifted down—Death! To decide about death! And no one to give him a hand. Life lost was lost for good. Let nothing go that you could keep; for, if it went, you couldn't get it back. It left you bare, like those trees when they lost their leaves; barer and barer until you, too, withered and came down. And, by a queer somersault of thought, he seemed to see not Annette lying up there behind that window-pane on which the sun was shining, but Irene lying in their bedroom in Montpellier Square, as it might conceivably have been her fate to lie, sixteen years ago. Would he have hesitated then? Not a moment! Operate, operate! Make certain of her life! No decision—a mere instinctive cry for help, in spite of his knowledge, even then, that she did not love him! But this! Ah! there was nothing overmastering in his feeling for Annette! Many times these last months, especially since she had been growing frightened, he had wondered. She had a will of her own, was selfish in her French way. And yet—so pretty! What would she wish—to take the risk. 'I know she wants the child,' he thought. 'If it's born dead, and no more chance afterwards—it'll upset her terribly. No more chance! All for nothing! Married life with her for years and years without a child. Nothing to steady her! She's too young. Nothing to look forward to, for her—for me! For me!' He struck his hands against his chest! Why couldn't he think without bringing himself in—get out of himself and see what he ought to do? The thought hurt him, then lost edge, as if it had come in contact with a breastplate. Out of oneself! Impossible! Out into soundless, scentless, touchless, sightless space! The very idea was ghastly, futile! And touching there the bedrock of reality, the bottom of his Forsyte spirit, Soames rested for a moment. When one ceased, all ceased; it might go on, but there'd be nothing in it!

He looked at his watch. In half an hour the doctor would be back. He must decide! If against the operation and she died, how face her mother and the doctor afterwards? How face his own conscience? It was his child that she was having. If for the operation—then he condemned them both to childlessness. And for what else had he married her but to have a lawful heir? And his father—at death's door, waiting for the news! 'It's cruel!' he thought; 'I ought never to have such a thing to settle! It's cruel!' He turned towards the house. Some deep, simple way of deciding! He took out a coin, and put it back. If he spun it, he knew he would not abide by what came up! He went into the dining-room, furthest away from that room whence the sounds issued. The doctor had said there was a chance. In here that chance seemed greater; the river did not flow, nor the leaves fall. A fire was burning. Soames unlocked the tantalus. He hardly ever touched spirits, but now—he poured himself out some whisky and drank it neat, craving a faster flow of blood. 'That fellow Jolyon,' he thought; 'he had children already. He has the woman I really loved; and now a son by her! And I—I'm asked to destroy my only child! Annette can't die; it's not possible. She's strong!'

He was still standing sullenly at the sideboard when he heard the doctor's carriage, and went out to him. He had to wait for him to come downstairs.

"Well, doctor?"

"The situation's the same. Have you decided?"

"Yes," said Soames; "don't operate!"

"Not? You understand—the risk's great?"

In Soames' set face nothing moved but the lips.

"You said there was a chance?"

"A chance, yes; not much of one."

"You say the baby must be born dead if you do?"

"Yes."

"Do you still think that in any case she can't have another?"

"One can't be absolutely sure, but it's most unlikely."

"She's strong," said Soames; "we'll take the risk."

The doctor looked at him very gravely. "It's on your shoulders," he said; "with my own wife, I couldn't."

Soames' chin jerked up as if someone had hit him.

"Am I of any use up there?" he asked.

"No; keep away."

"I shall be in my picture-gallery, then; you know where."

The doctor nodded, and went upstairs.

Soames continued to stand, listening. 'By this time to-morrow,' he thought, 'I may have her death on my hands.' No! it was unfair—monstrous, to put it that way! Sullenness dropped on him again, and he went up to the gallery. He stood at the window. The wind was in the north; it was cold, clear; very blue sky, heavy ragged white clouds chasing across; the river blue, too, through the screen of goldening trees; the woods all rich with colour, glowing, burnished-an early autumn. If it were his own life, would he be taking that risk? 'But she'd take the risk of losing me,' he thought, 'sooner than lose her child! She doesn't really love me!' What could one expect—a girl and French? The one thing really vital to them both, vital to their marriage and their futures, was a child! 'I've been through a lot for this,' he thought, 'I'll hold on—hold on. There's a chance of keeping both—a chance!' One kept till things were taken—one naturally kept! He began walking round the gallery. He had made one purchase lately which he knew was a fortune in itself, and he halted before it—a girl with dull gold hair which looked like filaments of metal gazing at a little golden monster she was holding in her hand. Even at this tortured moment he could just feel the extraordinary nature of the bargain he had made—admire the quality of the table, the floor, the chair, the girl's figure, the absorbed expression on her face, the dull gold filaments of her hair, the bright gold of the little monster. Collecting pictures; growing richer, richer! What use, if...! He turned his back abruptly on the picture, and went to the window. Some of his doves had flown up from their perches round the dovecot, and were stretching their wings in the wind. In the clear sharp sunlight their whiteness almost flashed. They flew far, making a flung-up hieroglyphic against the sky. Annette fed the doves; it was pretty to see her. They took it out of her hand; they knew she was matter-of-fact. A choking sensation came into his throat. She would not—could not die! She was too—too sensible; and she was strong, really strong, like her mother, in spite of her fair prettiness.

It was already growing dark when at last he opened the door, and stood listening. Not a sound! A milky twilight crept about the stairway and the landings below. He had turned back when a sound caught his ear. Peering down, he saw a black shape moving, and his heart stood still. What was it? Death? The shape of Death coming from her door? No! only a maid without cap or apron. She came to the foot of his flight of stairs and said breathlessly:

"The doctor wants to see you, sir."

He ran down. She stood flat against the wall to let him pass, and said:

"Oh, Sir! it's over."

"Over?" said Soames, with a sort of menace; "what d'you mean?"

"It's born, sir."

He dashed up the four steps in front of him, and came suddenly on the doctor in the dim passage. The man was wiping his brow.

"Well?" he said; "quick!"

"Both living; it's all right, I think."

Soames stood quite still, covering his eyes.

"I congratulate you," he heard the doctor say; "it was touch and go."

Soames let fall the hand which was covering his face.

"Thanks," he said; "thanks very much. What is it?"

"Daughter—luckily; a son would have killed her—the head."

A daughter!

"The utmost care of both," he hears the doctor say, "and we shall do. When does the mother come?"

"To-night, between nine and ten, I hope."

"I'll stay till then. Do you want to see them?"

"Not now," said Soames; "before you go. I'll have dinner sent up to you." And he went downstairs.

Relief unspeakable, and yet—a daughter! It seemed to him unfair. To have taken that risk—to have been through this agony—and what agony!—for a daughter! He stood before the blazing fire of wood logs in the hall, touching it with his toe and trying to readjust himself. 'My father!' he thought. A bitter disappointment, no disguising it! One never got all one wanted in this life! And there was no other—at least, if there was, it was no use!

While he was standing there, a telegram was brought him.

"Come up at once, your father sinking fast.—MOTHER."

He read it with a choking sensation. One would have thought he couldn't feel anything after these last hours, but he felt this. Half-past seven, a train from Reading at nine, and madame's train, if she had caught it, came in at eight-forty—he would meet that, and go on. He ordered the carriage, ate some dinner mechanically, and went upstairs. The doctor came out to him.

"They're sleeping."

"I won't go in," said Soames with relief. "My father's dying; I have to—go up. Is it all right?"

The doctor's face expressed a kind of doubting admiration. 'If they were all as unemotional' he might have been saying.

"Yes, I think you may go with an easy mind. You'll be down soon?"

"To-morrow," said Soames. "Here's the address."

The doctor seemed to hover on the verge of sympathy.

"Good-night!" said Soames abruptly, and turned away. He put on his fur coat. Death! It was a chilly business. He smoked a cigarette in the carriage—one of his rare cigarettes. The night was windy and flew on black wings; the carriage lights had to search out the way. His father! That old, old man! A comfortless night—to die!

The London train came in just as he reached the station, and Madame Lamotte, substantial, dark-clothed, very yellow in the lamplight, came towards the exit with a dressing-bag.

"This all you have?" asked Soames.

"But yes; I had not the time. How is my little one?"

"Doing well—both. A girl!"

"A girl! What joy! I had a frightful crossing!"

Her black bulk, solid, unreduced by the frightful crossing, climbed into the brougham.

"And you, mon cher?"

"My father's dying," said Soames between his teeth. "I'm going up. Give my love to Annette."

"Tiens!" murmured Madame Lamotte; "quel malheur!"

Soames took his hat off, and moved towards his train. 'The French!' he thought.

CHAPTER XIII—JAMES IS TOLD

A simple cold, caught in the room with double windows, where the air and the people who saw him were filtered, as it were, the room he had not left since the middle of September—and James was in deep waters. A little cold, passing his little strength and flying quickly to his lungs. "He mustn't catch cold," the doctor had declared, and he had gone and caught it. When he first felt it in his throat he had said to his nurse—for he had one now—"There, I knew how it would be, airing the room like that!" For a whole day he was highly nervous about himself and went in advance of all precautions and remedies; drawing every breath with extreme care and having his temperature taken every hour. Emily was not alarmed.

But next morning when she went in the nurse whispered: "He won't have his temperature taken."

Emily crossed to the side of the bed where he was lying, and said softly, "How do you feel, James?" holding the thermometer to his lips. James looked up at her.

"What's the good of that?" he murmured huskily; "I don't want to know."

Then she was alarmed. He breathed with difficulty, he looked terribly frail, white, with faint red discolorations. She had 'had trouble' with him, Goodness knew; but he was James, had been James for nearly fifty years; she couldn't remember or imagine life without James—James, behind all his fussiness, his pessimism, his crusty shell, deeply affectionate, really kind and generous to them all!

All that day and the next he hardly uttered a word, but there was in his eyes a noticing of everything done for him, a look on his face which told her he was fighting; and she did not lose hope. His very stillness, the way he conserved every little scrap of energy, showed the tenacity with which he was fighting. It touched her deeply; and though her face was composed and comfortable in the sick-room, tears ran down her cheeks when she was out of it.

About tea-time on the third day—she had just changed her dress, keeping her appearance so as not to alarm him, because he noticed everything—she saw a difference. 'It's no use; I'm tired,' was written plainly across that white face, and when she went up to him, he muttered: "Send for Soames."

"Yes, James," she said comfortably; "all right—at once." And she kissed his forehead. A tear dropped there, and as she wiped it off she saw that his eyes looked grateful. Much upset, and without hope now, she sent Soames the telegram.

When he entered out of the black windy night, the big house was still as a grave. Warmson's broad face looked almost narrow; he took the fur coat with a sort of added care, saying:

"Will you have a glass of wine, sir?"

Soames shook his head, and his eyebrows made enquiry.

Warmson's lips twitched. "He's asking for you, sir;" and suddenly he blew his nose. "It's a long time, sir," he said, "that I've been with Mr. Forsyte—a long time."

Soames left him folding the coat, and began to mount the stairs. This house, where he had been born and sheltered, had never seemed to him so warm, and rich, and cosy, as during this last pilgrimage to his father's room. It was not his taste; but in its own substantial, lincrusta way it was the acme of comfort and security. And the night was so dark and windy; the grave so cold and lonely!

He paused outside the door. No sound came from within. He turned the handle softly and was in the room before he was perceived. The light was shaded. His mother and Winifred were sitting on the far side of the bed; the nurse was moving away from the near side where was an empty chair. 'For me!' thought Soames. As he moved from the door his mother and sister rose, but he signed with his hand and they sat down again. He went up to the chair and stood looking at his father. James' breathing was as if strangled; his eyes were closed. And in Soames, looking on his father so worn and white and wasted, listening to his strangled breathing, there rose a passionate vehemence of anger against Nature, cruel, inexorable Nature, kneeling on the chest of that wisp of a body, slowly pressing out the breath, pressing out the life of the being who was dearest to him in the world. His father, of all men, had lived a careful life, moderate, abstemious, and this was his reward—to have life slowly, painfully squeezed out of him! And, without knowing that he spoke, he said: "It's cruel!"

He saw his mother cover her eyes and Winifred bow her face towards the bed. Women! They put up with things so much better than men. He took a step nearer to his father. For three days James had not been shaved, and his lips and chin were covered with hair, hardly more snowy than his forehead. It softened his face, gave it a queer look already not of this world. His eyes opened. Soames went quite close and bent over. The lips moved.

"Here I am, Father."

"Um—what—what news? They never tell...." the voice died, and a flood of emotion made Soames' face work so that he could not speak. Tell him?—yes. But what? He made a great effort, got his lips together, and said:

"Good news, dear, good—Annette, a son."

"Ah!" It was the queerest sound, ugly, relieved, pitiful, triumphant—like the noise a baby makes getting what it wants. The eyes closed, and that strangled sound of breathing began again. Soames recoiled to the chair and stonily sat down. The lie he had told, based, as it were, on some deep, temperamental instinct that after death James would not know the truth, had taken away all power of feeling for the moment. His arm brushed against something. It was his father's naked foot. In the struggle to breathe he had pushed it out from under the clothes. Soames took it in his hand, a cold foot, light and thin, white, very cold. What use to put it back, to wrap up that which must be colder soon! He warmed it mechanically with his hand, listening to his father's laboured breathing; while the power of feeling rose again within him. A little sob, quickly smothered, came from Winifred, but his mother sat unmoving with her eyes fixed on James. Soames signed to the nurse.

"Where's the doctor?" he whispered.

"He's been sent for."

"Can't you do anything to ease his breathing?"

"Only an injection; and he can't stand it. The doctor said, while he was fighting...."

"He's not fighting," whispered Soames, "he's being slowly smothered. It's awful."

James stirred uneasily, as if he knew what they were saying. Soames rose and bent over him. James feebly moved his two hands, and Soames took them.

"He wants to be pulled up," whispered the nurse.

Soames pulled. He thought he pulled gently, but a look almost of anger passed over James' face. The nurse plumped the pillows. Soames laid the hands down, and bending over kissed his father's forehead. As he was raising himself again, James' eyes bent on him a look which seemed to come from the very depths of what was left within. 'I'm done, my boy,' it seemed to say, 'take care of them, take care of yourself; take care—I leave it all to you.'

"Yes, Yes," Soames whispered, "yes, yes."

Behind him the nurse did he knew, not what, for his father made a tiny movement of repulsion as if resenting that interference; and almost at once his breathing eased away, became quiet; he lay very still. The strained expression on his face passed, a curious white tranquillity took its place. His eyelids quivered, rested; the whole face rested; at ease. Only by the faint puffing of his lips could they tell that he was breathing. Soames sank back on his chair, and fell to cherishing the foot again. He heard the nurse quietly crying over there by the fire; curious that she, a stranger, should be the only one of them who cried! He heard the quiet lick and flutter of the fire flames. One more old Forsyte going to his long rest—wonderful, they were!—wonderful how he had held on! His mother and Winifred were leaning forward, hanging on the sight of James' lips. But Soames bent sideways over the feet, warming them both; they gave him comfort, colder and colder though they grew. Suddenly he started up; a sound, a dreadful sound such as he had never heard, was coming from his father's lips, as if an outraged heart had broken with a long moan. What a strong heart, to have uttered that farewell! It ceased. Soames looked into the face. No motion; no breath! Dead! He kissed the brow, turned round and went out of the room. He ran upstairs to the bedroom, his old bedroom, still kept for him; flung himself face down on the bed, and broke into sobs which he stilled with the pillow....

A little later he went downstairs and passed into the room. James lay alone, wonderfully calm, free from shadow and anxiety, with the gravity on his ravaged face which underlies great age, the worn fine gravity of old coins.

Soames looked steadily at that face, at the fire, at all the room with windows thrown open to the London night.

"Good-bye!" he whispered, and went out.

CHAPTER XIV—HIS

He had much to see to, that night and all next day. A telegram at breakfast reassured him about Annette, and he only caught the last train back to Reading, with Emily's kiss on his forehead and in his ears her words:

"I don't know what I should have done without you, my dear boy."

He reached his house at midnight. The weather had changed, was mild again, as though, having finished its work and sent a Forsyte to his last account, it could relax. A second telegram, received at dinner-time, had confirmed the good news of Annette, and, instead of going in, Soames passed down through the garden in the moonlight to his houseboat. He could sleep there quite well. Bitterly tired, he lay down on the sofa in his fur coat and fell asleep. He woke soon after dawn and went on deck. He stood against the rail, looking west where the river swept round in a wide curve under the woods. In Soames, appreciation of natural beauty was curiously like that of his farmer ancestors, a sense of grievance if it wasn't there, sharpened, no doubt, and civilised, by his researches among landscape painting. But dawn has power to fertilise the most matter-of-fact vision, and he was stirred. It was another world from the river he knew, under that remote cool light; a world into which man had not entered, an unreal world, like some strange shore sighted by discovery. Its colour was not the colour of convention, was hardly colour at all; its shapes were brooding yet distinct; its silence stunning; it had no scent. Why it should move him he could not tell, unless it were that he felt so alone in it, bare of all relationship and all possessions. Into such a world his father might be voyaging, for all resemblance it had to the world he had left. And Soames took refuge from it in wondering what painter could have done it justice. The white-grey water was like—like the belly of a fish! Was it possible that this world on which he looked was all private property, except the water—and even that was tapped! No tree, no shrub, not a blade of grass, not a bird or beast, not even a fish that was not owned. And once on a time all this was jungle and marsh and water, and weird creatures roamed and sported without human cognizance to give them names; rotting luxuriance had rioted where those tall, carefully planted woods came down to the water, and marsh-misted reeds on that far side had covered all the pasture. Well! they had got it under, kennelled it all up, labelled it, and stowed it in lawyers' offices. And a good thing too! But once in a way, as now, the ghost of the past came out to haunt and brood and whisper to any human who chanced to be awake: 'Out of my unowned loneliness you all came, into it some day you will all return.'

And Soames, who felt the chill and the eeriness of that world-new to him and so very old: the world, unowned, visiting the scene of its past—went down and made himself tea on a spirit-lamp. When he had drunk it, he took out writing materials and wrote two paragraphs:

"On the 20th instant at his residence in Park Lane, James Forsyte, in his ninety-first year. Funeral at noon on the 24th at Highgate. No flowers by request."

"On the 20th instant at The Shelter; Mapledurham, Annette, wife of Soames Forsyte, of a daughter." And underneath on the blottingpaper he traced the word "son."

It was eight o'clock in an ordinary autumn world when he went across to the house. Bushes across the river stood round and bright-coloured out of a milky haze; the wood-smoke went up blue and straight; and his doves cooed, preening their feathers in the sunlight.

He stole up to his dressing-room, bathed, shaved, put on fresh linen and dark clothes.

Madame Lamotte was beginning her breakfast when he went down.

She looked at his clothes, said, "Don't tell me!" and pressed his hand. "Annette is prettee well. But the doctor say she can never have no more children. You knew that?" Soames nodded. "It's a pity. Mais la petite est adorable. Du cafe?"

Soames got away from her as soon as he could. She offended him—solid, matter-of-fact, quick, clear—French. He could not bear her vowels, her 'r's'; he resented the way she had looked at him, as if it were his fault that Annette could never bear him a son! His fault! He even resented her cheap adoration of the daughter he had not yet seen.

Curious how he jibbed away from sight of his wife and child!

One would have thought he must have rushed up at the first moment. On the contrary, he had a sort of physical shrinking from it—fastidious possessor that he was. He was afraid of what Annette was thinking of him, author of her agonies, afraid of the look of the baby, afraid of showing his disappointment with the present and—the future.

He spent an hour walking up and down the drawing-room before he could screw his courage up to mount the stairs and knock on the door of their room.

Madame Lamotte opened it.

"Ah! At last you come! Elle vous attend!" She passed him, and Soames went in with his noiseless step, his jaw firmly set, his eyes furtive.

Annette was very pale and very pretty lying there. The baby was hidden away somewhere; he could not see it. He went up to the bed, and with sudden emotion bent and kissed her forehead.

"Here you are then, Soames," she said. "I am not so bad now. But I suffered terribly, terribly. I am glad I cannot have any more. Oh! how I suffered!"

Soames stood silent, stroking her hand; words of endearment, of sympathy, absolutely would not come; the thought passed through him: 'An English girl wouldn't have said that!' At this moment he knew with certainty that he would never be near to her in spirit and in truth, nor she to him. He had collected her—that was all! And Jolyon's words came rushing into his mind: "I should imagine you will be glad to have your neck out of chancery." Well, he had got it out! Had he got it in again?

"We must feed you up," he said, "you'll soon be strong."

"Don't you want to see baby, Soames? She is asleep."

"Of course," said Soames, "very much."

He passed round the foot of the bed to the other side and stood staring. For the first moment what he saw was much what he had expected to see—a baby. But as he stared and the baby breathed and made little sleeping movements with its tiny features, it seemed to assume an individual shape, grew to be like a picture, a thing he would know again; not repulsive, strangely bud-like and touching. It had dark hair. He touched it with his finger, he wanted to see its eyes. They opened, they were dark—whether blue or brown he could not tell. The eyes winked, stared, they had a sort of sleepy depth in them. And suddenly his heart felt queer, warm, as if elated.

"Ma petite fleur!" Annette said softly.

"Fleur," repeated Soames: "Fleur! we'll call her that."

The sense of triumph and renewed possession swelled within him.

By God! this—this thing was his! By God! this—this thing was his!

THE FORSYTE SAGA

VOLUME III
AWAKENING
TO LET

BY
JOHN GALSWORTHY

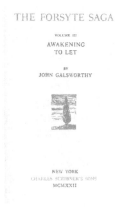

NEW YORK
CHARLES SCRIBNER'S SONS
MCMXXII

Soames at Highgate.

THE FORSYTE SAGA—VOLUME III.

By John Galsworthy

INTERLUDE. AWAKENING

TO CHARLES SCRIBNER

AWAKENING

Through the massive skylight illuminating the hall at Robin Hill, the July sunlight at five o'clock fell just where the broad stairway turned; and in that radiant streak little Jon Forsyte stood, blue-linen-suited. His hair was shining, and his eyes, from beneath a frown, for he was considering how to go downstairs, this last of innumerable times, before the car brought his father and mother home. Four at a time, and five at the bottom? Stale! Down the banisters? But in which fashion? On his face, feet foremost? Very stale. On his stomach, sideways? Paltry! On his back, with his arms stretched down on both sides?

385

Forbidden! Or on his face, head foremost, in a manner unknown as yet to any but himself? Such was the cause of the frown on the illuminated face of little Jon....

In that Summer of 1909 the simple souls who even then desired to simplify the English tongue, had, of course, no cognizance of little Jon, or they would have claimed him for a disciple. But one can be too simple in this life, for his real name was Jolyon, and his living father and dead half-brother had usurped of old the other shortenings, Jo and Jolly. As a fact little Jon had done his best to conform to convention and spell himself first Jhon, then John; not till his father had explained the sheer necessity, had he spelled his name Jon.

Up till now that father had possessed what was left of his heart by the groom, Bob, who played the concertina, and his nurse "Da," who wore the violet dress on Sundays, and enjoyed the name of Spraggins in that private life lived at odd moments even by domestic servants. His mother had only appeared to him, as it were in dreams, smelling delicious, smoothing his forehead just before he fell asleep, and sometimes docking his hair, of a golden brown colour. When he cut his head open against the nursery fender she was there to be bled over; and when he had nightmare she would sit on his bed and cuddle his head against her neck. She was precious but remote, because "Da" was so near, and there is hardly room for more than one woman at a time in a man's heart. With his father, too, of course, he had special bonds of union; for little Jon also meant to be a painter when he grew up—with the one small difference, that his father painted pictures, and little Jon intended to paint ceilings and walls, standing on a board between two step-ladders, in a dirty-white apron, and a lovely smell of whitewash. His father also took him riding in Richmond Park, on his pony, Mouse, so-called because it was so-coloured.

Little Jon had been born with a silver spoon in a mouth which was rather curly and large. He had never heard his father or his mother speak in an angry voice, either to each other, himself, or anybody else; the groom, Bob, Cook, Jane, Bella and the other servants, even "Da," who alone restrained him in his courses, had special voices when they talked to him. He was therefore of opinion that the world was a place of perfect and perpetual gentility and freedom.

A child of 1901, he had come to consciousness when his country, just over that bad attack of scarlet fever, the Boer War, was preparing for the Liberal revival of 1906. Coercion was unpopular, parents had exalted notions of giving their offspring a good time. They spoiled their rods, spared their children, and anticipated the results with enthusiasm. In choosing, moreover, for his father an amiable man of fifty-two, who had already lost an only son, and for his mother a woman of thirty-eight, whose first and only child he was, little Jon had done well and wisely. What had saved him from becoming a cross between a lap dog and a little prig, had been his father's adoration of his mother, for even little Jon could see that she was not merely just his mother, and that he played second fiddle to her in his father's heart: What he played in his mother's heart he knew not yet. As for "Auntie" June, his half-sister (but so old that she had grown out of the relationship) she loved him, of course, but was too sudden. His devoted "Da," too, had a Spartan touch. His bath was cold and his knees were bare; he was not encouraged to be sorry for himself. As to the vexed question of his education, little Jon shared the theory of those who considered that children should not be forced. He rather liked the Mademoiselle who came for two hours every morning to teach him her language, together with history, geography and sums; nor were the piano lessons which his mother gave him disagreeable, for she had a way of luring him from tune to tune, never making him practise one which did not give him pleasure, so that he remained eager to convert ten thumbs into eight fingers. Under his father he learned to draw pleasure-pigs and other animals. He was not a highly educated little boy. Yet, on the whole, the silver spoon stayed in his mouth without spoiling it, though "Da" sometimes said that other children would do him a "world of good."

It was a disillusionment, then, when at the age of nearly seven she held him down on his back, because he wanted to do something of which she did not approve. This first interference with the free individualism of a Forsyte drove him almost frantic. There was something appalling in the utter helplessness of that position, and the uncertainty as to whether it would ever come to an end. Suppose she never let him get up any more! He suffered torture at the top of his voice for fifty seconds. Worse than anything was his perception that "Da" had taken all that time to realise the agony of fear he was enduring. Thus, dreadfully, was revealed to him the lack of imagination in the human being.

When he was let up he remained convinced that "Da" had done a dreadful thing. Though he did not wish to bear witness against her, he had been compelled, by fear of repetition, to seek his mother and say: "Mum, don't let 'Da' hold me down on my back again."

His mother, her hands held up over her head, and in them two plaits of hair—"couleur de feuille morte," as little Jon had not yet learned to call it—had looked at him with eyes like little bits of his brown velvet tunic, and answered:

"No, darling, I won't."

She, being in the nature of a goddess, little Jon was satisfied; especially when, from under the dining-table at breakfast, where he happened to be waiting for a mushroom, he had overheard her say to his father:

"Then, will you tell 'Da,' dear, or shall I? She's so devoted to him"; and his father's answer:

"Well, she mustn't show it that way. I know exactly what it feels like to be held down on one's back. No Forsyte can stand it for a minute."

Conscious that they did not know him to be under the table, little Jon was visited by the quite new feeling of embarrassment, and stayed where he was, ravaged by desire for the mushroom.

Such had been his first dip into the dark abysses of existence. Nothing much had been revealed to him after that, till one day, having gone down to the cow-house for his drink of milk fresh from the cow, after Garratt had finished milking, he had seen Clover's calf, dead. Inconsolable, and followed by an upset Garratt, he had sought "Da"; but suddenly aware that she was not the person he wanted, had rushed away to find his father, and had run into the arms of his mother.

"Clover's calf's dead! Oh! Oh! It looked so soft!"

His mother's clasp, and her:

"Yes, darling, there, there!" had stayed his sobbing. But if Clover's calf could die, anything could—not only bees, flies, beetles and chickens—and look soft like that! This was appalling—and soon forgotten!

The next thing had been to sit on a bumble bee, a poignant experience, which his mother had understood much better than "Da"; and nothing of vital importance had happened after that till the year turned; when, following a day of utter wretchedness, he had enjoyed a disease composed of little spots, bed, honey in a spoon, and many Tangerine oranges. It was then that the world had flowered. To "Auntie" June he owed that flowering, for no sooner was he a little lame duck than she came rushing down from London, bringing with her the books which had nurtured her own Berserker spirit, born in the noted year of 1869. Aged, and of many colours, they were stored with the most formidable happenings. Of these she read to little Jon, till he was allowed to read to himself; whereupon she whisked back to London and left them with him in a heap. Those books cooked his fancy, till he thought and dreamed of nothing but midshipmen and dhows, pirates, rafts, sandal-wood traders, iron horses, sharks, battles, Tartars, Red Indians, balloons, North Poles and other extravagant delights. The moment he was suffered to get up, he rigged his bed fore and aft, and set out from it in a narrow bath across green seas of carpet, to a rock, which he climbed by means of its mahogany drawer knobs, to sweep the horizon with his drinking tumbler screwed to his eye, in search of rescuing sails. He made a daily raft out of the towel stand, the tea tray, and his pillows. He saved the juice from his French plums, bottled it in an empty medicine bottle, and provisioned the raft with the rum that it became; also with pemmican made out of little saved-up bits of chicken sat on and dried at the fire; and with lime juice against scurvy, extracted from the peel of his oranges and a little economised juice. He made a North Pole one morning from the whole of his bedclothes except the bolster, and reached it in a birch-bark canoe (in private life the fender), after a terrible encounter with a polar bear fashioned from the bolster and four skittles dressed up in "Da's" nightgown. After that, his father, seeking to steady his imagination, brought him Ivanhoe, Bevis, a book about King Arthur, and Tom Brown's Schooldays. He read the first, and for three days built, defended and stormed Front de Boeuf's castle, taking every part in the piece except those of Rebecca and Rowena; with piercing cries of: "En avant, de Bracy!" and similar utterances. After reading the book about King Arthur he became almost exclusively Sir Lamorac de Galis, because, though there was very little about him, he preferred his name to that of any other knight; and he rode his old rocking-horse to death, armed with a long bamboo. Bevis he found tame; besides, it required woods and animals, of which he had none in his nursery, except his two cats, Fitz and Puck Forsyte, who permitted no liberties. For Tom Brown he was as yet too young. There was relief in the house when, after the fourth week, he was permitted to go down and out.

The month being March the trees were exceptionally like the masts of ships, and for little Jon that was a wonderful Spring, extremely hard on his knees, suits, and the patience of "Da," who had the washing and reparation of his clothes. Every morning the moment his breakfast was over, he could be viewed by his mother and father, whose windows looked out that way, coming from the study, crossing the terrace, climbing the old oak tree, his face resolute and his hair bright. He began the day thus because there was not time to go far afield before his lessons. The old tree's variety never staled; it had mainmast, foremast, top-gallant mast, and he could always come down by the halyards—or ropes of the swing. After his lessons, completed by eleven, he would go to the kitchen for a thin piece of cheese, a biscuit and two French plums—provision enough for a jolly-boat at least—and eat it in some imaginative way; then, armed to the teeth with gun, pistols, and sword, he would begin the serious climbing of the morning, encountering by the way innumerable slavers, Indians, pirates, leopards, and bears. He was seldom seen at that hour of the day without a cutlass in his teeth (like Dick Needham) amid the rapid explosion of copper caps. And many were the gardeners he brought down with yellow peas shot out of his little gun. He lived a life of the most violent action.

"Jon," said his father to his mother, under the oak tree, "is terrible. I'm afraid he's going to turn out a sailor, or something hopeless. Do you see any sign of his appreciating beauty?"

"Not the faintest."

"Well, thank heaven he's no turn for wheels or engines! I can bear anything but that. But I wish he'd take more interest in Nature."

"He's imaginative, Jolyon."

"Yes, in a sanguinary way. Does he love anyone just now?"

"No; only everyone. There never was anyone born more loving or more lovable than Jon."

"Being your boy, Irene."

At this moment little Jon, lying along a branch high above them, brought them down with two peas; but that fragment of talk lodged, thick, in his small gizzard. Loving, lovable, imaginative, sanguinary!

The leaves also were thick by now, and it was time for his birthday, which, occurring every year on the twelfth of May, was always memorable for his chosen dinner of sweetbread, mushrooms, macaroons, and ginger beer.

Between that eighth birthday, however, and the afternoon when he stood in the July radiance at the turning of the stairway, several important things had happened.

"Da," worn out by washing his knees, or moved by that mysterious instinct which forces even nurses to desert their nurslings, left the very day after his birthday in floods of tears "to be married"—of all things—"to a man." Little Jon, from whom it had been kept, was inconsolable for an afternoon. It ought not to have been kept from him! Two large boxes of soldiers and some artillery, together with The Young Buglers, which had been among his birthday presents, cooperated with his grief in a sort of conversion, and instead of seeking adventures in person and risking his own life, he began to play imaginative games, in which he risked the lives of countless tin soldiers, marbles, stones and beans. Of these forms of "chair a canon" he made collections, and, using them alternately, fought the Peninsular, the Seven Years, the Thirty Years, and other wars, about which he had been reading of late in a big History of Europe which had been his grandfather's. He altered them to suit his genius, and fought them all over the floor in his day nursery, so that nobody could come in, for fearing of disturbing Gustavus Adolphus, King of Sweden, or treading on an army of Austrians. Because of the sound of the word he was passionately addicted to the Austrians, and finding there were so few battles in which they were successful he had to invent them in his games. His favourite generals were Prince Eugene, the Archduke Charles and Wallenstein. Tilly and Mack ("music-hall turns" he heard his father call them one day, whatever that might mean) one really could not love very much, Austrian though they were. For euphonic reasons, too, he doted on Turenne.

This phase, which caused his parents anxiety, because it kept him indoors when he ought to have been out, lasted through May and half of June, till his father killed it by bringing home to him Tom Sawyer and Huckleberry Finn. When he read those books something happened in him, and he went out of doors again in passionate quest of a river. There being none on the premises at Robin Hill, he had to make one out of the pond, which fortunately had water lilies, dragonflies, gnats, bullrushes, and three small willow trees. On this pond, after his father and Garratt had ascertained by sounding that it had a reliable bottom and was nowhere more than two feet deep, he was allowed a little collapsible canoe, in which he spent hours and hours paddling, and lying down out of sight of Indian Joe and other enemies. On the shore of the pond, too, he built himself a wigwam about four feet square, of old biscuit tins, roofed in by boughs. In this he would make little fires, and cook the birds he had not shot with his gun, hunting in the coppice and fields, or the fish he did not catch in the pond because there were none. This occupied the rest of June and that July, when his father and mother were away in Ireland. He led a lonely life of "make believe" during those five weeks of summer weather, with gun, wigwam, water and canoe; and, however hard his active little brain tried to keep the sense of beauty away, she did creep in on him for a second now and then, perching on the wing of a dragon-fly, glistening on the water lilies, or brushing his eyes with her blue as he lay on his back in ambush.

"Auntie" June, who had been left in charge, had a "grown-up" in the house, with a cough and a large piece of putty which he was making into a face; so she hardly ever came down to see him in the pond. Once, however, she brought with her two other "grown-ups." Little

Jon, who happened to have painted his naked self bright blue and yellow in stripes out of his father's water-colour box, and put some duck's feathers in his hair, saw them coming, and—ambushed himself among the willows. As he had foreseen, they came at once to his wigwam and knelt down to look inside, so that with a blood-curdling yell he was able to take the scalps of "Auntie" June and the woman "grown-up" in an almost complete manner before they kissed him. The names of the two grown-ups were "Auntie" Holly and "Uncle" Val, who had a brown face and a little limp, and laughed at him terribly. He took a fancy to "Auntie" Holly, who seemed to be a sister too; but they both went away the same afternoon and he did not see them again. Three days before his father and mother were to come home "Auntie" June also went off in a great hurry, taking the "grown-up" who coughed and his piece of putty; and Mademoiselle said: "Poor man, he was veree ill. I forbid you to go into his room, Jon." Little Jon, who rarely did things merely because he was told not to, refrained from going, though he was bored and lonely. In truth the day of the pond was past, and he was filled to the brim of his soul with restlessness and the want of something—not a tree, not a gun—something soft. Those last two days had seemed months in spite of Cast Up by the Sea, wherein he was reading about Mother Lee and her terrible wrecking bonfire. He had gone up and down the stairs perhaps a hundred times in those two days, and often from the day nursery, where he slept now, had stolen into his mother's room, looked at everything, without touching, and on into the dressing-room; and standing on one leg beside the bath, like Slingsby, had whispered:

"Ho, ho, ho! Dog my cats!" mysteriously, to bring luck. Then, stealing back, he had opened his mother's wardrobe, and taken a long sniff which seemed to bring him nearer to—he didn't know what.

He had done this just before he stood in the streak of sunlight, debating in which of the several ways he should slide down the banisters. They all seemed silly, and in a sudden languor he began descending the steps one by one. During that descent he could remember his father quite distinctly—the short grey beard, the deep eyes twinkling, the furrow between them, the funny smile, the thin figure which always seemed so tall to little Jon; but his mother he couldn't see. All that represented her was something swaying with two dark eyes looking back at him; and the scent of her wardrobe.

Bella was in the hall, drawing aside the big curtains, and opening the front door. Little Jon said, wheedling,

"Bella!"

"Yes, Master Jon."

"Do let's have tea under the oak tree when they come; I know they'd like it best."

"You mean you'd like it best."

Little Jon considered.

"No, they would, to please me."

Bella smiled. "Very well, I'll take it out if you'll stay quiet here and not get into mischief before they come."

Little Jon sat down on the bottom step, and nodded. Bella came close, and looked him over.

"Get up!" she said.

Little Jon got up. She scrutinized him behind; he was not green, and his knees seemed clean.

"All right!" she said. "My! Aren't you brown? Give me a kiss!"

And little Jon received a peck on his hair.

"What jam?" he asked. "I'm so tired of waiting."

"Gooseberry and strawberry."

Num! They were his favourites!

When she was gone he sat still for quite a minute. It was quiet in the big hall open to its East end so that he could see one of his trees, a brig sailing very slowly across the upper lawn. In the outer hall shadows were slanting from the pillars. Little Jon got up, jumped one of them, and walked round the clump of iris plants which filled the pool of grey-white marble in the centre. The flowers were pretty, but only smelled a very little. He stood in the open doorway and looked out. Suppose!—suppose they didn't come! He had waited so long that he felt he could not bear that, and his attention slid at once from such finality to the dust motes in the bluish sunlight coming in: Thrusting his hand up, he tried to catch some. Bella ought to have dusted that piece of air! But perhaps they weren't dust—only what sunlight was made of, and he looked to see whether the sunlight out of doors was the same. It was not. He had said he would stay quiet in the hall, but he simply couldn't any more; and crossing the gravel of the drive he lay down on the grass beyond. Pulling six daisies he named them carefully, Sir Lamorac, Sir Tristram, Sir Lancelot, Sir Palimedes, Sir Bors, Sir Gawain, and fought them in couples till only Sir Lamorac, whom he had selected for a specially stout stalk, had his head on, and even he, after three encounters, looked worn and waggly. A beetle was moving slowly in the grass, which almost wanted cutting. Every blade was a small tree, round whose trunk the beetle had to glide. Little Jon stretched out Sir Lamorac, feet foremost, and stirred the creature up. It scuttled painfully. Little Jon laughed, lost interest, and sighed. His heart felt empty. He turned over and lay on his back. There was a scent of honey from the lime trees in flower, and in the sky the blue was beautiful, with a few white clouds which looked and perhaps tasted like lemon ice. He could hear Bob playing: "Way down upon de Suwannee ribber" on his concertina, and it made him nice and sad. He turned over again and put his ear to the ground—Indians could hear things coming ever so far—but he could hear nothing—only the concertina! And almost instantly he did hear a grinding sound, a faint toot. Yes! it was a car—coming— coming! Up he jumped. Should he wait in the porch, or rush upstairs, and as they came in, shout: "Look!" and slide slowly down the banisters, head foremost? Should he? The car turned in at the drive. It was too late! And he only waited, jumping up and down in his excitement. The car came quickly, whirred, and stopped. His father got out, exactly like life. He bent down and little Jon bobbed up—they bumped. His father said,

"Bless us! Well, old man, you are brown!" Just as he would; and the sense of expectation— of something wanted—bubbled unextinguished in little Jon. Then, with a long, shy look he saw his mother, in a blue dress, with a blue motor scarf over her cap and hair, smiling. He jumped as high as ever he could, twined his legs behind her back, and hugged. He heard her gasp, and felt her hugging back. His eyes, very dark blue just then, looked into hers, very dark brown, till her lips closed on his eyebrow, and, squeezing with all his might, he heard her creak and laugh, and say:

"You are strong, Jon!"

He slid down at that, and rushed into the hall, dragging her by the hand.

While he was eating his jam beneath the oak tree, he noticed things about his mother that he had never seemed to see before, her cheeks for instance were creamy, there were silver threads in her dark goldy hair, her throat had no knob in it like Bella's, and she went in and out softly. He noticed, too, some little lines running away from the corners of her eyes, and a nice darkness under them. She was ever so beautiful, more beautiful than "Da" or Mademoiselle, or "Auntie" June or even "Auntie" Holly, to whom he had taken a fancy; even more beautiful than Bella, who had pink cheeks and came out too suddenly in places. This new beautifulness of his mother had a kind of particular importance, and he ate less than he had expected to.

When tea was over his father wanted him to walk round the gardens. He had a long conversation with his father about things in general, avoiding his private life—Sir Lamorac, the Austrians, and the emptiness he had felt these last three days, now so suddenly filled up. His father told him of a place called Glensofantrim, where he and his mother had been; and of the little people who came out of the ground there when it was very quiet. Little Jon came to a halt, with his heels apart.

"Do you really believe they do, Daddy?" "No, Jon, but I thought you might."

"Why?"

"You're younger than I; and they're fairies." Little Jon squared the dimple in his chin.

"I don't believe in fairies. I never see any." "Ha!" said his father.

"Does Mum?"

His father smiled his funny smile.

"No; she only sees Pan."

"What's Pan?"

"The Goaty God who skips about in wild and beautiful places."

"Was he in Glensofantrim?"

"Mum said so."

Little Jon took his heels up, and led on.

"Did you see him?"

"No; I only saw Venus Anadyomene."

Little Jon reflected; Venus was in his book about the Greeks and Trojans. Then Anna was her Christian and Dyomene her surname?

But it appeared, on inquiry, that it was one word, which meant rising from the foam.

"Did she rise from the foam in Glensofantrim?"

"Yes; every day."

"What is she like, Daddy?"

"Like Mum."

"Oh! Then she must be..." but he stopped at that, rushed at a wall, scrambled up, and promptly scrambled down again. The discovery that his mother was beautiful was one which he felt must absolutely be kept to himself. His father's cigar, however, took so long to smoke, that at last he was compelled to say:

"I want to see what Mum's brought home. Do you mind, Daddy?"

He pitched the motive low, to absolve him from unmanliness, and was a little disconcerted when his father looked at him right through, heaved an important sigh, and answered:

"All right, old man, you go and love her."

He went, with a pretence of slowness, and then rushed, to make up. He entered her bedroom from his own, the door being open. She was still kneeling before a trunk, and he stood close to her, quite still.

She knelt up straight, and said:

"Well, Jon?"

"I thought I'd just come and see."

Having given and received another hug, he mounted the window-seat, and tucking his legs up under him watched her unpack. He derived a pleasure from the operation such as he had not yet known, partly because she was taking out things which looked suspicious, and partly because he liked to look at her. She moved differently from anybody else, especially from Bella; she was certainly the refinedest-looking person he had ever seen. She finished the trunk at last, and knelt down in front of him.

"Have you missed us, Jon?"

Little Jon nodded, and having thus admitted his feelings, continued to nod.

"But you had 'Auntie' June?"

"Oh! she had a man with a cough."

His mother's face changed, and looked almost angry. He added hastily:

"He was a poor man, Mum; he coughed awfully; I—I liked him."

His mother put her hands behind his waist.

"You like everybody, Jon?"

Little Jon considered.

"Up to a point," he said: "Auntie June took me to church one Sunday."

"To church? Oh!"

"She wanted to see how it would affect me." "And did it?"

"Yes. I came over all funny, so she took me home again very quick. I wasn't sick after all. I went to bed and had hot brandy and water, and read The Boys of Beechwood. It was scrumptious."

His mother bit her lip.

"When was that?"

"Oh! about—a long time ago—I wanted her to take me again, but she wouldn't. You and Daddy never go to church, do you?"

"No, we don't."

"Why don't you?"

His mother smiled.

"Well, dear, we both of us went when we were little. Perhaps we went when we were too little."

"I see," said little Jon, "it's dangerous."

"You shall judge for yourself about all those things as you grow up."

Little Jon replied in a calculating manner:

"I don't want to grow up, much. I don't want to go to school." A sudden overwhelming desire to say something more, to say what he really felt, turned him red. "I—I want to stay with you, and be your lover, Mum."

Then with an instinct to improve the situation, he added quickly "I don't want to go to bed to-night, either. I'm simply tired of going to bed, every night."

"Have you had any more nightmares?"

"Only about one. May I leave the door open into your room to-night, Mum?"

"Yes, just a little." Little Jon heaved a sigh of satisfaction.

"What did you see in Glensofantrim?"

"Nothing but beauty, darling."

"What exactly is beauty?"

"What exactly is—Oh! Jon, that's a poser."

"Can I see it, for instance?" His mother got up, and sat beside him. "You do, every day. The sky is beautiful, the stars, and moonlit nights, and then the birds, the flowers, the trees—they're all beautiful. Look out of the window—there's beauty for you, Jon."

"Oh! yes, that's the view. Is that all?"

"All? no. The sea is wonderfully beautiful, and the waves, with their foam flying back."

"Did you rise from it every day, Mum?"

His mother smiled. "Well, we bathed."

Little Jon suddenly reached out and caught her neck in his hands.

"I know," he said mysteriously, "you're it, really, and all the rest is make-believe."

She sighed, laughed, said: "Oh! Jon!"

Little Jon said critically:

"Do you think Bella beautiful, for instance? I hardly do."

"Bella is young; that's something."

"But you look younger, Mum. If you bump against Bella she hurts."

"I don't believe 'Da' was beautiful, when I come to think of it; and Mademoiselle's almost ugly."

"Mademoiselle has a very nice face." "Oh! yes; nice. I love your little rays, Mum."

"Rays?"

Little Jon put his finger to the outer corner of her eye.

"Oh! Those? But they're a sign of age."

"They come when you smile."

"But they usen't to."

"Oh! well, I like them. Do you love me, Mum?"

"I do—I do love you, darling."

"Ever so?"

"Ever so!"

"More than I thought you did?"

"Much—much more."

"Well, so do I; so that makes it even."

Conscious that he had never in his life so given himself away, he felt a sudden reaction to the manliness of Sir Lamorac, Dick Needham, Huck Finn, and other heroes.

"Shall I show you a thing or two?" he said; and slipping out of her arms, he stood on his head. Then, fired by her obvious admiration, he mounted the bed, and threw himself head foremost from his feet on to his back, without touching anything with his hands. He did this several times.

That evening, having inspected what they had brought, he stayed up to dinner, sitting between them at the little round table they used when they were alone. He was extremely excited. His mother wore a French-grey dress, with creamy lace made out of little scriggly roses, round her neck, which was browner than the lace. He kept looking at her, till at last his father's funny smile made him suddenly attentive to his slice of pineapple. It was later than he had ever stayed up, when he went to bed. His mother went up with him, and he undressed very slowly so as to keep her there. When at last he had nothing on but his pyjamas, he said:

"Promise you won't go while I say my prayers!"

"I promise."

Kneeling down and plunging his face into the bed, little Jon hurried up, under his breath, opening one eye now and then, to see her standing perfectly still with a smile on her face. "Our Father"—so went his last prayer, "which art in heaven, hallowed be thy Mum, thy Kingdom Mum—on Earth as it is in heaven, give us this day our daily Mum and forgive us our trespasses on earth as it is in heaven and trespass against us, for thine is the evil the power and the glory for ever and ever. Amum! Look out!" He sprang, and for a long minute remained in her arms. Once in bed, he continued to hold her hand.

"You won't shut the door any more than that, will you? Are you going to be long, Mum?"

"I must go down and play to Daddy."

"Oh! well, I shall hear you."

"I hope not; you must go to sleep."

"I can sleep any night."

"Well, this is just a night like any other."

"Oh! no—it's extra special."

"On extra special nights one always sleeps soundest."

"But if I go to sleep, Mum, I shan't hear you come up."

"Well, when I do, I'll come in and give you a kiss, then if you're awake you'll know, and if you're not you'll still know you've had one."

Little Jon sighed, "All right!" he said: "I suppose I must put up with that. Mum?"

"Yes?"

"What was her name that Daddy believes in? Venus Anna Diomedes?"

"Oh! my angel! Anadyomene."

"Yes! but I like my name for you much better."

"What is yours, Jon?"

Little Jon answered shyly:

"Guinevere! it's out of the Round Table—I've only just thought of it, only of course her hair was down."

His mother's eyes, looking past him, seemed to float.

"You won't forget to come, Mum?"

"Not if you'll go to sleep."

"That's a bargain, then." And little Jon screwed up his eyes.

He felt her lips on his forehead, heard her footsteps; opened his eyes to see her gliding through the doorway, and, sighing, screwed them up again.

Then Time began.

For some ten minutes of it he tried loyally to sleep, counting a great number of thistles in a row, "Da's" old recipe for bringing slumber. He seemed to have been hours counting. It must, he thought, be nearly time for her to come up now. He threw the bedclothes back. "I'm hot!" he said, and his voice sounded funny in the darkness, like someone else's. Why didn't she come? He sat up. He must look! He got out of bed, went to the window and pulled the curtain a slice aside. It wasn't dark, but he couldn't tell whether because of daylight or the moon, which was very big. It had a funny, wicked face, as if laughing at him, and he did not want to look at it. Then, remembering that his mother had said moonlit nights were beautiful, he continued to stare out in a general way. The trees threw thick shadows, the lawn looked like spilt milk, and a long, long way he could see; oh! very far; right over the world, and it all looked different and swimmy. There was a lovely smell, too, in his open window.

'I wish I had a dove like Noah!' he thought.

"The moony moon was round and bright, It shone and shone and made it light."

After that rhyme, which came into his head all at once, he became conscious of music, very soft-lovely! Mum playing! He bethought himself of a macaroon he had, laid up in his chest of drawers, and, getting it, came back to the window. He leaned out, now munching, now holding his jaws to hear the music better. "Da" used to say that angels played on harps in heaven; but it wasn't half so lovely as Mum playing in the moony night, with him eating a macaroon. A cockchafer buzzed by, a moth flew in his face, the music stopped, and little Jon drew his head in. She must be coming! He didn't want to be found awake. He got back into bed and pulled the clothes nearly over his head; but he had left a streak of moonlight coming in. It fell across the floor, near the foot of the bed, and he watched it moving ever so slowly towards him, as if it were alive. The music began again, but he could only just hear it now; sleepy music, pretty—sleepy—music—sleepy—slee.....

And time slipped by, the music rose, fell, ceased; the moonbeam crept towards his face. Little Jon turned in his sleep till he lay on his back, with one brown fist still grasping the bedclothes. The corners of his eyes twitched—he had begun to dream. He dreamed he was drinking milk out of a pan that was the moon, opposite a great black cat which watched him with a funny smile like his father's. He heard it whisper: "Don't drink too much!" It was the cat's milk, of course, and he put out his hand amicably to stroke the creature; but it was no longer there; the pan had become a bed, in which he was lying, and when he tried to get out he couldn't find the edge; he couldn't find it—he—he—couldn't get out! It was dreadful!

He whimpered in his sleep. The bed had begun to go round too; it was outside him and inside him; going round and round, and getting fiery, and Mother Lee out of Cast up by the Sea was stirring it! Oh! so horrible she looked! Faster and faster!—till he and the bed and Mother Lee and the moon and the cat were all one wheel going round and round and up and up—awful—awful—awful!

He shrieked.

A voice saying: "Darling, darling!" got through the wheel, and he awoke, standing on his bed, with his eyes wide open.

There was his mother, with her hair like Guinevere's, and, clutching her, he buried his face in it.

"Oh! oh!"

"It's all right, treasure. You're awake now. There! There! It's nothing!"

But little Jon continued to say: "Oh! oh!"

Her voice went on, velvety in his ear:

"It was the moonlight, sweetheart, coming on your face."

Little Jon burbled into her nightgown

"You said it was beautiful. Oh!"

"Not to sleep in, Jon. Who let it in? Did you draw the curtains?"

"I wanted to see the time; I—I looked out, I—I heard you playing, Mum; I—I ate my macaroon." But he was growing slowly comforted; and the instinct to excuse his fear revived within him.

"Mother Lee went round in me and got all fiery," he mumbled.

"Well, Jon, what can you expect if you eat macaroons after you've gone to bed?"

"Only one, Mum; it made the music ever so more beautiful. I was waiting for you—I nearly thought it was to-morrow."

"My ducky, it's only just eleven now."

Little Jon was silent, rubbing his nose on her neck.

"Mum, is Daddy in your room?"

"Not to-night."

"Can I come?"

"If you wish, my precious."

Half himself again, little Jon drew back.

"You look different, Mum; ever so younger."

"It's my hair, darling."

Little Jon laid hold of it, thick, dark gold, with a few silver threads.

"I like it," he said: "I like you best of all like this."

Taking her hand, he had begun dragging her towards the door. He shut it as they passed, with a sigh of relief.

"Which side of the bed do you like, Mum?"

"The left side."

"All right."

Wasting no time, giving her no chance to change her mind, little Jon got into the bed, which seemed much softer than his own. He heaved another sigh, screwed his head into the pillow and lay examining the battle of chariots and swords and spears which always went on outside blankets, where the little hairs stood up against the light.

"It wasn't anything, really, was it?" he said.

From before her glass his mother answered:

"Nothing but the moon and your imagination heated up. You mustn't get so excited, Jon."

But, still not quite in possession of his nerves, little Jon answered boastfully:

"I wasn't afraid, really, of course!" And again he lay watching the spears and chariots. It all seemed very long.

"Oh! Mum, do hurry up!"

"Darling, I have to plait my hair."

"Oh! not to-night. You'll only have to unplait it again to-morrow. I'm sleepy now; if you don't come, I shan't be sleepy soon."

His mother stood up white and flowey before the winged mirror: he could see three of her, with her neck turned and her hair bright under the light, and her dark eyes smiling. It was unnecessary, and he said:

"Do come, Mum; I'm waiting."

"Very well, my love, I'll come."

Little Jon closed his eyes. Everything was turning out most satisfactory, only she must hurry up! He felt the bed shake, she was getting in. And, still with his eyes closed, he said sleepily: "It's nice, isn't it?"

He heard her voice say something, felt her lips touching his nose, and, snuggling up beside her who lay awake and loved him with her thoughts, he fell into the dreamless sleep, which rounded off his past.

VOLUME III. TO LET

"From out the fatal loins of those two foes

A pair of star-crossed lovers take their life."

—Romeo and Juliet.

TO CHARLES SCRIBNER

PART I

CHAPTER I.—ENCOUNTER

Soames Forsyte emerged from the Knightsbridge Hotel, where he was staying, in the afternoon of the 12th of May, 1920, with the intention of visiting a collection of pictures in a Gallery off Cork Street, and looking into the Future. He walked. Since the War he never took a cab if he could help it. Their drivers were, in his view, an uncivil lot, though now that the War was over and supply beginning to exceed demand again, getting more civil in accordance with the custom of human nature. Still, he had not forgiven them, deeply identifying them with gloomy memories, and now, dimly, like all members, of their class, with revolution. The considerable anxiety he had passed through during the War, and the more considerable anxiety he had since undergone in the Peace, had produced psychological consequences in a tenacious nature. He had, mentally, so frequently experienced ruin, that he had ceased to believe in its material probability. Paying away four thousand a year in income and super tax, one could not very well be worse off! A fortune of a quarter of a million, encumbered only by a wife and one daughter, and very diversely invested, afforded substantial guarantee even against that "wildcat notion" a levy on capital. And as to confiscation of war profits, he was entirely in favour of it, for he had none, and "serve the beggars right!" The price of pictures, moreover, had, if anything, gone up, and he had done better with his collection since the War began than ever before. Air-raids, also, had acted beneficially on a spirit congenitally cautious, and hardened a character already dogged. To be in danger of being entirely dispersed inclined one to be less apprehensive of the more partial dispersions involved in levies and taxation, while the habit of condemning the impudence of the Germans had led naturally to condemning that of Labour, if not openly at least in the sanctuary of his soul.

He walked. There was, moreover, time to spare, for Fleur was to meet him at the Gallery at four o'clock, and it was as yet but half-past two. It was good for him to walk—his liver was a little constricted, and his nerves rather on edge. His wife was always out when she was in Town, and his daughter would flibberty-gibbet all over the place like most young women since the War. Still, he must be thankful that she had been too young to do anything in that War itself. Not, of course, that he had not supported the War from its inception, with all his soul, but between that and supporting it with the bodies of his wife and daughter, there had been a gap fixed by something old-fashioned within him which abhorred emotional extravagance. He had, for instance, strongly objected to Annette, so attractive, and in 1914 only thirty-four, going to her native France, her "chere patrie" as, under the stimulus of war, she had begun to call it, to nurse her "braves poilus," forsooth! Ruining her health and her looks! As if she were really a nurse! He had put a stopper on it. Let her do needlework for them at home, or knit! She had not gone, therefore, and had never been quite the same woman since. A bad tendency of hers to mock at him, not openly, but in continual little ways, had grown. As for Fleur, the War had resolved the vexed problem whether or not she should go to school. She was better away from her mother in her war mood, from the chance of air-raids, and the impetus to do extravagant things; so he had placed her in a seminary as far West as had seemed to him compatible with excellence, and had missed her horribly. Fleur! He had never regretted the somewhat outlandish name by which at her birth he had decided so suddenly to call her—marked concession though it had been to the French. Fleur! A pretty name—a pretty child! But restless—too restless; and wilful! Knowing her power too over her father! Soames often reflected on the mistake it was to

399

dote on his daughter. To get old and dote! Sixty-five! He was getting on; but he didn't feel it, for, fortunately perhaps, considering Annette's youth and good looks, his second marriage had turned out a cool affair. He had known but one real passion in his life—for that first wife of his—Irene. Yes, and that fellow, his cousin Jolyon, who had gone off with her, was looking very shaky, they said. No wonder, at seventy-two, after twenty years of a third marriage!

Soames paused a moment in his march to lean over the railings of the Row. A suitable spot for reminiscence, half-way between that house in Park Lane which had seen his birth and his parents' deaths, and the little house in Montpellier Square where thirty-five years ago he had enjoyed his first edition of matrimony. Now, after twenty years of his second edition, that old tragedy seemed to him like a previous existence—which had ended when Fleur was born in place of the son he had hoped for. For many years he had ceased regretting, even vaguely, the son who had not been born; Fleur filled the bill in his heart. After all, she bore his name; and he was not looking forward at all to the time when she would change it. Indeed, if he ever thought of such a calamity, it was seasoned by the vague feeling that he could make her rich enough to purchase perhaps and extinguish the name of the fellow who married her—why not, since, as it seemed, women were equal to men nowadays? And Soames, secretly convinced that they were not, passed his curved hand over his face vigorously, till it reached the comfort of his chin. Thanks to abstemious habits, he had not grown fat and gabby; his nose was pale and thin, his grey moustache close-clipped, his eyesight unimpaired. A slight stoop closened and corrected the expansion given to his face by the heightening of his forehead in the recession of his grey hair. Little change had Time wrought in the "warmest" of the young Forsytes, as the last of the old Forsytes—Timothy—now in his hundred and first year, would have phrased it.

The shade from the plane-trees fell on his neat Homburg hat; he had given up top hats—it was no use attracting attention to wealth in days like these. Plane-trees! His thoughts travelled sharply to Madrid—the Easter before the War, when, having to make up his mind about that Goya picture, he had taken a voyage of discovery to study the painter on his spot. The fellow had impressed him—great range, real genius! Highly as the chap ranked, he would rank even higher before they had finished with him. The second Goya craze would be greater even than the first; oh, yes! And he had bought. On that visit he had—as never before—commissioned a copy of a fresco painting called "La Vendimia," wherein was the figure of a girl with an arm akimbo, who had reminded him of his daughter. He had it now in the Gallery at Mapledurham, and rather poor it was—you couldn't copy Goya. He would still look at it, however, if his daughter were not there, for the sake of something irresistibly reminiscent in the light, erect balance of the figure, the width between the arching eyebrows, the eager dreaming of the dark eyes. Curious that Fleur should have dark eyes, when his own were grey—no pure Forsyte had brown eyes—and her mother's blue! But of course her grandmother Lamotte's eyes were dark as treacle!

He began to walk on again toward Hyde Park Corner. No greater change in all England than in the Row! Born almost within hail of it, he could remember it from 1860 on. Brought there as a child between the crinolines to stare at tight-trousered dandies in whiskers, riding with a cavalry seat; to watch the doffing of curly-brimmed and white top hats; the leisurely air of it all, and the little bow-legged man in a long red waistcoat who used to come among the fashion with dogs on several strings, and try to sell one to his mother: King Charles spaniels, Italian greyhounds, affectionate to her crinoline—you never saw them now. You saw no quality of any sort, indeed, just working people sitting in dull rows with nothing to stare at but a few young bouncing females in pot hats, riding astride, or desultory Colonials charging up and down on dismal-looking hacks; with, here and there, little girls on ponies, or old gentlemen jogging their livers, or an orderly trying a great galumphing cavalry horse; no thoroughbreds, no grooms, no bowing, no scraping, no gossip—nothing; only the trees the same—the trees indifferent to the generations and declensions of mankind. A democratic England—dishevelled, hurried, noisy, and seemingly without an apex. And that something fastidious in the soul of Soames turned over within him. Gone forever, the close borough of rank and polish! Wealth there was—oh, yes! wealth—he himself was a richer man than his father had ever been; but manners, flavour, quality, all gone, engulfed in one vast, ugly, shoulder-rubbing, petrol-smelling Cheerio. Little half-beaten pockets of gentility and caste lurking here and there, dispersed and chetif, as Annette would say; but nothing ever again firm and coherent to look up to. And into this new hurly-burly of bad manners and loose morals his daughter—flower of his life— was flung! And when those Labour chaps got power—if they ever did—the worst was yet to come.

He passed out under the archway, at last no longer—thank goodness!—disfigured by the gungrey of its search-light. 'They'd better put a search-light on to where they're all going,' he thought, 'and light up their precious democracy!' And he directed his steps along the Club fronts of Piccadilly. George Forsyte, of course, would be sitting in the bay window of the Iseeum. The chap was so big now that he was there nearly all his time, like some immovable, sardonic, humorous eye noting the decline of men and things. And Soames hurried, ever constitutionally uneasy beneath his cousin's glance. George, who, as he had heard, had written a letter signed "Patriot" in the middle of the War, complaining of the Government's hysteria in docking the oats of race-horses. Yes, there he was, tall, ponderous, neat, clean-shaven, with his smooth hair, hardly thinned, smelling, no doubt, of the best hair-wash, and a pink paper in his hand. Well, he didn't change! And for perhaps the first time in his life Soames felt a kind of sympathy tapping in his waistcoat for that sardonic kinsman. With his weight, his perfectly parted hair, and bull-like gaze, he was a guarantee that the old order would take some shifting yet. He saw George move the pink paper as if inviting him to ascend—the chap must want to ask something about his property. It was still under Soames' control; for in the adoption of a sleeping partnership at that painful period twenty years back when he had divorced Irene, Soames had found himself almost insensibly retaining control of all purely Forsyte affairs.

Hesitating for just a moment, he nodded and went in. Since the death of his brother-in-law Montague Dartie, in Paris, which no one had quite known what to make of, except that it was certainly not suicide—the Iseeum Club had seemed more respectable to Soames. George, too, he knew, had sown the last of his wild oats, and was committed definitely to the joys of the table, eating only of the very best so as to keep his weight down, and owning, as he said, "just one or two old screws to give me an interest in life." He joined his cousin, therefore, in the bay window without the embarrassing sense of indiscretion he had been used to feel up there. George put out a well-kept hand.

"Haven't seen you since the War," he said. "How's your wife?"

"Thanks," said Soames coldly, "well enough."

Some hidden jest curved, for a moment, George's fleshy face, and gloated from his eye.

"That Belgian chap, Profond," he said, "is a member here now. He's a rum customer."

"Quite!" muttered Soames. "What did you want to see me about?"

"Old Timothy; he might go off the hooks at any moment. I suppose he's made his Will."
"Yes."

"Well, you or somebody ought to give him a look up—last of the old lot; he's a hundred, you know. They say he's like a mummy. Where are you goin' to put him? He ought to have a pyramid by rights."

Soames shook his head. "Highgate, the family vault."

"Well, I suppose the old girls would miss him, if he was anywhere else. They say he still takes an interest in food. He might last on, you know. Don't we get anything for the old Forsytes? Ten of them—average age eighty-eight—I worked it out. That ought to be equal to triplets."

"Is that all?" said Soames, "I must be getting on."

'You unsociable devil,' George's eyes seemed to answer. "Yes, that's all: Look him up in his mausoleum—the old chap might want to prophesy." The grin died on the rich curves of his face, and he added: "Haven't you attorneys invented a way yet of dodging this damned income tax? It hits the fixed inherited income like the very deuce. I used to have two thousand five hundred a year; now I've got a beggarly fifteen hundred, and the price of living doubled."

"Ah!" murmured Soames, "the turf's in danger."

Over George's face moved a gleam of sardonic self-defence.

"Well," he said, "they brought me up to do nothing, and here I am in the sear and yellow, getting poorer every day. These Labour chaps mean to have the lot before they've done. What are you going to do for a living when it comes? I shall work a six-hour day teaching politicians how to see a joke. Take my tip, Soames; go into Parliament, make sure of your four hundred—and employ me."

And, as Soames retired, he resumed his seat in the bay window.

Soames moved along Piccadilly deep in reflections excited by his cousin's words. He himself had always been a worker and a saver, George always a drone and a spender; and yet, if confiscation once began, it was he—the worker and the saver—who would be looted! That was the negation of all virtue, the overturning of all Forsyte principles. Could civilization be built on any other? He did not think so. Well, they wouldn't confiscate his pictures, for they wouldn't know their worth. But what would they be worth, if these maniacs once began to milk capital? A drug on the market. 'I don't care about myself,' he thought; 'I could live on five hundred a year, and never know the difference, at my age.' But Fleur! This fortune, so widely invested, these treasures so carefully chosen and amassed, were all for—her. And if it should turn out that he couldn't give or leave them to her—well, life had no meaning, and what was the use of going in to look at this crazy, futuristic stuff with the view of seeing whether it had any future?

Arriving at the Gallery off Cork Street, however, he paid his shilling, picked up a catalogue, and entered. Some ten persons were prowling round. Soames took steps and came on what looked to him like a lamp-post bent by collision with a motor omnibus. It was advanced some three paces from the wall, and was described in his catalogue as "Jupiter." He examined it with curiosity, having recently turned some of his attention to sculpture. 'If that's Jupiter,' he thought, 'I wonder what Juno's like.' And suddenly he saw her, opposite. She appeared to him like nothing so much as a pump with two handles, lightly clad in snow. He was still gazing at her, when two of the prowlers halted on his left. "Epatant!" he heard one say.

"Jargon!" growled Soames to himself.

The other's boyish voice replied

"Missed it, old bean; he's pulling your leg. When Jove and Juno created he them, he was saying: 'I'll see how much these fools will swallow.' And they've lapped up the lot."

"You young duffer! Vospovitch is an innovator. Don't you see that he's brought satire into sculpture? The future of plastic art, of music, painting, and even architecture, has set in satiric. It was bound to. People are tired—the bottom's tumbled out of sentiment."

"Well, I'm quite equal to taking a little interest in beauty. I was through the War. You've dropped your handkerchief, sir."

Soames saw a handkerchief held out in front of him. He took it with some natural suspicion, and approached it to his nose. It had the right scent—of distant Eau de Cologne—and his initials in a corner. Slightly reassured, he raised his eyes to the young man's face. It had rather fawn-like ears, a laughing mouth, with half a toothbrush growing out of it on each side, and small lively eyes, above a normally dressed appearance.

"Thank you," he said; and moved by a sort of irritation, added: "Glad to hear you like beauty; that's rare, nowadays."

"I dote on it," said the young man; "but you and I are the last of the old guard, sir."

Soames smiled.

"If you really care for pictures," he said, "here's my card. I can show you some quite good ones any Sunday, if you're down the river and care to look in."

"Awfully nice of you, sir. I'll drop in like a bird. My name's Mont-Michael." And he took off his hat.

Soames, already regretting his impulse, raised his own slightly in response, with a downward look at the young man's companion, who had a purple tie, dreadful little sluglike whiskers, and a scornful look—as if he were a poet!

It was the first indiscretion he had committed for so long that he went and sat down in an alcove. What had possessed him to give his card to a rackety young fellow, who went about with a thing like that? And Fleur, always at the back of his thoughts, started out like a filigree figure from a clock when the hour strikes. On the screen opposite the alcove was a large canvas with a great many square tomato-coloured blobs on it, and nothing else, so far as Soames could see from where he sat. He looked at his catalogue: "No. 32 'The Future Town'—Paul Post." 'I suppose that's satiric too,' he thought. 'What a thing!' But his second impulse was more cautious. It did not do to condemn hurriedly. There had been those stripey, streaky creations of Monet's, which had turned out such trumps; and then the stippled school; and Gauguin. Why, even since the Post-Impressionists there had been one or two painters not to be sneezed at. During the thirty-eight years of his connoisseur's life, indeed, he had marked so many "movements," seen the tides of taste and technique so ebb and flow, that there was really no telling anything except that there was money to be made out of every change of fashion. This too might quite well be a case where one must subdue primordial instinct, or lose the market. He got up and stood before the picture, trying hard to see it with the eyes of other people. Above the tomato blobs was what he took to be a sunset, till some one passing said: "He's got the airplanes wonderfully, don't you think!" Below the tomato blobs was a band of white with vertical black stripes, to which he could assign no meaning whatever, till some one else came by, murmuring: "What expression he gets with his foreground!" Expression? Of what? Soames went back to his seat. The thing was "rich," as his father would have said, and he wouldn't give a damn for it. Expression! Ah! they were all Expressionists now, he had heard, on the Continent. So it was coming here too, was it? He remembered the first wave of influenza in 1887—or '8—hatched in

China, so they said. He wondered where this—this Expressionism had been hatched. The thing was a regular disease!

He had become conscious of a woman and a youth standing between him and the "Future Town." Their backs were turned; but very suddenly Soames put his catalogue before his face, and drawing his hat forward, gazed through the slit between. No mistaking that back, elegant as ever though the hair above had gone grey. Irene! His divorced wife—Irene! And this, no doubt, was—her son—by that fellow Jolyon Forsyte—their boy, six months older than his own girl! And mumbling over in his mind the bitter days of his divorce, he rose to get out of sight, but quickly sat down again. She had turned her head to speak to her boy; her profile was still so youthful that it made her grey hair seem powdery, as if fancy-dressed; and her lips were smiling as Soames, first possessor of them, had never seen them smile. Grudgingly he admitted her still beautiful and in figure almost as young as ever. And how that boy smiled back at her! Emotion squeezed Soames' heart. The sight infringed his sense of justice. He grudged her that boy's smile—it went beyond what Fleur gave him, and it was undeserved. Their son might have been his son; Fleur might have been her daughter, if she had kept straight! He lowered his catalogue. If she saw him, all the better! A reminder of her conduct in the presence of her son, who probably knew nothing of it, would be a salutary touch from the finger of that Nemesis which surely must soon or late visit her! Then, half-conscious that such a thought was extravagant for a Forsyte of his age, Soames took out his watch. Past four! Fleur was late. She had gone to his niece Imogen Cardigan's, and there they would keep her smoking cigarettes and gossiping, and that. He heard the boy laugh, and say eagerly: "I say, Mum, is this by one of Auntie June's lame ducks?"

"Paul Post—I believe it is, darling."

The word produced a little shock in Soames; he had never heard her use it. And then she saw him. His eyes must have had in them something of George Forsyte's sardonic look; for her gloved hand crisped the folds of her frock, her eyebrows rose, her face went stony. She moved on.

"It is a caution," said the boy, catching her arm again.

Soames stared after them. That boy was good-looking, with a Forsyte chin, and eyes deep-grey, deep in; but with something sunny, like a glass of old sherry spilled over him; his smile perhaps, his hair. Better than they deserved—those two! They passed from his view into the next room, and Soames continued to regard the Future Town, but saw it not. A little smile snarled up his lips. He was despising the vehemence of his own feelings after all these years. Ghosts! And yet as one grew old—was there anything but what was ghost-like left? Yes, there was Fleur! He fixed his eyes on the entrance. She was due; but she would keep him waiting, of course! And suddenly he became aware of a sort of human breeze—a short, slight form clad in a sea-green djibbah with a metal belt and a fillet binding unruly red-gold hair all streaked with grey. She was talking to the Gallery attendants, and something familiar riveted his gaze—in her eyes, her chin, her hair, her spirit—something which suggested a thin Skye terrier just before its dinner. Surely June Forsyte! His cousin June—and coming straight to his recess! She sat down beside him, deep in thought, took out a tablet, and made a pencil note. Soames sat unmoving. A confounded thing, cousinship! "Disgusting!" he heard her murmur; then, as if resenting the presence of an overhearing stranger, she looked at him. The worst had happened.

"Soames!"

Soames turned his head a very little.

"How are you?" he said. "Haven't seen you for twenty years."

"No. Whatever made you come here?"

"My sins," said Soames. "What stuff!"

"Stuff? Oh, yes—of course; it hasn't arrived yet.

"It never will," said Soames; "it must be making a dead loss."

"Of course it is."

"How d'you know?"

"It's my Gallery."

Soames sniffed from sheer surprise.

"Yours? What on earth makes you run a show like this?"

"I don't treat Art as if it were grocery."

Soames pointed to the Future Town. "Look at that! Who's going to live in a town like that, or with it on his walls?"

June contemplated the picture for a moment.

"It's a vision," she said.

"The deuce!"

There was silence, then June rose. 'Crazylooking creature!' he thought.

"Well," he said, "you'll find your young stepbrother here with a woman I used to know. If you take my advice, you'll close this exhibition."

June looked back at him. "Oh! You Forsyte!" she said, and moved on. About her light, fly-away figure, passing so suddenly away, was a look of dangerous decisions. Forsyte! Of course, he was a Forsyte! And so was she! But from the time when, as a mere girl, she brought Bosinney into his life to wreck it, he had never hit it off with June and never would! And here she was, unmarried to this day, owning a Gallery!... And suddenly it came to Soames how little he knew now of his own family. The old aunts at Timothy's had been dead so many years; there was no clearing-house for news. What had they all done in the War? Young Roger's boy had been wounded, St. John Hayman's second son killed; young Nicholas' eldest had got an O. B. E., or whatever they gave them. They had all joined up somehow, he believed. That boy of Jolyon's and Irene's, he supposed, had been too young; his own generation, of course, too old, though Giles Hayman had driven a car for the Red Cross—and Jesse Hayman been a special constable—those "Dromios" had always been of a sporting type! As for himself, he had given a motor ambulance, read the papers till he was sick of them, passed through much anxiety, bought no clothes, lost seven pounds in weight; he didn't know what more he could have done at his age. Indeed, thinking it over, it struck him that he and his family had taken this war very differently to that affair with the Boers, which had been supposed to tax all the resources of the Empire. In that old war, of course, his nephew Val Dartie had been wounded, that fellow Jolyon's first son had died of enteric, "the Dromios" had gone out on horses, and June had been a nurse; but all that had seemed in the nature of a portent, while in this war everybody had done "their bit," so far as he could make out, as a matter of course. It seemed to show the growth of something or other—or perhaps the decline of something else. Had the Forsytes become less individual, or more Imperial, or less provincial? Or was it simply that one hated Germans?... Why didn't Fleur come, so that he could get away? He saw those three return together from the other room and pass back along the far side of the screen. The boy was standing before the Juno now. And, suddenly, on the other side of her, Soames saw—his daughter, with

405

eyebrows raised, as well they might be. He could see her eyes glint sideways at the boy, and the boy look back at her. Then Irene slipped her hand through his arm, and drew him on. Soames saw him glancing round, and Fleur looking after them as the three went out.

A voice said cheerfully: "Bit thick, isn't it, sir?"

The young man who had handed him his handkerchief was again passing. Soames nodded.

"I don't know what we're coming to."

"Oh! That's all right, sir," answered the young man cheerfully; "they don't either."

Fleur's voice said: "Hallo, Father! Here you are!" precisely as if he had been keeping her waiting.

The young man, snatching off his hat, passed on.

"Well," said Soames, looking her up and down, "you're a punctual sort of young woman!"

This treasured possession of his life was of medium height and colour, with short, dark chestnut hair; her wide-apart brown eyes were set in whites so clear that they glinted when they moved, and yet in repose were almost dreamy under very white, black-lashed lids, held over them in a sort of suspense. She had a charming profile, and nothing of her father in her face save a decided chin. Aware that his expression was softening as he looked at her, Soames frowned to preserve the unemotionalism proper to a Forsyte. He knew she was only too inclined to take advantage of his weakness.

Slipping her hand under his arm, she said:

"Who was that?"

"He picked up my handkerchief. We talked about the pictures."

"You're not going to buy that, Father?"

"No," said Soames grimly; "nor that Juno you've been looking at."

Fleur dragged at his arm. "Oh! Let's go! It's a ghastly show."

In the doorway they passed the young man called Mont and his partner. But Soames had hung out a board marked "Trespassers will be prosecuted," and he barely acknowledged the young fellow's salute.

"Well," he said in the street, "whom did you meet at Imogen's?"

"Aunt Winifred, and that Monsieur Profond."

"Oh!" muttered Soames; "that chap! What does your aunt see in him?"

"I don't know. He looks pretty deep—mother says she likes him."

Soames grunted.

"Cousin Val and his wife were there, too."

"What!" said Soames. "I thought they were back in South Africa."

"Oh, no! They've sold their farm. Cousin Val is going to train race-horses on the Sussex Downs. They've got a jolly old manor-house; they asked me down there."

Soames coughed: the news was distasteful to him. "What's his wife like now?"

"Very quiet, but nice, I think."

Soames coughed again. "He's a rackety chap, your Cousin Val."

"Oh! no, Father; they're awfully devoted. I promised to go—Saturday to Wednesday next."

"Training race-horses!" said Soames. It was extravagant, but not the reason for his distaste. Why the deuce couldn't his nephew have stayed out in South Africa? His own divorce had been bad enough, without his nephew's marriage to the daughter of the co-respondent; a half-sister too of June, and of that boy whom Fleur had just been looking at from under the pump-handle. If he didn't look out, she would come to know all about that old disgrace! Unpleasant things! They were round him this afternoon like a swarm of bees!

"I don't like it!" he said.

"I want to see the race-horses," murmured Fleur; "and they've promised I shall ride. Cousin Val can't walk much, you know; but he can ride perfectly. He's going to show me their gallops."

"Racing!" said Soames. "It's a pity the War didn't knock that on the head. He's taking after his father, I'm afraid."

"I don't know anything about his father."

"No," said Soames, grimly. "He took an interest in horses and broke his neck in Paris, walking down-stairs. Good riddance for your aunt." He frowned, recollecting the inquiry into those stairs which he had attended in Paris six years ago, because Montague Dartie could not attend it himself—perfectly normal stairs in a house where they played baccarat. Either his winnings or the way he had celebrated them had gone to his brother-in-law's head. The French procedure had been very loose; he had had a lot of trouble with it.

A sound from Fleur distracted his attention. "Look! The people who were in the Gallery with us."

"What people?" muttered Soames, who knew perfectly well.

"I think that woman's beautiful."

"Come into this pastry-cook's," said Soames abruptly, and tightening his grip on her arm he turned into a confectioner's. It was—for him—a surprising thing to do, and he said rather anxiously: "What will you have?"

"Oh! I don't want anything. I had a cocktail and a tremendous lunch."

"We must have something now we're here," muttered Soames, keeping hold of her arm.

"Two teas," he said; "and two of those nougat things."

But no sooner was his body seated than his soul sprang up. Those three—those three were coming in! He heard Irene say something to her boy, and his answer:

"Oh! no, Mum; this place is all right. My stunt." And the three sat down.

At that moment, most awkward of his existence, crowded with ghosts and shadows from his past, in presence of the only two women he had ever loved—his divorced wife and his daughter by her successor—Soames was not so much afraid of them as of his cousin June. She might make a scene—she might introduce those two children—she was capable of anything. He bit too hastily at the nougat, and it stuck to his plate. Working at it with his finger, he glanced at Fleur. She was masticating dreamily, but her eyes were on the boy. The Forsyte in him said: "Think, feel, and you're done for!" And he wiggled his finger desperately. Plate! Did Jolyon wear a plate? Did that woman wear a plate? Time had been when he had seen her wearing nothing! That was something, anyway, which had never been stolen from him. And she knew it, though she might sit there calm and self-possessed, as if she had never been his wife. An acid humour stirred in his Forsyte blood; a subtle pain divided by hair's breadth from pleasure. If only June did not suddenly bring her hornets about his ears! The boy was talking.

"Of course, Auntie June"—so he called his half-sister "Auntie," did he?—well, she must be fifty, if she was a day!—"it's jolly good of you to encourage them. Only—hang it all!" Soames stole a glance. Irene's startled eyes were bent watchfully on her boy. She—she had these devotions—for Bosinney—for that boy's father—for this boy! He touched Fleur's arm, and said:

"Well, have you had enough?"

"One more, Father, please."

She would be sick! He went to the counter to pay. When he turned round again he saw Fleur standing near the door, holding a handkerchief which the boy had evidently just handed to her.

"F. F.," he heard her say. "Fleur Forsyte—it's mine all right. Thank you ever so."

Good God! She had caught the trick from what he'd told her in the Gallery—monkey!

"Forsyte? Why—that's my name too. Perhaps we're cousins."

"Really! We must be. There aren't any others. I live at Mapledurham; where do you?"

"Robin Hill."

Question and answer had been so rapid that all was over before he could lift a finger. He saw Irene's face alive with startled feeling, gave the slightest shake of his head, and slipped his arm through Fleur's.

"Come along!" he said.

She did not move.

"Didn't you hear, Father? Isn't it queer—our name's the same. Are we cousins?"

"What's that?" he said. "Forsyte? Distant, perhaps."

"My name's Jolyon, sir. Jon, for short."

"Oh! Ah!" said Soames. "Yes. Distant. How are you? Very good of you. Good-bye!"

He moved on.

"Thanks awfully," Fleur was saying. "Au revoir!"

"Au revoir!" he heard the boy reply.

CHAPTER II.—FINE FLEUR FORSYTE

Emerging from the "pastry-cook's," Soames' first impulse was to vent his nerves by saying to his daughter: 'Dropping your hand-kerchief!' to which her reply might well be: 'I picked that up from you!' His second impulse therefore was to let sleeping dogs lie. But she would surely question him. He gave her a sidelong look, and found she was giving him the same. She said softly:

"Why don't you like those cousins, Father?" Soames lifted the corner of his lip.

"What made you think that?"

"Cela se voit."

'That sees itself!' What a way of putting it! After twenty years of a French wife Soames had still little sympathy with her language; a theatrical affair and connected in his mind with all the refinements of domestic irony.

"How?" he asked.

"You must know them; and you didn't make a sign. I saw them looking at you."

"I've never seen the boy in my life," replied Soames with perfect truth.

"No; but you've seen the others, dear."

Soames gave her another look. What had she picked up? Had her Aunt Winifred, or Imogen, or Val Dartie and his wife, been talking? Every breath of the old scandal had been carefully kept from her at home, and Winifred warned many times that he wouldn't have a whisper of it reach her for the world. So far as she ought to know, he had never been married before. But her dark eyes, whose southern glint and clearness often almost frightened him, met his with perfect innocence.

"Well," he said, "your grandfather and his brother had a quarrel. The two families don't know each other."

"How romantic!"

'Now, what does she mean by that?' he thought. The word was to him extravagant and dangerous—it was as if she had said: "How jolly!"

"And they'll continue not to know each, other," he added, but instantly regretted the challenge in those words. Fleur was smiling. In this age, when young people prided themselves on going their own ways and paying no attention to any sort of decent prejudice, he had said the very thing to excite her wilfulness. Then, recollecting the expression on Irene's face, he breathed again.

"What sort of a quarrel?" he heard Fleur say.

"About a house. It's ancient history for you. Your grandfather died the day you were born. He was ninety."

"Ninety? Are there many Forsytes besides those in the Red Book?"

"I don't know," said Soames. "They're all dispersed now. The old ones are dead, except Timothy."

Fleur clasped her hands.

"Timothy? Isn't that delicious?"

"Not at all," said Soames. It offended him that she should think "Timothy" delicious—a kind of insult to his breed. This new generation mocked at anything solid and tenacious. "You go and see the old boy. He might want to prophesy." Ah! If Timothy could see the disquiet England of his great-nephews and great-nieces, he would certainly give tongue. And involuntarily he glanced up at the Iseeum; yes—George was still in the window, with the same pink paper in his hand.

"Where is Robin Hill, Father?"

Robin Hill! Robin Hill, round which all that tragedy had centred! What did she want to know for?

"In Surrey," he muttered; "not far from Richmond. Why?"

"Is the house there?"

"What house?"

"That they quarrelled about."

"Yes. But what's all that to do with you? We're going home to-morrow—you'd better be thinking about your frocks."

"Bless you! They're all thought about. A family feud? It's like the Bible, or Mark Twain—awfully exciting. What did you do in the feud, Father?"

"Never you mind."

"Oh! But if I'm to keep it up?"

"Who said you were to keep it up?"

"You, darling."

"I? I said it had nothing to do with you."

"Just what I think, you know; so that's all right."

She was too sharp for him; fine, as Annette sometimes called her. Nothing for it but to distract her attention.

"There's a bit of rosaline point in here," he said, stopping before a shop, "that I thought you might like."

When he had paid for it and they had resumed their progress, Fleur said:

"Don't you think that boy's mother is the most beautiful woman of her age you've ever seen?"

Soames shivered. Uncanny, the way she stuck to it!

"I don't know that I noticed her."

"Dear, I saw the corner of your eye."

"You see everything—and a great deal more, it seems to me!"

"What's her husband like? He must be your first cousin, if your fathers were brothers."

"Dead, for all I know," said Soames, with sudden vehemence. "I haven't seen him for twenty years."

"What was he?"

"A painter."

"That's quite jolly."

The words: "If you want to please me you'll put those people out of your head," sprang to Soames' lips, but he choked them back—he must not let her see his feelings.

"He once insulted me," he said.

Her quick eyes rested on his face.

"I see! You didn't avenge it, and it rankles. Poor Father! You let me have a go!"

It was really like lying in the dark with a mosquito hovering above his face. Such pertinacity in Fleur was new to him, and, as they reached the hotel, he said grimly:

"I did my best. And that's enough about these people. I'm going up till dinner."

"I shall sit here."

With a parting look at her extended in a chair—a look half-resentful, half-adoring—Soames moved into the lift and was transported to their suite on the fourth floor. He stood by the window of the sitting-room which gave view over Hyde Park, and drummed a finger on its pane. His feelings were confused, tetchy, troubled. The throb of that old wound, scarred over by Time and new interests, was mingled with displeasure and anxiety, and a slight pain in his chest where that nougat stuff had disagreed. Had Annette come in? Not that she was any good to him in such a difficulty. Whenever she had questioned him about his first marriage, he had always shut her up; she knew nothing of it, save that it had been the great passion of his life, and his marriage with herself but domestic makeshift. She had always kept the grudge of that up her sleeve, as it were, and used it commercially. He listened. A sound—the vague murmur of a woman's movements—was coming through the door. She was in. He tapped.

"Who?"

"I," said Soames.

She had been changing her frock, and was still imperfectly clothed; a striking figure before her glass. There was a certain magnificence about her arms, shoulders, hair, which had darkened since he first knew her, about the turn of her neck, the silkiness of her garments, her dark-lashed, greyblue eyes—she was certainly as handsome at forty as she had ever been. A fine possession, an excellent housekeeper, a sensible and affectionate enough mother. If only she weren't always so frankly cynical about the relations between them! Soames, who had no more real affection for her than she had for him, suffered from a kind of English grievance in that she had never dropped even the thinnest veil of sentiment over their partnership. Like most of his countrymen and women, he held the view that marriage should be based on mutual love, but that when from a marriage love had disappeared, or, been found never to have really existed—so that it was manifestly not based on love—you must not admit it. There it was, and the love was not—but there you were, and must continue to be! Thus you had it both ways, and were not tarred with cynicism, realism, and immorality like the French. Moreover, it was necessary in the interests of property. He knew that she knew that they both knew there was no love between them, but he still expected her not to admit in words or conduct such a thing, and he could never understand what she meant when she talked of the hypocrisy of the English. He said:

"Whom have you got at 'The Shelter' next week?"

Annette went on touching her lips delicately with salve—he always wished she wouldn't do that.

"Your sister Winifred, and the Car-r-digans"—she took up a tiny stick of black—"and Prosper Profond."

"That Belgian chap? Why him?"

Annette turned her neck lazily, touched one eyelash, and said:

"He amuses Winifred."

"I want some one to amuse Fleur; she's restive."

"R-restive?" repeated Annette. "Is it the first time you see that, my friend? She was born r-restive, as you call it."

Would she never get that affected roll out of her r's?

He touched the dress she had taken off, and asked:

"What have you been doing?"

Annette looked at him, reflected in her glass. Her just-brightened lips smiled, rather full, rather ironical.

"Enjoying myself," she said.

"Oh!" answered Soames glumly. "Ribbandry, I suppose."

It was his word for all that incomprehensible running in and out of shops that women went in for. "Has Fleur got her summer dresses?"

"You don't ask if I have mine."

"You don't care whether I do or not."

"Quite right. Well, she has; and I have mine—terribly expensive."

"H'm!" said Soames. "What does that chap Profond do in England?"

Annette raised the eyebrows she had just finished.

"He yachts."

"Ah!" said Soames; "he's a sleepy chap."

"Sometimes," answered Annette, and her face had a sort of quiet enjoyment. "But sometimes very amusing."

"He's got a touch of the tar-brush about him."

Annette stretched herself.

"Tar-brush?" she said. "What is that? His mother was Armenienne."

"That's it, then," muttered Soames. "Does he know anything about pictures?"

"He knows about everything—a man of the world."

"Well, get some one for Fleur. I want to distract her. She's going off on Saturday to Val Dartie and his wife; I don't like it."

"Why not?"

Since the reason could not be explained without going into family history, Soames merely answered:

"Racketing about. There's too much of it."

"I like that little Mrs. Val; she is very quiet and clever."

"I know nothing of her except—This thing's new." And Soames took up a creation from the bed.

Annette received it from him.

"Would you hook me?" she said.

Soames hooked. Glancing once over her shoulder into the glass, he saw the expression on her face, faintly amused, faintly contemptuous, as much as to say: "Thanks! You will never learn!" No, thank God, he wasn't a Frenchman! He finished with a jerk, and the words: "It's too low here." And he went to the door, with the wish to get away from her and go down to Fleur again.

Annette stayed a powder-puff, and said with startling suddenness

"Que tu es grossier!"

He knew the expression—he had reason to. The first time she had used it he had thought it meant "What a grocer you are!" and had not known whether to be relieved or not when better informed. He resented the word—he was not coarse! If he was coarse, what was that chap in the room beyond his, who made those horrible noises in the morning when he cleared his throat, or those people in the Lounge who thought it well-bred to say nothing but what the whole world could hear at the top of their voices—quacking inanity! Coarse, because he had said her dress was low! Well, so it was! He went out without reply.

Coming into the Lounge from the far end, he at once saw Fleur where he had left her. She sat with crossed knees, slowly balancing a foot in silk stocking and grey shoe, sure sign that she was dreaming. Her eyes showed it too—they went off like that sometimes. And then, in a moment, she would come to life, and be as quick and restless as a monkey. And she knew so much, so self-assured, and not yet nineteen. What was that odious word? Flapper! Dreadful young creatures—squealing and squawking and showing their legs! The worst of them bad dreams, the best of them powdered angels! Fleur was not a flapper, not one of those slangy, ill-bred young females. And yet she was frighteningly self-willed, and full of life, and determined to enjoy it. Enjoy! The word brought no puritan terror to Soames; but it brought the terror suited to his temperament. He had always been afraid to enjoy to-day for fear he might not enjoy tomorrow so much. And it was terrifying to feel that his daughter was divested of that safeguard. The very way she sat in that chair showed it—lost in her dream. He had never been lost in a dream himself—there was nothing to be had out of it; and where she got it from he did not know! Certainly not from Annette! And yet Annette, as a young girl, when he was hanging about her, had once had a flowery look. Well, she had lost it now!

Fleur rose from her chair-swiftly, restlessly; and flung herself down at a writing-table. Seizing ink and writing paper, she began to write as if she had not time to breathe before she got her letter written. And suddenly she saw him. The air of desperate absorption vanished, she smiled, waved a kiss, made a pretty face as if she were a little puzzled and a little bored.

Ah! She was "fine"—"fine!"

CHAPTER III.—AT ROBIN HILL

Jolyon Forsyte had spent his boy's nineteenth birthday at Robin Hill, quietly going into his affairs. He did everything quietly now, because his heart was in a poor way, and, like all his family, he disliked the idea of dying. He had never realised how much till one day, two years ago, he had gone to his doctor about certain symptoms, and been told:

"At any moment, on any overstrain."

He had taken it with a smile—the natural Forsyte reaction against an unpleasant truth. But with an increase of symptoms in the train on the way home, he had realised to the full the sentence hanging over him. To leave Irene, his boy, his home, his work—though he did little enough work now! To leave them for unknown darkness, for the unimaginable state, for such nothingness that he would not even be conscious of wind stirring leaves above his grave, nor of the scent of earth and grass. Of such nothingness that, however hard he might try to conceive it, he never could, and must still hover on the hope that he might see again those he loved! To realise this was to endure very poignant spiritual anguish. Before he reached home that day he had determined to keep it from Irene. He would have to be more careful than man had ever been, for the least thing would give it away and make her

413

as wretched as himself, almost. His doctor had passed him sound in other respects, and seventy was nothing of an age—he would last a long time yet, if he could.

Such a conclusion, followed out for nearly two years, develops to the full the subtler side of character. Naturally not abrupt, except when nervously excited, Jolyon had become control incarnate. The sad patience of old people who cannot exert themselves was masked by a smile which his lips preserved even in private. He devised continually all manner of cover to conceal his enforced lack of exertion.

Mocking himself for so doing, he counterfeited conversion to the Simple Life; gave up wine and cigars, drank a special kind of coffee with no coffee in it. In short, he made himself as safe as a Forsyte in his condition could, under the rose of his mild irony. Secure from discovery, since his wife and son had gone up to Town, he had spent the fine May day quietly arranging his papers, that he might die to-morrow without inconveniencing any one, giving in fact a final polish to his terrestrial state. Having docketed and enclosed it in his father's old Chinese cabinet, he put the key into an envelope, wrote the words outside: "Key of the Chinese cabinet, wherein will be found the exact state of me, J. F.," and put it in his breast-pocket, where it would be always about him, in case of accident. Then, ringing for tea, he went out to have it under the old oak-tree.

All are under sentence of death; Jolyon, whose sentence was but a little more precise and pressing, had become so used to it that he thought habitually, like other people, of other things. He thought of his son now.

Jon was nineteen that day, and Jon had come of late to a decision. Educated neither at Eton like his father, nor at Harrow, like his dead half-brother, but at one of those establishments which, designed to avoid the evil and contain the good of the Public School system, may or may not contain the evil and avoid the good, Jon had left in April perfectly ignorant of what he wanted to become. The War, which had promised to go on for ever, had ended just as he was about to join the Army, six months before his time. It had taken him ever since to get used to the idea that he could now choose for himself. He had held with his father several discussions, from which, under a cheery show of being ready for anything—except, of course, the Church, Army, Law, Stage, Stock Exchange, Medicine, Business, and Engineering—Jolyon had gathered rather clearly that Jon wanted to go in for nothing. He himself had felt exactly like that at the same age. With him that pleasant vacuity had soon been ended by an early marriage, and its unhappy consequences. Forced to become an underwriter at Lloyd's, he had regained prosperity before his artistic talent had outcropped. But having—as the simple say—"learned" his boy to draw pigs and other animals, he knew that Jon would never be a painter, and inclined to the conclusion that his aversion from everything else meant that he was going to be a writer. Holding, however, the view that experience was necessary even for that profession, there seemed to Jolyon nothing in the meantime, for Jon, but University, travel, and perhaps the eating of dinners for the Bar. After that one would see, or more probably one would not. In face of these proffered allurements, however, Jon had remained undecided.

Such discussions with his son had confirmed in Jolyon a doubt whether the world had really changed. People said that it was a new age. With the profundity of one not too long for any age, Jolyon perceived that under slightly different surfaces the era was precisely what it had been. Mankind was still divided into two species: The few who had "speculation" in their souls, and the many who had none, with a belt of hybrids like himself in the middle. Jon appeared to have speculation; it seemed to his father a bad lookout.

With something deeper, therefore, than his usual smile, he had heard the boy say, a fortnight ago: "I should like to try farming, Dad; if it won't cost you too much. It seems to be about the only sort of life that doesn't hurt anybody; except art, and of course that's out of the question for me."

Jolyon subdued his smile, and answered:

"All right; you shall skip back to where we were under the first Jolyon in 1760. It'll prove the cycle theory, and incidentally, no doubt, you may grow a better turnip than he did."

A little dashed, Jon had answered:

"But don't you think it's a good scheme, Dad?"

"'Twill serve, my dear; and if you should really take to it, you'll do more good than most men, which is little enough."

To himself, however, he had said: 'But he won't take to it. I give him four years. Still, it's healthy, and harmless.'

After turning the matter over and consulting with Irene, he wrote to his daughter, Mrs. Val Dartie, asking if they knew of a farmer near them on the Downs who would take Jon as an apprentice. Holly's answer had been enthusiastic. There was an excellent man quite close; she and Val would love Jon to live with them.

The boy was due to go to-morrow.

Sipping weak tea with lemon in it, Jolyon gazed through the leaves of the old oak-tree at that view which had appeared to him desirable for thirty-two years. The tree beneath which he sat seemed not a day older! So young, the little leaves of brownish gold; so old, the whitey-grey-green of its thick rough trunk. A tree of memories, which would live on hundreds of years yet, unless some barbarian cut it down—would see old England out at the pace things were going! He remembered a night three years before, when, looking from his window, with his arm close round Irene, he had watched a German aeroplane hovering, it seemed, right over the old tree. Next day they had found a bomb hole in a field on Gage's farm. That was before he knew that he was under sentence of death. He could almost have wished the bomb had finished him. It would have saved a lot of hanging about, many hours of cold fear in the pit of his stomach. He had counted on living to the normal Forsyte age of eighty-five or more, when Irene would be seventy. As it was, she would miss him. Still there was Jon, more important in her life than himself; Jon, who adored his mother.

Under that tree, where old Jolyon—waiting for Irene to come to him across the lawn—had breathed his last, Jolyon wondered, whimsically, whether, having put everything in such perfect order, he had not better close his own eyes and drift away. There was something undignified in parasitically clinging on to the effortless close of a life wherein he regretted two things only—the long division between his father and himself when he was young, and the lateness of his union with Irene.

From where he sat he could see a cluster of apple-trees in blossom. Nothing in Nature moved him so much as fruit-trees in blossom; and his heart ached suddenly because he might never see them flower again. Spring! Decidedly no man ought to have to die while his heart was still young enough to love beauty! Blackbirds sang recklessly in the shrubbery, swallows were flying high, the leaves above him glistened; and over the fields was every imaginable tint of early foliage, burnished by the level sunlight, away to where the distant "smoke-bush" blue was trailed along the horizon. Irene's flowers in their narrow beds had startling individuality that evening, little deep assertions of gay life. Only Chinese and Japanese painters, and perhaps Leonardo, had known how to get that startling little ego into each painted flower, and bird, and beast—the ego, yet the sense of species, the universality of life as well. They were the fellows! 'I've made nothing that will live!' thought Jolyon; 'I've been an amateur—a mere lover, not a creator. Still, I shall leave Jon behind me when I go.' What luck that the boy had not been caught by that ghastly war! He might so easily have been killed, like poor Jolly twenty years ago out in the Transvaal. Jon would do something some day—if the Age didn't spoil him—an imaginative chap! His whim to take up farming was but a bit of sentiment, and about as likely to last. And just then he saw them coming up the field: Irene and the boy; walking from the station, with their arms linked. And getting up, he strolled down through the new rose garden to meet them....

Irene came into his room that night and sat down by the window. She sat there without speaking till he said:

"What is it, my love?"

"We had an encounter to-day."

"With whom?"

"Soames."

Soames! He had kept that name out of his thoughts these last two years; conscious that it was bad for him. And, now, his heart moved in a disconcerting manner, as if it had side-slipped within his chest.

Irene went on quietly:

"He and his daughter were in the Gallery, and afterward at the confectioner's where we had tea."

Jolyon went over and put his hand on her shoulder.

"How did he look?"

"Grey; but otherwise much the same."

"And the daughter?"

"Pretty. At least, Jon thought so."

Jolyon's heart side-slipped again. His wife's face had a strained and puzzled look.

"You didn't-?" he began.

"No; but Jon knows their name. The girl dropped her handkerchief and he picked it up."

Jolyon sat down on his bed. An evil chance!

"June was with you. Did she put her foot into it?"

"No; but it was all very queer and strained, and Jon could see it was."

Jolyon drew a long breath, and said:

"I've often wondered whether we've been right to keep it from him. He'll find out some day."

"The later the better, Jolyon; the young have such cheap, hard judgment. When you were nineteen what would you have thought of your mother if she had done what I have?"

Yes! There it was! Jon worshipped his mother; and knew nothing of the tragedies, the inexorable necessities of life, nothing of the prisoned grief in an unhappy marriage, nothing of jealousy or passion—knew nothing at all, as yet!

"What have you told him?" he said at last.

"That they were relations, but we didn't know them; that you had never cared much for your family, or they for you. I expect he will be asking you."

Jolyon smiled. "This promises to take the place of air-raids," he said. "After all, one misses them."

Irene looked up at him.

"We've known it would come some day."

He answered her with sudden energy:

"I could never stand seeing Jon blame you. He shan't do that, even in thought. He has imagination; and he'll understand if it's put to him properly. I think I had better tell him before he gets to know otherwise."

"Not yet, Jolyon."

That was like her—she had no foresight, and never went to meet trouble. Still—who knew?—she might be right. It was ill going against a mother's instinct. It might be well to let the boy go on, if possible, till experience had given him some touchstone by which he could judge the values of that old tragedy; till love, jealousy, longing, had deepened his charity. All the same, one must take precautions—every precaution possible! And, long after Irene had left him, he lay awake turning over those precautions. He must write to Holly, telling her that Jon knew nothing as yet of family history. Holly was discreet, she would make sure of her husband, she would see to it! Jon could take the letter with him when he went to-morrow.

And so the day on which he had put the polish on his material estate died out with the chiming of the stable clock; and another began for Jolyon in the shadow of a spiritual disorder which could not be so rounded off and polished....

But Jon, whose room had once been his day nursery, lay awake too, the prey of a sensation disputed by those who have never known it, "love at first sight!" He had felt it beginning in him with the glint of those dark eyes gazing into his athwart the Juno—a conviction that this was his 'dream'; so that what followed had seemed to him at once natural and miraculous. Fleur! Her name alone was almost enough for one who was terribly susceptible to the charm of words. In a homoeopathic Age, when boys and girls were co-educated, and mixed up in early life till sex was almost abolished, Jon was singularly old-fashioned. His modern school took boys only, and his holidays had been spent at Robin Hill with friends, or his parents alone. He had never, therefore, been inoculated against the germs of love by small doses of the poison. And now in the dark his temperature was mounting fast. He lay awake, featuring Fleur—as they called it—recalling her words, especially that "Au revoir!" so soft and sprightly.

He was still so wide awake at dawn that he got up, slipped on tennis shoes, trousers, and a sweater, and in silence crept downstairs and out through the study window. It was just light; there was a smell of grass. 'Fleur!' he thought; 'Fleur!' It was mysteriously white out of doors, with nothing awake except the birds just beginning to chirp. 'I'll go down into the coppice,' he thought. He ran down through the fields, reached the pond just as the sun rose, and passed into the coppice. Bluebells carpeted the ground there; among the larch-trees there was mystery—the air, as it were, composed of that romantic quality. Jon sniffed its freshness, and stared at the bluebells in the sharpening light. Fleur! It rhymed with her! And she lived at Mapledurham—a jolly name, too, on the river somewhere. He could find it in the atlas presently. He would write to her. But would she answer? Oh! She must. She had said "Au revoir!" Not good-bye! What luck that she had dropped her handkerchief! He would never have known her but for that. And the more he thought of that handkerchief, the more amazing his luck seemed. Fleur! It certainly rhymed with her! Rhythm thronged his head; words jostled to be joined together; he was on the verge of a poem.

Jon remained in this condition for more than half an hour, then returned to the house, and getting a ladder, climbed in at his bedroom window out of sheer exhilaration. Then, remembering that the study window was open, he went down and shut it, first removing the ladder, so as to obliterate all traces of his feeling. The thing was too deep to be revealed to mortal soul-even-to his mother.

CHAPTER IV.—THE MAUSOLEUM

There are houses whose souls have passed into the limbo of Time, leaving their bodies in the limbo of London. Such was not quite the condition of "Timothy's" on the Bayswater Road, for Timothy's soul still had one foot in Timothy Forsyte's body, and Smither kept the atmosphere unchanging, of camphor and port wine and house whose windows are only opened to air it twice a day.

To Forsyte imagination that house was now a sort of Chinese pill-box, a series of layers in the last of which was Timothy. One did not reach him, or so it was reported by members of the family who, out of old-time habit or absentmindedness, would drive up once in a blue moon and ask after their surviving uncle. Such were Francie, now quite emancipated from God (she frankly avowed atheism), Euphemia, emancipated from old Nicholas, and Winifred Dartie from her "man of the world." But, after all, everybody was emancipated now, or said they were—perhaps not quite the same thing!

When Soames, therefore, took it on his way to Paddington station on the morning after that encounter, it was hardly with the expectation of seeing Timothy in the flesh. His heart made a faint demonstration within him while he stood in full south sunlight on the newly whitened doorstep of that little house where four Forsytes had once lived, and now but one dwelt on like a winter fly; the house into which Soames had come and out of which he had gone times without number, divested of, or burdened with, fardels of family gossip; the house of the "old people" of another century, another age.

The sight of Smither—still corseted up to the armpits because the new fashion which came in as they were going out about 1903 had never been considered "nice" by Aunts Juley and Hester—brought a pale friendliness to Soames' lips; Smither, still faithfully arranged to old pattern in every detail, an invaluable servant—none such left—smiling back at him, with the words: "Why! it's Mr. Soames, after all this time! And how are you, sir? Mr. Timothy will be so pleased to know you've been."

"How is he?"

"Oh! he keeps fairly bobbish for his age, sir; but of course he's a wonderful man. As I said to Mrs. Dartie when she was here last: It would please Miss Forsyte and Mrs. Juley and Miss Hester to see how he relishes a baked apple still. But he's quite deaf. And a mercy, I always think. For what we should have done with him in the air-raids, I don't know."

"Ah!" said Soames. "What did you do with him?"

"We just left him in his bed, and had the bell run down into the cellar, so that Cook and I could hear him if he rang. It would never have done to let him know there was a war on. As I said to Cook, 'If Mr. Timothy rings, they may do what they like—I'm going up. My dear mistresses would have a fit if they could see him ringing and nobody going to him.' But he slept through them all beautiful. And the one in the daytime he was having his bath.

It was a mercy, because he might have noticed the people in the street all looking up—he often looks out of the window."

"Quite!" murmured Soames. Smither was getting garrulous! "I just want to look round and see if there's anything to be done."

"Yes, sir. I don't think there's anything except a smell of mice in the dining-room that we don't know how to get rid of. It's funny they should be there, and not a crumb, since Mr. Timothy took to not coming down, just before the War. But they're nasty little things; you never know where they'll take you next."

"Does he leave his bed?"—

"Oh! yes, sir; he takes nice exercise between his bed and the window in the morning, not to risk a change of air. And he's quite comfortable in himself; has his Will out every day regular. It's a great consolation to him—that."

"Well, Smither, I want to see him, if I can; in case he has anything to say to me."

Smither coloured up above her corsets.

"It will be an occasion!" she said. "Shall I take you round the house, sir, while I send Cook to break it to him?"

"No, you go to him," said Soames. "I can go round the house by myself."

One could not confess to sentiment before another, and Soames felt that he was going to be sentimental nosing round those rooms so saturated with the past. When Smither, creaking with excitement, had left him, Soames entered the dining-room and sniffed. In his opinion it wasn't mice, but incipient wood-rot, and he examined the panelling. Whether it was worth a coat of paint, at Timothy's age, he was not sure. The room had always been the most modern in the house; and only a faint smile curled Soames' lips and nostrils. Walls of a rich green surmounted the oak dado; a heavy metal chandelier hung by a chain from a ceiling divided by imitation beams. The pictures had been bought by Timothy, a bargain, one day at Jobson's sixty years ago—three Snyder "still lifes," two faintly coloured drawings of a boy and a girl, rather charming, which bore the initials "J. R."—Timothy had always believed they might turn out to be Joshua Reynolds, but Soames, who admired them, had discovered that they were only John Robinson; and a doubtful Morland of a white pony being shod. Deep-red plush curtains, ten high-backed dark mahogany chairs with deep-red plush seats, a Turkey carpet, and a mahogany dining-table as large as the room was small, such was an apartment which Soames could remember unchanged in soul or body since he was four years old. He looked especially at the two drawings, and thought: 'I shall buy those at the sale.'

From the dining-room he passed into Timothy's study. He did not remember ever having been in that room. It was lined from floor to ceiling with volumes, and he looked at them with curiosity. One wall seemed devoted to educational books, which Timothy's firm had published two generations back-sometimes as many as twenty copies of one book. Soames read their titles and shuddered. The middle wall had precisely the same books as used to be in the library at his own father's in Park Lane, from which he deduced the fancy that James and his youngest brother had gone out together one day and bought a brace of small libraries. The third wall he approached with more excitement. Here, surely, Timothy's own taste would be found. It was. The books were dummies. The fourth wall was all heavily curtained window. And turned toward it was a large chair with a mahogany reading-stand attached, on which a yellowish and folded copy of The Times, dated July 6, 1914, the day Timothy first failed to come down, as if in preparation for the War, seemed waiting for him still. In a corner stood a large globe of that world never visited by Timothy, deeply convinced of the unreality of everything but England, and permanently upset by the sea, on which he had been very sick one Sunday afternoon in 1836, out of a pleasure boat off the pier at Brighton, with Juley and Hester, Swithin and Hatty Chessman; all due to Swithin, who was always taking things into his head, and who, thank goodness, had been sick too. Soames knew all about it, having heard the tale fifty times at least from one or other of them. He went up to the globe, and gave it a spin; it emitted a faint creak and moved about an inch, bringing into his purview a daddy-long-legs which had died on it in latitude 44.

'Mausoleum!' he thought. 'George was right!' And he went out and up the stairs. On the half-landing he stopped before the case of stuffed humming-birds which had delighted his childhood. They looked not a day older, suspended on wires above pampas-grass. If the case were opened the birds would not begin to hum, but the whole thing would crumble, he suspected. It wouldn't be worth putting that into the sale! And suddenly he was caught by a memory of Aunt Ann—dear old Aunt Ann—holding him by the hand in front of that case and saying: "Look, Soamey! Aren't they bright and pretty, dear little humming-birds!" Soames remembered his own answer: "They don't hum, Auntie." He must have been six, in a black velveteen suit with a light-blue collar-he remembered that suit well! Aunt Ann with her ringlets, and her spidery kind hands, and her grave old aquiline smile—a fine old lady, Aunt Ann! He moved on up to the drawing-room door. There on each side of it were the groups of miniatures. Those he would certainly buy in! The miniatures of his four aunts, one of his Uncle Swithin adolescent, and one of his Uncle Nicholas as a boy. They had all been painted by a young lady friend of the family at a time, 1830, about, when miniatures were considered very genteel, and lasting too, painted as they were on ivory. Many a time had he heard the tale of that young lady: "Very talented, my dear; she had quite a weakness for Swithin, and very soon after she went into a consumption and died: so like Keats—we often spoke of it."

Well, there they were! Ann, Juley, Hester, Susan—quite a small child; Swithin, with sky-blue eyes, pink cheeks, yellow curls, white waistcoat-large as life; and Nicholas, like Cupid with an eye on heaven. Now he came to think of it, Uncle Nick had always been rather like that—a wonderful man to the last. Yes, she must have had talent, and miniatures always had a certain back-watered cachet of their own, little subject to the currents of competition on aesthetic Change. Soames opened the drawing-room door. The room was dusted, the furniture uncovered, the curtains drawn back, precisely as if his aunts still dwelt there patiently waiting. And a thought came to him: When Timothy died—why not? Would it not be almost a duty to preserve this house—like Carlyle's—and put up a tablet, and show it? "Specimen of mid-Victorian abode—entrance, one shilling, with catalogue." After all, it was the completest thing, and perhaps the deadest in the London of to-day. Perfect in its special taste and culture, if, that is, he took down and carried over to his own collection the four Barbizon pictures he had given them. The still sky-blue walls, tile green curtains patterned with red flowers and ferns; the crewel-worked fire-screen before the cast-iron grate; the mahogany cupboard with glass windows, full of little knickknacks; the beaded footstools; Keats, Shelley, Southey, Cowper, Coleridge, Byron's Corsair (but nothing else), and the Victorian poets in a bookshelf row; the marqueterie cabinet lined with dim red plush, full of family relics: Hester's first fan; the buckles of their mother's father's shoes; three bottled scorpions; and one very yellow elephant's tusk, sent home from India by Great-uncle Edgar Forsyte, who had been in jute; a yellow bit of paper propped up, with spidery writing on it, recording God knew what! And the pictures crowding on the walls—all water-colours save those four Barbizons looking like the foreigners they were, and doubtful customers at that—pictures bright and illustrative, "Telling the Bees," "Hey for the Ferry!" and two in the style of Frith, all thimblerig and crinolines, given them by

Swithin. Oh! many, many pictures at which Soames had gazed a thousand times in supercilious fascination; a marvellous collection of bright, smooth gilt frames.

And the boudoir-grand piano, beautifully dusted, hermetically sealed as ever; and Aunt Juley's album of pressed seaweed on it. And the gilt-legged chairs, stronger than they looked. And on one side of the fireplace the sofa of crimson silk, where Aunt Ann, and after her Aunt Juley, had been wont to sit, facing the light and bolt upright. And on the other side of the fire the one really easy chair, back to the light, for Aunt Hester. Soames screwed up his eyes; he seemed to see them sitting there. Ah! and the atmosphere—even now, of too many stuffs and washed lace curtains, lavender in bags, and dried bees' wings. 'No,' he thought, 'there's nothing like it left; it ought to be preserved.' And, by George, they might laugh at it, but for a standard of gentle life never departed from, for fastidiousness of skin and eye and nose and feeling, it beat to-day hollow—to-day with its Tubes and cars, its perpetual smoking, its cross-legged, bare-necked girls visible up to the knees and down to the waist if you took the trouble (agreeable to the satyr within each Forsyte but hardly his idea of a lady), with their feet, too, screwed round the legs of their chairs while they ate, and their "So longs," and their "Old Beans," and their laughter—girls who gave him the shudders whenever he thought of Fleur in contact with them; and the hard-eyed, capable, older women who managed life and gave him the shudders too. No! his old aunts, if they never opened their minds, their eyes, or very much their windows, at least had manners, and a standard, and reverence for past and future.

With rather a choky feeling he closed the door and went tiptoeing upstairs. He looked in at a place on the way: H'm! in perfect order of the eighties, with a sort of yellow oilskin paper on the walls. At the top of the stairs he hesitated between four doors. Which of them was Timothy's? And he listened. A sound, as of a child slowly dragging a hobby-horse about, came to his ears. That must be Timothy! He tapped, and a door was opened by Smither, very red in the face.

Mr. Timothy was taking his walk, and she had not been able to get him to attend. If Mr. Soames would come into the back-room, he could see him through the door.

Soames went into the back-room and stood watching.

The last of the old Forsytes was on his feet, moving with the most impressive slowness, and an air of perfect concentration on his own affairs, backward and forward between the foot of his bed and the window, a distance of some twelve feet. The lower part of his square face, no longer clean-shaven, was covered with snowy beard clipped as short as it could be, and his chin looked as broad as his brow where the hair was also quite white, while nose and cheeks and brow were a good yellow. One hand held a stout stick, and the other grasped the skirt of his Jaeger dressing-gown, from under which could be seen his bed-socked ankles and feet thrust into Jaeger slippers. The expression on his face was that of a crossed child, intent on something that he has not got. Each time he turned he stumped the stick, and then dragged it, as if to show that he could do without it:

"He still looks strong," said Soames under his breath.

"Oh! yes, sir. You should see him take his bath—it's wonderful; he does enjoy it so."

Those quite loud words gave Soames an insight. Timothy had resumed his babyhood.

"Does he take any interest in things generally?" he said, also loud.

"Oh! yes, sir; his food and his Will. It's quite a sight to see him turn it over and over, not to read it, of course; and every now and then he asks the price of Consols, and I write it on a slate for him—very large. Of course, I always write the same, what they were when he last took notice, in 1914. We got the doctor to forbid him to read the paper when the War broke out. Oh! he did take on about that at first. But he soon came round, because he knew it tired him; and he's a wonder to conserve energy as he used to call it when my dear mistresses were alive, bless their hearts! How he did go on at them about that; they were always so active, if you remember, Mr. Soames."

"What would happen if I were to go in?" asked Soames: "Would he remember me? I made his Will, you know, after Miss Hester died in 1907."

"Oh! that, sir," replied Smither doubtfully, "I couldn't take on me to say. I think he might; he really is a wonderful man for his age."

Soames moved into the doorway, and waiting for Timothy to turn, said in a loud voice: "Uncle Timothy!"

Timothy trailed back half-way, and halted.

"Eh?" he said.

"Soames," cried Soames at the top of his voice, holding out his hand, "Soames Forsyte!"

"No!" said Timothy, and stumping his stick loudly on the floor, he continued his walk.

"It doesn't seem to work," said Soames.

"No, sir," replied Smither, rather crestfallen; "you see, he hasn't finished his walk. It always was one thing at a time with him. I expect he'll ask me this afternoon if you came about the gas, and a pretty job I shall have to make him understand."

"Do you think he ought to have a man about him?"

Smither held up her hands. "A man! Oh! no. Cook and me can manage perfectly. A strange man about would send him crazy in no time. And my mistresses wouldn't like the idea of a man in the house. Besides, we're so—proud of him."

"I suppose the doctor comes?"

"Every morning. He makes special terms for such a quantity, and Mr. Timothy's so used, he doesn't take a bit of notice, except to put out his tongue."

"Well," said Soames, turning away, "it's rather sad and painful to me."

"Oh! sir," returned Smither anxiously, "you mustn't think that. Now that he can't worry about things, he quite enjoys his life, really he does. As I say to Cook, Mr. Timothy is more of a man than he ever was. You see, when he's not walkin', or takin' his bath, he's eatin', and when he's not eatin', he's sleepin'; and there it is. There isn't an ache or a care about him anywhere."

"Well," said Soames, "there's something in that. I'll go down. By the way, let me see his Will."

"I should have to take my time about that, sir; he keeps it under his pillow, and he'd see me, while he's active."

"I only want to know if it's the one I made," said Soames; "you take a look at its date some time, and let me know."

"Yes, sir; but I'm sure it's the same, because me and Cook witnessed, you remember, and there's our names on it still, and we've only done it once."

"Quite," said Soames. He did remember. Smither and Jane had been proper witnesses, having been left nothing in the Will that they might have no interest in Timothy's death. It had been—he fully admitted—an almost improper precaution, but Timothy had wished it, and, after all, Aunt Hester had provided for them amply.

"Very well," he said; "good-bye, Smither. Look after him, and if he should say anything at any time, put it down, and let me know."

"Oh! yes, Mr. Soames; I'll be sure to do that. It's been such a pleasant change to see you. Cook will be quite excited when I tell her."

Soames shook her hand and went down-stairs. He stood for fully two minutes by the hat-stand whereon he had hung his hat so many times. 'So it all passes,' he was thinking; 'passes and begins again. Poor old chap!' And he listened, if perchance the sound of Timothy trailing his hobby-horse might come down the well of the stairs; or some ghost of an old face show over the bannisters, and an old voice say: 'Why, it's dear Soames, and we were only saying that we hadn't seen him for a week!'

Nothing—nothing! Just the scent of camphor, and dust-motes in a sunbeam through the fanlight over the door. The little old house! A mausoleum! And, turning on his heel, he went out, and caught his train.

CHAPTER V.—THE NATIVE HEATH

"His foot's upon his native heath,

His name's—Val Dartie."

With some such feeling did Val Dartie, in the fortieth year of his age, set out that same Thursday morning very early from the old manor-house he had taken on the north side of the Sussex Downs. His destination was Newmarket, and he had not been there since the autumn of 1899, when he stole over from Oxford for the Cambridgeshire. He paused at the door to give his wife a kiss, and put a flask of port into his pocket.

"Don't overtire your leg, Val, and don't bet too much."

With the pressure of her chest against his own, and her eyes looking into his, Val felt both leg and pocket safe. He should be moderate; Holly was always right—she had a natural aptitude. It did not seem so remarkable to him, perhaps, as it might to others, that—half Dartie as he was—he should have been perfectly faithful to his young first cousin during the twenty years since he married her romantically out in the Boer War; and faithful without any feeling of sacrifice or boredom—she was so quick, so slyly always a little in front of his mood. Being first cousins they had decided, rather needlessly, to have no children; and, though a little sallower, she had kept her looks, her slimness, and the colour of her dark hair. Val particularly admired the life of her own she carried on, besides carrying on his, and riding better every year. She kept up her music, she read an awful lot—novels, poetry, all sorts of stuff. Out on their farm in Cape colony she had looked after all the "nigger" babies and women in a miraculous manner. She was, in fact, clever; yet made no fuss about it, and had no "side." Though not remarkable for humility, Val had come to have the feeling that she was his superior, and he did not grudge it—a great tribute. It might be noted that he never looked at Holly without her knowing of it, but that she looked at him sometimes unawares.

He had kissed her in the porch because he should not be doing so on the platform, though she was going to the station with him, to drive the car back. Tanned and wrinkled by Colonial weather and the wiles inseparable from horses, and handicapped by the leg which, weakened in the Boer War, had probably saved his life in the War just past, Val was still much as he had been in the days of his courtship; his smile as wide and charming, his eyelashes, if anything, thicker and darker, his eyes screwed up under them, as bright a grey, his freckles rather deeper, his hair a little grizzled at the sides. He gave the impression of one who has lived actively with horses in a sunny climate.

Twisting the car sharp round at the gate, he said:

"When is young Jon coming?"

"To-day."

"Is there anything you want for him? I could bring it down on Saturday."

"No; but you might come by the same train as Fleur—one-forty."

Val gave the Ford full rein; he still drove like a man in a new country on bad roads, who refuses to compromise, and expects heaven at every hole.

"That's a young woman who knows her way about," he said. "I say, has it struck you?"

"Yes," said Holly.

"Uncle Soames and your Dad—bit awkward, isn't it?"

"She won't know, and he won't know, and nothing must be said, of course. It's only for five days, Val."

"Stable secret! Righto!" If Holly thought it safe, it was. Glancing slyly round at him, she said: "Did you notice how beautifully she asked herself?"

"No!"

"Well, she did. What do you think of her, Val?"

"Pretty and clever; but she might run out at any corner if she got her monkey up, I should say."

"I'm wondering," Holly murmured, "whether she is the modern young woman. One feels at sea coming home into all this."

"You? You get the hang of things so quick."

Holly slid her hand into his coat-pocket.

"You keep one in the know," said Val encouraged. "What do you think of that Belgian fellow, Profond?"

"I think he's rather 'a good devil.'"

Val grinned.

"He seems to me a queer fish for a friend of our family. In fact, our family is in pretty queer waters, with Uncle Soames marrying a Frenchwoman, and your Dad marrying Soames's first. Our grandfathers would have had fits!"

"So would anybody's, my dear."

"This car," Val said suddenly, "wants rousing; she doesn't get her hind legs under her uphill. I shall have to give her her head on the slope if I'm to catch that train."

There was that about horses which had prevented him from ever really sympathising with a car, and the running of the Ford under his guidance compared with its running under that of Holly was always noticeable. He caught the train.

"Take care going home; she'll throw you down if she can. Good-bye, darling."

"Good-bye," called Holly, and kissed her hand.

In the train, after quarter of an hour's indecision between thoughts of Holly, his morning paper, the look of the bright day, and his dim memory of Newmarket, Val plunged into the recesses of a small square book, all names, pedigrees, tap-roots, and notes about the make and shape of horses. The Forsyte in him was bent on the acquisition of a certain strain of blood, and he was subduing resolutely as yet the Dartie hankering for a Nutter. On getting back to England, after the profitable sale of his South African farm and stud, and observing that the sun seldom shone, Val had said to himself: "I've absolutely got to have an interest in life, or this country will give me the blues. Hunting's not enough, I'll breed and I'll train." With just that extra pinch of shrewdness and decision imparted by long residence in a new country, Val had seen the weak point of modern breeding. They were all hypnotised by fashion and high price. He should buy for looks, and let names go hang! And here he was already, hypnotised by the prestige of a certain strain of blood! Half-consciously, he thought: 'There's something in this damned climate which makes one go round in a ring. All the same, I must have a strain of Mayfly blood.'

In this mood he reached the Mecca of his hopes. It was one of those quiet meetings favourable to such as wish to look into horses, rather than into the mouths of bookmakers; and Val clung to the paddock. His twenty years of Colonial life, divesting him of the dandyism in which he had been bred, had left him the essential neatness of the horseman, and given him a queer and rather blighting eye over what he called "the silly haw-haw" of some Englishmen, the "flapping cockatoory" of some English-women—Holly had none of that and Holly was his model. Observant, quick, resourceful, Val went straight to the heart of a transaction, a horse, a drink; and he was on his way to the heart of a Mayfly filly, when a slow voice said at his elbow:

"Mr. Val Dartie? How's Mrs. Val Dartie? She's well, I hope." And he saw beside him the Belgian he had met at his sister Imogen's.

"Prosper Profond—I met you at lunch," said the voice.

"How are you?" murmured Val.

"I'm very well," replied Monsieur Profond, smiling with a certain inimitable slowness. "A good devil," Holly had called him. Well! He looked a little like a devil, with his dark, clipped, pointed beard; a sleepy one though, and good-humoured, with fine eyes, unexpectedly intelligent.

"Here's a gentleman wants to know you—cousin of yours—Mr. George Forsyde."

Val saw a large form, and a face clean-shaven, bull-like, a little lowering, with sardonic humour bubbling behind a full grey eye; he remembered it dimly from old days when he would dine with his father at the Iseeum Club.

"I used to go racing with your father," George was saying: "How's the stud? Like to buy one of my screws?"

Val grinned, to hide the sudden feeling that the bottom had fallen out of breeding. They believed in nothing over here, not even in horses. George Forsyte, Prosper Profond! The devil himself was not more disillusioned than those two.

"Didn't know you were a racing man," he said to Monsieur Profond.

"I'm not. I don't care for it. I'm a yachtin' man. I don't care for yachtin' either, but I like to see my friends. I've got some lunch, Mr. Val Dartie, just a small lunch, if you'd like to 'ave some; not much—just a small one—in my car."

"Thanks," said Val; "very good of you. I'll come along in about quarter of an hour."

"Over there. Mr. Forsyde's comin'," and Monsieur Profond "poinded" with a yellow-gloved finger; "small car, with a small lunch"; he moved on, groomed, sleepy, and remote, George Forsyte following, neat, huge, and with his jesting air.

Val remained gazing at the Mayfly filly. George Forsyte, of course, was an old chap, but this Profond might be about his own age; Val felt extremely young, as if the Mayfly filly were a toy at which those two had laughed. The animal had lost reality.

"That 'small' mare"—he seemed to hear the voice of Monsieur Profond—"what do you see in her?—we must all die!"

And George Forsyte, crony of his father, racing still! The Mayfly strain—was it any better than any other? He might just as well have a flutter with his money instead.

"No, by gum!" he muttered suddenly, "if it's no good breeding horses, it's no good doing anything. What did I come for? I'll buy her."

He stood back and watched the ebb of the paddock visitors toward the stand. Natty old chips, shrewd portly fellows, Jews, trainers looking as if they had never been guilty of seeing a horse in their lives; tall, flapping, languid women, or brisk, loud-voiced women; young men with an air as if trying to take it seriously—two or three of them with only one arm.

'Life over here's a game!' thought Val. 'Muffin bell rings, horses run, money changes hands; ring again, run again, money changes back.'

But, alarmed at his own philosophy, he went to the paddock gate to watch the Mayfly filly canter down. She moved well; and he made his way over to the "small" car. The "small" lunch was the sort a man dreams of but seldom gets; and when it was concluded Monsieur Profond walked back with him to the paddock.

"Your wife's a nice woman," was his surprising remark.

"Nicest woman I know," returned Val dryly.

"Yes," said Monsieur Profond; "she has a nice face. I admire nice women."

Val looked at him suspiciously, but something kindly and direct in the heavy diabolism of his companion disarmed him for the moment.

"Any time you like to come on my yacht, I'll give her a small cruise."

"Thanks," said Val, in arms again, "she hates the sea."

"So do I," said Monsieur Profond.

"Then why do you yacht?"

The Belgian's eyes smiled. "Oh! I don't know. I've done everything; it's the last thing I'm doin'."

"It must be d-d expensive. I should want more reason than that."

Monsieur Prosper Profond raised his eyebrows, and puffed out a heavy lower lip.

"I'm an easy-goin' man," he said.

"Were you in the War?" asked Val.

"Ye-es. I've done that too. I was gassed; it was a small bit unpleasant." He smiled with a deep and sleepy air of prosperity, as if he had caught it from his name.

Whether his saying "small" when he ought to have said "little" was genuine mistake or affectation Val could not decide; the fellow was evidently capable of anything.

Among the ring of buyers round the Mayfly filly who had won her race, Monsieur Profond said:

"You goin' to bid?"

Val nodded. With this sleepy Satan at his elbow, he felt in need of faith. Though placed above the ultimate blows of Providence by the forethought of a grand-father who had tied him up a thousand a year to which was added the thousand a year tied up for Holly by her grand-father, Val was not flush of capital that he could touch, having spent most of what he had realised from his South African farm on his establishment in Sussex. And very soon he was thinking: 'Dash it! she's going beyond me!' His limit-six hundred-was exceeded; he dropped out of the bidding. The Mayfly filly passed under the hammer at seven hundred and fifty guineas. He was turning away vexed when the slow voice of Monsieur Profond said in his ear:

"Well, I've bought that small filly, but I don't want her; you take her and give her to your wife."

Val looked at the fellow with renewed suspicion, but the good humour in his eyes was such that he really could not take offence.

"I made a small lot of money in the War," began Monsieur Profond in answer to that look. "I 'ad armament shares. I like to give it away. I'm always makin' money. I want very small lot myself. I like my friends to 'ave it."

"I'll buy her of you at the price you gave," said Val with sudden resolution.

"No," said Monsieur Profond. "You take her. I don' want her."

"Hang it! one doesn't—"

"Why not?" smiled Monsieur Profond. "I'm a friend of your family."

"Seven hundred and fifty guineas is not a box of cigars," said Val impatiently.

"All right; you keep her for me till I want her, and do what you like with her."

"So long as she's yours," said Val. "I don't mind that."

"That's all right," murmured Monsieur Profond, and moved away.

Val watched; he might be "a good devil," but then again he might not. He saw him rejoin George Forsyte, and thereafter saw him no more.

He spent those nights after racing at his mother's house in Green Street.

Winifred Dartie at sixty-two was marvellously preserved, considering the three-and-thirty years during which she had put up with Montague Dartie, till almost happily released by a French staircase. It was to her a vehement satisfaction to have her favourite son back from South Africa after all this time, to feel him so little changed, and to have taken a fancy to his wife. Winifred, who in the late seventies, before her marriage, had been in the vanguard of freedom, pleasure, and fashion, confessed her youth outclassed by the donzellas of the day. They seemed, for instance, to regard marriage as an incident, and Winifred sometimes regretted that she had not done the same; a second, third, fourth incident might have secured her a partner of less dazzling inebriety; though, after all, he had left her Val, Imogen, Maud, Benedict (almost a colonel and unharmed by the War)—none of whom had been divorced as yet. The steadiness of her children often amazed one who remembered their father; but, as she was fond of believing, they were really all Forsytes, favouring herself, with the exception, perhaps, of Imogen. Her brother's "little girl" Fleur frankly puzzled Winifred. The child was as restless as any of these modern young women—"She's a small flame in a draught," Prosper Profond had said one day after dinner—but she did not flap, or talk at the top of her voice. The steady Forsyteism in Winifred's own character instinctively resented the feeling in the air, the modern girl's habits and her motto: "All's much of a muchness! Spend, to-morrow we shall be poor!" She found it a saving grace in Fleur that, having set her heart on a thing, she had no change of heart until she got it—though—what happened after, Fleur was, of course, too young to have made evident. The child was a "very pretty little thing," too, and quite a credit to take about, with her mother's French taste and gift for wearing clothes; everybody turned to look at Fleur—great consideration to Winifred, a lover of the style and distinction which had so cruelly deceived her in the case of Montague Dartie.

In discussing her with Val, at breakfast on Saturday morning, Winifred dwelt on the family skeleton.

"That little affair of your father-in-law and your Aunt Irene, Val—it's old as the hills, of course, Fleur need know nothing about it—making a fuss. Your Uncle Soames is very particular about that. So you'll be careful."

"Yes! But it's dashed awkward—Holly's young half-brother is coming to live with us while he learns farming. He's there already."

"Oh!" said Winifred. "That is a gaff! What is he like?"

"Only saw him once—at Robin Hill, when we were home in 1909; he was naked and painted blue and yellow in stripes—a jolly little chap."

Winifred thought that "rather nice," and added comfortably: "Well, Holly's sensible; she'll know how to deal with it. I shan't tell your uncle. It'll only bother him. It's a great comfort to have you back, my dear boy, now that I'm getting on."

"Getting on! Why! you're as young as ever. That chap Profond, Mother, is he all right?"

"Prosper Profond! Oh! the most amusing man I know."

Val grunted, and recounted the story of the Mayfly filly.

"That's so like him," murmured Winifred. "He does all sorts of things."

"Well," said Val shrewdly, "our family haven't been too lucky with that kind of cattle; they're too light-hearted for us."

It was true, and Winifred's blue study lasted a full minute before she answered:

"Oh! well! He's a foreigner, Val; one must make allowances."

"All right, I'll use his filly and make it up to him, somehow."

And soon after he gave her his blessing, received a kiss, and left her for his bookmaker's, the Iseeum Club, and Victoria station.

CHAPTER VI.—JON

Mrs. Val Dartie, after twenty years of South Africa, had fallen deeply in love, fortunately with something of her own, for the object of her passion was the prospect in front of her windows, the cool clear light on the green Downs. It was England again, at last! England more beautiful than she had dreamed. Chance had, in fact, guided the Val Darties to a spot where the South Downs had real charm when the sun shone. Holly had enough of her father's eye to apprehend the rare quality of their outlines and chalky radiance; to go up there by the ravine-like lane and wander along toward Chanctonbury or Amberley, was still a delight which she hardly attempted to share with Val, whose admiration of Nature was confused by a Forsyte's instinct for getting something out of it, such as the condition of the turf for his horses' exercise.

Driving the Ford home with a certain humouring, smoothness, she promised herself that the first use she would make of Jon would be to take him up there, and show him "the view" under this May-day sky.

She was looking forward to her young half-brother with a motherliness not exhausted by Val. A three-day visit to Robin Hill, soon after their arrival home, had yielded no sight of him—he was still at school; so that her recollection, like Val's, was of a little sunny-haired boy, striped blue and yellow, down by the pond.

Those three days at Robin Hill had been exciting, sad, embarrassing. Memories of her dead brother, memories of Val's courtship; the ageing of her father, not seen for twenty years, something funereal in his ironic gentleness which did not escape one who had much subtle instinct; above all, the presence of her stepmother, whom she could still vaguely remember as the "lady in grey" of days when she was little and grandfather alive and Mademoiselle Beauce so cross because that intruder gave her music lessons—all these confused and tantalised a spirit which had longed to find Robin Hill untroubled. But Holly was adept at keeping things to herself, and all had seemed to go quite well.

Her father had kissed her when she left him, with lips which she was sure had trembled.

"Well, my dear," he said, "the War hasn't changed Robin Hill, has it? If only you could have brought Jolly back with you! I say, can you stand this spiritualistic racket? When the oak-tree dies, it dies, I'm afraid."

From the warmth of her embrace he probably divined that he had let the cat out of the bag, for he rode off at once on irony.

"Spiritualism—queer word, when the more they manifest the more they prove that they've got hold of matter."

"How?" said Holly.

"Why! Look at their photographs of auric presences. You must have something material for light and shade to fall on before you can take a photograph. No, it'll end in our calling all matter spirit, or all spirit matter—I don't know which."

"But don't you believe in survival, Dad?"

Jolyon had looked at her, and the sad whimsicality of his face impressed her deeply.

"Well, my dear, I should like to get something out of death. I've been looking into it a bit. But for the life of me I can't find anything that telepathy, sub-consciousness, and emanation from the storehouse of this world can't account for just as well. Wish I could! Wishes father thought but they don't breed evidence." Holly had pressed her lips again to his forehead with the feeling that it confirmed his theory that all matter was becoming spirit—his brow felt, somehow, so insubstantial.

But the most poignant memory of that little visit had been watching, unobserved, her stepmother reading to herself a letter from Jon. It was—she decided—the prettiest sight she had ever seen. Irene, lost as it were in the letter of her boy, stood at a window where the light fell on her face and her fine grey hair; her lips were moving, smiling, her dark eyes laughing, dancing, and the hand which did not hold the letter was pressed against her breast. Holly withdrew as from a vision of perfect love, convinced that Jon must be nice.

When she saw him coming out of the station with a kit-bag in either hand, she was confirmed in her predisposition. He was a little like Jolly, that long-lost idol of her childhood, but eager-looking and less formal, with deeper eyes and brighter-coloured hair, for he wore no hat; altogether a very interesting "little" brother!

His tentative politeness charmed one who was accustomed to assurance in the youthful manner; he was disturbed because she was to drive him home, instead of his driving her. Shouldn't he have a shot? They hadn't a car at Robin Hill since the War, of course, and he had only driven once, and landed up a bank, so she oughtn't to mind his trying. His laugh, soft and infectious, was very attractive, though that word, she had heard, was now quite old-fashioned. When they reached the house he pulled out a crumpled letter which she read while he was washing—a quite short letter, which must have cost her father many a pang to write.

"MY DEAR,

"You and Val will not forget, I trust, that Jon knows nothing of family history. His mother and I think he is too young at present. The boy is very dear, and the apple of her eye. Verbum sapientibus,

"Your loving father,

"J. F."

That was all; but it renewed in Holly an uneasy regret that Fleur was coming.

After tea she fulfilled that promise to herself and took Jon up the hill. They had a long talk, sitting above an old chalk-pit grown over with brambles and goosepenny. Milkwort and liverwort starred the green slope, the larks sang, and thrushes in the brake, and now and then a gull flighting inland would wheel very white against the paling sky, where the vague moon was coming up. Delicious fragrance came to them, as if little invisible creatures were running and treading scent out of the blades of grass.

Jon, who had fallen silent, said rather suddenly:

"I say, this is wonderful! There's no fat on it at all. Gull's flight and sheep-bells."

"'Gull's flight and sheep-bells'! You're a poet, my dear!"

Jon sighed.

"Oh, Golly! No go!"

"Try! I used to at your age."

"Did you? Mother says 'try' too; but I'm so rotten. Have you any of yours for me to see?"

"My dear," Holly murmured, "I've been married nineteen years. I only wrote verses when I wanted to be."

"Oh!" said Jon, and turned over on his face: the one cheek she could see was a charming colour. Was Jon "touched in the wind," then, as Val would have called it? Already? But, if so, all the better, he would take no notice of young Fleur. Besides, on Monday he would begin his farming. And she smiled. Was it Burns who followed the plough, or only Piers Plowman? Nearly every young man and most young women seemed to be poets now, judging from the number of their books she had read out in South Africa, importing them from Hatchus and Bumphards; and quite good—oh! quite; much better than she had been herself! But then poetry had only really come in since her day—with motor-cars. Another long talk after dinner over a wood fire in the low hall, and there seemed little left to know about Jon except anything of real importance. Holly parted from him at his bedroom door, having seen twice over that he had everything, with the conviction that she would love him, and Val would like him. He was eager, but did not gush; he was a splendid listener, sympathetic, reticent about himself. He evidently loved their father, and adored his mother. He liked riding, rowing, and fencing better than games. He saved moths from candles, and couldn't bear spiders, but put them out of doors in screws of paper sooner than kill them. In a word, he was amiable. She went to sleep, thinking that he would suffer horribly if anybody hurt him; but who would hurt him?

Jon, on the other hand, sat awake at his window with a bit of paper and a pencil, writing his first "real poem" by the light of a candle because there was not enough moon to see by, only enough to make the night seem fluttery and as if engraved on silver. Just the night for Fleur to walk, and turn her eyes, and lead on-over the hills and far away. And Jon, deeply furrowed in his ingenuous brow, made marks on the paper and rubbed them out and wrote them in again, and did all that was necessary for the completion of a work of art; and he had a feeling such as the winds of Spring must have, trying their first songs among the coming blossom. Jon was one of those boys (not many) in whom a home-trained love of beauty had survived school life. He had had to keep it to himself, of course, so that not even the drawing-master knew of it; but it was there, fastidious and clear within him. And his poem seemed to him as lame and stilted as the night was winged. But he kept it, all the same. It was a "beast," but better than nothing as an expression of the inexpressible. And he thought with a sort of discomfiture: 'I shan't be able to show it to Mother.' He slept terribly well, when he did sleep, overwhelmed by novelty.

CHAPTER VII.—FLEUR

To avoid the awkwardness of questions which could not be answered, all that had been told Jon was:

"There's a girl coming down with Val for the week-end."

For the same reason, all that had been told Fleur was: "We've got a youngster staying with us."

The two yearlings, as Val called them in his thoughts, met therefore in a manner which for unpreparedness left nothing to be desired. They were thus introduced by Holly:

"This is Jon, my little brother; Fleur's a cousin of ours, Jon."

Jon, who was coming in through a French window out of strong sunlight, was so confounded by the providential nature of this miracle, that he had time to hear Fleur say calmly: "Oh, how do you do?" as if he had never seen her, and to understand dimly from the quickest imaginable little movement of her head that he never had seen her. He bowed therefore over her hand in an intoxicated manner, and became more silent than the grave. He knew better than to speak. Once in his early life, surprised reading by a nightlight, he had said fatuously "I was just turning over the leaves, Mum," and his mother had replied: "Jon, never tell stories, because of your face nobody will ever believe them."

The saying had permanently undermined the confidence necessary to the success of spoken untruth. He listened therefore to Fleur's swift and rapt allusions to the jolliness of everything, plied her with scones and jam, and got away as soon as might be. They say that in delirium tremens you see a fixed object, preferably dark, which suddenly changes shape and position. Jon saw the fixed object; it had dark eyes and passably dark hair, and changed its position, but never its shape. The knowledge that between him and that object there was already a secret understanding (however impossible to understand) thrilled him so that he waited feverishly, and began to copy out his poem—which of course he would never dare to—show her—till the sound of horses' hoofs roused him, and, leaning from his window, he saw her riding forth with Val. It was clear that she wasted no time, but the sight filled him with grief. He wasted his. If he had not bolted, in his fearful ecstasy, he might have been asked to go too. And from his window he sat and watched them disappear, appear again in the chine of the road, vanish, and emerge once more for a minute clear on the outline of the Down. 'Silly brute!' he thought; 'I always miss my chances.'

Why couldn't he be self-confident and ready? And, leaning his chin on his hands, he imagined the ride he might have had with her. A week-end was but a week-end, and he had missed three hours of it. Did he know any one except himself who would have been such a flat? He did not.

He dressed for dinner early, and was first down. He would miss no more. But he missed Fleur, who came down last. He sat opposite her at dinner, and it was terrible—impossible to say anything for fear of saying the wrong thing, impossible to keep his eyes fixed on her in the only natural way; in sum, impossible to treat normally one with whom in fancy he had already been over the hills and far away; conscious, too, all the time, that he must seem to her, to all of them, a dumb gawk. Yes, it was terrible! And she was talking so well—swooping with swift wing this way and that. Wonderful how she had learned an art which he found so disgustingly difficult. She must think him hopeless indeed!

His sister's eyes, fixed on him with a certain astonishment, obliged him at last to look at Fleur; but instantly her eyes, very wide and eager, seeming to say, "Oh! for goodness' sake!" obliged him to look at Val, where a grin obliged him to look at his cutlet—that, at least, had no eyes, and no grin, and he ate it hastily.

"Jon is going to be a farmer," he heard Holly say; "a farmer and a poet."

He glanced up reproachfully, caught the comic lift of her eyebrow just like their father's, laughed, and felt better.

Val recounted the incident of Monsieur Prosper Profond; nothing could have been more favourable, for, in relating it, he regarded Holly, who in turn regarded him, while Fleur seemed to be regarding with a slight frown some thought of her own, and Jon was really free to look at her at last. She had on a white frock, very simple and well made; her arms were bare, and her hair had a white rose in it. In just that swift moment of free vision, after such intense discomfort, Jon saw her sublimated, as one sees in the dark a slender white fruit-tree; caught her like a verse of poetry flashed before the eyes of the mind, or a tune which floats out in the distance and dies. He wondered giddily how old she was—she seemed so much more self-possessed and experienced than himself. Why mustn't he say they had met? He remembered suddenly his mother's face; puzzled, hurt-looking, when she answered: "Yes, they're relations, but we don't know them." Impossible that his mother, who loved beauty, should not admire Fleur if she did know her.

Alone with Val after dinner, he sipped port deferentially and answered the advances of this new-found brother-in-law. As to riding (always the first consideration with Val) he could have the young chestnut, saddle and unsaddle it himself, and generally look after it when he brought it in. Jon said he was accustomed to all that at home, and saw that he had gone up one in his host's estimation.

"Fleur," said Val, "can't ride much yet, but she's keen. Of course, her father doesn't know a horse from a cart-wheel. Does your Dad ride?"

"He used to; but now he's—you know, he's—" He stopped, so hating the word "old." His father was old, and yet not old; no—never!

"Quite," muttered Val. "I used to know your brother up at Oxford, ages ago, the one who died in the Boer War. We had a fight in New College Gardens. That was a queer business," he added, musing; "a good deal came out of it."

Jon's eyes opened wide; all was pushing him toward historical research, when his sister's voice said gently from the doorway:

"Come along, you two," and he rose, his heart pushing him toward something far more modern.

Fleur having declared that it was "simply too wonderful to stay indoors," they all went out. Moonlight was frosting the dew, and an old sundial threw a long shadow. Two box hedges at right angles, dark and square, barred off the orchard. Fleur turned through that angled opening.

"Come on!" she called. Jon glanced at the others, and followed. She was running among the trees like a ghost. All was lovely and foamlike above her, and there was a scent of old trunks, and of nettles. She vanished. He thought he had lost her, then almost ran into her standing quite still.

"Isn't it jolly?" she cried, and Jon answered:

"Rather!"

She reached up, twisted off a blossom and, twirling it in her fingers, said:

"I suppose I can call you Jon?"

"I should think so just."

"All right! But you know there's a feud between our families?"

Jon stammered: "Feud? Why?"

"It's ever so romantic and silly. That's why I pretended we hadn't met. Shall we get up early to-morrow morning and go for a walk before breakfast and have it out? I hate being slow about things, don't you?"

Jon murmured a rapturous assent.

"Six o'clock, then. I think your mother's beautiful"

Jon said fervently: "Yes, she is."

"I love all kinds of beauty," went on Fleur, "when it's exciting. I don't like Greek things a bit."

"What! Not Euripides?"

"Euripides? Oh! no, I can't bear Greek plays; they're so long. I think beauty's always swift. I like to look at one picture, for instance, and then run off. I can't bear a lot of things together. Look!" She held up her blossom in the moonlight. "That's better than all the orchard, I think."

And, suddenly, with her other hand she caught Jon's.

"Of all things in the world, don't you think caution's the most awful? Smell the moonlight!"

She thrust the blossom against his face; Jon agreed giddily that of all things in the world caution was the worst, and bending over, kissed the hand which held his.

"That's nice and old-fashioned," said Fleur calmly. "You're frightfully silent, Jon. Still I like silence when it's swift." She let go his hand. "Did you think I dropped my handkerchief on purpose?"

"No!" cried Jon, intensely shocked.

"Well, I did, of course. Let's get back, or they'll think we're doing this on purpose too." And again she ran like a ghost among the trees. Jon followed, with love in his heart, Spring in his heart, and over all the moonlit white unearthly blossom. They came out where they had gone in, Fleur walking demurely.

"It's quite wonderful in there," she said dreamily to Holly.

Jon preserved silence, hoping against hope that she might be thinking it swift.

She bade him a casual and demure good-night, which made him think he had been dreaming....

In her bedroom Fleur had flung off her gown, and, wrapped in a shapeless garment, with the white flower still in her hair, she looked like a mousme, sitting cross-legged on her bed, writing by candlelight.

"DEAREST CHERRY,

"I believe I'm in love. I've got it in the neck, only the feeling is really lower down. He's a second cousin-such a child, about six months older and ten years younger than I am. Boys always fall in love with their seniors, and girls with their juniors or with old men of forty. Don't laugh, but his eyes are the truest things I ever saw; and he's quite divinely silent! We had a most romantic first meeting in London under the Vospovitch Juno. And now he's sleeping in the next room and the moonlight's on the blossom; and to-morrow morning, before anybody's awake, we're going to walk off into Down fairyland. There's a feud between our families, which makes it really exciting. Yes! and I may have to use subterfuge and come on you for invitations—if so, you'll know why! My father doesn't want us to know each other, but I can't help that. Life's too short. He's got the most beautiful mother, with lovely silvery hair and a young face with dark eyes. I'm staying with his sister—who married my cousin; it's all mixed up, but I mean to pump her to-morrow. We've often talked about love being a spoil-sport; well, that's all tosh, it's the beginning of sport, and the sooner you feel it, my dear, the better for you.

"Jon (not simplified spelling, but short for Jolyon, which is a name in my family, they say) is the sort that lights up and goes out; about five feet ten, still growing, and I believe he's going to be a poet. If you laugh at me I've done with you forever. I perceive all sorts of difficulties, but you know when I really want a thing I get it. One of the chief effects of love is that you see the air sort of inhabited, like seeing a face in the moon; and you feel— you feel dancey and soft at the same time, with a funny sensation—like a continual first sniff of orange—blossom—Just above your stays. This is my first, and I feel as if it were going to be my last, which is absurd, of course, by all the laws of Nature and morality. If you mock me I will smite you, and if you tell anybody I will never forgive you. So much so, that I almost don't think I'll send this letter. Anyway, I'll sleep over it. So good-night, my Cherry—oh!

"Your,

"FLEUR."

CHAPTER VIII.—IDYLL ON GRASS

When those two young Forsytes emerged from the chine lane, and set their faces east toward the sun, there was not a cloud in heaven, and the Downs were dewy. They had come at a good bat up the slope and were a little out of breath; if they had anything to say they did not say it, but marched in the early awkwardness of unbreakfasted morning under the songs of the larks. The stealing out had been fun, but with the freedom of the tops the sense of conspiracy ceased, and gave place to dumbness.

"We've made one blooming error," said Fleur, when they had gone half a mile. "I'm hungry."

Jon produced a stick of chocolate. They shared it and their tongues were loosened. They discussed the nature of their homes and previous existences, which had a kind of fascinating unreality up on that lonely height. There remained but one thing solid in Jon's past—his mother; but one thing solid in Fleur's—her father; and of these figures, as though seen in the distance with disapproving faces, they spoke little.

The Down dipped and rose again toward Chanctonbury Ring; a sparkle of far sea came into view, a sparrow-hawk hovered in the sun's eye so that the blood-nourished brown of his wings gleamed nearly red. Jon had a passion for birds, and an aptitude for sitting very still to watch them; keen-sighted, and with a memory for what interested him, on birds he was almost worth listening to. But in Chanctonbury Ring there were none—its great beech temple was empty of life, and almost chilly at this early hour; they came out willingly again into the sun on the far side. It was Fleur's turn now. She spoke of dogs, and the way people treated them. It was wicked to keep them on chains! She would like to flog people who did that. Jon was astonished to find her so humanitarian. She knew a dog, it seemed, which some farmer near her home kept chained up at the end of his chicken run, in all weathers, till it had almost lost its voice from barking!

"And the misery is," she said vehemently, "that if the poor thing didn't bark at every one who passes it wouldn't be kept there. I do think men are cunning brutes. I've let it go twice, on the sly; it's nearly bitten me both times, and then it goes simply mad with joy; but it always runs back home at last, and they chain it up again. If I had my way, I'd chain that man up." Jon saw her teeth and her eyes gleam. "I'd brand him on his forehead with the word 'Brute'; that would teach him!"

Jon agreed that it would be a good remedy.

"It's their sense of property," he said, "which makes people chain things. The last generation thought of nothing but property; and that's why there was the War."

"Oh!" said Fleur, "I never thought of that. Your people and mine quarrelled about property. And anyway we've all got it—at least, I suppose your people have."

"Oh! yes, luckily; I don't suppose I shall be any good at making money."

"If you were, I don't believe I should like you."

Jon slipped his hand tremulously under her arm. Fleur looked straight before her and chanted:

"Jon, Jon, the farmer's son, Stole a pig, and away he run!"

Jon's arm crept round her waist.

"This is rather sudden," said Fleur calmly; "do you often do it?"

Jon dropped his arm. But when she laughed his arm stole back again; and Fleur began to sing:

"O who will oer the downs so free, O who will with me ride? O who will up and follow me—"

"Sing, Jon!"

Jon sang. The larks joined in, sheep-bells, and an early morning church far away over in Steyning. They went on from tune to tune, till Fleur said:

"My God! I am hungry now!"

"Oh! I am sorry!"

She looked round into his face.

"Jon, you're rather a darling."

And she pressed his hand against her waist. Jon almost reeled from happiness. A yellow-and-white dog coursing a hare startled them apart. They watched the two vanish down the slope, till Fleur said with a sigh: "He'll never catch it, thank goodness! What's the time? Mine's stopped. I never wound it."

Jon looked at his watch. "By Jove!" he said, "mine's stopped; too."

They walked on again, but only hand in hand.

"If the grass is dry," said Fleur, "let's sit down for half a minute."

Jon took off his coat, and they shared it.

"Smell! Actually wild thyme!"

With his arm round her waist again, they sat some minutes in silence.

"We are goats!" cried Fleur, jumping up; "we shall be most fearfully late, and look so silly, and put them on their guard. Look here, Jon We only came out to get an appetite for breakfast, and lost our way. See?"

"Yes," said Jon.

"It's serious; there'll be a stopper put on us. Are you a good liar?"

"I believe not very; but I can try."

Fleur frowned.

"You know," she said, "I realize that they don't mean us to be friends."

"Why not?"

"I told you why."

"But that's silly."

"Yes; but you don't know my father!"

"I suppose he's fearfully fond of you."

"You see, I'm an only child. And so are you—of your mother. Isn't it a bore? There's so much expected of one. By the time they've done expecting, one's as good as dead."

"Yes," muttered Jon, "life's beastly short. One wants to live forever, and know everything."

"And love everybody?"

"No," cried Jon; "I only want to love once—you."

"Indeed! You're coming on! Oh! Look! There's the chalk-pit; we can't be very far now. Let's run."

Jon followed, wondering fearfully if he had offended her.

The chalk-pit was full of sunshine and the murmuration of bees. Fleur flung back her hair.

"Well," she said, "in case of accidents, you may give me one kiss, Jon," and she pushed her cheek forward. With ecstasy he kissed that hot soft cheek.

"Now, remember! We lost our way; and leave it to me as much as you can. I'm going to be rather beastly to you; it's safer; try and be beastly to me!"

Jon shook his head. "That's impossible."

"Just to please me; till five o'clock, at all events."

"Anybody will be able to see through it," said Jon gloomily.

"Well, do your best. Look! There they are! Wave your hat! Oh! you haven't got one. Well, I'll cooee! Get a little away from me, and look sulky."

Five minutes later, entering the house and doing his utmost to look sulky, Jon heard her clear voice in the dining-room:

"Oh! I'm simply ravenous! He's going to be a farmer—and he loses his way! The boy's an idiot!"

CHAPTER IX. GOYA

Lunch was over and Soames mounted to the picture-gallery in his house near Mapleduram. He had what Annette called "a grief." Fleur was not yet home. She had been expected on Wednesday; had wired that it would be Friday; and again on Friday that it would be Sunday afternoon; and here were her aunt, and her cousins the Cardigans, and this fellow Profond, and everything flat as a pancake for the want of her. He stood before his Gauguin—sorest point of his collection. He had bought the ugly great thing with two early Matisses before the War, because there was such a fuss about those Post-Impressionist chaps. He was wondering whether Profond would take them off his hands—the fellow seemed not to know what to do with his money—when he heard his sister's voice say: "I think that's a horrid thing, Soames," and saw that Winifred had followed him up.

"Oh! you do?" he said dryly; "I gave five hundred for it."

"Fancy! Women aren't made like that even if they are black."

Soames uttered a glum laugh. "You didn't come up to tell me that."

"No. Do you know that Jolyon's boy is staying with Val and his wife?"

Soames spun round.

"What?"

"Yes," drawled Winifred; "he's gone to live with them there while he learns farming."

Soames had turned away, but her voice pursued him as he walked up and down. "I warned Val that neither of them was to be spoken to about old matters."

"Why didn't you tell me before?"

Winifred shrugged her substantial shoulders.

"Fleur does what she likes. You've always spoiled her. Besides, my dear boy, what's the harm?"

"The harm!" muttered Soames. "Why, she—" he checked himself. The Juno, the handkerchief, Fleur's eyes, her questions, and now this delay in her return—the symptoms seemed to him so sinister that, faithful to his nature, he could not part with them.

"I think you take too much care," said Winifred. "If I were you, I should tell her of that old matter. It's no good thinking that girls in these days are as they used to be. Where they pick up their knowledge I can't tell, but they seem to know everything."

Over Soames' face, closely composed, passed a sort of spasm, and Winifred added hastily:

"If you don't like to speak of it, I could for you."

Soames shook his head. Unless there was absolute necessity the thought that his adored daughter should learn of that old scandal hurt his pride too much.

"No," he said, "not yet. Never if I can help it.

"Nonsense, my dear. Think what people are!"

"Twenty years is a long time," muttered Soames. "Outside our family, who's likely to remember?"

Winifred was silenced. She inclined more and more to that peace and quietness of which Montague Dartie had deprived her in her youth. And, since pictures always depressed her, she soon went down again.

Soames passed into the corner where, side by side, hung his real Goya and the copy of the fresco "La Vendimia." His acquisition of the real Goya rather beautifully illustrated the cobweb of vested interests and passions which mesh the bright-winged fly of human life. The real Goya's noble owner's ancestor had come into possession of it during some Spanish war—it was in a word loot. The noble owner had remained in ignorance of its value until in the nineties an enterprising critic discovered that a Spanish painter named Goya was a genius. It was only a fair Goya, but almost unique in England, and the noble owner became a marked man. Having many possessions and that aristocratic culture which, independent of mere sensuous enjoyment, is founded on the sounder principle that one must know everything and be fearfully interested in life, he had fully intended to keep an article which contributed to his reputation while he was alive, and to leave it to the nation after he was dead. Fortunately for Soames, the House of Lords was violently attacked in 1909, and the noble owner became alarmed and angry. 'If,' he said to himself, 'they think they can have it both ways they are very much mistaken. So long as they leave me in quiet enjoyment the nation can have some of my pictures at my death. But if the nation is going to bait me, and rob me like this, I'm damned if I won't sell the lot. They can't have my private property and my public spirit—both.' He brooded in this fashion for several months till one morning, after reading the speech of a certain statesman, he telegraphed to his agent to come down and bring Bodkin. On going over the collection Bodkin, than whose opinion on market values none was more sought, pronounced that with a free hand to sell to America, Germany, and other places where there was an interest in art, a lot more money could be made than by selling in England. The noble owner's public spirit—he said—was well known but the pictures were unique. The noble owner put this opinion in his pipe and smoked it for a year. At the end of that time he read another speech by the same statesman, and telegraphed to his agents: "Give Bodkin a free hand." It was at this juncture that Bodkin conceived the idea which saved the Goya and two other unique pictures for the native country of the noble owner. With one hand Bodkin proffered the pictures to the foreign market, with the other he formed a list of private British collectors. Having obtained what he considered the highest possible bids from across the seas, he submitted pictures and bids to the private British collectors, and invited them, of their public spirit, to outbid. In three instances (including the Goya) out of twenty-one he was successful. And why? One of the private collectors made buttons—he had made so many that he desired that his wife should be called Lady "Buttons." He therefore bought a unique picture at great cost, and gave it to the nation. It was "part," his friends said, "of his general game." The second of the private collectors was an Americophobe, and bought an unique picture to "spite the damned Yanks." The third of the private collectors was Soames, who—more sober than either of the, others—bought after a visit to Madrid, because he was certain that Goya was still on the up grade. Goya was not booming at the moment, but he would come again; and, looking at that portrait, Hogarthian, Manetesque in its directness, but with its own queer sharp beauty of paint, he was perfectly satisfied still that he had made no error, heavy though the price had been—heaviest he had ever paid. And next to it was hanging the copy of "La Vendimia." There she was—the little wretch—looking back at him in her dreamy mood, the mood he loved best because he felt so much safer when she looked like that.

He was still gazing when the scent of a cigar impinged on his nostrils, and a voice said:

"Well, Mr. Forsyde, what you goin' to do with this small lot?"

That Belgian chap, whose mother—as if Flemish blood were not enough—had been Armenian! Subduing a natural irritation, he said:

"Are you a judge of pictures?"

"Well, I've got a few myself."

"Any Post-Impressionists?"

"Ye-es, I rather like them."

"What do you think of this?" said Soames, pointing to the Gauguin.

Monsieur Profond protruded his lower lip and short pointed beard.

"Rather fine, I think," he said; "do you want to sell it?"

Soames checked his instinctive "Not particularly"—he would not chaffer with this alien.

"Yes," he said.

"What do you want for it?"

"What I gave."

"All right," said Monsieur Profond. "I'll be glad to take that small picture. Post-Impressionists—they're awful dead, but they're amusin'. I don' care for pictures much, but I've got some, just a small lot."

"What do you care for?"

Monsieur Profond shrugged his shoulders.

"Life's awful like a lot of monkeys scramblin' for empty nuts."

"You're young," said Soames. If the fellow must make a generalization, he needn't suggest that the forms of property lacked solidity!

"I don' worry," replied Monsieur Profond smiling; "we're born, and we die. Half the world's starvin'. I feed a small lot of babies out in my mother's country; but what's the use? Might as well throw my money in the river."

Soames looked at him, and turned back toward his Goya. He didn't know what the fellow wanted.

"What shall I make my cheque for?" pursued Monsieur Profond.

"Five hundred," said Soames shortly; "but I don't want you to take it if you don't care for it more than that."

"That's all right," said Monsieur Profond; "I'll be 'appy to 'ave that picture."

He wrote a cheque with a fountain-pen heavily chased with gold. Soames watched the process uneasily. How on earth had the fellow known that he wanted to sell that picture? Monsieur Profond held out the cheque.

"The English are awful funny about pictures," he said. "So are the French, so are my people. They're all awful funny."

"I don't understand you," said Soames stiffly.

"It's like hats," said Monsieur Profond enigmatically, "small or large, turnin' up or down—just the fashion. Awful funny." And, smiling, he drifted out of the gallery again, blue and solid like the smoke of his excellent cigar.

Soames had taken the cheque, feeling as if the intrinsic value of ownership had been called in question. 'He's a cosmopolitan,' he thought, watching Profond emerge from under the verandah with Annette, and saunter down the lawn toward the river. What his wife saw in the fellow he didn't know, unless it was that he could speak her language; and there passed in Soames what Monsieur Profond would have called a "small doubt" whether Annette was not too handsome to be walking with any one so "cosmopolitan." Even at that distance he could see the blue fumes from Profond's cigar wreath out in the quiet sunlight; and his grey buckskin shoes, and his grey hat—the fellow was a dandy! And he could see the quick turn of his wife's head, so very straight on her desirable neck and shoulders. That turn of her neck always seemed to him a little too showy, and in the "Queen of all I survey" manner—not quite distinguished. He watched them walk along the path at the bottom of the garden. A young man in flannels joined them down there—a Sunday caller no doubt, from up the river. He went back to his Goya. He was still staring at that replica of Fleur, and worrying over Winifred's news, when his wife's voice said:

"Mr. Michael Mont, Soames. You invited him to see your pictures."

There was the cheerful young man of the Gallery off Cork Street!

"Turned up, you see, sir; I live only four miles from Pangbourne. Jolly day, isn't it?"

Confronted with the results of his expansiveness, Soames scrutinized his visitor. The young man's mouth was excessively large and curly—he seemed always grinning. Why didn't he grow the rest of those idiotic little moustaches, which made him look like a music-hall buffoon? What on earth were young men about, deliberately lowering their class with these tooth-brushes, or little slug whiskers? Ugh! Affected young idiots! In other respects he was presentable, and his flannels very clean.

"Happy to see you!" he said.

The young man, who had been turning his head from side to side, became transfixed. "I say!" he said, "'some' picture!"

Soames saw, with mixed sensations, that he had addressed the remark to the Goya copy.

"Yes," he said dryly, "that's not a Goya. It's a copy. I had it painted because it reminded me of my daughter."

"By Jove! I thought I knew the face, sir. Is she here?"

The frankness of his interest almost disarmed Soames.

"She'll be in after tea," he said. "Shall we go round the pictures?"

And Soames began that round which never tired him. He had not anticipated much intelligence from one who had mistaken a copy for an original, but as they passed from section to section, period to period, he was startled by the young man's frank and relevant remarks. Natively shrewd himself, and even sensuous beneath his mask, Soames had not spent thirty-eight years over his one hobby without knowing something more about pictures than their market values. He was, as it were, the missing link between the artist and the commercial public. Art for art's sake and all that, of course, was cant. But aesthetics and good taste were necessary. The appreciation of enough persons of good taste was what gave a work of art its permanent market value, or in other words made it "a work of art." There was no real cleavage. And he was sufficiently accustomed to sheep-like and unseeing visitors, to be intrigued by one who did not hesitate to say of Mauve: "Good old haystacks!" or of James Maris: "Didn't he just paint and paper 'em! Mathew was the real swell, sir; you could dig into his surfaces!" It was after the young man had whistled before a Whistler, with the words, "D'you think he ever really saw a naked woman, sir?" that Soames remarked:

"What are you, Mr. Mont, if I may ask?"

"I, sir? I was going to be a painter, but the War knocked that. Then in the trenches, you know, I used to dream of the Stock Exchange, snug and warm and just noisy enough. But the Peace knocked that, shares seem off, don't they? I've only been demobbed about a year. What do you recommend, sir?"

"Have you got money?"

"Well," answered the young man, "I've got a father; I kept him alive during the War, so he's bound to keep me alive now. Though, of course, there's the question whether he ought to be allowed to hang on to his property. What do you think about that, sir?"

Soames, pale and defensive, smiled.

"The old man has fits when I tell him he may have to work yet. He's got land, you know; it's a fatal disease."

"This is my real Goya," said Soames dryly.

"By George! He was a swell. I saw a Goya in Munich once that bowled me middle stump. A most evil-looking old woman in the most gorgeous lace. He made no compromise with the public taste. That old boy was 'some' explosive; he must have smashed up a lot of convention in his day. Couldn't he just paint! He makes Velasquez stiff, don't you think?"

"I have no Velasquez," said Soames.

The young man stared. "No," he said; "only nations or profiteers can afford him, I suppose. I say, why shouldn't all the bankrupt nations sell their Velasquez and Titians and other swells to the profiteers by force, and then pass a law that any one who holds a picture by an Old Master—see schedule—must hang it in a public gallery? There seems something in that."

"Shall we go down to tea?" said Soames.

The young man's ears seemed to droop on his skull. 'He's not dense,' thought Soames, following him off the premises.

Goya, with his satiric and surpassing precision, his original "line," and the daring of his light and shade, could have reproduced to admiration the group assembled round Annette's tea-tray in the inglenook below. He alone, perhaps, of painters would have done justice to the sunlight filtering through a screen of creeper, to the lovely pallor of brass, the old cut glasses, the thin slices of lemon in pale amber tea; justice to Annette in her black lacey dress; there was something of the fair Spaniard in her beauty, though it lacked the spirituality of that rare type; to Winifred's grey-haired, corseted solidity; to Soames, of a certain grey and flat-checked distinction; to the vivacious Michael Mont, pointed in ear and eye; to Imogen, dark, luscious of glance, growing a little stout; to Prosper Profond, with his expression as who should say, "Well, Mr. Goya, what's the use of paintin' this small party?" finally, to Jack Cardigan, with his shining stare and tanned sanguinity betraying the moving principle: "I'm English, and I live to be fit."

Curious, by the way, that Imogen, who as a girl had declared solemnly one day at Timothy's that she would never marry a good man—they were so dull—should have married Jack Cardigan, in whom health had so destroyed all traces of original sin, that she might have retired to rest with ten thousand other Englishmen without knowing the difference from the one she had chosen to repose beside. "Oh!" she would say of him, in her "amusing" way, "Jack keeps himself so fearfully fit; he's never had a day's illness in his life. He went right through the War without a finger-ache. You really can't imagine how fit he is!" Indeed, he was so "fit" that he couldn't see when she was flirting, which was such a comfort in a way. All the same she was quite fond of him, so far as one could be of a sports-machine, and of the two little Cardigans made after his pattern. Her eyes just then were comparing him maliciously with Prosper Profond. There was no "small" sport or game which Monsieur Profond had not played at too, it seemed, from skittles to tarpon-fishing, and worn out every one. Imogen would sometimes wish that they had worn out Jack, who continued to play at them and talk of them with the simple zeal of a school-girl learning hockey; at the age of Great-uncle Timothy she well knew that Jack would be playing carpet golf in her bedroom, and "wiping somebody's eye."

He was telling them now how he had "pipped the pro—a charmin' fellow, playin' a very good game," at the last hole this morning; and how he had pulled down to Caversham since lunch, and trying to incite Prosper Profond to play him a set of tennis after tea—do him good—"keep him fit.

"But what's the use of keepin' fit?" said Monsieur Profond.

"Yes, sir," murmured Michael Mont, "what do you keep fit for?"

"Jack," cried Imogen, enchanted, "what do you keep fit for?"

Jack Cardigan stared with all his health. The questions were like the buzz of a mosquito, and he put up his hand to wipe them away. During the War, of course, he had kept fit to kill Germans; now that it was over he either did not know, or shrank in delicacy from explanation of his moving principle.

"But he's right," said Monsieur Profond unexpectedly, "there's nothin' left but keepin' fit."

The saying, too deep for Sunday afternoon, would have passed unanswered, but for the mercurial nature of young Mont.

"Good!" he cried. "That's the great discovery of the War. We all thought we were progressing—now we know we're only changing."

"For the worse," said Monsieur Profond genially.

"How you are cheerful, Prosper!" murmured Annette.

"You come and play tennis!" said Jack Cardigan; "you've got the hump. We'll soon take that down. D'you play, Mr. Mont?"

"I hit the ball about, sir."

At this juncture Soames rose, ruffled in that deep instinct of preparation for the future which guided his existence.

"When Fleur comes—" he heard Jack Cardigan say.

Ah! and why didn't she come? He passed through drawing-room, hall, and porch out on to the drive, and stood there listening for the car. All was still and Sundayfied; the lilacs in full flower scented the air. There were white clouds, like the feathers of ducks gilded by the sunlight. Memory of the day when Fleur was born, and he had waited in such agony with her life and her mother's balanced in his hands, came to him sharply. He had saved her then, to be the flower of his life. And now! was she going to give him trouble—pain—give him trouble? He did not like the look of things! A blackbird broke in on his reverie with an evening song—a great big fellow up in that acacia-tree. Soames had taken quite an interest in his birds of late years; he and Fleur would walk round and watch them; her eyes were sharp as needles, and she knew every nest. He saw her dog, a retriever, lying on the drive in a patch of sunlight, and called to him. "Hallo, old fellow-waiting for her too!" The dog came slowly with a grudging tail, and Soames mechanically laid a pat on his head. The dog, the bird, the lilac, all were part of Fleur for him; no more, no less. "Too fond of her!' he thought, 'too fond!' He was like a man uninsured, with his ships at sea. Uninsured again—as in that other time, so long ago, when he would wander dumb and jealous in the wilderness of London, longing for that woman—his first wife—the mother of this infernal boy. Ah! There was the car at last! It drew up, it had luggage, but no Fleur.

"Miss Fleur is walking up, sir, by the towing-path."

Walking all those miles? Soames stared. The man's face had the beginning of a smile on it. What was he grinning at? And very quickly he turned, saying, "All right, Sims!" and went into the house. He mounted to the picture-gallery once more. He had from there a view of the river bank, and stood with his eyes fixed on it, oblivious of the fact that it would be an hour at least before her figure showed there. Walking up! And that fellow's grin! The boy—! He turned abruptly from the window. He couldn't spy on her. If she wanted to keep things from him—she must; he could not spy on her. His heart felt empty, and bitterness mounted from it into his very mouth. The staccato shouts of Jack Cardigan pursuing the ball, the laugh of young Mont rose in the stillness and came in. He hoped they were making that chap Profond run. And the girl in "La Vendimia" stood with her arm akimbo and her dreamy eyes looking past him. 'I've done all I could for you,' he thought, 'since you were no higher than my knee. You aren't going to—to—hurt me, are you?'

But the Goya copy answered not, brilliant in colour just beginning to tone down. 'There's no real life in it,' thought Soames. 'Why doesn't she come?'

CHAPTER X.—TRIO

Among those four Forsytes of the third, and, as one might say, fourth generation, at Wansdon under the Downs, a week-end prolonged unto the ninth day had stretched the crossing threads of tenacity almost to snapping-point. Never had Fleur been so "fine," Holly so watchful, Val so stable-secretive, Jon so silent and disturbed. What he learned of farming in that week might have been balanced on the point of a penknife and puffed off. He, whose nature was essentially averse from intrigue, and whose adoration of Fleur disposed him to think that any need for concealing it was "skittles," chafed and fretted, yet obeyed, taking what relief he could in the few moments when they were alone. On Thursday, while they were standing in the bay window of the drawing-room, dressed for dinner, she said to him:

"Jon, I'm going home on Sunday by the 3.40 from Paddington; if you were to go home on Saturday you could come up on Sunday and take me down, and just get back here by the last train, after. You were going home anyway, weren't you?"

Jon nodded.

"Anything to be with you," he said; "only why need I pretend—"

Fleur slipped her little finger into his palm:

"You have no instinct, Jon; you must leave things to me. It's serious about our people. We've simply got to be secret at present, if we want to be together." The door was opened, and she added loudly: "You are a duffer, Jon."

Something turned over within Jon; he could not bear this subterfuge about a feeling so natural, so overwhelming, and so sweet.

On Friday night about eleven he had packed his bag, and was leaning out of his window, half miserable, and half lost in a dream of Paddington station, when he heard a tiny sound, as of a finger-nail tapping on his door. He rushed to it and listened. Again the sound. It was a nail. He opened. Oh! What a lovely thing came in!

"I wanted to show you my fancy dress," it said, and struck an attitude at the foot of his bed.

Jon drew a long breath and leaned against the door. The apparition wore white muslin on its head, a fichu round its bare neck over a wine-coloured dress, fulled out below its slender waist.

It held one arm akimbo, and the other raised, right-angled, holding a fan which touched its head.

"This ought to be a basket of grapes," it whispered, "but I haven't got it here. It's my Goya dress. And this is the attitude in the picture. Do you like it?"

"It's a dream."

The apparition pirouetted. "Touch it, and see."

Jon knelt down and took the skirt reverently.

"Grape colour," came the whisper, "all grapes—La Vendimia—the vintage."

Jon's fingers scarcely touched each side of the waist; he looked up, with adoring eyes.

"Oh! Jon," it whispered; bent, kissed his forehead, pirouetted again, and, gliding out, was gone.

Jon stayed on his knees, and his head fell forward against the bed. How long he stayed like that he did not know. The little noises—of the tapping nail, the feet, the skirts rustling—as in a dream—went on about him; and before his closed eyes the figure stood and smiled and whispered, a faint perfume of narcissus lingering in the air. And his forehead where it had been kissed had a little cool place between the brows, like the imprint of a flower. Love filled his soul, that love of boy for girl which knows so little, hopes so much, would not brush the down off for the world, and must become in time a fragrant memory—a searing passion—a humdrum mateship—or, once in many times, vintage full and sweet with sunset colour on the grapes.

Enough has been said about Jon Forsyte here and in another place to show what long marches lay between him and his great-great-grandfather, the first Jolyon, in Dorset down by the sea. Jon was sensitive as a girl, more sensitive than nine out of ten girls of the day; imaginative as one of his half-sister June's "lame duck" painters; affectionate as a son of his father and his mother naturally would be. And yet, in his inner tissue, there was something of the old founder of his family, a secret tenacity of soul, a dread of showing his feelings, a determination not to know when he was beaten. Sensitive, imaginative, affectionate boys get a bad time at school, but Jon had instinctively kept his nature dark, and been but normally unhappy there. Only with his mother had he, up till then, been absolutely frank and natural; and when he went home to Robin Hill that Saturday his heart was heavy because Fleur had said that he must not be frank and natural with her from whom he had never yet kept anything, must not even tell her that they had met again, unless he found that she knew already. So intolerable did this seem to him that he was very near to telegraphing an excuse and staying up in London. And the first thing his mother said to him was:

"So you've had our little friend of the confectioner's there, Jon. What is she like on second thoughts?"

With relief, and a high colour, Jon answered:

"Oh! awfully jolly, Mum."

Her arm pressed his.

Jon had never loved her so much as in that minute which seemed to falsify Fleur's fears and to release his soul. He turned to look at her, but something in her smiling face—something which only he perhaps would have caught—stopped the words bubbling up in him. Could fear go with a smile? If so, there was fear in her face. And out of Jon tumbled quite other words, about farming, Holly, and the Downs. Talking fast, he waited for her to come back to Fleur. But she did not. Nor did his father mention her, though of course he, too, must know. What deprivation, and killing of reality was in his silence about Fleur— when he was so full of her; when his mother was so full of Jon, and his father so full of his mother! And so the trio spent the evening of that Saturday.

After dinner his mother played; she seemed to play all the things he liked best, and he sat with one knee clasped, and his hair standing up where his fingers had run through it. He gazed at his mother while she played, but he saw Fleur—Fleur in the moonlit orchard, Fleur in the sunlit gravel-pit, Fleur in that fancy dress, swaying, whispering, stooping, kissing his forehead. Once, while he listened, he forgot himself and glanced at his father in that other easy chair. What was Dad looking like that for? The expression on his face was so sad and puzzling. It filled him with a sort of remorse, so that he got up and went and sat on the arm of his father's chair. From there he could not see his face; and again he saw Fleur—in his mother's hands, slim and white on the keys, in the profile of her face and her powdery hair; and down the long room in the open window where the May night walked outside.

When he went up to bed his mother came into his room. She stood at the window, and said:

"Those cypresses your grandfather planted down there have done wonderfully. I always think they look beautiful under a dropping moon. I wish you had known your grandfather, Jon."

"Were you married to father when he was alive?" asked Jon suddenly.

"No, dear; he died in '92—very old—eighty-five, I think."

"Is Father like him?"

"A little, but more subtle, and not quite so solid."

"I know, from grandfather's portrait; who painted that?"

"One of June's 'lame ducks.' But it's quite good."

Jon slipped his hand through his mother's arm. "Tell me about the family quarrel, Mum."

He felt her arm quivering. "No, dear; that's for your Father some day, if he thinks fit."

"Then it was serious," said Jon, with a catch in his breath.

"Yes." And there was a silence, during which neither knew whether the arm or the hand within it were quivering most.

"Some people," said Irene softly, "think the moon on her back is evil; to me she's always lovely. Look at those cypress shadows! Jon, Father says we may go to Italy, you and I, for two months. Would you like?"

Jon took his hand from under her arm; his sensation was so sharp and so confused. Italy with his mother! A fortnight ago it would have been perfection; now it filled him with dismay; he felt that the sudden suggestion had to do with Fleur. He stammered out:

"Oh! yes; only—I don't know. Ought I—now I've just begun? I'd like to think it over."

Her voice answered, cool and gentle:

"Yes, dear; think it over. But better now than when you've begun farming seriously. Italy with you! It would be nice!"

Jon put his arm round her waist, still slim and firm as a girl's.

"Do you think you ought to leave Father?" he said feebly, feeling very mean.

"Father suggested it; he thinks you ought to see Italy at least before you settle down to anything."

The sense of meanness died in Jon; he knew, yes—he knew—that his father and his mother were not speaking frankly, no more than he himself. They wanted to keep him from Fleur. His heart hardened. And, as if she felt that process going on, his mother said:

"Good-night, darling. Have a good sleep and think it over. But it would be lovely!"

She pressed him to her so quickly that he did not see her face. Jon stood feeling exactly as he used to when he was a naughty little boy; sore because he was not loving, and because he was justified in his own eyes.

But Irene, after she had stood a moment in her own room, passed through the dressing-room between it and her husband's.

"Well?"

"He will think it over, Jolyon."

Watching her lips that wore a little drawn smile, Jolyon said quietly:

"You had better let me tell him, and have done with it. After all, Jon has the instincts of a gentleman. He has only to understand—"

"Only! He can't understand; that's impossible."

"I believe I could have at his age."

Irene caught his hand. "You were always more of a realist than Jon; and never so innocent."

"That's true," said Jolyon. "It's queer, isn't it? You and I would tell our stories to the world without a particle of shame; but our own boy stumps us."

"We've never cared whether the world approves or not."

"Jon would not disapprove of us!"

"Oh! Jolyon, yes. He's in love, I feel he's in love. And he'd say: 'My mother once married without love! How could she have!' It'll seem to him a crime! And so it was!"

Jolyon took her hand, and said with a wry smile:

"Ah! why on earth are we born young? Now, if only we were born old and grew younger year by year, we should understand how things happen, and drop all our cursed intolerance. But you know if the boy is really in love, he won't forget, even if he goes to Italy. We're a tenacious breed; and he'll know by instinct why he's being sent. Nothing will really cure him but the shock of being told."

"Let me try, anyway."

Jolyon stood a moment without speaking. Between this devil and this deep sea—the pain of a dreaded disclosure and the grief of losing his wife for two months—he secretly hoped for the devil; yet if she wished for the deep sea he must put up with it. After all, it would be training for that departure from which there would be no return. And, taking her in his arms, he kissed her eyes, and said:

"As you will, my love."

CHAPTER XI.—DUET

That "small" emotion, love, grows amazingly when threatened with extinction. Jon reached Paddington station half an hour before his time and a full week after, as it seemed to him. He stood at the appointed bookstall, amid a crowd of Sunday travellers, in a Harris tweed suit exhaling, as it were, the emotion of his thumping heart. He read the names of the novels on the book-stall, and bought one at last, to avoid being regarded with suspicion by the book-stall clerk. It was called "The Heart of the Trail!" which must mean something, though it did not seem to. He also bought "The Lady's Mirror" and "The Landsman." Every minute was an hour long, and full of horrid imaginings. After nineteen had passed, he saw her with a bag and a porter wheeling her luggage. She came swiftly; she came cool. She greeted him as if he were a brother.

"First class," she said to the porter, "corner seats; opposite."

Jon admired her frightful self-possession.

"Can't we get a carriage to ourselves," he whispered.

"No good; it's a stopping train. After Maidenhead perhaps. Look natural, Jon."

Jon screwed his features into a scowl. They got in—with two other beasts!—oh! heaven! He tipped the porter unnaturally, in his confusion. The brute deserved nothing for putting them in there, and looking as if he knew all about it into the bargain.

Fleur hid herself behind "The Lady's Mirror." Jon imitated her behind "The Landsman." The train started. Fleur let "The Lady's Mirror" fall and leaned forward.

"Well?" she said.

"It's seemed about fifteen days."

She nodded, and Jon's face lighted up at once.

"Look natural," murmured Fleur, and went off into a bubble of laughter. It hurt him. How could he look natural with Italy hanging over him? He had meant to break it to her gently, but now he blurted it out.

"They want me to go to Italy with Mother for two months."

Fleur drooped her eyelids; turned a little pale, and bit her lips. "Oh!" she said. It was all, but it was much.

That "Oh!" was like the quick drawback of the wrist in fencing ready for riposte. It came.

"You must go!"

"Go?" said Jon in a strangled voice.

"Of course."

"But—two months—it's ghastly."

"No," said Fleur, "six weeks. You'll have forgotten me by then. We'll meet in the National Gallery the day after you get back."

Jon laughed.

"But suppose you've forgotten me," he muttered into the noise of the train.

Fleur shook her head.

"Some other beast—" murmured Jon.

Her foot touched his.

"No other beast," she said, lifting "The Lady's Mirror."

The train stopped; two passengers got out, and one got in.

'I shall die,' thought Jon, 'if we're not alone at all.'

The train went on; and again Fleur leaned forward.

"I never let go," she said; "do you?"

Jon shook his head vehemently.

"Never!" he said. "Will you write to me?"

"No; but you can—to my Club."

She had a Club; she was wonderful!

"Did you pump Holly?" he muttered.

"Yes, but I got nothing. I didn't dare pump hard."

"What can it be?" cried Jon.

"I shall find out all right."

A long silence followed till Fleur said: "This is Maidenhead; stand by, Jon!"

The train stopped. The remaining passenger got out. Fleur drew down her blind.

"Quick!" she cried. "Hang out! Look as much of a beast as you can."

Jon blew his nose, and scowled; never in all his life had he scowled like that! An old lady recoiled, a young one tried the handle. It turned, but the door would not open. The train moved, the young lady darted to another carriage.

"What luck!" cried Jon. "It Jammed."

"Yes," said Fleur; "I was holding it."

The train moved out, and Jon fell on his knees.

"Look out for the corridor," she whispered; "and—quick!"

Her lips met his. And though their kiss only lasted perhaps ten seconds, Jon's soul left his body and went so far beyond, that, when he was again sitting opposite that demure figure, he was pale as death. He heard her sigh, and the sound seemed to him the most precious he had ever heard—an exquisite declaration that he meant something to her.

"Six weeks isn't really long," she said; "and you can easily make it six if you keep your head out there, and never seem to think of me."

Jon gasped.

"This is just what's really wanted, Jon, to convince them, don't you see? If we're just as bad when you come back they'll stop being ridiculous about it. Only, I'm sorry it's not Spain; there's a girl in a Goya picture at Madrid who's like me, Father says. Only she isn't—we've got a copy of her."

It was to Jon like a ray of sunshine piercing through a fog. "I'll make it Spain," he said, "Mother won't mind; she's never been there. And my Father thinks a lot of Goya."

"Oh! yes, he's a painter—isn't he?"

"Only water-colour," said Jon, with honesty.

"When we come to Reading, Jon, get out first and go down to Caversham lock and wait for me. I'll send the car home and we'll walk by the towing-path."

Jon seized her hand in gratitude, and they sat silent, with the world well lost, and one eye on the corridor. But the train seemed to run twice as fast now, and its sound was almost lost in that of Jon's sighing.

"We're getting near," said Fleur; "the towing-path's awfully exposed. One more! Oh! Jon, don't forget me."

Jon answered with his kiss. And very soon, a flushed, distracted-looking youth could have been seen—as they say—leaping from the train and hurrying along the platform, searching his pockets for his ticket.

When at last she rejoined him on the towing-path a little beyond Caversham lock he had made an effort, and regained some measure of equanimity. If they had to part, he would not make a scene! A breeze by the bright river threw the white side of the willow leaves up into the sunlight, and followed those two with its faint rustle.

"I told our chauffeur that I was train-giddy," said Fleur. "Did you look pretty natural as you went out?"

"I don't know. What is natural?"

"It's natural to you to look seriously happy. When I first saw you I thought you weren't a bit like other people."

"Exactly what I thought when I saw you. I knew at once I should never love anybody else."

Fleur laughed.

"We're absurdly young. And love's young dream is out of date, Jon. Besides, it's awfully wasteful. Think of all the fun you might have. You haven't begun, even; it's a shame, really. And there's me. I wonder!"

Confusion came on Jon's spirit. How could she say such things just as they were going to part?

"If you feel like that," he said, "I can't go. I shall tell Mother that I ought to try and work. There's always the condition of the world!"

"The condition of the world!"

Jon thrust his hands deep into his pockets.

"But there is," he said; "think of the people starving!"

Fleur shook her head. "No, no, I never, never will make myself miserable for nothing."

"Nothing! But there's an awful state of things, and of course one ought to help."

"Oh! yes, I know all that. But you can't help people, Jon; they're hopeless. When you pull them out they only get into another hole. Look at them, still fighting and plotting and struggling, though they're dying in heaps all the time. Idiots!"

"Aren't you sorry for them?"

"Oh! sorry—yes, but I'm not going to make myself unhappy about it; that's no good."

And they were silent, disturbed by this first glimpse of each other's natures.

"I think people are brutes and idiots," said Fleur stubbornly.

"I think they're poor wretches," said Jon. It was as if they had quarrelled—and at this supreme and awful moment, with parting visible out there in that last gap of the willows!

"Well, go and help your poor wretches, and don't think of me."

Jon stood still. Sweat broke out on his forehead, and his limbs trembled. Fleur too had stopped, and was frowning at the river.

"I must believe in things," said Jon with a sort of agony; "we're all meant to enjoy life."

Fleur laughed. "Yes; and that's what you won't do, if you don't take care. But perhaps your idea of enjoyment is to make yourself wretched. There are lots of people like that, of course."

She was pale, her eyes had darkened, her lips had thinned. Was it Fleur thus staring at the water? Jon had an unreal feeling as if he were passing through the scene in a book where the lover has to choose between love and duty. But just then she looked round at him. Never was anything so intoxicating as that vivacious look. It acted on him exactly as the tug of a chain acts on a dog—brought him up to her with his tail wagging and his tongue out.

"Don't let's be silly," she said, "time's too short. Look, Jon, you can just see where I've got to cross the river. There, round the bend, where the woods begin."

Jon saw a gable, a chimney or two, a patch of wall through the trees—and felt his heart sink.

"I mustn't dawdle any more. It's no good going beyond the next hedge, it gets all open. Let's get on to it and say good-bye."

They went side by side, hand in hand, silently toward the hedge, where the may-flower, both pink and white, was in full bloom.

"My Club's the 'Talisman,' Stratton Street, Piccadilly. Letters there will be quite safe, and I'm almost always up once a week."

Jon nodded. His face had become extremely set, his eyes stared straight before him.

"To-day's the twenty-third of May," said Fleur; "on the ninth of July I shall be in front of the 'Bacchus and Ariadne' at three o'clock; will you?"

"I will."

"If you feel as bad as I it's all right. Let those people pass!"

A man and woman airing their children went by strung out in Sunday fashion.

The last of them passed the wicket gate.

"Domesticity!" said Fleur, and blotted herself against the hawthorn hedge. The blossom sprayed out above her head, and one pink cluster brushed her cheek. Jon put up his hand jealously to keep it off.

"Good-bye, Jon." For a second they stood with hands hard clasped. Then their lips met for the third time, and when they parted Fleur broke away and fled through the wicket gate. Jon stood where she had left him, with his forehead against that pink cluster. Gone! For an eternity—for seven weeks all but two days! And here he was, wasting the last sight of her! He rushed to the gate. She was walking swiftly on the heels of the straggling children. She turned her head, he saw her hand make a little flitting gesture; then she sped on, and the trailing family blotted her out from his view.

The words of a comic song—

"Paddington groan-worst ever known

He gave a sepulchral Paddington groan—"

came into his head, and he sped incontinently back to Reading station. All the way up to London and down to Wansdon he sat with "The Heart of the Trail" open on his knee, knitting in his head a poem so full of feeling that it would not rhyme.

CHAPTER XII.—CAPRICE

Fleur sped on. She had need of rapid motion; she was late, and wanted all her wits about her when she got in. She passed the islands, the station, and hotel, and was about to take the ferry, when she saw a skiff with a young man standing up in it, and holding to the bushes.

"Miss Forsyte," he said; "let me put you across. I've come on purpose."

She looked at him in blank amazement.

451

"It's all right, I've been having tea with your people. I thought I'd save you the last bit. It's on my way, I'm just off back to Pangbourne. My name's Mont. I saw you at the picture-gallery—you remember—when your father invited me to see his pictures."

"Oh!" said Fleur; "yes—the handkerchief."

To this young man she owed Jon; and, taking his hand, she stepped down into the skiff. Still emotional, and a little out of breath, she sat silent; not so the young man. She had never heard any one say so much in so short a time. He told her his age, twenty-four; his weight, ten stone eleven; his place of residence, not far away; described his sensations under fire, and what it felt like to be gassed; criticized the Juno, mentioned his own conception of that goddess; commented on the Goya copy, said Fleur was not too awfully like it; sketched in rapidly the condition of England; spoke of Monsieur Profond—or whatever his name was—as "an awful sport"; thought her father had some "ripping" pictures and some rather "dug-up"; hoped he might row down again and take her on the river because he was quite trustworthy; inquired her opinion of Tchekov, gave her his own; wished they could go to the Russian ballet together some time—considered the name Fleur Forsyte simply topping; cursed his people for giving him the name of Michael on the top of Mont; outlined his father, and said that if she wanted a good book she should read "Job"; his father was rather like Job while Job still had land.

"But Job didn't have land," Fleur murmured; "he only had flocks and herds and moved on."

"Ah!" answered Michael Mont, "I wish my gov'nor would move on. Not that I want his land. Land's an awful bore in these days, don't you think?"

"We never have it in my family," said Fleur. "We have everything else. I believe one of my great-uncles once had a sentimental farm in Dorset, because we came from there originally, but it cost him more than it made him happy."

"Did he sell it?"

"No; he kept it."

"Why?"

"Because nobody would buy it."

"Good for the old boy!"

"No, it wasn't good for him. Father says it soured him. His name was Swithin."

"What a corking name!"

"Do you know that we're getting farther off, not nearer? This river flows."

"Splendid!" cried Mont, dipping his sculls vaguely; "it's good to meet a girl who's got wit."

"But better to meet a young man who's got it in the plural."

Young Mont raised a hand to tear his hair.

"Look out!" cried Fleur. "Your scull!"

"All right! It's thick enough to bear a scratch."

"Do you mind sculling?" said Fleur severely. "I want to get in."

"Ah!" said Mont; "but when you get in, you see, I shan't see you any more to-day. Fini, as the French girl said when she jumped on her bed after saying her prayers. Don't you bless the day that gave you a French mother, and a name like yours?"

"I like my name, but Father gave it me. Mother wanted me called Marguerite."

"Which is absurd. Do you mind calling me M. M. and letting me call you F. F.? It's in the spirit of the age."

"I don't mind anything, so long as I get in."

Mont caught a little crab, and answered: "That was a nasty one!"

"Please row."

"I am." And he did for several strokes, looking at her with rueful eagerness. "Of course, you know," he ejaculated, pausing, "that I came to see you, not your father's pictures."

Fleur rose.

"If you don't row, I shall get out and swim."

"Really and truly? Then I could come in after you."

"Mr. Mont, I'm late and tired; please put me on shore at once."

When she stepped out on to the garden landing-stage he rose, and grasping his hair with both hands, looked at her.

Fleur smiled.

"Don't!" cried the irrepressible Mont. "I know you're going to say: 'Out, damned hair!'"

Fleur whisked round, threw him a wave of her hand. "Good-bye, Mr. M.M.!" she called, and was gone among the rose-trees. She looked at her wrist-watch and the windows of the house. It struck her as curiously uninhabited. Past six! The pigeons were just gathering to roost, and sunlight slanted on the dovecot, on their snowy feathers, and beyond in a shower on the top boughs of the woods. The click of billiard-balls came from the ingle-nook—Jack Cardigan, no doubt; a faint rustling, too, from an eucalyptus-tree, startling Southerner in this old English garden. She reached the verandah and was passing in, but stopped at the sound of voices from the drawing-room to her left. Mother! Monsieur Profond! From behind the verandah screen which fenced the ingle-nook she heard these words:

"I don't, Annette."

Did Father know that he called her mother "Annette"? Always on the side of her Father— as children are ever on one side or the other in houses where relations are a little strained— she stood, uncertain. Her mother was speaking in her low, pleasing, slightly metallic voice—one word she caught: "Demain." And Profond's answer: "All right." Fleur frowned. A little sound came out into the stillness. Then Profond's voice: "I'm takin' a small stroll."

Fleur darted through the window into the morning-room. There he came from the drawing-room, crossing the verandah, down the lawn; and the click of billiard-balls which, in listening for other sounds, she had ceased to hear, began again. She shook herself, passed into the hall, and opened the drawing-room door. Her mother was sitting on the sofa between the windows, her knees crossed, her head resting on a cushion, her lips half parted, her eyes half closed. She looked extraordinarily handsome.

"Ah! Here you are, Fleur! Your father is beginning to fuss."

"Where is he?"

"In the picture-gallery. Go up!"

"What are you going to do to-morrow, Mother?"

"To-morrow? I go up to London with your aunt."

"I thought you might be. Will you get me a quite plain parasol?"

"What colour?"

"Green. They're all going back, I suppose."

"Yes, all; you will console your father. Kiss me, then."

Fleur crossed the room, stooped, received a kiss on her forehead, and went out past the impress of a form on the sofa-cushions in the other corner. She ran up-stairs.

Fleur was by no means the old-fashioned daughter who demands the regulation of her parents' lives in accordance with the standard imposed upon herself. She claimed to regulate her own life, not those of others; besides, an unerring instinct for what was likely to advantage her own case was already at work. In a disturbed domestic atmosphere the heart she had set on Jon would have a better chance. None the less was she offended, as a flower by a crisping wind. If that man had really been kissing her mother it was—serious, and her father ought to know. "Demain!" "All right!" And her mother going up to Town! She turned into her bedroom and hung out of the window to cool her face, which had suddenly grown very hot. Jon must be at the station by now! What did her father know about Jon? Probably everything—pretty nearly!

She changed her dress, so as to look as if she had been in some time, and ran up to the gallery.

Soames was standing stubbornly still before his Alfred Stevens—the picture he loved best. He did not turn at the sound of the door, but she knew he had heard, and she knew he was hurt. She came up softly behind him, put her arms round his neck, and poked her face over his shoulder till her cheek lay against his. It was an advance which had never yet failed, but it failed her now, and she augured the worst. "Well," he said stonily, "so you've come!"

"Is that all," murmured Fleur, "from a bad parent?" And she rubbed her cheek against his.

Soames shook his head so far as that was possible.

"Why do you keep me on tenterhooks like this, putting me off and off?"

"Darling, it was very harmless."

"Harmless! Much you know what's harmless and what isn't."

Fleur dropped her arms.

"Well, then, dear, suppose you tell me; and be quite frank about it."

And she went over to the window-seat.

Her father had turned from his picture, and was staring at his feet. He looked very grey. 'He has nice small feet,' she thought, catching his eye, at once averted from her.

"You're my only comfort," said Soames suddenly, "and you go on like this."

Fleur's heart began to beat.

"Like what, dear?"

Again Soames gave her a look which, but for the affection in it, might have been called furtive.

"You know what I told you," he said. "I don't choose to have anything to do with that branch of our family."

"Yes, ducky, but I don't know why I shouldn't."

Soames turned on his heel.

"I'm not going into the reasons," he said; "you ought to trust me, Fleur!"

The way he spoke those words affected Fleur, but she thought of Jon, and was silent, tapping her foot against the wainscot. Unconsciously she had assumed a modern attitude, with one leg twisted in and out of the other, with her chin on one bent wrist, her other arm across her chest, and its hand hugging her elbow; there was not a line of her that was not involuted, and yet—in spite of all—she retained a certain grace.

"You knew my wishes," Soames went on, "and yet you stayed on there four days. And I suppose that boy came with you to-day."

Fleur kept her eyes on him.

"I don't ask you anything," said Soames; "I make no inquisition where you're concerned."

Fleur suddenly stood up, leaning out at the window with her chin on her hands. The sun had sunk behind trees, the pigeons were perched, quite still, on the edge of the dove-cot; the click of the billiard-balls mounted, and a faint radiance shone out below where Jack Cardigan had turned the light up.

"Will it make you any happier," she said suddenly, "if I promise you not to see him for say—the next six weeks?" She was not prepared for a sort of tremble in the blankness of his voice.

"Six weeks? Six years—sixty years more like. Don't delude yourself, Fleur; don't delude yourself!"

Fleur turned in alarm.

"Father, what is it?"

Soames came close enough to see her face.

"Don't tell me," he said, "that you're foolish enough to have any feeling beyond caprice. That would be too much!" And he laughed.

Fleur, who had never heard him laugh like that, thought: 'Then it is deep! Oh! what is it?' And putting her hand through his arm she said lightly:

"No, of course; caprice. Only, I like my caprices and I don't like yours, dear."

"Mine!" said Soames bitterly, and turned away.

The light outside had chilled, and threw a chalky whiteness on the river. The trees had lost all gaiety of colour. She felt a sudden hunger for Jon's face, for his hands, and the feel of his lips again on hers. And pressing her arms tight across her breast she forced out a little light laugh.

"O la! la! What a small fuss! as Profond would say. Father, I don't like that man."

She saw him stop, and take something out of his breast pocket.

"You don't?" he said. "Why?"

"Nothing," murmured Fleur; "just caprice!"

"No," said Soames; "not caprice!" And he tore what was in his hands across. "You're right. I don't like him either!"

"Look!" said Fleur softly. "There he goes! I hate his shoes; they don't make any noise."

Down in the failing light Prosper Profond moved, his hands in his side pockets, whistling softly in his beard; he stopped, and glanced up at the sky, as if saying: "I don't think much of that small moon."

Fleur drew back. "Isn't he a great cat?" she whispered; and the sharp click of the billiard-balls rose, as if Jack Cardigan had capped the cat, the moon, caprice, and tragedy with: "In off the red!"

Monsieur Profond had resumed his stroll, to a teasing little tune in his beard. What was it? Oh! yes, from "Rigoletto": "Donna a mobile." Just what he would think! She squeezed her father's arm.

"Prowling!" she muttered, as he turned the corner of the house. It was past that disillusioned moment which divides the day and night-still and lingering and warm, with hawthorn scent and lilac scent clinging on the riverside air. A blackbird suddenly burst out. Jon would be in London by now; in the Park perhaps, crossing the Serpentine, thinking of her! A little sound beside her made her turn her eyes; her father was again tearing the paper in his hands. Fleur saw it was a cheque.

"I shan't sell him my Gauguin," he said. "I don't know what your aunt and Imogen see in him."

"Or Mother."

"Your mother!" said Soames.

'Poor Father!' she thought. 'He never looks happy—not really happy. I don't want to make him worse, but of course I shall have to, when Jon comes back. Oh! well, sufficient unto the night!'

"I'm going to dress," she said.

In her room she had a fancy to put on her "freak" dress. It was of gold tissue with little trousers of the same, tightly drawn in at the ankles, a page's cape slung from the shoulders, little gold shoes, and a gold-winged Mercury helmet; and all over her were tiny gold bells, especially on the helmet; so that if she shook her head she pealed. When she was dressed she felt quite sick because Jon could not see her; it even seemed a pity that the sprightly young man Michael Mont would not have a view. But the gong had sounded, and she went down.

She made a sensation in the drawing-room. Winifred thought it "Most amusing." Imogen was enraptured. Jack Cardigan called it "stunning," "ripping," "topping," and "corking."

Monsieur Profond, smiling with his eyes, said: "That's a nice small dress!" Her mother, very handsome in black, sat looking at her, and said nothing. It remained for her father to apply the test of common sense. "What did you put on that thing for? You're not going to dance."

Fleur spun round, and the bells pealed.

"Caprice!"

Soames stared at her, and, turning away, gave his arm to Winifred. Jack Cardigan took her mother. Prosper Profond took Imogen. Fleur went in by herself, with her bells jingling....

The "small" moon had soon dropped down, and May night had fallen soft and warm, enwrapping with its grape-bloom colour and its scents the billion caprices, intrigues, passions, longings, and regrets of men and women. Happy was Jack Cardigan who snored into Imogen's white shoulder, fit as a flea; or Timothy in his "mausoleum," too old for anything but baby's slumber. For so many lay awake, or dreamed, teased by the criss-cross of the world.

The dew fell and the flowers closed; cattle grazed on in the river meadows, feeling with their tongues for the grass they could not see; and the sheep on the Downs lay quiet as stones. Pheasants in the tall trees of the Pangbourne woods, larks on their grassy nests above the gravel-pit at Wansdon, swallows in the eaves at Robin Hill, and the sparrows of Mayfair, all made a dreamless night of it, soothed by the lack of wind. The Mayfly filly, hardly accustomed to her new quarters, scraped at her straw a little; and the few night-flitting things—bats, moths, owls—were vigorous in the warm darkness; but the peace of night lay in the brain of all day-time Nature, colourless and still. Men and women, alone, riding the hobby-horses of anxiety or love, burned their wavering tapers of dream and thought into the lonely hours.

Fleur, leaning out of her window, heard the hall clock's muffled chime of twelve, the tiny splash of a fish, the sudden shaking of an aspen's leaves in the puffs of breeze that rose along the river, the distant rumble of a night train, and time and again the sounds which none can put a name to in the darkness, soft obscure expressions of uncatalogued emotions from man and beast, bird and machine, or, maybe, from departed Forsytes, Darties, Cardigans, taking night strolls back into a world which had once suited their embodied spirits. But Fleur heeded not these sounds; her spirit, far from disembodied, fled with swift wing from railway-carriage to flowery hedge, straining after Jon, tenacious of his forbidden image, and the sound of his voice, which was taboo. And she crinkled her nose, retrieving from the perfume of the riverside night that moment when his hand slipped between the mayflowers and her cheek. Long she leaned out in her freak dress, keen to burn her wings at life's candle; while the moths brushed her cheeks on their pilgrimage to the lamp on her dressing-table, ignorant that in a Forsyte's house there is no open flame. But at last even she felt sleepy, and, forgetting her bells, drew quickly in.

Through the open window of his room, alongside Annette's, Soames, wakeful too, heard their thin faint tinkle, as it might be shaken from stars, or the dewdrops falling from a flower, if one could hear such sounds.

'Caprice!' he thought. 'I can't tell. She's wilful. What shall I do? Fleur!'

And long into the "small" night he brooded.

PART II

CHAPTER I.—MOTHER AND SON

To say that Jon Forsyte accompanied his mother to Spain unwillingly would scarcely have been adequate. He went as a well-natured dog goes for a walk with its mistress, leaving a choice mutton-bone on the lawn. He went looking back at it. Forsytes deprived of their mutton-bones are wont to sulk. But Jon had little sulkiness in his composition. He adored his mother, and it was his first travel. Spain had become Italy by his simply saying: "I'd rather go to Spain, Mum; you've been to Italy so many times; I'd like it new to both of us."

The fellow was subtle besides being naive. He never forgot that he was going to shorten the proposed two months into six weeks, and must therefore show no sign of wishing to do so. For one with so enticing a mutton-bone and so fixed an idea, he made a good enough travelling companion, indifferent to where or when he arrived, superior to food, and thoroughly appreciative of a country strange to the most travelled Englishman. Fleur's wisdom in refusing to write to him was profound, for he reached each new place entirely without hope or fever, and could concentrate immediate attention on the donkeys and tumbling bells, the priests, patios, beggars, children, crowing cocks, sombreros, cactus-hedges, old high white villages, goats, olive-trees, greening plains, singing birds in tiny cages, watersellers, sunsets, melons, mules, great churches, pictures, and swimming grey-brown mountains of a fascinating land.

It was already hot, and they enjoyed an absence of their compatriots. Jon, who, so far as he knew, had no blood in him which was not English, was often innately unhappy in the presence of his own countrymen. He felt they had no nonsense about them, and took a more practical view of things than himself. He confided to his mother that he must be an unsociable beast—it was jolly to be away from everybody who could talk about the things people did talk about. To which Irene had replied simply:

"Yes, Jon, I know."

In this isolation he had unparalleled opportunities of appreciating what few sons can apprehend, the whole-heartedness of a mother's love. Knowledge of something kept from her made him, no doubt, unduly sensitive; and a Southern people stimulated his admiration for her type of beauty, which he had been accustomed to hear called Spanish, but which he now perceived to be no such thing. Her beauty was neither English, French, Spanish, nor Italian—it was special! He appreciated, too, as never before, his mother's subtlety of instinct. He could not tell, for instance, whether she had noticed his absorption in that Goya picture, "La Vendimia," or whether she knew that he had slipped back there after lunch and again next morning, to stand before it full half an hour, a second and third time. It was not Fleur, of course, but like enough to give him heartache—so dear to lovers—remembering her standing at the foot of his bed with her hand held above her head. To keep a postcard reproduction of this picture in his pocket and slip it out to look at became for Jon one of those bad habits which soon or late disclose themselves to eyes sharpened by love, fear, or jealousy. And his mother's were sharpened by all three. In Granada he was fairly caught, sitting on a sun-warmed stone bench in a little battlemented garden on the Alhambra hill, whence he ought to have been looking at the view. His mother, he had thought, was examining the potted stocks between the polled acacias, when her voice said:

"Is that your favourite Goya, Jon?"

He checked, too late, a movement such as he might have made at school to conceal some surreptitious document, and answered: "Yes."

"It certainly is most charming; but I think I prefer the 'Quitasol' Your father would go crazy about Goya; I don't believe he saw them when he was in Spain in '92."

In '92—nine years before he had been born! What had been the previous existences of his father and his mother? If they had a right to share in his future, surely he had a right to share in their pasts. He looked up at her. But something in her face—a look of life hard-lived, the mysterious impress of emotions, experience, and suffering-seemed, with its incalculable depth, its purchased sanctity, to make curiosity impertinent. His mother must have had a wonderfully interesting life; she was so beautiful, and so—so—but he could not frame what he felt about her. He got up, and stood gazing down at the town, at the plain all green with crops, and the ring of mountains glamorous in sinking sunlight. Her life was like the past of this old Moorish city, full, deep, remote—his own life as yet such a baby of a thing, hopelessly ignorant and innocent! They said that in those mountains to the West, which rose sheer from the blue-green plain, as if out of a sea, Phoenicians had dwelt—a dark, strange, secret race, above the land! His mother's life was as unknown to him, as secret, as that Phoenician past was to the town down there, whose cocks crowed and whose children played and clamoured so gaily, day in, day out. He felt aggrieved that she should know all about him and he nothing about her except that she loved him and his father, and was beautiful. His callow ignorance—he had not even had the advantage of the War, like nearly everybody else!—made him small in his own eyes.

That night, from the balcony of his bedroom, he gazed down on the roof of the town—as if inlaid with honeycomb of jet, ivory, and gold; and, long after, he lay awake, listening to the cry of the sentry as the hours struck, and forming in his head these lines:

"Voice in the night crying, down in the old sleeping

Spanish city darkened under her white stars!

"What says the voice-its clear-lingering anguish?

Just the watchman, telling his dateless tale of safety?

Just a road-man, flinging to the moon his song?

"No! 'Tis one deprived, whose lover's heart is weeping,

Just his cry: 'How long?'"

The word "deprived" seemed to him cold and unsatisfactory, but "bereaved" was too final, and no other word of two syllables short-long came to him, which would enable him to keep "whose lover's heart is weeping." It was past two by the time he had finished it, and past three before he went to sleep, having said it over to himself at least twenty-four times. Next day he wrote it out and enclosed it in one of those letters to Fleur which he always finished before he went down, so as to have his mind free and companionable.

About noon that same day, on the tiled terrace of their hotel, he felt a sudden dull pain in the back of his head, a queer sensation in the eyes, and sickness. The sun had touched him too affectionately. The next three days were passed in semi-darkness, and a dulled, aching indifference to all except the feel of ice on his forehead and his mother's smile. She never moved from his room, never relaxed her noiseless vigilance, which seemed to Jon angelic. But there were moments when he was extremely sorry for himself, and wished terribly that Fleur could see him. Several times he took a poignant imaginary leave of her and of the earth, tears oozing out of his eyes. He even prepared the message he would send to her by his mother—who would regret to her dying day that she had ever sought to separate them—his poor mother! He was not slow, however, in perceiving that he had now his excuse for going home.

Toward half-past six each evening came a "gasgacha" of bells—a cascade of tumbling chimes, mounting from the city below and falling back chime on chime. After listening to them on the fourth day he said suddenly:

"I'd like to be back in England, Mum, the sun's too hot."

"Very well, darling. As soon as you're fit to travel!" And at once he felt better, and—meaner.

They had been out five weeks when they turned toward home. Jon's head was restored to its pristine clarity, but he was confined to a hat lined by his mother with many layers of orange and green silk and he still walked from choice in the shade. As the long struggle of discretion between them drew to its close, he wondered more and more whether she could

459

see his eagerness to get back to that which she had brought him away from. Condemned by Spanish Providence to spend a day in Madrid between their trains, it was but natural to go again to the Prado. Jon was elaborately casual this time before his Goya girl. Now that he was going back to her, he could afford a lesser scrutiny. It was his mother who lingered before the picture, saying:

"The face and the figure of the girl are exquisite."

Jon heard her uneasily. Did she understand? But he felt once more that he was no match for her in self-control and subtlety. She could, in some supersensitive way, of which he had not the secret, feel the pulse of his thoughts; she knew by instinct what he hoped and feared and wished. It made him terribly uncomfortable and guilty, having, beyond most boys, a conscience. He wished she would be frank with him, he almost hoped for an open struggle. But none came, and steadily, silently, they travelled north. Thus did he first learn how much better than men women play a waiting game. In Paris they had again to pause for a day. Jon was grieved because it lasted two, owing to certain matters in connection with a dressmaker; as if his mother, who looked beautiful in anything, had any need of dresses! The happiest moment of his travel was that when he stepped on to the Folkestone boat.

Standing by the bulwark rail, with her arm in his, she said

"I'm afraid you haven't enjoyed it much, Jon. But you've been very sweet to me."

Jon squeezed her arm.

"Oh! yes, I've enjoyed it awfully-except for my head lately."

And now that the end had come, he really had, feeling a sort of glamour over the past weeks—a kind of painful pleasure, such as he had tried to screw into those lines about the voice in the night crying; a feeling such as he had known as a small boy listening avidly to Chopin, yet wanting to cry. And he wondered why it was that he couldn't say to her quite simply what she had said to him:

"You were very sweet to me." Odd—one never could be nice and natural like that! He substituted the words: "I expect we shall be sick."

They were, and reached London somewhat attenuated, having been away six weeks and two days, without a single allusion to the subject which had hardly ever ceased to occupy their minds.

CHAPTER II.—FATHERS AND DAUGHTERS

Deprived of his wife and son by the Spanish adventure, Jolyon found the solitude at Robin Hill intolerable. A philosopher when he has all that he wants is different from a philosopher when he has not. Accustomed, however, to the idea, if not to the reality of resignation, he would perhaps have faced it out but for his daughter June. He was a "lame duck" now, and on her conscience. Having achieved—momentarily—the rescue of an etcher in low circumstances, which she happened to have in hand, she appeared at Robin Hill a fortnight after Irene and Jon had gone. June was living now in a tiny house with a big studio at Chiswick. A Forsyte of the best period, so far as the lack of responsibility was concerned, she had overcome the difficulty of a reduced income in a manner satisfactory to herself and her father. The rent of the Gallery off Cork Street which he had bought for her and her increased income tax happening to balance, it had been quite simple—she no longer paid him the rent. The Gallery might be expected now at any time, after eighteen years of barren usufruct, to pay its way, so that she was sure her father would not feel it. Through this device she still had twelve hundred a year, and by reducing what she ate, and, in place of two Belgians in a poor way, employing one Austrian in a poorer, practically the same surplus for the relief of genius. After three days at Robin Hill she carried her father back with her to Town. In those three days she had stumbled on the secret he had kept for two years, and had instantly decided to cure him. She knew, in fact, the very man. He had done wonders with. Paul Post—that painter a little in advance of Futurism; and she was impatient with her father because his eyebrows would go up, and because he had heard of neither. Of course, if he hadn't "faith" he would never get well! It was absurd not to have faith in the man who had healed Paul Post so that he had only just relapsed, from having overworked, or overlived, himself again. The great thing about this healer was that he relied on Nature. He had made a special study of the symptoms of Nature—when his patient failed in any natural symptom he supplied the poison which caused it—and there you were! She was extremely hopeful. Her father had clearly not been living a natural life at Robin Hill, and she intended to provide the symptoms. He was—she felt—out of touch with the times, which was not natural; his heart wanted stimulating. In the little Chiswick house she and the Austrian—a grateful soul, so devoted to June for rescuing her that she was in danger of decease from overwork—stimulated Jolyon in all sorts of ways, preparing him for his cure. But they could not keep his eyebrows down; as, for example, when the Austrian woke him at eight o'clock just as he was going to sleep, or June took The Times away from him, because it was unnatural to read "that stuff" when he ought to be taking an interest in "life." He never failed, indeed, to be astonished at her resource, especially in the evenings. For his benefit, as she declared, though he suspected that she also got something out of it, she assembled the Age so far as it was satellite to genius; and with some solemnity it would move up and down the studio before him in the Fox-trot, and that more mental form of dancing—the One-step—which so pulled against the music, that Jolyon's eyebrows would be almost lost in his hair from wonder at the strain it must impose on the dancer's will-power. Aware that, hung on the line in the Water Colour Society, he was a back number to those with any pretension to be called artists, he would sit in the darkest corner he could find, and wonder about rhythm, on which so long ago he had been raised. And when June brought some girl or young man up to him, he would rise humbly to their level so far as that was possible, and think: 'Dear me! This is very dull for them!' Having his father's perennial sympathy with Youth, he used to get very tired from entering into their points of view. But it was all stimulating, and he never failed in admiration of his daughter's indomitable spirit. Even genius itself attended these gatherings now and then, with its nose on one side; and June always introduced it to her father. This, she felt, was exceptionally good for him, for genius was a natural symptom he had never had—fond as she was of him.

Certain as a man can be that she was his own daughter, he often wondered whence she got herself—her red-gold hair, now greyed into a special colour; her direct, spirited face, so different from his own rather folded and subtilised countenance, her little lithe figure, when he and most of the Forsytes were tall. And he would dwell on the origin of species, and debate whether she might be Danish or Celtic. Celtic, he thought, from her pugnacity, and her taste in fillets and djibbahs. It was not too much to say that he preferred her to the Age with which she was surrounded, youthful though, for the greater part, it was. She took, however, too much interest in his teeth, for he still had some of those natural symptoms. Her dentist at once found "Staphylococcus aureus present in pure culture" (which might cause boils, of course), and wanted to take out all the teeth he had and supply him with two complete sets of unnatural symptoms. Jolyon's native tenacity was roused, and in the studio that evening he developed his objections. He had never had any boils, and his own teeth would last his time. Of course—June admitted—they would last his time if he didn't have them out! But if he had more teeth he would have a better heart and his time would be longer. His recalcitrance—she said—was a symptom of his whole attitude; he was taking it lying down. He ought to be fighting. When was he going to see the man who had cured Paul Post? Jolyon was very sorry, but the fact was he was not going to see him. June chafed. Pondridge—she said—the healer, was such a fine man, and he had such difficulty in making two ends meet, and getting his theories recognised. It was just such indifference and prejudice as her father manifested which was keeping him back. It would be so splendid for both of them!

"I perceive," said Jolyon, "that you are trying to kill two birds with one stone."

"To cure, you mean!" cried June.

"My dear, it's the same thing."

June protested. It was unfair to say that without a trial.

Jolyon thought he might not have the chance, of saying it after.

"Dad!" cried June, "you're hopeless."

"That," said Jolyon, "is a fact, but I wish to remain hopeless as long as possible. I shall let sleeping dogs lie, my child. They are quiet at present."

"That's not giving science a chance," cried June. "You've no idea how devoted Pondridge is. He puts his science before everything."

"Just," replied Jolyon, puffing the mild cigarette to which he was reduced, "as Mr. Paul Post puts his art, eh? Art for Art's sake—Science for the sake of Science. I know those enthusiastic egomaniac gentry. They vivisect you without blinking. I'm enough of a Forsyte to give them the go-by, June."

"Dad," said June, "if you only knew how old-fashioned that sounds! Nobody can afford to be half-hearted nowadays."

"I'm afraid," murmured Jolyon, with his smile, "that's the only natural symptom with which Mr. Pondridge need not supply me. We are born to be extreme or to be moderate, my dear; though, if you'll forgive my saying so, half the people nowadays who believe they're extreme are really very moderate. I'm getting on as well as I can expect, and I must leave it at that."

June was silent, having experienced in her time the inexorable character of her father's amiable obstinacy so far as his own freedom of action was concerned.

How he came to let her know why Irene had taken Jon to Spain puzzled Jolyon, for he had little confidence in her discretion. After she had brooded on the news, it brought a rather sharp discussion, during which he perceived to the full the fundamental opposition between her active temperament and his wife's passivity. He even gathered that a little soreness still remained from that generation-old struggle between them over the body of Philip Bosinney, in which the passive had so signally triumphed over the active principle.

According to June, it was foolish and even cowardly to hide the past from Jon. Sheer opportunism, she called it.

"Which," Jolyon put in mildly, "is the working principle of real life, my dear."

"Oh!" cried June, "you don't really defend her for not telling Jon, Dad. If it were left to you, you would."

"I might, but simply because I know he must find out, which will be worse than if we told him."

"Then why don't you tell him? It's just sleeping dogs again."

"My dear," said Jolyon, "I wouldn't for the world go against Irene's instinct. He's her boy."

"Yours too," cried June.

"What is a man's instinct compared with a mother's?"

"Well, I think it's very weak of you."

"I dare say," said Jolyon, "I dare say."

And that was all she got from him; but the matter rankled in her brain. She could not bear sleeping dogs. And there stirred in her a tortuous impulse to push the matter toward decision. Jon ought to be told, so that either his feeling might be nipped in the bud, or, flowering in spite of the past, come to fruition. And she determined to see Fleur, and judge for herself. When June determined on anything, delicacy became a somewhat minor consideration. After all, she was Soames' cousin, and they were both interested in pictures. She would go and tell him that he ought to buy a Paul Post, or perhaps a piece of sculpture by Boris Strumolowski, and of course she would say nothing to her father. She went on the following Sunday, looking so determined that she had some difficulty in getting a cab at Reading station. The river country was lovely in those days of her own month, and June ached at its loveliness. She who had passed through this life without knowing what union was had a love of natural beauty which was almost madness. And when she came to that choice spot where Soames had pitched his tent, she dismissed her cab, because, business over, she wanted to revel in the bright water and the woods. She appeared at his front door, therefore, as a mere pedestrian, and sent in her card. It was in June's character to know that when her nerves were fluttering she was doing something worth while. If one's nerves did not flutter, she was taking the line of least resistance, and knew that nobleness was not obliging her. She was conducted to a drawing-room, which, though not in her style, showed every mark of fastidious elegance. Thinking, 'Too much taste—too many knick-knacks,' she saw in an old lacquer-framed mirror the figure of a girl coming in from the verandah. Clothed in white, and holding some white roses in her hand, she had, reflected in that silvery-grey pool of glass, a vision-like appearance, as if a pretty ghost had come out of the green garden.

"How do you do?" said June, turning round. "I'm a cousin of your father's."

"Oh, yes; I saw you in that confectioner's."

"With my young stepbrother. Is your father in?"

"He will be directly. He's only gone for a little walk."

June slightly narrowed her blue eyes, and lifted her decided chin.

"Your name's Fleur, isn't it? I've heard of you from Holly. What do you think of Jon?"

The girl lifted the roses in her hand, looked at them, and answered calmly:

"He's quite a nice boy."

"Not a bit like Holly or me, is he?"

"Not a bit."

'She's cool,' thought June.

And suddenly the girl said: "I wish you'd tell me why our families don't get on?"

Confronted with the question she had advised her father to answer, June was silent; whether because this girl was trying to get something out of her, or simply because what one would do theoretically is not always what one will do when it comes to the point.

"You know," said the girl, "the surest way to make people find out the worst is to keep them ignorant. My father's told me it was a quarrel about property. But I don't believe it; we've both got heaps. They wouldn't have been so bourgeois as all that."

June flushed. The word applied to her grandfather and father offended her.

"My grandfather," she said, "was very generous, and my father is, too; neither of them was in the least bourgeois."

"Well, what was it then?" repeated the girl: Conscious that this young Forsyte meant having what she wanted, June at once determined to prevent her, and to get something for herself instead.

"Why do you want to know?"

The girl smelled at her roses. "I only want to know because they won't tell me."

"Well, it was about property, but there's more than one kind."

"That makes it worse. Now I really must know."

June's small and resolute face quivered. She was wearing a round cap, and her hair had fluffed out under it. She looked quite young at that moment, rejuvenated by encounter.

"You know," she said, "I saw you drop your handkerchief. Is there anything between you and Jon? Because, if so, you'd better drop that too."

The girl grew paler, but she smiled.

"If there were, that isn't the way to make me."

At the gallantry of that reply, June held out her hand.

"I like you; but I don't like your father; I never have. We may as well be frank."

"Did you come down to tell him that?"

June laughed. "No; I came down to see you."

"How delightful of you."

This girl could fence.

"I'm two and a half times your age," said June, "but I quite sympathize. It's horrid not to have one's own way."

The girl smiled again. "I really think you might tell me."

How the child stuck to her point

"It's not my secret. But I'll see what I can do, because I think both you and Jon ought to be told. And now I'll say good-bye."

"Won't you wait and see Father?"

June shook her head. "How can I get over to the other side?"

"I'll row you across."

"Look!" said June impulsively, "next time you're in London, come and see me. This is where I live. I generally have young people in the evening. But I shouldn't tell your father that you're coming."

The girl nodded.

Watching her scull the skiff across, June thought: 'She's awfully pretty and well made. I never thought Soames would have a daughter as pretty as this. She and Jon would make a lovely couple.

The instinct to couple, starved within herself, was always at work in June. She stood watching Fleur row back; the girl took her hand off a scull to wave farewell, and June walked languidly on between the meadows and the river, with an ache in her heart. Youth to youth, like the dragon-flies chasing each other, and love like the sun warming them through and through. Her youth! So long ago—when Phil and she—And since? Nothing—no one had been quite what she had wanted. And so she had missed it all. But what a coil was round those two young things, if they really were in love, as Holly would have it—as her father, and Irene, and Soames himself seemed to dread. What a coil, and what a barrier! And the itch for the future, the contempt, as it were, for what was overpast, which forms the active principle, moved in the heart of one who ever believed that what one wanted was more important than what other people did not want. From the bank, awhile, in the warm summer stillness, she watched the water-lily plants and willow leaves, the fishes rising; sniffed the scent of grass and meadow-sweet, wondering how she could force everybody to be happy. Jon and Fleur! Two little lame ducks—charming callow yellow little ducks! A great pity! Surely something could be done! One must not take such situations lying down. She walked on, and reached a station, hot and cross.

That evening, faithful to the impulse toward direct action, which made many people avoid her, she said to her father:

"Dad, I've been down to see young Fleur. I think she's very attractive. It's no good hiding our heads under our wings, is it?"

The startled Jolyon set down his barley-water, and began crumbling his bread.

"It's what you appear to be doing," he said. "Do you realise whose daughter she is?"

"Can't the dead past bury its dead?"

Jolyon rose.

"Certain things can never be buried."

"I disagree," said June. "It's that which stands in the way of all happiness and progress. You don't understand the Age, Dad. It's got no use for outgrown things. Why do you think it matters so terribly that Jon should know about his mother? Who pays any attention to that sort of thing now? The marriage laws are just as they were when Soames and Irene couldn't get a divorce, and you had to come in. We've moved, and they haven't. So nobody cares. Marriage without a decent chance of relief is only a sort of slave-owning; people oughtn't to own each other. Everybody sees that now. If Irene broke such laws, what does it matter?"

"It's not for me to disagree there," said Jolyon; "but that's all quite beside the mark. This is a matter of human feeling."

"Of course it is," cried June, "the human feeling of those two young things."

"My dear," said Jolyon with gentle exasperation; "you're talking nonsense."

"I'm not. If they prove to be really fond of each other, why should they be made unhappy because of the past?"

"You haven't lived that past. I have—through the feelings of my wife; through my own nerves and my imagination, as only one who is devoted can."

June, too, rose, and began to wander restlessly.

"If," she said suddenly, "she were the daughter of Philip Bosinney, I could understand you better. Irene loved him, she never loved Soames."

Jolyon uttered a deep sound-the sort of noise an Italian peasant woman utters to her mule. His heart had begun beating furiously, but he paid no attention to it, quite carried away by his feelings.

"That shows how little you understand. Neither I nor Jon, if I know him, would mind a love-past. It's the brutality of a union without love. This girl is the daughter of the man who once owned Jon's mother as a negro-slave was owned. You can't lay that ghost; don't try to, June! It's asking us to see Jon joined to the flesh and blood of the man who possessed Jon's mother against her will. It's no good mincing words; I want it clear once for all. And now I mustn't talk any more, or I shall have to sit up with this all night." And, putting his hand over his heart, Jolyon turned his back on his daughter and stood looking at the river Thames.

June, who by nature never saw a hornet's nest until she had put her head into it, was seriously alarmed. She came and slipped her arm through his. Not convinced that he was right, and she herself wrong, because that was not natural to her, she was yet profoundly impressed by the obvious fact that the subject was very bad for him. She rubbed her cheek against his shoulder, and said nothing.

After taking her elderly cousin across, Fleur did not land at once, but pulled in among the reeds, into the sunshine. The peaceful beauty of the afternoon seduced for a little one not much given to the vague and poetic. In the field beyond the bank where her skiff lay up, a machine drawn by a grey horse was turning an early field of hay. She watched the grass cascading over and behind the light wheels with fascination—it looked so cool and fresh. The click and swish blended with the rustle of the willows and the poplars, and the cooing of a wood-pigeon, in a true river song. Alongside, in the deep green water, weeds, like yellow snakes, were writhing and nosing with the current; pied cattle on the farther side stood in the shade lazily swishing their tails. It was an afternoon to dream. And she took out Jon's letters—not flowery effusions, but haunted in their recital of things seen and done by a longing very agreeable to her, and all ending "Your devoted J." Fleur was not sentimental, her desires were ever concrete and concentrated, but what poetry there was in the daughter of Soames and Annette had certainly in those weeks of waiting gathered round her memories of Jon. They all belonged to grass and blossom, flowers and running water. She enjoyed him in the scents absorbed by her crinkling nose. The stars could persuade her that she was standing beside him in the centre of the map of Spain; and of an early morning the dewy cobwebs, the hazy sparkle and promise of the day down in the garden, were Jon personified to her.

Two white swans came majestically by, while she was reading his letters, followed by their brood of six young swans in a line, with just so much water between each tail and head, a flotilla of grey destroyers. Fleur thrust her letters back, got out her sculls, and pulled up to the landing-stage. Crossing the lawn, she wondered whether she should tell her father of June's visit. If he learned of it from the butler, he might think it odd if she did not. It gave her, too, another chance to startle out of him the reason of the feud. She went, therefore, up the road to meet him.

Soames had gone to look at a patch of ground on which the Local Authorities were proposing to erect a Sanatorium for people with weak lungs. Faithful to his native individualism, he took no part in local affairs, content to pay the rates which were always going up. He could not, however, remain indifferent to this new and dangerous scheme.

The site was not half a mile from his own house. He was quite of opinion that the country should stamp out tuberculosis; but this was not the place. It should be done farther away. He took, indeed, an attitude common to all true Forsytes, that disability of any sort in other people was not his affair, and the State should do its business without prejudicing in any way the natural advantages which he had acquired or inherited. Francie, the most free-spirited Forsyte of his generation (except perhaps that fellow Jolyon) had once asked him in her malicious way: "Did you ever see the name Forsyte in a subscription list, Soames?" That was as it might be, but a Sanatorium would depreciate the neighbourhood, and he should certainly sign the petition which was being got up against it. Returning with this decision fresh within him, he saw Fleur coming.

She was showing him more affection of late, and the quiet time down here with her in this summer weather had been making him feel quite young; Annette was always running up to Town for one thing or another, so that he had Fleur to himself almost as much as he could wish. To be sure, young Mont had formed a habit of appearing on his motor-cycle almost every other day. Thank goodness, the young fellow had shaved off his half-toothbrushes, and no longer looked like a mountebank! With a girl friend of Fleur's who was staying in the house, and a neighbouring youth or so, they made two couples after dinner, in the hall, to the music of the electric pianola, which performed Fox-trots unassisted, with a surprised shine on its expressive surface. Annette, even, now and then passed gracefully up and down in the arms of one or other of the young men. And Soames, coming to the drawing-room door, would lift his nose a little sideways, and watch them, waiting to catch a smile from Fleur; then move back to his chair by the drawing-room hearth, to peruse The Times or some other collector's price list. To his ever-anxious eyes Fleur showed no signs of remembering that caprice of hers.

When she reached him on the dusty road, he slipped his hand within her arm.

"Who, do you think, has been to see you, Dad? She couldn't wait! Guess!"

"I never guess," said Soames uneasily. "Who?"

"Your cousin, June Forsyte."

Quite unconsciously Soames gripped her arm. "What did she want?"

"I don't know. But it was rather breaking through the feud, wasn't it?"

"Feud? What feud?"

"The one that exists in your imagination, dear."

Soames dropped her arm. Was she mocking, or trying to draw him on?

"I suppose she wanted me to buy a picture," he said at last.

"I don't think so. Perhaps it was just family affection."

"She's only a first cousin once removed," muttered Soames.

"And the daughter of your enemy."

"What d'you mean by that?"

"I beg your pardon, dear; I thought he was."

"Enemy!" repeated Soames. "It's ancient history. I don't know where you get your notions."

"From June Forsyte."

It had come to her as an inspiration that if he thought she knew, or were on the edge of knowledge, he would tell her.

Soames was startled, but she had underrated his caution and tenacity.

"If you know," he said coldly, "why do you plague me?"

Fleur saw that she had overreached herself.

"I don't want to plague you, darling. As you say, why want to know more? Why want to know anything of that 'small' mystery—Je m'en fiche, as Profond says?"

"That chap!" said Soames profoundly.

That chap, indeed, played a considerable, if invisible, part this summer—for he had not turned up again. Ever since the Sunday when Fleur had drawn attention to him prowling on the lawn, Soames had thought of him a good deal, and always in connection with Annette, for no reason, except that she was looking handsomer than for some time past. His possessive instinct, subtle, less formal, more elastic since the War, kept all misgiving underground. As one looks on some American river, quiet and pleasant, knowing that an alligator perhaps is lying in the mud with his snout just raised and indistinguishable from a snag of wood—so Soames looked on the river of his own existence, subconscious of Monsieur Profond, refusing to see more than the suspicion of his snout. He had at this epoch in his life practically all he wanted, and was as nearly happy as his nature would permit. His senses were at rest; his affections found all the vent they needed in his daughter; his collection was well known, his money well invested; his health excellent, save for a touch of liver now and again; he had not yet begun to worry seriously about what would happen after death, inclining to think that nothing would happen. He resembled one of his own gilt-edged securities, and to knock the gilt off by seeing anything he could avoid seeing would be, he felt instinctively, perverse and retrogressive. Those two crumpled rose-leaves, Fleur's caprice and Monsieur Profond's snout, would level away if he lay on them industriously.

That evening Chance, which visits the lives of even the best-invested Forsytes, put a clue into Fleur's hands. Her father came down to dinner without a handkerchief, and had occasion to blow his nose.

"I'll get you one, dear," she had said, and ran upstairs. In the sachet where she sought for it—an old sachet of very faded silk—there were two compartments: one held handkerchiefs; the other was buttoned, and contained something flat and hard. By some childish impulse Fleur unbuttoned it. There was a frame and in it a photograph of herself as a little girl. She gazed at it, fascinated, as one is by one's own presentment. It slipped under her fidgeting thumb, and she saw that another photograph was behind. She pressed her own down further, and perceived a face, which she seemed to know, of a young woman, very good-looking, in a very old style of evening dress. Slipping her own photograph up over it again, she took out a handkerchief and went down. Only on the stairs did she identify that face. Surely—surely Jon's mother! The conviction came as a shock. And she stood still in a flurry of thought. Why, of course! Jon's father had married the woman her father had wanted to marry, had cheated him out of her, perhaps. Then, afraid of showing by her manner that she had lighted on his secret, she refused to think further, and, shaking out the silk handkerchief, entered the dining-room.

"I chose the softest, Father."

"H'm!" said Soames; "I only use those after a cold. Never mind!"

That evening passed for Fleur in putting two and two together; recalling the look on her father's face in the confectioner's shop—a look strange and coldly intimate, a queer look. He must have loved that woman very much to have kept her photograph all this time, in spite of having lost her. Unsparing and matter-of-fact, her mind darted to his relations with her own mother. Had he ever really loved her? She thought not. Jon was the son of the woman he had really loved. Surely, then, he ought not to mind his daughter loving him; it only wanted getting used to. And a sigh of sheer relief was caught in the folds of her nightgown slipping over her head.

CHAPTER III.—MEETINGS

Youth only recognises Age by fits and starts. Jon, for one, had never really seen his father's age till he came back from Spain. The face of the fourth Jolyon, worn by waiting, gave him quite a shock—it looked so wan and old. His father's mask had been forced awry by the emotion of the meeting, so that the boy suddenly realised how much he must have felt their absence. He summoned to his aid the thought: 'Well, I didn't want to go!' It was out of date for Youth to defer to Age. But Jon was by no means typically modern. His father had always been "so jolly" to him, and to feel that one meant to begin again at once the conduct which his father had suffered six weeks' loneliness to cure was not agreeable.

At the question, "Well, old man, how did the great Goya strike you?" his conscience pricked him badly. The great Goya only existed because he had created a face which resembled Fleur's.

On the night of their return, he went to bed full of compunction; but awoke full of anticipation. It was only the fifth of July, and no meeting was fixed with Fleur until the ninth. He was to have three days at home before going back to farm. Somehow he must contrive to see her!

In the lives of men an inexorable rhythm, caused by the need for trousers, not even the fondest parents can deny. On the second day, therefore, Jon went to Town, and having satisfied his conscience by ordering what was indispensable in Conduit Street, turned his face toward Piccadilly. Stratton Street, where her Club was, adjoined Devonshire House. It would be the merest chance that she should be at her Club. But he dawdled down Bond Street with a beating heart, noticing the superiority of all other young men to himself. They wore their clothes with such an air; they had assurance; they were old. He was suddenly overwhelmed by the conviction that Fleur must have forgotten him. Absorbed in his own feeling for her all these weeks, he had mislaid that possibility. The corners of his mouth drooped, his hands felt clammy. Fleur with the pick of youth at the beck of her smile-Fleur incomparable! It was an evil moment. Jon, however, had a great idea that one must be able to face anything. And he braced himself with that dour reflection in front of a bric-a-brac shop. At this high-water mark of what was once the London season, there was nothing to mark it out from any other except a grey top hat or two, and the sun. Jon moved on, and turning the corner into Piccadilly, ran into Val Dartie moving toward the Iseeum Club, to which he had just been elected.

"Hallo! young man! Where are you off to?"

Jon gushed. "I've just been to my tailor's."

Val looked him up and down. "That's good! I'm going in here to order some cigarettes; then come and have some lunch."

Jon thanked him. He might get news of her from Val!

The condition of England, that nightmare of its Press and Public men, was seen in different perspective within the tobacconist's which they now entered.

"Yes, sir; precisely the cigarette I used to supply your father with. Bless me! Mr. Montague Dartie was a customer here from—let me see—the year Melton won the Derby. One of my very best customers he was." A faint smile illumined the tobacconist's face. "Many's the tip he's given me, to be sure! I suppose he took a couple of hundred of these every week, year in, year out, and never changed his cigarette. Very affable gentleman, brought me a lot of custom. I was sorry he met with that accident. One misses an old customer like him."

Val smiled. His father's decease had closed an account which had been running longer, probably, than any other; and in a ring of smoke puffed out from that time-honoured cigarette he seemed to see again his father's face, dark, good-looking, moustachioed, a little puffy, in the only halo it had earned. His father had his fame here, anyway—a man who smoked two hundred cigarettes a week, who could give tips, and run accounts for ever! To his tobacconist a hero! Even that was some distinction to inherit!

"I pay cash," he said; "how much?"

"To his son, sir, and cash—ten and six. I shall never forget Mr. Montague Dartie. I've known him stand talkin' to me half an hour. We don't get many like him now, with everybody in such a hurry. The War was bad for manners, sir—it was bad for manners. You were in it, I see."

"No," said Val, tapping his knee, "I got this in the war before. Saved my life, I expect. Do you want any cigarettes, Jon?"

Rather ashamed, Jon murmured, "I don't smoke, you know," and saw the tobacconist's lips twisted, as if uncertain whether to say "Good God!" or "Now's your chance, sir!"

"That's right," said Val; "keep off it while you can. You'll want it when you take a knock. This is really the same tobacco, then?"

"Identical, sir; a little dearer, that's all. Wonderful staying power—the British Empire, I always say."

"Send me down a hundred a week to this address, and invoice it monthly. Come on, Jon."

Jon entered the Iseeum with curiosity. Except to lunch now and then at the Hotch-Potch with his father, he had never been in a London Club. The Iseeum, comfortable and unpretentious, did not move, could not, so long as George Forsyte sat on its Committee, where his culinary acumen was almost the controlling force. The Club had made a stand against the newly rich, and it had taken all George Forsyte's prestige, and praise of him as a "good sportsman," to bring in Prosper Profond.

The two were lunching together when the half-brothers-in-law entered the dining-room, and attracted by George's forefinger, sat down at their table, Val with his shrewd eyes and charming smile, Jon with solemn lips and an attractive shyness in his glance. There was an air of privilege around that corner table, as though past masters were eating there. Jon was fascinated by the hypnotic atmosphere. The waiter, lean in the chaps, pervaded with such free-masonical deference. He seemed to hang on George Forsyte's lips, to watch the gloat in his eye with a kind of sympathy, to follow the movements of the heavy club-marked silver fondly. His liveried arm and confidential voice alarmed Jon, they came so secretly over his shoulder.

Except for George's "Your grandfather tipped me once; he was a deuced good judge of a cigar!" neither he nor the other past master took any notice of him, and he was grateful for this. The talk was all about the breeding, points, and prices of horses, and he listened to it vaguely at first, wondering how it was possible to retain so much knowledge in a head. He could not take his eyes off the dark past master—what he said was so deliberate and discouraging—such heavy, queer, smiled-out words. Jon was thinking of butterflies, when he heard him say:

"I want to see Mr. Soames Forsyde take an interest in 'orses."

"Old Soames! He's too dry a file!"

With all his might Jon tried not to grow red, while the dark past master went on.

"His daughter's an attractive small girl. Mr. Soames Forsyde is a bit old-fashioned. I want to see him have a pleasure some day." George Forsyte grinned.

"Don't you worry; he's not so miserable as he looks. He'll never show he's enjoying anything—they might try and take it from him. Old Soames! Once bit, twice shy!"

"Well, Jon," said Val, hastily, "if you've finished, we'll go and have coffee."

"Who were those?" Jon asked, on the stairs. "I didn't quite——"

"Old George Forsyte is a first cousin of your father's and of my Uncle Soames. He's always been here. The other chap, Profond, is a queer fish. I think he's hanging round Soames' wife, if you ask me!"

Jon looked at him, startled. "But that's awful," he said: "I mean—for Fleur."

"Don't suppose Fleur cares very much; she's very up-to-date."

"Her mother!"

"You're very green, Jon."

Jon grew red. "Mothers," he stammered angrily, "are different."

"You're right," said Val suddenly; "but things aren't what they were when I was your age. There's a 'To-morrow we die' feeling. That's what old George meant about my Uncle Soames. He doesn't mean to die to-morrow."

Jon said, quickly: "What's the matter between him and my father?"

"Stable secret, Jon. Take my advice, and bottle up. You'll do no good by knowing. Have a liqueur?"

Jon shook his head.

"I hate the way people keep things from one," he muttered, "and then sneer at one for being green."

"Well, you can ask Holly. If she won't tell you, you'll believe it's for your own good, I suppose."

Jon got up. "I must go now; thanks awfully for the lunch."

Val smiled up at him half-sorry, and yet amused. The boy looked so upset.

"All right! See you on Friday."

"I don't know," murmured Jon.

And he did not. This conspiracy of silence made him desperate. It was humiliating to be treated like a child! He retraced his moody steps to Stratton Street. But he would go to her Club now, and find out the worst! To his enquiry the reply was that Miss Forsyte was not in the Club. She might be in perhaps later. She was often in on Monday—they could not say. Jon said he would call again, and, crossing into the Green Park, flung himself down under a tree. The sun was bright, and a breeze fluttered the leaves of the young lime-tree beneath which he lay; but his heart ached. Such darkness seemed gathered round his happiness. He heard Big Ben chime "Three" above the traffic. The sound moved something in him, and, taking out a piece of paper, he began to scribble on it with a pencil. He had jotted a stanza, and was searching the grass for another verse, when something hard touched his shoulder-a green parasol. There above him stood Fleur!

"They told me you'd been, and were coming back. So I thought you might be out here; and you are—it's rather wonderful!"

"Oh, Fleur! I thought you'd have forgotten me."

"When I told you that I shouldn't!"

Jon seized her arm.

"It's too much luck! Let's get away from this side." He almost dragged her on through that too thoughtfully regulated Park, to find some cover where they could sit and hold each other's hands.

"Hasn't anybody cut in?" he said, gazing round at her lashes, in suspense above her cheeks.

"There is a young idiot, but he doesn't count."

Jon felt a twitch of compassion for the-young idiot.

"You know I've had sunstroke; I didn't tell you."

"Really! Was it interesting?"

"No. Mother was an angel. Has anything happened to you?"

"Nothing. Except that I think I've found out what's wrong between our families, Jon."

His heart began beating very fast.

"I believe my father wanted to marry your mother, and your father got her instead."

"Oh!"

"I came on a photo of her; it was in a frame behind a photo of me. Of course, if he was very fond of her, that would have made him pretty mad, wouldn't it?"

Jon thought for a minute. "Not if she loved my father best."

"But suppose they were engaged?"

"If we were engaged, and you found you loved somebody better, I might go cracked, but I shouldn't grudge it you."

"I should. You mustn't ever do that with me, Jon.

"My God! Not much!"

"I don't believe that he's ever really cared for my mother."

Jon was silent. Val's words—the two past masters in the Club!

"You see, we don't know," went on Fleur; "it may have been a great shock. She may have behaved badly to him. People do."

"My mother wouldn't."

Fleur shrugged her shoulders. "I don't think we know much about our fathers and mothers. We just see them in the light of the way they treat us; but they've treated other people, you know, before we were born-plenty, I expect. You see, they're both old. Look at your father, with three separate families!"

"Isn't there any place," cried Jon, "in all this beastly London where we can be alone?"

"Only a taxi."

"Let's get one, then."

When they were installed, Fleur asked suddenly: "Are you going back to Robin Hill? I should like to see where you live, Jon. I'm staying with my aunt for the night, but I could get back in time for dinner. I wouldn't come to the house, of course."

Jon gazed at her enraptured.

"Splendid! I can show it you from the copse, we shan't meet anybody. There's a train at four."

The god of property and his Forsytes great and small, leisured, official, commercial, or professional, like the working classes, still worked their seven hours a day, so that those two of the fourth generation travelled down to Robin Hill in an empty first-class carriage, dusty and sun-warmed, of that too early train. They travelled in blissful silence, holding each other's hands.

At the station they saw no one except porters, and a villager or two unknown to Jon, and walked out up the lane, which smelled of dust and honeysuckle.

For Jon—sure of her now, and without separation before him—it was a miraculous dawdle, more wonderful than those on the Downs, or along the river Thames. It was love-in-a-mist—one of those illumined pages of Life, where every word and smile, and every light touch they gave each other were as little gold and red and blue butterflies and flowers and birds scrolled in among the text—a happy communing, without afterthought, which lasted thirty-seven minutes. They reached the coppice at the milking hour. Jon would not take her as far as the farmyard; only to where she could see the field leading up to the gardens, and the house beyond. They turned in among the larches, and suddenly, at the winding of the path, came on Irene, sitting on an old log seat.

There are various kinds of shocks: to the vertebrae; to the nerves; to moral sensibility; and, more potent and permanent, to personal dignity. This last was the shock Jon received, coming thus on his mother. He became suddenly conscious that he was doing an indelicate thing. To have brought Fleur down openly—yes! But to sneak her in like this! Consumed with shame, he put on a front as brazen as his nature would permit.

Fleur was smiling, a little defiantly; his mother's startled face was changing quickly to the impersonal and gracious. It was she who uttered the first words:

"I'm very glad to see you. It was nice of Jon to think of bringing you down to us."

"We weren't coming to the house," Jon blurted out. "I just wanted Fleur to see where I lived."

His mother said quietly:

"Won't you come up and have tea?"

Feeling that he had but aggravated his breach of breeding, he heard Fleur answer:

"Thanks very much; I have to get back to dinner. I met Jon by accident, and we thought it would be rather jolly just to see his home."

How self-possessed she was!

"Of course; but you must have tea. We'll send you down to the station. My husband will enjoy seeing you."

The expression of his mother's eyes, resting on him for a moment, cast Jon down level with the ground—a true worm. Then she led on, and Fleur followed her. He felt like a child, trailing after those two, who were talking so easily about Spain and Wansdon, and the house up there beyond the trees and the grassy slope. He watched the fencing of their eyes, taking each other in—the two beings he loved most in the world.

He could see his father sitting under the oaktree; and suffered in advance all the loss of caste he must go through in the eyes of that tranquil figure, with his knees crossed, thin, old, and elegant; already he could feel the faint irony which would come into his voice and smile.

"This is Fleur Forsyte, Jolyon; Jon brought her down to see the house. Let's have tea at once—she has to catch a train. Jon, tell them, dear, and telephone to the Dragon for a car."

To leave her alone with them was strange, and yet, as no doubt his mother had foreseen, the least of evils at the moment; so he ran up into the house. Now he would not see Fleur alone again—not for a minute, and they had arranged no further meeting! When he returned under cover of the maids and teapots, there was not a trace of awkwardness beneath the tree; it was all within himself, but not the less for that. They were talking of the Gallery off Cork Street.

"We back numbers," his father was saying, "are awfully anxious to find out why we can't appreciate the new stuff; you and Jon must tell us."

"It's supposed to be satiric, isn't it?" said Fleur.

He saw his father's smile.

"Satiric? Oh! I think it's more than that. What do you say, Jon?"

"I don't know at all," stammered Jon. His father's face had a sudden grimness.

"The young are tired of us, our gods and our ideals. Off with their heads, they say—smash their idols! And let's get back to-nothing! And, by Jove, they've done it! Jon's a poet. He'll be going in, too, and stamping on what's left of us. Property, beauty, sentiment—all smoke. We mustn't own anything nowadays, not even our feelings. They stand in the way of—Nothing."

Jon listened, bewildered, almost outraged by his father's words, behind which he felt a meaning that he could not reach. He didn't want to stamp on anything!

"Nothing's the god of to-day," continued Jolyon; "we're back where the Russians were sixty years ago, when they started Nihilism."

"No, Dad," cried Jon suddenly, "we only want to live, and we don't know how, because of the Past—that's all!"

"By George!" said Jolyon, "that's profound, Jon. Is it your own? The Past! Old ownerships, old passions, and their aftermath. Let's have cigarettes."

Conscious that his mother had lifted her hand to her lips, quickly, as if to hush something, Jon handed the cigarettes. He lighted his father's and Fleur's, then one for himself. Had he taken the knock that Val had spoken of? The smoke was blue when he had not puffed, grey when he had; he liked the sensation in his nose, and the sense of equality it gave him. He was glad no one said: "So you've begun!" He felt less young.

Fleur looked at her watch, and rose. His mother went with her into the house. Jon stayed with his father, puffing at the cigarette.

"See her into the car, old man," said Jolyon; "and when she's gone, ask your mother to come back to me."

Jon went. He waited in the hall. He saw her into the car. There was no chance for any word; hardly for a pressure of the hand. He waited all that evening for something to be said to him. Nothing was said. Nothing might have happened. He went up to bed, and in the mirror on his dressing-table met himself. He did not speak, nor did the image; but both looked as if they thought the more.

CHAPTER IV.—IN GREEN STREET

Uncertain whether the impression that Prosper Profond was dangerous should be traced to his attempt to give Val the Mayfly filly; to a remark of Fleur's: "He's like the hosts of Midian—he prowls and prowls around"; to his preposterous inquiry of Jack Cardigan: "What's the use of keepin' fit?" or, more simply, to the fact that he was a foreigner, or alien as it was now called. Certain, that Annette was looking particularly handsome, and that Soames—had sold him a Gauguin and then torn up the cheque, so that Monsieur Profond himself had said: "I didn't get that small picture I bought from Mr. Forsyde."

However suspiciously regarded, he still frequented Winifred's evergreen little house in Green Street, with a good-natured obtuseness which no one mistook for naivete, a word hardly applicable to Monsieur Prosper Profond. Winifred still found him "amusing," and would write him little notes saying: "Come and have a 'jolly' with us"—it was breath of life to her to keep up with the phrases of the day.

The mystery, with which all felt him to be surrounded, was due to his having done, seen, heard, and known everything, and found nothing in it—which was unnatural. The English type of disillusionment was familiar enough to Winifred, who had always moved in fashionable circles. It gave a certain cachet or distinction, so that one got something out of it. But to see nothing in anything, not as a pose, but because there was nothing in anything, was not English; and that which was not English one could not help secretly feeling dangerous, if not precisely bad form. It was like having the mood which the War had left, seated—dark, heavy, smiling, indifferent—in your Empire chair; it was like listening to that mood talking through thick pink lips above a little diabolic beard. It was, as Jack Cardigan expressed it—for the English character at large—"a bit too thick"—for if nothing was really worth getting excited about, there were always games, and one could make it so! Even Winifred, ever a Forsyte at heart, felt that there was nothing to be had out of such a mood of disillusionment, so that it really ought not to be there. Monsieur Profond, in fact, made the mood too plain in a country which decently veiled such realities.

When Fleur, after her hurried return from Robin Hill, came down to dinner that evening, the mood was standing at the window of Winifred's little drawing-room, looking out into Green Street, with an air of seeing nothing in it. And Fleur gazed promptly into the fireplace with an air of seeing a fire which was not there.

Monsieur Profond came from the window. He was in full fig, with a white waistcoat and a white flower in his buttonhole.

"Well, Miss Forsyde," he said, "I'm awful pleased to see you. Mr. Forsyde well? I was sayin' to-day I want to see him have some pleasure. He worries."

"You think so?" said Fleur shortly.

"Worries," repeated Monsieur Profond, burring the r's.

Fleur spun round. "Shall I tell you," she said, "what would give him pleasure?" But the words, "To hear that you had cleared out," died at the expression on his face. All his fine white teeth were showing.

"I was hearin' at the Club to-day about his old trouble." Fleur opened her eyes. "What do you mean?"

Monsieur Profond moved his sleek head as if to minimize his statement.

"Before you were born," he said; "that small business."

Though conscious that he had cleverly diverted her from his own share in her father's worry, Fleur was unable to withstand a rush of nervous curiosity. "Tell me what you heard."

"Why!" murmured Monsieur Profond, "you know all that."

"I expect I do. But I should like to know that you haven't heard it all wrong."

"His first wife," murmured Monsieur Profond.

Choking back the words, "He was never married before," she said: "Well, what about her?"

"Mr. George Forsyde was tellin' me about your father's first wife marryin' his cousin Jolyon afterward. It was a small bit unpleasant, I should think. I saw their boy—nice boy!"

Fleur looked up. Monsieur Profond was swimming, heavily diabolical, before her. That— the reason! With the most heroic effort of her life so far, she managed to arrest that swimming figure. She could not tell whether he had noticed. And just then Winifred came in.

"Oh! here you both are already; Imogen and I have had the most amusing afternoon at the Babies' bazaar."

"What babies?" said Fleur mechanically.

"The 'Save the Babies.' I got such a bargain, my dear. A piece of old Armenian work— from before the Flood. I want your opinion on it, Prosper."

"Auntie," whispered Fleur suddenly.

At the tone in the girl's voice Winifred closed in on her.'

"What's the matter? Aren't you well?"

Monsieur Profond had withdrawn into the window, where he was practically out of hearing.

"Auntie, he-he told me that father has been married before. Is it true that he divorced her, and she married Jon Forsyte's father?"

Never in all the life of the mother of four little Darties had Winifred felt more seriously embarrassed. Her niece's face was so pale, her eyes so dark, her voice so whispery and strained.

"Your father didn't wish you to hear," she said, with all the aplomb she could muster. "These things will happen. I've often told him he ought to let you know."

"Oh!" said Fleur, and that was all, but it made Winifred pat her shoulder—a firm little shoulder, nice and white! She never could help an appraising eye and touch in the matter of her niece, who would have to be married, of course—though not to that boy Jon.

"We've forgotten all about it years and years ago," she said comfortably. "Come and have dinner!"

"No, Auntie. I don't feel very well. May I go upstairs?"

"My dear!" murmured Winifred, concerned, "you're not taking this to heart? Why, you haven't properly come out yet! That boy's a child!"

"What boy? I've only got a headache. But I can't stand that man to-night."

"Well, well," said Winifred, "go and lie down. I'll send you some bromide, and I shall talk to Prosper Profond. What business had he to gossip? Though I must say I think it's much better you should know."

Fleur smiled. "Yes," she said, and slipped from the room.

She went up with her head whirling, a dry sensation in her throat, a guttered frightened feeling in her breast. Never in her life as yet had she suffered from even momentary fear that she would not get what she had set her heart on. The sensations of the afternoon had been full and poignant, and this gruesome discovery coming on the top of them had really made her head ache. No wonder her father had hidden that photograph, so secretly behind her own-ashamed of having kept it! But could he hate Jon's mother and yet keep her photograph? She pressed her hands over her forehead, trying to see things clearly. Had they told Jon—had her visit to Robin Hill forced them to tell him? Everything now turned on that! She knew, they all knew, except—perhaps—Jon!

She walked up and down, biting her lip and thinking desperately hard. Jon loved his mother. If they had told him, what would he do? She could not tell. But if they had not told him, should she not—could she not get him for herself—get married to him, before he knew? She searched her memories of Robin Hill. His mother's face so passive—with its dark eyes and as if powdered hair, its reserve, its smile—baffled her; and his father's—kindly, sunken, ironic. Instinctively she felt they would shrink from telling Jon, even now, shrink from hurting him—for of course it would hurt him awfully to know!

Her aunt must be made not to tell her father that she knew. So long as neither she herself nor Jon were supposed to know, there was still a chance—freedom to cover one's tracks, and get what her heart was set on. But she was almost overwhelmed by her isolation. Every one's hand was against her—every one's! It was as Jon had said—he and she just wanted to live and the past was in their way, a past they hadn't shared in, and didn't understand! Oh! What a shame! And suddenly she thought of June. Would she help them? For somehow June had left on her the impression that she would be sympathetic with their love, impatient of obstacle. Then, instinctively, she thought: 'I won't give anything away, though, even to her. I daren't. I mean to have Jon; against them all.'

Soup was brought up to her, and one of Winifred's pet headache cachets. She swallowed both. Then Winifred herself appeared. Fleur opened her campaign with the words:

"You know, Auntie, I do wish people wouldn't think I'm in love with that boy. Why, I've hardly seen him!"

Winifred, though experienced, was not "fine." She accepted the remark with considerable relief. Of course, it was not pleasant for the girl to hear of the family scandal, and she set herself to minimise the matter, a task for which she was eminently qualified, "raised" fashionably under a comfortable mother and a father whose nerves might not be shaken, and for many years the wife of Montague Dartie. Her description was a masterpiece of understatement. Fleur's father's first wife had been very foolish. There had been a young man who had got run over, and she had left Fleur's father. Then, years after, when it might all have come—right again, she had taken up with their cousin Jolyon; and, of course, her father had been obliged to have a divorce. Nobody remembered anything of it now, except just the family. And, perhaps, it had all turned out for the best; her father had Fleur; and Jolyon and Irene had been quite happy, they said, and their boy was a nice boy. "Val having Holly, too, is a sort of plaster, don't you know?" With these soothing words, Winifred patted her niece's shoulder; thought: 'She's a nice, plump little thing!' and went back to Prosper Profond, who, in spite of his indiscretion, was very "amusing" this evening.

For some minutes after her aunt had gone Fleur remained under influence of bromide material and spiritual. But then reality came back. Her aunt had left out all that mattered—all the feeling, the hate, the love, the unforgivingness of passionate hearts. She, who knew so little of life, and had touched only the fringe of love, was yet aware by instinct that words have as little relation to fact and feeling as coin to the bread it buys. 'Poor Father!' she thought. 'Poor me! Poor Jon! But I don't care, I mean to have him!' From the window of her darkened room she saw "that man" issue from the door below and "prowl" away. If he and her mother—how would that affect her chance? Surely it must make her father cling to her more closely, so that he would consent in the end to anything she wanted, or become reconciled the sooner to what she did without his knowledge.

She took some earth from the flower-box in the window, and with all her might flung it after that disappearing figure. It fell short, but the action did her good.

And a little puff of air came up from Green Street, smelling of petrol, not sweet.

CHAPTER V.—PURELY FORSYTE AFFAIRS

Soames, coming up to the City, with the intention of calling in at Green Street at the end of his day and taking Fleur back home with him, suffered from rumination. Sleeping partner that he was, he seldom visited the City now, but he still had a room of his own at Cuthcott, Kingson and Forsyte's, and one special clerk and a half assigned to the management of purely Forsyte affairs. They were somewhat in flux just now—an auspicious moment for the disposal of house property. And Soames was unloading the estates of his father and Uncle Roger, and to some extent of his Uncle Nicholas. His shrewd and matter-of-course probity in all money concerns had made him something of an autocrat in connection with these trusts. If Soames thought this or thought that, one had better save oneself the bother of thinking too. He guaranteed, as it were, irresponsibility to numerous Forsytes of the third and fourth generations. His fellow trustees, such as his cousins Roger or Nicholas, his cousins-in-law Tweetyman and Spender, or his sister Cicely's husband, all trusted him; he signed first, and where he signed first they signed after, and nobody was a penny the worse. Just now they were all a good many pennies the better, and Soames was beginning to see the close of certain trusts, except for distribution of the income from securities as gilt-edged as was compatible with the period.

Passing the more feverish parts of the City toward the most perfect backwater in London, he ruminated. Money was extraordinarily tight; and morality extraordinarily loose! The War had done it. Banks were not lending; people breaking contracts all over the place. There was a feeling in the air and a look on faces that he did not like. The country seemed in for a spell of gambling and bankruptcies. There was satisfaction in the thought that neither he nor his trusts had an investment which could be affected by anything less maniacal than national repudiation or a levy on capital. If Soames had faith, it was in what he called "English common sense"—or the power to have things, if not one way then another. He might—like his father James before him—say he didn't know what things were coming to, but he never in his heart believed they were. If it rested with him, they wouldn't—and, after all, he was only an Englishman like any other, so quietly tenacious of what he had that he knew he would never really part with it without something more or less equivalent in exchange. His mind was essentially equilibristic in material matters, and his way of putting the national situation difficult to refute in a world composed of human beings. Take his own case, for example! He was well off. Did that do anybody harm? He did not eat ten meals a day; he ate no more than, perhaps not so much as, a poor man. He spent no money on vice; breathed no more air, used no more water to speak of than the mechanic or the porter. He certainly had pretty things about him, but they had given employment in the making, and somebody must use them. He bought pictures, but Art must be encouraged. He was, in fact, an accidental channel through which money flowed, employing labour. What was there objectionable in that? In his charge money was in quicker and more useful flux than it would be in charge of the State and a lot of slow-fly money-sucking officials. And as to what he saved each year—it was just as much in flux as what he didn't save, going into Water Board or Council Stocks, or something sound and useful. The State paid him no salary for being trustee of his own or other people's money he did all that for nothing. Therein lay the whole case against nationalisation—owners of private property were unpaid, and yet had every incentive to quicken up the flux. Under nationalisation—just the opposite! In a country smarting from officialism he felt that he had a strong case.

It particularly annoyed him, entering that backwater of perfect peace, to think that a lot of unscrupulous Trusts and Combinations had been cornering the market in goods of all kinds, and keeping prices at an artificial height. Such abusers of the individualistic system were the ruffians who caused all the trouble, and it was some satisfaction to see them getting into a stew at last lest the whole thing might come down with a run—and land them in the soup.

The offices of Cuthcott, Kingson and Forsyte occupied the ground and first floors of a house on the right-hand side; and, ascending to his room, Soames thought: 'Time we had a coat of paint.'

His old clerk Gradman was seated, where he always was, at a huge bureau with countless pigeonholes. Half-the-clerk stood beside him, with a broker's note recording investment of the proceeds from sale of the Bryanston Square house, in Roger Forsyte's estate. Soames took it, and said:

"Vancouver City Stock. H'm. It's down today!"

With a sort of grating ingratiation old Gradman answered him:

"Ye-es; but everything's down, Mr. Soames." And half-the-clerk withdrew.

Soames skewered the document on to a number of other papers and hung up his hat.

"I want to look at my Will and Marriage Settlement, Gradman."

Old Gradman, moving to the limit of his swivel chair, drew out two drafts from the bottom lefthand drawer. Recovering his body, he raised his grizzle-haired face, very red from stooping.

"Copies, Sir."

Soames took them. It struck him suddenly how like Gradman was to the stout brindled yard dog they had been wont to keep on his chain at The Shelter, till one day Fleur had come and insisted it should be let loose, so that it had at once bitten the cook and been destroyed. If you let Gradman off his chain, would he bite the cook?

Checking this frivolous fancy, Soames unfolded his Marriage Settlement. He had not looked at it for over eighteen years, not since he remade his Will when his father died and Fleur was born. He wanted to see whether the words "during coverture" were in. Yes, they were—odd expression, when you thought of it, and derived perhaps from horse-breeding! Interest on fifteen thousand pounds (which he paid her without deducting income tax) so long as she remained his wife, and afterward during widowhood "dum casta"—old-fashioned and rather pointed words, put in to insure the conduct of Fleur's mother. His Will made it up to an annuity of a thousand under the same conditions. All right! He returned the copies to Gradman, who took them without looking up, swung the chair, restored the papers to their drawer, and went on casting up.

"Gradman! I don't like the condition of the country; there are a lot of people about without any common sense. I want to find a way by which I can safeguard Miss Fleur against anything which might arise."

Gradman wrote the figure "2" on his blotting-paper.

"Ye-es," he said; "there's a nahsty spirit."

"The ordinary restraint against anticipation doesn't meet the case."

"Nao," said Gradman.

"Suppose those Labour fellows come in, or worse! It's these people with fixed ideas who are the danger. Look at Ireland!"

"Ah!" said Gradman.

"Suppose I were to make a settlement on her at once with myself as beneficiary for life, they couldn't take anything but the interest from me, unless of course they alter the law."

Gradman moved his head and smiled.

"Ah!" he said, "they wouldn't do tha-at!"

"I don't know," muttered Soames; "I don't trust them."

"It'll take two years, sir, to be valid against death duties."

Soames sniffed. Two years! He was only sixty-five!

"That's not the point. Draw a form of settlement that passes all my property to Miss Fleur's children in equal shares, with antecedent life-interests first to myself and then to her without power of anticipation, and add a clause that in the event of anything happening to divert her life-interest, that interest passes to the trustees, to apply for her benefit, in their absolute discretion."

Gradman grated: "Rather extreme at your age, sir; you lose control."

"That's my business," said Soames sharply.

Gradman wrote on a piece of paper: "Life-interest—anticipation—divert interest—absolute discretion...." and said:

"What trustees? There's young Mr. Kingson; he's a nice steady young fellow."

"Yes, he might do for one. I must have three. There isn't a Forsyte now who appeals to me."

"Not young Mr. Nicholas? He's at the Bar. We've given 'im briefs."

"He'll never set the Thames on fire," said Soames.

A smile oozed out on Gradman's face, greasy from countless mutton-chops, the smile of a man who sits all day.

"You can't expect it, at his age, Mr. Soames."

"Why? What is he? Forty?"

"Ye-es, quite a young fellow."

"Well, put him in; but I want somebody who'll take a personal interest. There's no one that I can see."

"What about Mr. Valerius, now he's come home?"

"Val Dartie? With that father?"

"We-ell," murmured Gradman, "he's been dead seven years—the Statute runs against him."

"No," said Soames. "I don't like the connection." He rose. Gradman said suddenly:

"If they were makin' a levy on capital, they could come on the trustees, sir. So there you'd be just the same. I'd think it over, if I were you."

"That's true," said Soames. "I will. What have you done about that dilapidation notice in Vere Street?"

"I 'aven't served it yet. The party's very old. She won't want to go out at her age."

"I don't know. This spirit of unrest touches every one."

"Still, I'm lookin' at things broadly, sir. She's eighty-one."

"Better serve it," said Soames, "and see what she says. Oh! and Mr. Timothy? Is everything in order in case of—"

"I've got the inventory of his estate all ready; had the furniture and pictures valued so that we know what reserves to put on. I shall be sorry when he goes, though. Dear me! It is a time since I first saw Mr. Timothy!"

"We can't live for ever," said Soames, taking down his hat.

"Nao," said Gradman; "but it'll be a pity—the last of the old family! Shall I take up the matter of that nuisance in Old Compton Street? Those organs—they're nahsty things."

"Do. I must call for Miss Fleur and catch the four o'clock. Good-day, Gradman."

"Good-day, Mr. Soames. I hope Miss Fleur—"

"Well enough, but gads about too much."

"Ye-es," grated Gradman; "she's young."

Soames went out, musing: "Old Gradman! If he were younger I'd put him in the trust. There's nobody I can depend on to take a real interest."

Leaving the bilious and mathematical exactitude, the preposterous peace of that backwater, he thought suddenly: 'During coverture! Why can't they exclude fellows like Profond, instead of a lot of hard-working Germans?' and was surprised at the depth of uneasiness which could provoke so unpatriotic a thought. But there it was! One never got a moment of real peace. There was always something at the back of everything! And he made his way toward Green Street.

Two hours later by his watch, Thomas Gradman, stirring in his swivel chair, closed the last drawer of his bureau, and putting into his waistcoat pocket a bunch of keys so fat that they gave him a protuberance on the liver side, brushed his old top hat round with his sleeve, took his umbrella, and descended. Thick, short, and buttoned closely into his old frock coat, he walked toward Covent Garden market. He never missed that daily promenade to the Tube for Highgate, and seldom some critical transaction on the way in connection with vegetables and fruit. Generations might be born, and hats might change, wars be fought, and Forsytes fade away, but Thomas Gradman, faithful and grey, would take his daily walk and buy his daily vegetable. Times were not what they were, and his son had lost a leg, and they never gave him those nice little plaited baskets to carry the stuff in now, and these Tubes were convenient things—still he mustn't complain; his health was good considering his time of life, and after fifty-four years in the Law he was getting a round eight hundred a year and a little worried of late, because it was mostly collector's commission on the rents, and with all this conversion of Forsyte property going on, it looked like drying up, and the price of living still so high; but it was no good worrying—"The good God made us all"—as he was in the habit of saying; still, house property in London—he didn't know what Mr. Roger or Mr. James would say if they could see it being sold like this—seemed to show a lack of faith; but Mr. Soames—he worried. Life and lives in being and twenty-one years after—beyond that you couldn't go; still, he kept his health wonderfully—and Miss Fleur was a pretty little thing—she was; she'd marry; but lots of people had no children nowadays—he had had his first child at twenty-two; and Mr. Jolyon, married while he was at Cambridge, had his child the same year—gracious Peter! That was back in '69, a long time before old Mr. Jolyon—fine judge of property—had taken his Will away from Mr. James—dear, yes! Those were the days when they were buyin' property right and left, and none of this khaki and fallin' over one another to get out of things; and cucumbers at twopence; and a melon—the old melons, that made your mouth water! Fifty years since he went into Mr. James' office, and Mr. James had said to him: "Now, Gradman, you're only a shaver—you pay attention, and you'll make your five hundred a year before you've done." And he had, and feared God, and served the Forsytes, and kept a vegetable diet at night. And, buying a copy of John Bull—not that he approved of it, an extravagant affair—he entered the Tube elevator with his mere brown-paper parcel, and was borne down into the bowels of the earth.

CHAPTER VI.—SOAMES' PRIVATE LIFE

On his way to Green Street it occurred to Soames that he ought to go into Dumetrius' in Suffolk Street about the possibility of the Bolderby Old Crome. Almost worth while to have fought the war to have the Bolderby Old Crome, as it were, in flux! Old Bolderby had died, his son and grandson had been killed—a cousin was coming into the estate, who meant to sell it, some said because of the condition of England, others said because he had asthma.

If Dumetrius once got hold of it the price would become prohibitive; it was necessary for Soames to find out whether Dumetrius had got it, before he tried to get it himself. He therefore confined himself to discussing with Dumetrius whether Monticellis would come again now that it was the fashion for a picture to be anything except a picture; and the future of Johns, with a side-slip into Buxton Knights. It was only when leaving that he added: "So they're not selling the Bolderby Old Crome, after all?" In sheer pride of racial superiority, as he had calculated would be the case, Dumetrius replied:

"Oh! I shall get it, Mr. Forsyte, sir!"

The flutter of his eyelid fortified Soames in a resolution to write direct to the new Bolderby, suggesting that the only dignified way of dealing with an Old Crome was to avoid dealers. He therefore said, "Well, good-day!" and went, leaving Dumetrius the wiser.

At Green Street he found that Fleur was out and would be all the evening; she was staying one more night in London. He cabbed on dejectedly, and caught his train.

He reached his house about six o'clock. The air was heavy, midges biting, thunder about. Taking his letters he went up to his dressing-room to cleanse himself of London.

An uninteresting post. A receipt, a bill for purchases on behalf of Fleur. A circular about an exhibition of etchings. A letter beginning:

"SIR,

"I feel it my duty..."

That would be an appeal or something unpleasant. He looked at once for the signature. There was none! Incredulously he turned the page over and examined each corner. Not being a public man, Soames had never yet had an anonymous letter, and his first impulse was to tear it up, as a dangerous thing; his second to read it, as a thing still more dangerous.

"SIR,

"I feel it my duty to inform you that having no interest in the matter your lady is carrying on with a foreigner—"

Reaching that word Soames stopped mechanically and examined the postmark. So far as he could pierce the impenetrable disguise in which the Post Office had wrapped it, there was something with a "sea" at the end and a "t" in it. Chelsea? No! Battersea? Perhaps! He read on.

"These foreigners are all the same. Sack the lot. This one meets your lady twice a week. I know it of my own knowledge—and to see an Englishman put on goes against the grain. You watch it and see if what I say isn't true. I shouldn't meddle if it wasn't a dirty foreigner that's in it.

"Yours obedient."

The sensation with which Soames dropped the letter was similar to that he would have had entering his bedroom and finding it full of black-beetles. The meanness of anonymity gave a shuddering obscenity to the moment. And the worst of it was that this shadow had been at the back of his mind ever since the Sunday evening when Fleur had pointed down at Prosper Profond strolling on the lawn, and said: "Prowling cat!" Had he not in connection therewith, this very day, perused his Will and Marriage Settlement? And now this anonymous ruffian, with nothing to gain, apparently, save the venting of his spite against foreigners, had wrenched it out of the obscurity in which he had hoped and wished it would remain. To have such knowledge forced on him, at his time of life, about Fleur's mother! He picked the letter up from the carpet, tore it across, and then, when it hung together by just the fold at the back, stopped tearing, and reread it. He was taking at that moment one of the decisive resolutions of his life. He would not be forced into another scandal. No! However he decided to deal with this matter—and it required the most far-sighted and careful consideration he would do nothing that might injure Fleur. That resolution taken, his mind answered the helm again, and he made his ablutions. His hands trembled as he dried them. Scandal he would not have, but something must be done to stop this sort of thing! He went into his wife's room and stood looking around him. The idea of searching for anything which would incriminate, and entitle him to hold a menace over her, did not even come to him. There would be nothing—she was much too practical. The idea of having her watched had been dismissed before it came—too well he remembered his previous experience of that. No! He had nothing but this torn-up letter from some anonymous ruffian, whose impudent intrusion into his private life he so violently resented. It was repugnant to him to make use of it, but he might have to. What a mercy Fleur was not at home to-night! A tap on the door broke up his painful cogitations.

"Mr. Michael Mont, sir, is in the drawing-room. Will you see him?"

"No," said Soames; "yes. I'll come down."

Anything that would take his mind off for a few minutes!

Michael Mont in flannels stood on the verandah smoking a cigarette. He threw it away as Soames came up, and ran his hand through his hair.

Soames' feeling toward this young man was singular. He was no doubt a rackety, irresponsible young fellow according to old standards, yet somehow likeable, with his extraordinarily cheerful way of blurting out his opinions.

"Come in," he said; "have you had tea?"

Mont came in.

"I thought Fleur would have been back, sir; but I'm glad she isn't. The fact is, I—I'm fearfully gone on her; so fearfully gone that I thought you'd better know. It's old-fashioned, of course, coming to fathers first, but I thought you'd forgive that. I went to my own Dad, and he says if I settle down he'll see me through. He rather cottons to the idea, in fact. I told him about your Goya."

"Oh!" said Soames, inexpressibly dry. "He rather cottons?"

"Yes, sir; do you?"

Soames smiled faintly.

"You see," resumed Mont, twiddling his straw hat, while his hair, ears, eyebrows, all seemed to stand up from excitement, "when you've been through the War you can't help being in a hurry."

"To get married; and unmarried afterward," said Soames slowly.

"Not from Fleur, sir. Imagine, if you were me!"

Soames cleared his throat. That way of putting it was forcible enough.

"Fleur's too young," he said.

"Oh! no, sir. We're awfully old nowadays. My Dad seems to me a perfect babe; his thinking apparatus hasn't turned a hair. But he's a Baronight, of course; that keeps him back."

"Baronight," repeated Soames; "what may that be?"

"Bart, sir. I shall be a Bart some day. But I shall live it down, you know."

"Go away and live this down," said Soames.

Young Mont said imploringly: "Oh! no, sir. I simply must hang around, or I shouldn't have a dog's chance. You'll let Fleur do what she likes, I suppose, anyway. Madame passes me."

"Indeed!" said Soames frigidly.

"You don't really bar me, do you?" and the young man looked so doleful that Soames smiled.

"You may think you're very old," he said; "but you strike me as extremely young. To rattle ahead of everything is not a proof of maturity."

"All right, sir; I give you our age. But to show you I mean business—I've got a job."

"Glad to hear it."

"Joined a publisher; my governor is putting up the stakes."

Soames put his hand over his mouth—he had so very nearly said: "God help the publisher!" His grey eyes scrutinised the agitated young man.

"I don't dislike you, Mr. Mont, but Fleur is everything to me: Everything—do you understand?"

"Yes, sir, I know; but so she is to me."

"That's as may be. I'm glad you've told me, however. And now I think there's nothing more to be said."

"I know it rests with her, sir."

"It will rest with her a long time, I hope."

"You aren't cheering," said Mont suddenly.

"No," said Soames, "my experience of life has not made me anxious to couple people in a hurry. Good-night, Mr. Mont. I shan't tell Fleur what you've said."

"Oh!" murmured Mont blankly; "I really could knock my brains out for want of her. She knows that perfectly well."

"I dare say." And Soames held out his hand. A distracted squeeze, a heavy sigh, and soon after sounds from the young man's motor-cycle called up visions of flying dust and broken bones.

'The younger generation!' he thought heavily, and went out on to the lawn. The gardeners had been mowing, and there was still the smell of fresh-cut grass—the thundery air kept all scents close to earth. The sky was of a purplish hue—the poplars black. Two or three boats passed on the river, scuttling, as it were, for shelter before the storm. 'Three days' fine weather,' thought Soames, 'and then a storm!' Where was Annette? With that chap, for all he knew—she was a young woman! Impressed with the queer charity of that thought, he entered the summerhouse and sat down. The fact was—and he admitted it—Fleur was so much to him that his wife was very little—very little; French—had never been much more than a mistress, and he was getting indifferent to that side of things! It was odd how, with all this ingrained care for moderation and secure investment, Soames ever put his emotional eggs into one basket. First Irene—now Fleur. He was dimly conscious of it, sitting there, conscious of its odd dangerousness. It had brought him to wreck and scandal once, but now—now it should save him! He cared so much for Fleur that he would have no further scandal. If only he could get at that anonymous letter-writer, he would teach him not to meddle and stir up mud at the bottom of water which he wished should remain stagnant!... A distant flash, a low rumble, and large drops of rain spattered on the thatch above him. He remained indifferent, tracing a pattern with his finger on the dusty surface of a little rustic table. Fleur's future! 'I want fair sailing for her,' he thought. 'Nothing else matters at my time of life.' A lonely business—life! What you had you never could keep to yourself! As you warned one off, you let another in. One could make sure of nothing! He reached up and pulled a red rambler rose from a cluster which blocked the window.

Flowers grew and dropped—Nature was a queer thing! The thunder rumbled and crashed, travelling east along a river, the paling flashes flicked his eyes; the poplar tops showed sharp and dense against the sky, a heavy shower rustled and rattled and veiled in the little house wherein he sat, indifferent, thinking.

When the storm was over, he left his retreat and went down the wet path to the river bank.

Two swans had come, sheltering in among the reeds. He knew the birds well, and stood watching the dignity in the curve of those white necks and formidable snake-like heads. 'Not dignified—what I have to do!' he thought. And yet it must be tackled, lest worse befell. Annette must be back by now from wherever she had gone, for it was nearly dinner-time, and as the moment for seeing her approached, the difficulty of knowing what to say and how to say it had increased. A new and scaring thought occurred to him. Suppose she wanted her liberty to marry this fellow! Well, if she did, she couldn't have it. He had not married her for that. The image of Prosper Profond dawdled before him reassuringly. Not a marrying man! No, no! Anger replaced that momentary scare. 'He had better not come my way,' he thought. The mongrel represented—! But what did Prosper Profond represent? Nothing that mattered surely. And yet something real enough in the world— unmorality let off its chain, disillusionment on the prowl! That expression Annette had caught from him: "Je m'en fiche!" A fatalistic chap! A continental—a cosmopolitan—a product of the age! If there were condemnation more complete, Soames felt that he did not know it.

The swans had turned their heads, and were looking past him into some distance of their own. One of them uttered a little hiss, wagged its tail, turned as if answering to a rudder, and swam away. The other followed. Their white bodies, their stately necks, passed out of his sight, and he went toward the house.

Annette was in the drawing-room, dressed for dinner, and he thought as he went up-stairs 'Handsome is as handsome does.' Handsome! Except for remarks about the curtains in the drawing-room, and the storm, there was practically no conversation during a meal distinguished by exactitude of quantity and perfection of quality. Soames drank nothing. He followed her into the drawing-room afterward, and found her smoking a cigarette on the sofa between the two French windows. She was leaning back, almost upright, in a low black frock, with her knees crossed and her blue eyes half-closed; grey-blue smoke issued from her red, rather full lips, a fillet bound her chestnut hair, she wore the thinnest silk stockings, and shoes with very high heels showing off her instep. A fine piece in any room! Soames, who held that torn letter in a hand thrust deep into the side-pocket of his dinner-jacket, said:

"I'm going to shut the window; the damp's lifting in."

He did so, and stood looking at a David Cox adorning the cream-panelled wall close by.

What was she thinking of? He had never understood a woman in his life—except Fleur— and Fleur not always! His heart beat fast. But if he meant to do it, now was the moment. Turning from the David Cox, he took out the torn letter.

"I've had this."

Her eyes widened, stared at him, and hardened.

Soames handed her the letter.

"It's torn, but you can read it." And he turned back to the David Cox—a sea-piece, of good tone—but without movement enough. 'I wonder what that chap's doing at this moment?' he thought. 'I'll astonish him yet.' Out of the corner of his eye he saw Annette holding the letter rigidly; her eyes moved from side to side under her darkened lashes and frowning darkened eyes. She dropped the letter, gave a little shiver, smiled, and said:

"Dirrty!"

"I quite agree," said Soames; "degrading. Is it true?"

A tooth fastened on her red lower lip. "And what if it were?"

She was brazen!

"Is that all you have to say?"

"No."

"Well, speak out!"

"What is the good of talking?"

Soames said icily: "So you admit it?"

"I admit nothing. You are a fool to ask. A man like you should not ask. It is dangerous."

Soames made a tour of the room, to subdue his rising anger.

"Do you remember," he said, halting in front of her, "what you were when I married you? Working at accounts in a restaurant."

"Do you remember that I was not half your age?"

Soames broke off the hard encounter of their eyes, and went back to the David Cox.

"I am not going to bandy words. I require you to give up this—friendship. I think of the matter entirely as it affects Fleur."

"Ah!—Fleur!"

"Yes," said Soames stubbornly; "Fleur. She is your child as well as mine."

"It is kind to admit that!"

"Are you going to do what I say?"

"I refuse to tell you."

"Then I must make you."

Annette smiled.

"No, Soames," she said. "You are helpless. Do not say things that you will regret."

Anger swelled the veins on his forehead. He opened his mouth to vent that emotion, and could not. Annette went on:

"There shall be no more such letters, I promise you. That is enough."

Soames writhed. He had a sense of being treated like a child by this woman who had deserved he did not know what.

"When two people have married, and lived like us, Soames, they had better be quiet about each other. There are things one does not drag up into the light for people to laugh at. You will be quiet, then; not for my sake for your own. You are getting old; I am not, yet. You have made me ver-ry practical"

Soames, who had passed through all the sensations of being choked, repeated dully:

"I require you to give up this friendship."

"And if I do not?"

"Then—then I will cut you out of my Will."

Somehow it did not seem to meet the case. Annette laughed.

"You will live a long time, Soames."

"You—you are a bad woman," said Soames suddenly.

Annette shrugged her shoulders.

"I do not think so. Living with you has killed things in me, it is true; but I am not a bad woman. I am sensible—that is all. And so will you be when you have thought it over."

"I shall see this man," said Soames sullenly, "and warn him off."

"Mon cher, you are funny. You do not want me, you have as much of me as you want; and you wish the rest of me to be dead. I admit nothing, but I am not going to be dead, Soames, at my age; so you had better be quiet, I tell you. I myself will make no scandal; none. Now, I am not saying any more, whatever you do."

She reached out, took a French novel off a little table, and opened it. Soames watched her, silenced by the tumult of his feelings. The thought of that man was almost making him want her, and this was a revelation of their relationship, startling to one little given to introspective philosophy. Without saying another word he went out and up to the picture-gallery. This came of marrying a Frenchwoman! And yet, without her there would have been no Fleur! She had served her purpose.

'She's right,' he thought; 'I can do nothing. I don't even know that there's anything in it.' The instinct of self-preservation warned him to batten down his hatches, to smother the fire with want of air. Unless one believed there was something in a thing, there wasn't.

That night he went into her room. She received him in the most matter-of-fact way, as if there had been no scene between them. And he returned to his own room with a curious sense of peace. If one didn't choose to see, one needn't. And he did not choose—in future he did not choose. There was nothing to be gained by it—nothing! Opening the drawer he took from the sachet a handkerchief, and the framed photograph of Fleur. When he had looked at it a little he slipped it down, and there was that other one—that old one of Irene. An owl hooted while he stood in his window gazing at it. The owl hooted, the red climbing roses seemed to deepen in colour, there came a scent of lime-blossom. God! That had been a different thing! Passion—Memory! Dust!

CHAPTER VII.—JUNE TAKES A HAND

One who was a sculptor, a Slav, a sometime resident in New York, an egoist, and impecunious, was to be found of an evening in June Forsyte's studio on the bank of the Thames at Chiswick. On the evening of July 6, Boris Strumolowski—several of whose works were on show there because they were as yet too advanced to be on show anywhere else—had begun well, with that aloof and rather Christ-like silence which admirably suited his youthful, round, broad cheek-boned countenance framed in bright hair banged like a girl's. June had known him three weeks, and he still seemed to her the principal embodiment of genius, and hope of the future; a sort of Star of the East which had strayed into an unappreciative West. Until that evening he had conversationally confined himself to recording his impressions of the United States, whose dust he had just shaken from off his feet—a country, in his opinion, so barbarous in every way that he had sold practically nothing there, and become an object of suspicion to the police; a country, as he said, without a race of its own, without liberty, equality, or fraternity, without principles, traditions, taste, without—in a word—a soul. He had left it for his own good, and come to the only other country where he could live well. June had dwelt unhappily on him in her lonely moments, standing before his creations—frightening, but powerful and symbolic once they had been explained! That he, haloed by bright hair like an early Italian painting, and absorbed in his genius to the exclusion of all else—the only sign of course by which real genius could be told—should still be a "lame duck" agitated her warm heart almost to the exclusion of Paul Post. And she had begun to take steps to clear her Gallery, in order to fill it with Strumolowski masterpieces. She had at once encountered trouble. Paul Post had kicked; Vospovitch had stung. With all the emphasis of a genius which she did not as yet deny them, they had demanded another six weeks at least of her Gallery. The American stream, still flowing in, would soon be flowing out. The American stream was their right, their only hope, their salvation—since nobody in this "beastly" country cared for Art. June had yielded to the demonstration. After all Boris would not mind their having the full benefit of an American stream, which he himself so violently despised.

This evening she had put that to Boris with nobody else present, except Hannah Hobdey, the mediaeval black-and-whitist, and Jimmy Portugal, editor of the Neo-Artist. She had put it to him with that sudden confidence which continual contact with the neo-artistic world had never been able to dry up in her warm and generous nature. He had not broken his Christ-like silence, however, for more than two minutes before she began to move her blue eyes from side to side, as a cat moves its tail. This—he said—was characteristic of England, the most selfish country in the world; the country which sucked the blood of other countries; destroyed the brains and hearts of Irishmen, Hindus, Egyptians, Boers, and Burmese, all the best races in the world; bullying, hypocritical England! This was what he had expected, coming to, such a country, where the climate was all fog, and the people all tradesmen perfectly blind to Art, and sunk in profiteering and the grossest materialism. Conscious that Hannah Hobdey was murmuring, "Hear, hear!" and Jimmy Portugal sniggering, June grew crimson, and suddenly rapped out:

"Then why did you ever come? We didn't ask you."

The remark was so singularly at variance with all she had led him to expect from her, that Strumolowski stretched out his hand and took a cigarette.

"England never wants an idealist," he said.

But in June something primitively English was thoroughly upset; old Jolyon's sense of justice had risen, as it were, from bed. "You come and sponge on us," she said, "and then abuse us. If you think that's playing the game, I don't."

She now discovered that which others had discovered before her—the thickness of hide beneath which the sensibility of genius is sometimes veiled. Strumolowski's young and ingenuous face became the incarnation of a sneer.

"Sponge, one does not sponge, one takes what is owing—a tenth part of what is owing. You will repent to say that, Miss Forsyte."

"Oh, no," said June, "I shan't."

"Ah! We know very well, we artists—you take us to get what you can out of us. I want nothing from you"—and he blew out a cloud of June's smoke.

Decision rose in an icy puff from the turmoil of insulted shame within her. "Very well, then, you can take your things away."

And, almost in the same moment, she thought: 'Poor boy! He's only got a garret, and probably not a taxi fare. In front of these people, too; it's positively disgusting!'

Young Strumolowski shook his head violently; his hair, thick, smooth, close as a golden plate, did not fall off.

"I can live on nothing," he said shrilly; "I have often had to for the sake of my Art. It is you bourgeois who force us to spend money."

The words hit June like a pebble, in the ribs. After all she had done for Art, all her identification with its troubles and lame ducks. She was struggling for adequate words when the door was opened, and her Austrian murmured:

"A young lady, gnädiges Fräulein."

"Where?"

"In the little meal-room."

With a glance at Boris Strumolowski, at Hannah Hobdey, at Jimmy Portugal, June said nothing, and went out, devoid of equanimity. Entering the "little meal-room," she perceived the young lady to be Fleur—looking very pretty, if pale. At this disenchanted moment a little lame duck of her own breed was welcome to June, so homoeopathic by instinct.

The girl must have come, of course, because of Jon; or, if not, at least to get something out of her. And June felt just then that to assist somebody was the only bearable thing.

"So you've remembered to come," she said.

"Yes. What a jolly little duck of a house! But please don't let me bother you, if you've got people."

"Not at all," said June. "I want to let them stew in their own juice for a bit. Have you come about Jon?"

"You said you thought we ought to be told. Well, I've found out."

"Oh!" said June blankly. "Not nice, is it?"

They were standing one on each side of the little bare table at which June took her meals. A vase on it was full of Iceland poppies; the girl raised her hand and touched them with a gloved finger. To her new-fangled dress, frilly about the hips and tight below the knees, June took a sudden liking—a charming colour, flax-blue.

'She makes a picture,' thought June. Her little room, with its whitewashed walls, its floor and hearth of old pink brick, its black paint, and latticed window athwart which the last of the sunlight was shining, had never looked so charming, set off by this young figure, with the creamy, slightly frowning face. She remembered with sudden vividness how nice she herself had looked in those old days when her heart was set on Philip Bosinney, that dead lover, who had broken from her to destroy for ever Irene's allegiance to this girl's father. Did Fleur know of that, too?

"Well," she said, "what are you going to do?"

It was some seconds before Fleur answered.

"I don't want Jon to suffer. I must see him once more to put an end to it."

"You're going to put an end to it!"

"What else is there to do?"

The girl seemed to June, suddenly, intolerably spiritless.

"I suppose you're right," she muttered. "I know my father thinks so; but—I should never have done it myself. I can't take things lying down."

How poised and watchful that girl looked; how unemotional her voice sounded!

"People will assume that I'm in love."

"Well, aren't you?"

Fleur shrugged her shoulders. 'I might have known it,' thought June; 'she's Soames' daughter—fish! And yet—he!'

"What do you want me to do then?" she said with a sort of disgust.

"Could I see Jon here to-morrow on his way down to Holly's? He'd come if you sent him a line to-night. And perhaps afterward you'd let them know quietly at Robin Hill that it's all over, and that they needn't tell Jon about his mother."

"All right!" said June abruptly. "I'll write now, and you can post it. Half-past two tomorrow. I shan't be in, myself."

She sat down at the tiny bureau which filled one corner. When she looked round with the finished note Fleur was still touching the poppies with her gloved finger.

June licked a stamp. "Well, here it is. If you're not in love, of course, there's no more to be said. Jon's lucky."

Fleur took the note. "Thanks awfully!"

'Cold-blooded little baggage!' thought June. Jon, son of her father, to love, and not to be loved by the daughter of—Soames! It was humiliating!

"Is that all?"

Fleur nodded; her frills shook and trembled as she swayed toward the door.

"Good-bye!"

"Good-bye!... Little piece of fashion!" muttered June, closing the door. "That family!" And she marched back toward her studio. Boris Strumolowski had regained his Christ-like silence and Jimmy Portugal was damning everybody, except the group in whose behalf he ran the Neo-Artist. Among the condemned were Eric Cobbley, and several other "lame-duck" genii who at one time or another had held first place in the repertoire of June's aid and adoration. She experienced a sense of futility and disgust, and went to the window to let the river-wind blow those squeaky words away.

But when at length Jimmy Portugal had finished, and gone with Hannah Hobdey, she sat down and mothered young Strumolowski for half an hour, promising him a month, at least, of the American stream; so that he went away with his halo in perfect order. 'In spite of all,' June thought, 'Boris is wonderful.'

CHAPTER VIII.—THE BIT BETWEEN THE TEETH

To know that your hand is against every one's is—for some natures—to experience a sense of moral release. Fleur felt no remorse when she left June's house. Reading condemnatory resentment in her little kinswoman's blue eyes-she was glad that she had fooled her, despising June because that elderly idealist had not seen what she was after.

End it, forsooth! She would soon show them all that she was only just beginning. And she smiled to herself on the top of the bus which carried her back to Mayfair. But the smile died, squeezed out by spasms of anticipation and anxiety. Would she be able to manage Jon? She had taken the bit between her teeth, but could she make him take it too? She knew the truth and the real danger of delay—he knew neither; therein lay all the difference in the world.

'Suppose I tell him,' she thought; 'wouldn't it really be safer?' This hideous luck had no right to spoil their love; he must see that! They could not let it! People always accepted an accomplished fact in time! From that piece of philosophy—profound enough at her age—she passed to another consideration less philosophic. If she persuaded Jon to a quick and secret marriage, and he found out afterward that she had known the truth. What then? Jon hated subterfuge. Again, then, would it not be better to tell him? But the memory of his mother's face kept intruding on that impulse. Fleur was afraid. His mother had power over him; more power perhaps than she herself. Who could tell? It was too great a risk. Deep-sunk in these instinctive calculations she was carried on past Green Street as far as the Ritz Hotel. She got down there, and walked back on the Green Park side. The storm had washed every tree; they still dripped. Heavy drops fell on to her frills, and to avoid them she crossed over under the eyes of the Iseeum Club. Chancing to look up she saw Monsieur Profond with a tall stout man in the bay window. Turning into Green Street she heard her name called, and saw "that prowler" coming up. He took off his hat—a glossy "bowler" such as she particularly detested.

"Good evenin'! Miss Forsyde. Isn't there a small thing I can do for you?"

"Yes, pass by on the other side."

"I say! Why do you dislike me?"

"Do I?"

"It looks like it."

"Well, then, because you make me feel life isn't worth living."

Monsieur Profond smiled.

"Look here, Miss Forsyde, don't worry. It'll be all right. Nothing lasts."

"Things do last," cried Fleur; "with me anyhow—especially likes and dislikes."

"Well, that makes me a bit un'appy."

"I should have thought nothing could ever make you happy or unhappy."

"I don't like to annoy other people. I'm goin' on my yacht."

Fleur looked at him, startled.

"Where?"

"Small voyage to the South Seas or somewhere," said Monsieur Profond.

Fleur suffered relief and a sense of insult. Clearly he meant to convey that he was breaking with her mother. How dared he have anything to break, and yet how dared he break it?

"Good-night, Miss Forsyde! Remember me to Mrs. Dartie. I'm not so bad really. Good-night!" Fleur left him standing there with his hat raised. Stealing a look round, she saw him stroll—immaculate and heavy—back toward his Club.

'He can't even love with conviction,' she thought. 'What will Mother do?'

Her dreams that night were endless and uneasy; she rose heavy and unrested, and went at once to the study of Whitaker's Almanac. A Forsyte is instinctively aware that facts are the real crux of any situation. She might conquer Jon's prejudice, but without exact machinery to complete their desperate resolve, nothing would happen. From the invaluable tome she learned that they must each be twenty-one; or some one's consent would be necessary, which of course was unobtainable; then she became lost in directions concerning licenses, certificates, notices, districts, coming finally to the word "perjury." But that was nonsense! Who would really mind their giving wrong ages in order to be married for love! She ate hardly any breakfast, and went back to Whitaker. The more she studied the less sure she became; till, idly turning the pages, she came to Scotland. People could be married there without any of this nonsense. She had only to go and stay there twenty-one days, then Jon could come, and in front of two people they could declare themselves married. And what was more—they would be! It was far the best way; and at once she ran over her schoolfellows. There was Mary Lambe who lived in Edinburgh and was "quite a sport!"

She had a brother too. She could stay with Mary Lambe, who with her brother would serve for witnesses. She well knew that some girls would think all this unnecessary, and that all she and Jon need do was to go away together for a weekend and then say to their people: "We are married by Nature, we must now be married by Law." But Fleur was Forsyte enough to feel such a proceeding dubious, and to dread her father's face when he heard of it. Besides, she did not believe that Jon would do it; he had an opinion of her such as she could not bear to diminish. No! Mary Lambe was preferable, and it was just the time of year to go to Scotland. More at ease now she packed, avoided her aunt, and took a bus to Chiswick. She was too early, and went on to Kew Gardens. She found no peace among its flower-beds, labelled trees, and broad green spaces, and having lunched off anchovy-paste sandwiches and coffee, returned to Chiswick and rang June's bell. The Austrian admitted her to the "little meal-room." Now that she knew what she and Jon were up against, her longing for him had increased tenfold, as if he were a toy with sharp edges or dangerous paint such as they had tried to take from her as a child. If she could not have her way, and get Jon for good and all, she felt like dying of privation. By hook or crook she must and would get him! A round dim mirror of very old glass hung over the pink brick hearth. She stood looking at herself reflected in it, pale, and rather dark under the eyes; little shudders kept passing through her nerves. Then she heard the bell ring, and, stealing to the window, saw him standing on the doorstep smoothing his hair and lips, as if he too were trying to subdue the fluttering of his nerves.

She was sitting on one of the two rush-seated chairs, with her back to the door, when he came in, and she said at once—

"Sit down, Jon, I want to talk seriously."

Jon sat on the table by her side, and without looking at him she went on:

"If you don't want to lose me, we must get married."

Jon gasped.

"Why? Is there anything new?"

"No, but I felt it at Robin Hill, and among my people."

"But—" stammered Jon, "at Robin Hill—it was all smooth—and they've said nothing to me."

"But they mean to stop us. Your mother's face was enough. And my father's."

"Have you seen him since?"

Fleur nodded. What mattered a few supplementary lies?

"But," said Jon eagerly, "I can't see how they can feel like that after all these years."

Fleur looked up at him.

"Perhaps you don't love me enough." "Not love you enough! Why—!"

"Then make sure of me."

"Without telling them?"

"Not till after."

Jon was silent. How much older he looked than on that day, barely two months ago, when she first saw him—quite two years older!

"It would hurt Mother awfully," he said.

Fleur drew her hand away.

"You've got to choose."

Jon slid off the table on to his knees.

"But why not tell them? They can't really stop us, Fleur!"

"They can! I tell you, they can."

"How?"

"We're utterly dependent—by putting money pressure, and all sorts of other pressure. I'm not patient, Jon."

"But it's deceiving them."

Fleur got up.

"You can't really love me, or you wouldn't hesitate. 'He either fears his fate too much!'"

Lifting his hands to her waist, Jon forced her to sit down again. She hurried on:

"I've planned it all out. We've only to go to Scotland. When we're married they'll soon come round. People always come round to facts. Don't you see, Jon?"

"But to hurt them so awfully!"

So he would rather hurt her than those people of his! "All right, then; let me go!"

Jon got up and put his back against the door.

"I expect you're right," he said slowly; "but I want to think it over."

She could see that he was seething with feelings he wanted to express; but she did not mean to help him. She hated herself at this moment and almost hated him. Why had she to do all the work to secure their love? It wasn't fair. And then she saw his eyes, adoring and distressed.

"Don't look like that! I only don't want to lose you, Jon."

"You can't lose me so long as you want me."

"Oh, yes, I can."

Jon put his hands on her shoulders.

"Fleur, do you know anything you haven't told me?"

It was the point-blank question she had dreaded. She looked straight at him, and answered: "No." She had burnt her boats; but what did it matter, if she got him? He would forgive her. And throwing her arms round his neck, she kissed him on the lips. She was winning! She felt it in the beating of his heart against her, in the closing of his eyes. "I want to make sure! I want to make sure!" she whispered. "Promise!"

Jon did not answer. His face had the stillness of extreme trouble. At last he said:

"It's like hitting them. I must think a little, Fleur. I really must."

Fleur slipped out of his arms.

"Oh! Very well!" And suddenly she burst into tears of disappointment, shame, and overstrain. Followed five minutes of acute misery. Jon's remorse and tenderness knew no bounds; but he did not promise. Despite her will to cry, "Very well, then, if you don't love me enough-goodbye!" she dared not. From birth accustomed to her own way, this check from one so young, so tender, so devoted, baffled and surprised her. She wanted to push him away from her, to try what anger and coldness would do, and again she dared not. The knowledge that she was scheming to rush him blindfold into the irrevocable weakened everything—weakened the sincerity of pique, and the sincerity of passion; even her kisses had not the lure she wished for them. That stormy little meeting ended inconclusively.

"Will you some tea, gnadiges Fraulein?"

Pushing Jon from her, she cried out:

"No-no, thank you! I'm just going."

And before he could prevent her she was gone.

She went stealthily, mopping her gushed, stained cheeks, frightened, angry, very miserable. She had stirred Jon up so fearfully, yet nothing definite was promised or arranged! But the more uncertain and hazardous the future, the more "the will to have" worked its tentacles into the flesh of her heart—like some burrowing tick!

No one was at Green Street. Winifred had gone with Imogen to see a play which some said was allegorical, and others "very exciting, don't you know." It was because of what others said that Winifred and Imogen had gone. Fleur went on to Paddington. Through the carriage the air from the brick-kilns of West Drayton and the late hayfields fanned her still gushed cheeks. Flowers had seemed to be had for the picking; now they were all thorned and prickled. But the golden flower within the crown of spikes seemed to her tenacious spirit all the fairer and more desirable.

CHAPTER IX.—THE FAT IN THE FIRE

On reaching home Fleur found an atmosphere so peculiar that it penetrated even the perplexed aura of her own private life. Her mother was inaccessibly entrenched in a brown study; her father contemplating fate in the vinery. Neither of them had a word to throw to a dog. 'Is it because of me?' thought Fleur. 'Or because of Profond?' To her mother she said:

"What's the matter with Father?"

Her mother answered with a shrug of her shoulders.

To her father:

"What's the matter with Mother?"

Her father answered:

"Matter? What should be the matter?" and gave her a sharp look.

"By the way," murmured Fleur, "Monsieur Profond is going a 'small' voyage on his yacht, to the South Seas."

Soames examined a branch on which no grapes were growing.

"This vine's a failure," he said. "I've had young Mont here. He asked me something about you."

"Oh! How do you like him, Father?"

"He—he's a product—like all these young people."

"What were you at his age, dear?"

Soames smiled grimly.

"We went to work, and didn't play about—flying and motoring, and making love."

"Didn't you ever make love?"

She avoided looking at him while she said that, but she saw him well enough. His pale face had reddened, his eyebrows, where darkness was still mingled with the grey, had come close together.

"I had no time or inclination to philander."

"Perhaps you had a grand passion."

Soames looked at her intently.

"Yes—if you want to know—and much good it did me." He moved away, along by the hot-water pipes. Fleur tiptoed silently after him.

"Tell me about it, Father!"

Soames became very still.

"What should you want to know about such things, at your age?"

"Is she alive?"

He nodded.

"And married?"

"Yes."

"It's Jon Forsyte's mother, isn't it? And she was your wife first."

It was said in a flash of intuition. Surely his opposition came from his anxiety that she should not know of that old wound to his pride. But she was startled. To see some one so old and calm wince as if struck, to hear so sharp a note of pain in his voice!

"Who told you that? If your aunt! I can't bear the affair talked of."

"But, darling," said Fleur, softly, "it's so long ago."

"Long ago or not, I...."

Fleur stood stroking his arm.

"I've tried to forget," he said suddenly; "I don't wish to be reminded." And then, as if venting some long and secret irritation, he added: "In these days people don't understand. Grand passion, indeed! No one knows what it is."

"I do," said Fleur, almost in a whisper.

Soames, who had turned his back on her, spun round.

"What are you talking of—a child like you!"

"Perhaps I've inherited it, Father."

"What?"

"For her son, you see."

He was pale as a sheet, and she knew that she was as bad. They stood staring at each other in the steamy heat, redolent of the mushy scent of earth, of potted geranium, and of vines coming along fast.

"This is crazy," said Soames at last, between dry lips.

Scarcely moving her own, she murmured:

"Don't be angry, Father. I can't help it."

But she could see he wasn't angry; only scared, deeply scared.

"I thought that foolishness," he stammered, "was all forgotten."

"Oh, no! It's ten times what it was."

Soames kicked at the hot-water pipe. The hapless movement touched her, who had no fear of her father—none.

"Dearest!" she said. "What must be, must, you know."

"Must!" repeated Soames. "You don't know what you're talking of. Has that boy been told?"

The blood rushed into her cheeks.

"Not yet."

He had turned from her again, and, with one shoulder a little raised, stood staring fixedly at a joint in the pipes.

"It's most distasteful to me," he said suddenly; "nothing could be more so. Son of that fellow! It's—it's—perverse!"

She had noted, almost unconsciously, that he did not say "son of that woman," and again her intuition began working.

Did the ghost of that grand passion linger in some corner of his heart?

She slipped her hand under his arm.

"Jon's father is quite ill and old; I saw him."

"You—?"

"Yes, I went there with Jon; I saw them both."

"Well, and what did they say to you?"

"Nothing. They were very polite."

"They would be." He resumed his contemplation of the pipe-joint, and then said suddenly: "I must think this over—I'll speak to you again to-night."

She knew this was final for the moment, and stole away, leaving him still looking at the pipe-joint. She wandered into the fruit-garden, among the raspberry and currant bushes, without impetus to pick and eat. Two months ago—she was light-hearted! Even two days ago—light-hearted, before Prosper Profond told her. Now she felt tangled in a web-of passions, vested rights, oppressions and revolts, the ties of love and hate. At this dark moment of discouragement there seemed, even to her hold-fast nature, no way out. How deal with it—how sway and bend things to her will, and get her heart's desire? And, suddenly, round the corner of the high box hedge, she came plump on her mother, walking swiftly, with an open letter in her hand. Her bosom was heaving, her eyes dilated, her cheeks flushed. Instantly Fleur thought: 'The yacht! Poor Mother!'

Annette gave her a wide startled look, and said:

"J'ai la migraine."

"I'm awfully sorry, Mother."

"Oh, yes! you and your father—sorry!"

"But, Mother—I am. I know what it feels like."

Annette's startled eyes grew wide, till the whites showed above them.

"Poor innocent!" she said.

Her mother—so self-possessed, and commonsensical—to look and speak like this! It was all frightening! Her father, her mother, herself! And only two months back they had seemed to have everything they wanted in this world.

Annette crumpled the letter in her hand. Fleur knew that she must ignore the sight.

"Can't I do anything for your head, Mother?"

Annette shook that head and walked on, swaying her hips.

'It's cruel,' thought Fleur, 'and I was glad! That man! What do men come prowling for, disturbing everything! I suppose he's tired of her. What business has he to be tired of my mother? What business!' And at that thought, so natural and so peculiar, she uttered a little choked laugh.

She ought, of course, to be delighted, but what was there to be delighted at? Her father didn't really care! Her mother did, perhaps? She entered the orchard, and sat down under a cherry-tree. A breeze sighed in the higher boughs; the sky seen through their green was very blue and very white in cloud—those heavy white clouds almost always present in river landscape. Bees, sheltering out of the wind, hummed softly, and over the lush grass fell the thick shade from those fruit-trees planted by her father five-and-twenty, years ago. Birds were almost silent, the cuckoos had ceased to sing, but wood-pigeons were cooing. The breath and drone and cooing of high summer were not for long a sedative to her excited nerves. Crouched over her knees she began to scheme. Her father must be made to back her up. Why should he mind so long as she was happy? She had not lived for nearly nineteen years without knowing that her future was all he really cared about. She had, then, only to convince him that her future could not be happy without Jon. He thought it a mad fancy. How foolish the old were, thinking they could tell what the young felt! Had not he confessed that he—when young—had loved with a grand passion? He ought to understand! 'He piles up his money for me,' she thought; 'but what's the use, if I'm not going to be happy?' Money, and all it bought, did not bring happiness. Love only brought that. The ox-eyed daisies in this orchard, which gave it such a moony look sometimes, grew wild and happy, and had their hour. 'They oughtn't to have called me Fleur,' she mused, 'if they didn't mean me to have my hour, and be happy while it lasts.' Nothing real stood in the way, like poverty, or disease—sentiment only, a ghost from the unhappy past! Jon was right. They wouldn't let you live, these old people! They made mistakes, committed crimes, and wanted their children to go on paying! The breeze died away; midges began to bite. She got up, plucked a piece of honeysuckle, and went in.

It was hot that night. Both she and her mother had put on thin, pale low frocks. The dinner flowers were pale. Fleur was struck with the pale look of everything; her father's face, her mother's shoulders; the pale panelled walls, the pale grey velvety carpet, the lamp-shade, even the soup was pale. There was not one spot of colour in the room, not even wine in the pale glasses, for no one drank it. What was not pale was black—her father's clothes, the butler's clothes, her retriever stretched out exhausted in the window, the curtains black with a cream pattern. A moth came in, and that was pale. And silent was that half-mourning dinner in the heat.

Her father called her back as she was following her mother out.

She sat down beside him at the table, and, unpinning the pale honeysuckle, put it to her nose.

"I've been thinking," he said.

"Yes, dear?"

"It's extremely painful for me to talk, but there's no help for it. I don't know if you understand how much you are to me I've never spoken of it, I didn't think it necessary; but—but you're everything. Your mother—" he paused, staring at his finger-bowl of Venetian glass.

"Yes?"'

"I've only you to look to. I've never had—never wanted anything else, since you were born."

"I know," Fleur murmured.

Soames moistened his lips.

"You may think this a matter I can smooth over and arrange for you. You're mistaken. I'm helpless."

Fleur did not speak.

"Quite apart from my own feelings," went on Soames with more resolution, "those two are not amenable to anything I can say. They—they hate me, as people always hate those whom they have injured." "But he—Jon—"

"He's their flesh and blood, her only child. Probably he means to her what you mean to me. It's a deadlock."

"No," cried Fleur, "no, Father!"

Soames leaned back, the image of pale patience, as if resolved on the betrayal of no emotion.

"Listen!" he said. "You're putting the feelings of two months—two months—against the feelings of thirty-five years! What chance do you think you have? Two months—your very first love affair, a matter of half a dozen meetings, a few walks and talks, a few kisses—

against, against what you can't imagine, what no one could who hasn't been through it. Come, be reasonable, Fleur! It's midsummer madness!"

Fleur tore the honeysuckle into little, slow bits.

"The madness is in letting the past spoil it all.

"What do we care about the past? It's our lives, not yours."

Soames raised his hand to his forehead, where suddenly she saw moisture shining.

"Whose child are you?" he said. "Whose child is he? The present is linked with the past, the future with both. There's no getting away from that."

She had never heard philosophy pass those lips before. Impressed even in her agitation, she leaned her elbows on the table, her chin on her hands.

"But, Father, consider it practically. We want each other. There's ever so much money, and nothing whatever in the way but sentiment. Let's bury the past, Father."

His answer was a sigh.

"Besides," said Fleur gently, "you can't prevent us."

"I don't suppose," said Soames, "that if left to myself I should try to prevent you; I must put up with things, I know, to keep your affection. But it's not I who control this matter. That's what I want you to realise before it's too late. If you go on thinking you can get your way and encourage this feeling, the blow will be much heavier when you find you can't."

"Oh!" cried Fleur, "help me, Father; you can help me, you know."

Soames made a startled movement of negation. "I?" he said bitterly. "Help? I am the impediment—the just cause and impediment—isn't that the jargon? You have my blood in your veins."

He rose.

"Well, the fat's in the fire. If you persist in your wilfulness you'll have yourself to blame. Come! Don't be foolish, my child—my only child!"

Fleur laid her forehead against his shoulder.

All was in such turmoil within her. But no good to show it! No good at all! She broke away from him, and went out into the twilight, distraught, but unconvinced. All was indeterminate and vague within her, like the shapes and shadows in the garden, except— her will to have. A poplar pierced up into the dark-blue sky and touched a white star there. The dew wetted her shoes, and chilled her bare shoulders. She went down to the river bank, and stood gazing at a moonstreak on the darkening water. Suddenly she smelled tobacco smoke, and a white figure emerged as if created by the moon. It was young Mont in flannels, standing in his boat. She heard the tiny hiss of his cigarette extinguished in the water.

"Fleur," came his voice, "don't be hard on a poor devil! I've been waiting hours."

"For what?"

"Come in my boat!"

"Not I."

"Why not?"

"I'm not a water-nymph."

"Haven't you any romance in you? Don't be modern, Fleur!"

He appeared on the path within a yard of her.

"Go away!"

"Fleur, I love you. Fleur!"

Fleur uttered a short laugh.

"Come again," she said, "when I haven't got my wish."

"What is your wish?"

"Ask another."

"Fleur," said Mont, and his voice sounded strange, "don't mock me! Even vivisected dogs are worth decent treatment before they're cut up for good."

Fleur shook her head; but her lips were trembling.

"Well, you shouldn't make me jump. Give me a cigarette."

Mont gave her one, lighted it, and another for himself.

"I don't want to talk rot," he said, "but please imagine all the rot that all the lovers that ever were have talked, and all my special rot thrown in."

"Thank you, I have imagined it. Good-night!" They stood for a moment facing each other in the shadow of an acacia-tree with very moonlit blossoms, and the smoke from their cigarettes mingled in the air between them.

"Also ran: 'Michael Mont'?" he said. Fleur turned abruptly toward the house. On the lawn she stopped to look back. Michael Mont was whirling his arms above him; she could see them dashing at his head; then waving at the moonlit blossoms of the acacia. His voice just reached her. "Jolly-jolly!" Fleur shook herself. She couldn't help him, she had too much trouble of her own! On the verandah she stopped very suddenly again. Her mother was sitting in the drawing-room at her writing bureau, quite alone. There was nothing remarkable in the expression of her face except its utter immobility. But she looked desolate! Fleur went upstairs. At the door of her room she paused. She could hear her father walking up and down, up and down the picture-gallery.

'Yes,' she thought, jolly! Oh, Jon!'

CHAPTER X.—DECISION

When Fleur left him Jon stared at the Austrian. She was a thin woman with a dark face and the concerned expression of one who has watched every little good that life once had slip from her, one by one. "No tea?" she said.

Susceptible to the disappointment in her voice, Jon murmured:

"No, really; thanks."

"A lil cup—it ready. A lil cup and cigarette."

Fleur was gone! Hours of remorse and indecision lay before him! And with a heavy sense of disproportion he smiled, and said:

"Well—thank you!"

She brought in a little pot of tea with two little cups, and a silver box of cigarettes on a little tray.

"Sugar? Miss Forsyte has much sugar—she buy my sugar, my friend's sugar also. Miss Forsyte is a veree kind lady. I am happy to serve her. You her brother?"

"Yes," said Jon, beginning to puff the second cigarette of his life.

"Very young brother," said the Austrian, with a little anxious smile, which reminded him of the wag of a dog's tail.

"May I give you some?" he said. "And won't you sit down, please?"

The Austrian shook her head.

"Your father a very nice old man—the most nice old man I ever see. Miss Forsyte tell me all about him. Is he better?"

Her words fell on Jon like a reproach. "Oh Yes, I think he's all right."

"I like to see him again," said the Austrian, putting a hand on her heart; "he have veree kind heart."

"Yes," said Jon. And again her words seemed to him a reproach.

"He never give no trouble to no one, and smile so gentle."

"Yes, doesn't he?"

"He look at Miss Forsyte so funny sometimes. I tell him all my story; he so sympatisch. Your mother—she nice and well?"

"Yes, very."

"He have her photograph on his dressing-table. Veree beautiful"

Jon gulped down his tea. This woman, with her concerned face and her reminding words, was like the first and second murderers.

"Thank you," he said; "I must go now. May—may I leave this with you?"

He put a ten-shilling note on the tray with a doubting hand and gained the door. He heard the Austrian gasp, and hurried out. He had just time to catch his train, and all the way to Victoria looked at every face that passed, as lovers will, hoping against hope. On reaching Worthing he put his luggage into the local train, and set out across the Downs for Wansdon, trying to walk off his aching irresolution. So long as he went full bat, he could enjoy the beauty of those green slopes, stopping now and again to sprawl on the grass, admire the perfection of a wild rose or listen to a lark's song. But the war of motives within him was but postponed—the longing for Fleur, and the hatred of deception. He came to the old chalk-pit above Wansdon with his mind no more made up than when he started. To see both sides of a question vigorously was at once Jon's strength and weakness. He tramped in, just as the first dinner-bell rang. His things had already been brought up. He had a hurried bath and came down to find Holly alone—Val had gone to Town and would not be back till the last train.

Since Val's advice to him to ask his sister what was the matter between the two families, so much had happened—Fleur's disclosure in the Green Park, her visit to Robin Hill, to-day's meeting—that there seemed nothing to ask. He talked of Spain, his sunstroke, Val's horses, their father's health. Holly startled him by saying that she thought their father not at all well. She had been twice to Robin Hill for the week-end. He had seemed fearfully languid, sometimes even in pain, but had always refused to talk about himself.

"He's awfully dear and unselfish—don't you think, Jon?"

Feeling far from dear and unselfish himself, Jon answered: "Rather!"

"I think, he's been a simply perfect father, so long as I can remember."

"Yes," answered Jon, very subdued.

"He's never interfered, and he's always seemed to understand. I shall never forget his letting me go to South Africa in the Boer War when I was in love with Val."

"That was before he married Mother, wasn't it?" said Jon suddenly.

"Yes. Why?"

"Oh! nothing. Only, wasn't she engaged to Fleur's father first?"

Holly put down the spoon she was using, and raised her eyes. Her stare was circumspect. What did the boy know? Enough to make it better to tell him? She could not decide. He looked strained and worried, altogether older, but that might be the sunstroke.

"There was something," she said. "Of course we were out there, and got no news of anything." She could not take the risk.

It was not her secret. Besides, she was in the dark about his feelings now. Before Spain she had made sure he was in love; but boys were boys; that was seven weeks ago, and all Spain between.

She saw that he knew she was putting him off, and added:

"Have you heard anything of Fleur?"

"Yes."

His face told her, then, more than the most elaborate explanations. So he had not forgotten!

She said very quietly: "Fleur is awfully attractive, Jon, but you know—Val and I don't really like her very much."

"Why?"

"We think she's got rather a 'having' nature."

"'Having'? I don't know what you mean. She—she——" he pushed his dessert plate away, got up, and went to the window.

Holly, too, got up, and put her arm round his waist.

"Don't be angry, Jon dear. We can't all see people in the same light, can we? You know, I believe each of us only has about one or two people who can see the best that's in us, and bring it out. For you I think it's your mother. I once saw her looking at a letter of yours; it was wonderful to see her face. I think she's the most beautiful woman I ever saw—Age doesn't seem to touch her."

Jon's face softened; then again became tense. Everybody—everybody was against him and Fleur! It all strengthened the appeal of her words: "Make sure of me—marry me, Jon!"

Here, where he had passed that wonderful week with her—the tug of her enchantment, the ache in his heart increased with every minute that she was not there to make the room, the garden, the very air magical. Would he ever be able to live down here, not seeing her? And he closed up utterly, going early to bed. It would not make him healthy, wealthy, and wise, but it closeted him with memory of Fleur in her fancy frock. He heard Val's arrival—the Ford discharging cargo, then the stillness of the summer night stole back—with only the bleating of very distant sheep, and a night-jar's harsh purring. He leaned far out. Cold moon—warm air—the Downs like silver! Small wings, a stream bubbling, the rambler roses! God—how empty all of it without her! In the Bible it was written: Thou shalt leave father and mother and cleave to—Fleur!

Let him have pluck, and go and tell them! They couldn't stop him marrying her—they wouldn't want to stop him when they knew how he felt. Yes! He would go! Bold and open—Fleur was wrong!

The night-jar ceased, the sheep were silent; the only sound in the darkness was the bubbling of the stream. And Jon in his bed slept, freed from the worst of life's evils—indecision.

CHAPTER XI.—TIMOTHY PROPHESIES

On the day of the cancelled meeting at the National Gallery began the second anniversary of the resurrection of England's pride and glory—or, more shortly, the top hat. "Lord's"—that festival which the War had driven from the field—raised its light and dark blue flags for the second time, displaying almost every feature of a glorious past. Here, in the luncheon interval, were all species of female and one species of male hat, protecting the multiple types of face associated with "the classes." The observing Forsyte might discern in the free or unconsidered seats a certain number of the squash-hatted, but they hardly ventured on the grass; the old school—or schools—could still rejoice that the proletariat was not yet paying the necessary half-crown. Here was still a close borough, the only one left on a large scale—for the papers were about to estimate the attendance at ten thousand. And the ten thousand, all animated by one hope, were asking each other one question: "Where are you lunching?" Something wonderfully uplifting and reassuring in that query and the sight of so many people like themselves voicing it! What reserve power in the British realm—enough pigeons, lobsters, lamb, salmon mayonnaise, strawberries, and bottles of champagne to feed the lot! No miracle in prospect—no case of seven loaves and a few fishes—faith rested on surer foundations. Six thousand top hats, four thousand parasols would be doffed and furled, ten thousand mouths all speaking the same English would be filled. There was life in the old dog yet! Tradition! And again Tradition! How strong and how elastic! Wars might rage, taxation prey, Trades Unions take toll, and Europe perish of starvation; but the ten thousand would be fed; and, within their ring fence, stroll upon green turf, wear their top hats, and meet—themselves. The heart was sound, the pulse still regular. E-ton! E-ton! Har-r-o-o-o-w!

Among the many Forsytes, present on a hunting-ground theirs, by personal prescriptive right, or proxy, was Soames with his wife and daughter. He had not been at either school, he took no interest in cricket, but he wanted Fleur to show her frock, and he wanted to wear his top hat parade it again in peace and plenty among his peers. He walked sedately with Fleur between him and Annette. No women equalled them, so far as he could see. They could walk, and hold themselves up; there was substance in their good looks; the modern woman had no build, no chest, no anything! He remembered suddenly with what intoxication of pride he had walked round with Irene in the first years of his first marriage. And how they used to lunch on the drag which his mother would make his father have, because it was so "chic"—all drags and carriages in those days, not these lumbering great Stands! And how consistently Montague Dartie had drunk too much. He supposed that people drank too much still, but there was not the scope for it there used to be. He remembered George Forsyte—whose brothers Roger and Eustace had been at Harrow and

Eton—towering up on the top of the drag waving a light-blue flag with one hand and a dark-blue flag with the other, and shouting "Etroow-Harrton!" Just when everybody was silent, like the buffoon he had always been; and Eustace got up to the nines below, too dandified to wear any colour or take any notice. Hm! Old days, and Irene in grey silk shot with palest green. He looked, sideways, at Fleur's face. Rather colourless-no light, no eagerness! That love affair was preying on her—a bad business! He looked beyond, at his wife's face, rather more touched up than usual, a little disdainful—not that she had any business to disdain, so far as he could see. She was taking Profond's defection with curious quietude; or was his "small" voyage just a blind? If so, he should refuse to see it! Having promenaded round the pitch and in front of the pavilion, they sought Winifred's table in the Bedouin Club tent. This Club—a new "cock and hen"—had been founded in the interests of travel, and of a gentleman with an old Scottish name, whose father had somewhat strangely been called Levi. Winifred had joined, not because she had travelled, but because instinct told her that a Club with such a name and such a founder was bound to go far; if one didn't join at once one might never have the chance. Its tent, with a text from the Koran on an orange ground, and a small green camel embroidered over the entrance, was the most striking on the ground. Outside it they found Jack Cardigan in a dark blue tie (he had once played for Harrow), batting with a Malacca cane to show how that fellow ought to have hit that ball. He piloted them in. Assembled in Winifred's corner were Imogen, Benedict with his young wife, Val Dartie without Holly, Maud and her husband, and, after Soames and his two were seated, one empty place.

"I'm expecting Prosper," said Winifred, "but he's so busy with his yacht."

Soames stole a glance. No movement in his wife's face! Whether that fellow were coming or not, she evidently knew all about it. It did not escape him that Fleur, too, looked at her mother. If Annette didn't respect his feelings, she might think of Fleur's! The conversation, very desultory, was syncopated by Jack Cardigan talking about "mid-off." He cited all the "great mid-offs" from the beginning of time, as if they had been a definite racial entity in the composition of the British people. Soames had finished his lobster, and was beginning on pigeon-pie, when he heard the words, "I'm a small bit late, Mrs. Dartie," and saw that there was no longer any empty place. That fellow was sitting between Annette and Imogen. Soames ate steadily on, with an occasional word to Maud and Winifred. Conversation buzzed around him. He heard the voice of Profond say:

"I think you're mistaken, Mrs. Forsyde; I'll—I'll bet Miss Forsyde agrees with me."

"In what?" came Fleur's clear voice across the table.

"I was sayin', young gurls are much the same as they always were—there's very small difference."

"Do you know so much about them?"

That sharp reply caught the ears of all, and Soames moved uneasily on his thin green chair.

"Well, I don't know, I think they want their own small way, and I think they always did."

"Indeed!"

"Oh, but—Prosper," Winifred interjected comfortably, "the girls in the streets—the girls who've been in munitions, the little flappers in the shops; their manners now really quite hit you in the eye."

At the word "hit" Jack Cardigan stopped his disquisition; and in the silence Monsieur Profond said:

"It was inside before, now it's outside; that's all."

"But their morals!" cried Imogen.

"Just as moral as they ever were, Mrs. Cardigan, but they've got more opportunity."

The saying, so cryptically cynical, received a little laugh from Imogen, a slight opening of Jack Cardigan's mouth, and a creak from Soames' chair.

Winifred said: "That's too bad, Prosper."

"What do you say, Mrs. Forsyde; don't you think human nature's always the same?"

Soames subdued a sudden longing to get up and kick the fellow. He heard his wife reply:

"Human nature is not the same in England as anywhere else." That was her confounded mockery!

"Well, I don't know much about this small country"—'No, thank God!' thought Soames— "but I should say the pot was boilin' under the lid everywhere. We all want pleasure, and we always did."

Damn the fellow! His cynicism was—was outrageous!

When lunch was over they broke up into couples for the digestive promenade. Too proud to notice, Soames knew perfectly that Annette and that fellow had gone prowling round together. Fleur was with Val; she had chosen him, no doubt, because he knew that boy. He himself had Winifred for partner. They walked in the bright, circling stream, a little flushed and sated, for some minutes, till Winifred sighed:

"I wish we were back forty years, old boy!"

Before the eyes of her spirit an interminable procession of her own "Lord's" frocks was passing, paid for with the money of her father, to save a recurrent crisis. "It's been very amusing, after all. Sometimes I even wish Monty was back. What do you think of people nowadays, Soames?"

"Precious little style. The thing began to go to pieces with bicycles and motor-cars; the War has finished it."

"I wonder what's coming?" said Winifred in a voice dreamy from pigeon-pie. "I'm not at all sure we shan't go back to crinolines and pegtops. Look at that dress!"

Soames shook his head.

"There's money, but no faith in things. We don't lay by for the future. These youngsters— it's all a short life and a merry one with them."

"There's a hat!" said Winifred. "I don't know—when you come to think of the people killed and all that in the War, it's rather wonderful, I think. There's no other country— Prosper says the rest are all bankrupt, except America; and of course her men always took their style in dress from us."

"Is that chap," said Soames, "really going to the South Seas?"

"Oh! one never knows where Prosper's going!"

"He's a sign of the times," muttered Soames, "if you like."

Winifred's hand gripped his arm.

"Don't turn your head," she said in a low voice, "but look to your right in the front row of the Stand."

Soames looked as best he could under that limitation. A man in a grey top hat, grey-bearded, with thin brown, folded cheeks, and a certain elegance of posture, sat there with a woman in a lawn-coloured frock, whose dark eyes were fixed on himself. Soames looked quickly at his feet. How funnily feet moved, one after the other like that! Winifred's voice said in his ear:

"Jolyon looks very ill; but he always had style. She doesn't change—except her hair."

"Why did you tell Fleur about that business?"

"I didn't; she picked it up. I always knew she would."

"Well, it's a mess. She's set her heart upon their boy."

"The little wretch," murmured Winifred. "She tried to take me in about that. What shall you do, Soames?"

"Be guided by events."

They moved on, silent, in the almost solid crowd.

"Really," said Winifred suddenly; "it almost seems like Fate. Only that's so old-fashioned. Look! there are George and Eustace!"

George Forsyte's lofty bulk had halted before them.

"Hallo, Soames!" he said. "Just met Profond and your wife. You'll catch 'em if you put on pace. Did you ever go to see old Timothy?"

Soames nodded, and the streams forced them apart.

"I always liked old George," said Winifred. "He's so droll."

"I never did," said Soames. "Where's your seat? I shall go to mine. Fleur may be back there."

Having seen Winifred to her seat, he regained his own, conscious of small, white, distant figures running, the click of the bat, the cheers and counter-cheers. No Fleur, and no Annette! You could expect nothing of women nowadays! They had the vote. They were "emancipated," and much good it was doing them! So Winifred would go back, would she, and put up with Dartie all over again? To have the past once more—to be sitting here as he had sat in '83 and '84, before he was certain that his marriage with Irene had gone all wrong, before her antagonism had become so glaring that with the best will in the world he could not overlook it. The sight of her with that fellow had brought all memory back. Even now he could not understand why she had been so impracticable. She could love other men; she had it in her! To himself, the one person she ought to have loved, she had chosen to refuse her heart. It seemed to him, fantastically, as he looked back, that all this modern relaxation of marriage—though its forms and laws were the same as when he married her—that all this modern looseness had come out of her revolt; it seemed to him, fantastically, that she had started it, till all decent ownership of anything had gone, or was on the point of going. All came from her! And now—a pretty state of things! Homes! How could you have them without mutual ownership? Not that he had ever had a real home! But had that been his fault? He had done his best. And his rewards were—those two sitting in that Stand, and this affair of Fleur's!

And overcome by loneliness he thought: 'Shan't wait any longer! They must find their own way back to the hotel—if they mean to come!' Hailing a cab outside the ground, he said:

"Drive me to the Bayswater Road." His old aunts had never failed him. To them he had meant an ever-welcome visitor. Though they were gone, there, still, was Timothy!

Smither was standing in the open doorway.

"Mr. Soames! I was just taking the air. Cook will be so pleased."

"How is Mr. Timothy?"

"Not himself at all these last few days, sir; he's been talking a great deal. Only this morning he was saying: 'My brother James, he's getting old.' His mind wanders, Mr. Soames, and then he will talk of them. He troubles about their investments. The other day he said: 'There's my brother Jolyon won't look at Consols'—he seemed quite down about it. Come in, Mr. Soames, come in! It's such a pleasant change!"

"Well," said Soames, "just for a few minutes."

"No," murmured Smither in the hall, where the air had the singular freshness of the outside day, "we haven't been very satisfied with him, not all this week. He's always been one to leave a titbit to the end; but ever since Monday he's been eating it first. If you notice a dog, Mr. Soames, at its dinner, it eats the meat first. We've always thought it such a good sign of Mr. Timothy at his age to leave it to the last, but now he seems to have lost all his self-control; and, of course, it makes him leave the rest. The doctor doesn't make anything of it, but"—Smither shook her head—"he seems to think he's got to eat it first, in case he shouldn't get to it. That and his talking makes us anxious."

"Has he said anything important?"

"I shouldn't like to say that, Mr. Soames; but he's turned against his Will. He gets quite pettish—and after having had it out every morning for years, it does seem funny. He said the other day: 'They want my money.' It gave me such a turn, because, as I said to him, nobody wants his money, I'm sure. And it does seem a pity he should be thinking about money at his time of life. I took my courage in my 'ands. 'You know, Mr. Timothy,' I said, 'my dear mistress'—that's Miss Forsyte, Mr. Soames, Miss Ann that trained me—'she never thought about money,' I said, 'it was all character with her.' He looked at me, I can't tell you how funny, and he said quite dry: 'Nobody wants my character.' Think of his saying a thing like that! But sometimes he'll say something as sharp and sensible as anything."

Soames, who had been staring at an old print by the hat-rack, thinking, 'That's got value!' murmured: "I'll go up and see him, Smither."

"Cook's with him," answered Smither above her corsets; "she will be pleased to see you."

He mounted slowly, with the thought: 'Shan't care to live to be that age.'

On the second floor, he paused, and tapped. The door was opened, and he saw the round homely face of a woman about sixty.

"Mr. Soames!" she said: "Why! Mr. Soames!"

Soames nodded. "All right, Cook!" and entered.

Timothy was propped up in bed, with his hands joined before his chest, and his eyes fixed on the ceiling, where a fly was standing upside down. Soames stood at the foot of the bed, facing him.

"Uncle Timothy," he said, raising his voice. "Uncle Timothy!"

Timothy's eyes left the fly, and levelled themselves on his visitor. Soames could see his pale tongue passing over his darkish lips.

"Uncle Timothy," he said again, "is there anything I can do for you? Is there anything you'd like to say?"

"Ha!" said Timothy.

"I've come to look you up and see that everything's all right."

Timothy nodded. He seemed trying to get used to the apparition before him.

"Have you got everything you want?"

"No," said Timothy.

"Can I get you anything?"

"No," said Timothy.

"I'm Soames, you know; your nephew, Soames Forsyte. Your brother James' son."

Timothy nodded.

"I shall be delighted to do anything I can for you."

Timothy beckoned. Soames went close to him:

"You—" said Timothy in a voice which seemed to have outlived tone, "you tell them all from me—you tell them all—" and his finger tapped on Soames' arm, "to hold on—hold on—Consols are goin' up," and he nodded thrice.

"All right!" said Soames; "I will."

"Yes," said Timothy, and, fixing his eyes again on the ceiling, he added: "That fly!"

Strangely moved, Soames looked at the Cook's pleasant fattish face, all little puckers from staring at fires.

"That'll do him a world of good, sir," she said.

A mutter came from Timothy, but he was clearly speaking to himself, and Soames went out with the cook.

"I wish I could make you a pink cream, Mr. Soames, like in old days; you did so relish them. Good-bye, sir; it has been a pleasure."

"Take care of him, Cook, he is old."

And, shaking her crumpled hand, he went down-stairs. Smither was still taking the air in the doorway.

"What do you think of him, Mr. Soames?"

"H'm!" Soames murmured: "He's lost touch."

"Yes," said Smither, "I was afraid you'd think that coming fresh out of the world to see him like."

"Smither," said Soames, "we're all indebted to you."

"Oh, no, Mr. Soames, don't say that! It's a pleasure—he's such a wonderful man."

"Well, good-bye!" said Soames, and got into his taxi.

'Going up!' he thought; 'going up!'

Reaching the hotel at Knightsbridge he went to their sitting-room, and rang for tea. Neither of them were in. And again that sense of loneliness came over him. These hotels. What monstrous great places they were now! He could remember when there was nothing bigger than Long's or Brown's, Morley's or the Tavistock, and the heads that were shaken over the Langham and the Grand. Hotels and Clubs—Clubs and Hotels; no end to them now! And Soames, who had just been watching at Lord's a miracle of tradition and continuity, fell into reverie over the changes in that London where he had been born five-

and-sixty years before. Whether Consols were going up or not, London had become a terrific property. No such property in the world, unless it were New York! There was a lot of hysteria in the papers nowadays; but any one who, like himself, could remember London sixty years ago, and see it now, realised the fecundity and elasticity of wealth. They had only to keep their heads, and go at it steadily. Why! he remembered cobblestones, and stinking straw on the floor of your cab. And old Timothy—what could he not have told them, if he had kept his memory! Things were unsettled, people in a funk or in a hurry, but here were London and the Thames, and out there the British Empire, and the ends of the earth. "Consols are goin' up!" He should n't be a bit surprised. It was the breed that counted. And all that was bull-dogged in Soames stared for a moment out of his grey eyes, till diverted by the print of a Victorian picture on the walls. The hotel had bought three dozen of that little lot! The old hunting or "Rake's Progress" prints in the old inns were worth looking at—but this sentimental stuff—well, Victorianism had gone! "Tell them to hold on!" old Timothy had said. But to what were they to hold on in this modern welter of the "democratic principle"? Why, even privacy was threatened! And at the thought that privacy might perish, Soames pushed back his teacup and went to the window. Fancy owning no more of Nature than the crowd out there owned of the flowers and trees and waters of Hyde Park! No, no! Private possession underlay everything worth having. The world had slipped its sanity a bit, as dogs now and again at full moon slipped theirs and went off for a night's rabbiting; but the world, like the dog, knew where its bread was buttered and its bed warm, and would come back sure enough to the only home worth having—to private ownership. The world was in its second childhood for the moment, like old Timothy—eating its titbit first!

He heard a sound behind him, and saw that his wife and daughter had come in.

"So you're back!" he said.

Fleur did not answer; she stood for a moment looking at him and her mother, then passed into her bedroom. Annette poured herself out a cup of tea.

"I am going to Paris, to my mother, Soames."

"Oh! To your mother?"

"Yes."

"For how long?"

"I do not know."

"And when are you going?"

"On Monday."

Was she really going to her mother? Odd, how indifferent he felt! Odd, how clearly she had perceived the indifference he would feel so long as there was no scandal. And suddenly between her and himself he saw distinctly the face he had seen that afternoon—Irene's.

"Will you want money?"

"Thank you; I have enough."

"Very well. Let us know when you are coming back."

Annette put down the cake she was fingering, and, looking up through darkened lashes, said:

"Shall I give Maman any message?"

"My regards."

Annette stretched herself, her hands on her waist, and said in French:

"What luck that you have never loved me, Soames!" Then rising, she too left the room. Soames was glad she had spoken it in French—it seemed to require no dealing with. Again that other face—pale, dark-eyed, beautiful still! And there stirred far down within him the ghost of warmth, as from sparks lingering beneath a mound of flaky ash. And Fleur infatuated with her boy! Queer chance! Yet, was there such a thing as chance? A man went down a street, a brick fell on his head. Ah! that was chance, no doubt. But this! "Inherited," his girl had said. She—she was "holding on"!

PART III

CHAPTER I.—OLD JOLYON WALKS

Twofold impulse had made Jolyon say to his wife at breakfast "Let's go up to Lord's!"

"Wanted"—something to abate the anxiety in which those two had lived during the sixty hours since Jon had brought Fleur down. "Wanted"—too, that which might assuage the pangs of memory in one who knew he might lose them any day!

Fifty-eight years ago Jolyon had become an Eton boy, for old Jolyon's whim had been that he should be canonised at the greatest possible expense. Year after year he had gone to Lord's from Stanhope Gate with a father whose youth in the eighteen-twenties had been passed without polish in the game of cricket. Old Jolyon would speak quite openly of swipes, full tosses, half and three-quarter balls; and young Jolyon with the guileless snobbery of youth had trembled lest his sire should be overheard. Only in this supreme matter of cricket he had been nervous, for his father—in Crimean whiskers then—had ever impressed him as the beau ideal. Though never canonised himself, Old Jolyon's natural fastidiousness and balance had saved him from the errors of the vulgar. How delicious, after bowling in a top hat and a sweltering heat, to go home with his father in a hansom cab, bathe, dress, and forth to the "Disunion" Club, to dine off white bait, cutlets, and a tart, and go—two "swells," old and young, in lavender kid gloves—to the opera or play. And on Sunday, when the match was over, and his top hat duly broken, down with his father in a special hansom to the "Crown and Sceptre," and the terrace above the river— the golden sixties when the world was simple, dandies glamorous, Democracy not born, and the books of Whyte Melville coming thick and fast.

A generation later, with his own boy, Jolly, Harrow-buttonholed with corn-flowers—by old Jolyon's whim his grandson had been canonised at a trifle less expense—again Jolyon had experienced the heat and counter-passions of the day, and come back to the cool and the strawberry beds of Robin Hill, and billiards after dinner, his boy making the most heart-breaking flukes and trying to seem languid and grown-up. Those two days each year he and his son had been alone together in the world, one on each side—and Democracy just born!

And so, he had unearthed a grey top hat, borrowed a tiny bit of light-blue ribbon from Irene, and gingerly, keeping cool, by car and train and taxi, had reached Lord's Ground. There, beside her in a lawn-coloured frock with narrow black edges, he had watched the game, and felt the old thrill stir within him.

When Soames passed, the day was spoiled. Irene's face was distorted by compression of the lips. No good to go on sitting here with Soames or perhaps his daughter recurring in front of them, like decimals. And he said:

"Well, dear, if you've had enough—let's go!"

That evening Jolyon felt exhausted. Not wanting her to see him thus, he waited till she had begun to play, and stole off to the little study. He opened the long window for air, and the door, that he might still hear her music drifting in; and, settled in his father's old armchair, closed his eyes, with his head against the worn brown leather. Like that passage of the Cesar Franck Sonata—so had been his life with her, a divine third movement. And now this business of Jon's—this bad business! Drifted to the edge of consciousness, he hardly knew if it were in sleep that he smelled the scent of a cigar, and seemed to see his father in the blackness before his closed eyes. That shape formed, went, and formed again; as if in the very chair where he himself was sitting, he saw his father, black-coated, with knees crossed, glasses balanced between thumb and finger; saw the big white moustaches, and the deep eyes looking up below a dome of forehead and seeming to search his own, seeming to speak. "Are you facing it, Jo? It's for you to decide. She's only a woman!" Ah! how well he knew his father in that phrase; how all the Victorian Age came up with it! And his answer "No, I've funked it—funked hurting her and Jon and myself. I've got a heart; I've funked it." But the old eyes, so much older, so much younger than his own, kept at it; "It's your wife; your son; your past. Tackle it, my boy!" Was it a message from walking spirit; or but the instinct of his sire living on within him? And again came that scent of cigar smoke-from the old saturated leather. Well! he would tackle it, write to Jon, and put the whole thing down in black and white! And suddenly he breathed with difficulty, with a sense of suffocation, as if his heart were swollen. He got up and went out into the air. The stars were very bright. He passed along the terrace round the corner of the house, till, through the window of the music-room, he could see Irene at the piano, with lamp-light falling on her powdery hair; withdrawn into herself she seemed, her dark eyes staring straight before her, her hands idle. Jolyon saw her raise those hands and clasp them over her breast. 'It's Jon, with her,' he thought; 'all Jon! I'm dying out of her—it's natural!'

And, careful not to be seen, he stole back.

Next day, after a bad night, he sat down to his task. He wrote with difficulty and many erasures.

"MY DEAREST BOY,

"You are old enough to understand how very difficult it is for elders to give themselves away to their young. Especially when—like your mother and myself, though I shall never think of her as anything but young—their hearts are altogether set on him to whom they must confess. I cannot say we are conscious of having sinned exactly—people in real life very seldom are, I believe—but most persons would say we had, and at all events our conduct, righteous or not, has found us out. The truth is, my dear, we both have pasts, which it is now my task to make known to you, because they so grievously and deeply affect your future. Many, very many years ago, as far back indeed as 1883, when she was only twenty, your mother had the great and lasting misfortune to make an unhappy marriage—no, not with me, Jon. Without money of her own, and with only a stepmother—closely related to Jezebel—she was very unhappy in her home life. It was Fleur's father that she married, my cousin Soames Forsyte. He had pursued her very tenaciously and to do him justice was deeply in love with her. Within a week she knew the fearful mistake she had made. It was not his fault; it was her error of judgment—her misfortune."

So far Jolyon had kept some semblance of irony, but now his subject carried him away.

"Jon, I want to explain to you if I can—and it's very hard—how it is that an unhappy marriage such as this can so easily come about. You will of course say: 'If she didn't really love him how could she ever have married him?' You would be right if it were not for one or two rather terrible considerations. From this initial mistake of hers all the subsequent trouble, sorrow, and tragedy have come, and so I must make it clear to you if I can. You see, Jon, in those days and even to this day—indeed, I don't see, for all the talk of enlightenment, how it can well be otherwise—most girls are married ignorant of the sexual side of life. Even if they know what it means they have not experienced it. That's the crux. It is this actual lack of experience, whatever verbal knowledge they have, which makes all the difference and all the trouble. In a vast number of marriages-and your mother's was one—girls are not and cannot be certain whether they love the man they marry or not; they do not know until after that act of union which makes the reality of marriage. Now, in many, perhaps in most doubtful cases, this act cements and strengthens the attachment, but in other cases, and your mother's was one, it is a revelation of mistake, a destruction of such attraction as there was. There is nothing more tragic in a woman's life than such a revelation, growing daily, nightly clearer. Coarse-grained and unthinking people are apt to laugh at such a mistake, and say, 'What a fuss about nothing!' Narrow and self-righteous people, only capable of judging the lives of others by their own, are apt to condemn those who make this tragic error, to condemn them for life to the dungeons they have made for themselves. You know the expression: 'She has made her bed, she must lie on it!' It is a hard-mouthed saying, quite unworthy of a gentleman or lady in the best sense of those words; and I can use no stronger condemnation. I have not been what is called a moral man, but I wish to use no words to you, my dear, which will make you think lightly of ties or contracts into which you enter. Heaven forbid! But with the experience of a life behind me I do say that those who condemn the victims of these tragic mistakes, condemn them and hold out no hands to help them, are inhuman, or rather they would be if they had the understanding to know what they are doing. But they haven't! Let them go! They are as much anathema to me as I, no doubt, am to them. I have had to say all this, because I am going to put you into a position to judge your mother, and you are very young, without experience of what life is. To go on with the story. After three years of effort to subdue her shrinking—I was going to say her loathing and it's not too strong a word, for shrinking soon becomes loathing under such circumstances—three years of what to a sensitive, beauty-loving nature like your mother's, Jon, was torment, she met a young man who fell in love with her. He was the architect of this very house that we live in now, he was building it for her and Fleur's father to live in, a new prison to hold her, in place of the one she inhabited with him in London. Perhaps that fact played some part in what came of it. But in any case she, too, fell in love with him. I know it's not necessary to explain to you that one does not precisely choose with whom one will fall in love. It comes. Very well! It came. I can imagine—though she never said much to me about it—the struggle that then took place in her, because, Jon, she was brought up strictly and was not light in her ideas—not at all. However, this was an overwhelming feeling, and it came to pass that they loved in deed as well as in thought. Then came a fearful tragedy. I must tell you of it because if I don't you will never understand the real situation that you have now to face. The man whom she had married—Soames Forsyte, the father of Fleur one night, at the height of her passion for this young man, forcibly reasserted his rights over her. The next day she met her lover and told him of it. Whether he committed suicide or whether he was accidentally run over in his distraction, we never knew; but so it was. Think of your mother as she was that evening when she heard of his death. I happened to see her. Your grandfather sent me to help her if I could. I only just saw her, before the door was shut against me by her husband. But I have never forgotten her face, I can see it now. I was not in love with her then, not for twelve years after, but I have never forgotten. My dear boy—it is not easy to write like this. But you see, I must. Your mother is wrapped up in you, utterly, devotedly. I don't wish to write harshly of Soames Forsyte. I don't think harshly of him. I have long been sorry for him; perhaps I was sorry even then. As the world judges she was in error, he within his rights. He loved her—in his way. She was his property. That is the view he holds of life—of human feelings and hearts—property. It's not his fault—so was he born. To me it is a view that has always been abhorrent—so was I born! Knowing you as I do, I feel it cannot be otherwise than abhorrent to you. Let me go on with the story. Your mother fled from his house that night; for twelve years she lived quietly alone without companionship of any sort, until in 1899 her husband—you see, he was still her husband, for he did not attempt to divorce her, and she of course had no right to divorce him—became conscious, it seems, of the want of children, and commenced a long attempt to induce her to go back to him and give him a child. I was her trustee then, under your Grandfather's Will, and I watched this going on. While watching, I became attached to her, devotedly attached. His pressure increased, till one day she came to me here and practically put herself under my protection. Her husband, who was kept informed of all her movements, attempted to force us apart by bringing a divorce suit, or possibly he really meant it, I don't know; but anyway our names were publicly joined. That decided us, and we became united in fact. She was divorced, married me, and you were born. We have lived in perfect happiness, at least I have, and I believe your mother also. Soames, soon after the divorce, married Fleur's mother, and she was born. That is the story, Jon. I have told it you, because by the affection which we see you have formed for this man's daughter you are blindly moving toward what must utterly destroy your mother's happiness, if not your own. I don't wish to speak of myself, because at my age there's no use supposing I shall cumber the ground much longer, besides, what I should suffer would be mainly on her account, and on yours. But what I want you to realise is that feelings of horror and aversion such as those can never be buried or forgotten. They are alive in her to-day. Only yesterday at Lord's we happened to see Soames Forsyte. Her face, if you had seen it, would have convinced you. The idea that you should marry his daughter is a nightmare to her, Jon. I have nothing to say against Fleur save that she is his daughter. But your children, if you married her, would be the grandchildren of Soames, as much as of your mother, of a man who once owned your mother as a man might own a slave. Think what that would mean. By such a marriage you enter the camp which held your mother prisoner and wherein she ate her heart out. You are just on the threshold of life, you have only known this girl two months, and however deeply you think you love her, I appeal to you to break it off at once. Don't give your mother this rankling pain and humiliation during the rest of her life. Young though she will always seem to me, she is fifty-seven. Except for us two she has no one in the world. She will soon have only you. Pluck up your spirit, Jon, and break away. Don't put this cloud and barrier between you. Don't break her heart! Bless you, my dear boy, and again forgive me for all the pain this letter must bring you—we tried to spare it you, but Spain—it seems—was no good.

"Ever your devoted father,

"JOLYON FORSYTE."

Having finished his confession, Jolyon sat with a thin cheek on his hand, re-reading. There were things in it which hurt him so much, when he thought of Jon reading them, that he nearly tore the letter up. To speak of such things at all to a boy—his own boy—to speak of them in relation to his own wife and the boy's own mother, seemed dreadful to the reticence of his Forsyte soul. And yet without speaking of them how make Jon understand the reality, the deep cleavage, the ineffaceable scar? Without them, how justify this stifling of the boy's love? He might just as well not write at all!

He folded the confession, and put it in his pocket. It was—thank Heaven!—Saturday; he had till Sunday evening to think it over; for even if posted now it could not reach Jon till Monday. He felt a curious relief at this delay, and at the fact that, whether sent or not, it was written.

In the rose garden, which had taken the place of the old fernery, he could see Irene snipping and pruning, with a little basket on her arm. She was never idle, it seemed to him, and he envied her now that he himself was idle nearly all his time. He went down to her. She held up a stained glove and smiled. A piece of lace tied under her chin concealed her hair, and her oval face with its still dark brows looked very young.

"The green-fly are awful this year, and yet it's cold. You look tired, Jolyon."

Jolyon took the confession from his pocket. "I've been writing this. I think you ought to see it?"

"To Jon?" Her whole face had changed, in that instant, becoming almost haggard.

"Yes; the murder's out."

He gave it to her, and walked away among the roses. Presently, seeing that she had finished reading and was standing quite still with the sheets of the letter against her skirt, he came back to her.

"Well?"

"It's wonderfully put. I don't see how it could be put better. Thank you, dear."

"Is there anything you would like left out?"

She shook her head.

"No; he must know all, if he's to understand."

"That's what I thought, but—I hate it!"

He had the feeling that he hated it more than she—to him sex was so much easier to mention between man and woman than between man and man; and she had always been more natural and frank, not deeply secretive like his Forsyte self.

"I wonder if he will understand, even now, Jolyon? He's so young; and he shrinks from the physical."

"He gets that shrinking from my father, he was as fastidious as a girl in all such matters. Would it be better to rewrite the whole thing, and just say you hated Soames?"

Irene shook her head.

"Hate's only a word. It conveys nothing. No, better as it is."

"Very well. It shall go to-morrow."

She raised her face to his, and in sight of the big house's many creepered windows, he kissed her.

CHAPTER II.—CONFESSION

Late that same afternoon, Jolyon had a nap in the old armchair. Face down on his knee was La Rotisserie de la Refine Pedauque, and just before he fell asleep he had been thinking: 'As a people shall we ever really like the French? Will they ever really like us!' He himself had always liked the French, feeling at home with their wit, their taste, their cooking. Irene and he had paid many visits to France before the War, when Jon had been at his private school. His romance with her had begun in Paris—his last and most enduring romance. But the French—no Englishman could like them who could not see them in some sort with the detached aesthetic eye! And with that melancholy conclusion he had nodded off.

When he woke he saw Jon standing between him and the window. The boy had evidently come in from the garden and was waiting for him to wake. Jolyon smiled, still half asleep. How nice the chap looked—sensitive, affectionate, straight! Then his heart gave a nasty jump; and a quaking sensation overcame him. Jon! That confession! He controlled himself with an effort. "Why, Jon, where did you spring from?"

Jon bent over and kissed his forehead.

Only then he noticed the look on the boy's face.

"I came home to tell you something, Dad."

With all his might Jolyon tried to get the better of the jumping, gurgling sensations within his chest.

"Well, sit down, old man. Have you seen your mother?"

"No." The boy's flushed look gave place to pallor; he sat down on the arm of the old chair, as, in old days, Jolyon himself used to sit beside his own father, installed in its recesses. Right up to the time of the rupture in their relations he had been wont to perch there—had he now reached such a moment with his own son? All his life he had hated scenes like poison, avoided rows, gone on his own way quietly and let others go on theirs. But now— it seemed—at the very end of things, he had a scene before him more painful than any he had avoided. He drew a visor down over his emotion, and waited for his son to speak.

"Father," said Jon slowly, "Fleur and I are engaged."

'Exactly!' thought Jolyon, breathing with difficulty.

"I know that you and Mother don't like the idea. Fleur says that Mother was engaged to her father before you married her. Of course I don't know what happened, but it must be ages ago. I'm devoted to her, Dad, and she says she is to me."

Jolyon uttered a queer sound, half laugh, half groan.

"You are nineteen, Jon, and I am seventy-two. How are we to understand each other in a matter like this, eh?"

"You love Mother, Dad; you must know what we feel. It isn't fair to us to let old things spoil our happiness, is it?"

Brought face to face with his confession, Jolyon resolved to do without it if by any means he could. He laid his hand on the boy's arm.

"Look, Jon! I might put you off with talk about your both being too young and not knowing your own minds, and all that, but you wouldn't listen, besides, it doesn't meet the case—Youth, unfortunately, cures itself. You talk lightly about 'old things like that,' knowing nothing—as you say truly—of what happened. Now, have I ever given you reason to doubt my love for you, or my word?"

At a less anxious moment he might have been amused by the conflict his words aroused— the boy's eager clasp, to reassure him on these points, the dread on his face of what that reassurance would bring forth; but he could only feel grateful for the squeeze.

"Very well, you can believe what I tell you. If you don't give up this love affair, you will make Mother wretched to the end of her days. Believe me, my dear, the past, whatever it was, can't be buried—it can't indeed."

Jon got off the arm of the chair.

'The girl'—thought Jolyon—'there she goes—starting up before him—life itself—eager, pretty, loving!'

"I can't, Father; how can I—just because you say that? Of course, I can't!"

"Jon, if you knew the story you would give this up without hesitation; you would have to! Can't you believe me?"

"How can you tell what I should think? Father, I love her better than anything in the world."

Jolyon's face twitched, and he said with painful slowness:

"Better than your mother, Jon?"

From the boy's face, and his clenched fists Jolyon realised the stress and struggle he was going through.

"I don't know," he burst out, "I don't know! But to give Fleur up for nothing—for something I don't understand, for something that I don't believe can really matter half so much, will make me—make me...."

"Make you feel us unjust, put a barrier—yes. But that's better than going on with this."

"I can't. Fleur loves me, and I love her. You want me to trust you; why don't you trust me, Father? We wouldn't want to know anything—we wouldn't let it make any difference. It'll only make us both love you and Mother all the more."

Jolyon put his hand into his breast pocket, but brought it out again empty, and sat, clucking his tongue against his teeth.

"Think what your mother's been to you, Jon! She has nothing but you; I shan't last much longer."

"Why not? It isn't fair to—Why not?"

"Well," said Jolyon, rather coldly, "because the doctors tell me I shan't; that's all."

"Oh, Dad!" cried Jon, and burst into tears.

This downbreak of his son, whom he had not seen cry since he was ten, moved Jolyon terribly. He recognised to the full how fearfully soft the boy's heart was, how much he would suffer in this business, and in life generally. And he reached out his hand helplessly—not wishing, indeed not daring to get up.

"Dear man," he said, "don't—or you'll make me!"

Jon smothered down his paroxysm, and stood with face averted, very still.

'What now?' thought Jolyon. 'What can I say to move him?'

"By the way, don't speak of that to Mother," he said; "she has enough to frighten her with this affair of yours. I know how you feel. But, Jon, you know her and me well enough to be sure we wouldn't wish to spoil your happiness lightly. Why, my dear boy, we don't care for anything but your happiness—at least, with me it's just yours and Mother's and with her just yours. It's all the future for you both that's at stake."

Jon turned. His face was deadly pale; his eyes, deep in his head, seemed to burn.

517

"What is it? What is it? Don't keep me like this!"

Jolyon, who knew that he was beaten, thrust his hand again into his breast pocket, and sat for a full minute, breathing with difficulty, his eyes closed. The thought passed through his mind: 'I've had a good long innings—some pretty bitter moments—this is the worst!' Then he brought his hand out with the letter, and said with a sort of fatigue: "Well, Jon, if you hadn't come to-day, I was going to send you this. I wanted to spare you—I wanted to spare your mother and myself, but I see it's no good. Read it, and I think I'll go into the garden." He reached forward to get up.

Jon, who had taken the letter, said quickly, "No, I'll go"; and was gone.

Jolyon sank back in his chair. A blue-bottle chose that moment to come buzzing round him with a sort of fury; the sound was homely, better than nothing.... Where had the boy gone to read his letter? The wretched letter—the wretched story! A cruel business—cruel to her—to Soames—to those two children—to himself!... His heart thumped and pained him. Life—its loves—its work—its beauty—its aching, and—its end! A good time; a fine time in spite of all; until—you regretted that you had ever been born. Life—it wore you down, yet did not make you want to die—that was the cunning evil! Mistake to have a heart! Again the blue-bottle came buzzing—bringing in all the heat and hum and scent of summer—yes, even the scent—as of ripe fruits, dried grasses, sappy shrubs, and the vanilla breath of cows. And out there somewhere in the fragrance Jon would be reading that letter, turning and twisting its pages in his trouble, his bewilderment and trouble—breaking his heart about it! The thought made Jolyon acutely miserable. Jon was such a tender-hearted chap, affectionate to his bones, and conscientious, too—it was so unfair, so damned unfair! He remembered Irene saying to him once: "Never was any one born more loving and lovable than Jon." Poor little Jon! His world gone up the spout, all of a summer afternoon! Youth took things so hard! And stirred, tormented by that vision of Youth taking things hard, Jolyon got out of his chair, and went to the window. The boy was nowhere visible. And he passed out. If one could take any help to him now—one must!

He traversed the shrubbery, glanced into the walled garden—no Jon! Nor where the peaches and the apricots were beginning to swell and colour. He passed the Cupressus trees, dark and spiral, into the meadow. Where had the boy got to? Had he rushed down to the coppice—his old hunting-ground? Jolyon crossed the rows of hay. They would cock it on Monday and be carrying the day after, if rain held off. Often they had crossed this field together—hand in hand, when Jon was a little chap. Dash it! The golden age was over by the time one was ten! He came to the pond, where flies and gnats were dancing over a bright reedy surface; and on into the coppice. It was cool there, fragrant of larches. Still no Jon! He called. No answer! On the log seat he sat down, nervous, anxious, forgetting his own physical sensations. He had been wrong to let the boy get away with that letter; he ought to have kept him under his eye from the start! Greatly troubled, he got up to retrace his steps. At the farm-buildings he called again, and looked into the dark cow-house. There in the cool, and the scent of vanilla and ammonia, away from flies, the three Alderneys were chewing the quiet cud; just milked, waiting for evening, to be turned out again into the lower field. One turned a lazy head, a lustrous eye; Jolyon could see the slobber on its grey lower lip. He saw everything with passionate clearness, in the agitation of his nerves— all that in his time he had adored and tried to paint—wonder of light and shade and colour. No wonder the legend put Christ into a manger—what more devotional than the eyes and moon-white horns of a chewing cow in the warm dusk! He called again. No answer! And he hurried away out of the coppice, past the pond, up the hill. Oddly ironical—now he came to think of it—if Jon had taken the gruel of his discovery down in the coppice where his mother and Bosinney in those old days had made the plunge of acknowledging their love. Where he himself, on the log seat the Sunday morning he came back from Paris, had realised to the full that Irene had become the world to him. That would have been the place for Irony to tear the veil from before the eyes of Irene's boy! But he was not here! Where had he got to? One must find the poor chap!

A gleam of sun had come, sharpening to his hurrying senses all the beauty of the afternoon, of the tall trees and lengthening shadows, of the blue, and the white clouds, the scent of the hay, and the cooing of the pigeons; and the flower shapes standing tall. He came to the rosery, and the beauty of the roses in that sudden sunlight seemed to him unearthly. "Rose, you Spaniard!" Wonderful three words! There she had stood by that bush of dark red roses; had stood to read and decide that Jon must know it all! He knew all now! Had she chosen wrong? He bent and sniffed a rose, its petals brushed his nose and trembling lips; nothing so soft as a rose-leaf's velvet, except her neck—Irene! On across the lawn he went, up the slope, to the oak-tree. Its top alone was glistening, for the sudden sun was away over the house; the lower shade was thick, blessedly cool—he was greatly overheated. He paused a minute with his hand on the rope of the swing—Jolly, Holly— Jon! The old swing! And suddenly, he felt horribly—deadly ill. 'I've over done it!' he thought: 'by Jove! I've overdone it—after all!' He staggered up toward the terrace, dragged himself up the steps, and fell against the wall of the house. He leaned there gasping, his face buried in the honey-suckle that he and she had taken such trouble with that it might sweeten the air which drifted in. Its fragrance mingled with awful pain. 'My love!' he thought; 'the boy!' And with a great effort he tottered in through the long window, and sank into old Jolyon's chair. The book was there, a pencil in it; he caught it up, scribbled a word on the open page.... His hand dropped.... So it was like this—was it?...

There was a great wrench; and darkness....

CHAPTER III.—IRENE

When Jon rushed away with the letter in his hand, he ran along the terrace and round the corner of the house, in fear and confusion. Leaning against the creepered wall he tore open the letter. It was long—very long! This added to his fear, and he began reading. When he came to the words: "It was Fleur's father that she married," everything seemed to spin before him. He was close to a window, and entering by it, he passed, through music-room and hall, up to his bedroom. Dipping his face in cold water, he sat on his bed, and went on reading, dropping each finished page on the bed beside him. His father's writing was easy to read—he knew it so well, though he had never had a letter from him one quarter so long. He read with a dull feeling—imagination only half at work. He best grasped, on that first reading, the pain his father must have had in writing such a letter. He let the last sheet fall, and in a sort of mental, moral helplessness began to read the first again. It all seemed to him disgusting—dead and disgusting. Then, suddenly, a hot wave of horrified emotion tingled through him. He buried his face in his hands. His mother! Fleur's father! He took up the letter again, and read on mechanically. And again came the feeling that it was all dead and disgusting; his own love so different! This letter said his mother—and her father! An awful letter!

Property! Could there be men who looked on women as their property? Faces seen in street and countryside came thronging up before him—red, stock-fish faces; hard, dull faces; prim, dry faces; violent faces; hundreds, thousands of them! How could he know what men who had such faces thought and did? He held his head in his hands and groaned. His mother! He caught up the letter and read on again: "horror and aversion-alive in her to-day.... your children.... grandchildren.... of a man who once owned your mother as a man

519

might own a slave...." He got up from his bed. This cruel shadowy past, lurking there to murder his love and Fleur's, was true, or his father could never have written it. 'Why didn't they tell me the first thing,' he thought, 'the day I first saw Fleur? They knew I'd seen her. They were afraid, and—now—I've—got it!' Overcome by misery too acute for thought or reason, he crept into a dusky corner of the room and sat down on the floor. He sat there, like some unhappy little animal. There was comfort in dusk, and the floor—as if he were back in those days when he played his battles sprawling all over it. He sat there huddled, his hair ruffled, his hands clasped round his knees, for how long he did not know. He was wrenched from his blank wretchedness by the sound of the door opening from his mother's room. The blinds were down over the windows of his room, shut up in his absence, and from where he sat he could only hear a rustle, her footsteps crossing, till beyond the bed he saw her standing before his dressing-table. She had something in her hand. He hardly breathed, hoping she would not see him, and go away. He saw her touch things on the table as if they had some virtue in them, then face the window-grey from head to foot like a ghost. The least turn of her head, and she must see him! Her lips moved: "Oh! Jon!" She was speaking to herself; the tone of her voice troubled Jon's heart. He saw in her hand a little photograph. She held it toward the light, looking at it—very small. He knew it—one of himself as a tiny boy, which she always kept in her bag. His heart beat fast. And, suddenly as if she had heard it, she turned her eyes and saw him. At the gasp she gave, and the movement of her hands pressing the photograph against her breast, he said:

"Yes, it's me."

She moved over to the bed, and sat down on it, quite close to him, her hands still clasping her breast, her feet among the sheets of the letter which had slipped to the floor. She saw them, and her hands grasped the edge of the bed. She sat very upright, her dark eyes fixed on him. At last she spoke.

"Well, Jon, you know, I see."

"Yes."

"You've seen Father?"

"Yes."

There was a long silence, till she said:

"Oh! my darling!"

"It's all right." The emotions in him were so, violent and so mixed that he dared not move—resentment, despair, and yet a strange yearning for the comfort of her hand on his forehead.

"What are you going to do?"

"I don't know."

There was another long silence, then she got up. She stood a moment, very still, made a little movement with her hand, and said: "My darling boy, my most darling boy, don't think of me—think of yourself," and, passing round the foot of the bed, went back into her room.

Jon turned—curled into a sort of ball, as might a hedgehog—into the corner made by the two walls.

He must have been twenty minutes there before a cry roused him. It came from the terrace below. He got up, scared. Again came the cry: "Jon!" His mother was calling! He ran out and down the stairs, through the empty dining-room into the study. She was kneeling before the old armchair, and his father was lying back quite white, his head on his breast, one of his hands resting on an open book, with a pencil clutched in it—more strangely still than anything he had ever seen. She looked round wildly, and said:

"Oh! Jon—he's dead—he's dead!"

Jon flung himself down, and reaching over the arm of the chair, where he had lately been sitting, put his lips to the forehead. Icy cold! How could—how could Dad be dead, when only an hour ago—! His mother's arms were round the knees; pressing her breast against them. "Why—why wasn't I with him?" he heard her whisper. Then he saw the tottering word "Irene" pencilled on the open page, and broke down himself. It was his first sight of human death, and its unutterable stillness blotted from him all other emotion; all else, then, was but preliminary to this! All love and life, and joy, anxiety, and sorrow, all movement, light and beauty, but a beginning to this terrible white stillness. It made a dreadful mark on him; all seemed suddenly little, futile, short. He mastered himself at last, got up, and raised her.

"Mother! don't cry—Mother!"

Some hours later, when all was done that had to be, and his mother was lying down, he saw his father alone, on the bed, covered with a white sheet. He stood for a long time gazing at that face which had never looked angry—always whimsical, and kind. "To be kind and keep your end up—there's nothing else in it," he had once heard his father say. How wonderfully Dad had acted up to that philosophy! He understood now that his father had known for a long time past that this would come suddenly—known, and not said a word. He gazed with an awed and passionate reverence. The loneliness of it—just to spare his mother and himself! His own trouble seemed small while he was looking at that face. The word scribbled on the page! The farewell word! Now his mother had no one but himself! He went up close to the dead face—not changed at all, and yet completely changed. He had heard his father say once that he did not believe in consciousness surviving death, or that if it did it might be just survival till the natural age limit of the body had been reached—the natural term of its inherent vitality; so that if the body were broken by accident, excess, violent disease, consciousness might still persist till, in the course of Nature uninterfered with, it would naturally have faded out. It had struck him because he had never heard any one else suggest it. When the heart failed like this—surely it was not quite natural! Perhaps his father's consciousness was in the room with him. Above the bed hung a picture of his father's father. Perhaps his consciousness, too, was still alive; and his brother's—his half-brother, who had died in the Transvaal. Were they all gathered round this bed? Jon kissed the forehead, and stole back to his own room. The door between it and his mother's was ajar; she had evidently been in—everything was ready for him, even some biscuits and hot milk, and the letter no longer on the floor. He ate and drank, watching the last light fade. He did not try to see into the future—just stared at the dark branches of the oak-tree, level with his window, and felt as if life had stopped. Once in the night, turning in his heavy sleep, he was conscious of something white and still, beside his bed, and started up.

His mother's voice said:

"It's only I, Jon dear!" Her hand pressed his forehead gently back; her white figure disappeared.

Alone! He fell heavily asleep again, and dreamed he saw his mother's name crawling on his bed.

CHAPTER IV.—SOAMES COGITATES

The announcement in The Times of his cousin Jolyon's death affected Soames quite simply. So that chap was gone! There had never been a time in their two lives when love had not been lost between them. That quick-blooded sentiment hatred had run its course long since in Soames' heart, and he had refused to allow any recrudescence, but he considered this early decease a piece of poetic justice. For twenty years the fellow had enjoyed the reversion of his wife and house, and—he was dead! The obituary notice, which appeared a little later, paid Jolyon—he thought—too much attention. It spoke of that "diligent and agreeable painter whose work we have come to look on as typical of the best late-Victorian water-colour art." Soames, who had almost mechanically preferred Mole, Morpin, and Caswell Baye, and had always sniffed quite audibly when he came to one of his cousin's on the line, turned The Times with a crackle.

He had to go up to Town that morning on Forsyte affairs, and was fully conscious of Gradman's glance sidelong over his spectacles. The old clerk had about him an aura of regretful congratulation. He smelled, as it were, of old days. One could almost hear him thinking: "Mr. Jolyon, ye-es—just my age, and gone—dear, dear! I dare say she feels it. She was a nice-lookin' woman. Flesh is flesh! They've given 'im a notice in the papers. Fancy!" His atmosphere in fact caused Soames to handle certain leases and conversions with exceptional swiftness.

"About that settlement on Miss Fleur, Mr. Soames?"

"I've thought better of that," answered Soames shortly.

"Ah! I'm glad of that. I thought you were a little hasty. The times do change."

How this death would affect Fleur had begun to trouble Soames. He was not certain that she knew of it—she seldom looked at the paper, never at the births, marriages, and deaths.

He pressed matters on, and made his way to Green Street for lunch. Winifred was almost doleful. Jack Cardigan had broken a splashboard, so far as one could make out, and would not be "fit" for some time. She could not get used to the idea.

"Did Profond ever get off?" he said suddenly.

"He got off," replied Winifred, "but where—I don't know."

Yes, there it was—impossible to tell anything! Not that he wanted to know. Letters from Annette were coming from Dieppe, where she and her mother were staying.

"You saw that fellow's death, I suppose?"

"Yes," said Winifred. "I'm sorry for—for his children. He was very amiable." Soames uttered a rather queer sound. A suspicion of the old deep truth—that men were judged in this world rather by what they were than by what they did—crept and knocked resentfully at the back doors of his mind.

"I know there was a superstition to that effect," he muttered.

"One must do him justice now he's dead."

"I should like to have done him justice before," said Soames; "but I never had the chance. Have you got a 'Baronetage' here?"

"Yes; in that bottom row."

Soames took out a fat red book, and ran over the leaves.

"Mont-Sir Lawrence, 9th Bt., cr. 1620, e. s. of Geoffrey, 8th Bt., and Lavinia, daur. of Sir Charles Muskham, Bt., of Muskham Hall, Shrops: marr. 1890 Emily, daur. of Conway Charwell, Esq., of Condaford Grange, co. Oxon; 1 son, heir Michael Conway, b. 1895, 2 daurs. Residence: Lippinghall Manor, Folwell, Bucks. Clubs: Snooks': Coffee House: Aeroplane. See Bidicott."

"H'm!" he said. "Did you ever know a publisher?"

"Uncle Timothy."

"Alive, I mean."

"Monty knew one at his Club. He brought him here to dinner once. Monty was always thinking of writing a book, you know, about how to make money on the turf. He tried to interest that man."

"Well?"

"He put him on to a horse—for the Two Thousand. We didn't see him again. He was rather smart, if I remember."

"Did it win?"

"No; it ran last, I think. You know Monty really was quite clever in his way."

"Was he?" said Soames. "Can you see any connection between a sucking baronet and publishing?"

"People do all sorts of things nowadays," replied Winifred. "The great stunt seems not to be idle—so different from our time. To do nothing was the thing then. But I suppose it'll come again."

"This young Mont that I'm speaking of is very sweet on Fleur. If it would put an end to that other affair I might encourage it."

"Has he got style?" asked Winifred.

"He's no beauty; pleasant enough, with some scattered brains. There's a good deal of land, I believe. He seems genuinely attached. But I don't know."

"No," murmured Winifred; "it's—very difficult. I always found it best to do nothing. It is such a bore about Jack; now we shan't get away till after Bank Holiday. Well, the people are always amusing, I shall go into the Park and watch them."

"If I were you," said Soames, "I should have a country cottage, and be out of the way of holidays and strikes when you want."

"The country bores me," answered Winifred, "and I found the railway strike quite exciting." Winifred had always been noted for sang-froid.

Soames took his leave. All the way down to Reading he debated whether he should tell Fleur of that boy's father's death. It did not alter the situation except that he would be independent now, and only have his mother's opposition to encounter. He would come into a lot of money, no doubt, and perhaps the house—the house built for Irene and himself—the house whose architect had wrought his domestic ruin. His daughter—mistress of that house! That would be poetic justice! Soames uttered a little mirthless laugh. He had designed that house to re-establish his failing union, meant it for the seat of his descendants, if he could have induced Irene to give him one! Her son and Fleur! Their children would be, in some sort, offspring of the union between himself and her!

The theatricality in that thought was repulsive to his sober sense. And yet—it would be the easiest and wealthiest way out of the impasse, now that Jolyon was gone. The juncture of two Forsyte fortunes had a kind of conservative charm. And she—Irene-would be linked to him once more. Nonsense! Absurd! He put the notion from his head.

On arriving home he heard the click of billiard-balls, and through the window saw young Mont sprawling over the table. Fleur, with her cue akimbo, was watching with a smile. How pretty she looked! No wonder that young fellow was out of his mind about her. A title—land! There was little enough in land, these days; perhaps less in a title. The old Forsytes had always had a kind of contempt for titles, rather remote and artificial things—not worth the money they cost, and having to do with the Court. They had all had that feeling in differing measure—Soames remembered. Swithin, indeed, in his most expansive days had once attended a Levee. He had come away saying he shouldn't go again—"all that small fry." It was suspected that he had looked too big in knee-breeches. Soames remembered how his own mother had wished to be presented because of the fashionable nature of the performance, and how his father had put his foot down with unwonted decision. What did she want with that peacocking—wasting time and money; there was nothing in it!

The instinct which had made and kept the English Commons the chief power in the State, a feeling that their own world was good enough and a little better than any other because it was their world, had kept the old Forsytes singularly free of "flummery," as Nicholas had been wont to call it when he had the gout. Soames' generation, more self-conscious and ironical, had been saved by a sense of Swithin in knee-breeches. While the third and the fourth generation, as it seemed to him, laughed at everything.

However, there was no harm in the young fellow's being heir to a title and estate—a thing one couldn't help. He entered quietly, as Mont missed his shot. He noted the young man's eyes, fixed on Fleur bending over in her turn; and the adoration in them almost touched him.

She paused with the cue poised on the bridge of her slim hand, and shook her crop of short dark chestnut hair.

"I shall never do it."

"'Nothing venture.'"

"All right." The cue struck, the ball rolled. "'There!"

"Bad luck! Never mind!"

Then they saw him, and Soames said:

"I'll mark for you."

He sat down on the raised seat beneath the marker, trim and tired, furtively studying those two young faces. When the game was over Mont came up to him.

"I've started in, sir. Rum game, business, isn't it? I suppose you saw a lot of human nature as a solicitor."

"I did."

"Shall I tell you what I've noticed: People are quite on the wrong tack in offering less than they can afford to give; they ought to offer more, and work backward."

Soames raised his eyebrows.

"Suppose the more is accepted?"

"That doesn't matter a little bit," said Mont; "it's much more paying to abate a price than to increase it. For instance, say we offer an author good terms—he naturally takes them. Then we go into it, find we can't publish at a decent profit and tell him so. He's got confidence in us because we've been generous to him, and he comes down like a lamb, and bears us no malice. But if we offer him poor terms at the start, he doesn't take them, so we have to advance them to get him, and he thinks us damned screws into the bargain.

"Try buying pictures on that system," said Soames; "an offer accepted is a contract—haven't you learned that?"

Young Mont turned his head to where Fleur was standing in the window.

"No," he said, "I wish I had. Then there's another thing. Always let a man off a bargain if he wants to be let off."

"As advertisement?" said Soames dryly.

"Of course it is; but I meant on principle."

"Does your firm work on those lines?"

"Not yet," said Mont, "but it'll come."

"And they will go."

"No, really, sir. I'm making any number of observations, and they all confirm my theory. Human nature is consistently underrated in business, people do themselves out of an awful lot of pleasure and profit by that. Of course, you must be perfectly genuine and open, but that's easy if you feel it. The more human and generous you are the better chance you've got in business."

Soames rose.

"Are you a partner?"

"Not for six months, yet."

"The rest of the firm had better make haste and retire."

Mont laughed.

"You'll see," he said. "There's going to be a big change. The possessive principle has got its shutters up."

"What?" said Soames.

"The house is to let! Good-bye, sir; I'm off now."

Soames watched his daughter give her hand, saw her wince at the squeeze it received, and distinctly heard the young man's sigh as he passed out. Then she came from the window, trailing her finger along the mahogany edge of the billiard-table. Watching her, Soames knew that she was going to ask him something. Her finger felt round the last pocket, and she looked up.

"Have you done anything to stop Jon writing to me, Father?"

Soames shook his head.

"You haven't seen, then?" he said. "His father died just a week ago to-day."

"Oh!"

In her startled, frowning face he saw the instant struggle to apprehend what this would mean.

"Poor Jon! Why didn't you tell me, Father?"

"I never know!" said Soames slowly; "you don't confide in me."

"I would, if you'd help me, dear."

"Perhaps I shall."

Fleur clasped her hands. "Oh! darling—when one wants a thing fearfully, one doesn't think of other people. Don't be angry with me."

Soames put out his hand, as if pushing away an aspersion.

"I'm cogitating," he said. What on earth had made him use a word like that! "Has young Mont been bothering you again?"

Fleur smiled. "Oh! Michael! He's always bothering; but he's such a good sort—I don't mind him."

"Well," said Soames, "I'm tired; I shall go and have a nap before dinner."

He went up to his picture-gallery, lay down on the couch there, and closed his eyes. A terrible responsibility this girl of his—whose mother was—ah! what was she? A terrible responsibility! Help her—how could he help her? He could not alter the fact that he was her father. Or that Irene—! What was it young Mont had said—some nonsense about the possessive instinct—shutters up—To let? Silly!

The sultry air, charged with a scent of meadow-sweet, of river and roses, closed on his senses, drowsing them.

CHAPTER V.—THE FIXED IDEA

"The fixed idea," which has outrun more constables than any other form of human disorder, has never more speed and stamina than when it takes the avid guise of love. To hedges and ditches, and doors, to humans without ideas fixed or otherwise, to perambulators and the contents sucking their fixed ideas, even to the other sufferers from this fast malady—the fixed idea of love pays no attention. It runs with eyes turned inward to its own light, oblivious of all other stars. Those with the fixed ideas that human happiness depends on their art, on vivisecting dogs, on hating foreigners, on paying supertax, on remaining Ministers, on making wheels go round, on preventing their neighbours from being divorced, on conscientious objection, Greek roots, Church dogma, paradox and superiority to everybody else, with other forms of ego-mania—all are unstable compared with him or her whose fixed idea is the possession of some her or him. And though Fleur, those chilly summer days, pursued the scattered life of a little Forsyte whose frocks are paid for, and whose business is pleasure, she was—as Winifred would have said in the latest fashion of speech—"honest to God" indifferent to it all. She wished and wished for the moon, which sailed in cold skies above the river or the Green Park when she went to Town. She even kept Jon's letters, covered with pink silk, on her heart, than which in days when corsets were so low, sentiment so despised, and chests so out of fashion, there could, perhaps, have been no greater proof of the fixity of her idea.

After hearing of his father's death, she wrote to Jon, and received his answer three days later on her return from a river picnic. It was his first letter since their meeting at June's. She opened it with misgiving, and read it with dismay.

"Since I saw you I've heard everything about the past. I won't tell it you—I think you knew when we met at June's. She says you did. If you did, Fleur, you ought to have told me. I expect you only heard your father's side of it. I have heard my mother's. It's dreadful. Now that she's so sad I can't do anything to hurt her more. Of course, I long for you all day, but I don't believe now that we shall ever come together—there's something too strong pulling us apart."

So! Her deception had found her out. But Jon—she felt—had forgiven that. It was what he said of his mother which caused the guttering in her heart and the weak sensation in her legs.

Her first impulse was to reply—her second, not to reply. These impulses were constantly renewed in the days which followed, while desperation grew within her. She was not her father's child for nothing. The tenacity which had at once made and undone Soames was her backbone, too, frilled and embroidered by French grace and quickness. Instinctively she conjugated the verb "to have" always with the pronoun "I." She concealed, however, all signs of her growing desperation, and pursued such river pleasures as the winds and rain of a disagreeable July permitted, as if she had no care in the world; nor did any "sucking baronet" ever neglect the business of a publisher more consistently than her attendant spirit, Michael Mont.

To Soames she was a puzzle. He was almost deceived by this careless gaiety. Almost—because he did not fail to mark her eyes often fixed on nothing, and the film of light shining from her bedroom window late at night. What was she thinking and brooding over into small hours when she ought to have been asleep? But he dared not ask what was in her mind; and, since that one little talk in the billiard-room, she said nothing to him.

In this taciturn condition of affairs it chanced that Winifred invited them to lunch and to go afterward to "a most amusing little play, 'The Beggar's Opera'" and would they bring a man to make four? Soames, whose attitude toward theatres was to go to nothing, accepted, because Fleur's attitude was to go to everything. They motored up, taking Michael Mont, who, being in his seventh heaven, was found by Winifred "very amusing." "The Beggar's Opera" puzzled Soames. The people were very unpleasant, the whole thing very cynical. Winifred was "intrigued"—by the dresses. The music, too, did not displease her. At the Opera, the night before, she had arrived too early for the Russian Ballet, and found the stage occupied by singers, for a whole hour pale or apoplectic from terror lest by some dreadful inadvertence they might drop into a tune. Michael Mont was enraptured with the whole thing. And all three wondered what Fleur was thinking of it. But Fleur was not thinking of it. Her fixed idea stood on the stage and sang with Polly Peachum, mimed with Filch, danced with Jenny Diver, postured with Lucy Lockit, kissed, trolled, and cuddled with Macheath. Her lips might smile, her hands applaud, but the comic old masterpiece made no more impression on her than if it had been pathetic, like a modern "Revue." When they embarked in the car to return, she ached because Jon was not sitting next her instead of Michael Mont. When, at some jolt, the young man's arm touched hers as if by accident, she only thought: 'If that were Jon's arm!' When his cheerful voice, tempered by her proximity, murmured above the sound of the car's progress, she smiled and answered, thinking: 'If that were Jon's voice!' and when once he said, "Fleur, you look a perfect angel in that dress!" she answered, "Oh, do you like it?" thinking, 'If only Jon could see it!'

During this drive she took a resolution. She would go to Robin Hill and see him—alone; she would take the car, without word beforehand to him or to her father. It was nine days since his letter, and she could wait no longer. On Monday she would go! The decision made her well disposed toward young Mont. With something to look forward to she could afford to tolerate and respond. He might stay to dinner; propose to her as usual; dance with her, press her hand, sigh—do what he liked. He was only a nuisance when he interfered with her fixed idea. She was even sorry for him so far as it was possible to be sorry for anybody but herself just now. At dinner he seemed to talk more wildly than usual about what he called "the death of the close borough"—she paid little attention, but her father seemed paying a good deal, with the smile on his face which meant opposition, if not anger.

"The younger generation doesn't think as you do, sir; does it, Fleur?"

Fleur shrugged her shoulders—the younger generation was just Jon, and she did not know what he was thinking.

"Young people will think as I do when they're my age, Mr. Mont. Human nature doesn't change."

"I admit that, sir; but the forms of thought change with the times. The pursuit of self-interest is a form of thought that's going out."

"Indeed! To mind one's own business is not a form of thought, Mr. Mont, it's an instinct."

Yes, when Jon was the business!

"But what is one's business, sir? That's the point. Everybody's business is going to be one's business. Isn't it, Fleur?"

Fleur only smiled.

"If not," added young Mont, "there'll be blood."

"People have talked like that from time immemorial"

"But you'll admit, sir, that the sense of property is dying out?"

"I should say increasing among those who have none."

"Well, look at me! I'm heir to an entailed estate. I don't want the thing; I'd cut the entail to-morrow."

"You're not married, and you don't know what you're talking about."

Fleur saw the young man's eyes turn rather piteously upon her.

"Do you really mean that marriage—?" he began.

"Society is built on marriage," came from between her father's close lips; "marriage and its consequences. Do you want to do away with it?"

Young Mont made a distracted gesture. Silence brooded over the dinner table, covered with spoons bearing the Forsyte crest—a pheasant proper—under the electric light in an alabaster globe. And outside, the river evening darkened, charged with heavy moisture and sweet scents.

'Monday,' thought Fleur; 'Monday!'

CHAPTER VI.—DESPERATE

The weeks which followed the death of his father were sad and empty to the only Jolyon Forsyte left. The necessary forms and ceremonies—the reading of the Will, valuation of the estate, distribution of the legacies—were enacted over the head, as it were, of one not yet of age. Jolyon was cremated. By his special wish no one attended that ceremony, or wore black for him. The succession of his property, controlled to some extent by old Jolyon's Will, left his widow in possession of Robin Hill, with two thousand five hundred pounds a year for life. Apart from this the two Wills worked together in some complicated way to insure that each of Jolyon's three children should have an equal share in their grandfather's and father's property in the future as in the present, save only that Jon, by virtue of his sex, would have control of his capital when he was twenty-one, while June and Holly would only have the spirit of theirs, in order that their children might have the body after them. If they had no children, it would all come to Jon if he outlived them; and since June was fifty, and Holly nearly forty, it was considered in Lincoln's Inn Fields that but for the cruelty of income tax, young Jon would be as warm a man as his grandfather when he died. All this was nothing to Jon, and little enough to his mother. It was June who did everything needful for one who had left his affairs in perfect order. When she had gone, and those two were alone again in the great house, alone with death drawing them together, and love driving them apart, Jon passed very painful days secretly disgusted and disappointed with himself. His mother would look at him with such a patient sadness which yet had in it an instinctive pride, as if she were reserving her defence. If she smiled he was angry that his answering smile should be so grudging and unnatural. He did not judge or condemn her; that was all too remote—indeed, the idea of doing so had never come to him. No! he was grudging and unnatural because he couldn't have what he wanted because of her. There was one alleviation—much to do in connection with his father's career, which could not be safely entrusted to June, though she had offered to undertake it. Both Jon and his mother had felt that if she took his portfolios, unexhibited drawings and unfinished matter, away with her, the work would encounter such icy blasts from Paul Post and other frequenters of her studio, that it would soon be frozen out even of her warm heart. On its old-fashioned plane and of its kind the work was good, and they could not bear the thought of its subjection to ridicule. A one-man exhibition of his work was the least testimony they could pay to one they had loved; and on preparation for this they spent many hours together. Jon came to have a curiously increased respect for his father. The quiet tenacity with which he had converted a mediocre talent into something really individual was disclosed by these researches. There was a great mass of work with a rare continuity of growth in depth and reach of vision. Nothing certainly went very deep, or reached very high—but such as the work was, it was thorough, conscientious, and complete. And, remembering his father's utter absence of "side" or self-assertion, the chaffing humility with which he had always spoken of his own efforts, ever calling himself "an amateur," Jon could not help feeling that he had never really known his father. To take himself seriously, yet never that he did so, seemed to have been his ruling principle. There was something in this which appealed to the boy, and made him heartily endorse his mother's comment: "He had true refinement; he couldn't help thinking of others, whatever he did. And when he took a resolution which went counter, he did it with the minimum of defiance—not like the Age, is it? Twice in his life he had to go against everything; and yet it never made him bitter." Jon saw tears running down her face, which she at once turned away from him. She was so quiet about her loss that sometimes he had thought she didn't feel it much. Now, as he looked at her, he felt how far he fell short of the reserve power and dignity in both his father and his mother. And, stealing up to her, he put his arm round her waist. She kissed him swiftly, but with a sort of passion, and went out of the room.

The studio, where they had been sorting and labelling, had once been Holly's schoolroom, devoted to her silkworms, dried lavender, music, and other forms of instruction. Now, at the end of July, despite its northern and eastern aspects, a warm and slumberous air came in between the long-faded lilac linen curtains. To redeem a little the departed glory, as of a field that is golden and gone, clinging to a room which its master has left, Irene had placed on the paint-stained table a bowl of red roses. This, and Jolyon's favourite cat, who still clung to the deserted habitat, were the pleasant spots in that dishevelled, sad workroom. Jon, at the north window, sniffing air mysteriously scented with warm strawberries, heard a car drive up. The lawyers again about some nonsense! Why did that scent so make one ache? And where did it come from—there were no strawberry beds on this side of the house. Instinctively he took a crumpled sheet of paper from his pocket, and wrote down some broken words. A warmth began spreading in his chest; he rubbed the palms of his hands together. Presently he had jotted this:

"If I could make a little song A little song to soothe my heart! I'd make it all of little things The plash of water, rub of wings, The puffing-off of dandies crown, The hiss of raindrop spilling down, The purr of cat, the trill of bird, And ev'ry whispering I've heard From willy wind in leaves and grass, And all the distant drones that pass. A song as tender and as light As flower, or butterfly in flight; And when I saw it opening, I'd let it fly and sing!"

He was still muttering it over to himself at the window, when he heard his name called, and, turning round, saw Fleur. At that amazing apparition, he made at first no movement and no sound, while her clear vivid glance ravished his heart. Then he went forward to the table, saying, "How nice of you to come!" and saw her flinch as if he had thrown something at her.

"I asked for you," she said, "and they showed me up here. But I can go away again."

Jon clutched the paint-stained table. Her face and figure in its frilly frock photographed itself with such startling vividness upon his eyes, that if she had sunk through the floor he must still have seen her.

"I know I told you a lie, Jon. But I told it out of love."

"Yes, oh! yes! That's nothing!"

"I didn't answer your letter. What was the use—there wasn't anything to answer. I wanted to see you instead." She held out both her hands, and Jon grasped them across the table. He tried to say something, but all his attention was given to trying not to hurt her hands. His own felt so hard and hers so soft. She said almost defiantly:

"That old story—was it so very dreadful?"

"Yes." In his voice, too, there was a note of defiance.

She dragged her hands away. "I didn't think in these days boys were tied to their mothers' apron-strings."

Jon's chin went up as if he had been struck.

"Oh! I didn't mean it, Jon. What a horrible thing to say!" Swiftly she came close to him. "Jon, dear; I didn't mean it."

"All right."

She had put her two hands on his shoulder, and her forehead down on them; the brim of her hat touched his neck, and he felt it quivering. But, in a sort of paralysis, he made no response. She let go of his shoulder and drew away.

"Well, I'll go, if you don't want me. But I never thought you'd have given me up."

"I haven't," cried Jon, coming suddenly to life. "I can't. I'll try again."

Her eyes gleamed, she swayed toward him. "Jon—I love you! Don't give me up! If you do, I don't know what—I feel so desperate. What does it matter—all that past-compared with this?"

She clung to him. He kissed her eyes, her cheeks, her lips. But while he kissed her he saw, the sheets of that letter fallen down on the floor of his bedroom—his father's white dead face—his mother kneeling before it. Fleur's whispered, "Make her! Promise! Oh! Jon, try!" seemed childish in his ear. He felt curiously old.

"I promise!" he muttered. "Only, you don't understand."

"She wants to spoil our lives, just because—"

"Yes, of what?"

Again that challenge in his voice, and she did not answer. Her arms tightened round him, and he returned her kisses; but even while he yielded, the poison worked in him, the poison of the letter. Fleur did not know, she did not understand—she misjudged his mother; she came from the enemy's camp! So lovely, and he loved her so—yet, even in her embrace, he could not help the memory of Holly's words: "I think she has a 'having' nature," and his mother's "My darling boy, don't think of me—think of yourself!"

When she was gone like a passionate dream, leaving her image on his eyes, her kisses on his lips, such an ache in his heart, Jon leaned in the window, listening to the car bearing her away. Still the scent as of warm strawberries, still the little summer sounds that should make his song; still all the promise of youth and happiness in sighing, floating, fluttering July—and his heart torn; yearning strong in him; hope high in him yet with its eyes cast down, as if ashamed. The miserable task before him! If Fleur was desperate, so was he—watching the poplars swaying, the white clouds passing, the sunlight on the grass.

He waited till evening, till after their almost silent dinner, till his mother had played to him and still he waited, feeling that she knew what he was waiting to say. She kissed him and went up-stairs, and still he lingered, watching the moonlight and the moths, and that unreality of colouring which steals along and stains a summer night. And he would have given anything to be back again in the past—barely three months back; or away forward, years, in the future. The present with this dark cruelty of a decision, one way or the other, seemed impossible. He realised now so much more keenly what his mother felt than he had at first; as if the story in that letter had been a poisonous germ producing a kind of fever of partisanship, so that he really felt there were two camps, his mother's and his—Fleur's and her father's. It might be a dead thing, that old tragic ownership and enmity, but dead things were poisonous till time had cleaned them away. Even his love felt tainted, less illusioned, more of the earth, and with a treacherous lurking doubt lest Fleur, like her father, might want to own; not articulate, just a stealing haunt, horribly unworthy, which crept in and about the ardour of his memories, touched with its tarnishing breath the vividness and grace of that charmed face and figure—a doubt, not real enough to convince him of its presence, just real enough to deflower a perfect faith. And perfect faith, to Jon, not yet twenty, was essential. He still had Youth's eagerness to give with both hands, to take with neither—to give lovingly to one who had his own impulsive generosity. Surely she had! He got up from the window-seat and roamed in the big grey ghostly room, whose walls were hung with silvered canvas. This house his father said in that death-bed letter—had been built for his mother to live in—with Fleur's father! He put out his hand in the half-dark, as if to grasp the shadowy hand of the dead. He clenched, trying to feel the thin vanished fingers of his father; to squeeze them, and reassure him that he—he was on his father's side. Tears, prisoned within him, made his eyes feel dry and hot. He went back to the window. It was warmer, not so eerie, more comforting outside, where the moon hung golden, three days off full; the freedom of the night was comforting. If only Fleur and he had met on some desert island without a past—and Nature for their house! Jon had still his high regard for desert islands, where breadfruit grew, and the water was blue above the coral. The night was deep, was free—there was enticement in it; a lure, a promise, a refuge

531

from entanglement, and love! Milksop tied to his mother's...! His cheeks burned. He shut the window, drew curtains over it, switched off the lighted sconce, and went up-stairs.

The door of his room was open, the light turned up; his mother, still in her evening gown, was standing at the window. She turned and said:

"Sit down, Jon; let's talk." She sat down on the window-seat, Jon on his bed. She had her profile turned to him, and the beauty and grace of her figure, the delicate line of the brow, the nose, the neck, the strange and as it were remote refinement of her, moved him. His mother never belonged to her surroundings. She came into them from somewhere—as it were! What was she going to say to him, who had in his heart such things to say to her?

"I know Fleur came to-day. I'm not surprised." It was as though she had added: "She is her father's daughter!" And Jon's heart hardened. Irene went on quietly:

"I have Father's letter. I picked it up that night and kept it. Would you like it back, dear?"

Jon shook his head.

"I had read it, of course, before he gave it to you. It didn't quite do justice to my criminality."

"Mother!" burst from Jon's lips.

"He put it very sweetly, but I know that in marrying Fleur's father without love I did a dreadful thing. An unhappy marriage, Jon, can play such havoc with other lives besides one's own. You are fearfully young, my darling, and fearfully loving. Do you think you can possibly be happy with this girl?"

Staring at her dark eyes, darker now from pain, Jon answered

"Yes; oh! yes—if you could be."

Irene smiled.

"Admiration of beauty and longing for possession are not love. If yours were another case like mine, Jon—where the deepest things are stifled; the flesh joined, and the spirit at war!"

"Why should it, Mother? You think she must be like her father, but she's not. I've seen him."

Again the smile came on Irene's lips, and in Jon something wavered; there was such irony and experience in that smile.

"You are a giver, Jon; she is a taker."

That unworthy doubt, that haunting uncertainty again! He said with vehemence:

"She isn't—she isn't. It's only because I can't bear to make you unhappy, Mother, now that Father—" He thrust his fists against his forehead.

Irene got up.

"I told you that night, dear, not to mind me. I meant it. Think of yourself and your own happiness! I can stand what's left—I've brought it on myself."

Again the word "Mother!" burst from Jon's lips.

She came over to him and put her hands over his.

"Do you feel your head, darling?"

Jon shook it. What he felt was in his chest—a sort of tearing asunder of the tissue there, by the two loves.

"I shall always love you the same, Jon, whatever you do. You won't lose anything." She smoothed his hair gently, and walked away.

He heard the door shut; and, rolling over on the bed, lay, stifling his breath, with an awful held-up feeling within him.

CHAPTER VII.—EMBASSY

Enquiring for her at tea time Soames learned that Fleur had been out in the car since two. Three hours! Where had she gone? Up to London without a word to him? He had never become quite reconciled with cars. He had embraced them in principle—like the born empiricist, or Forsyte, that he was—adopting each symptom of progress as it came along with: "Well, we couldn't do without them now." But in fact he found them tearing, great, smelly things. Obliged by Annette to have one—a Rollhard with pearl-grey cushions, electric light, little mirrors, trays for the ashes of cigarettes, flower vases—all smelling of petrol and stephanotis—he regarded it much as he used to regard his brother-in-law, Montague Dartie. The thing typified all that was fast, insecure, and subcutaneously oily in modern life. As modern life became faster, looser, younger, Soames was becoming older, slower, tighter, more and more in thought and language like his father James before him. He was almost aware of it himself. Pace and progress pleased him less and less; there was an ostentation, too, about a car which he considered provocative in the prevailing mood of Labour. On one occasion that fellow Sims had driven over the only vested interest of a working man. Soames had not forgotten the behaviour of its master, when not many people would have stopped to put up with it. He had been sorry for the dog, and quite prepared to take its part against the car, if that ruffian hadn't been so outrageous. With four hours fast becoming five, and still no Fleur, all the old car-wise feelings he had experienced in person and by proxy balled within him, and sinking sensations troubled the pit of his stomach. At seven he telephoned to Winifred by trunk call. No! Fleur had not been to Green Street. Then where was she? Visions of his beloved daughter rolled up in her pretty frills, all blood and dust-stained, in some hideous catastrophe, began to haunt him. He went to her room and spied among her things. She had taken nothing—no dressing-case, no Jewellery. And this, a relief in one sense, increased his fears of an accident. Terrible to be helpless when his loved one was missing, especially when he couldn't bear fuss or publicity of any kind! What should he do if she were not back by nightfall?

At a quarter to eight he heard the car. A great weight lifted from off his heart; he hurried down. She was getting out—pale and tired-looking, but nothing wrong. He met her in the hall.

"You've frightened me. Where have you been?"

"To Robin Hill. I'm sorry, dear. I had to go; I'll tell you afterward." And, with a flying kiss, she ran up-stairs.

Soames waited in the drawing-room. To Robin Hill! What did that portend?

It was not a subject they could discuss at dinner—consecrated to the susceptibilities of the butler. The agony of nerves Soames had been through, the relief he felt at her safety, softened his power to condemn what she had done, or resist what she was going to do; he waited in a relaxed stupor for her revelation. Life was a queer business. There he was at sixty-five and no more in command of things than if he had not spent forty years in building up security-always something one couldn't get on terms with! In the pocket of his dinner-jacket was a letter from Annette. She was coming back in a fortnight. He knew nothing of what she had been doing out there. And he was glad that he did not. Her absence had been a relief. Out of sight was out of mind! And now she was coming back. Another worry! And the Bolderby Old Crome was gone—Dumetrius had got it—all because that anonymous letter had put it out of his thoughts. He furtively remarked the strained look on his daughter's face, as if she too were gazing at a picture that she couldn't buy. He almost wished the War back. Worries didn't seem, then, quite so worrying. From the caress in her voice, the look on her face, he became certain that she wanted something from him, uncertain whether it would be wise of him to give it her. He pushed his savoury away uneaten, and even joined her in a cigarette.

After dinner she set the electric piano-player going. And he augured the worst when she sat down on a cushion footstool at his knee, and put her hand on his.

"Darling, be nice to me. I had to see Jon—he wrote to me. He's going to try what he can do with his mother. But I've been thinking. It's really in your hands, Father. If you'd persuade her that it doesn't mean renewing the past in any way! That I shall stay yours, and Jon will stay hers; that you need never see him or her, and she need never see you or me! Only you could persuade her, dear, because only you could promise. One can't promise for other people. Surely it wouldn't be too awkward for you to see her just this once now that Jon's father is dead?"

"Too awkward?" Soames repeated. "The whole thing's preposterous."

"You know," said Fleur, without looking up, "you wouldn't mind seeing her, really."

Soames was silent. Her words had expressed a truth too deep for him to admit. She slipped her fingers between his own—hot, slim, eager, they clung there. This child of his would corkscrew her way into a brick wall!

"What am I to do if you won't, Father?" she said very softly.

"I'll do anything for your happiness," said Soames; "but this isn't for your happiness."

"Oh! it is; it is!"

"It'll only stir things up," he said grimly.

"But they are stirred up. The thing is to quiet them. To make her feel that this is just our lives, and has nothing to do with yours or hers. You can do it, Father, I know you can."

"You know a great deal, then," was Soames' glum answer.

"If you will, Jon and I will wait a year—two years if you like."

"It seems to me," murmured Soames, "that you care nothing about what I feel."

Fleur pressed his hand against her cheek.

"I do, darling. But you wouldn't like me to be awfully miserable."

How she wheedled to get her ends! And trying with all his might to think she really cared for him—he was not sure—not sure. All she cared for was this boy! Why should he help her to get this boy, who was killing her affection for himself? Why should he? By the laws of the Forsytes it was foolish! There was nothing to be had out of it—nothing! To give her to that boy! To pass her into the enemy's camp, under the influence of the woman who had injured him so deeply! Slowly—inevitably—he would lose this flower of his life! And suddenly he was conscious that his hand was wet. His heart gave a little painful jump. He couldn't bear her to cry. He put his other hand quickly over hers, and a tear dropped on that, too. He couldn't go on like this! "Well, well," he said, "I'll think it over, and do what I can. Come, come!" If she must have it for her happiness—she must; he couldn't refuse to help her. And lest she should begin to thank him he got out of his chair and went up to the piano-player—making that noise! It ran down, as he reached it, with a faint buzz. That musical box of his nursery days: "The Harmonious Blacksmith," "Glorious Port"—the thing had always made him miserable when his mother set it going on Sunday afternoons. Here it was again—the same thing, only larger, more expensive, and now it played "The Wild, Wild Women," and "The Policeman's Holiday," and he was no longer in black velvet with a sky blue collar. 'Profond's right,' he thought, 'there's nothing in it! We're all progressing to the grave!' And with that surprising mental comment he walked out.

He did not see Fleur again that night. But, at breakfast, her eyes followed him about with an appeal he could not escape—not that he intended to try. No! He had made up his mind to the nerve-racking business. He would go to Robin Hill—to that house of memories. Pleasant memory—the last! Of going down to keep that boy's father and Irene apart by threatening divorce. He had often thought, since, that it had clinched their union. And, now, he was going to clinch the union of that boy with his girl. 'I don't know what I've done,' he thought, 'to have such things thrust on me!' He went up by train and down by train, and from the station walked by the long rising lane, still very much as he remembered it over thirty years ago. Funny—so near London! Some one evidently was holding on to the land there. This speculation soothed him, moving between the high hedges slowly, so as not to get overheated, though the day was chill enough. After all was said and done there was something real about land, it didn't shift. Land, and good pictures! The values might fluctuate a bit, but on the whole they were always going up—worth holding on to, in a world where there was such a lot of unreality, cheap building, changing fashions, such a "Here to-day and gone to-morrow" spirit. The French were right, perhaps, with their peasant proprietorship, though he had no opinion of the French. One's bit of land! Something solid in it! He had heard peasant proprietors described as a pig-headed lot; had heard young Mont call his father a pigheaded Morning Poster—disrespectful young devil. Well, there were worse things than being pig-headed or reading the Morning Post. There was Profond and his tribe, and all these Labour chaps, and loud-mouthed politicians and 'wild, wild women'! A lot of worse things! And suddenly Soames became conscious of feeling weak, and hot, and shaky. Sheer nerves at the meeting before him! As Aunt Juley might have said—quoting "Superior Dosset"—his nerves were "in a proper fautigue." He could see the house now among its trees, the house he had watched being built, intending it for himself and this woman, who, by such strange fate, had lived in it with another after all! He began to think of Dumetrius, Local Loans, and other forms of investment. He could not afford to meet her with his nerves all shaking; he who represented the Day of Judgment for her on earth as it was in heaven; he, legal ownership, personified, meeting lawless beauty, incarnate. His dignity demanded impassivity during this embassy designed to link their offspring, who, if she had behaved herself, would have been brother and sister. That wretched tune, "The Wild, Wild Women," kept running in his head, perversely, for tunes did not run there as a rule. Passing the poplars in front of the house, he thought: 'How they've grown; I had them planted!' A maid answered his ring.

"Will you say—Mr. Forsyte, on a very special matter."

If she realised who he was, quite probably she would not see him. 'By George!' he thought, hardening as the tug came. 'It's a topsy-turvy affair!'

The maid came back. "Would the gentleman state his business, please?"

"Say it concerns Mr. Jon," said Soames.

And once more he was alone in that hall with the pool of grey-white marble designed by her first lover. Ah! she had been a bad lot—had loved two men, and not himself! He must remember that when he came face to face with her once more. And suddenly he saw her in the opening chink between the long heavy purple curtains, swaying, as if in hesitation; the old perfect poise and line, the old startled dark-eyed gravity, the old calm defensive voice: "Will you come in, please?"

He passed through that opening. As in the picture-gallery and the confectioner's shop, she seemed to him still beautiful. And this was the first time—the very first—since he married her seven-and-thirty years ago, that he was speaking to her without the legal right to call her his. She was not wearing black—one of that fellow's radical notions, he supposed.

"I apologise for coming," he said glumly; "but this business must be settled one way or the other."

"Won't you sit down?"

"No, thank you."

Anger at his false position, impatience of ceremony between them, mastered him, and words came tumbling out:

"It's an infernal mischance; I've done my best to discourage it. I consider my daughter crazy, but I've got into the habit of indulging her; that's why I'm here. I suppose you're fond of your son."

"Devotedly."

"Well?"

"It rests with him."

He had a sense of being met and baffled. Always—always she had baffled him, even in those old first married days.

"It's a mad notion," he said.

"It is."

"If you had only—! Well—they might have been—" he did not finish that sentence "brother and sister and all this saved," but he saw her shudder as if he had, and stung by the sight he crossed over to the window. Out there the trees had not grown—they couldn't, they were old!

"So far as I'm concerned," he said, "you may make your mind easy. I desire to see neither you nor your son if this marriage comes about. Young people in these days are—are unaccountable. But I can't bear to see my daughter unhappy. What am I to say to her when I go back?"

"Please say to her as I said to you, that it rests with Jon."

"You don't oppose it?"

"With all my heart; not with my lips."

Soames stood, biting his finger.

"I remember an evening—" he said suddenly; and was silent. What was there—what was there in this woman that would not fit into the four corners of his hate or condemnation? "Where is he—your son?"

"Up in his father's studio, I think."

"Perhaps you'd have him down."

He watched her ring the bell, he watched the maid come in.

"Please tell Mr. Jon that I want him."

"If it rests with him," said Soames hurriedly, when the maid was gone, "I suppose I may take it for granted that this unnatural marriage will take place; in that case there'll be formalities. Whom do I deal with—Herring's?"

Irene nodded.

"You don't propose to live with them?"

Irene shook her head.

"What happens to this house?"

"It will be as Jon wishes."

"This house," said Soames suddenly: "I had hopes when I began it. If they live in it—their children! They say there's such a thing as Nemesis. Do you believe in it?"

"Yes."

"Oh! You do!"

He had come back from the window, and was standing close to her, who, in the curve of her grand piano, was, as it were, embayed.

"I'm not likely to see you again," he said slowly. "Will you shake hands"—his lip quivered, the words came out jerkily—"and let the past die." He held out his hand. Her pale face grew paler, her eyes so dark, rested immovably on his, her hands remained clasped in front of her. He heard a sound and turned. That boy was standing in the opening of the curtains. Very queer he looked, hardly recognisable as the young fellow he had seen in the Gallery off Cork Street—very queer; much older, no youth in the face at all—haggard, rigid, his hair ruffled, his eyes deep in his head. Soames made an effort, and said with a lift of his lip, not quite a smile nor quite a sneer:

"Well, young man! I'm here for my daughter; it rests with you, it seems—this matter. Your mother leaves it in your hands."

The boy continued staring at his mother's face, and made no answer.

"For my daughter's sake I've brought myself to come," said Soames. "What am I to say to her when I go back?"

Still looking at his mother, the boy said, quietly:

"Tell Fleur that it's no good, please; I must do as my father wished before he died."

"Jon!"

"It's all right, Mother."

In a kind of stupefaction Soames looked from one to the other; then, taking up hat and umbrella which he had put down on a chair, he walked toward the curtains. The boy stood aside for him to go by. He passed through and heard the grate of the rings as the curtains were drawn behind him. The sound liberated something in his chest.

'So that's that!' he thought, and passed out of the front door.

CHAPTER VIII.—THE DARK TUNE

As Soames walked away from the house at Robin Hill the sun broke through the grey of that chill afternoon, in smoky radiance. So absorbed in landscape painting that he seldom looked seriously for effects of Nature out of doors—he was struck by that moody effulgence—it mourned with a triumph suited to his own feeling. Victory in defeat. His embassy had come to naught. But he was rid of those people, had regained his daughter at the expense of—her happiness. What would Fleur say to him? Would she believe he had done his best? And under that sunlight faring on the elms, hazels, hollies of the lane and those unexploited fields, Soames felt dread. She would be terribly upset! He must appeal to her pride. That boy had given her up, declared part and lot with the woman who so long ago had given her father up! Soames clenched his hands. Given him up, and why? What had been wrong with him? And once more he felt the malaise of one who contemplates himself as seen by another—like a dog who chances on his refection in a mirror and is intrigued and anxious at the unseizable thing.

Not in a hurry to get home, he dined in town at the Connoisseurs. While eating a pear it suddenly occurred to him that, if he had not gone down to Robin Hill, the boy might not have so decided. He remembered the expression on his face while his mother was refusing the hand he had held out. A strange, an awkward thought! Had Fleur cooked her own goose by trying to make too sure?

He reached home at half-past nine. While the car was passing in at one drive gate he heard the grinding sputter of a motor-cycle passing out by the other. Young Mont, no doubt, so Fleur had not been lonely. But he went in with a sinking heart. In the cream-panelled drawing-room she was sitting with her elbows on her knees, and her chin on her clasped hands, in front of a white camellia plant which filled the fireplace. That glance at her before she saw him renewed his dread. What was she seeing among those white camellias?

"Well, Father!"

Soames shook his head. His tongue failed him. This was murderous work! He saw her eyes dilate, her lips quivering.

"What? What? Quick, Father!"

"My dear," said Soames, "I—I did my best, but—" And again he shook his head.

Fleur ran to him, and put a hand on each of his shoulders.

"She?"

"No," muttered Soames; "he. I was to tell you that it was no use; he must do what his father wished before he died." He caught her by the waist. "Come, child, don't let them hurt you. They're not worth your little finger."

Fleur tore herself from his grasp.

"You didn't you—couldn't have tried. You—you betrayed me, Father!"

Bitterly wounded, Soames gazed at her passionate figure writhing there in front of him.

"You didn't try—you didn't—I was a fool! I won't believe he could—he ever could! Only yesterday he—! Oh! why did I ask you?"

"Yes," said Soames, quietly, "why did you? I swallowed my feelings; I did my best for you, against my judgment—and this is my reward. Good-night!"

With every nerve in his body twitching he went toward the door.

Fleur darted after him.

"He gives me up? You mean that? Father!"

Soames turned and forced himself to answer:

"Yes."

"Oh!" cried Fleur. "What did you—what could you have done in those old days?"

The breathless sense of really monstrous injustice cut the power of speech in Soames' throat. What had he done! What had they done to him!

And with quite unconscious dignity he put his hand on his breast, and looked at her.

"It's a shame!" cried Fleur passionately.

Soames went out. He mounted, slow and icy, to his picture gallery, and paced among his treasures. Outrageous! Oh! Outrageous! She was spoiled! Ah! and who had spoiled her? He stood still before the Goya copy. Accustomed to her own way in everything. Flower of his life! And now that she couldn't have it! He turned to the window for some air. Daylight was dying, the moon rising, gold behind the poplars! What sound was that? Why! That piano thing! A dark tune, with a thrum and a throb! She had set it going—what comfort could she get from that? His eyes caught movement down there beyond the lawn, under the trellis of rambler roses and young acacia-trees, where the moonlight fell. There she was, roaming up and down. His heart gave a little sickening jump. What would she do under this blow? How could he tell? What did he know of her—he had only loved her all his life— looked on her as the apple of his eye! He knew nothing—had no notion. There she was— and that dark tune—and the river gleaming in the moonlight!

'I must go out,' he thought.

He hastened down to the drawing-room, lighted just as he had left it, with the piano thrumming out that waltz, or fox-trot, or whatever they called it in these days, and passed through on to the verandah.

Where could he watch, without her seeing him? And he stole down through the fruit garden to the boat-house. He was between her and the river now, and his heart felt lighter. She was his daughter, and Annette's—she wouldn't do anything foolish; but there it was— he didn't know! From the boat house window he could see the last acacia and the spin of her skirt when she turned in her restless march. That tune had run down at last—thank goodness! He crossed the floor and looked through the farther window at the water slow-flowing past the lilies. It made little bubbles against them, bright where a moon-streak fell. He remembered suddenly that early morning when he had slept on the house-boat after his father died, and she had just been born—nearly nineteen years ago! Even now he recalled the unaccustomed world when he woke up, the strange feeling it had given him. That day the second passion of his life began—for this girl of his, roaming under the acacias. What a comfort she had been to him! And all the soreness and sense of outrage left him. If he could make her happy again, he didn't care! An owl flew, queeking, queeking; a bat flitted by; the moonlight brightened and broadened on the water. How long was she going to roam about like this! He went back to the window, and suddenly saw her coming down to the bank. She stood quite close, on the landing-stage. And Soames watched, clenching his hands. Should he speak to her? His excitement was intense. The stillness of her figure, its youth, its absorption in despair, in longing, in—itself. He would always remember it, moonlit like that; and the faint sweet reek of the river and the shivering of the willow leaves. She had everything in the world that he could give her, except the one thing that she could not have because of him! The perversity of things hurt him at that moment, as might a fish-bone in his throat.

Then, with an infinite relief, he saw her turn back toward the house. What could he give her to make amends? Pearls, travel, horses, other young men—anything she wanted—that he might lose the memory of her young figure lonely by the water! There! She had set that tune going again! Why—it was a mania! Dark, thrumming, faint, travelling from the house. It was as though she had said: "If I can't have something to keep me going, I shall die of this!" Soames dimly understood. Well, if it helped her, let her keep it thrumming on all night! And, mousing back through the fruit garden, he regained the verandah. Though he meant to go in and speak to her now, he still hesitated, not knowing what to say, trying hard to recall how it felt to be thwarted in love. He ought to know, ought to remember— and he could not! Gone—all real recollection; except that it had hurt him horribly. In this blankness he stood passing his handkerchief over hands and lips, which were very dry. By craning his head he could just see Fleur, standing with her back to that piano still grinding out its tune, her arms tight crossed on her breast, a lighted cigarette between her lips, whose smoke half veiled her face. The expression on it was strange to Soames, the eyes shone and stared, and every feature was alive with a sort of wretched scorn and anger. Once or twice he had seen Annette look like that—the face was too vivid, too naked, not his daughter's at that moment. And he dared not go in, realising the futility of any attempt at consolation. He sat down in the shadow of the ingle-nook.

Monstrous trick, that Fate had played him! Nemesis! That old unhappy marriage! And in God's name-why? How was he to know, when he wanted Irene so violently, and she consented to be his, that she would never love him? The tune died and was renewed, and died again, and still Soames sat in the shadow, waiting for he knew not what. The fag of Fleur's cigarette, flung through the window, fell on the grass; he watched it glowing, burning itself out. The moon had freed herself above the poplars, and poured her unreality on the garden. Comfortless light, mysterious, withdrawn—like the beauty of that woman who had never loved him—dappling the nemesias and the stocks with a vesture not of earth. Flowers! And his flower so unhappy! Ah! Why could one not put happiness into Local Loans, gild its edges, insure it against going down?

Light had ceased to flow out now from the drawing-room window. All was silent and dark in there. Had she gone up? He rose, and, tiptoeing, peered in. It seemed so! He entered. The verandah kept the moonlight out; and at first he could see nothing but the outlines of furniture blacker than the darkness. He groped toward the farther window to shut it. His foot struck a chair, and he heard a gasp. There she was, curled and crushed into the corner of the sofa! His hand hovered. Did she want his consolation? He stood, gazing at that ball of crushed frills and hair and graceful youth, trying to burrow its way out of sorrow. How leave her there? At last he touched her hair, and said:

"Come, darling, better go to bed. I'll make it up to you, somehow." How fatuous! But what could he have said?

CHAPTER IX.—UNDER THE OAK-TREE

When their visitor had disappeared Jon and his mother stood without speaking, till he said suddenly:

"I ought to have seen him out."

But Soames was already walking down the drive, and Jon went upstairs to his father's studio, not trusting himself to go back.

The expression on his mother's face confronting the man she had once been married to, had sealed a resolution growing within him ever since she left him the night before. It had put the finishing touch of reality. To marry Fleur would be to hit his mother in the face; to betray his dead father! It was no good! Jon had the least resentful of natures. He bore his parents no grudge in this hour of his distress. For one so young there was a rather strange power in him of seeing things in some sort of proportion. It was worse for Fleur, worse for his mother even, than it was for him. Harder than to give up was to be given up, or to be the cause of some one you loved giving up for you. He must not, would not behave grudgingly! While he stood watching the tardy sunlight, he had again that sudden vision of the world which had come to him the night before. Sea on sea, country on country, millions on millions of people, all with their own lives, energies, joys, griefs, and suffering—all with things they had to give up, and separate struggles for existence. Even though he might be willing to give up all else for the one thing he couldn't have, he would be a fool to think his feelings mattered much in so vast a world, and to behave like a cry-baby or a cad. He pictured the people who had nothing—the millions who had given up life in the War, the millions whom the War had left with life and little else; the hungry children he had read of, the shattered men; people in prison, every kind of unfortunate. And—they did not help him much. If one had to miss a meal, what comfort in the knowledge that many others had to miss it too? There was more distraction in the thought of getting away out into this vast world of which he knew nothing yet. He could not go on staying here, walled in and sheltered, with everything so slick and comfortable, and nothing to do but brood and think what might have been. He could not go back to Wansdon, and the memories of Fleur. If he saw her again he could not trust himself; and if he stayed here or went back there, he would surely see her. While they were within reach of each other that must happen. To go far away and quickly was the only thing to do. But, however much he loved his mother, he did not want to go away with her. Then feeling that was brutal, he made up his mind desperately to propose that they should go to Italy. For two hours in that melancholy room he tried to master himself, then dressed solemnly for dinner.

His mother had done the same. They ate little, at some length, and talked of his father's catalogue. The show was arranged for October, and beyond clerical detail there was nothing more to do.

After dinner she put on a cloak and they went out; walked a little, talked a little, till they were standing silent at last beneath the oak-tree. Ruled by the thought: 'If I show anything, I show all,' Jon put his arm through hers and said quite casually:

"Mother, let's go to Italy."

Irene pressed his arm, and said as casually:

"It would be very nice; but I've been thinking you ought to see and do more than you would if I were with you."

"But then you'd be alone."

"I was once alone for more than twelve years. Besides, I should like to be here for the opening of Father's show."

Jon's grip tightened round her arm; he was not deceived.

"You couldn't stay here all by yourself; it's too big."

"Not here, perhaps. In London, and I might go to Paris, after the show opens. You ought to have a year at least, Jon, and see the world."

"Yes, I'd like to see the world and rough it. But I don't want to leave you all alone."

"My dear, I owe you that at least. If it's for your good, it'll be for mine. Why not start tomorrow? You've got your passport."

"Yes; if I'm going it had better be at once. Only—Mother—if—if I wanted to stay out somewhere—America or anywhere, would you mind coming presently?"

"Wherever and whenever you send for me. But don't send until you really want me."

Jon drew a deep breath.

"I feel England's choky."

They stood a few minutes longer under the oak-tree—looking out to where the grand stand at Epsom was veiled in evening. The branches kept the moonlight from them, so that it only fell everywhere else—over the fields and far away, and on the windows of the creepered house behind, which soon would be to let.

CHAPTER X.—FLEUR'S WEDDING

The October paragraphs describing the wedding of Fleur Forsyte to Michael Mont hardly conveyed the symbolic significance of this event. In the union of the great-granddaughter of "Superior Dosset" with the heir of a ninth baronet was the outward and visible sign of that merger of class in class which buttresses the political stability of a realm. The time had come when the Forsytes might resign their natural resentment against a "flummery" not theirs by birth, and accept it as the still more natural due of their possessive instincts. Besides, they had to mount to make room for all those so much more newly rich. In that quiet but tasteful ceremony in Hanover Square, and afterward among the furniture in Green Street, it had been impossible for those not in the know to distinguish the Forsyte troop from the Mont contingent—so far away was "Superior Dosset" now. Was there, in the crease of his trousers, the expression of his moustache, his accent, or the shine on his top-hat, a pin to choose between Soames and the ninth baronet himself? Was not Fleur as self-possessed, quick, glancing, pretty, and hard as the likeliest Muskham, Mont, or Charwell filly present? If anything, the Forsytes had it in dress and looks and manners. They had become "upper class" and now their name would be formally recorded in the Stud Book, their money joined to land. Whether this was a little late in the day, and those rewards of the possessive instinct, lands and money, destined for the melting-pot—was still a question so moot that it was not mooted. After all, Timothy had said Consols were goin' up. Timothy, the last, the missing link; Timothy, in extremis on the Bayswater Road—so Francie had reported. It was whispered, too, that this young Mont was a sort of socialist—strangely wise of him, and in the nature of insurance, considering the days they lived in. There was no uneasiness on that score. The landed classes produced that sort of amiable foolishness at times, turned to safe uses and confined to theory. As George remarked to his sister Francie: "They'll soon be having puppies—that'll give him pause."

The church with white flowers and something blue in the middle of the East window looked extremely chaste, as though endeavouring to counteract the somewhat lurid phraseology of a Service calculated to keep the thoughts of all on puppies. Forsytes, Haymans, Tweetymans, sat in the left aisle; Monts, Charwells; Muskhams in the right; while a sprinkling of Fleur's fellow-sufferers at school, and of Mont's fellow-sufferers in, the War, gaped indiscriminately from either side, and three maiden ladies, who had dropped in on their way from Skyward's brought up the rear, together with two Mont retainers and Fleur's old nurse. In the unsettled state of the country as full a house as could be expected.

Mrs. Val Dartie, who sat with her husband in the third row, squeezed his hand more than once during the performance. To her, who knew the plot of this tragi-comedy, its most dramatic moment was well-nigh painful. 'I wonder if Jon knows by instinct,' she thought—

Jon, out in British Columbia. She had received a letter from him only that morning which had made her smile and say:

"Jon's in British Columbia, Val, because he wants to be in California. He thinks it's too nice there."

"Oh!" said Val, "so he's beginning to see a joke again."

"He's bought some land and sent for his mother."

"What on earth will she do out there?"

"All she cares about is Jon. Do you still think it a happy release?"

Val's shrewd eyes narrowed to grey pin-points between their dark lashes.

"Fleur wouldn't have suited him a bit. She's not bred right."

"Poor little Fleur!" sighed Holly. Ah! it was strange—this marriage. The young man, Mont, had caught her on the rebound, of course, in the reckless mood of one whose ship has just gone down. Such a plunge could not but be—as Val put it—an outside chance. There was little to be told from the back view of her young cousin's veil, and Holly's eyes reviewed the general aspect of this Christian wedding. She, who had made a love-match which had been successful, had a horror of unhappy marriages. This might not be one in the end—but it was clearly a toss-up; and to consecrate a toss-up in this fashion with manufactured unction before a crowd of fashionable free-thinkers—for who thought otherwise than freely, or not at all, when they were "dolled" up—seemed to her as near a sin as one could find in an age which had abolished them. Her eyes wandered from the prelate in his robes (a Charwell-the Forsytes had not as yet produced a prelate) to Val, beside her, thinking—she was certain—of the Mayfly filly at fifteen to one for the Cambridgeshire. They passed on and caught the profile of the ninth baronet, in counterfeitment of the kneeling process. She could just see the neat ruck above his knees where he had pulled his trousers up, and thought: 'Val's forgotten to pull up his!' Her eyes passed to the pew in front of her, where Winifred's substantial form was gowned with passion, and on again to Soames and Annette kneeling side by side. A little smile came on her lips—Prosper Profond, back from the South Seas of the Channel, would be kneeling too, about six rows behind. Yes! This was a funny "small" business, however it turned out; still it was in a proper church and would be in the proper papers to-morrow morning.

They had begun a hymn; she could hear the ninth baronet across the aisle, singing of the hosts of Midian. Her little finger touched Val's thumb—they were holding the same hymn-book—and a tiny thrill passed through her, preserved—from twenty years ago. He stooped and whispered:

"I say, d'you remember the rat?" The rat at their wedding in Cape Colony, which had cleaned its whiskers behind the table at the Registrar's! And between her little and third forgers she squeezed his thumb hard.

The hymn was over, the prelate had begun to deliver his discourse. He told them of the dangerous times they lived in, and the awful conduct of the House of Lords in connection with divorce. They were all soldiers—he said—in the trenches under the poisonous gas of the Prince of Darkness, and must be manful. The purpose of marriage was children, not mere sinful happiness.

An imp danced in Holly's eyes—Val's eyelashes were meeting. Whatever happened; he must not snore. Her finger and thumb closed on his thigh till he stirred uneasily.

The discourse was over, the danger past. They were signing in the vestry; and general relaxation had set in.

A voice behind her said:

"Will she stay the course?"

"Who's that?" she whispered.

"Old George Forsyte!"

Holly demurely scrutinized one of whom she had often heard. Fresh from South Africa, and ignorant of her kith and kin, she never saw one without an almost childish curiosity. He was very big, and very dapper; his eyes gave her a funny feeling of having no particular clothes.

"They're off!" she heard him say.

They came, stepping from the chancel. Holly looked first in young Mont's face. His lips and ears were twitching, his eyes, shifting from his feet to the hand within his arm, stared suddenly before them as if to face a firing party. He gave Holly the feeling that he was spiritually intoxicated. But Fleur! Ah! That was different. The girl was perfectly composed, prettier than ever, in her white robes and veil over her banged dark chestnut hair; her eyelids hovered demure over her dark hazel eyes. Outwardly, she seemed all there. But inwardly, where was she? As those two passed, Fleur raised her eyelids—the restless glint of those clear whites remained on Holly's vision as might the flutter of caged bird's wings.

In Green Street Winifred stood to receive, just a little less composed than usual. Soames' request for the use of her house had come on her at a deeply psychological moment. Under the influence of a remark of Prosper Profond, she had begun to exchange her Empire for Expressionistic furniture. There were the most amusing arrangements, with violet, green, and orange blobs and scriggles, to be had at Mealard's. Another month and the change would have been complete. Just now, the very "intriguing" recruits she had enlisted, did not march too well with the old guard. It was as if her regiment were half in khaki, half in scarlet and bearskins. But her strong and comfortable character made the best of it in a drawing-room which typified, perhaps, more perfectly than she imagined, the semi-bolshevized imperialism of her country. After all, this was a day of merger, and you couldn't have too much of it! Her eyes travelled indulgently among her guests. Soames had gripped the back of a buhl chair; young Mont was behind that "awfully amusing" screen, which no one as yet had been able to explain to her. The ninth baronet had shied violently at a round scarlet table, inlaid under glass with blue Australian butteries' wings, and was clinging to her Louis-Quinze cabinet; Francie Forsyte had seized the new mantel-board, finely carved with little purple grotesques on an ebony ground; George, over by the old spinet, was holding a little sky-blue book as if about to enter bets; Prosper Profond was twiddling the knob of the open door, black with peacock-blue panels; and Annette's hands, close by, were grasping her own waist; two Muskhams clung to the balcony among the plants, as if feeling ill; Lady Mont, thin and brave-looking, had taken up her long-handled glasses and was gazing at the central light shade, of ivory and orange dashed with deep magenta, as if the heavens had opened. Everybody, in fact, seemed holding on to something. Only Fleur, still in her bridal dress, was detached from all support, flinging her words and glances to left and right.

The room was full of the bubble and the squeak of conversation. Nobody could hear anything that anybody said; which seemed of little consequence, since no one waited for anything so slow as an answer. Modern conversation seemed to Winifred so different from the days of her prime, when a drawl was all the vogue. Still it was "amusing," which, of course, was all that mattered. Even the Forsytes were talking with extreme rapidity—Fleur and Christopher, and Imogen, and young Nicholas's youngest, Patrick. Soames, of course, was silent; but George, by the spinet, kept up a running commentary, and Francie, by her mantel-shelf. Winifred drew nearer to the ninth baronet. He seemed to promise a certain repose; his nose was fine and drooped a little, his grey moustaches too; and she said, drawling through her smile:

"It's rather nice, isn't it?"

His reply shot out of his smile like a snipped bread pellet

"D'you remember, in Frazer, the tribe that buries the bride up to the waist?"

He spoke as fast as anybody! He had dark lively little eyes, too, all crinkled round like a Catholic priest's. Winifred felt suddenly he might say things she would regret.

"They're always so amusing—weddings," she murmured, and moved on to Soames. He was curiously still, and Winifred saw at once what was dictating his immobility. To his right was George Forsyte, to his left Annette and Prosper Profond. He could not move without either seeing those two together, or the reflection of them in George Forsyte's japing eyes. He was quite right not to be taking notice.

"They say Timothy's sinking;" he said glumly.

"Where will you put him, Soames?"

"Highgate." He counted on his fingers. "It'll make twelve of them there, including wives. How do you think Fleur looks?"

"Remarkably well."

Soames nodded. He had never seen her look prettier, yet he could not rid himself of the impression that this business was unnatural—remembering still that crushed figure burrowing into the corner of the sofa. From that night to this day he had received from her no confidences. He knew from his chauffeur that she had made one more attempt on Robin Hill and drawn blank—an empty house, no one at home. He knew that she had received a letter, but not what was in it, except that it had made her hide herself and cry. He had remarked that she looked at him sometimes when she thought he wasn't noticing, as if she were wondering still what he had done—forsooth—to make those people hate him so. Well, there it was! Annette had come back, and things had worn on through the summer—very miserable, till suddenly Fleur had said she was going to marry young Mont. She had shown him a little more affection when she told him that. And he had yielded— what was the good of opposing it? God knew that he had never wished to thwart her in anything! And the young man seemed quite delirious about her. No doubt she was in a reckless mood, and she was young, absurdly young. But if he opposed her, he didn't know what she would do; for all he could tell she might want to take up a profession, become a doctor or solicitor, some nonsense. She had no aptitude for painting, writing, music, in his view the legitimate occupations of unmarried women, if they must do something in these days. On the whole, she was safer married, for he could see too well how feverish and restless she was at home. Annette, too, had been in favour of it—Annette, from behind the veil of his refusal to know what she was about, if she was about anything. Annette had said: "Let her marry this young man. He is a nice boy—not so highty-flighty as he seems." Where she got her expressions, he didn't know—but her opinion soothed his doubts. His wife, whatever her conduct, had clear eyes and an almost depressing amount of common sense. He had settled fifty thousand on Fleur, taking care that there was no cross settlement in case it didn't turn out well. Could it turn out well? She had not got over that other boy— he knew. They were to go to Spain for the honeymoon. He would be even lonelier when she was gone. But later, perhaps, she would forget, and turn to him again! Winifred's voice broke on his reverie.

"Why! Of all wonders-June!"

There, in a djibbah—what things she wore!—with her hair straying from under a fillet, Soames saw his cousin, and Fleur going forward to greet her. The two passed from their view out on to the stairway.

"Really," said Winifred, "she does the most impossible things! Fancy her coming!"

"What made you ask her?" muttered Soames.

"Because I thought she wouldn't accept, of course."

Winifred had forgotten that behind conduct lies the main trend of character; or, in other words, omitted to remember that Fleur was now a "lame duck."

On receiving her invitation, June had first thought, 'I wouldn't go near them for the world!' and then, one morning, had awakened from a dream of Fleur waving to her from a boat with a wild unhappy gesture. And she had changed her mind.

When Fleur came forward and said to her, "Do come up while I'm changing my dress," she had followed up the stairs. The girl led the way into Imogen's old bedroom, set ready for her toilet.

June sat down on the bed, thin and upright, like a little spirit in the sear and yellow. Fleur locked the door.

The girl stood before her divested of her wedding dress. What a pretty thing she was!

"I suppose you think me a fool," she said, with quivering lips, "when it was to have been Jon. But what does it matter? Michael wants me, and I don't care. It'll get me away from home." Diving her hand into the frills on her breast, she brought out a letter. "Jon wrote me this."

June read: "Lake Okanagen, British Columbia. I'm not coming back to England. Bless you always. Jon."

"She's made safe, you see," said Fleur.

June handed back the letter.

"That's not fair to Irene," she said, "she always told Jon he could do as he wished."

Fleur smiled bitterly. "Tell me, didn't she spoil your life too?" June looked up. "Nobody can spoil a life, my dear. That's nonsense. Things happen, but we bob up."

With a sort of terror she saw the girl sink on her knees and bury her face in the djibbah. A strangled sob mounted to June's ears.

"It's all right—all right," she murmured, "Don't! There, there!"

But the point of the girl's chin was pressed ever closer into her thigh, and the sound was dreadful of her sobbing.

Well, well! It had to come. She would feel better afterward! June stroked the short hair of that shapely head; and all the scattered mother-sense in her focussed itself and passed through the tips of her fingers into the girl's brain.

"Don't sit down under it, my dear," she said at last. "We can't control life, but we can fight it. Make the best of things. I've had to. I held on, like you; and I cried, as you're crying now. And look at me!"

Fleur raised her head; a sob merged suddenly into a little choked laugh. In truth it was a thin and rather wild and wasted spirit she was looking at, but it had brave eyes.

"All right!" she said. "I'm sorry. I shall forget him, I suppose, if I fly fast and far enough."

And, scrambling to her feet, she went over to the wash-stand.

June watched her removing with cold water the traces of emotion. Save for a little becoming pinkness there was nothing left when she stood before the mirror. June got off the bed and took a pin-cushion in her hand. To put two pins into the wrong places was all the vent she found for sympathy.

"Give me a kiss," she said when Fleur was ready, and dug her chin into the girl's warm cheek.

"I want a whiff," said Fleur; "don't wait."

June left her, sitting on the bed with a cigarette between her lips and her eyes half closed, and went down-stairs. In the doorway of the drawing-room stood Soames as if unquiet at his daughter's tardiness. June tossed her head and passed down on to the half-landing. Her cousin Francie was standing there.

"Look!" said June, pointing with her chin at Soames. "That man's fatal!"

"How do you mean," said Francie, "fatal?"

June did not answer her. "I shan't wait to see them off," she said. "Good-bye!"

"Good-bye!" said Francie, and her eyes, of a Celtic grey, goggled. That old feud! Really, it was quite romantic!

Soames, moving to the well of the staircase, saw June go, and drew a breath of satisfaction. Why didn't Fleur come? They would miss their train. That train would bear her away from him, yet he could not help fidgeting at the thought that they would lose it. And then she did come, running down in her tan-coloured frock and black velvet cap, and passed him into the drawing-room. He saw her kiss her mother, her aunt, Val's wife, Imogen, and then come forth, quick and pretty as ever. How would she treat him at this last moment of her girlhood? He couldn't hope for much!

Her lips pressed the middle of his cheek.

"Daddy!" she said, and was past and gone! Daddy! She hadn't called him that for years. He drew a long breath and followed slowly down. There was all the folly with that confetti stuff and the rest of it to go through with yet. But he would like just to catch her smile, if she leaned out, though they would hit her in the eye with the shoe, if they didn't take care. Young Mont's voice said fervently in his ear:

"Good-bye, sir; and thank you! I'm so fearfully bucked."

"Good-bye," he said; "don't miss your train."

He stood on the bottom step but three, whence he could see above the heads—the silly hats and heads. They were in the car now; and there was that stuff, showering, and there went the shoe. A flood of something welled up in Soames, and—he didn't know—he couldn't see!

CHAPTER XI.—THE LAST OF THE OLD FORSYTES

When they came to prepare that terrific symbol Timothy Forsyte—the one pure individualist left, the only man who hadn't heard of the Great War—they found him wonderful—not even death had undermined his soundness.

To Smither and Cook that preparation came like final evidence of what they had never believed possible—the end of the old Forsyte family on earth. Poor Mr. Timothy must now take a harp and sing in the company of Miss Forsyte, Mrs. Julia, Miss Hester; with Mr. Jolyon, Mr. Swithin, Mr. James, Mr. Roger, and Mr. Nicholas of the party. Whether Mrs. Hayman would be there was more doubtful, seeing that she had been cremated. Secretly Cook thought that Mr. Timothy would be upset—he had always been so set against barrel organs. How many times had she not said: "Drat the thing! There it is again! Smither, you'd better run up and see what you can do." And in her heart she would so have enjoyed the tunes, if she hadn't known that Mr. Timothy would ring the bell in a minute and say: "Here, take him a halfpenny and tell him to move on." Often they had been obliged to add threepence of their own before the man would go—Timothy had ever underrated the value of emotion. Luckily he had taken the organs for blue-bottles in his last years, which had been a comfort, and they had been able to enjoy the tunes. But a harp! Cook wondered. It was a change! And Mr. Timothy had never liked change. But she did not speak of this to Smither, who did so take a line of her own in regard to heaven that it quite put one about sometimes.

She cried while Timothy was being prepared, and they all had sherry afterward out of the yearly Christmas bottle, which would not be needed now. Ah! dear! She had been there five-and-forty years and Smither three-and-forty! And now they would be going to a tiny house in Tooting, to live on their savings and what Miss Hester had so kindly left them— for to take fresh service after the glorious past—No! But they would like just to see Mr. Soames again, and Mrs. Dartie, and Miss Francie, and Miss Euphemia. And even if they had to take their own cab, they felt they must go to the funeral. For six years Mr. Timothy had been their baby, getting younger and younger every day, till at last he had been too young to live.

They spent the regulation hours of waiting in polishing and dusting, in catching the one mouse left, and asphyxiating the last beetle so as to leave it nice, discussing with each other what they would buy at the sale. Miss Ann's workbox; Miss Juley's (that is Mrs. Julia's) seaweed album; the fire-screen Miss Hester had crewelled; and Mr. Timothy's hair—little golden curls, glued into a black frame. Oh! they must have those—only the price of things had gone up so!

It fell to Soames to issue invitations for the funeral. He had them drawn up by Gradman in his office—only blood relations, and no flowers. Six carriages were ordered. The Will would be read afterward at the house.

He arrived at eleven o'clock to see that all was ready. At a quarter past old Gradman came in black gloves and crape on his hat. He and Soames stood in the drawing-room waiting. At half-past eleven the carriages drew up in a long row. But no one else appeared. Gradman said:

"It surprises me, Mr. Soames. I posted them myself."

"I don't know," said Soames; "he'd lost touch with the family." Soames had often noticed in old days how much more neighbourly his family were to the dead than to the living. But, now, the way they had flocked to Fleur's wedding and abstained from Timothy's funeral, seemed to show some vital change. There might, of course, be another reason; for Soames felt that if he had not known the contents of Timothy's Will, he might have stayed away himself through delicacy. Timothy had left a lot of money, with nobody in particular to leave it to. They mightn't like to seem to expect something.

At twelve o'clock the procession left the door; Timothy alone in the first carriage under glass. Then Soames alone; then Gradman alone; then Cook and Smither together. They started at a walk, but were soon trotting under a bright sky. At the entrance to Highgate Cemetery they were delayed by service in the Chapel. Soames would have liked to stay outside in the sunshine. He didn't believe a word of it; on the other hand, it was a form of insurance which could not safely be neglected, in case there might be something in it after all.

They walked up two and two—he and Gradman, Cook and Smither—to the family vault. It was not very distinguished for the funeral of the last old Forsyte.

He took Gradman into his carriage on the way back to the Bayswater Road with a certain glow in his heart. He had a surprise in pickle for the old chap who had served the Forsytes four-and-fifty years-a treat that was entirely his doing. How well he remembered saying to Timothy the day—after Aunt Hester's funeral: "Well; Uncle Timothy, there's Gradman. He's taken a lot of trouble for the family. What do you say to leaving him five thousand?" and his surprise, seeing the difficulty there had been in getting Timothy to leave anything, when Timothy had nodded. And now the old chap would be as pleased as Punch, for Mrs. Gradman, he knew, had a weak heart, and their son had lost a leg in the War. It was extraordinarily gratifying to Soames to have left him five thousand pounds of Timothy's money. They sat down together in the little drawing-room, whose walls—like a vision of heaven—were sky-blue and gold with every picture-frame unnaturally bright, and every speck of dust removed from every piece of furniture, to read that little masterpiece—the Will of Timothy. With his back to the light in Aunt Hester's chair, Soames faced Gradman with his face to the light, on Aunt Ann's sofa; and, crossing his legs, began:

"This is the last Will and Testament of me Timothy Forsyte of The Bower Bayswater Road, London I appoint my nephew Soames Forsyte of The Shelter Mapleduram and Thomas Gradman of 159 Folly Road Highgate (hereinafter called my Trustees) to be the trustees and executors of this my Will To the said Soames Forsyte I leave the sum of one thousand pounds free of legacy duty and to the said Thomas Gradman I leave the sum of five thousand pounds free of legacy duty."

Soames paused. Old Gradman was leaning forward, convulsively gripping a stout black knee with each of his thick hands; his mouth had fallen open so that the gold fillings of three teeth gleamed; his eyes were blinking, two tears rolled slowly out of them. Soames read hastily on.

"All the rest of my property of whatsoever description I bequeath to my Trustees upon Trust to convert and hold the same upon the following trusts namely To pay thereout all my debts funeral expenses and outgoings of any kind in connection with my Will and to hold the residue thereof in trust for that male lineal descendant of my father Jolyon Forsyte by his marriage with Ann Pierce who after the decease of all lineal descendants whether male or female of my said father by his said marriage in being at the time of my death shall last attain the age of twenty-one years absolutely it being my desire that my property shall be nursed to the extreme limit permitted by the laws of England for the benefit of such male lineal descendant as aforesaid."

Soames read the investment and attestation clauses, and, ceasing, looked at Gradman. The old fellow was wiping his brow with a large handkerchief, whose brilliant colour supplied a sudden festive tinge to the proceedings.

"My word, Mr. Soames!" he said, and it was clear that the lawyer in him had utterly wiped out the man: "My word! Why, there are two babies now, and some quite young children— if one of them lives to be eighty—it's not a great age—and add twenty-one—that's a hundred years; and Mr. Timothy worth a hundred and fifty thousand pound net if he's worth a penny. Compound interest at five per cent. doubles you in fourteen years. In fourteen years three hundred thousand-six hundred thousand in twenty-eight—twelve hundred thousand in forty-two—twenty-four hundred thousand in fifty-six—four million eight hundred thousand in seventy—nine million six hundred thousand in eighty-four— Why, in a hundred years it'll be twenty million! And we shan't live to use it! It is a Will!"

Soames said dryly: "Anything may happen. The State might take the lot; they're capable of anything in these days."

"And carry five," said Gradman to himself. "I forgot—Mr. Timothy's in Consols; we shan't get more than two per cent. with this income tax. To be on the safe side, say eight millions. Still, that's a pretty penny."

Soames rose and handed him the Will. "You're going into the City. Take care of that, and do what's necessary. Advertise; but there are no debts. When's the sale?"

"Tuesday week," said Gradman. "Life or lives in bein' and twenty-one years afterward—it's a long way off. But I'm glad he's left it in the family...."

The sale—not at Jobson's, in view of the Victorian nature of the effects—was far more freely attended than the funeral, though not by Cook and Smither, for Soames had taken it on himself to give them their heart's desires. Winifred was present, Euphemia, and Francie, and Eustace had come in his car. The miniatures, Barbizons, and J. R. drawings had been bought in by Soames; and relics of no marketable value were set aside in an off-room for members of the family who cared to have mementoes. These were the only restrictions upon bidding characterised by an almost tragic languor. Not one piece of furniture, no picture or porcelain figure appealed to modern taste. The humming birds had fallen like autumn leaves when taken from where they had not hummed for sixty years. It was painful to Soames to see the chairs his aunts had sat on, the little grand piano they had practically never played, the books whose outsides they had gazed at, the china they had dusted, the curtains they had drawn, the hearth-rug which had warmed their feet; above all, the beds they had lain and died in—sold to little dealers, and the housewives of Fulham. And yet— what could one do? Buy them and stick them in a lumber-room? No; they had to go the way of all flesh and furniture, and be worn out. But when they put up Aunt Ann's sofa and were going to knock it down for thirty shillings, he cried out, suddenly: "Five pounds!" The sensation was considerable, and the sofa his.

When that little sale was over in the fusty saleroom, and those Victorian ashes scattered, he went out into the misty October sunshine feeling as if cosiness had died out of the world, and the board "To Let" was up, indeed. Revolutions on the horizon; Fleur in Spain; no comfort in Annette; no Timothy's on the Bayswater Road. In the irritable desolation of his soul he went into the Goupenor Gallery. That chap Jolyon's watercolours were on view there. He went in to look down his nose at them—it might give him some faint satisfaction. The news had trickled through from June to Val's wife, from her to Val, from Val to his mother, from her to Soames, that the house—the fatal house at Robin Hill—was for sale, and Irene going to join her boy out in British Columbia, or some such place. For one wild moment the thought had come to Soames: 'Why shouldn't I buy it back? I meant it for my!' No sooner come than gone. Too lugubrious a triumph; with too many humiliating memories for himself and Fleur. She would never live there after what had happened. No, the place must go its way to some peer or profiteer. It had been a bone of contention from the first, the shell of the feud; and with the woman gone, it was an empty shell. "For Sale or To Let." With his mind's eye he could see that board raised high above the ivied wall which he had built.

He passed through the first of the two rooms in the Gallery. There was certainly a body of work! And now that the fellow was dead it did not seem so trivial. The drawings were pleasing enough, with quite a sense of atmosphere, and something individual in the brush work. 'His father and my father; he and I; his child and mine!' thought Soames. So it had gone on! And all about that woman! Softened by the events of the past week, affected by the melancholy beauty of the autumn day, Soames came nearer than he had ever been to realisation of that truth—passing the understanding of a Forsyte pure—that the body of Beauty has a spiritual essence, uncapturable save by a devotion which thinks not of self. After all, he was near that truth in his devotion to his daughter; perhaps that made him understand a little how he had missed the prize. And there, among the drawings of his kinsman, who had attained to that which he had found beyond his reach, he thought of him and her with a tolerance which surprised him. But he did not buy a drawing.

Just as he passed the seat of custom on his return to the outer air he met with a contingency which had not been entirely absent from his mind when he went into the Gallery—Irene, herself, coming in. So she had not gone yet, and was still paying farewell visits to that fellow's remains! He subdued the little involuntary leap of his subconsciousness, the mechanical reaction of his senses to the charm of this once-owned woman, and passed her with averted eyes. But when he had gone by he could not for the life of him help looking back. This, then, was finality—the heat and stress of his life, the madness and the longing thereof, the only defeat he had known, would be over when she faded from his view this time; even such memories had their own queer aching value.

She, too, was looking back. Suddenly she lifted her gloved hand, her lips smiled faintly, her dark eyes seemed to speak. It was the turn of Soames to make no answer to that smile and that little farewell wave; he went out into the fashionable street quivering from head to foot. He knew what she had meant to say: "Now that I am going for ever out of the reach of you and yours—forgive me; I wish you well." That was the meaning; last sign of that terrible reality—passing morality, duty, common sense—her aversion from him who had owned her body, but had never touched her spirit or her heart. It hurt; yes—more than if she had kept her mask unmoved, her hand unlifted.

Three days later, in that fast-yellowing October, Soames took a taxi-cab to Highgate Cemetery and mounted through its white forest to the Forsyte vault. Close to the cedar, above catacombs and columbaria, tall, ugly, and individual, it looked like an apex of the competitive system. He could remember a discussion wherein Swithin had advocated the addition to its face of the pheasant proper. The proposal had been rejected in favour of a wreath in stone, above the stark words: "The family vault of Jolyon Forsyte: 1850." It was in good order. All trace of the recent interment had been removed, and its sober grey gloomed reposefully in the sunshine. The whole family lay there now, except old Jolyon's wife, who had gone back under a contract to her own family vault in Suffolk; old Jolyon himself lying at Robin Hill; and Susan Hayman, cremated so that none knew where she might be. Soames gazed at it with satisfaction—massive, needing little attention; and this was important, for he was well aware that no one would attend to it when he himself was gone, and he would have to be looking out for lodgings soon. He might have twenty years before him, but one never knew. Twenty years without an aunt or uncle, with a wife of whom one had better not know anything, with a daughter gone from home. His mood inclined to melancholy and retrospection.

This cemetery was full, they said—of people with extraordinary names, buried in extraordinary taste. Still, they had a fine view up here, right over London. Annette had once given him a story to read by that Frenchman, Maupassant, most lugubrious concern, where all the skeletons emerged from their graves one night, and all the pious inscriptions on the stones were altered to descriptions of their sins. Not a true story at all. He didn't know about the French, but there was not much real harm in English people except their teeth and their taste, which was certainly deplorable. "The family vault of Jolyon Forsyte: 1850." A lot of people had been buried here since then—a lot of English life crumbled to mould and dust! The boom of an airplane passing under the gold-tinted clouds caused him to lift his eyes. The deuce of a lot of expansion had gone on. But it all came back to a cemetery— to a name and a date on a tomb. And he thought with a curious pride that he and his family had done little or nothing to help this feverish expansion. Good solid middlemen, they had gone to work with dignity to manage and possess. "Superior Dosset," indeed, had built in a dreadful, and Jolyon painted in a doubtful, period, but so far as he remembered not another of them all had soiled his hands by creating anything—unless you counted Val Dartie and his horse-breeding. Collectors, solicitors, barristers, merchants, publishers, accountants, directors, land agents, even soldiers—there they had been! The country had expanded, as it were, in spite of them. They had checked, controlled, defended, and taken advantage of the process and when you considered how "Superior Dosset" had begun life with next to nothing, and his lineal descendants already owned what old Gradman estimated at between a million and a million and a half, it was not so bad! And yet he sometimes felt as if the family bolt was shot, their possessive instinct dying out. They seemed unable to make money—this fourth generation; they were going into art, literature, farming, or the army; or just living on what was left them—they had no push and no tenacity. They would die out if they didn't take care.

Soames turned from the vault and faced toward the breeze. The air up here would be delicious if only he could rid his nerves of the feeling that mortality was in it. He gazed restlessly at the crosses and the urns, the angels, the "immortelles," the flowers, gaudy or withering; and suddenly he noticed a spot which seemed so different from anything else up there that he was obliged to walk the few necessary yards and look at it. A sober corner, with a massive queer-shaped cross of grey rough-hewn granite, guarded by four dark yew-trees. The spot was free from the pressure of the other graves, having a little box-hedged garden on the far side, and in front a goldening birch-tree. This oasis in the desert of conventional graves appealed to the aesthetic sense of Soames, and he sat down there in the sunshine. Through those trembling gold birch leaves he gazed out at London, and yielded to the waves of memory. He thought of Irene in Montpellier Square, when her hair was rusty-golden and her white shoulders his—Irene, the prize of his love-passion, resistant to his ownership. He saw Bosinney's body lying in that white mortuary, and Irene sitting on the sofa looking at space with the eyes of a dying bird. Again he thought of her by the little green Niobe in the Bois de Boulogne, once more rejecting him. His fancy took him on beside his drifting river on the November day when Fleur was to be born, took him to the dead leaves floating on the green-tinged water and the snake-headed weed for ever swaying and nosing, sinuous, blind, tethered. And on again to the window opened to the cold starry night above Hyde Park, with his father lying dead. His fancy darted to that picture of "the future town," to that boy's and Fleur's first meeting; to the bluish trail of Prosper Profond's cigar, and Fleur in the window pointing down to where the fellow prowled. To the sight of Irene and that dead fellow sitting side by side in the stand at Lord's. To her and that boy at Robin Hill. To the sofa, where Fleur lay crushed up in the corner; to her lips pressed into his cheek, and her farewell "Daddy." And suddenly he saw again Irene's grey-gloved hand waving its last gesture of release.

He sat there a long time dreaming his career, faithful to the scut of his possessive instinct, warming himself even with its failures.

"To Let"—the Forsyte age and way of life, when a man owned his soul, his investments, and his woman, without check or question. And now the State had, or would have, his investments, his woman had herself, and God knew who had his soul. "To Let"—that sane and simple creed!

The waters of change were foaming in, carrying the promise of new forms only when their destructive flood should have passed its full. He sat there, subconscious of them, but with his thoughts resolutely set on the past—as a man might ride into a wild night with his face to the tail of his galloping horse. Athwart the Victorian dykes the waters were rolling on property, manners, and morals, on melody and the old forms of art—waters bringing to his mouth a salt taste as of blood, lapping to the foot of this Highgate Hill where Victorianism lay buried. And sitting there, high up on its most individual spot, Soames—like a figure of Investment—refused their restless sounds. Instinctively he would not fight them—there was in him too much primeval wisdom, of Man the possessive animal. They would quiet down when they had fulfilled their tidal fever of dispossessing and destroying; when the creations and the properties of others were sufficiently broken and defected—they would lapse and ebb, and fresh forms would rise based on an instinct older than the fever of change—the instinct of Home.

"Je m'en fiche," said Prosper Profond. Soames did not say "Je m'en fiche"—it was French, and the fellow was a thorn in his side—but deep down he knew that change was only the interval of death between two forms of life, destruction necessary to make room for fresher property. What though the board was up, and cosiness to let?—some one would come along and take it again some day.

And only one thing really troubled him, sitting there—the melancholy craving in his heart—because the sun was like enchantment on his face and on the clouds and on the golden birch leaves, and the wind's rustle was so gentle, and the yewtree green so dark, and the sickle of a moon pale in the sky.

He might wish and wish and never get it—the beauty and the loving in the world!

THE END

Made in the USA
Coppell, TX
24 June 2020